Nyx throws back her head in a peal of exultant laughter. Around her pulses a ghastly grey light that hints at cosmic energies at her command. Above, the darkness in the depths of the sky heaves and crawls like an expectant creature waiting to be born.

In this moment you finally understand. What she brings is the threat of unbeing, the sure annihilation that leads to total emptiness forever. Her power lies in humanity's horror of the void. She is night as the source of unreasoning fear, the harbinger of panic even in the hearts of those who never shrink from any danger they can see and touch. She is the foe who cannot be faced. And yet you must face her.

For the sake of all existence you must conquer unconquerable Night.

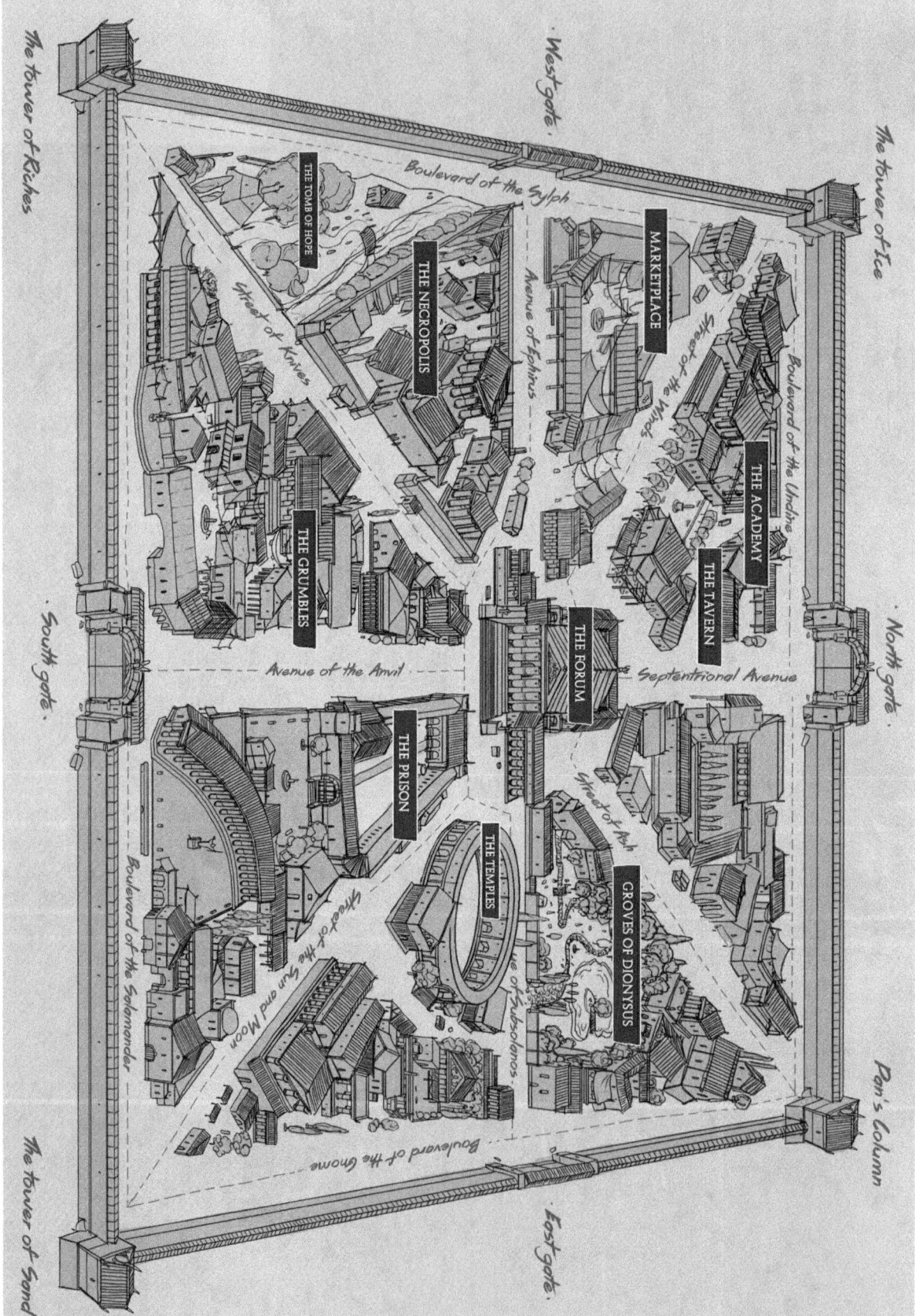

WORKSHOP OF THE GODS

Dave Morris

Cover by Mattia Simone

Fabled Lands Publishing

VulcanVerse Solo Roleplaying Adventures

The Houses of the Dead
The Hammer of the Sun
The Wild Woods
The Pillars of the Sky
Workshop of the Gods

The dragon wing of Night o'erspreads the earth...

Darkness casts a baleful shadow over the Vulcanverse, threatening all who dwell in the five realms. Queen Nyx, with her dread sons Death and Sleep at her side, unleashes a devastating war that will sweep away both gods and titans and leave her the unchallenged monarch of all creation.

You set out on a perilous journey on which you must hone your skills, win over allies, and gather the secrets that will make you into the Hero of the Age, the only mortal capable of opposing the Night Queen.

Traverse the vast expanse of Vulcan's world, confronting battle-hardened foes and cunning rivals at every turn. You will make friends for whom you are willing to risk everything and enemies whose treachery will make your blood boil. Restore the fortunes of ruined lands, giving heart to their people, as you encounter gods and monsters and unravel mysteries that may hold the key to your destiny.

Among your many fantastic experiences you will be drawn into worlds steeped in sinister dream and dark myth. Are you ready to brave the grimy alleyways of the criminal underworld and the treacherous intrigues of the great palaces? To plunge back through time to take part in the eternal battle and to witness the first dawn? To set sail across the celestial void? Are you willing to face murderous androids that can kill with a scream? Can you outrun the terrible hounds of death? Do you have the courage and tenacity to break through the skin of existence to find the workshop of the gods where new realities are born?

With thanks to John Jones for unpicking most of the Gordian knots I had managed to tie myself up in while gathering the threads of all the Vulcanverse books. If there are any corners of these Augean stables that still need sweeping, it's my oversight and not his.

Published 2024 by Fabled Lands Publishing,
an imprint of Fabled Lands LLP

ISBN 978-1-909905-42-9

Text © Dave Morris 2024

Illustrations copyright © Mattia Simone 2024

Your Vulcanverse Adventure Starts Here

Vulcanverse is an open-world solo role-playing game. You can play the books in any order, coming back to earlier books whenever you travel to the region they cover. Instead of a single storyline, there are virtually unlimited adventures. If you like to be given quests, *Workshop of the Gods* is a good book to start in. You'll also have the advantage of having grown up in the city, so you'll be familiar with the streets and landmarks.

To play all you need is two dice, an eraser and a pencil. You only need one book to start, but by collecting other books in the series you can explore more of the Vulcanverse.

If you have already adventured using other books in the series, you will know your entry point into this book. Turn to that section now.

If this is your first Vulcanverse book, read the rest of the rules before starting at section **1**. You will keep the same adventuring persona throughout the books – starting out as a novice but gradually gaining in power, wealth, prestige and experience throughout the series.

ADVENTURE SHEET

Your Adventure Sheet lists everything you'll need to keep track of while playing. Don't fill it in yet. That will happen as you begin your adventure.

ATTRIBUTES

You have four attributes whose values typically range from −1 to +2 as you're starting out. You will discover your attribute scores as you play. They are:

CHARM	Your understanding of people and their motives.
GRACE	How agile, supple and quick you are.
INGENUITY	Cunning and reasoning, and your ability to think on your feet.
STRENGTH	Physical might and endurance.

The maximum possible innate score in an attribute is +5. If you are at maximum and are told to add to your score, it has no effect.

Items that augment attributes

There are items you can acquire that boost your attributes while you have them. These are:

CHARM:	**laurel wreath** (+1)
	golden lyre (+2)
GRACE:	**recurve bow** (+1)
	winged sandals (+2)
INGENUITY:	**hornbook** (+1)
	abacus (+2)
STRENGTH:	**hardwood club** (+1)
	iron spear (+2)

You can only use the bonus from one such item at a time. So if you had a **laurel wreath** that gives CHARM +1 and a **golden lyre** that gives CHARM +2, you'd only get the CHARM bonus from the latter. Similarly, two **laurel wreaths** still only give you a +1.

An item can augment your attribute score above the innate limit of +5. If you have a STRENGTH score of +5 and you possess an iron spear, your total STRENGTH bonus when making a roll counts as +7.

Making an attribute roll

Attribute rolls are made to see if you succeed at a task. These are rolls of two dice with a difficulty that you must equal or beat to succeed.

For instance, you might be told: 'Make a STRENGTH roll at difficulty 7'. You roll two dice, add your STRENGTH score (including the modifiers for any one possession that boosts STRENGTH) and to succeed you need to get 7 or more.

*Example: You are at the bottom of a cliff. To climb it you need to make a GRACE roll at difficulty 5. You roll two dice and score 4. Your GRACE attribute is −1 but luckily you have **winged sandals** which give a +2 GRACE bonus, so your modified GRACE is +1, just enough to make the roll a success.*

A roll of double 6 ('boxcars') is always a success regardless of difficulty. A roll of double 1 ('snake eyes') is always a failure regardless of modifiers.

WOUNDS

The Adventure Sheet has a box labelled Wound. This is unticked at the start of the adventure. From time to time you may be asked to put a tick in it. You only have one Wounded tick at a time; if you're asked to tick the box when it is already ticked, you don't add another.

While the Wound box is ticked you have injuries, and these will cause you to deduct 1 from any attribute roll until the box is unticked.

If you have an item such as **tincture of healing** that allows you to untick the Wound box, you cannot use it to avoid taking a wound, only to remove a wound after you have taken it. So if you do take a wound, apply any effects listed and when you turn to the next section you can then use the item to heal.

SCARS

You begin with no scars, but may acquire them from lasting injuries or from returning from the afterlife. Scars are a mixed blessing. Many people will shun you because of them, but others will admire or fear you more.

POSSESSIONS

Possessions are always marked in bold text, like this: **iron spear**. If you come across an item marked like this you can pick it up and add it to your list of possessions.

You can carry up to twenty possessions at a time. If you come across an item you want when already at your limit, you'll have to discard something to make room. There are places in the Vulcanverse where you can leave possessions and come back for them later.

MONEY

You can carry any sum of money (measured in a coinage called pyr). You'll discover as you play whether you have any money to start off with.

GLORY

Glory starts at 0 but will grow as you perform deeds that increase your renown. With high Glory you will be recognized as a hero and given more respect by those you meet.

CODEWORDS

There is a list of codewords at the back of the book. Sometimes you will be told you have acquired a codeword. When this happens, put a tick in the box next to that codeword. If you later lose the codeword, erase the tick.

The codewords are arranged alphabetically for each book in the series. In this book, for example, all codewords begin with R. This makes it easy to check if you picked up a codeword from a book you played previously. For instance, you might be asked if you have picked up a codeword in a book you have already adventured in. The letter of that codeword will tell you which book to check (eg if it begins with N, it is from Book 1: *The Houses of the Dead*).

TITLES

Titles record the achievements you have earned, marking you as the champion of a city, protector of a temple, admiral of a fleet, or even a monarch. You will be told when you acquire a title.

BLESSINGS

If you fail an attribute roll, you can use up a blessing to roll the dice again. You can only do that once per roll, so you cannot use a second blessing to get another reroll if the first one fails.

You can have up to three blessings at a time. You start the adventure with no blessings. Usually the place to get blessings is at a shrine or temple, but you may find other opportunities to acquire them.

COMPANION

As you travel the Vulcanverse, you will meet some people who are willing to journey with you. You can have one companion at a time. When you pick up a new companion you must remove your current companion, if any, from the Companion box. You can also part company with a companion at any time just by deleting their name from the box. You do not have a companion at the start of the adventure.

A companion is not necessarily at your side every minute of the day. There will be times when you face trouble on your own and wonder why your companion doesn't help out. They could have wandered off to look in a shop window. They might be elsewhere and planning to meet up with you later. You can get temporarily separated from a companion, but don't delete them from your Adventure Sheet unless told to, or unless you want to.

CURRENT LOCATION

You'll use this box from time to time to keep track of where you are. You will be told when to use it. Whenever you are told to record an entry number in your Current Location box, first delete any number that was already there.

NOTES

Use this box on your Adventure Sheet to keep a record of quests, clues or other things you need to remember.

Lastly, if 'Is this book suitable for children or the nervous?' is a question you might ask, the answer is emphatically, 'No.'

That's all you need to know to get started on your adventure. Now turn to **1**.

"Night, resistless vanquisher of all,
Both gods and men."

1

Time is a river, they say, and it is not possible to step into the same river twice. But you can swim upstream in memory and in dreams, treading water to revisit the moments that time has swept away.

Begin by setting your four attribute scores on your Adventure Sheet: CHARM, GRACE, INGENUITY and STRENGTH are all at 0. The scores may change depending on your choices growing up.

Yours is a large family. Your parents are active members of the community and you have many sisters, yet when your brother is born it is for some reason assumed that he is your special responsibility. You make sure he is safe in his cradle. Later, when he is old enough to wander off, you are the one who makes sure the yard gate stays closed.

What do you think about these duties?

Looking after him is a chore	▶ 247
It's fine – you love him	▶ 83

2

'Hey!'

You whirl around. The voice came from nearby but you don't see anyone.

'Down here.'

A trapdoor opens by your feet and a man beckons you. You hoist Dunamis down first. 'We're right outside the tavern,' she realises. 'This is the beer cellar.'

'The tavern's gone,' says the man, glancing at the gutted ruins nearby. 'Hurry, or you won't fare any better.'

You look back at the approaching Keres. 'Maybe I should – '

'Don't even think of fighting them,' says the man. 'They'll skewer you before you can say ouch.'

A hail of rocks and lumps of wood comes pouring from the tops of the buildings opposite. You see a few figures darting along the broken walls, keeping up a barrage of missiles to distract the Keres while you get away.

The man slams the trapdoor shut behind you and points to a narrow torchlit tunnel through the cellar. 'They're too big to get down here, but even so we shouldn't hang around.'

'You took a risk saving us,' you say as you follow him through a warren of brick-lined passageways.

'Folks around here owe you,' he says. 'We don't forget a good deed.'

He takes you to a set of makeshift wooden steps that end in a door. 'This leads into the undercroft of the Academy,' he says.

'Thanks.' You shake his hand.

'I'd wish you luck,' he says unsentimentally, 'but you won't need it. You're the new hero of Temesa. The good one.'

▶ 93

3

A man strolls past giving you a sidelong appraisal. He isn't tall, but he has powerful shoulders and moves with an athlete's grace. You might not even notice him except for the way everybody else on the street is being so careful not to meet his eye or get in his way.

You glance at him. 'Something you want to say?'

'Zinc would like to meet you,' he says with a broad grin. He has a scar across his lips that pulls his mouth into a wry expression.

'What if I don't want to meet him?'

'Then you shouldn't hang around here, I'd say. Eventually everybody in the Grumbles gets to know Zinc. One way or another.'

You notice he's brought along some muscle. Hard, capable-looking men who are waiting at a discreet distance. If you don't go with him to meet Zinc, they will escort you out of the Grumbles and back to the main streets.

Accept Zinc's invitation	▶ 675
Refuse	▶ 1617

4

If you have both the codewords *Oasis* and *Quiddity* ▶ 1394

Otherwise ▶ 573

Right beside you a boulder opens its eyes – two vast glassy green orbs with deep black vertical slashes for pupils. A split tongue flicks between what you thought were cracks in the rock. Glistening fangs, ivory-yellow and sharp as flakes of flint, reveal themselves in a gaping wet maw.

You whirl, reappraising your surroundings in a glance. A giant grey-skinned snake, perfectly camouflaged against the stone of the pass, completely surrounds you. It slithers down off the rocks, encircling you in tightening bands of scale-armoured muscle.

Make a GRACE roll at difficulty 12.

Succeed ▶ 893
Fail   ▶ 1479

It is a damp day with an overcast that the sun fails to burn off. By late afternoon a mist is rising, giving a picturesque cast to the glades, ponds and leafy avenues of the cemetery. The surrounding sepulchres, wreathed in smoky white fumes, could be the buildings of an uninhabited city through which you wander as a giant.

The fog grows thick, and as you retrace your steps you realize you are lost. Trees loom against the drifting grey. You call out, but all sounds are muffled. Seeing a figure with upraised arm, you take it for a watchman beckoning visitors to the gate. You hurry forward only to find it's a statue with death's face, placed as sentinel at the entrance to a vault.

A sound – the scrape of a metal shovel on dirt and stone. Surely one of the gravediggers working late? You pick your way between the tombs. Out of the fog a shape appears – a hunched figure hauling a coffin out of a tomb whose door has been broken open. The figure uses its spade to smash the hasp of the coffin, and with a cry of horrible glee falls upon the body and begins to gnaw at its arm.

Attack this ghoul ▶ 969
Get away before it sees you ▶ 1191
Creep closer to spy on it ▶ 1348

You see a shoal of glowing red fish that swim through the air. They disappear into a gaping hole in the ground. From far below in the darkness comes the echoing drip of water. Bronze rungs form a ladder leading to the bottom of this well.

If you climb down, record **472** as your Current Location and then ▶ 252

Otherwise ▶ 472

'Then you would turn on us just as readily,' says Thanatos. 'And we have no use for minions who calculate the rationing of their loyalty.'

He starts to draw back his cowl.

▶ 147

'Is that supposed to be wiring?' pipes up the Face. 'Or is it just a pile of uncooked spaghetti?'

The Dactyls stiffen indignantly. Thumb leans over to glare at the Face. 'Take that back, chrome dome,' he growls. 'We're doing our best here.'

'You think there's a pat on the back for trying, you big lug?' snaps the Face. 'It's the fate of the world we're talking about.'

'Oh, and you could do better, could you, you brass bigmouth?'

'You bet I could, you pollical plodder.'

'That's enough,' says Psyche, stepping between them. She asks the Face, 'What are you proposing?'

'If you switch out those circuits, princess, you can set up a parallel processor that's not part of the matrix rebuild.'

'What's it talking about?' mutters Pinkie.

'Wait,' says Psyche, holding up her hand for silence. She stares at the wiring, brow creased in thought. 'That makes sense. It wouldn't be very powerful. Just enough to tweak the odds very, very slightly. But if that came at just the right time…'

'You mean it might be possible to arrange a miracle?' you ask.

'A very minor one.' She turns to you. 'I can isolate this unit from the main workshop machinery, that's easy enough. The problem is the interface.'

'How do you mean?'

Psyche disconnects a wire. 'I don't have a socket in my head to plug this into. To directly control reality in real time, we'd need…' She looks at the Face.

'A cranium filled with several miles of copper wiring,' it says. 'I guess that'd be me, then.'

Psyche explains that if she connects the Face to the parallel processor, it would be able to monitor what you're doing and at opportune moments could tweak reality in your favour.

'But it would mean leaving the Face here,' she concludes.

Do that ▶ 1026

No, you might need it later ▶ 1511

'Politics doesn't have to be dull,' Kazala tells the assembled guests. 'What if I told you that a plan for lasting peace began with me crouching in a pit in the eastern desert, breaking teeth out of a fossilized dragon while skeletal sentries prowled the dunes? If they'd caught me I'd have been flayed alive. Look.' She pulls her robe off her shoulder to reveal a long scar. 'That's from one time I wasn't quite quick enough. I left some blood behind on the Spartoi's swords that day, but I got away with – ' She opens her hand, revealing a few nuts she took earlier from a bowl. 'Well, these are just snacks, but I left the desert with a handful of dragon's teeth.'

'What use are dragon's teeth?' asks a rotund gentleman with a beard like a dirty white octopus. 'I've heard that if you sow them you get a crop of Spartoi, and they're as likely to murder you as do you a favour.'

'Exactly right, sir!' says Kazala, jabbing her finger at him as if he'd managed to answer a trick question. 'Who'd want such a thing? I wandered high and low wondering what to do with my clutch of dragon's teeth. Such a hard-won prize – ' again she displays her scar, giving the men in the audience a longer look at her shapely back – 'I couldn't bear to sell them, though I had no use for them until I came to Sarpedon on the southern edge of the Borean plateau…'

She goes on to tell of negotiations with the council of Sarpedon, but even though her story is winding down now you can see it will be hard to win the audience round. You make the most of her low-key denouement, opening an account of your own with dangerous intrigues, violent arguments, tense discussions, and knife-edge diplomacy.

Make a CHARM roll at difficulty 9. You can add an additional +1 to your dice score if you have a Glory of 10 or more.

Success: your story is judged more interesting ▶ 868
Failure: Kazala has won this round ▶ 785

11

A golden fist swings around with the force of a sledgehammer. Reeling, you spit out a mouthful of teeth and blood.

If the Wound box on your Adventure Sheet was unticked, put a tick in it now and then ▶ 890
If you were already injured ▶ 671

12

As you touch the syndic he cries out in his sleep, a chilling moan that is magnified in the dark so that it makes your hair stand on end. The embryonic dream floating him bursts into life with a blossom of nascent green flame that is visible even in the darkness. It reaches for you with half-formed fingers…

You are in the library in Iskandria. The place is deserted.

You are hurrying from room to room, scanning the shelves. There's a book you must find. It has the answer to everything. You pull down one volume after another, desperately searching, but the pages of every book are charred black. They turn to ashes in your hand.

Lose 1 point from any of your attributes (CHARM, GRACE, INGENUITY or STRENGTH, you decide which) and then ▶ 431

13

'What a pity,' says Bosk. 'But I expect you'll end up doing it anyway, and if you do then I recommend coming back here for a dip in the lake. It's so refreshing.'

He gathers his clothes and puts them on, even though he's still damp from his swim, and jogs off across the grass.
▶ 806

14

'Are you familiar with the artefact locally referred to as the Tomb of Hope?' asks Myletes.

'On the Boulevard of the Sylph. Sure.'

'I have begun an investigation into the nature of its construction and why it bears that name.'

'Shall we walk over there now and take a look? I've got some time to spare.'

Myletes shakes his head vigorously. 'Oh, no no no. I don't want to actually see it. That could prejudice my studies disastrously.'

You're puzzled. 'So how are you going to find out anything about it?'

'By pure reason, of course. Everything that is important is written in the texts we have here in the library, and by a process of deduction I shall gradually uncover the truth.'

Though unconvinced, you decide against arguing the point with him. After a short while some younger scholars arrive for a tutorial and you take your leave.
▶ 1062

15

Note 1544 as your Current Location, then ▶ 1269 and tick the box next to the Academy of Philosophers. From now on you will always be able to find your way back here.

16

At first you think they're too far gone to listen. They stare back, crouching fearfully behind the broken timbers and bricks. Wind-whipped fires send dancing streaks of light across their faces.

Then one old lady creeps out into the street. 'That's right,' she says, her voice barely audible over the howl of the wind. She turns to the others, shouting to be heard. 'What are we doing, skulking about while this poor lady is trapped under there? We're not beasts. This is our city, isn't it? So do something!'

She limps over and starts helping to clear the pile of bricks and beams. Others follow, ashamed to see a feeble old woman showing more courage than them. Working together, they soon clear away the debris. The woman who was trapped is helped to her feet, scratched and bruised but alive.

Get the title **Local Hero** and ▶ **233**

17

□ □

Do not tick either of the boxes unless you were told to do so in the section you just turned from.

Neither of the boxes is ticked	▶ **540**
One box is now ticked	▶ **468**
Two boxes are ticked	▶ **890**

18

If you have the codeword **Royal** and you possess the **Panoply of the Lost Hero** ▶ **1139**

Otherwise ▶ **666**

19

It's the work of a moment. Her unclean diet leaves her too weak to resist. Or perhaps it's simply that she welcomes death. As you grab the shovel and stand over her, she only gazes up with an abject look of resignation.

Your savage blow cracks her skull and she slumps, as dead as the carrion she was feasting on. Disgusted by the slime of blood and brains on your hands, you throw the shovel into the bushes. Stumbling blindly, you race through the fog until brought up short by the cemetery wall. You follow it to the gate.

'I was just locking up,' grumbles the watchman, loosening the chain to let you out. Too numb with horror to reply, and fighting the urge to be sick, you push past him into the street.

Get the codeword **Reef** and ▶ **1617**

20

Lose the codeword **Rogue**.

The girl leads you away from the crowded streets and through an area of derelict tenements. As you turn a corner you catch a glimpse of her red cloak disappearing through a doorway.

'Wait – !'

She doesn't seem to hear you. She races up a narrow staircase of half-rotten timbers that twists up and up until you come to a cavernous loft filled with darkness and cobwebs. The roof tiles are cracked in many places, allowing daylight to poke long pallid fingers through the dust-filled air.

She is standing in the middle of the loft with her back to you. You approach, reaching for her. 'I've come to take you back to your daddy.'

'And I have come to send you to Hell!' rasps a guttural voice.

The figure turns. It's not a little girl. It's a dwarf whose face is contorted with hatred.

A blur of motion. A warm trickling. His knife has slashed you across the stomach. Only lightning-fast reflexes saved you from being gutted where you stand. Tick the Wound box on your Adventure Sheet.

'Don't make it too quick,' says a voice from the shadows. 'Leave some for me.'

It is the café owner. He treads closer, a meat cleaver in his hand. The floorboards creak under his bulk. Under his bulging brow, his eyes glint like chips of dirty ice.

'I suppose there's no chance of a double decaff to go,' you say.

'That's right,' he sneers, 'now I have to pander to the tastes of you idle foreigners with your herbal teas and your effete little biscuits. Once I was the richest slave trader in Boreas. That's down to you.'

'Just doing my bit for humanity.'

'Humanity?' He spits. 'We are Gargareans. The rest are mere animals for us to use as we will.'

He and the dwarf are coming at you from both sides.

Fight them ▶ 1363
Outthink them ▶ 131

21

Swinging his massive club ahead of him in a whooshing figure-of-eight motion, Enceladus charges forward bellowing a war-cry that shakes you to the core. The air around him is thick with the sour smell of sweat and the scorching reek of his fiery slobber.

Make a STRENGTH roll at difficulty 10.

Succeed ▶ 878
Fail ▶ 943

22

If you are female and Chipos is your companion ▶ 286

If you are male and Loutro is your companion ▶ 503

Otherwise, if you have the codeword *Quench* and do not have *Rigor* ▶ 1049

Otherwise, if you have the title **Persona Non Grata** ▶ 1352

Otherwise, if you have the **Face of Wisdom** (INGENUITY +3) ▶ 742

If none of the above ▶ 562

23

A tall figure is standing at the parapet gazing out over the cloying mists and flame-shot peaks of Hades.

'Greetings, Lord Xechasiaris,' you say.

He turns slowly, as if not quite sure you're talking to him, although there is no one else here.

'I never forget a face,' he says. 'Only the name that goes with it.'

Lose the codeword *Roar* and ▶ 1011

24

The sun appears over the garden wall, sending a blaze of daylight through the drenched and sagging ivy.

Tritona's mouth forms a perfect O of surprise. You feel the shudder that runs through her. As the sunbeams touch her face she dissolves like a painting being washed away by turpentine. You are left holding empty air.

Lose the codeword *Ruffle* and ▶ 38

25

You embrace. He heaves a deep sigh.

'What? Still heavy of heart, my love?'

'All the more so,' he says with a sad smile, 'for I know that when we have visited the cataracts of Notus and I have imparted the mysteries of the goddess's cult, then we must part – perhaps forever.'

'Then let us never go to Notus again. The gods can settle their own affairs, leaving us to live our lives together.'

He shakes his head. 'You know that cannot be. Heroes do not get to enjoy free will, and your destiny is like a meteor blazing across the sky. But until the moment of our parting, we have each other.'

If you have the codeword *Ruby* ▶ 601

If not ▶ 97

26

It starts to get dark. There are a few deliveries to the house, and various tenants come and go, but nobody resembling Autolycus or his automaton companion.

At last you're forced to give up. When you come by the next day, the garret room has been cleaned out.

'Is the caretaker not on duty today?' you ask the thickset woman who tells you she's the landlady.

'Caretaker?' She snorts with laughter. 'It's not one of your fancy hostelries, this. If anything needs fixing the tenants have to sort it out for themselves.'

▶ 771

27

'Good luck!' shouts Dunamis.

You look back. 'You're not coming?'

'Remember Zinc's note? While you're looking for Vulcan's workshop, I'm going to go and find whatever it was Zinc left.'

'What makes you think it'll be any use now?'

'Zinc ran crime in this city for twenty years. He did that by always thinking three steps ahead of everyone else. Him and me, we had our differences, but I know enough not to underestimate him.'

You see she's determined. 'All right. Be careful.'

She smiles – a genuine smile, it doesn't come easily to her. With a quick wave she's gone. You continue down.

▶ 1082

28

A search of their pockets turns up a **lava gem**, a **honey cake**, and a **winding key** for a music box, which you can add to your possessions. There's also a note written in a crude hand:

'Dear Braxus, I hope your master is treating you well and you're getting enough to eat. Tell him you are a growing boy, just not by much. If you should manage to buy your freedom, or alternatively knife the fat bastard in the night and the filth don't round you up, get your stubby arse over to Mount Helikon in Boreas where there's a mad coot with a boat on a mountain. Sounds daft, I know, but you might get a steady job if he needs a mascot. Remember to pack a tarbrush – I mean, a toothbrush. Your loving mum.'

Leaving the bodies for the rats, you make your way back down to the street.

▶ 571

29

The wings spread like living appendages, carrying you high over the dour peaks that ring the shadowed land of the dead. A veil of white mist undulates below, shot through with flickers of fire and darkness. The wind wafts up a faint fetor as of things that should have been buried long ago.

If you were with a companion, delete them from your Adventure Sheet. Also remove the **beeswax** that you have used.

You begin to descend – towards where?

The Plains of Howling Darkness ▶ 412 in *The Houses of the Dead*

    The Slimeswamp   ▶ 38 in *The Houses of the Dead*

    The Delta of Darkness ▶ 493 in *The Houses of the Dead*

    The Black Bayou   ▶ 273 in *The Houses of the Dead*

    The River Acheron   ▶ 588 in *The Houses of the Dead*

    The River Styx   ▶ 330 in *The Houses of the Dead*

    The City of the Dead ▶ 696 in *The Houses of the Dead*

30

Your foes are swift and agile, but you have the advantage of desperation. You race along the road, not caring that the pebbles tear at your bare feet, and gradually the sounds of pursuit dwindle behind you.

A blue lamp flashes against the wall from a side street. It's a patrol of the night watch – half a dozen stalwart fellows with cudgels.

'Ah, officers – '

It's only as you raise your arm to accost them that you remember you've come out in just a nightgown. This will take some fast talking.

To influence them you need to make a CHARM roll at a difficulty of 15 minus your Glory score. For instance, if you have Glory of 10 then the CHARM roll is at difficulty 5. You cannot use an item such as a **laurel wreath** or **golden lyre** to influence this roll, but you can use a blessing to reroll.

A natural leader ▶ 1393

A mumbling ninny ▶ 588

31

This is the Boulevard of the Salamander, a street given over to warehouses, specialty shops, and a number of tenement blocks where clerks, storekeepers and petty officials have their lodgings.

You pass a curious row of shops stacked on top of each other. Ladders connect between galleries, each giving access to a different set of shops. On the ground level are barbers, on the level above the windows display all manner of wigs, and the top storey consists of stores selling hats.

If you have a **sulky head** among your possessions ▶ 1611; otherwise read on.

To go straight to a city location that you already know about, note **31** as your Current Location, then ▶ 1432

Or you can go:

East ▶ 570

West ▶ 555

32

By now there's a milling throng of pursuers pressed right up to the edge of the roof. You can see the pallid, worm-gnawed features of the vampires, the red eyes and spittle-flecked jaws of the were-creatures, the misshapen features of capering nightmare demons. Baying and snarling, they are so intent on getting to you that some even get jostled over the edge and fall flailing to the street far below.

There's a commotion at the back of the horde, near the stairs up onto the roof. Some of the rear ranks are turning in confusion. A vampire spins, a spear thrust into its chest, and disintegrates in a tattered cloud of dust and rags and old bones. A slim hand reaches out, pulls back the spear, and swings it in a wide arc to keep the nearest monsters at bay.

As the rabble parts you see a lithe figure in studded

leather armour. In one hand she has the spear, in the other a sword that's already slick with blood. Behind her are a band of stalwart fighters, each holding their own against the night creatures that come rushing and snapping at them from all sides.

'Zoë?' You turn to the Minotaur. 'Look! It's the Princess of the Golden Band.'

The Minotaur chops a leaping were-ape off the ship's rail. 'Guess I won't begrudge them a piece of the action,' he grunts.

Zoë is too far off to hear you over the thunderous storm, but she sees your look of recognition and raises her hand in salute. She and her companions swore to come to your aid when you needed it most, and they are as good as their word.

Her surprise attack has divided the monstrous horde. Half of them turn to fight Zoë and her men. Others are still leaping from the parapet trying to get aboard, but her arrival has bought you some time. Meanwhile, the *Sunrise* continues to lose altitude.

'I can handle this mob,' shouts the Minotaur. 'Go make yourself useful.'

The crew are still trying to raise the sails, no easy feat in this wind. And the helmsman is struggling to fix the buoyancy rotor. Should you see what you can do to help them, or stay shoulder-to-shoulder with the Minotaur?

Keep fighting at the rail ▶ **453**
Help with the rigging ▶ **776**
Take a look at the buoyancy rotor ▶ **829**

33

'Oi, wanker! Get your arse back here!' roars Chipos at the top of his lungs.

Sphikos halts and looks around in perplexity. You wave for him to come back.

'Watch your step!' Chipos calls out. 'You could fall right through this gunk.'

Sphikos joins you. He's a little breathless, more with excitement than exertion. 'We're at the dawn of creation,' he says.

▶ **1044**

34

'This always was the most unfinished part of the Vulcanverse,' you say, noticing that the buildings here in the Grumbles are now no more than glowing green wireframes.

'People used to say Vulcan couldn't be bothered to polish this bit of the city,' says Dunamis. 'Looks smaller now you can see through all the houses, doesn't it?'

'So where's this package Zinc left for me?'

Dunamis leads you through a maze of glowing lines till you come to a patch of ground marked out by the luminous edges of vanished buildings.

'Recognize it?'

'Zinc's little kitchen garden.'

She nods. 'And somewhere about here, according to the note – ' she digs around in the soil and picks out an object wrapped in dirty cloth – 'is the prize marrow.'

You take it from her. Nestled inside the scrap of cloth is an object that shines with inner light. You unwrap it. A sphere of gleaming yellow amber.

Get the **Eye of Hyperion** and lose the codeword *Radiant*.

'Satisfied with your freebie?' says Dunamis with all the withering impatience of a typical teenage girl. 'Coz we still have to save the world.'

Where now?
The nearest gate ▶ **723**
The nearest tower ▶ **171**
The Avenue of the Anvil ▶ **1632**
Your mansion (only if you have the title **The Unexpected Heir**) ▶ **1257**
Your family home (only if you have the codeword *Reverie*) ▶ **1385**
The Academy of Philosophers ▶ **1510**
The temple district ▶ **1326**
The Forum ▶ **981**

35

No one will accompany you into Hades, so if you have a companion and wish to press on you will have to delete them from your Adventure Sheet.

Continue into Hades ▶ **72** in *The Houses of the Dead*
Turn back into the city ▶ **555**

36

Lord Xechasiaris is sitting on a marble bench at the side of the entrance. He gives you a vacant smile as you walk over.

'You look nice. Cute as a baby's bottom. Do I know you?'

'My lord, you sent me to find your lost youth.'

'I lost it, did I? How careless. What's this?'

'Sometimes scent is the key to memory,' you suggest.

You hand him the flower you have brought. Remove it from your list of possessions. He puts it to his nose, inhales, and –

'Gods above! It's all coming back to me. There was a light rainfall that day, so soft it was just a spray on your face, but it woke up the ground. Petrichor, they call that. Little green shoots everywhere. I remember one of the waggoneers had a bitch who'd had puppies and she let me play with a spotted black and white one. Poor little runt, I fed him milk soaked on a dry crust but he didn't make it. To humour me the waggoneers buried him, bet they'd have just chucked him in a ditch otherwise, and this flower was nearby and I plucked it to put on the grave.'

'Fascinating, my lord. Obviously an important chapter for your memoirs.'

He gives you a shrewd look, quite different from his vagueness of a few minutes earlier. 'No need to humour me, youngster. I'm old, not stupid. Now, thank you for this, but I need to get going. Lots of things to catch up on.'

As he walks away, he looks back and adds, 'My parents had been worried out of their wits, of course, but they were so happy to have me back that I was never scolded for running away. I must have felt guilty about it, though, because I never travelled again. Would have loved to see other lands, but I spent my whole life here in the city. Funny, that.'

Get the codeword **Rain** and ▶ 187

37

You are turning away when it strikes you: you've seen this armour before. It is the panoply of the Lost Hero, which you recovered and returned to her in a series of arduous quests.

Strange – you remember collecting the pieces of armour, but you have no memory of the Lost Hero herself. Her face and the things she said to you are a blur. But wasn't that the curse that the gods placed on her, doomed to be forgotten by future generations?

▶ Current Location

38

You look for the treasure where Tritona told you it was hidden. In the bottom of the pots you find a total of fifty **lava gems**. Note 515 as your Current Location and then ▶ 1402 and record them in the box there.

39

If you have the title **Witness of the First Dawn** ▶ 1059
    If not ▶ 580

40

A second guard appears in a doorway at the far end of the passage. He hesitates, unsure whether to help his colleague or go for reinforcements.

Stop him before he can run off ▶ 1656
Concentrate on the one you're already fighting ▶ 523

Note that your Current Location is now **140**.

You are up long before dawn. As the Achaean camp stirs into life, you go to gaze across the plain where today's battle will be fought. A bank of sea mist, a white wall between the two hosts of heroes, has detached Ilion from its earthly moorings. The gleaming towers, more golden lace than stone, float in the crystalline air.

If you have the codeword **Ramrod** ▶ 465; otherwise read on.

All along the shore, men are strapping on armour or harnessing horses to chariots. At the outskirts of the Myrmidon enclosure, the strange armour broods on its stand like a sentinel from another world.

Will you fight with the Achaeans today, or do you intend to stand aloof from this war?

Prepare yourself for battle ▶ 727
Stay out of it; it's not your fight ▶ 823
Take a closer look at the armour ▶ 306
Speak with Achilles ▶ 766

42

Eros takes your limp body in his arms, raising your head so that you can see the rout of the fallen Night Queen's army. On the eastern horizon, a red glow shows that the day is coming back.

'What about…?' your voice trails off, your throat too dry for words.

'Her progeny?' says Eros. 'Driven back to the furthest abyss. Without their dread dam they'll never dare to return.'

'You did it,' says Dunamis, running up. 'You killed Nyx!'

She looks at you breathlessly, tears in her eyes. You want to tell her to get herself home to Iskandria. It's too much effort even to keep your eyes open. A stillness folds around you, an eternal rest. You feel yourself drifting, seemingly weightless.

It's like being born. Not a thing to fear.

43

The brilliantly polished armour shines as if with inner fire. Stirred gently on its frame by the wind off the sea, it produces a faint clanging, like the quietest note that could be sounded from an immense bell.

▶ Current Location

44

Two remain, scuttling about the lawn to try and get on either side of you. Their mandibles are churning like oiled and polished knives. Their limbs, each lined with razor

sharp flanges, scrape against the armoured carapaces with a hollow sound like bamboo trees swaying in a strong wind.

Make a STRENGTH or GRACE roll (your choice) at difficulty 13.

Succeed ▶ **1608**
Fail ▶ **1587**

45

Delicate hands take the webbing from you. Swift and shimmering in the low shafts of sunset, the dryads flit back and forth between the rows of tall topiary. They move almost too fast to perceive, back and forth, weaving a net of fine strands across the avenue.

The insect-creatures sense something, but the dryads are of too subtle a stuff for their compound eyes to see. Alarmed by the invisible danger, they rear up on their chitinous legs, braced like huge spring-loaded machines of war, feelers twitching.

In a moment the dryads have finished their work and are back beside you, giggling to themselves. To them it is a game. They point out the impenetrable gossamer strands, so thin that even the raindrops now falling barely touch them.

The insects, hearing something moving in the bushes, lose all caution. They charge forwards only to blunder into the strands of webbing strung between the trees on either side of the avenue. They lash out blindly and loops of web catch around their claws, their legs, their antennae. In struggling to break free they are getting more and more entangled.

'Go now, mortal friend,' say the laughing dryads, thrusting you out of the green haven. You are once more standing in the cold evening rain. Topiary beasts sway on either side in the rising wind.

The giant insects are held rigid, wrapped like insectoid mummies in a shroud of glistening silk. Helpless as they are, you despatch them easily.

Delete the **attercop silk** from your possessions and ▶ **143**

46

You leap to your feet but fatigue and stress have sapped your resolve. You are too slow. Nyx sweeps your attack aside with contemptuous ease.

'You have heart, at least,' she says, opening her grip to show it to you – your red, throbbing heart, plucked from your chest.

The world around you wobbles as though it were projected on the surface of a bubble. Flakes of darkness swim across the bubble's surface. All grows dull. You know no more.

▶ **666**

47

Xechasiaris weighs up what you've told him. 'Your words have the ring of truth,' he says with a wistful smile. 'Even the Speaker of the Syndics has never argued a point so well. I will go to my final rest, then. After all, it's only another adventure.'

He walks slowly away, actually seeming to dissolve into nothingness now that he has made up his mind to accept death.

▶ **351**

48

❑

This is the north-east corner of the city. The tall tower known as Pan's Column rises above the ramparts. If you do not have the codeword *Reverie* and the box above is empty, put a tick in it and ▶ **369**; otherwise read on.

The tower is of polished brown marble shot through with swirls of glaucous crystal. The sides are deeply grooved so that the whole structure resembles a giant Ionic column, with clusters of ivy sculpted into the stone around the door and windows and a massive coronet of stone acanthus leaves supporting the parapet.

To go straight to a city location that you already know about, note **48** as your Current Location, then ▶ **1432**

Or you can go:

West along the Boulevard of the Undine ▶ **970**
South-west along the Street of Ash ▶ **232**
South down the Boulevard of the Gnome ▶ **1534**
Up the tower ▶ **1629**

49

The person you're trying to creep up on has senses as keen as a cat. You'll need a GRACE roll at difficulty 13. Don't apply any item bonuses to the roll – you are in your nightgown, and your possessions are back in your bedroom. However, if you fail and you have a blessing you can use it to reroll the dice once.

Quieter than any mouse ▶ **1161**
Louder than a clumsy dog ▶ **1641**

50

'You have already met the Celedons,' says Eos. 'Nyx has subverted them to her will. No longer pliant servitors, but deadly hunters whose screams have the power to stun or kill.'

If you have the **voicebox remote** ▶ **110**
Otherwise ▶ **1105**

51

He might be right. Why take the risk?

As you turn away, you distinctly hear a chuckle in the gurgling water of the fountain. Gain a blessing if you are not currently at your maximum limit.

Might you have gained a greater boon if you hadn't vacillated over taking back your offering? You may never know.

▶ **806**

52

Zinc is sitting at a plain table at the back of a small café. If not for the metal mask you wouldn't give him a second glance. As you step in off the street, the men at the neighbouring tables discreetly size you up. They are burly, capable-looking toughs alert to any threat to their boss.

'There you are.' Zinc waves you over, points to the chair opposite him. 'About time. We have things to talk about.'

If you have the title **The Chosen One** and this box ❑ is empty, tick it and ▶ **798**; otherwise read on.

If you have the codeword *Plundered* but not *Rink* and this box ❑ is empty, tick it and ▶ **149**; otherwise read on.

If you don't have the codeword *Robber* ▶ **1270**; otherwise read on.

If you possess the **scrimshaw hourglass** and this box ❑ is empty, tick it and ▶ **685**; otherwise read on.

Other people are waiting to talk to Zinc, but he sets aside his criminal enterprises for a short while to chat to you. ▶ **326**

53

The Archon of the Moon beckons from a doorway off the main hall. She steps towards you, seeming almost to glide in the trailing silver robes that barely sway with her movements.

'You carry an interesting piece of embroidery,' she says, her voice pitched so low that you have to lean close to catch her words.

'I'm told it depicts the Olympian gods, Your Grace.'

'You're a collector?'

'Not really. I won it in a quest.'

She runs her fingers over the fabric. 'There is powerful magic in this. It could serve as a portal for travel between worlds, perhaps to Olympus itself.'

'How would I open such a portal, Your Grace?'

Her smile is as inscrutable as the face of the Moon on her headdress. 'If the need is there, you'll find a way.'

▶ **1642**

54

You explore a vast palace with vaulted ceilings like a marble sky, pearl-coloured and shot with veins of gold. The floor is beaten copper that shimmers in the reflected light of the snow that rings the mountain peak. Yet here the aether that you inhale, though so pure that it makes you gasp for breath, carries no arctic chill. There are fragrances of blossom, honey, fresh leaves. The music of dancing fountains and wind chimes drifts softly from far away.

Magnificent as it is, the palace shows signs of a terrible

battle. Angry scorch-marks blasted across walls as big as cliff-faces. Chipped bas-relief friezes. Torn tapestries whose beauty is only enhanced by being brutally defaced. Chunks gouged out of monumental pillars. These marks of damage can only have been inflicted by titanic weapons – swords like storm waves and maces the size of a war-galley's battering ram.

'What's happened here?' you ask.

Bosk points to splashes of golden ichor on the metal floor. 'The titans have already attacked once. The gods fought them off, but the fight was long and wearying. Now the titans are regrouping at the mouth of Tartarus.'

The deeper you venture into the palace, the more fragmented and dreamlike it feels. Often you get the sense of entering a room a moment after somebody has left it. Turning down an avenue-sized corridor, you catch a fleeting glimpse of beings too huge for you to fully comprehend, like mountaintops momentarily revealed through a gap in drifting clouds.

'It's all so huge. I feel like an ant here. What can I possibly do to affect a war between gods and titans?'

'What's that?' Bosk grabs your arm and gives you a shaking that rattles your teeth. 'That's no kind of talk for the hero of the age. It just takes a little time for mortals to push through into the reality of Olympus. Trust me, you'll soon find your groove.'

He's right. Entering a banquet hall, you find the alabaster table only slightly bigger than you'd expect. On this scale you are no longer an insect, more like a child standing beside adult-sized furniture.

Now you hear voices, muttering echoes along the colonnaded gallery at the back of the room. Sandalled footsteps are coming closer. The air grows charged with a numinous energy that makes your scalp tingle – or perhaps it's just your own nervousness at the thought of meeting the gods.

'Here they come,' says Bosk. 'They know the titans are mustering for another attack. They need to restore their strength before then.'

'With what?' You gesture at the golden plates and bowls on the table – all empty.

'That's up to you. Make your choice and make it well.'

Put out some **food of the gods** ▶ 298

Serve **poisoned ambrosia** ▶ 492

Neither ▶ 1186

55

By now a gibbering throng of monsters is pressed right up to the edge of the roof. You can see the pallid, worm-gnawed features of the vampires, the red eyes and spittle-flecked jaws of the were-creatures, the misshapen features of capering nightmare demons. Baying and snarling, they are so intent on getting to you that some get jostled over the edge and fall flailing to the street far below.

Each time a grapple lodges on the ship's rail, instantly a stream of attackers comes scrabbling along it to get aboard. Careless of the wind, rain and the lethal drop below, their only thought is to continue their wild onslaught. Even the Minotaur, whose blade flashes and spills blood and guts with every swing, must eventually tire and then the monstrous tide will overwhelm the ship.

Should you stay to help the Minotaur fight them off, or go to help get the buoyancy rotor working before the *Sunrise* loses any more height?

Fight to repel boarders ▶ 583

Help fix the buoyancy rotor ▶ 1630

56

The noticeboard is a black mirror in whose depths swim luminous messages. As you concentrate, each message in turn comes into sharp focus.

You can select any mission whose box is unticked – just tick the box and turn to the corresponding section.

❑ Reputation at stake ▶ 749

❑ Missing person ▶ 991

❑ A matter of honour ▶ 1504

❑ A culinary problem ▶ 263

If you don't want to choose a mission, or if all missions have now been taken ▶ Current Location

57

She fights back with redoubled ferocity, desperate to escape before the dawn strikes her dead forever. Make a STRENGTH roll at difficulty 8 to stop her breaking free.

Success ▶ 1250

Failure ▶ 1036

58

Your CHARM score isn't only about cajolery. It's also a measure of how well you can judge the effect of your words on someone, whether that's sweet talk or threats or deception.

In this case you've badly misread your man. The attempt to scare him stings his pride. In a bold voice he declares, 'You and your thugs may do your worst, but I am an honest man and I intend to stand up for what's right.'

You can't follow through on your threats in case the White Guard have someone keeping an eye on their witness, so you have to go back and report failure. Zinc shakes his head sadly. 'It's not Moose getting locked up that bothers me,' he says. 'He's a liability as much as he's an asset. I had you pegged as smarter than that, though.'

▶ 326

59

There's no place like home. You are curled up in a basket by the hearth – which is odd, because that's where the family dog slept. What was his name? In fact there were several dogs, growing up. They're a bit of a blur now.

Your mother is pounding dough to make bread. It sounds like somebody being bludgeoned to death. Your father and aunts and uncles are outside inspecting the vines that grow around the walls and lend a green tint to the sunlight pouring through doors and windows.

You look around the room. Something is missing. You were never an only child, but where are your siblings?

If you worship Ares and do not have the codeword *Ostrich* ▶ 1418

Otherwise ▶ 757

60

He holds the **masterpiece by Apelles** up to the daylight and nods appreciatively. 'I don't know much about art, as they say, but I can read a signature. I'll give you 200 pyr for the painting right now, or maybe you'd rather have credit on a future purchase?'

Take the cash	▶ 1447
Take the credit	▶ 1372
No deal	▶ 828

61

The storm batters at the window and casts ripples of rainwater shadow over the walls as you close in a death-struggle with the vampire.

Though she is slight, apparently no more than a frail wisp of a girl, her undead body is animated by the overpowering vigour of the eternally damned. You wrestle with her and her grip is as hard as cold iron. Make a STRENGTH roll at difficulty 11.

| Succeed | ▶ 628 |
| Fail | ▶ 248 |

62

A giant figure strides down from the sky. His naked frame dwarfs even the other titans. If you have the codeword *Rhombus* ▶ 1275 immediately; otherwise read on.

'I said I would come when you needed me,' he booms, 'and Prometheus keeps his word.'

So saying, he stands shoulder to shoulder with Eros confronting the spawn of Nyx. Get the codeword *Rhapsody*.

Now if you have the codeword *Quake* ▶ 553

If not but you have the codeword *Pumped* ▶ 720

Otherwise, if you have the codeword *Nanny* ▶ 1637

Otherwise ▶ 1183

63

The Avenue of the Anvil is the artisans' quarter of the city. Smithies and potteries shoulder in among high peak-gabled houses and open onto side alleys where tufts of grass poke up from the cobblestones. One of the side streets here is known as Turnagain Lane – ironically a cul-de-sac ending in the dark granite walls of the prison.

If you have the codeword *Rendezvous* ▶ 1323

If not ▶ 502

64

The mutated tower contorts ever more frantically, like a giant slug rearing up in torment at the burning touch of salt.

Where will you head next?

The nearest gate ▶ 723

The Avenue of the Anvil ▶ 1632

Your mansion (only if you have the title **The Unexpected Heir**) ▶ 1257

Your family home (only if you have the codeword *Reverie*) ▶ 1385

The Academy of Philosophers ▶ 1510

The temple district ▶ 1326

The Forum ▶ 981

65

Priests of your own deity will treat your injuries for free. At any other temple you must pay a **lava gem**.

The salves and bandages they apply allow you to untick the Wound box on your Adventure Sheet

'Go home and rest,' advises the infirmarian, a priest whom the deity has granted curative skills. 'And next time: duck.'

▶ 103

66

Deeds speak louder than words. You join the small band of rescuers. The woman is groaning in pain from a heavy roof beam that has pinned her to the ground. You help clear away the rubble. That leaves only the roof beam.

'We can't lift it,' hisses a man through clenched teeth. 'There aren't enough of us.'

'There will be.' You bend, taking hold of one end of the beam. The other three rescuers obviously think it's hopeless, but they pitch in. Muscles straining, all heaving together you barely shift it by an inch.

Make an INGENUITY roll. Renown helps, so the difficulty of the roll is 24 minus your Glory score; for instance, with a Glory of 13 you'd make the roll at difficulty 11. (Difficulty cannot go below 0.)

Succeed ▶ 291
Fail ▶ 930

67

You expected him to be offended, but he accepts your money with a hangdog look and apologises all the way to the door. 'I should not have come. I see now that I've put you in a very difficult spot. Rest assured I shall depart the city this very day.'

'Where will you go?'

He stares blindly up and down the street. 'I always wanted a simple rural life. Perhaps with your generous gift I can buy a small inn.' He bows and turns away to hide his tears. 'I swear I'll never bring shame on you, your grace. May the gods protect you.'

As it happens, if the gods have any opinion on the affair it is one of disapproval. Lose one blessing if you have any (excepting the permanent blessing granted by Demeter) then ▶ 97

68

'I never forget a face,' says the sergeant on duty.

If you have the title **Public-Spirited** ▶ 402
Otherwise ▶ 302

69

You talk the looters round and send them off to rally the populace. They're a rabble rather than an army, but at this point any organized resistance against Nyx is better than nothing.

'We ought to look for the nearest city gate,' says Dunamis. 'I can show you how I hack the noticeboards.'

▶ Current Location

70

'You think death is bad?' you ask him. 'Hang around here and you'll face much worse.'

He looks at you, a flicker of doubt in his eyes. 'In what way?'

'Have you ever come across the skeleton of a moth? Just tiny filaments held together by gossamer and dust. That's what you'll become if you insist on remaining. Gradually you're going to decay, losing substance every day, getting abraded away till you're less than a ghost. Unable to speak with anyone, unable to touch or even see the world around

you. Then it'll be too late to move on. You'll be reduced to wandering in the unending grey forever.'

To convince him you'll need a CHARM roll at difficulty 9. Add 1 to the number rolled for each of the following titles or codewords that you have:

Accursed of Ares
Grief Stricken
Ostrich
Persona Non Grata
Pursued by Nemesis
Quaff
Quiver
Unfriended by Apollo
Walking Wounded

If you succeed ▶ 1585
If you fail ▶ 660

71

You are quite satisfied with the forged orders when you send them to Sakan, but when days go by without any result you start to brood. Did you spell his name right? Was the wax you used for the seal the right shade of purple? Should you have spent a bit more to get the high-quality vellum that senior officials prefer?

Later you hear a rumour that Sakan has been telling everyone that a fellow officer tried forging orders to get him out of the way. He hints at a dark secret that the other officer wants to keep covered up, and the story is that he'll reveal the forger's identity in a few days.

Poor Viranos, you think. In trying to help him, you've just added forgery to the list of slanders that Sakan will use to besmirch his standing in the city.

▶ 1432

72

The story involves a couple of travellers who keep getting to within sight of their destination, only to be chased away by a wolf that they avoid by jumping off cliffs or into rivers.

'Boring!' yell several onlookers when the wolf shows up for the third time.

'Does the story go anywhere?' you ask the woman standing next to you.

'No,' she says glumly. 'Bit aimless, this one. They just wanted an excuse to show off the wolf puppet now that they've made it.'

'It would be better without the wolf,' says her friend. 'Just have the two guys expecting it and it never shows up. "Waiting For Lobo", I'd call it.'

'Congratulations,' says the woman. 'You've thought of a story even more tedious than the one they've got.'

As the crowd disperses, some of the audience drop coins in a box in front of the booth. You can leave some money yourself if you think the show was worth it.

▶ 232

73

'I don't like it, Onco. Shouldn't we be getting out of the city while we still can?'

'With nothing in our pockets but fluff? Don't be a dope, Croton. Wherever we go we'll need cash to get started.'

'But "Tomb of Hope"... You have to admit, it smacks of something sinister.'

'Always kylix-half-empty with you, isn't it. What about the "hope" bit? Haven't you passed this a thousand times and wondered what treasures might be inside? Well, now we're going to find out.'

The voices are muffled, punctuated by a chipping sound. You hear the scrape of a heavy block being levered free. Lamplight flickers around you, stirred into swirling patterns by thick walls of green glass.

A face presses up against the wall next to you. Imperfections in the glass make his features look like a painting that has run in the rain.

'What can you see?' hisses Croton.

'Gimme the lamp. Hard to say. I think it's a mummy.'

'Oh... oh no. No. Come on, let's get out of here.'

'Stop your whining,' snaps Onco. 'What did you think we were going to find in a tomb? Mummies are buried with gold and gems, aren't they. Now help me loosen this last block.'

A chisel clinks against the glass, which instantly clouds over with a cobwebbing of tiny cracks. Rolling over, you push against the block. It disintegrates into tiny splinters. You are face to face with the two tomb robbers.

'Aiee!' shrieks Croton, dropping the lantern. In the guttering light they scurry back along the tunnel they've dug. You hear running feet disappearing down the street outside.

You wriggle along the narrow tunnel and pull yourself into the open air. From the robbers' remarks you already realized you'd arrived inside the Tomb of Hope, but the scene that meets your eyes is very different from the familiar city you left behind. It is a bleak vista of abandonment and devastation. In place of shopfronts and teeming crowds, you are confronted by a blighted ruin with the taste of smoke and brick dust in the air.

High winds rip at your clothes. The stars overhead are faint and flickering embers in the ashes of the cosmos, racing madly through torn strips of cloud. Pearl-coloured light shines down feebly from the remote crescent of the moon, casting trembling shadows in the wreckage.

What has happened in your absence? Entire roofs have been swept away as if by an apocalyptic storm, revealing timbers like the bones of a decaying carcass. Windows are just a few splinters of glass. A street sign hanging on a single chain bangs fretfully against the wall. Fires have broken out among the darkened ruins, flattened by the wind into crouching animals with their ferocity cowed.

There is no sign of life anywhere. It looks like the end of the world.

▶ 156

74

As you wait to enter the palace, if you have the title **Earth Mother's Herald** ▶ 1213

Otherwise read on.

The porters insist that you hand over any attribute-boosting items 'to prevent cheating at the gambling tables, unfairly achieved seduction, or other peccadilloes of that sort.'

Note **207** as your Current Location and then ▶ 964

75

You go to stand in the centre of the room, directly under the dome. Hushed echoes merge into a continuous muttering. After a moment you hear a voice that seems to be whispering right by your ear:

'These shoes are killing me. Should never have worn them. Why didn't I pick the sensible pair? It's an all-night ball, for Hera's sake. No good catching a guy's eye if I'm limping around by midnight like I've got mousetraps on my toes. And I might as well be wearing skates on that slippery ballroom floor. If I take a tumble they'll all remember me as the clumsy clodhopper, not the stunner in spectacular sandals.'

You had thought you were alone in the building, but when you look round you see a young woman in silver high-heeled shoes carefully supporting herself against the wall. 'They're really for sitting down in,' she says with a nervous laugh.

'Dancing barefoot is all the rage in Iskandria,' you tell her.

At that her face lights up. 'Is it? How marvellous. I might just take these and throw them in the lake.'

'There's a lake?'

'Beyond the trees in the garden,' she says, pointing out of the door to a stone-flagged passageway that leads off the side of this courtyard. 'You can cut through there if you don't want to go back to the main quad.'

Go along the passage to the garden ▶ 1415

Back towards the gate ▶ **750**
Look at the hand-shaped fountain ▶ **489**

76

You position yourself in a side alley from where you can keep watch on Naft's warehouse. Later in a the afternoon a tall but obviously female figure comes along the street swathed from head to foot in a brightly patterned silk gown that veils even her face. She goes into Naft's yard and reappears a few moments later carrying the straw-packed jar of amaranth oil, heading west down the street.

Accost her ▶ **514**
Follow her ▶ **787**

77

❏ ❏

Tick one of the boxes above.

If both boxes were already ticked ▶ **1595**
If not and you have the codeword *Recite* ▶ **1640**
Otherwise ▶ **950**

78

Hundreds fall dying as flashing swords hew limbs and heads asunder, but neither your side nor Nyx's can gain ground. The forces are equally matched in strength.

A Myrmidon officer, staggering back to catch his breath, turns to you. 'Show yourself at the head of the troops!' he cries. 'They yearn for their champion.'

He's right. Inspiring leadership can turn the tide of even the most hopeless battle. You hurl yourself into the front line, calling to your soldiers to join you in a push aimed at splitting Nyx's ranks.

Make a CHARM roll at difficulty 18. You can add 1 to your dice score if your Glory is at least 16.

Fire in their bellies ▶ **1243**
Faint hearts ▶ **322**

79

'My mother exiled me here' says Eos.

'Why?'

'She is ashamed of me,' says Eos, hanging her head as though she feels deserving of blame. 'Imagine if Ares had a child who loved peace, or Athena gave birth to one who was reckless and unthinking.'

▶ **262**

80

Deep in the warren of streets running through the Grumbles, you find the nook in the alley wall where a locked grating leads to a narrow tunnel reeking of brimstone and decay.

If you have an **iron key** you can unlock the grating and crawl through to Hades – but if you do that you must part ways with your companion, if any, as no one will voluntarily travel there.

Follow the tunnel to Hades (if you have an **iron key**) ▶ **713** in *The Houses of the Dead*
Stay in the city ▶ **571**

81

'Hey, if you don't mind…'

'Crying like a Halizon girl, I mean. Women back home tend to be fragile, wilting types. We expect men always to be the tough and stoic ones.'

'Maybe that's your problem right there.'

▶ **1093**

82

You make your way towards a crowd of bystanders. Roll one die:

score 1	A mugging	▶ **406**
score 2	Seditious graffiti	▶ **339**
score 3	A firebrand speaker	▶ **154**
score 4	A strange animal	▶ **1296**
score 5	Distressed refugees	▶ **1307**
score 6	A miraculous fountain	▶ **360**

83

When your brother is old enough to go to school, you take it on yourself to walk with him each morning. At first he chatters to you about his day, all the new things he has seen and learned about and the friends he is making. It is a delight to experience the world made afresh in his eyes.

After only a few weeks, though, his usual outgoing nature changes. He drags his feet on the way to school, keeping his eyes on the ground, and replies to your attempts to draw him out with a few mumbled words.

You make enquiries and discover he is being picked on by a boy of about your own age named Nihakos, a sullen brute whom you have never liked.

How do you deal with it?

Challenge Nihakos to a fight ▶ **288**
Humiliate the bully ▶ **329**
Teach your brother to defend himself ▶ **739**
Do nothing; your brother
must fight his own battles ▶ **247**

84

Eros carries you to Olympus. The hallowed halls have been restored. Golden sunlight slants down from a sky of perfect blue. Fountains send a million sparkling diamonds dancing. Ethereal music drifts on the air.

'The titans have been cast back into their pit,' says Zeus.

You notice he addresses Eros rather than you. Eros notices it too. 'The hero of the age overcame Nyx,' he says, pointing to you. 'What hope did the other titans have without the Queen of Night to lead them? Majestic one, it is this mortal we must thank for the restoration of the natural order.'

Zeus gazes out from the peak across gulfs of space to the distant hills and plains of the Vulcanverse. There mortals have resumed their brief uncosseted lives under the pitiless and whimsical rulership of the gods – or so it seems. But all of the beings he is looking down on are just zombies, no more real than the marionettes of the Street of Ash. The real inhabitants of the Vulcanverse are hidden in another parallel world that lies beyond.

Zeus' glance brushes you, a sensation as if you were almost struck by lightning. 'Well done. You are a credit to your deity.'

He turns his back, and Eros draws you away out of the throne room. 'You see?' he says. 'The semblance of a world of subservient mortals is enough to keep the Olympians happy.'

'And you?'

He smiles. 'I like a world of passions raw, lusts unbridled, a place where feelings boil over and make a beautiful mess. In short, let us return to the real Vulcan City and leave the gods to their delusions.'

▶ **1667**

85

The first falls gurgling, his blood foaming into the surf around your feet. The second lunges in furiously, so eager for the fight that he slips on the dank seaweed clinging to the shore. You lean back, his sword clatters against the rock, and you smash his throat with a blow that leaves him gasping his last breath.

You are not so lucky with the third. You parry his sword easily enough. It's the burning torch in his other hand that you forgot. He presses it to your shoulder. There's a hiss, the stink of burnt flesh.

'Cry out, damn you,' he mutters, eyes wide in fear.

'Because of this? Pain is meat and drink to an Amazon.'

So saying you snap his neck. The others have had enough. On hearing you are an Amazon, they throw down their weapons and flee back to the boats.

Tick the Wound box on your Adventure Sheet unless you have the **Panoply of the Lost Hero**, then ▶ **1288**

86

The meal was as nutritious as it was flavoursome. If the Wound box on your Adventure Sheet was ticked, you can untick it. Then ▶ **232**

87

It takes all your will simply to drag yourself to your feet. You raise your hand to strike her but you are unable to act. Her mesmeric gaze is a dark green pool in which your willpower is drowning.

If either Loutro or Chipos is your current companion ▶ **1277**

If not but you have a **mirror shield** ▶ **228**

Otherwise make an INGENUITY roll at difficulty 10:

Succeed ▶ **1265**

Fail ▶ **858**

88
❑

If the box is empty, tick it and ▶ **434**; otherwise read on.

You stand beside the pyramid of green glass known as the Tomb of Hope. Locals say it existed before the city was built, and some even claim that Vulcan was unable to overwrite it when he established his own reality here.

If you have the codeword *Quill* and this box ❑ is empty, tick it and ▶ **640**

If you have the codeword *Quill* and the box was already ticked ▶ **1279**

Otherwise you see only your own shadowy reflection in the dark vitrine surface.

▶ **325**

89

'We're sitting ducks here,' says Ancaeus, his face taught with urgency. The ship is swaying on the wind, incredibly floating fifty metres above the ground, but seems unable to make headway.

'So let's get going.'

'I second that!' bellows the Minotaur as he swings his axe in a huge figure-of-eight cut. Two were-creatures who had leapt from the roof are cut apart in mid-air and fall away in bloody chunks.

'Not so easy,' says Ancaeus. 'We don't have enough crewmen to do everything.' He turns and shouts to a few sailors in the rigging, 'Get the mainsail up! Helmsman, see to the buoyancy rotor – get us clear of this roof!'

Even as he says that, the *Sunrise* lurches and drops a couple of metres. Ancaeus turns back to you. 'If we lose altitude they won't even need ropes to get aboard. They can just jump down onto the deck.'

Thunder booms ominously across the sky. Directly astern along the street, your attention is caught by the gash in the fabric of space itself. It's bigger than before and a greyish-blue glow begins to flicker around the edges. In the midst of the now-blinding light, a shadowy shape is wading or clawing its way through into reality.

'It's a portal to Death's kingdom,' shouts Ancaeus over the storm. 'He's coming. Thanatos himself. We don't have much time.'

If you have either or both of the codewords **Retract** and **Remedy** ▶ 388

If you have neither ▶ 691

90

You hesitate for a moment on the edge of the shimmering pool. The streams in its depths will carry you back to Vulcan City to face – what? Nyx. Her sons, Death and Sleep. Her army of night creatures.

You have had many lives. Opportunities and adventures that no other mortal has experienced. If you have to give your life to save your people, no one can say that isn't a fair bargain.

You dive in. Beneath the glittering surface, the water swirls with patterns of faint light. You plunge deeper. A vitrine darkness closes around you. Space and time dissolve as you feel yourself being borne back on the undercurrents that flow between the worlds.

▶ 73

91

Going from street to street, you show the silk robes to a succession of storekeepers, shoppers, beggars, idlers, workmen and even a militia patrol. It takes all your social skills to coax them to talk and you have to give away strips of silk as bribes to help nudge their memory, but in a few hours you are able to trace the metal maiden's route back from Naft's warehouse to a lane in the Grumbles.

'She lives in there,' says a street musician with a monkey on his shoulder. He points to a narrow tenement building with high, narrow gables pressing against the sky.

'You're sure?'

He strokes his chin. 'Now, let me see…' You thrust the last scrap of the silken robe into his hands. He makes it into a little scarf for the monkey and adds, 'Yes. I see her come out of there most days. Lives with a guy who looks like a fox that's found the farmer's keys.'

▶ 1547

92

'You know the Street of Ash, over on the far side of town?' she says.

'I know where it is.'

'La-di-da restaurants you get over there. Much nicer than a stolen scrap of stale bread and a dollop of gravy like we have to put up with in this dump.'

'Other people's apples make a nice change, though, don't they? But I thought we were talking about Autolycus.'

'Maybe we are. Five coins for a starter, main course,

pudding, and I bet you get cheese and crackers to follow. All of it fresh produce shipped in daily from Arcadia. Man, I'm getting hungry just thinking about it. If I had any money I'd stroll over there myself.'

You nod. Obviously she's hinting at something, but having grown up on the streets it's not Dunamis's way to say anything straight out.

'I could get some lunch if I'm over that way,' you tell her.

'Do that. Oh, and you might as well have this.'

She presses a small paper envelope into your hand. You glance inside to see a handful of hard, black, gritty powder.

'Emery, isn't it? What's it for?'

'In case you need to throw a spanner in the works. You'll know when the time comes.'

She suddenly darts off down a side alley, a movement as lithe and impulsive as a wild animal bolting.

Add the **packet of emery dust** to your possessions if you decide to keep it, then ▶ **571**

93

Do you have the title **Giant Slayer**? If so and if this box ❑ is empty, put a tick in it now and ▶ **486**

Otherwise read on.

The Academy is deserted. Not even looters have been here. The lightless windows around the courtyard stand almost as a symbol of the benighted ignorance that Nyx wants to bring upon the human race.

'There's nothing here,' whispers Dunamis, feeling the same sense of daunting unease. 'Where shall we head now?'

The nearest gate ▶ **723**

The nearest tower ▶ **171**

The Avenue of the Anvil ▶ **1632**

Your mansion (only if you have the title **The Unexpected Heir**) ▶ **1257**

Your family home (only if you have the codeword *Reverie*) ▶ **1385**

The temple district ▶ **1326**

The Forum ▶ **981**

94

The stairs wind up and up. You continue until you hear Dunamis starting to drag her feet behind you.

'We're wearing ourselves out,' she grumbles, 'and we're getting exactly nowhere.'

Keep going ▶ **517**

Listen to Dunamis's advice ▶ **699**

95

If you have the codeword *Root* ▶ **250**

If not but you have the title **The Liberator** ▶ **1079**

If you have neither of those but you have the codeword *Nibble* ▶ **619**

Otherwise, if you ever found a **baby in a basket** ▶ **1452**

And if not ▶ **1336**

96

It's not like other times you've been brought back to life. A current of coruscating energy envelops you, moulding new limbs and organs. It sears and stings.

You see a crackling image of Vulcan, fading and distorting and flaring like a broken magic lantern whose light is in danger of burning out.

He glances away from an array of flickering screens just long enough to shout to you, 'The very matrix of reality is under threat. I have no more energy to spare. Don't get killed again. This is the last resurrection you'll get.'

If you were injured, untick your Wound box and then ▶ Current Location

97

You are served the finest foods, bathed and massaged with aromatic oils by well-trained servants, and you sleep on sheets of cool silk. A few days here, browsing the library shelves or relaxing in your leafy garden listening to the drone of bees, is like a tonic for the mind and body alike. If you are injured, you can untick the Wound box on your Adventure Sheet.

To store things here or retrieve them, note **515** as your Current Location and ▶ **1402**

To go out into the city ▶ **515**

98

'Ever been in the deserts west of Iskandria?' he asks. 'Lots of interesting stuff buried in the dunes there.'

You laugh. 'Yeah, old stone tablets, broken clay jars, bones of the adventurers who didn't make it...'

'Second chances too. Helps if you travel with somebody who can keep their eyes open, though.'

You chat for a little longer but Ptolemos seems distracted by his memories. You are not even sure if he notices when you leave.

▶ 806

99

A chariot veers out of the Achaean lines and veers towards you in a plume of dust. Time seems to flow unevenly. You're aware of the hurtling chariot and a figure jumping down. He's running across the advancing front, dodging chariot wheels and thundering hooves, while you stand transfixed by the tiny black fleck in the immense vault of the sky.

A jolt as the normal flow of time resumes. Your eyes make sense of that fleck — an arrow, heading straight for you. At the same instant, glancing sideways, you see the onrushing figure is Achilles. His arm is outstretched towards you. With a prodigious leap he scythes through the air, braces his foot on the still-spinning wheel of your chariot, flings himself full-length in front of you, reaching for the hurtling arrow. His fingers start to close. The shaft of the arrow is in his palm. His grip tightens. He catches the arrow in mid-flight. You hear his gasp of pain through clenched teeth as it burns his hand.

But he was a split-second too late. The impact jerks his arm back. The point of the arrow is still headed for you. Too late to dodge. Achilles deflects it just enough. It tears painfully at the corner of your eye, leaving a deep gash across your cheek right back to the jawline.

Gain 1 scar. It could be worse. You could have lost the eye.

'Apollo guided that archer's aim,' says Achilles.

If you are a worshipper of Apollo ▶ 983

If you follow another god ▶ 1327

100

A high-pitched mechanical whirring comes from the chrysalis you are carrying. It splits apart, releasing a swarm of tiny glowing beetles, each a masterpiece of craftsmanship with copper elytra and fine mica wings driven by miniature cogwheels.

The beetles zip through the air around you, moving so fast that they create a cocoon of golden light that completely encloses you. A sense of dislocation follows as you realize that the cocoon is sinking through the stone of the floor. You are carried downwards, drifting ghost-like in between the very atoms of rock until you come to rest in another chamber below the first.

If you have the title **Soul Bearer** and the codeword *Remedy* ▶ 1493

If you have **Soul Bearer** but you don't have *Remedy* ▶ 442

Otherwise ▶ 1347

101

Achilles is still furious at Agamemnon. 'Let him try to take anything of mine, that's the moment he'd get an unwanted gift — my spear in his heart, black blood spurting. The dog-faced thief. I see more action in a week than he has in the ten years of this war.'

'Few of the Achaean generals seem to have much love for Agamemnon, so why do you fight for him?'

'It's not that simple. Many of them swore an oath to support Menelaus, Agamemnon's brother, if anyone challenged his position as Helen's husband. That oath was Odysseus's idea. It came back to bite him when Paris of Ilion made off with her. Odysseus tried to feign madness to get out of coming, knowing full well we'd be away from home ten years or more.'

'So you're here on account of that oath?'

He gives you a strange, luminously searching look. 'No, I wasn't one of those who wanted to marry Helen. I love another, one not even dreamt of in those days. When I came here I was just a boy, barely sixteen years old. I've spent my whole adult life at war.'

'Then why did you come?'

'Sometimes I ask myself that.' He smiles bitterly. 'I was told: choose glory or choose long life. And I was sixteen.'

It's late. Following Achilles's gaze, you look out into the night.

▶ 572

102

As you're making your way out of the palace, she puts her hand on your arm. You glance across and see that she's got her eyes closed — which is odd, considering the crowds of officials and citizens thronging the halls here.

'Careful. You'll bump into someone. Or trip over and hurt yourself.'

She draws in a deep breath, savouring it like a rich bouquet. 'I'm just thinking how much you miss when you go about with your eyes open.'

'Exactly. Slipping on banana peels, stepping on

discarded rakes, walking in front of runaway carts, barging into angry people twice your size…'

'Listening's distracting too. There's so much to be got just from tastes and smells. That's a whole world right there.'

'Says the girl who was brought to life by a magic grape.'

'There, you see. That's my point.'

▶ **187**

103

❑

If you do not have the codeword *Reverie* and the box above is empty, put a tick in it and ▶ **1190**; otherwise read on.

You are on a broad marble thoroughfare lined with temples. The temples are monuments to the grandeur of the Olympian gods. They stand on a sweeping crescent that connects two of the main thoroughfares of the city, majestically aloof from the surrounding buildings and of a cyclopean scale calculated to instil awe.

Which will you enter?

The temple of Apollo, the Shining Hero ▶ **510**

The temple of Athena, Goddess of Wisdom ▶ **374**

The temple of Ares, God of Strife ▶ **788**

The temple of Artemis, Goddess of the Hunt ▶ **409**

Or continue on your way:

To the Avenue of Subsolanus ▶ **625**

To the Street of the Sun and Moon ▶ **1324**

104

You find the bench, but there is no sign of Ptolemos. A woman is pulling up weeds by the side of the path. You ask her if she knows him.

'Old blind man? Scars down his neck?'

'That's him.'

'I remember. He used to come and sit here every day when I was a girl. Always reminiscing about the wars. He used to scare me at first, but later he'd ask me to describe the flowers and you could see him painting a picture in his head. Fancy you knowing about him. You look too young.'

'I don't understand. I wanted to tell him something.'

She straightens up, still holding her trowel, and gives you an odd look. 'He died years ago.'

Lose the codeword *Ripple* and ▶ **806**

105

The reply comes like a pulse beating inside your head: 'If you have been swept and stranded by the tides of time, perhaps it is because your destiny has brought you here.'

'But you must have planned it, surely?'

'You can go back, if it is your wish. Or you can wait and see if fate has greater plans for you.'

'I must stop Nyx. She –'

'The quickest road is not always the straightest. You must decide. Will you be sent back now, at once, or hold on here in the mythic past?'

What will you reply?

'Send me back now.' ▶ **792**

'I'll wait.' ▶ **179**

106

❑ ❑

Tick the next empty box above.

Just ticked the first box ▶ **632**

Just ticked the second box ▶ **508**

Both boxes were already ticked ▶ **1600**

107

Try a CHARM roll at difficulty 7. If you succeed ▶ **740**

If you fail, read on.

Either you'll have to kill him (▶ **1586**) or you'll have to relinquish the **fish-headed standard** (in which case delete it from your possessions and return to the city ▶ **555**).

108

You kick out blindly and hear the satisfying crunch of bone. The lycanthrope gives a yelp and releases its grip. Striking out at the nearest vampire, your blow caves in its mouldering rib cage. It shows no sign of pain but the impact throws it back. You plant your foot on its shoulder and launch yourself up around the curve of the dome.

Slipping and skinning your shins, you claw your way to the top. From here you can see the whole city cowering under the fury of the storm. Across the rain-lashed roof, converging on you from all sides, the hellish rabble of night creatures surge around the base of the dome like a dark tide.

And beyond them, vast and terrible against the roiling clouds, comes Thanatos, the angel of death with his sword that even the Olympians fear.

If you have the **wings of Icarus** ▶ **193**

Otherwise ▶ **755**

109

'Doesn't everyone know that? Helen of Sparta ran away with an Ilionic prince. Or perhaps she was abducted; that's a detail. The complication was that she was already married, and her husband was the Menelaus – the brother of Agamemnon, the high king.'

'And he's ordered you all to go to war over it.'

Odysseus snorts. 'Order us? We're kings in our own

right. No, somebody was too clever by half. To stop all Helen's many suitors from causing trouble once she wed, this busybody said we should all swear to defend her husband against any who tried to take her away. Well, that came back to bite us when she was bundled off to Ilion. Now we've been fighting here for nearly ten years and not seen our homes and loved ones in all that time.'

'You must be so pissed off at the guy who suggested the mutual support pact.'

'Every time I look in the damned mirror.'

Ask if Achilles was one of Helen's suitors ▶ **1331**

Talk about something else ▶ **204**

Continue on your way ▶ **735**

110

'This little gadget will soon shut them up,' you say, patting the box on your belt.

'Don't rely on it too much,' cautions Eos. 'It can only be used a few times. In any case, there are worse things awaiting you than the Celedons.'

No more delays – you need to get going ▶ **90**

Ask what she means ▶ **1105**

111

If you have the codewords **Ruffle** or **Rabbit** but do not have the codeword **Reef** ▶ **527**; otherwise read on.

From a period of complete nonbeing you drift into darkness. Sounds, shapes, colours loom and fade. Gradually your senses begin to filter the surroundings through a semblance of consciousness. A hum emerges, a harmonic oscillation like a gentle electronic heartbeat. Voices sharpened by hard metallic surfaces.

'The template is stabilizing.'

'Delete recent history, reinitialize operating parameters at standard values.'

'Reset complete. What about associated objects?'

'Retain them. No, wait. Delete currency objects. If we leave those it could mess up the economic modelling.'

Lose all pyr and cross off your companion, if you had one, but retain your possessions, blessings, codewords and titles. You can untick the Wound box on your Adventure Sheet. Unlike resurrection in other books, there is no need to add a scar.

'Subject is ready for reification. Is there a preferred insertion point?'

'Access its neural patterns, run a simulation. In effect, just ask it where it wants to go.'

Where *do* you want to go?

Arcadia ▶ **500** in *The Wild Woods*

Boreas ▶ **500** in *The Pillars of the Sky*

Hades ▶ **500** in *The Houses of the Dead*

Notus ▶ **500** in *The Hammer of the Sun*

Vulcan City ▶ **1642** in this book

112

If you have the **sceptre of Agamemnon** and you don't have the title **Witness of the First Dawn** ▶ **796**

Otherwise ▶ **1163**

113

'From an alchemist I have obtained a potation…' His eyes flick evasively to the side.

'A potation?'

'A decoction, if you prefer. A tincture of certain herbs. It slows the heart to the point that even a doctor might take you for dead. Reposing here in the bed beside my wife, your dream-self uncoupled from the mortal clay, you will be able to follow her path into the dreamlands and bring her back to me.'

He waits for your decision, his expression caught between patrician haughtiness and broken pleading.

'All right, I'll do it.' ▶ **423**

'No, I'm not interested.' ▶ **515**

114

There's a blinding flash of lightning followed by a peal of thunder that shakes the house. In that instantaneous white blaze, an image is stamped on your vision that will haunt you forever. You see the vampire now as she really is – not a pale and beautiful woman, but a rotted corpse with maggots writhing in her pock-marked cheeks and lustreless eyes that leak brown slime. Clammy strips of dead flesh hang from her bones. Her appearance before was an illusion born of dream, but now your eyes have been opened to full wakefulness and you must confront the true horror.

She lurches forward, swollen grey fingers reaching for you, her lipless teeth clacking eagerly. Make a STRENGTH roll at difficulty 10.

Succeed ▶ **946**

Fail ▶ **866**

115

The Minotaur hears you running up behind him. Pivoting on one foot, he spins around, seizing you bodily and lifting you off your feet. 'Oh no,' he bellows. 'I'm not going to let your grandstanding spoil my one noble gesture.'

'What are you doing? Put me down!'

'You bet I will. I'm expendable, hero, but you've got a bigger job to do.'

He flings you back into the glowing pool. The last thing

you see before the water closes over your head is the howling horde pouring over him, engulfing him as a wave engulfs a lone swimmer.

The gleeful shrieks of Nyx's minions are cut off as watery darkness closes around you. Space and time dissolve as you feel yourself being borne back on the undercurrents that flow between the worlds.

► 73

116

Lose the codeword *Robber* unless you also have the codeword *Recursive*.

One of Zinc's men brings you the stolen purse a few hours later. 'Don't make a habit of being a do-gooder, eh?' he says. 'It's bad for business.'

The purse contains 50 pyr. If you decide to keep it, add it to the money on your Adventure Sheet. Or you can return it to the young man who was mugged.

► 806

117

A bell-like voice calls to you through the charred skeleton of a fire-gutted ruin. The figure moves closer, past the flames still licking over the building's timbers, and molten light and shade splashes over her golden frame. A face of terrible inhuman beauty floats out of the darkness. As she advances, the sustained note of her voice begins to change from a sweet clear chime into a discordant shriek.

'A Celedon!' gasps Dunamis.

If you have the **voicebox remote** and want to use it ► 77

Otherwise you can make a run for it (► 1176) or stand and fight (► 1303).

118

'Consider the impermanence of death,' she says. 'A body may be slain, but if strong passions linger that is not the end. So it was for the nameless wanderer they call the Hero of Temesa. He came to the city long ago, and in a drunken madness he attacked a girl. Her brothers caught him and stoned him to death, but this stranger was a creature of brooding resentment who hated the people of the city. His spirit returned in the body of a wild beast and slaughtered many – not only those who had murdered him, but their neighbours too. Finally the citizens came and asked my predecessor what could be done, and through her lips the god told them to build a shrine to the vengeful ghost and make an offering to it every new moon.'

'What kind of offering?'

'A comely maiden. There is a ritual in which she is

"wed" to the ghost and left inside its shrine.'

'Where is this shrine? Not here in the temple?'

'Of course not. The creature is evil. To propitiate it here would be an act of gross profanity.'

'So where?'

'You wish to exorcize the ghost? Then your destiny leads you to the Street of the Winds.' She gestures for you to leave.

► 510

119

The topiary avenue forms a kind of bower, an avenue of grass leading to a pavilion that gleams against the darkening sky.

If you have the **heart of oak** or the **heart of ash** ► 1097

If not ► 738

120

You'll need to make both a powerful leap and a your mightiest blow. Attempt two rolls, STRENGTH and GRACE, both at difficulty 11.

Both rolls are successful	► 1095
Either or both fail	► 1179

121

'Wait! You don't realize – I've got control of Vulcan's matrix. Once we've dealt with Nyx we can reshape the world however we see fit. Mortals won't need to bow down to the gods anymore.'

For once Daedalus actually looks impressed. 'I really want to see the look on Zeus's big fuzzy face when he hears about that. All right, so what are we waiting for?' He reaches into the hatch and pulls out a bag full of strange devices. 'I've got some gadgets here that make Zeus's thunderbolts look like pea-shooters.'

'This is it, then,' you say, surveying your forces. 'It's too bad we don't have a catchy rallying-cry.'

'Don't worry about it,' says Daedalus. 'The poets will make something up when they sing about this day.'

► 804

122

'Ah, it's you,' says a portly figure you've never seen in your life. Holding his robe bunched up in his hands, he hurries across the courtyard to accost you.

'Eh?'

'Are you you?'

'Of course.'

'*Quod erat demonstrandum.* Now, enough chit-chat. This

is serious. We have lost three philosophers of the peripatetic school. Peripatetic – that means they like to walk around while they're pondering a problem.'

'And they've just, what, vanished?'

'They must have got lost in thought and just wandered off.'

'A constant risk, I suppose.'

'Quite so. Anyway, we'd like you to bring them back.'

'Where would I find them?'

He blinks. 'If I knew that, they wouldn't be lost.'

Get the codeword *Razor* and ▶ **1544**

123

A grey dawn filters into the alcove. Consciousness seeps back sluggishly. Every inch of you is scratched and bruised, and when you try to get to your feet you are almost felled by a wave of nausea and pain. You have taken a hard pummelling and will bear the marks for weeks to come.

Stumbling to the door, you hammer at it until somebody comes with the key. The flood of daylight stabs at your eyes. Or is it shame that sends you scurrying into a corner to hug your knees, shivering, until the landlord brings you some breakfast?

'Guess you saw him then. The Hero.'

Your voice is hoarse, though you don't remember screaming. 'Tougher… than I thought.'

'At least you're alive. And still got your wits. Better than any girl who's been through that before you.'

'So you'll go on appeasing the monster? Month after month, a new helpless unfortunate?'

'Don't think I like it, do you? I count the days till a champion turns up who can throttle the fiend and send it back to whatever unholy pit it came from.'

▶ **764**

124

Simple relaxation does not come naturally to you. When you are at home, you find the sense of comfort and security chafes on your nerves until you want to scream. Having your family around you, much as you love them, saps your strength. You would rather be out in the dark, maze-like warrens of the city's criminal quarter, where danger is a taste on the air and any corner might conceal a threat. Only then do you feel truly alive, your blood quickening with the promise of strife and violence. Despite your youth, would-be muggers have only to see your wolfish smile and sharp eyes to back away in search of an easier victim.

'That one belongs to the wild lord,' you hear one gang member mutter to another.

You stride boldly up to them. 'Who is that who claims to own me?'

He laughs, but not without a tremor of unease. 'Ares, the blood-stained bane of mortals. He's in your heart, youngster, and you'll know no rest this side of the grave.'

Record on your Adventure Sheet that Ares is your god, then ▶ **452**

125

The monster shudders and thrashes as your thrust splinters its thorax. Its mandibles open and close with a rattling noise before seizing up like a broken piece of machinery. Twitching, it sinks to the ground and lies still.

▶ **143**

126

Grinning, Ancaeus slaps you on the back. 'So you've come to your senses. Good. Let's get back to the *Sunrise*.'

You escort Eos to the edge of the island where the ship is moored. She moves with faltering steps at first, but soon picks up the pace.

'It's been a long time since I walked on solid ground,' she explains.

Ancaeus laughs. 'I don't think anyone could describe the deck of a ship that way, goddess, but you'll get your sea legs in no time.'

The crew have filled the water barrels and repairs are soon complete. As they come back aboard they look in awe on the slim figure of Eos standing in the prow.

'None of the usual griping and swearing, you notice,' Ancaeus whispers to you. 'I think having a goddess on board is going to bring us good luck.'

Are you determined to abandon the Vulcanverse to its fate and seek new worlds with Ancaeus? If so ▶ **379**

If not ▶ **297**

127

You are falling, spinning, hurtling through howling darkness. Images loom in front of your eyes and then are snatched away. A ritual on a dried-up river bed. It seemed hopeless, just a child wishing something wasn't so, but then came the tang of storm rain and a surging torrent that swept across the land and made it green again.

Now an image of the glorious city by the bay. Ships with blazing sails. Sunshine turning the sea to a billion diamonds. A paradise coveted by brutish raiders, damaged and fire-blacked by war, until new scenes flash by that show it rebuilt, grander and more magnificent even than in days of yore. A place more beautiful to you than Olympus.

Now a balcony with views across the city. A cool breeze up off the harbour. Dark marble floor and pillars fired with honey light. The rustle of silken robes. A voice:

'Sister, as I was made, so you can be made again. As you restored the land, the goddess now restores you. Return to the living world, reborn, and sweep away the dark queen's evil. She is twenty centuries of choking dust. You are the flood that brings hope.'

Lose any blessings or benisons, with the exception of Demeter's permanent blessing if you have it, and then ▶ 73

128

'What are you doing?' growls the slaver. 'Come on, help me roll this carrion into the water.'

'Might have something worth keeping,' whines the dwarf, patting your pockets. He strips off your knapsack and starts pulling out items. 'What's this? Ooh, it's all slimy. Heh heh.'

He's holding a long rubbery tube that coils and twitches of its own accord. The tentacle that you lopped off in the swamps of Hades.

'Give me that, you disgusting little cockroach.' The slaver snatches it from him and tosses it into the water.

The dwarf's face registers petulant irritation, but a moment later that emotion is washed away by an expression of staring terror. He is pointing at something behind the slaver. 'Ah... ah...' he gasps.

You cannot raise your head, but you see a glittering silvery light and a huge shadow spreading up the brickwork of the tunnel wall.

'What is this outrage?' echoes a voice like the torrent of drain water after a flood.

The slaver turns. 'Who are you?'

You still can't see anything but that blaze of silvery light. Whoever he is talking to must have risen directly out of the sewer water.

'I am the goddess Cloacina, guardian of these subterranean culverts. And I demand to know how you dare to pollute my sacred waters with this detritus.'

The slaver shrinks back, but despite the quiver in his voice he answers firmly. 'Er... that tentacle? It's... an offering to you, my lady. And see, we also have this half-dead body that I was about to sacrifice in your honour.'

'This tentacle,' snaps the voice of the goddess, 'was cut from the kraken. It has no place in the mythology of this universe. It is an aberration.'

'But...' The slaver's courage is giving way now. 'The sacrifice...'

'You are the sacrifice!'

Thin translucent feelers shoot out, glistening in the silver glow like the pleopods of a huge crustacean. The slaver and the dwarf are seized and lifted off the floor. Their shadows sway across the wall like broken puppets swinging on a tangle of strings. Then they drop out of sight and their screams are swallowed up by the foul water.

The silvery light shrinks. You lie on the cold stone. Slowly the torch in the wall-bracket burns lower. You must get out of here or be left in pitch darkness. By sheer will rather than physical strength, you crawl up the stairs and stagger out into the street.

Delete the **kraken's tentacle** from your possessions and ▶ 571

129

Zagreus has the diadem in his lap. You take it. As you do, the thick darkness drains away. Dunamis swings the lantern beam around and it shines on the Speaker, who has jerked upright.

'You are too late,' crackles the mechanical voice. 'The world is about to be reborn in Night's image.'

Smoke starts pouring from the Speaker's joints. There are sparks, a smell of burning, and then it blows apart. Lumps of tin clatter across the dais.

Even the din of the explosion is not enough to wake Zagreus and the other syndics. The half-formed dream above him winks open its eye and glares at you balefully.

'I think we should probably get going,' calls out Dunamis.

You're already heading down the aisle towards the door. 'I second the motion.'

Note that you possess **Vulcan's diadem** and then ▶ 820

130

You lean close to the merchant's ear and explain quietly and reasonably what will happen to him if he doesn't retract his charge against Moose.

Try a CHARM roll at difficulty 8 by rolling two dice, adding your CHARM modifier (including a bonus for any one attribute-boosting item) and you need a total of 8 or more.

Genuine menace ▶ 1145
Empty threats ▶ 58

131

The dwarf is circling warily. You already know how sharp his knife is. As you glance towards him, the slave trader's hatred gets the better of him. Snarling, he raises the meat cleaver and runs straight at you.

This will take quick thinking and split-second timing. If you get it wrong you are dead.

Make an INGENUITY roll at difficulty 8.

Succeed ▶ 1449
Fail ▶ 643

They're fanning out. You notice the quick hand signals they're using to time their attacks. They remain eerily silent, entirely focussed on the business of killing you.

Attempt a STRENGTH or GRACE roll (your choice) at difficulty 11. You cannot use any items to get a bonus to the roll because you aren't carrying your possessions.

Succeed ▶ **775**
Fail ▶ **456**

Get the codeword **Roar**.

The drizzle is turning to pounding rain. You glance back from the graveyard gate and the family now look like ghosts themselves in the grey watery haze.

You look along the rain-lashed street, which is all but deserted. A few forlorn shoppers huddle under sagging awnings weighing up whether to wait out the downpour or run for home. Xechasiaris is somewhere out there in the city. But where?

Turn onto the Avenue of Ephirus ▶ **613**
Go along the Street of Knives ▶ **1617**

Achilles is not in his tent. His slaves bow deferentially, but are close-lipped as to where their master has gone.

▶ **140**

Even with your ears plugged with wax, the high-pitched shriek of the Celedons is almost too painful to bear. You strike out at them, but your mightiest blows only serve to dent their metal bodies.

Switching strategy, you aim at their joints in the hope that you can break their gears and cripple them. Attempt a STRENGTH or GRACE roll (your choice) at difficulty 14.

Succeed ▶ **582**
Fail ▶ **259**

The pain stops. You lie nerveless, limp as a shipwreck survivor pounded by storm waves before being flung up on a dismal shore. As a pall of darkness closes over the sky, Oizys begins to shriek in excitement. 'She comes! She comes! The sable liege behold of Night primeval, and of Chaos old.'

The gods turn, grim-faced, to watch as the faint red sun trembles briefly on the western edge of the world before sinking out of sight. Across the heavens comes a rush of icy blackness, twisting and thickening, pouring through the open windows of the banquet hall.

Night has come, for the first time ever, to Olympus. She towers over the wounded gods as they tower over mortals. And you see a look in their eyes that is almost inconceivable. The gods are afraid.

Ares's tension snaps into instant violence. He charges down the hall, sword swinging. Nyx spreads her arms. For a moment she stands like a lover welcoming an embrace. Then a bolt of darkness floods out of her, swatting the god of war away with such irresistible force that he smashes through the marble wall and lies with his neck at a broken angle.

Undeterred, Artemis and Apollo loose arrows. They fly swiftly to strike the night queen but have no more effect than stones thrown into a whirlwind. Twin tendrils of darkness snake out from Nyx's robes, impaling the twin gods. They fall twitching, their golden blood spreading across the metal floor.

Athena runs forward in a crouch so that the banquet table shields her from Nyx's attacks. She leaps out of cover, her face a mask of concentrated fury. For a moment it looks as if nothing can stop her spear from piercing Nyx's breast – until a yawning void opens into which Athena is sucked, as helpless as a leaf in a storm. Her flung spear grazes Nyx's arm. Blood like smoke flows from the wound, but Nyx only laughs.

Others fare no better. Hermes, Hera and Aphrodite attack together, each scoring just a glancing blow before Nyx blasts them apart. They fall butchered, severed limbs like the sculpted fragments of beautiful statues.

'Witch,' roars Zeus, summoning a thunderbolt in each giant fist. 'You only dare attack when we are already weakened.'

'Weakened? In my eyes you are already dead.'

Zeus flings the bolts. They shoot towards their target, twin lances of crackling white fire. Nyx meets them with a conjured shield of darkness. The very air screams in pain as Nyx trades coruscating attacks with Zeus and his brother Poseidon, the two standing shoulder to shoulder in a desperate last defence. The battle becomes a vortex of darkness that surrounds them all, a darkness shot with fiery blasts and the howl of twisted metal. Pressure builds in the room until you feel as if a single breath would crush your lungs.

Oizys watches through your eyes, tittering in glee. 'The deathless ones will die today!'

A final explosion sweeps you off your feet. The massive banquet table crashes down. You roll aside. A split-second slower and it would have cut you in half. Looking up from the rubble, you see Nyx standing triumphant in the carnage.

The broken and burnt bodies of the gods surround her.

'The time of the Olympians is ended,' she cries exultantly. Seeing you, she narrows her eyes. 'I expected better things of you, but I am in a giving mood and I will let you live on as my servant in the new world I am forging. Come forth now, Oizys.'

'Yes, Majesty.' Out of the corner of your eye you see a twiglike scrap of a woman dart from behind you – or inside you. She scurries nervously to the side of the room.

Nyx sways as she surveys the ruins of the hall. She is injured. Even in their debilitated state, all the Olympians fighting her together were able to inflict some damage. But still, what could you do to oppose her – even assuming you want to?

Declare yourself her loyal follower ▶ 1594

Oppose her at any cost ▶ 834

137

You hand him the **fish-headed standard**. Delete it from your possessions.

He seems surprised that you didn't fight him. Perhaps even a little disappointed. 'Well… that's the right thing to do,' he says at last.

'It's no use to me,' you say with a shrug, walking back towards the city gate.

As it was the revered standard of the Murmillones, probably it was the right thing to do. Nonetheless the story of how you meekly handed it over is bound to get out. Lose 1 Glory and ▶ 555

138

'It's you!' she says.

It's only when you hear her voice that you recognize her. Life on the streets in Vulcan City has made her leaner and sharper-featured, but there's no mistaking the girl you freed from slavery among the Gargareans.

'Dunamis! You were supposed to go straight home to Iskandria. Not take up a career as a thief.'

She gives you a wink. 'How else was I supposed to make ends meet? I got hungry, stole a loaf of bread, and I guess I got a taste for it.'

'A loaf of bread is one thing. With those rubies you could buy the whole bakery.'

Insist she gives the hairclip back ▶ 300

Let her keep it ▶ 1061

139

If Loutro is your companion ▶ 568

If not but you have the codeword *Oyster* ▶ 436

If you do not have *Oyster* but have the title **Initiate of the Tethysian Mysteries** ▶ 680

Otherwise ▶ 665

140

The morning is beautiful like a tightened bow, the soft light of sunrise as serene as the silence of a crouching lion. Across the wide plain, hazed in gold, the glorious walls of Ilion already seem half unreal, a sad mirage from the world of myth.

If you have the codeword **Ramrod** ▶ 465; otherwise read on.

'Oh, what a day, eh, Amazon?' says a soldier as he walks past towards the waiting chariots. 'What a lovely day. Will you be fighting with us?'

Get yourself ready for battle ▶ **727**
Just watch from the sidelines ▶ **823**
Take a closer look at the armour ▶ **306**
Speak with Achilles ▶ **766**

141

The story is a dramatic one. The goddess Demeter has come to the mortal world to search for her daughter, who has been abducted by the god Hades. The marionette depicting Demeter is bigger than all the rest, but when she stoops and puts on a shawl the audience understands that she is using a glamour to disguise herself.

Taken in by a poor cottager and his wife, she does various chores around their farm with her divine magic. A lot of comedy derives from the couple always just missing the clues that show she has supernatural power.

Their baby son, however, discovers Demeter is a goddess. Taking a shine to him, she holds him over a fire — which is cleverly represented by fluttering strips of red and yellow paper — to burn away his mortality. The couple discover her doing this and think she is trying to murder the baby. They try to wrestle him away, and he ends up falling into the fire and burning to death. Demeter reveals her identity and before she leaves she turns the baby's spirit into a star that will watch over the cottage in future.

'I don't understand,' shouts a youngster as the curtain falls. 'Is that the end? Did she find her daughter? Aren't we going to get a scene in the underworld?'

'Everyone's a critic,' remarks the man standing next to you.

Some of the audience leave some money in a box in front of the booth. You can do so if you wish.

▶ **232**

142

By now there's a milling throng of pursuers pressed right up to the edge of the roof. Through curtains of slashing rain you can see the pallid, worm-gnawed faces of the vampires, the red eyes and spittle-flecked jaws of the were-creatures, the misshapen features of capering nightmare demons. Shrieking and snarling, they are so intent on getting to you that some even get jostled over the edge and fall flailing to the street far below.

There's a commotion at the back of the horde, near the stairs up onto the roof. Some of the rear ranks are turning in confusion. A vampire falls, a spear protruding from its chest, and disintegrates in a tattered cloud of dust and rags and old bones. A slim hand reaches out, pulls back the spear, and swings it in a wide arc to keep the nearest monsters at bay.

As the rabble parts you see a lithe figure in studded leather armour. In one hand she has the spear, in the other a sword that's already slick with blood. Behind her are a band of stalwart fighters, each holding their own against the night creatures that come rushing and snapping at them from all sides.

'Zoë?' You turn to the Minotaur. 'Look there! It's the daughter of King Midas.'

The Minotaur chops a leaping were-ape off the ship's rail. 'A little helping hand can't hurt,' he grunts.

You shout a greeting. Zoë is too far off to hear you over the raging storm, but she sees your look of recognition and raises her hand in salute. You don't know what has brought her here at this moment, or who her companions are, but you'll take all the help you can get.

Her surprise attack has divided the monstrous horde. Half of them turn to fight Zoë and her men. Others are still leaping from the parapet trying to get aboard, but her arrival has bought you some time. Should you stay to help the Minotaur repel boarders, or go to help get the buoyancy rotor working before the *Sunrise* loses any more height?

Stay at the rail ▶ **761**
Help with the buoyancy rotor ▶ **1220**

143

The rain is spattering down now in fat cold drops from an inky sky. The grass looks like long undulating wet hair that glistens darkly in the dull storm-light.

A slow handclap from one end of the patio draws your attention to the big bearded man who spoke to you earlier. 'I knew those bugs wouldn't give you much of a fight. Just warming up, eh?'

▶ **1263**

144

'I was high in the mountains of north-east Boreas,' begins Kazala, 'where I had come seeking the fabled cyclops. But when I looked up and saw it outlined against a frost-bright sky awash with stars, I knew that it was far stranger and more mysterious than I could have imagined. And so began the most thrilling escapade of my career.'

She goes on to relate a story of a deserted citadel high in the mountains, where automated servants swept and cleaned but no life stirred. A flashback to the western Badlands of Notus involves her stalking a cockatrice, slaying it in battle, and draining its blood to use as an antidote for sickness and poison.

You hardly listen to the rest of her tale as you're trying to concoct an equally enthralling yarn from some of your old adventures. Make a CHARM roll at difficulty 10. You can add an additional +1 to your dice score if you have a Glory of 10 or more.

Success means that the audience likes your story best ▶ 1195

Failure means that the applause they give Kazala is louder ▶ 1119

145

A sharp, horn-hard forelimb drives towards you. With a desperate effort you twist out of the way, but not quite fast enough. The spiked claw tears a lump of flesh out of your arm. You stagger, pain washing in blurry waves across your vision.

If the Wound box on your Adventure Sheet was unticked, put a tick in it now and then ▶ 1047

If you were already injured, you sink to the ground as your blood spills out ▶ 666

146

If you have the codeword *Oyster* ▶ 939

If not ▶ 118

147

Even before you meet Death's stare, you sense the hideous energy crackling within the shadows of the cowl. There is a sharp taste on the air as of storms and searing heat.

If you have the codeword *Recursive* ▶ 395; otherwise read on

If you have the **scrimshaw hourglass** ▶ 475

Otherwise ▶ 340

148

You're knocked off your feet by the force of Nyx's blow. Your armour saved you from injury but the breastplate is now laid open, your bare flesh exposed to her next attack.

'You will not be so lucky again,' says Nyx.

She raises the sword of darkness, which writhes in her hand like a living thing. But before she can strike, lights flicker amid the ruins – more and more of them, like fireflies in the dark. The ordinary citizens of Vulcan City are emerging from hiding, filled now with hope. They come forward, marching defiantly to join your army. Your courage has given them faith that victory is possible.

Each citizen carries a candle or a flaming torch. Individually they are mere glimmers, but together they merge into a bright radiance. For a moment Nyx is distracted, shielding her eyes against the glare. But you can see that it's not enough. No more than a spark that she can snuff out with a gesture.

'Fools,' she says, 'I'll uncreate you all. You will return to the primordial clay.'

If you have the **kingslayer dagger** and want to use it ▶ 1133

If you have the **Eye of Hyperion** and want to use that ▶ 1083

If you have the **tapestry of Arachne** and want to use that ▶ 273

If none of the above but you have the codeword *Radiant* ▶ 311

Otherwise, if you have the title **Godslayer** ▶ 600 and if not ▶ 182

149

You ask Zinc if he knows the whereabouts of the master thief, Autolycus.

'Why? Got a beef with him?'

'He robbed my palace in Arcadia.'

Zinc's expression is unreadable behind his mask, making his silent scrutiny disconcerting. After a long pause he says, 'Sometimes he shacks up hereabouts with his mechanical squeeze. But I don't want him bothered. He pays his dues in return for my protection. Seeing as he's the greatest thief of all time, it's a good income and I won't be happy if anything happens to jeopardize that.'

If you have the codeword *Rigor* ▶ 277

If not ▶ 605

150

'Never thought you'd let feelings get in the way of the smart choice.'

Daedalus was about to lower his armour's visor and fly off. He pauses, needled by your remark. 'How do you see that?' he says.

'If I lose today, Nyx definitely wipes out this reality. She'll be undisputed ruler of the universe forevermore.'

'Right. And if you win, Zeus will step in. Same deal.'

'But that's not a dead certainty.'

'Ninety-nine percent,' he insists. But even as he says it you can see a cloud of doubt in his eyes.

'Smart money plays the odds, right? One percent chance of an outcome where we come out on top – even if it's only that, which I doubt, it's worth shooting for.'

He heaves a sigh. 'I just know this is a mistake. All right, let's do it before I come to my senses.'

He turns towards the two titans, spreads his armoured wings, and surges into the air on invisible jets of force.

▶ **804**

151

❑

Do not tick the box unless you were told to in the section you've just turned from.

The box is empty   ▶ **359**
You just ticked it   ▶ **1157**
It was ticked already ▶ **1137**

152

'I just did it to see if I could, Your Honour.'

'Like climbing a mountain? Because it was there?'

You're kicking yourself that you didn't come up with a better excuse, but now you'll have to run with it. 'I'm used to a life of high adventure, Your Honour. Saving kingdoms, rescuing those in distress, battling monsters.'

She nods. 'Boredom, then? Life in the city a bit humdrum for you?'

'Exactly. I need to keep my hand in, you see. Practice makes perfect, and a hero needs stealth and cunning as much as a strong sword-arm.'

'So assaulting the appointed officers of the city prison, that was in the nature of a workout, was it?'

'Um...'

'If it was all worth it to hone your skills, you won't mind making a contribution to civic funds.' She makes a note in a ledger. 'Fined 500 pyr. Pay up the next time you're coming into the city – or you can save your money by staying away in future.'

You are set free with the fine marked as owing. Get the

codeword *Ridge* and lose 2 Glory.

▶ **1642**

153

'How you doing?' Dunamis calls out of the darkness.

'Third row back. Hang on – seat six, right? I've got him.'

Now ▶ **294** and tick the box there before you read on.

154

A crowd has gathered around a young man standing on a overturned bucket.

'Friends!' he is saying, waving his arms as he speaks. 'Are we the subjects of a king? No. Are we the playthings of the gods? The vassals of the aristocracy? No. We are free citizens. Let us cast off the fetters of government, the shackles of worship, the bonds of serfdom. This very day I say we must declare Vulcan City to be Anthropolis. Today is the first day of the new order! Rule of mortals by mortals for mortals. Who's with me?'

A man with a squinting expression raises his hand.

'Well done!' cries the speaker.

'I just wanted to ask if you were on all day,' says the man in a querulous tone, 'or if there'd be a different speaker this afternoon.'

'Is this revolution all that urgent?' pipes up a woman with two children. 'I could do it next week, but right now I've got to get the kiddies home.'

'There isn't a king in Vulcan City anyway,' points out a park keeper who has taken some time off from sweeping leaves to listen in. 'No point in using the same speech here that you'd give in Saesara.'

The crowd starts to disperse. Still, you have noticed a few effective tricks of rhetoric that the young man used. If your CHARM is currently less than +1 you can increase it by 1.

▶ **806**

155

You wait for them go past before slipping out of the protective limbo where they could not sense you. 'Take care, mortal friend,' say the dryads as they recede back into the green. 'These foes are as nothing compared to the dangers that lie ahead of you this night.'

With that parting advice they are gone. You are once more standing between the swaying topiary hedges with cold rain gusting on your face.

The three insectoid monsters are just ahead of you. The rearmost one waves its antennae, tasting the wind, and starts to turn. You run forward and drive a killing blow through the chitin plates of its neck. The head rolls twitching across the grass. But as that one gives a dying spasm and curls up, the others dart back towards you.

Now ▶ **738** and tick one of the boxes there before reading on.

156

A roaring wind tears through the ruins. Engulfed in darkness, lit only by scattered fires and billowing red sparks, the city could be the last fragment of creation left adrift in an infinite sea of darkness.

Where are you trying to get to?
The nearest gate ▶ **723**
The nearest tower ▶ **171**
The Avenue of the Anvil ▶ **1632**
Your mansion (only if you have the title **The Unexpected Heir**) ▶ **1257**
Your family home (only if you have the codeword *Reverie*) ▶ **1385**
The Academy of Philosophers ▶ **1510**
The temple district ▶ **1326**
The Forum ▶ **981**

157

There's a sickeningly loud crack. Almost fainting with pain, unable to breathe, for a moment you think it must have been the sound of your bones breaking. But the cold trickle of oil across your legs reminds you of the flask tucked into your belt. You slip out of the snake's coils like a wet bar of soap snatched at in the bath.

Cross off the **jar of amaranth oil**, then make a STRENGTH roll at difficulty 9.
Succeed ▶ **1571**
Fail ▶ **1550**

158

'On the contrary,' says the third philosopher when you go up to him in the street, 'I am not lost. Not anymore. I was lost, for a time, but then I realized a great truth. Thinking about life is not the answer. We must simply live!'

'I can't argue with that. But have you thought it through? You're wandering the streets of Vulcan City without money or belongings.'

'What does that matter? Everything I need to enjoy life is around me in abundance.'

He reaches to take an orange from a fruit stall.

'Oi, you have to pay for that.'

He regards the stall holder with astonishment. 'So if I have no money I must starve?'

'That's how it works. Go on, shove off.'

'Oh, unjust world!' wails the philosopher. 'Take me

back to the Academy. I miss my ivory tower.'

You escort him back and are pleased to see that a baby gate has been installed on the doorway of the peripatetic school.

'Thank you for rounding up our strays,' says the philosopher who originally gave you this task. 'You're obviously a highly resourceful individual.'

Get the title **Sage Herder**. Also, if your INGENUITY is +2 or less, increase it by +1 and then ▶ **1544**

159

'Next stop the Avenue of Ephirus, then,' says the head.

'Why?'

'I refuse to answer that. I simply cannot be owned by a dolt.'

If Galatea is with you ▶ **102**
Otherwise ▶ **187**

160

You have the beginnings of an idea. There's no time to think it through. Already the armies are mustering for the final battle. The situation is desperate so you'll just have to play it by ear.

'You're not going to let Nyx rule?' you say to Daedalus.

'Obviously not, but it's less effort to let her get rid of all the other trouble-makers before I step in and take charge.'

Make an INGENUITY roll at difficulty 12.
Brainwave ▶ **809**
Coming up blank ▶ **1574**

161

The Boulevard of the Gnome has a central line of dark green cypress trees that provide shade and a cool freshness. Street-sweepers with palm-frond brooms are busy from dawn to dusk clearing away the ochre sand trodden in by merchants arriving from the land of Notus. The merchants' camels press in eagerly around the brimming water-troughs to wash the desert's dust from their mouths.

If you have the title **Favoured by Orion** and this box ❑ is empty, tick it and ▶ **1365**; otherwise read on.

To go straight to a city location that you already know about, note **161** as your Current Location, then ▶ **1432**

Or you can go:
North ▶ **333**
South ▶ **570**

162

What detail did you get wrong? Were the coins scattered in too regular a pattern? Were they too new and shiny to be in a lowlife's pocket? Did you overdo it with the lava gems? Or was it as simple as not sounding like a convincing drunk to Sakan's practiced ear? Whatever the reason, as you spring up he already has his sword in his hand.

'Mugger, eh?' he says derisively. 'You picked the wrong victim.'

'Excuse me. This is no mugging, it's an assassination.'

He actually laughs at that. 'It's going to be a slaughter, that's for sure.'

Make a STRENGTH or GRACE roll (your choice) at difficulty 9.

Succeed ▶ 1040

Fail ▶ 900

163

The cramped space and low ceiling here makes manoeuvring impossible. It is a contest of raw strength, and as the demon locks its powerful arms around you it is already hard to draw breath. Your bones and sinews begin to ache under the strain as it draws you closer to its eager, ravening mouth.

Make a STRENGTH roll at difficulty 12. You cannot use a blessing in this fight because the gods turn a blind eye to the doings of the Hero of Temesa.

Succeed ▶ 177

Fail ▶ 564

164

'I will rescue the boy!'

A bronzed, athletic fellow steps forward, throwing off his shirt to reveal an impressive gym-sculpted torso. He throws back his long fair hair, spits on his palms, grips the rope and shins up it, vanishing through the hole in thin air just as Sphikos did.

'Who was that?' you wonder.

'Actor,' drawls a man with a perpetual expression as if he's sucked a lemon. 'Really, that's his name. Actor. He's such a show-off.'

Minutes pass. No one speaks. There's a gust of chill air through the room. You catch the sharp, pungent odour of the air after a thunderstorm. At the same moment feet appear on the rope, sliding down to reveal the rest of Actor and, under one muscular arm, the limp form of Sphikos.

'He's only fainted,' says Actor, laying him on the rug. 'Stand back. Give the lad some air.'

'My dear boy,' admonishes Lady Pemphreda as Sphikos opens his eyes. 'That last trick needs more work.'

'Sorry, aunty. The thing is, the chap who taught it me disappeared just like that, so I never got to hear how to get back.'

While all eyes are on Sphikos and his saviour, you spot something else drifting down from the ceiling – a **phoenix feather**. Add it to your possessions if you decide to keep it.

▶ 1324

165

'Melt it down for the silver,' says Uncle Nicomachus, observing your interest in the coin. 'That's all it's good for these days.'

'Is beauty worth nothing, then?' chuckles Sophos. 'I would have thought a soldier like you would appreciate this coin as a memento of greater days, Nicomachus.'

'Is this an ant?' you ask.

'The insignia of the Myrmidons,' says Sophos.

Nicomachus rolls his eyes, exasperated at the interruption to the game, but he can't help himself. 'The Myrmidons were Achilles's men. Fierce, hardy, industrious and loyal. They wore black armour. Imagine looking down from the walls of Troy and seeing that gleaming horde arrayed against you.'

'What happened to them?'

'An army is nothing without its people,' says Sophos, 'and people need crops. The mighty river of Notus sustained the city of Iskandria, but when the river dried up the crops started to wither – and so did the civilization of the Myrmidons.'

'Ancient history,' growls Nicomachus. 'Now go away and let us enjoy our game.' But later, at supper, he says, 'If you're interested in the Myrmidons I could introduce you to an old army buddy of mine who spent some time in Iskandria.'

'I'd like to meet him.' ▶ 698

'Maybe some other time.' ▶ 575

166

The Achaean chariots roll out eastwards, a thunderous horde. Across the plain but drawing nearer come the troops of Ilion, the rumbling of their wheels and the shouted war-cries still faint at this distance yet swollen with the coming violence of battle.

The early sea mist has burnt off. Brilliant sunshine paints the plain. Above, a few wisps of white cloud make you think of the peaks of Olympus. Are the gods watching as these teeming armies of ants rush together yelling threats and boasts?

What's that? A dark speck out of the corner of your eye. You turn to face it.

If you have the codeword *Rage* ▶ 192

If not ▶ 99

167

'Stand there, keep quiet, and you won't get hurt,' snaps one of the intruders.

A third man steps into the room from behind you. 'Nobody else stirring,' he tells the others.

'Good.' The first man points at you. 'Our only beef is with the scum who owns this place.'

'Well,' says the remaining man, 'we are going to burn the whole house to the ground, so in fairness the servants are going to die too. But that's just bad luck.'

The man who came in after you is standing within reach. You swing your arm in a rapid arc, twisting your hips into the blow, driving the edge of your hand like a hatchet into his larynx. He had no time to react and drops choking. The others are instantly ready with knives in their hands.

You smile a predator's smile. 'You're the ones who are out of luck, gentlemen.'

▶ 1023 and tick one of the boxes there before reading on.

168

It's the third and last round. You can't hope to win now, but at least you might go out on a high note.

Do you have the codeword *Quill*? If so ▶ 935

If not ▶ 304

169

The Minotaur turns, bellows a ferocious battle-cry, and throws his axe in your direction. The blade scythes through the air, faint starlight striking a glimmering arc along its razor-sharp edge.

Catch it in mid-flight	▶ 1046
Dodge it	▶ 669
Stand your ground without flinching	▶ 382

170

'I know what endless night is like,' she says. 'That's how it feels for ever and ever before the spark of life gets put into you. Is that what you'd wish on everybody?'

'Listen to this statue putting on the airs of a living being,' sneers Hypnos. With the slightest of gestures he waves away Galatea's humanity, transforming her back into ivory. She is frozen in the act of reaching to touch your hand.

Remove Galatea from the Companion box on your Adventure Sheet. Does her fate make you change your mind about siding with Nyx?

| Yes | ▶ 236 |
| Not at all | ▶ 688 |

171

The wind throws dust and litter along the empty street. A pall of thick black smoke stings your eyes. All around you, stark in the wan moonlight, is a scene of terrible desolation.

Note **412** as your Current Location and then ▶ 549

172

You race to the stern, where the helmsman is bent over a device like a ship's compass. He prises off the copper lid on the top of the housing to reveal a spinning disk of tangled geometric lines. It makes you feel slightly sick to look at it because of how it's continually shifting, unfolding and refolding, apparently in impossible shapes.

'You have to get your head around it existing in other dimensions,' says the helmsman, hesitantly reaching towards the glowing disk with a strangely shaped spanner. 'Got much experience with buoyancy rotors?'

'That what this is? I thought I was looking at a migraine aura.'

If you have the codeword *Recursive* ▶ 1417 now; otherwise read on.

'It's out of alignment,' says the helmsman. 'See those sparks? It's dragging against the side of the containment vessel. That's why we're losing altitude.'

'So you need to adjust it? That's what the spanner's for?'

'I'm a navigator, not a handyman. How would I know how to adjust it? Brute force might do the trick.'

He lunges for the glittering disk as if it's a rare butterfly he's trying to catch in a net. There's a protesting screech as the disk grinds against the spanner head. The deck lurches under you. Arcs of disturbing light splash and play around your head.

'Little help here…' grunts the helmsman, straining with all his might to twist the disk back into alignment.

Make a STRENGTH roll at difficulty 14.

| Succeed | ▶ 1318 |
| Fail | ▶ 216 |

173

The perruquier smiles as broadly as his narrow face will allow and shows you to the door. Delete the **sulky head** and in its place get the **Face of Wisdom (INGENUITY +3)**.

'Happy now?' you ask the head.

'Much better. At last I can show my face in public. Now, let's establish some ground rules. I will answer questions about any plans you may come up with, and I advise you to listen to my advice because I am always right.'

'A little tautological, but – '

'Furthermore, I don't mind helping you wherever you go, but I abhor the regions outside the city. They are incorrigibly uncivilized. So if you insist on carrying me with you on your travels, bear in mind that I will stay in your backpack.'

'Actually, I – '

'Or whatever you carry your chattels in. And I refuse to speak other than to say yes or no. If you want a proper conversation it will have to wait until we come home.'

'Home being..?'

'Here in the city, of course. It's the only bit of the world Vulcan lavished any care or attention on. The rest of it – well, you've got a sandpit, a patch of weeds, a bunch of icy crags, and that other place we don't want to be seen dead in.'

▶ 31

174

It races forward on hard drumming legs, raising its pincers high to strike down at your head. Instead of ducking away, you throw your body directly at it, twisting in mid-air so that you hit the wet grass on your back. Momentum carries you sliding under its thorax. Thrusting up with all your strength, you burst the smaller plates of chitin there, slicing through the soft inner organs.

Fetid slime and pale viscous blood rush out in a torrent. Bracing high on its rear legs, the creature emits a horrible juddering howl and falls in a hollow clatter to the ground.

▶ 143

175

Darkness swells up from within your heart, cracking through the bulwark of your sanity in the same way that a tidal wave sweeps away a settlement's fragile man-made defences.

If you already had the codeword *Rug* ▶ 1226

If not, acquire the codeword *Rug* now and ▶ 239

176

'You can't stay here,' Ancaeus says to Eos. 'Nyx won't be content just leave you in exile now. As long as there's the threat of a new dawn she'll hunt you down.'

A frown clouds her sublime brow. 'Where would I go?'

'Go with Ancaeus,' you tell her.

'What about you?' says the Minotaur gruffly.

Good question. What will it be?

'I'm right behind you. Nyx can have the old world, we'll find a new one.' ▶ 379

'I'm going back to Vulcan City.' ▶ 90

177

Pressed up against the hot, hard, bristling body of the demon, you plunge your weapon deep into its heart. There comes a howl like the opening of Hades's vaults, a swirling rush of darkness, a smell of stagnant gas and old spilled blood – and then nothing. The Hero of Temesa is no more.

Gain the codeword **Rune** and lose the title **Walking Wounded** if you have it. Also gain 1 Glory.

The next morning, when the tavern door is unlocked, the locals are astonished to find you tucking into a hearty breakfast. In the alcove where sacrifices used to be made to the demon you have built a roaring fire.

'You'll have to repaint the sign,' you tell the landlord.

'No need to change the name,' he says, pulling you a pint on the house.

'But the Hero's been exorcized.'

'Way I see it, we've got a new one. You're the Hero of Temesa from now on.'

▶ 764

178

You race along the beach, waving your arms to alert the sentries. 'Saboteurs! They're torching the ships.'

It takes too long. By the time you've gathered a small band of sentries, thick black smoke is already billowing up from the Myrmidon ships. You lead the men past the burning hulls, orange flames licking and roaring at the dry wood. The saboteurs have fallen back to their own ships. You call for archers, but the ships are too far out. The arrows fall uselessly into the choppy waters, provoking mirth from your enemies and an even greater despair in your own heart.

At the close of day, Achilles and his Myrmidons return from battle to find their ships and supplies lost in the inferno.

'I'm sorry,' you tell him.

He shakes his head. 'It doesn't matter. I was never going home anyway. I'm just glad you weren't hurt.'

▶ 1500

179

You crouch with your head pressed to the rug in front of the altar. Eventually the priests draw back the drapes. Sunlight streams into the kiosk that is their makeshift temple. The incense fumes are swept away on a sharp brine-fresh breeze.

'You spoke to the god,' says a priest, helping you to your feet. 'So now you must know what to do.'

▶ Current Location

180

A man in a feathered cloak stalks past you with the ochre dust of Notus still on his feet. His face is extraordinary, as hard as something cured in the sun and with cactus spines driven through his earlobes, lips, and septum in the painful fashion of the desert nomads. The fetishes around his neck and pouches of astringent herbs at his belt mark him as a shaman.

He stares around him has if outraged by the very existence of the city-dwellers jostling around him on the street, then his eyes alight on the metal head slung across your shoulder. His arm shoots out like a cobra, his long tapering fingers stroking the object's cranium.

'This is a vessel waiting for a spirit to inhabit it,' he says.

'Interesting you should say that. By the way, I'm – '

'I know who you are.' He turns his gaze on you, eyes as unyielding as agate; this man could stare down the sun. 'Go west to the tower that overlooks Hades. A little to the north is an obsidian pyramid like the tombs of the kings of old. Seek one who will give the head life.'

He turns and strides off without another word.

► 570

181

A round object the size of a melon comes rolling and bouncing out of the shadows, stopping short with a hollow metallic clang against a pile of rubble. Cables unspool, releasing the globe's contents: a swarm of whirring cobalt-winged hornets with luminous eyes. As one streaks past your face you have a momentary glimpse of mechanical cogs and etched circuitry.

'Works of art, if I say so myself.'

You whirl around. 'Daedalus!'

'You didn't think I'd miss this?'

More of the metal-coiled nests drop from the ruins, opening to release angry seething clouds of the robotic insects.

'And I see you brought some… iron wasps.'

'Not technically accurate. They're a cobalt-titanium alloy.' He shrugs. 'But wasps, yeah. Don't let the small size throw you off. These are my best weapon ever.'

A cloud of a few dozen wasps snap into formation and fly like an arrow at Hypnos. He bares his teeth in a derisory grin. 'Little gnats. Is that really the best you can do against titans, mortal?' The wasps cannon into him, unleashing a flurry of tiny metal-barbed stings. 'Ah!' cries Hypnos, slapping the swarm away with his giant hand. His grin has been wiped away by a wince of pain.

'Hydra venom,' Daedalus calls out to him. 'Hurts like a bitch, I hear.'

It's unlikely that Daedalus's mechanical insects can do any real harm to Hypnos and Thanatos, but while they're having to fend off the swarms they'll be distracted from fighting back.

► 804

182

You have nothing that can overcome Nyx. For all the courage of your allies, theirs is a hopeless cause. Her demonic legions will slaughter them. Her sons will consign any survivors to eternal torment.

She turns to you. In her eyes you are no more than last niggling detail to be dealt with before her reign of eternal night can begin.

'You will not merely cease to be,' she says. 'You will never have been. Your whole life will be unmade. Such is the power of Night.'

A strand of black vapour curls towards you. There is nowhere to run. You shut your eyes. There is a moment of – what? Anticipation? Terror? Acceptance?

Then you are wiped out of existence.

► 666

183

You scramble away through the rubble. Unable to see, you trip and fall headlong but instantly you're up again. Dunamis is just ahead, the lantern bobbing as she leaps fallen timbers and clambers over walls. You keep running until the Celedon's shrill cry fades into the distance.

'I'd forgotten about those metal muthas,' says Dunamis, leaning against a lamppost to get her breath back. 'If they're loose on the streets, no wonder everybody's in hiding.'

'Yeah. Unless what they're hiding from is something even worse.'

She gives a snort of wry laughter. 'Cheery thought.'

► Current Location

184

Psyche steps out from behind a house-sized piece of machinery. She has dishevelled hair and a smudge of engine oil on the end of her nose, but somehow they only accentuate her breathtaking beauty.

'It's good to see you again,' she says, 'but we don't have a lot of time. I've been trying to abort the rebuild.'

'Pressed for time or not, I'm going to need a primer.'

She nods. 'Of course. Eros often chides me for racing ahead of everyone else. What you see around you is the workshop of the gods, the crucible in which every element of this world is mixed and shaped.'

'Vulcan's control centre, you mean?'

Psyche looks as if she's about to correct you, then catches herself. 'Near enough. Anyway, Vulcan is busy with the other gods fighting off an attack by the titans. Or he could already be dead for all I know. In his absence, Nyx gained control of the workshop and she has set it to rebuild the world in her image.'

'Thank goodness you're here to throw a spanner in the works.'

'Ah…' She winces. 'It's not quite that simple. 'Look at this dial. It shows Nyx's new pattern loading into the universe matrix.'

You gasp in shock. 'It's already at ninety percent! Hand me a wrench. I'll smash it.'

'No,' she says, jumping in front of you. 'That will destroy everything that exists. We have to wait for this build to complete first.'

'Then what?'

'Now that you've found Vulcan's diadem, I can get access to the matrix's command interface. That's why Nyx wanted the diadem. Her agents planned to seize it at the ball, but your young friend got to it first. When this build is complete, I'll use the diadem to force a reset.'

'I think I see a flaw in that plan. Once Nyx is mistress of the universe, she won't leave you alive long enough to do it.'

'You've caught up fast,' says Psyche with a wry smile. 'If I'm going to make this work, you've got to buy me some time.'

If you have the codeword *Riven* ▶ 614
If not ▶ 352

185

A metal fist catches you in the ribs. There's a sickening crack and you curl up around the blow, stabbing pain robbing you for a moment of all your strength. At all costs you have to stay conscious. If you pass out, all is lost.

If the Wound box on your Adventure Sheet was unticked, put a tick in it now and then ▶ 17

If you were already injured ▶ 671

186

The strange glow in the sky is a portal opening into the gulfs beyond the world. Taking shape from it are the figures of Queen Nyx and her hellish progeny, Death and Sleep. They step forth and at their heels, pouring in a darkling tide, come the hordes of Nyx's legions – howling beast-men, lurching undead, creatures left half-formed and gibbering, demons whose gaping maws are foaming with mortal blood.

'Run,' you say, pushing Dunamis behind you.

'Run where?' she says.

You don't look round, but you sense her slip away through the ruins. Just as well. You couldn't have answered her question. Where in the universe could she be safe if Nyx triumphs?

'The matrix of reality is almost recast,' says Nyx, gazing upon you as if you were no more than an insect to be trodden underfoot. 'My world is about to be born. You can do nothing now to prevent it.'

She sweeps her hand, and darkest night comes rushing over the city. There are no stars, no moon, not even clouds – nothing overhead now but a fathomless abyss. The wind dies away to a dead calm. This is the eye of the storm.

▶ 249

187

The Palace of the Syndics is a baroque structure of polished grey and brown stone. Barrel vaults along the front lead into a semicircular chamber built in tiers that correspond to the ever-changing factions within the government. Throughout the day the halls and passages swarm with functionaries, lobbyists and petitioners, their voices turned into an ever-present echoing murmur by the hard stone walls.

The syndics comprise a council of forty-nine members picked from the aristocracy and the priesthood. Their job is to formulate the laws that will enact the decrees of the Archons, whose palace faces this one.

None of the syndics speaks during a debate. Instead, he or she submits an argument in writing to the Speaker, a mechanical automaton that stands at the front of the debating chamber. The Speaker then reads the syndic's opinions aloud. This is supposed to prevent any syndic from using their personal charisma and oratory to sway a vote.

If your Glory is 8 or more and you have the codeword *Rhyme* or either of the titles **Repairer of Reputations** or **Informant** and this box ❑ is empty, tick it and ▶ 398

Otherwise, if you have a **hellebore flower**, a **bunch of poppies** or a **rosebud** and this box ❑ is empty, tick it and ▶ 36

Otherwise if you have Glory of 14 or more and do not have the codeword *Ritual* ▶ 942

Otherwise there's nothing for you to do here and you may as well leave ▶ 1642

188

Myletes's study is at the back of a cobbled courtyard where the air is freshened by a sparkling fountain and the hard green foliage of bergamot trees. As you enter the cool book-lined study Myletes is bent over his desk. He looks up, blinks at you with furrowed brow, then remembers to take off his reading spectacles and gives a delighted cry of welcome.

'Come in! Sit! Tell me all your news,' he says, lifting a stack of books off the only other chair in the room.

If this box ❑ is empty, tick it and ▶ 1043; otherwise read on.

If you have the **Precepts of Chiron** ▶ 1188
Otherwise ▶ 1202

189

Note **571** as your Current Location.

Then if you have the codeword *Reverie* ▶ **520** and tick the box next to the tunnel straight to hell.

If you don't have *Reverie* ▶ **1269** and tick the box there next to the tunnel straight to hell.

190

'Here in the city you will confront your ultimate destiny,' says the Oracle in a droning voice. 'Attend the masked ball at the palace of Vulcan. That is where the end begins.'

'How do I get in? Am I invited?'

'Your deity will see to that. I can tell you no more. All our fates depend on you now.'

She waves you away, back to the main hall of the temple.
▶ **510**

191

Get the codeword *Radish*.

'Where do you get this stuff from?' you ask the restaurant owner.

'A supplier called Naft the Lean. He has a warehouse near the Tower of Riches. But if you want a bottle – '

'No, thank you. I was just curious.'
▶ **86**

192

It takes you a moment to recognize it. A black dot. An arrow tilting straight down out of the sky.

'Apollo must have loosed that,' you hear somebody cry. But there is no time to say or think any more.

If you have the **Panoply of the Lost Hero** ▶ **377**

If not ▶ **1024**

193

From all around they come, the yammering hordes of night: vampires with paste-white faces like drowned corpses in the pouring rain, red-eyed werewolves whose pelts gleam in the flickering lightning, and darting hellions on their spiky bat-like wings.

They are surging up the dome. No time to bother with waxing the wings. You just have to hope the flight will be short enough that they don't seize up. You hurriedly strap them on, fixing one buckle in three. It'll have to do.

Poising like a diver on the summit of the dome, you wait for a fierce blast of wind and launch yourself off into space. Make a GRACE roll at difficulty 7.

Succeed ▶ **931**

Fail ▶ **726**

194

'About that,' says Pug, 'you know that sometimes you have to take a leap of faith? Just take a run at the edge, jump, and trust that somebody will be waiting there to catch you.'

'Got anything specific in mind?'

He shakes off his inner reverie and smiles. 'Don't mind me, I'm just a sculptor. We artists can get imagination and prophecy mixed up.'
▶ **480**

195

A misstep! You lunge, grasping desperately, but there's nothing solid to catch hold of. You're plunging down and down towards a darker mass of cloud where the mutter and flash of a storm is brewing.

Sure enough, a sheet of lightning spits out of the thundercloud. An instant of blinding white pain – and then oblivion. ▶ **111**

196

You stop for a cup of tea outside a fashionable café.

'No charge,' says the proprietor, a bald man with deep-set brooding eyes.

'That's very kind.'

'Nothing is too good for the hero of the Myrmidons.'

'Is that what they're calling me?' you say with a smile.

He wipes his hands on his apron. 'Your fame has spread even to this city. Not all would recognize you, but I was there at the battle on the inland sea. You liberated all the slaves of the Gargareans. All except one.'

You were getting up to leave, but that stops you. 'What do you mean. Which one?'

'My little daughter, sad to say.'

'She's still enslaved by the Gargareans? Impossible. The Iskandrian authorities keep a close eye on that regime.'

'Oh, I misspoke. She is no longer captive there. Physically she was freed with their other slaves, but there is not only bondage of the body. In spirit she remained cowed, trapped even when we came to safety here in the city.' His shoulders slump. 'Now she has run away. I can only hope that in time the cloud of terror will lift from her mind and she will find her way back home to me.'

'If I see her – '

He musters a hopeful smile. 'She wears a red hooded cape. About so high. She's hard to miss.'

Get the codeword *Rogue*.

To go straight to a city location that you already know about, note **515** as your Current Location, then ▶ **1432**

Or you can go:

North ▶ **222**

South ▶ **1642**

'Made for him, isn't it? Divine craftsmanship, I call it. A perfect fit – or it would be, if he ever wore it.'

'Why doesn't he?'

'What's the point? You see, before we set sail, a prophecy told Achilles he could either have a short life filled with glory or a long life of obscurity and ease. He chose to burn brightly but not for long.'

'So he doesn't wear armour?'

'Not that armour. It's supposed to be all but invulnerable. He prefers to strap on the same basic kit as his men. You can see why. The Myrmidons don't go in for pampering their leaders.'

Ask him a different question ▶ **204**

Bid him farewell for now ▶ **735**

You walk along the blue-green tiles of the Boulevard of the Undine. On either side of the street, the plaster façades of the buildings are moulded into almost organic shapes, streaked with blue and green dye, the windows bordered with seashells and crushed pearl that glint like silver coins on a submerged wreck seen half-buried in the sea bed.

If you have a **bone knife** and this box ❑ is empty, tick it and ▶ **1502**; otherwise read on.

If you have the codeword **Rumour** and this box ❑ is empty, tick it and ▶ **396**; otherwise read on.

To go straight to a city location that you already know about, note **198** as your Current Location, then ▶ **1432**

East towards the city gates ▶ **222**

West ▶ **451**

'If you're going to kill me, at least let me be the first to bow to you as King Daedalus.'

'That's how you want to go out? Really? Not fighting to the bitter end?'

'This way I get to be remembered forever, as your first subject.'

'Have it your own way.' He starts to tighten his grip on your windpipe.

'Wait,' you gurgle. 'What about your coronation?'

'Oh, I'll need time to plan that out properly. But don't worry, I'll let everyone know it was your idea.'

His armoured fingers are digging into your throat. You can't breathe. A wave of dizziness drags you into oblivion.

▶ **666**

A heavy-set man comes running across the plaza behind you. Barging through the doorway, he reaches over Dunamis's shoulder and shutters the lantern.

'Hey!' she says.

Ignoring her, he slams the door of the tower behind him, blotting out the violet nebula that was forming in the sky. You are plunged into total darkness.

'You idiot, now we can't see it!' shouts Dunamis.

Tensed for a blow from your shadow-self, you raise your hands defensively. You strain your ears but there's no sound at all.

'It's all right now,' chuckles the heavy-set man. 'It's gone.'

Dunamis slides up the shutter and in the lantern-light you recognize the newcomer. 'Sisyphus!'

'I got here just in time,' he says. 'No point in fighting your own shadow. All you needed to do was put out the light. No light, no shadow, see? Oh, am I a mastermind or what?'

'You've put on weight,' you tell him.

He pulls a chagrined face. 'Pushing that big old rock uphill kept me fit as a butcher's dog. Now all those muscles have run to fat.'

'How did you find us?' says Dunamis, ever suspicious.

'I'm smart, young lady. I was going to clear out of town. Don't need an instruction manual to tell me somebody is remaking reality, and I don't want to be around when it happens – but I knew you'd be right in the thick of it, old friend. Saving the world, that's your jam. Me, I'm off.'

'Where can you go that's safe?' you ask.

'Back to Hades, that's where. Rock-rolling's not so bad. Well, toodle-pip.'

He flings open the tower door and gives you a cheery wave as he heads off down the street.

Lose the title **Hero Without A Shadow** and ▶ 392

201

An enigmatic message directs you to a rendezvous just outside the south gate of the city. You go at dusk, trying to ignore a niggling sense of doubt.

You wait near a broken stone arch overgrown with ivy. The road at this hour is deserted. Just when you think no one is coming, there is a glitter of metal in the shadows and an armoured warrior approaches. He wears steel scale and his helmet is shaped like a fish's head with a high dorsal crest. In his right hand he grips a wide-bladed sword.

'Nobody told me it was fancy dress,' you say.

'I am a Murmillo,' he rasps. 'The fish is sacred to my people. You have no right to that standard you bear.'

He lifts the sword and you see that its edge is serrated like the sharp fin of a predatory fish. What will you reply?

'If you want it you'll have to fight for it.' ▶ 887

'You're welcome to it.' ▶ 137

202

A stabbing pain in your leg jerks you awake. All around you a pitched battle rages across the deck. The crew are fighting a swarm of thorny-armoured insects as big as wolfhounds. Snatching up a weapon, you see the Minotaur covered in green slime from the pile of insects he's killed. He's crunching one of them underfoot as he cleaves a couple more in pieces with his axe.

'What's going on?' you ask, staggering to his side.

'These fuckers came out of the hold. Luckily your pal Zoë noticed them and raised the alarm.' He glances down at the bite on your leg. 'That's got to hurt.'

The wound is inflamed and already the torn flesh is turning black. Make a STRENGTH roll at difficulty 11 to resist the corrosive venom.

If you succeed ▶ 1322

If you fail, note **1012** as your Current Location and then ▶ 670

203

You awaken to a new day. Note **1500** in the Current Location box on your Adventure Sheet.

The dawn, an opening furnace, spills molten gold along the horizon and fires the walls of proud Ilion across the plain. All along the shore, the Achaeans are mustering for battle, helmet plumes swaying in the white wave-glancing sun like an endless field of ripe corn. Hot-blooded horses are harnessed to gleaming chariots. They rear impatiently and paw the ground.

A league away, under the windy heights of Ilion's walls, another force is gathering – the legions of King Priam under the command of his son, Prince Hektor. You watch the Achaean lines sweep out across the plain to meet them, soon swallowed up in clouds of sun-blazoned yellow dust. Only the servants and slave girls are left in camp, along with a handful of sentries stationed here to guard the Achaean ships from any attackers who might manage to break through.

Like those Achaean horses you are champing at the bit, frustrated to think of the battle raging only a mile away. You can hear the shouts and the clangour of arms, the heavy rumbling of chariot wheels that rolls faintly like far-off thunder through the churned-up dust. But you are still not fully recovered from your ordeal. A brisk run along the beach will help tone up your bed-weakened muscles so that you will be ready for action when needed.

Towards midday you decide to get some exercise climbing the rocks at the end of the beach beyond the Myrmidon ships. The sun is beating down and you are soon slick with sweat. This is how to get the kinks out.

Cresting the ridge, you see three longships in the surf of a small cove. The Achaeans must have ignored this cove as there is no room to beach a large fleet. You duck out of sight, observing a squad of soldiers wading ashore with swords and flaming brands. They glance around, confer for a moment, and one leads the way towards the main stretch of beach. They must be allies of Ilion who are here to put the Achaean ships to the torch. In moments they will reach the first ships, those of Achilles and his men. The hulls, dried by years of blistering sun and salt-laced wind, will go up like matchwood.

Stop them ▶ 1428

Go for help ▶ 1626

Ignore them; it's not your fight ▶ 1310

204

Odysseus is always ready to talk to you, seemingly as impressed by your martial prowess as he is attracted to your healthy good looks. You can ask him any question below for which the box is not yet ticked – first tick the box, then turn to the section indicated.

❑ 'How do I get to speak to the gods?' ▶ 1521

❑ 'What's that strange
    armour outside Achilles' tent?' ▶ 197

❑ 'Tell me about the war.' ▶ 109

If all the boxes are now ticked ▶ 1623

205

She turns her face to you. The burning look in her eyes conveys both shame and fury. 'Whatever I become,' she says in a snarl that belies her earlier whimpering, 'it is because of you.'

She wrenches her hands away, jumps up, and darts off. As the mist swallows her it's as if a dream had ended – except that the mauled corpse still lies beside you in the wreckage of its coffin.

You grope your way to the necropolis wall and follow it round to the gate. Outside in the street, people are hurrying to their homes. All seems normal. Only you know that within the walls a lone figure prowls and preys upon the dead.

Get the codeword *Reef* and ▶ **1617**

206

You overhear a group of philosophers arguing about the concept of free will. 'It is an illusion,' maintains one. 'Our choices are determined by rules over which we have no control.'

'Not at all!' shouts another. 'I choose to refute you, but I might equally have remained silent and allowed you to keep your delusion.'

'Why should you not both be right?' says a third. 'If I am perfectly logical, I will always make the correct choice. That choice is therefore decided by an external set of rules, namely logic, but behaving logically is my conscious decision.'

In a lull in the debate, you venture a question: 'Do you know of any experiment that would show the difference between free will and determinism?'

'All things being exactly equal,' replies the first philosopher, 'a person will always make the same choice.'

'Pish and tosh,' grumbles the second. 'I might eat toast for breakfast today and porridge tomorrow.'

'But you remember having toast today,' you point out. 'That will influence your choice tomorrow. And all you are doing is asserting a point of view, not providing evidence for it. So is there any way of testing these theories?'

'Who taught you to think in this way?' wonders the third philosopher.

'Nobody taught me. It's obvious.'

'The child is inspired by the goddess,' declares another scholar who has been listening to the debate.

'Which goddess?' you ask.

'The most beauteous and wise Athena, of course.'

Record on your Adventure Sheet that Athena is your god and then ▶ **452**

207

A short, high-arched tunnel leads through from the street to the palace courtyard. Along it echo sounds of music and gaiety. The warm evening breeze brings perfume, laughter, blossom scents, song and the clink of glasses.

If Polymnia is your companion ▶ **591**
If she's not with you ▶ **941**

208

You take the butterfly carefully out of your pocket. Although made of cogs and flywheels, it is a fragile device with wings of beaten metal foil.

Do you want to send it up to the prisoner who has sent you the message?

Yes ▶ **1301** and tick the box there before reading on
Not at the moment ▶ **63**

209

The puppets are made of ivory, wood and papier-mâché decorated with sequins and bits of coloured glass. They are operated by strings, presumably run over pulleys because the stage is at the top of each booth, leaving no room for the puppeteers.

If you do *not* have any of the codewords *Oedipus*, *Olifant* or *Other* and this box ❑ is empty, tick it and ▶ **141**; otherwise read on.

If you do *not* have either of the codewords *Remedy* or *Retract* and this box ❑ is empty, tick it and ▶ **234**; otherwise read on.

If you have the codeword *Quest* and this box ❑ is empty, tick it and ▶ **1205**; otherwise read on.

If you have the codeword *Phosphoric* and this box ❑ is empty, tick it and ▶ **948**; otherwise read on.

If you have the codeword *Neverending* and this box ❑ is empty, tick it and ▶ **72**

Otherwise ▶ **1135**

210

'Are you lost?' you say to a short man in white robes who is muttering as he meanders down the street.

'I don't know where I am,' he says. 'But if you know where you are, and you know that I am here too, then I can only be said to be lost from my own subjective viewpoint.'

You resist an urge to punch him. 'You'll notice that your two colleagues are lost also. One of them I already sent back to the Academy, but the other is as lost as it is possible to be.'

'I don't think that can be true. We can conceive of a person who is completely lost, but that idealized lost individual is still located in our mind. It follows that there must exist an even more lost person in reality.'

'And where would that person be?' You briefly cling to the hope that philosophy might actually prove useful in your task.

'He or she would be in literally the last place you'd look.'

You sigh. 'Every lost thing is in the last place you look for it, obviously, because having found it you stop looking.' He starts to consider that, until you snap at him to stop thinking. 'Getting lost in thought is how you came to be lost in reality. So don't think of anything else till you get back to the Academy.'

You give him directions home and watch him till the end of the street, where he hesitates trying to remember whether to turn left or right.

▶ Current Location

211

'Have you ever spoken to any other Amazon in that way?' you ask him. 'It would explain how you lost your eye.'

His mouth drops open in astonishment. As he draws in a deep breath it seems he's building to an explosion of rage, but instead he releases it in a thunderous bellow of laughter.

'Hah, that's a spirit we could do with in our ranks,' he says, looking around him at his generals. 'See this woman? She has more guts than the whole pack of you.'

With a contemptuous sweep of his hand he dismisses the old priest, Chryses.

Follow Chryses   ▶ **1624**
Stay to speak with Agamemnon   ▶ **1529**

212

'Then come with us,' implores Ancaeus. 'We are bound for the shores on the far side of the Ocean of Night. There await new worlds beyond counting. You can be the spirit of a thousand dawns, out where your mother's anger can never reach you.'

Will you say anything to that?

'Ancaeus is right. Come with us.' ▶ **126**
'No. The world we left behind has greater need.' ▶ **1100**
Stay silent ▶ **390**

213

Remove the **copper casket of doom** from your list of possessions and get the codeword *Remedy*.

'Curious little doohickey,' says Daedalus, turning the box in his hands. 'What's this combination puzzle? Oh, I get it. The tiles are sized according to a Fibonacci series. Ingenious. So the tile to open it would be this one here.'

As he touches it there's a blinding flash. The wall slams you in the back and you slump like a broken puppet. Through falling mortar and thick black smoke you see a chink of daylight. The explosion has collapsed the ceiling. There's shouting but it seems to come from far off, muffled by a ringing noise. You cough and a hot copper-smelling

taste fills your mouth.

Dizziness and nausea give way to semi-consciousness. It's only when people start lifting broken masonry off your body that you're aware of any pain. They haul you out of the rubble and carry you to your temple. There you lie in bandages for a day or more, sipping the bitter medicine the acolytes bring you, until your senses come back. Tick the Wound box on your Adventure Sheet if it wasn't ticked already.

If you have a companion other than Tomyios ▶ **384**
Otherwise ▶ **313**

214

'Do you like it? I had it made of ivory. It's Dolos, the smiling one of tricks. He used to be Prometheus's apprentice, but there was no future in it after that business with giving fire to mortals.'

'I didn't know we were supposed to come masked.'

'It's optional.' As you go to move away, he closes a vice-like grip on your arm. 'And I'd recognize you anywhere, bare-faced or masked.'

'You have the advantage of me. I don't remember us having met.'

'Perhaps if I told you that Dolos is my half-brother? Or that my twin brother is one you have met many times, though the fact that you're here now shows that you've always refused his hospitality.'

▶ **827**

215

She moved the cups so fast, you have no idea which one the ruby is under. It's a stab in the dark. Which cup will you pick?

The first   ▶ **801**
The second   ▶ **658**
The third   ▶ **1419**

216

You wrench frantically at the disk, but it is too little and too late. The spanner shears off in your hand, part of the handle lodging against the rotor housing and slowing the spinning disk even more. The ship falters, dipping in the sky. You look up in time to see Thanatos outlined against the storm, his giant hand swinging around to splinter the hull. Crippled, its sails torn and flapping in the wind, the *Sunrise* spins out of control. It lurches to one side. Sailors scream as they are flung overboard. You cling to the wheel as the ship drops in a helpless spiral, breaking up on the ground as surely as if a gale had swept her onto rocks.

You lie stunned in the wreckage. A few people have

remained in the street, too paralyzed with terror to run. One edges nervously past where you are lying, perhaps hoping to bolt and run. Then he turns his face upwards and gives a despairing moan. Slipping on the wet cobblestones, he starts to scramble away. A sliver of deathly white light stabs down, touching him for just an instant, and he is gone. All that remains of him is a wisp of dark vapour that is blown away on the wind.

A colossal foot descends to the street beside you, landing with a tremor that dislodges bricks and sends cracks spreading through the flagstones. Painfully you rise to behold pitiless Thanatos standing like a mountain against the raging storm.

▶ **595**

217

'One of my guys, I call him Moose, got himself picked up by the White Guard. And what sticks in my craw is it was for something so petty, just 50 pyr he stole off a spice merchant.'

'Can't he stomach a few weeks in jail, then? Can't be much of a penalty for something like that.'

Zinc taps his metal chin. 'Normally, but Moose is a three-time loser. His previous convictions are a bit more serious. They'll throw the book at him this time, and Moose, he's not much of a reader.'

'What do you need me to do?' you ask. 'If it's a jailbreak, I can't see that working.'

'Of course not,' agrees Zinc. 'Not from the White Guard barracks. No, what I want you to do is confess to the crime. Take the rap on Moose's behalf. They'll go easy on you seeing as you've got no criminal record, just a short spell behind bars, and they'll have to let Moose go.'

He waves at someone over your shoulder and they come forward to pay their weekly cut. Your audience is at an end. As you walk home you ponder what you should do.

Nothing – let Moose face the music ▶ **1539**

Confess to the crime ▶ **1218**

Go and talk to the spice merchant ▶ **915**

See a friend in the White Guard (only if you have the codeword *Rhyme*) ▶ **1590**

218

'How long can we remain here?' frets the woman.

'As long as we like, my love.'

'He won't stand for it. He'll find a way to wake me up.'

The young man shakes his head. 'He doesn't dare. I bribed the Oracle to put the fear of the gods into him if he tried that.'

'Then he'll put my sleeping form out in the street,' she

wails. 'Or he'll tattoo my body with obscenities. He'll beat me where I lie and I'll feel the blows even here in the dreamlands. You don't know him.'

'I know he's a cold-hearted monster, but you're safe from him here.'

'What was that? Oh, see how I start at shadows. I feel so helpless. Hold me, my darling.'

Well, this is a surprise. Perhaps the account the merchant gave you was coloured by his own interpretation of events. Certainly it doesn't seem that the young man has taken her away against her will.

Speak to them ▶ **1639**

Attack the man ▶ **786**

219

Too slow. She steps inside the arc of your attack, slices her knife across your chest, and spins away before your blow can connect.

If the Wound box on your Adventure Sheet was not already ticked, put a tick in it now and ▶ **1349**

If you were already injured and you have any companion except Tomyios ▶ **968**

Otherwise ▶ **111**

220

'You think Zeus is the lesser of two evils?' Prometheus shakes his head vehemently. 'Mortal, you are deluded. He and Nyx are alike in tyranny. If you fight for his cause you've allowed yourself to become a pawn in their cosmic game.'

So saying, he withdraws into the sky until all that can be seen of him is a constellation dimly shining high in the heavens.

If you have the codeword *Quake* ▶ **553**

If not but you have the codeword *Pumped* ▶ **720**

Otherwise, if you have the codeword *Nanny* ▶ **1637**

Otherwise ▶ **1183**

221

'Hey, there's a couple of likely pigeons. Coo-ee!'

You turn. A gang of looters are rampaging between the dark, dingy buildings. They're dressed in a strange combination of filthy rags covered with silk gowns, furs and fistfuls of jewellery, making them look like overgrown street kids who have ransacked an expensive wardrobe.

The nearest looter comes weaving towards you, a flagon of wine sloshing in one hand. You're more interested in what he's holding in the other: a long curved knife.

'We'll have your money, then,' he says as the others fan

out around you. He picks with the tip of the knife at the buttons on Dunamis's jerkin. 'Might take payment in lieu, if you catch my drift.'

So the survivors of the cataclysm are giving in to fear and selfishness. You might have expected it. That's what night does, awakening men's darkest fears and most bestial nature.

'Get off, pig!' shouts Dunamis as the gang leader slices away her top button.

'Oh, now that's not very nice, is it?' he says. 'Might have to scrub your mouth out, using language like that.'

If you have the title **Local Hero** ▶ 871

Otherwise you can reason with them (▶ 892) or you can fight (▶ 554).

222

❏

You are at the North Gate. If you do not have the codeword **Reverie** and the box above is empty, put a tick in it and ▶ 433; otherwise read on.

If you have the codeword **Ridge**, note 222 as your Current Location and ▶ 1064; otherwise read on.

Between colossal pillars of cedarwood trundle carts bearing timber, meat, grain, wine and herbs from the lush woods and fields of Arcadia. As each cart enters the city, its contents disappear to be replaced with a glowing quantity of pyr which its owner can use as cash.

Beside the teeming thoroughfare is a noticeboard on which are posted missions to be undertaken by those who are willing to take risks.

To go straight to a city location that you already know about, note 222 as your Current Location, then ▶ 1432

Otherwise you can take a look at the noticeboard, in which case note 222 as your Current Location, then ▶ 56

Or you can go:

West along the Boulevard of the Undine ▶ 198
South along Septentrional Avenue ▶ 515
East along the Boulevard of the Undine ▶ 970
North out of the city ▶ 804 in *The Wild Woods*

223

Make an INGENUITY roll at difficulty 12.
Succeed ▶ 1580
Fail ▶ 642

224

Beyond the courtyard, visible through a wide archway, there is a rotunda surmounted by a gilded dome that blazes furnace-white against the evening sky. Further on, water sprays up from a fountain sculpted like the raised fingers of a giant hand.

Take a look in the rotunda ▶ 1530
Go over to the fountain ▶ 489

225

The caretaker shows you into a room at the very top of the house. It is sparsely furnished but with tables and chairs that gleam with the beaten golden metal that covers them. The walls are painted white to make the most of the light that penetrates the narrow gable windows.

'At least you can see the sky up here,' you remark, glancing out across the closely-packed rooftops of the Grumbles.

'That's what I tell him,' wheezes the old caretaker, recovering from the climb. 'He should pay more rent for this room, even if it is right up in the attic. He could afford it, too. Look at these fancy bits and pieces. You ever hear of a gold-topped table? And that metal chair. There's avant-garde and then there's plain uncomfortable.'

'It can't be real gold, surely?'

'Fake gold, he calls it. Just copper, brass and zinc, he says. But even so he can't be short of a coin or two, can he?'

Have a look around ▶ 773
Sit and wait for Autolycus to return ▶ 922
Leave and watch the house from a distance ▶ 603

226

You shrug, having no logical answer to give her. 'There has to be justice, as the saying goes, even if the heavens fall. Also, you saddled me with that spiteful termagant chowing down on my viscera. You bet I want payback.'

She shakes her head, beginning to turn away even as tendrils of smoky darkness reach from her robes towards you. As the tendrils pass through the wreckage from the table, metal goblets and broken chunks of stone evaporate into nothingness at their touch.

'You will not merely cease to exist,' murmurs Nyx. 'You will be expunged from reality. You will never have been.'

A black tendril curls towards you. Backed against the wall, there is nowhere to run. You shut your eyes.

The sound of a sword slicing through the air. A hissing like a white-hot poker plunged into a water bucket. You look up to the window, where a mighty figure stands in a defiant pose, sword in hand, great wings outstretched behind him. A golden aura flickers around his blade as it sucks in the fumes of the severed tendril.

'Eros!' laughs Nyx. 'You'd do better not to interfere, my boy.'

'Given all the abandonment issues, mother, it feels like my fight too,' says Eros, stepping down into the room.

'And I didn't come alone.'

A giant figure strides down from the ink-black sky outside. His naked frame is as big as Nyx herself. 'I said I would come when you needed me,' he says to you, his voice booming like thunder, 'and Prometheus keeps his word.'

So saying, he steps forward to stand shoulder to shoulder with Eros.

If you have the **Eye of Hyperion** ▶ 919

If not but you have the **kingslayer dagger** ▶ 1138

Otherwise ▶ 1440

227

'You know the child of whom I speak,' says the Oracle.

'Yes, but I fail to see – '

'In saving her you have entwined her future with yours. She is now as much an instrument of fate as you are.'

'Is that what I am? The instrument of fate?' You smile uncertainly.

The Oracle seems to look right through you. 'Go now. Reflect on what I've told you.'

Bowing, you return to the outer temple.

▶ 510

228

As lightning splinters the darkness outside, there's an answering flash of light from the corner of the room. It's where you left the shield propped against the wall. Tritona casts no reflection in its surface. That doesn't come as a surprise – vampires are widely known not to appear in a mirror – but what you can't at first understand is why you cast no reflection either.

A second flicker of lightning reveals the truth. Your image is there, but it's the reflection of you lying in your bed. You're still asleep. The you that is standing in front of Tritona is just your dream-self.

You can't attack her. Those glowing green eyes prevent you taking even a step nearer. Instead you throw yourself back to the bed and pull away the sheets, willing yourself to wake up.

Sleep peels away from you like an entangling net. With a mighty effort you surface from slumber and jump up – the real you, now – to face Tritona.

▶ 114

229

You are eating lunch at a street food stall when a man sits down at your table. You look up into world-weary eyes that are watching you with calm professionalism. He is bald, short but taut-framed, with a battered, sun-blistered face that speaks of a man who has seen a lot of action.

'Zinc'd like to see you when you have time,' he says in a gravelly, offhand tone that sounds uninterested to the point of boredom.

'Or what? You going to drag me there, old man?'

'Do I look like I'm packing a weapon?'

You shrug, ladling more chilli syrup onto your waffle. 'Maybe you should, given the neighbourhood.'

'Anybody gives me any trouble, I take their weapon off them and show them how to use it.' He gets up and starts to walk away. 'You coming?'

Go with him to meet Zinc ▶ 675

Not right now ▶ 1425

230

'There's something you don't know,' you tell him. 'I already hacked Vulcan's matrix.'

He throws you a startled look. 'Even if that's true, you're not going to be able to do much while I've got my fingers around your windpipe.'

'Your mistake, genius, is thinking everybody's a fool. I left somebody in charge of the matrix for me. You think you've got me. Truth is, I've got you.'

Tell the Face of Wisdom to deactivate Daedalus's armoured suit ▶ 445

Or melt it ▶ 1174

231

Ancaeus stands at the prow and casts an eye around the deck. Satisfied that everything is squared away, he summons the crew around him.

'Comrades! You have endured perils without number to be here. Now, while breath remains to us, let's forge on into the unpeopled universe that lies beyond the sun.' He sweeps his arm at the dark void that lies ahead. 'Sons of heroes, that's what you are – not born to live like brutes under the heel of the titan queen. No, your fate is far more glorious. Together we'll make a new life of hope and virtue at our journey's end.'

'Are you telling us there'll be no weevils in the ship's biscuits, skipper?' calls out one man, provoking high-spirited laughter.

'There's better than biscuits ahead of us,' cries Ancaeus, grinning. 'Wine and feasting, boys! I'm talking about the chance to begin again in a golden land of opportunity.'

With that he dismisses them. Murmuring excitedly, they go back to their duties with rekindled enthusiasm.

'Good to give them a little pep talk after what they've been through,' you say to Ancaeus as he comes over to join you.

'Yes, it was a close-run thing back there. Still, we came

through it. Just a little damage, easily repaired. Now we're on the Ocean of Night, nothing can catch us.'

You nod. 'That breathing space will help. We're going to need a base where we can rally forces to oppose Nyx.' You call to the helmsman, 'Plot a course for Iskandria. We can enlist the Myrmidon army on our side.'

'Belay that order, helm!' snaps Ancaeus. 'Hold her steady for infinity.'

You're puzzled. 'But what's the plan? Recover our strength and launch a surprise attack? Pick up some allies? We can't do that out here in the void.'

'Weren't you listening to what I told the crew?' says Ancaeus, shaking his head in amazement. 'We're not going back.'

Maybe he's right   ▶ **1107**
No! You must return and face Nyx   ▶ **1486**

232

You are on the Street of Ash. Fresh scents of green leaves and blossoms dispel the usual dusty smells of the city, for on the south side of the street are the railings that look out over a wide expanse of nemoral parkland. The park is known as the Groves of Dionysus.

Along the street you pass leaf-shaded shops and restaurants. The many fountains freshen the air and make this a favourite spot for outdoor entertainment, including a number of puppet-show booths and street musicians.

To go straight to a city location that you already know about, note **232** as your Current Location, then ▶ **1432**

Watch a puppet show ▶ **209**

Eat at a restaurant (costs 5 pyr) ▶ **800**

Visit the house of the inventor (if you have the codeword **Retract**) ▶ **1553**

Or you can go:

North-east to the watchtower   ▶ **48**
South-west to the Forum   ▶ **1642**
Into the Groves of Dionysus   ▶ **806**

233

As you hurry along the rubble-strewn street, a slight figure darts nimbly out of a doorway to join you. She holds up a lantern to show you her face. It's Dunamis, the gamine street thief.

'Thought you might have skipped town,' she says. Her tone is nonchalant, but from the way her eyes keep scanning the shadows you can tell she's on edge.

'The old place sure has changed while I was away. Which was how long, incidentally?'

'Huh?' She tenses at something in a side alley. 'False alarm, it's just a cat. What do you mean, how long? I just

saw you a few hours ago.'

'You mean – '

'Keep moving. There are patrols sweeping through all the time.' She tugs at your sleeve.

'You mean all of this – the whole city in ruins? That only took *a few hours?*'

Dunamis shrugs. 'Maybe. It's hard to keep track of time now. A priest back there, he said this is the eternal night. It's going to spread over the whole world and we'll never see another day.' She looks at you, all her streetwise bravado swept away for a moment so she just looks like any dismayed young girl. 'What do you think? Is that true? It's all over?'

'Not a chance. Nyx is a force to be reckoned with, sure, but she's made one big mistake.'

'What's that?'

'She left the two of us alive.'

▶ Current Location

234

The play concerns a prisoner in a garret cell who spies on the people outside the prison and, amid many sighs and occasional banter with his guards, discourses on the nature of freedom. There is also a puppet who may be the prisoner's daughter who sends him messages tied to a butterfly.

The puppeteers have a reputation for weaving interruptions into the story. When a portly child starts giggling, the prisoner asks one of his guards, 'Are you keeping pigs in the next cell? I can hardly hear myself over the oinking.' Later on a man in the crowd blows his nose loudly, prompting a puppet to remark on how that's reminded him to get the drains unblocked.

The audience are so taken by these improvisations that they forget all about the story and vie with each other to come up with excuses for the puppets to make funny asides. At the end the prisoner makes a direct appeal to the audience:

'Our play is over, now 'tis true
I must be here confined by you,
Or set free. It's for you to choose:
Keep me locked up – or screw the screws?'

'It's funny because it's so true,' remarks a scraggy, lantern-jawed woman next to you. 'I used to work as a cook in the prison and half of them in there reckon they're philosophers.'

She tosses a copper coin into the hat in front of the booth. You can leave a pyr or two yourself if you think it was worth it, then ▶ **232**

You and Ancaeus hurry the confused goddess back towards the waiting *Sunrise*. 'Get ready to cast off!' shouts Ancaeus to the crew.

Eos glances back across the island to where the Minotaur stands, a lone figure against an onrushing tide of macabre creatures. 'Shouldn't we help your friend?'

'Don't waste time!' snaps Ancaeus. Then, remembering himself, he takes her hand and guides her up the gangplank. 'Forgive me, O divinity, but he's sacrificing himself to buy us these extra seconds. We mustn't waste them.'

▶ 379

236

For a moment you stand as immobile as Galatea herself. Then cold horror gives way to hot rage.

'I was a fool to think the brood of Nyx could be anything other than monsters,' you say, lunging for him. 'I curse myself for that, and my mistake has doomed my loyal friend. But her bravery has shown me the right path. Whatever happens, I'll destroy you.'

▶ 803

237

Get the codeword **Robber**.

'Dunamis?' says Zinc. '*You're* the pickpocket who's taking more in a day than my best dippers can filch in a week?'

'In a fortnight, more like,' she says.

They obviously know each other quite well. You listen to them arguing over whether Dunamis should pay a tithe for being allowed to work the Street of Knives.

'Nope,' she says with a child's obstinacy.

'No?' Zinc's tin mask remains impassive, but his tone and body language express astonishment. 'Think carefully, girl. I've had people thrown off rooftops for less.'

'Yeah, yeah. You won't do that to me. I'll tell you why – I'm going to teach your other cutpurses how to do their job. You'll double your takings, but what I steal I get to keep. Deal?'

They shake on it, and it occurs to you that in thirty years' time Dunamis might well be the crime boss of Vulcan City.

If you have the codeword *Recursive* ▶ 645

Otherwise ▶ 326

238

Strolling through the market, you're struck by the rich array of colourful regional costumes on display: the bright felts of mountain nomads, the billowing robes of desert dwellers, the intricately worked leather jerkins of foresters, the feather headdresses of mammoth hunters, the blazing silks and filigree silver ornaments of seafaring merchants, the pattern-bordered togas of wandering scholars, and many others.

You take out the drawings Xechasiaris gave you, glancing from them to the people teeming all around. Maybe you can spot some detail that will tell you where he travelled all those years ago.

'Hey, watch where you're going!'

The drawings are knocked from your hands. Quickly gathering them up before they get trodden into the ground, you get up to find the man you bumped into looking at one.

He hands it to you. 'Clumsy so-and-so, aren't you?' But already his anger is cooling.

'Sorry. I was distracted.'

'That picture, it's meant to be Saesara, isn't it?'

'Is it?' You peer at the drawing he noticed.

'That's a field of poppies in front of the royal palace.'

'What? These red dots and that blob?'

He sighs. 'Everyone's a critic. I'm just saying I like your faux-primitive style.'

'I didn't do these. A seven-year-old boy drew them.'

He strokes his chin. 'He'll go far.'

'Yeah… no, he's peaked, put it that way. But he did go far, back then. These red blotches are poppies, you reckon?'

'Come along and see them for yourself. I'm taking a trade caravan out to Saesara this afternoon. It's just a few days' journey.'

Take him up on his offer   ▶ 842

Refuse   ▶ 613

239

As you writhe in psychic agony, Nyx reaches her fingers into your very soul, tearing out strands of vital essence. She drains your attributes (CHARM, GRACE, INGENUITY, and STRENGTH) by a total of 10 points. You can choose which attributes to lose points from. For example, you could lose 4 points from STRENGTH and 2 points from each of the others. Remember that attributes can go negative.

If you still have the courage to fight on ▶ 399

240

If you have the title **Witness of the First Dawn** and this box ❑ is empty, tick it and ▶ 1193

Otherwise ▶ 1384

241

Again the scene changes. You're back in the Achaean camp, walking unnoticed between the tents as dusk falls. The sea breeze is cold. The surf rattles and sighs between the pebbles. Out on the far horizon, the sea bears the red track of the setting sun like a bloodstain.

A squad of Achaeans are carrying a limp figure atop their outstretched arms like a fallen hero being borne to a funeral pyre. They take her to Achilles's tent and lay her down on a trestle. You are swept closer with no more volition than a dandelion blown on the wind.

You are not surprised to see that the figure has your face. You reach out. Soul and body reunite. You fight to return to life as voices surge and babble in the throng that's gathered around you.

'I heard she was a princess.'

'An Amazon and all.'

'So why did she fight on our side?'

'She fell in love with Achilles.'

'They say she broke Poseidon's trident.'

'And Apollo shot her in the eye, but she just laughed it off.'

'Taking on the goddess Aphrodite, though…'

'Chopped her down like an oak. I can still feel the ground shake.'

'The gods can't forgive that.'

'What's her name?'

'Forgot.'

Crystal-clear water gently laps the shore. With a mighty effort you draw breath into your lungs, force open your eyes.

'She's alive!' gasps a soldier. 'Get Achilles.'

He comes at once. You are already on your feet. 'I feared the gods had decided to kill you,' he says, clasping your arm.

'They still have a use for me,' you say bitterly. 'You know – bad mortal, you hurt one of us, now can you do it again to the Queen of Night?'

'True, the gods are cruel. I'm proud of what you did. If you can make the gods bleed, it gives us hope that one day we needn't believe in them. All the same, you'd better come and make an offering at the shrine. And I will too. Even if the gods only spared you for their own reasons, I'm thankful you're all right.'

▶ 357

242

Pandora is not keen to remain another minute in Vulcan City. 'It's ersatz. A mechanical fabrication.'

'Aren't *you* artificial? A fabrication yourself?'

She winces. 'I thought I had explained that to you. Come and see me in Iskandria, where we can talk in comfort.'

So saying, her outlines blur and she dissolves back into the interior of the glass pyramid. ▶ 325

243

A search of their pockets turns up a **winding key** for a music box, a **lava gem** and a **honey cake**, which you can add to your possessions. There's also a note written in a crude hand:

'Hey, you hairy old knob, do you remember that priest of the Dark Lady who I got a prophecy off? He said there was something down in the desert east of the Sacred Way that would mean we could undo all the bad times. Put everything back the way it was supposed to be, he reckoned. I spent weeks down there, ended up with more sand in my teeth than you'd get in a bushel of spinach, but I came back empty-handed. "Well, you should have had another pair of eyes with you," said the seer. Now he tells me! I can't get back to Notus for months, but if you want to pop down there with your pet midget maybe you can find it. Your loving brother Kinaukas.'

Leaving the bodies for the rats, you make your way back down to the street.

▶ 571

244

'The future is not a single length of string,' she says, 'but a web of possibilities. Some fates are conditional on others. I advise you to scale the peaks of Boreas before you go looking for these two.'

'And then?'

'Once you have befriended the last of the Argonauts, then it will be time to help the prisoners. But beware, for he lives as a hermit now and is distrustful of all outsiders.'

She hangs her head, exhausted by the effort of piercing the veil of time. You return to the main hall.

▶ 510

245

The sergeant's expression changes almost to one of respect. A glance is enough to tell the men to let you go. He makes out a receipt and hands it to you.

'I'm sure you'll toe the straight and narrow from now on,' he says, indicating with a wave that you are free to go.

Lose the codeword *Ridge* and ▶ 1642

246

'They say you're the boss of this place. Hence the mask?'

His mask is unmistakably modelled on the design of the mechanical Speaker who announces the proclamations of the city's syndics.

'This?' The inscrutable stare looks back at you. 'I've got my own reasons for wearing it.'

▶ 1487

247

As you get older you spend more time with your friends and less at home. You become familiar with the streets of your city, even the districts that your parents never brought you to.

Where are you most often to be found?

The Forum	▶ **370**
The Academy of Philosophers	▶ **206**
The Groves of Dionysus	▶ **780**
The slums and backstreets	▶ **124**

248

Her nails rip at your flesh. Blood spurts and she drinks it, grinning at you gruesomely with gore dripping from her chin.

If the Wound box on your Adventure Sheet is not ticked, put a tick in it now and ▶ **1612**

If you were already injured ▶ **858**

249

All around you the ruined city crawls with unclean life. From the rubble and fused glass, where shadows move like oil spills, the forces of the night gather. Creatures slither out of broken sewer pipes, claw their way up from under the earth, come stalking through the broken shells of buildings, and swoop out of the muttering storm clouds overhead. Grinning skulls, feral snouts, and faces like leather fright-masks confront you in a seething fuligin mass.

'Behold my army,' says Nyx. 'A thousand demons, a thousand devils ready to usher in an eternity of endless night. Nothing can stand against them.'

'Perhaps,' you say. 'They'll have to fight to prove it.'

As if in answer to your defiant words, the booming cry of a battle-horn sounds through the ruins. The tramp of feet echoes between the stone columns as legions of bronze-armoured warriors march to back you up. Their commander calls them to halt and salutes you, saying, 'The Myrmidons of Iskandria are here to fight for you.'

'The men of Sarpedon too,' calls out another warrior, leading his own troops to join ranks with the Iskandrians. 'Though we are not so fearsome in battle as the fabled Myrmidons, yet we are sworn to repay our debt to you and we will give our lives if need be.'

'Two battalions of mortals,' sneers Nyx. 'Is that all you can muster against my atramentous hordes?'

There is a hollow clattering as of a thousand dry sticks being smashed together. Along the avenues march phalanx after phalanx of skeletal warriors, their ranks bristling with spears and swords.

'The Spartoi!' says Nyx. For the first time she seems taken aback. 'You fleshless monsters, you should side with me.'

'We hate all,' snaps the Spartoi commander. 'Every living thing, mortal or titan, is our sworn foe. But we fight today beside these, our former enemies, to defend the world Vulcan made. Miserable as it is, it is ours.'

Now your own ranks are swelling, presenting Nyx's legions with a force to match their own. Do you have other allies flocking to your cause?

If you have the title **Amazonian Queen** ▶ **1581**

Otherwise ▶ **954**

250

Daedalus shows you what he's working on. It's a suit of gleaming articulated armour with razor-edged metallic wings on the back.

'Never thought of you as an angel,' you say.

He laughs. 'The beauty of it is the inbuilt regeneration system. Short of being instantaneously vaporized, nothing can kill me once I'm wearing this. We can take on the gods themselves.'

'Are the gods our enemies now? I thought the threat was Nyx.'

'It's a sliding scale. She's way up at the top, though, that's true.'

If you have the **copper casket of doom** and want to give it to him ▶ **213**

If not, Daedalus can program the golden beetles to carry you anywhere you want to go.

To Boreas ▶ **1053** in *The Pillars of the Sky*

To Arcadia ▶ **266** in *The Wild Woods*

To Notus ▶ **436** in *The Hammer of the Sun*

To Hades ▶ **493** in *The Houses of the Dead* (but you must lose any companion as no one will accompany you to that realm)

Back up to the city streets ▶ **806** in this book

251

The serpent tightens its hold. There's a sickening crack and a convulsive shudder goes through your body. But even as it releases your dying form, the serpent realizes its mistake. Your last action was to dig your fingers into the soft tissue of its throat, so that as it pulls away your death-grip tears out its windpipe

Note your Current Location as **683** and then ▶ **670**

252

You are at the bottom of the well. There is a stone alcove behind a grating in the wall.

You can leave possessions and money in the alcove to

save having to carry them around with you. Write in the box anything you are leaving – or you can recover items you left here earlier by writing them on your Adventure Sheet and erasing them from the box.

```
ITEMS IN THE WELL
```

Leave the well ▶ Current Location

253

Your servants creep in, having been woken by the commotion. 'Call the militia,' you tell them.

'That one's still alive,' says your valet, pointing from a safe distance to a figure sprawling in the hearth.

'Who sent you?' you say, lifting the assailant's head. 'Might as well own up to it now. I'll tell the militia to go easy on you.'

'The burghers of a village called Bridgadoom,' he says. 'You stole their savings. This was meant to be payback.'

Strange – you probably spent that money without a second thought, but the villagers have harboured a grudge all this time. You tell the militia captain to keep an eye out for anyone from Bridgadoom.

If you have the codeword **Robber** and want to call in a favour from Zinc to have the Bridgadoomians dealt with
▶ 290

If not ▶ 97

254

There is an expectant hush as Lady Pemphreda and her guests wait for you to tell your next tale. Only Kazala looks distracted, fidgeting impatiently for you to stumble in your storytelling so that she gets a chance to show you up.

If you have the codeword **Query** ▶ 522

If not ▶ 10

255

You laugh scornfully, and for the first time Hypnos looks astonished.

'You think I'm doing this for the gods?' you say to him. 'The gods don't care what happens to mortals. Nor do the titans. Let them destroy each other. As for your mother – too long have human beings lived in fear of the dark. Prometheus gave us fire to banish those fears. I oppose you because it is mankind's destiny to drive back superstition and hate. I choose to side with the forces of light.'

▶ 803

256

You struggle on with strength born of desperation, but there are too many. The Minotaur falls under the onslaught of a dozen misshapen monsters. Your own weapons are knocked from your hands and you are pulled down with a storm of claws and fangs tearing at you. Pinned to the blood-soaked deck, you look up to see Thanatos outlined against the storm, his giant hand swinging around to splinter the hull. Crippled, its sails torn and flapping in the wind, the *Sunrise* spins out of control. It lurches to one side. Sailors scream as they are flung overboard. You cling to the rail as the ship drops in a helpless spiral, breaking up on the ground as surely as if a gale had swept her onto rocks.

You lie stunned in the wreckage. A few people have remained in the street, too paralyzed with terror to run. One edges nervously past where you are lying, perhaps hoping to bolt and run. Then he turns his face upwards and gives a despairing moan. Slipping on the wet cobblestones, he starts to scramble away. A sliver of deathly white light stabs down, touching him for just an instant, and he is gone. All that remains of him is a wisp of dark vapour that is blown away on the wind.

A colossal foot descends to the street beside you, landing with a tremor that dislodges bricks and sends cracks spreading through the flagstones. Painfully you rise to behold pitiless Thanatos standing like a mountain against the raging storm.

▶ 595

257

There's a sizzle accompanied by the stench of scorched cloth and burning flesh as you drive the point of the poker into her flesh. With a scream she doubles around the pain, the knife balanced in limp fingers.

Now's your chance, before she can recover. Make a STRENGTH roll at difficulty 7 without any item bonus.

Success ▶ 1335

Failure ▶ 902

258

Note that your Current Location is **1642**.

If you have the codeword *Rebuke* or either of the titles **Paladin** or **The Unexpected Heir** ▶ 1106

If not but you have the codeword *Robber* and want to call in a favour ▶ 953

Otherwise you will need to forge a letter convincing enough to entice him away – make an INGENUITY roll at a difficulty of 10.

A work of art ▶ 886

A blot of ink ▶ 71

259

A metallic fist crunches into your cheek. It's like an anvil smacking you in the face. You reel back, tasting blood. If not for the bracing cold of the night air you'd have passed out already.

If the Wound box on your Adventure Sheet was unticked, put a tick in it now and then ▶ 437

If you were already injured ▶ 671

260

All along the shore outside Agamemnon's command tent, hundreds of high-prowed black ships rest like sleeping dragons, an impression only strengthened by the eternally vigilant eye that most of the ships have painted on their prow. Around the beached hulls laps the human tide of soldiers – cooking, brooding, laughing, wenching, praying, tending the injured, drinking, pissing, polishing their armour, training, planning for the next day's struggle, or just lying on the sand by their shelters like men already sunk in death.

Staring out to sea, you think of the distance that separates these men from their homes and families. How much greater the gulf back to your own time and place. The stars are beginning to appear, beacons that sailors use to plot their course when out of sight of land. But what course could you take to return – and should you, given that your fate is to stand alone against the titan whom even Zeus fears? Night, whose cloak is even now settling over the world.

The reddening light of sunset reminds you that you are feeling weary. It has been a long day.

Make your way back through the camp to Achilles' tent ▶ 535

Find a place to sleep on the beach ▶ 572

261

'It was worth getting these blessed,' you tell Ptolemos. 'Each one heals an injury.'

'Don't waste them, chucklehead. Keep one at least for doing something useful.'

'Listen, if you got in as many fights as I do, you wouldn't think instant first aid was such a bad idea. Also they taste amazing.'

'I've no doubt they do. You might even call them miraculous. Get yourself down to that headland south-west of Iskandria, take a look at the city from there. Got to be an impressive sight now it's rebuilding. You did that. It might inspire you to have a crack at some more great deeds.'

'I ought to do that sometime.'

'Not sometime. Now.' He gives you a shove that sends you stumbling away from the bench. 'And you can go for a paddle in the sea while you're there.'

'Be like that,' you tell him, rubbing your arm.

As you walk away, he calls out and you turn. 'You did a pretty good job for a know-nothing kid,' he says. ▶ 806

262

Eos's voice grows even quieter as she reveals her innermost heart. 'It has always been my dearest wish to be the first dawn of a new world. Why else was I born with the power of the rising sun in my heart? But while my mother reigns I am banished to this far corner of the universe.'

If you have the codeword *Quiddity* ▶ 212

If not ▶ 1100

263

You are directed to a house on the Street of the Winds, where a skinny middle-aged woman is fussing over a dozen pots and frying-pans. As you are shown into the kitchen she claps her hands, dismissing all her servants.

'Are you having a dinner party?' you ask, gazing around the large and well-stocked kitchen strung with onions, tomatoes and bunches of herbs. A brace of geese hang in one corner alongside a butcher's block on which rests a huge haunch of venison. The aromas seething out of the simmering saucepans make your stomach rumble.

'This is just a light supper,' she says, her lip curling slightly in a bitter smile. 'My husband always comes home from his excursions with a hearty appetite.'

'Your husband? Would I know him?'

'I call him the Grumble King,' she says with a short, enigmatic laugh.

'Because he's a crime lord?'

'Crime lord? He spends the whole day at the theatre flirting with the dancing girls. No, I call him that because nothing's ever good enough for him.'

'Under the circumstances, it's generous of you to welcome him home with such an appetizing feast.'

'Isn't it? And that's why I asked you here. I want to cook him some very special dishes, and to get them just right I need an ingredient that can't be found anywhere but Arcadia. It's called ophidiaroot. If you should happen to come across some on your travels, I'd be most grateful.'

Get the codeword *Retrieve* and ▶ 1062

264

Note **509** as your Current Location, then ▶ 1269 and tick the box next to the West Gate. From now on you will always be able to find your way back here.

265

Shrieking and wailing, a crowd of people run pell-mell past you along the street. As they go by, one of them grabs your arm and tries to pull you along with them. It's a priestess of Demeter in torn, soot-smirched robes.

'Can't you hear it?' she shouts over the howling wind.

'What?'

'The end of the world! The titans have got loose from Tartarus. They are laying siege to Olympus.'

You don't ask how she knows. She's a priestess, after all.

If you have the permanent blessing of Demeter and do not have the codeword *Rhombus* ▶ 1278

Otherwise ▶ 1619

266

The Celedons stalk confidently towards you, their slender metal bodies gleaming liquidly in the dancing lamplight. Their combined screams are growing in intensity, causing a pulsing pressure inside your skull.

If you have any **beeswax**   ▶ 341

If not   ▶ 17

267

You cry out as a hissing circle of black fire tightens around you, burning through your flesh and bones and right into your soul. Mortally wounded, you collapse to the ground.

With a last spiteful smile, Nyx slumps lifeless in front of you. A grey bloom spreads across her limbs. A howl goes up from her demonic legions as they see their mistress's body break apart into fragments of cindery ash that are scattered by the breeze.

The sky is growing lighter, but your own vision dims. You have slain the Night Queen, but at the cost of your own life.

▶ 42

Marija leads the way up three flights of stairs, silk skirts swishing softly, her hips swaying with limber grace just ahead of you. Her perfume trails on the air, musky as delicate spices. You wonder if she makes her living as a prostitute. Zinc didn't tell you much about her, but using her figure and her charm to seduce men seems like a plausible occupation. The pillow talk would provide her with the secrets that are an informant's stock in trade.

You shake your head. What difference does it make what she does? Or did? All that is about to end.

Her room is large and airy, with tall windows through which the afternoon light streams in golden shafts. At one end is a chaise longue strewn with plump velvet pillows. Embroidered screens separate the space into areas for sleeping, eating and entertaining. In the middle of the floor is a brightly patterned circular rug with the spiral design often seen in Boreas.

'You're from the north – ?' you begin, then catch yourself. What does it matter?

'Darling, I'm from all over.' She shrugs the silk robe off her slim shoulders and lets it slide to the floor. 'No sense in ruining a perfectly good dress,' she says with a lingering smile. 'Now, I'll just purify myself in the sight of the goddess and we can get down to it.'

She crosses to a large mirror in an ornate ivory frame in the shape of many smooth arms clasping each other, slender white fingers beringed with garlands of carved leaves. Projecting from the bottom of the frame is a small bronze dish into which Marija sprinkles a few grey-green dittany leaves. The bronzed surface of the mirror has flaked away with antiquity so that it reflects her face only in enigmatic kaleidoscope fragments – a heavy-lashed almond eye, smiling red lips, a flashing crystal earring.

She sets a burning taper to the leaves. They must have been dried, because they catch light at once. She mutters a prayer as a wild scent fills the room suggestive of dazzling mountain streams and thick dark forests.

'Which goddess?' you say, feeling as if your reply has been blundering lost through dim mental caverns.

Her response seems to take even longer. 'The Protectress. The Lady of the Keys. She Who Waits at the Three-Fold Crossroads.' Marija turns, her nakedness half-veiled by threads of white smoke from the burning plants, and raises her voice. 'Hekate, Mistress of Mysteries, deliver me from this evil!'

She touches a section of the mirror frame and there is a mechanical click. Try for a CHARM roll at difficulty 14. That is, roll two dice and add your CHARM modifier (including the bonus from one attribute-boosting item if you have it with you) and you need a total of at least 14.

Succeed ▶ **407**
Fail ▶ **544**

269

'What's got you so scared?'

You approach a man who's staring in petrified horror into the darkness beyond the fires. When you shake him, he seems to surface slowly out of a trance. He turns to you wide-eyed.

'The metal women,' he gasps. 'I saw them kill a man with a scream.'

You turn to others hiding nearby. 'Listen to me, all of you. We have to stick together, look out for each other. Animals cower alone in the dark and that's how predators get to pick them off one by one. But we're human beings. This is our city. Whatever we have to face, if we face it side by side we can survive any danger. Together we win, alone we die.'

Make a CHARM roll at difficulty 12.

Succeed ▶ **16**
Fail ▶ **748**

270

❑

If the box above is empty, tick it and ▶ **1035**

If the box was already ticked, erase the tick and then ▶ **733**

271

Zinc says that this time you have to decide if you're going to do the job and then he'll tell you what it is. What's your response to that?

'Whatever it is I'll do it.' ▶ **217**
'No thanks. Too risky.' ▶ **326**

272

A maid brings you a parcel that has just been delivered. From the scuffed and dusty wrapping it looks as if it has come from far away.

If you have the title **Steward of the Summer Palace** and this box ❑ is empty, tick it and ▶ **836**

Otherwise, if you have the title **Champion of the Amazons** and this box ❑ is empty, tick it and ▶ **448**

Otherwise, if you have the title **The Liberator** and this box ❑ is empty, tick it and ▶ **1579**

Otherwise, if you have the codeword *Quail* and this box ❑ is empty, tick it and ▶ **1333**

Otherwise, if you have the codewords *Nadir*, *Pheon* and *Rye* and this box ❑ is empty, tick it and ▶ **1662**

Otherwise ▶ **880**

273

Sweeping the tapestry in both arms, you give it a sharp snap, unfurling it like a banner over Nyx's head.

You have never seen the tapestry look as vivid. Normally the images are so close to abstract that you need

to stare at it to unpick the interlocking spirals into recognizable images. But now it seems almost alive. Curling patterns of waves, delicately hued in blue and green, mark out the god Poseidon in his watery kingdom. His brother Zeus, in the centre of the image looking down on all creation, wields dazzling bolts of electric flame. On the far side, flickering mauve and grey beams illuminate dread Hades where he stands thrusting open the doors of his realm. And between them the tapestry teems with all the gods, sparked into a semblance of animation by the magic that crackles on the very air.

A gale springs up, catching Nyx's robe and her long black hair, pulling her towards the tapestry you are brandishing before her. It has become a gateway between the worlds that has the power to carry you both far away from here.

If you have the codeword *Rhombus* ▶ 1070
If not but you have the codeword *Rudiment* ▶ 579
Otherwise ▶ 826

274

You race your horse towards the giant figure. It swims in and out of reality before your vision. As you draw close her scale becomes clear. This is a colossus you are attacking, but there's no chance to back out now.

Bracing your foot on the horse's back, you launch yourself up towards the giant figure, legs scything as you draw back your sword. A shimmering aurora hangs around her, her celestial robe whose billowing gossamer folds shield her from sight of mortal eyes. You must aim your blow between those folds, at the fleeting moment her marble-white flesh is exposed.

If your Glory score is 18 or more ▶ 1095
Otherwise, if you have the codeword *Royal* ▶ 1535
Otherwise ▶ 120

275

The purse contains 50 pyr but if you accept a monetary reward your reputation will suffer and you'll lose 1 Glory. Of course, if you have 0 Glory then there's no reputation to worry about.

Decide if you'd rather have the money or the Glory, adjust your Adventure Sheet accordingly, and ▶ 806

276

Where the house used to stand is just a crater.

'Did they find any bodies?' you ask a passer-by.

'Huh?'

'After the house collapsed. There was a workshop in the basement. I wondered if anyone was down there when the

explosion went off.'

He scratches his head. 'Don't think so. The authorities cleared it all, like you can see. There was a family lived here – Glauco the carpenter along with his wife and kids. They're all dead, the roof fell on them. Nobody in the basement, though, as far as I know. No sign of any workshop, neither.'

▶ 232

277

You haven't gone far from Zinc's door when a voice calls out: 'Hey there.'

You turn around, seeing no one nearby, then look up to a windowsill above the street where Dunamis is sitting eating an apple.

'Is that your room up there?' you ask her.

She shakes her head. 'Not my apple, either. And you might say this isn't my business, but I heard you're looking for Autolycus.'

'What's it to you?'

She pitches the apple core across the street, then swings nimbly down beside you. 'You don't trust advice if it doesn't have a price tag, is that the problem?'

Decline her help ▶ 571

Ask her what she knows ▶ 955 if you have the codeword *Radish*; otherwise ▶ 92

278

By now there's a teeming horde of nightmare creatures pressed right up to the edge of the roof, close enough for you to make out every detail in the pallid, worm-gnawed faces of the vampires, the red eyes and spittle-flecked jaws of the were-beasts, the misshapen features of capering nightmare demons. Baying and snarling, they are so intent on getting to you that some even get jostled over the edge and fall flailing to the street far below.

Each time a grapple lodges on the ship's rail, a stream of attackers instantly comes scrabbling along it to get aboard. Heedless of the wind, rain and the lethal drop below, their only thought is to press their wild onslaught. Even the Minotaur, whose blade flashes and spills blood and guts with every swing, must eventually tire and then the monstrous tide will overwhelm the ship.

There's a commotion at the back of the horde, near the stairs up onto the roof. Some of the rear ranks are turning in confusion. A vampire staggers, a spear sticking out of its chest, and disintegrates in a tattered cloud of dust and rags and old bones. A slim hand reaches out, retrieves the spear, and swings it in a wide arc to keep the nearest monsters at bay.

As the rabble parts you see a lithe figure in studded leather armour. In one hand she has the spear, in the other a sword that's already slick with blood. Behind her are a band of stalwart fighters, each holding their own against the night creatures that come rushing and snapping at them from all sides.

'Zoë..?'

She's too far off to hear you over the raging storm, but she sees your look of recognition and raises her hand in salute. She and her companions swore to come to your aid when you needed it most, and they are as good as their word. You only hope they are enough to swing the tide of battle.

Her surprise attack has distracted the vampires who were manning the grapple-line cannon. There are still plenty of were-beasts leaping across to the ship, but not so many that the Minotaur can't hold them off. Meanwhile the *Sunrise* is stalled in mid-air and gradually losing altitude. Should you go to help Ancaeus raise the sails, or help the helmsman with the buoyancy rotor?

Get up in the rigging	▶ **1540**
Help out with the buoyancy rotor	▶ **172**

279

The revenant forces you to the floor. A flash of lightning illuminates the last thing you will see in this existence: her ravaged dead face, lit up with unholy glee, as she presses her yellow fangs to your exposed flesh.

Lose the codewords **Rabbit** and **Ruffle** if you have them. Also lose 1 from your STRENGTH score, as even after coming back to life you will continue to feel the ache of the vampire's bite.

▶ **111**

280

'Will you take breakfast here on the rug, excellency?'

It's morning. Your valet is standing over you.

'What am I doing on the floor? Ow, my head.'

'I assume you drank a little too much brandy and decided to sleep there,' says the valet sniffily.

You jump up in alarm. 'The safe!'

Running to check on your valuables, you discover the worst. Orphea has taken the lot. Any possessions marked on your Adventure Sheet were stored in your bedroom, so you retain those, but your storeroom has been ransacked; note **515** as your Current Location and then ▶ **1402** and delete anything written in the box there.

281

Somehow you find your voice. 'She's really gone?'

Vulcan nods. 'Thanks to you, mortal.'

'And the Olympian gods?'

'All dead, except for me. I shall send out my automata to drive the titans back into Tartarus. Nyx's twin whelps along with them.'

'What will happen to the mortal world?'

'The Vulcanverse, it has been called. I have already restored it. No one there will remember the awful horrors of Nyx's brief reign. And more than that – I see now it is wrong for me to use it as my laboratory experiment. You mortals have earned the right to decide your own destiny. I shall relinquish my control of events there. Henceforth humanity's future is in their own hands.'

He runs his fingers over another bank of switches and dials. The scene melts away. You no longer stand in the rarefied air of Olympus but back on the streets of Vulcan City with the smells of camel dung, fruit stalls, roasting street food, spices, perfumes, sweat, woodsmoke, and livestock. Instead of the murmur of soft empyrean music your ears are filled with the chatter of passers-by, lusty shouts, hawkers' cries, snatches of birdsong, spirited haggling, children's laughter, rattling cartwheels, the clang of a temple bell, the panting of a dog as it runs past in the gutter.

'Hey!' yells a man driving a wagon piled high with wares. 'You going to stand gawping in the middle of the street all day?'

You move to the side of the road to let him past. As he goes he casts a sullen glance at you over his shoulder. 'All right for some, eh? The rest of us have work to do.'

He stares in astonishment as you roar with laughter. You are home.

282

You run yelling towards the Myrmidon tents. Achilles is sitting there, listening with heavy heart to the battle being waged far across the plain. Seeing you with the saboteurs hard on your heels, he springs up and grabs two spears, flinging one to you.

Your pursuers skid to a halt in the sand as you turn to face them. 'Big deal,' sneers their leader, putting on a show of bravado. 'Are we supposed to be afraid of a couple of Achaeans?'

'Sorry to disappoint, but I'm no Achaean,' you say, driving the spear into his guts to emphasize the point. 'I'm an Amazon.'

'And I,' says Achilles, racing up to join you, 'am the prince of the Myrmidons.'

That's enough for them. They throw down their swords and make a run for it. It doesn't save them. Swift-footed

Achilles is the master of fighting on the move. He chases them down, slaying almost without effort, his spear swinging and thrusting till the beach is gory with blood. Even you, who have witnessed and dealt out much slaughter, are shocked by his savagery. Yet when the foes are all slain, he turns to you with a look of tenderness and says, 'Are you hurt?'

'Not a scratch.'

'That's all that matters.' He drops the spear and wades into the surf to wash off the blood.

▶ 1288

283

'You do not travel alone.'

The invisible creature clamped around your brow gives a minatory twitch. 'Unfortunately not,' you say, grimacing.

'Climb to the peak of Mount Atos, then descend to the plateau in the centre of Boreas. Fear no challenge. Then you will be rid of the burden you bear.'

That's all she has to say. You say a short prayer and leave.

▶ 510

284

He blows into the **bone flute of Koré**, then peers along it. 'I'm no musician, but I have a customer who has been looking for something like this. I can give you 200 pyr. Or, if you'd rather, instead of cash I can open you a line of credit to spend here in the shop.'

Take the cash   ▶ 1447
Take the credit   ▶ 1372
No deal   ▶ 828

285

'I can at least assure you that you're on the right track,' you tell Pug. 'The hourglass does have the power to go back in time.'

He looks at you, forgetting his own troubles as he senses that you have far greater concerns than his. 'You do realize,' he says after a time, 'that you can only use it once?'

'What's that?'

'I'm saying: don't waste the chance it's given you, because you won't get another.'

If you have the **scrimshaw hourglass** and want to give it to him ▶ 321

If not ▶ 480

286

You are roused from sleep one night by Chipos climbing into bed with you. 'I can't resist your come-hither looks any longer,' he growls in what he must think is a seductive murmur. 'Me and you, babe. It's meant to be.'

What's your response?

'Get the hell out of here.'   ▶ 1334
'About time too.'   ▶ 443

287

A hatch opens in the rubble nearby. Some new and unexpected threat? You drop into a crouch, but the figure who emerges is no demon or chthonic menace.

'Daedalus!'

He's brandishing a map and a device that looks like a large crystalline compass. 'How about that? Pinpointed your location to within a couple of metres.'

'A handy little gadget,' you admit. 'I hope you brought some ingenious weapons too.'

'About that...' He shakes his head. 'I just came to wish you luck, but I'm sitting this one out.'

'The final battle? You're staying on the sidelines?'

'He's bothered by the deal you made with the Olympians,' roars Thanatos in delight. 'The inventor has no love for Zeus and his brood.'

Daedalus nods. 'I hate to say it, but the long goodbye guy has it right. Nyx wins, Zeus wins – either way it's a lose for humanity.'

He turns and starts to descend back into the tunnels below the city. If you have the codeword *Rudiment* ▶ 121 now.

Otherwise to convince him to fight you're going to need a CHARM roll at difficulty 16:

Succeed   ▶ 659
Fail   ▶ 1342

288

'Standing up for your weakling kid brother, eh?' he sneers.

'No. I just feel like giving you a pasting.'

After school the two of you meet behind a wall in the necropolis to settle the matter. Most of your schoolmates have come to cheer you on. Everybody would like to see Nihakos taken down a peg or two.

Do you win the fight?

Of course   ▶ 616
It's more or less a draw   ▶ 411
Nihakos kicks your butt   ▶ 821

289

'Guess we'll see you next visiting day,' says Daedalus. 'Don't take too long. Night's coming.'

'Dad doesn't mean sunset,' says Icarus, glancing out of the barred window. 'He means – '

'Yeah, I get it. World in the balance.'

You head for the door. 'Take Ari,' says Daedalus, winding the robot spider and setting it down. 'He'll spring all the doors for you and watch till the coast is clear.'

What do you say?

'OK, thanks.' ▶ 637

'I don't need your robot's help.' ▶ 947

290

Lose the codeword *Robber* unless you also have the codeword *Recursive*.

A few days later, as you stop to look in a shop window, a small ferret of a man sidles up to you across the street and slouches against the wall, gesturing with his long-stemmed pipe as though the two of you were old friends chatting in a taproom.

'Zinc must have a real soft spot for you,' he says with a tobacco-roughened cackle.

'What makes you say that?'

'Two tourists will be going back home to Arcadia in a box. Civilians, you get me? Normally he prefers to leave civilians alone.'

'Maybe he had as big a grudge against them as I did.'

You turn and walk away.

▶ 1617

291

Another pair of hands grips the beam. And another. It begins to shift. Encouraged, more and more of the onlookers dart forward to join the rescue effort. Your combined strength lifts the beam high enough that the injured woman is able to squirm out. A priest in torn and soot-smeared robes pulls her to safety. You and the others let go and the beam crunches back to the ground.

'Can you walk?' the priest is asking the woman. 'We can't stay here.'

'Your holiness,' hisses one of the rescuers urgently, 'they're coming.'

The priest turns to you. 'You taught us a priceless lesson tonight.'

'What's happened here?'

He cocks his head as a long ringing note echoes over the howl of the wind. 'No time to explain. Trust in the gods, friend, but also – '

'Yes?'

'Run!'

He takes to his heels and the others follow, two men supporting the limping woman. In moments they've vanished into the darkness. You are alone.

Get the title **Local Hero** and ▶ 233

292

Note that your Current Location is **1642**.

Officers of the Guard share sets of rooms, four to a set, each with his own bedroom leading off a sitting room common to the four. You blunder into Sakan's rooms at a time you know his three roommates are out on patrol.

'Viranos, yeah?' you say, careful to keep your shoulders hunched in a servile posture while drawling with the kind of dumb insolence that only servants can muster. 'Package for you. Sign here.'

Sakan barely glances at you. 'Get lost.'

'You don't want it, Mr Viranos?'

'I'm not Viranos, damn your eyes.'

You crane your neck to look again at the number on the door. 'Oh, right. My mistake.'

You are hefting the parcel back out into the corridor when Sakan calls you back. 'What have you got there?'

'A suit for Mr Viranos to wear at Lady Amythita's dinner party. She sent it with her compliments and the express wish that he mustn't turn up in anything else. "Don't come scruffy," the lady said.'

Sakan twists his lips in something like a laugh. 'Oh, he's a yokel, all right. Give it here, I'll see he gets it.'

'I'm supposed to give it direct to him,' you say, putting on a show of reluctance.

Sakan snatches away the parcel and tosses you a coin. 'You can take that or you can take my boot up your arse. Now clear off.'

A few hours later the news is all over town. Sakan has been found dead. 'Looked like he was boiled from the inside,' says the alewife who is telling you. 'My niece works at the barracks and she said there was blood and shit everywhere. They'll have to burn the rug and scrub the floorboards with bleach.'

'What was he wearing?' you ask nonchalantly.

'Funny you should ask. A bright green tunic, my niece said. Seared right into his flesh, it was. I expect they'll have to burn that too.'

'Probably just as well.'

Lose the **tunic of Nessus** and get the codeword *Rock*, then ▶ 1432

293

If you have a **packet of emery dust** ▶ 1249

If not but you have the **Face of Wisdom** (INGENUITY +3) ▶ 725

Otherwise attempt a CHARM roll at difficulty 10.

Succeed ▶ 1051

Fail ▶ 1030

294

☐

Do not put a tick in the box unless you were told to do so in the section you just turned from.

If the box is empty ▶ 846
If you have just put a tick in it ▶ 129
If it was already ticked ▶ 1491

295

You take your mother's hand and tell her, 'Be comforted. His death has been avenged.'

She gives you an unfathomable look. 'Avenged?' she says. 'What difference does that make? He's dead. Nothing else matters.'

▶ 1411

296

One left – but you can't afford to take any chances. He looks to be the toughest of them.

Make a STRENGTH roll at difficulty 8. You cannot use any items to get a bonus to the roll because you aren't carrying your possessions.

Succeed ▶ 845
Fail ▶ 456

297

The sailors are ready to cast off. You run to the side, jump up on the rail, and leap across to the island.

'What are you doing?' growls the Minotaur.

'It's something stupid and heroic, isn't it?' says Ancaeus.

'Probably,' you call back. 'But I figure why break the habit of a lifetime?'

'How will you even get home?' says Ancaeus. 'You could wait millennia for another ship to dock here.'

Eos smiles. 'Go to the pool in the middle of the island, valiant one. Dive deep. The waters will carry you back.'

'You're an idiot,' says Ancaeus as he pulls in the last mooring rope, 'but good luck.' ▶ 90

298

If you want to sprinkle the **food of the gods** with **abysm toxin**, cross both off your possessions and ▶ 492

If you leave it untainted ▶ 1621

299

There are smears of blood on the fingerprints dug into his neck. The murderer and the burglar who cut themself breaking in are one and the same person.

You also notice soot under the corpse's fingernails, just on his right hand.

Look around for the letters ▶ 1431
Make yourself scarce ▶ 988

300

Get the codeword **Rose**.

Dunamis pouts, but when she sees you won't be swayed she slinks back to the sundial and replaces the hairclip before the owner notices it was missing.

Returning, she plucks a handful of foliage off the bushes and starts shredding it. 'You think I should turn over a new leaf?'

'What kind of life is it, making your way by petty robbery?'

She throws you a sly smile. 'That's a very good point. Little trinkets like that won't make me rich. I'll aim higher in future.'

Before you can say another word, she has slipped away through the partygoers thronging the courtyard.

▶ 808

301

You walk through a garden overhung with heavy boughs. The moon is a huge pale green apple waiting to be plucked. On the trees around you hang dazzling cream-white crescent-shaped fruits. The clear high notes of the nightingale's song die away, leaving only the scented night breeze and a waiting silence.

A tingle on the back of your neck makes you look up. A large spider is inching its way towards the ground on a thread that might go all the way up to the moon.

Brush it aside ▶ 1429
Watch it spin its web ▶ 1654

302

'You owe quite a tidy sum, don't you?' says the sergeant chidingly. 'You must've been very, very naughty. Now it's time to cough up.'

He gestures to some of his men and they come forward, seizing you in firm hands. The sergeant swaggers around his desk and snatches the money pouch from your belt. 'This will do as a down payment,' he sneers.

Delete any money you were carrying.

If you had less than 40 pyr ▶ 1096
If you had 500 pyr or more ▶ 245
Otherwise they are content to shove you out into the street ▶ 1642

303

If you have the codeword **Quench** and this box ☐ is empty, tick it and ▶ 330

Otherwise, if you do not have the codeword *Razor* and this box ❑ is empty, tick it and ▶ 1430

Otherwise, if you have *Razor* but do not have the title **Sage Herder** and this box ❑ is empty, tick it and ▶ 607

Otherwise, if you do not have the codeword *Rune* and this box ❑ is empty, tick it and ▶ 146

Otherwise, if you do have the codeword *Neural* but not the title **Soul Bearer** and this box ❑ is empty, tick it and ▶ 323

Otherwise if you have the title **The Chosen One** ▶ 190

Otherwise ▶ 816

304

You get a few sympathetic pats on the shoulder as Kazala takes a bow. Afterwards, as people go back to their drinks and conversations, she comes over and raises her glass.

'You had the best three stories in all of Vulcan City,' she says. 'I just told mine with a bit more brio.'

'Let me get out on a few more adventures,' you say, returning her toast, 'and then we can have a rematch.'

Although you accepted defeat gracefully, your reputation takes a hit. Lose 1 Glory and ▶ 1324

305

Look at your codewords and titles. Check a box for each of the following that applies:
- ❑ The codeword *Rhapsody*
- ❑ The codeword *Quake*
- ❑ The codeword *Pumped*
- ❑ The codeword *Nanny* or the title **Godslayer**

If all four boxes are now ticked ▶ 1160

If three or fewer are ticked ▶ 1072

306

❑

If the box above was already ticked ▶ 1460

Otherwise, tick the box now and read on.

It's made of – you're not sure what. Metal would surely be bulkier, more cumbersome; leather less hardy. It has hung in the spray and sea winds yet at all times it gleams as if freshly forged. The plates of the armour are like the stuff of beetles' wings, glossy and durable, burnished and brighter than fire.

And the design is almost unearthly. It seems fashioned for Achilles, so close a fit for his broad shoulders and strong athletic frame that it might have been grown as his twin. And yet here it stands in the open, untended, unclaimed, and Achilles when he enters and leaves the enclosure spares it not so much as a glance.

Beside it rests a great shield glittering with silver. Few mortal warriors could lift it. On its shining face, impervious to ordinary weapons, are embossed constellations and intricate scenes that seem to shimmer and change in the light, depicting the destiny of empires, and all encircled by an azure rim evoking the Ocean that girds the world.

If you have the **Panoply of the Lost Hero** among your possessions ▶ 413

If not but you have the codeword *Nanny* ▶ 37

Otherwise ▶ 1460

307

The odds are all against you. You have one last chance. Make a GRACE roll at difficulty 16.

Succeed ▶ 978

Fail ▶ 46

308

By now there's a teeming horde of night-creatures pressed right up to the edge of the roof, so close that you can see the pallid, worm-gnawed features of the vampires, the red eyes and spittle-flecked jaws of the were-beasts, the misshapen faces of capering nightmare demons. Baying and snarling, they are so intent on getting to you that some get jostled over the edge and fall flailing to the street far below.

Each time a grapple lodges on the ship's rail, instantly a stream of attackers comes scrabbling along it to get aboard. Careless of the wind, rain and the lethal drop below, their only thought is to continue their wild onslaught. Even the Minotaur, whose blade flashes and spills blood and guts with every swing, must eventually tire and then the monstrous tide will overwhelm the ship.

The mainsail is still only half-raised, the wet canvas flapping uselessly in the wind as Ancaeus tugs at the ropes. Not only is there no forward momentum, but the ship is listing and beginning to lose altitude as the helmsman bends helplessly over the buoyancy rotor. But can you afford to help either of them when it means leaving the Minotaur alone to repel boarders?

Stay at the rail	▶ 487
Help fix the buoyancy rotor	▶ 854
Get up in the rigging	▶ 1375

309

The priests gather in a wooden kiosk at the end of the beach. Drawing curtains to blot of the daylight, they burn tapers that fill the interior with richly scented smoke. As your senses reel from the overpowering vapour, you feel the presence of your deity. Bowing, you wait to hear the voice of the god.

'Speak.'

What will you say?

'Can you return me to my own time?'	▶ 105
'Should I fight in this war?'	▶ 1130

If you have the codewords **Ratchet** and **Quiddity** ▶ 934

If you have **Ratchet** but not **Quiddity** ▶ 1355

Otherwise, if you have **Rug** ▶ 973

Otherwise ▶ 1531

310

Even as she slumps lifeless to the ground, Nyx flings a last tendril of searing darkness. You are too badly injured to evade it. Unless you can think of something fast, you're doomed.

You need to make an INGENUITY roll at difficulty 16.

Succeed	▶ 401
Fail	▶ 267

311

Among the crowd there is a familiar gamine face. Nyx has no reason to notice her, but you do. 'Here,' calls Dunamis. 'Zinc left this. You might need it.' She runs forward and tosses something to you. You catch it – a ball of yellow amber about four inches across.

'What trinket have you there?' snarls Nyx. But you see her frown as recognition dawns.

'Hyperion was the original sun god,' shouts Dunamis. 'It's his eye.'

Hearing that, Nyx reacts with desperate speed. Her hands sweep up, summoning a dark mist that billows out around you. You're engulfed in a black void. Ancient fear of the unknown raises the hairs on the back of your neck. But you're given hope by the look you saw in Nyx's eyes before the darkness fell. She is afraid.

The Eye of Hyperion begins to glow. At first it's no more than a faint spark, but it grows brighter, golden light streaming from it and pushing back the encircling darkness. Nyx's face, dimly outlined by the light, contorts as she focuses on summoning all her power. Torrents of black nullity pour down onto the glowing Eye. It gutters, dimming, and you fear it's about to be extinguished. But within it lies the essence of the titan of the sun, once almost the equal of the queen of night. Pulsing, the golden light flares up, resisting Nyx's power for a moment more.

Her face looms huge and white in the abyssal darkness, etched with strain as she summons all her might. Beads of sweat stand out glistening on her brow.

'You will learn,' she mutters between clenched teeth. 'I am Night. I am unconquerable.'

She may well be right. In this struggle between light and dark, she's gradually gaining the upper hand. The beams of light from the Eye are sputtering, growing dimmer, no brighter than a candleflame now in the immensity of utter darkness.

312

You're walking past the hatch to the hold when you hear a series of thuds from below.

'Sounds like some of the cargo's rolling about down there,' says a sailor who is winding up a coil of rope.

You look around. Whatever you heard, it can't be any of the crew – they're all on deck. Could it be a stowaway? A saboteur?

Go down and take a look	▶ 618
Tell Ancaeus	▶ 843
Ignore it	▶ 438

313

You haul yourself painfully out of bed and accost the priest in charge of the infirmary. 'Were there any other survivors of the explosion?' you ask.

'If so they weren't brought here.'

'There was a man I was talking to. He was holding the device that exploded.'

The priest shrugs. 'He might have been taken to a different temple. Which god did he revere?'

'He's not really a fan of the gods, come to think of it.'

'In that case,' says the priest loftily, 'he will have suffered the just deserts of mortal pride. Unless he has the power to work his own miracles.'

That's a worrying thought. He just might – in which case you have made a very powerful enemy.

Seeing that you are well enough to walk, the priests tell you that they need the bed for other patients. You make your way outside, still brooding on Daedalus's fate.

▶ 625

314

Along the street lope a pack of Keres, the terrible hunting dogs of Thanatos. Their great grey wings are folded tight around their skeletally thin bodies, leaving them with immensely long stilt-like forelegs with which they pick their way through the rubble. Their snouts are long and crammed with needle-sharp teeth, superficially wolf-like but with the warty leather skin of huge lizards.

Most horribly, speared on those long legs each of the Keres has a series of victims, some still alive and squirming with the hard claw of the forelimb driven right though them like birds on a spit.

The Keres sniff the air. Little eyes like flakes of spite bore into you. It's too late to run.

If your Current Location is **93** and you have the codeword *Rune* and this box ❑ is empty, tick it and ▶ **2**

Otherwise, if your Current Location is **881** and you have the title **Friend of the Forest** and this box ❑ is empty, tick it and ▶ **1426**

Otherwise, if your Current Location is **1175** and you have the title **Repairer of Reputations** and this box ❑ is empty, tick it and ▶ **998**

Otherwise, if you have the codeword *Pledged* and this box ❑ is empty, tick it and ▶ **1567**

Otherwise ▶ **1047**

315

'The lord of that region is bound by forces inimical to life. Your destiny is to set him free.'

'How?' you ask, though hesitating to question the mouthpiece of a god.

'Obtain a gift from the goddess Nysa and take it to each of the other three mountain deities to be blessed. Then journey to the Fortress of the Wind, but be sure you don't go there alone.'

That's all she has to say. You murmur a short prayer to Apollo and leave.

▶ **510**

316

The Palace of the Archons comprises an open hall behind a colonnade of fluted white pillars. The floor of the hall is a polished surface that continually swirls in a mobile pattern of gold, rust and grey-white. In the rafters high above are immense eyes that occasionally blink – mechanical contrivances, you assume, but they serve to remind the Archons that there are greater powers than them in this world.

Seven Archons rule the city in the name of the Olympian gods. These seven wear crowns that correspond to the sun, the moon and the five classical planets. By consulting the heavens they learn the wishes of the gods, periodically issuing edicts to ensure those wishes are fulfilled.

Symbolically the Archons embody the seven qualities believed essential for good governance: intelligence, skill, intuition, leadership, knowledge, willpower and resources.

To gain entry into the Palace you must have no scars and a Glory score of at least 10. Failing that, the guards turn you away at the door as unworthy to walk in these sacred precincts – unless you have the title of **Paladin**, in which case the normal rules don't apply.

Walk in   ▶ **713**
Turn away   ▶ **1642**

317

The night watchmen are hauling your uninvited visitor off to jail. 'Don't you want to know what I came here for?' he calls back to you from the doorway.

Tell them to wait; you want to hear his story ▶ **811**
They can take him away; you go back to bed ▶ **97**

A horrible big dog comes bounding along the street. Only it's not actually bounding, it's more like scuttling. And it's not a dog, it's a very big black ant. Its mandibles are snapping like garden shears, and you don't like the look of it at all, but other people on the street seem to think it's cute and you don't want to be left out, so you reach down to pet it.

Snick! The serrated mandibles saw through your flesh like a knife cutting cabbage. The ant scurries on. You are left looking at your fingers as they roll into the gutter.

'That's why I prefer a cat,' says a burly quarryman standing nearby.

You look sadly at your mutilated hand. 'It's not as painful as I thought, but I miss them. Those fingers had done things you people wouldn't believe.'

'Don't be a cry baby,' says the man, not unkindly. 'Here.'

He pulls a pat of butter out of his pocket, brushing stone dust off it before putting it into your good hand.

'Isn't butter for burns?'

'Not even,' he says. 'But you're right, it's a salve.'

'So my fingers will just grow back again, then, will they?'

'Oh, you don't want to get too attached to them. It's only magnets, you know, that holds them on. You can keep the butter. Any that's left over, make a sand – '

'A sandwich?'

'Whatever. I better get going. Those rocks won't break themselves.'

As he strolls off, you see the ant coming back so you push open a gate in the wall and dive through into a garden.

▶ 301

Write in the box anything you are leaving – or you can recover items you left here earlier by writing them on your Adventure Sheet and erasing them from the box.

ITEMS AT HOME

Go out ▶ Current Location

'You are in the wrong place,' says the Oracle, her voice so low that you have to lean forward to hear her.

'Where should I be?'

'You seek insight regarding the region of Arcadia? Look for it either in the Groves of Dionysus or among the wine jugs of the Pygmaioi Odos.'

'What's that? A name? A place?'

Her eyes flutter, the pupils flickering as she struggles between another world and this one. 'The Pygmaioi are what you know today as gnomes.'

She gives a gasp and falls forward off her stool.

'Are you all right?'

You would help her up, but profane hands are not permitted to touch her while the god's spirit still lingers. She motions you away. 'Leave me now. I have told you all I can.'

▶ 510

321

Delete the **scrimshaw hourglass** from your possessions.

'It's never just about changing one decision,' you point out. 'You have to live a different life. Otherwise there'll just be another mistake waiting down the road.'

If you have the codeword *Quiddity* ▶ 194

If not ▶ 676

322

It's not enough. With faltering morale your troops begin to buckle under the sheer weight of numbers on the enemy side. As they fall back into a last-ditch defence, you realize your only hope is to strike directly at Nyx herself.

Struggling through the melee, you hack down a succession of slavering foes until you break through their lines. There ahead of you stands the towering figure of Nyx, majestic and seemingly as unassailable as an obelisk of black granite. And yet you must try. If you fail, she will usher in a reign of darkness and terror for all time.

Get the codeword *Romance* and ▶ 344

323

'I see a cell high up under the eaves of a baleful prison. Two men are incarcerated there, a father and son.'

'Do I free them?'

She peers into the invisible future. 'The gods have given you the means to do so. But it is the pleasure of the gods to grant us free will. Perhaps you will free them, perhaps harm them, perhaps leave them there to rot.'

You could almost scream in frustration. 'You're telling me nothing. Is this what you call a prophecy?'

If you have the codeword *Quiddity* ▶ 355

If not but you have the codeword *Noisome* ▶ 244

Otherwise ▶ 629

324

Look at your codewords and titles. Check a box for each of the following that applies:

❑ The codeword *Rhapsody*
❑ The codeword *Quake*
❑ The codeword *Pumped*
❑ The codeword *Nanny* or the title **Godslayer**

If all four boxes are now ticked ▶ 875

If three or fewer are ticked ▶ 1160

325

Towards its southern end, the Boulevard of the Sylph is shabbier, with smaller shops and houses crowded in together. An inexpungible stain mottles the city wall here, a grey-brown mould that thrives on the cadaverous exhalations that blow in off the realm of Hades.

This corner of the city is steeped in perpetual twilight. Swiftly moving pearlescent shadows create a disturbing sense of dislocation. You are constantly catching a furtive movement in the corner of your eye, only to turn and face an empty doorway or alley.

To go straight to a city location that you already know about, note **325** as your Current Location, then ▶ 1432

Or you can go:

North	▶ 509
South	▶ 1222
To the Tomb of Hope	▶ 88
Into a curio shop	▶ 1320

326

Zinc loses interest in you as other matters press for his attention. With a wave of his hand he either bids you farewell or dismisses you – take it however you wish – and one of his gang escorts you out of the Grumbles.

'Which way you wanna go?' says your guide, pausing at the junction of two narrow, twisting alleys.

The Street of Knives	▶ 1617
The Avenue of the Anvil	▶ 63

327

You and Achilles help each other with the straps of your armour. He picks out a team of horses and orders one of his men to harness them to a chariot.

'Any tips?' you ask him.

'Don't get killed.' He cracks a smile. The imminence of battle is like a drug to him, firing his blood and giving him a vitality he rarely reveals at other times.

'Nor you.'

'I won't die before Ilion falls,' he says. 'You know, destiny. Takes the shine off a good fight, if you want the truth.'

▶ 166

328

'Turns out there's some reward money for you,' he says, opening a safe at the back of his office. 'Ten percent of what we were able to recover of Autolycus's ill-gotten gains.'

'And how's Autolycus doing?'

'Couldn't tell you. He escaped the day after you brought him in. We still got his tin squeeze, though, so I don't think he'll give us any more trouble.'

He hands you a bag containing 150 pyr. Add it to the money on your Adventure Sheet. Thanking the sergeant, you go back out to the Forum.

▶ 1642

329

One morning you send your brother to school on his own. He takes a route that runs past Nihakos's house, and as Nihakos comes out of his gate he gets a rotten tomato smack in his face. After a moment of blank astonishment he chases after your brother, calling out almost lascivious promises of bloody revenge.

Your brother darts down the street you told him to take, leaping at just the right moment. Nihakos charges on in his heavy flat-footed way and falls right through the carpet of palm leaves you positioned over an open sewer cover. There is a splash, a frenzied bubbling cry, and then vile sucking sounds as Nihakos tries to heave himself out of the slime.

He plods back home past walls lined with the schoolkids he has lorded it over in the past – all jeering at the excrement-covered bully. You never see him again. Perhaps his family moved away. You never bother to find out.

Increase your GRACE or your INGENUITY by +1 (you decide which) but reduce your CHARM to −1.

▶ **247**

330

'When you save a life, does that person owe you? Or are you responsible for them?'

'Perhaps a little of both.'

If you have the codeword *Rigor* ▶ 227
If not but you have the codeword *Reflection* ▶ 690
Otherwise ▶ 1509

331

'You and I have met every night, did you but know it. And you are almost as familiar with my dear brother, though perhaps your experiences with him have been less agreeable.'

'And your brother is..?'

He claps you heartily on the back, a friendly enough gesture though it knocks the wind out of you. 'A gentle soul, for all that his reputation's so fearsome. He'll be along shortly. He wouldn't want to miss the ball at the end of time.'

▶ **827**

332

Seeing their queen defeated, Nyx's forces melt away like dew against the rising light of dawn. Your own allies cheer your grand and total triumph. Among their ranks you see many old friends. To know they have stayed at your side through the darkest times is reward enough.

If you have the codeword *Rhombus* ▶ 1538
Otherwise ▶ 1667

333

❏

You are at the East Gate of the city. If you do not have the codeword *Reverie* and the box above is empty, put a tick in it and ▶ 1562; otherwise read on.

If you have the codeword *Ridge*, note **333** as your Current Location and ▶ 1064; otherwise read on.

Between tall pylons of red granite trundle carts that carry spices, stone, jewels, ivory and fruit from the land of

Notus. As each cart enters the city, the wares vanish and are replaced with a glowing quantity of pyr which the trader can use as cash.

Beside the gate is a noticeboard on which prospective employers post missions that a daring adventurer can undertake for gold and glory.

To go straight to a city location that you already know about, note **333** as your Current Location, then ▶ **1432**

Otherwise you can take a look at the noticeboard, in which case note **333** as your Current Location, then ▶ **56**

Or you can go:

North along the Boulevard of the Gnome ▶ **1534**

West along the Avenue of Subsolanus ▶ **625**

South along the Boulevard of the Gnome ▶ **161**

East out of the city ▶ **333** in *The Hammer of the Sun*

334

The sheets are slick with rain and the mast keeps pitching to and fro as gusts of wind batter the hull. As you climb you glance down to see the small figure of the Minotaur struggling against what looks like an endless black tide of monsters pouring from the rooftop.

The sail is tangled on the furthest spar. You stagger out, clutching desperately to the rigging and trying to keep your footing on the slippery timber. Tugging at the trapped sail, you manage to drag part of it free but the canvas rips and hangs flapping uselessly in the wind. The ship continues to sink inexorably.

A shadow blots out the flickering sky. You look up to see Thanatos outlined against the storm, his giant hand swinging around to splinter the hull. Crippled, the *Sunrise* spins out of control. It lurches to one side. Sailors are flung overboard, falling to their death on the street below. You cling to the yard as the ship drops in a helpless spiral, breaking up on the ground as surely as if a gale had swept her onto rocks.

You lie stunned in the wreckage. A few people have remained in the street, too paralyzed with terror to run. One edges nervously past where you are lying, perhaps hoping to bolt and run. Then he turns his face upwards and gives a despairing moan. Slipping on the wet cobblestones, he starts to scramble away. A sliver of deathly white light stabs down, touching him for just an instant, and he is gone. All that remains of him is a wisp of dark vapour that is blown away on the wind.

A colossal foot descends to the street beside you, landing with a tremor that dislodges bricks and sends cracks spreading through the flagstones. Painfully you rise to behold pitiless Thanatos standing like a mountain against the raging storm. ▶ **595**

335

'Any idea where he'd have gone?'

They look at you indignantly. Finally one of the sisters speaks for them all. 'There was no way of telling what was going on in his head,' she says. 'He used to be one of the sharpest minds in city politics, can you believe, but by the end he'd wander out of the house in his birthday suit and sit in the yard having a long conversation with an old cartwheel he called Shanks.'

'He was a barmy bird and no mistake,' ventures one of the grandkids. 'Finding him will be hard enough, and good luck convincing the old coot that he's dead.'

If Galatea is your companion ▶ **1555**

If Polymnia is your companion ▶ **1475**

If neither of those is with you but you have the **Face of Wisdom** (INGENUITY +3) ▶ **1319**

Otherwise ▶ **133**

336

'I see the Delta of Darkness,' intones the Oracle. 'There – a hut. Inside, a ladder. And down and down and down you climb, even under the underworld.'

'What will I find there?'

'Lost voyagers, becalmed in the bowels of the earth.'

She goes silent, staring at you. Being scrutinized by the whites of her eyes makes you uncomfortable, so you mutter your thanks and retreat out of her presence.

▶ **510**

337

The sun appears over the trees, sending a blaze of warm clean light through the rain-spattered windows.

The effect on the vampire is ghastly. With a sound like a foul drain clearing, she spews maggots onto the carpet. Corruption spreads over her like a mould, turning the rotted white flesh a poisonous dark grey. Her eyes sink and shrivel in her sockets. Her hair falls away in clumps.

With a last shudder and a gust of foetid breath that might be either a curse or a sigh, she collapses into a shapeless mound of decayed bones and dirt-smeared rags.

The smell lingers for days, even after you've had the rug removed and burned. Finally you have to move to another bedroom. The door to the room where you slew the vampire is kept locked, and after a time the servants take to calling it Tritona's room. Thus in death she returns as a presence to the house she was exiled from in life.

Lose the codewords *Rabbit* and *Ruffle* if you have them and then ▶ **97**

338

'I thought nobody could see the palace unless Vulcan wanted them to,' you say.

Dunamis nods. 'There's a way around that using the noticeboards by the city gates. You can glitch the simulation.'

'That's a lot of effort to go to just to slit a few purses.'

'Well…' She scuffs at the grass with her foot, suddenly a bashful young girl rather than a street-smart thief. 'Zinc told me to keep an eye on you.'

'Does he think I'll cause trouble?'

'More like trouble will happen to you. Anyway, we should mingle. Maybe I'll catch you later.'

She slips away across the courtyard, which by now is filled with groups of party guests. Over the mutter of conversation the Celedons continue their sublime singing. A colonnade runs the length of one wall of the courtyard. At the back of it, open doors reveal a high-ceilinged ballroom within.

Get the codeword *Rose* and ▶ **224**

339

You squeeze through to the front of the crowd, coming face to face with a bearded priest who is glaring at you in outrage.

'So you admit it!' he says, pointing an indignant finger at a defaced stone plinth that stands at the meeting point of four paths.

'Admit it? I just got here.'

'I asked the gods to send the miscreant forth, and here you are. Do you wish to add blasphemy to your crime of vandalism?'

'This is ridiculous,' you protest, but one look at the faces around you shows that they are all on the priest's side.

'Pay a fine to the temples and we'll say no more about it,' says the priest with a condescending sneer.

'How big a fine?'

He strokes his long beard. 'We'll call it 20 pyr.'

If you have no money or refuse to pay ▶ **861**

Otherwise cross off 20 pyr and ▶ **806**

340

Myth speaks of a cold clutch at the end, but Death's gaze is a white-hot magnesium fire – searing, blinding, like a rip in the world through to the volcanic light beyond. In that pitiless blaze nothing can survive.

▶ **666**

341

Hurriedly you cram the **beeswax** into your ears; delete it from your possessions. You can still hear the piercing cry of the Celedons, but it's less painful than before.

▶ **437**

342

❑

If the box above was already ticked ▶ **1293** immediately; otherwise put a tick in it now and then read on.

Achilles has been waiting for you to share his evening meal. 'We have eaten together for all the time you've been here,' he says with an almost diffident smile, 'but usually it's just been a few bits of broth-soaked bread for you.'

'Don't apologize. It's hard feeding somebody when they don't have the good manners to stay conscious.'

'It hasn't stopped me from getting to know you. You talked in your delirium.'

'Oh dear.' You pour a goblet of wine. 'Perhaps better to draw a veil over anything I said.'

'No man will hear aught of it from these lips,' says Achilles seriously. 'But I heard enough to think you know something of the loneliness of destiny. I share that curse. The gods have decreed my life will be short but filled with glory. By my hand Ilion will fall, but I will not survive to carry any of the spoils back home to Phthia.'

'I thought the city of the Myrmidons was called Iskandria.'

He looks deep into your eyes, a secret pain clouding his youthful brow. 'You may know it by another name. I heard enough to know that your home is worlds away from here.'

'And I must get back.'

'I know. I'll be sad to part from you. Your presence here has been a shaft of light piercing the unending cloud of this damned war. We're never free of it – after dinner I must check on the horses and chariot. There's to be a battle tomorrow.'

What will you say?

'Shall I take part?' ► **766**

'Why do you fight, Achilles?' ► **609**

'Do you know how I can get home?' ► **1526**

343

You while away a few pleasant hours conversing with Lady Pemphreda's witty guests. Even so, it is hard to hide your disappointment.

'You sigh like the end of summer,' says a freckled woman with silver bangles that rattle on her wrists as she talks. 'Troubles?'

You shrug. 'I hoped for a little fun here, that's all. A diverting adventure, a game, some juicy gossip. Something like that.'

'Maybe next time,' she says with a smile.

► **1324**

344

The closer you get to Nyx, the more daunting she becomes. This is the titan queen whom even Zeus feared. With her cloak of night around her she is a blot of utter darkness, blacker than the dour sky behind her.

You snatch up a sword, running up a makeshift ramp of rubble to gain height. Perhaps you can launch yourself at her, a human missile.

She throws you a scornful look and starts to turn away, not even deigning to raise her hand against you. 'One mortal? Hero though you may be in your own world, you are less than an ant to me. I will grant you one boon for your courage, however. You may decide which of my sons gets to claim your soul.'

Her sons? Of course, Hypnos and Thanatos. Sleep and Death. They converge upon you, looming giants as mighty as their mother. Even as you leap, you see the gap between them closing. Their swords present a whirling wall of steel directly in your path.

But then another figure arises from nowhere, equal to them in stature, blazing with a golden hue, great wings outstretched against the ink-black sky. He stands ready to do battle with the twin sons of Night.

'Eros,' Thanatos sneers, recognizing him. 'You are no match for Death.'

Eros laughs back in his face. 'I am Love, and Love is unconquerable.'

You run to join him. 'Thanks for showing up, but we're still outmatched.'

'Wait,' says Eros. 'I have summoned other allies to our cause. If they join us we will give these whelps a fight they'll remember.'

If you have the title **The Liberator** ► **62**

If not but you have the codeword *Quake* ► **553**

If not but you have the codeword *Pumped* ► **720**

Otherwise, if you have the codeword *Nanny* ► **1637**

Otherwise ► **1183**

345

'I can counsel men to keep their heads. I can advise how to array forces for battle, how to rule wisely, how to treat with enemies and how to reward friends. But, dear lady, you ask of things far beyond my ken.'

'You are said to be the most knowledgeable man here. If you cannot advise me then I am stranded.'

'Perhaps your destiny has led you here to Ilion, for this is the Eternal Battle, waged endlessly on the outskirts of time and space.'

You shake your head. 'Your war is a local squabble. No matter what happens here, unless I get back the whole of eternity is doomed to be swallowed by fathomless Night.'

Nestor's bushy eyebrows raise in alarm. 'You speak of one whom even storm-wielding Zeus fears. Listen, Amazon, if your quest is of such paramount import then you cannot seek counsel from any less than the gods themselves. Go to the priests. Buy a tripod and make a sacrifice. If your god has not abandoned you, that way you will come by the answers you seek.'

Ask another question ► **724**

Thank him and leave ► **735**

346

The *Sunrise* draws alongside an island floating in the emptiness of space. Grappling hooks are flung across to moor the ship in place, then the sailors push out a gangplank. It creaks and sways as you walk down it. You try not to look over the side, where under a sheer precipice of suspended rock there are stars stretching off into infinity.

Ancaeus joins you. 'The Isle of the Dawn,' he says. 'The last outpost of the reality we know. After carrying out repairs and stocking up on supplies, we'll be sailing on into the unknown.'

'If I come with you.'

'If you do.'

The terrain here is not like a regular landscape, more like a vast flat pavement of stone that over the aeons has subsided into jumbled slabs. The few trees are dead and bare, fossilized into tortuous twisted shapes.

'I don't know if you're going to find much in the way of

supplies here,' you say to Ancaeus as you look out across this desolate scene.

'We'll see.' He directs the crew to start fixing up the ship, detailing a search party to look for water.

'There's your water,' you say, pointing. 'Or some sort of liquid, anyway.'

A glimmer of silver in the middle of the island marks a lake from which streams meander out in all directions to the edge, where they cascade in a spray of faint light into the airless void. An outcropping of rock rises out of the lake, the only feature in the flat landscape.

'Let's find out,' says Ancaeus.

The Minotaur joins you, his axe slung casually across his bulky shoulders. 'Just in case of trouble,' he says, seeing you looking at it.

The three of you set off with Ancaeus hurrying ahead. Having finally reached these places he's been dreaming of and working towards for years, his eagerness to explore lends him the sprightliness of youth.

The island isn't big. A few minutes' walk brings you to the shore of the lake.

▶ **539**

347

You languish in chains, growing steadily weaker. From time to time the guards send you down to the torture chamber for interrogation, but after a while they lose interest in asking you questions. Not long after that they forget to bring you food – or perhaps there is a deliberate policy to starve you. No magistrate ever convicted you, so perhaps the prison authorities simply regard you as an inconvenient detail to be got rid of.

Eventually the squalid conditions, the beatings and the lack of food take their toll. You succumb to fever and die alone in the dark.

▶ **111**

348

'That's probably at the Syndics' palace,' ventures Dunamis.

'Good to know, my dear!' declares Myletes. 'All right, and tell me, where would you take it?'

Dunamis pokes her toe into the carpet. 'Er... well... I suppose perhaps one of the noticeboards..?'

'Where did you get this girl?' Myletes says. 'She's much smarter than you. Yes, that's exactly right. Use the noticeboard, get into Vulcan's workshop, and see if you can undo Nyx's changes.'

If you have the **Face of Wisdom** (INGENUITY +3) ▶ **646**

Otherwise ▶ **1290**

349

You remove the antlers. The young man jumps back in astonishment. The girl gives a gasp and jumps to the ground.

'You are a wizard,' says Dydkos.

'In dreams, isn't everybody?'

'Why reveal your true nature, then? If you came here to steal Roxana back to that venomous toad she's wedded to, you had only to carry her off.'

You shrug. 'It seemed too easy. Anyway, who said I'd come here to take her back?'

They wait while you weigh up your options.

If you agree to side with them against the merchant ▶ **763**

If not then you will have to fight Dydkos to get to her. Make a STRENGTH or GRACE roll (your choice) at difficulty 14.

Succeed ▶ **1149**

Fail ▶ **863**

350
❑

The last stretch of tunnel is so narrow that you almost have to dislocate your shoulders to squeeze through. Clods of clay entwined with tree roots give way to a trickle of foul sewer water, and you emerge in a rubbish-strewn alley. The grating you have come through is set in a niche in the brickwork.

If the box above is empty, put a tick in it and ▶ **189**

If it was already ticked ▶ **571**

351

The funeral party is waiting for you outside their ancestral tomb, a massive edifice of gleaming marble whose sheer excess and bad taste stand in insolent defiance of death.

'He's gone,' you tell them.

The eldest son looks at the coffin. The lid is now fixed on. 'We thought we'd have to put it in the vault empty,' he says.

'It seems a bit heavier now,' says one of the pallbearers.

They open the coffin, and Xechasiaris's body lies there, just a grey lump of mortal clay now that his spirit has gone on to the afterlife.

'What's this?' says a pallbearer, reaching to tug a scroll from the corpse's hands. 'Huh. It's a codicil to his will. And signed too.'

'What nonsense!' The family all try to snatch the scroll from him, but only succeed in getting in each other's way. The pallbearer shows it to you.

'But – this grants me ownership of a house on Septentrional Avenue!'

The family, who were all talking at once, go silent and stare at you like a pack of hyenas. 'Impossible,' says the eldest daughter. 'That's our family home.'

'It's got a witness seal from the temple of Hades,' says the pallbearer. 'All looks above board to me.'

'You can't take our home,' says the youngest daughter, bursting into tears. 'We've just lost our father. We can't lose our home too.'

Well?

| Tear up the codicil | ▶ 851 |
| Evict them and move in | ▶ 1217 |

352

Psyche adjusts some dials on the equipment beside her. 'I've isolated this somatic fabricator from the rest of the matrix. If you're ready, I'll use it to make some enhancements.'

You look at her askance. 'Enhancements to me, do you mean?'

'No need to look so fretful,' she says impatiently. 'You've been brought back to life, haven't you? And every time you hone your strength or speed, those are changes that the workshop of the gods is making to your basic template.'

Agree to have Psyche modify your abilities ▶ 1628

Decline the offer ▶ 1171

353

The intruder is a slim athletic man in snug-fitting black burglar's clothes. He's still holding the jemmy he used to get the window open. A movement in the far corner of the room alerts you that he's not alone. There's at least one more.

It occurs to you with an icy shock that you don't have your possessions, including any items that normally give you attribute bonuses. Those are in the bedroom upstairs. You're facing them in just your nightgown.

Act dumb	▶ 1517
Fight	▶ 1369
Run to get the night watch	▶ 648

354

You smash the last of the Celedons, breaking the rivets that hold her torso together so that her backplate pops off. Cables and gears spill out and her screeching cry dies away to a final grinding click.

You snatch up a loose brick to batter her head in, but Dunamis catches your arm. 'Easy, tiger. Nyx couldn't even make a decent alarm clock out of what's left of that lot. Let's get going.'

▶ Current Location

355

'If you free them you will make a powerful ally,' she concedes grudgingly.

Petulant at being forced to make an unequivocal statement, she points to the door. You are dismissed.

▶ 510

356

Cross off what you paid, either 100 pyr or a **curio credit**. Also delete the **winding key** from your possessions and record the **Box of the Music of the Spheres** instead.

Sell him another item	▶ 526
Look for something to buy	▶ 496
Leave	▶ 325

357

Achilles accompanies you along the beach to the makeshift temple where the Achaean priests sacrifice to the gods. You walk in silence, feet crunching on the pebble-strewn sand. All around, soldiers are settling down to their evening meal. After the ferocity of the day's fighting, each is sunk in his own thoughts so that an unearthly hush has descended on the camp, broken only by occasional snatches of murmured conversation.

Achilles takes your arm and leads you towards one of the campfires. The knot of men around it look up with startled expressions, self-conscious to have two such renowned heroes in their midst. Achilles nods to them absently, hardly aware of their presence. He gestures at the leaping flames that daub dancing patterns of light and darkness on your faces.

'Great an event as this war may be,' he says, 'it is but one fire in the whole of eternity. See along the shore – the constellation of fires in the night, they are like the great tumults and tragedies in history, all-consuming if you are close to them, but in the vast ocean of darkness they are merely pinpricks.'

'I wouldn't have taken you for a poet.'

'Any man is a poet if love inspires him.' He looks towards the shrine. 'I have a feeling we must part soon.'

You nod. 'Our mortal lives are like these sparks rising from the fire. See how each swirls on the wind, burns bright, and then is snuffed out.'

'And so we are forgotten, our lives without meaning?'

'We must make our own meaning.'

Out over the sea, limpid stars hang in the darkness. A voice is softly calling your name. Looking to see if Achilles and the others hear it too, you notice they are motionless. The flames too stand fixed in place. The waves are no longer sighing but quiet and still. Time holds its breath.

Squinting into the dark you can make out the face of

your god against the sky. The god's voice is the only sound in all this frozen stillness. 'Come.'

You wade out into the water. It closes silently over your head like black oil. Guided by the protective hand of your god, you swim through the waiting centuries back to your own time.

If you have the codeword *Nanny* ▶ 709

If not ▶ 73

358

'I'll only climb over the wall again,' Dunamis says breezily as you march her to the gate.

'Don't be greedy. You've already got a pocketful of jewellery. That should be enough to be going on with.'

'Easy to say when you're the sort who gets invited to hobnob with the swells.'

A thought strikes you as she's walking away. 'How did you even find this place? Doesn't Vulcan conceal it from most people's eyes?'

'Oh, that?' She glances over her shoulder and gives you a wink. 'You've just got to know which button to press – if you can find the buttons in the first place.'

You return to the courtyard pondering what she meant. ▶ 808

359

If this box ❑ was already ticked ▶ 1267

If the box is empty, put a tick in it now and then read on.

The ground shakes, dislodging pebbles that tumble down the slope of the hill. Ahead of you, a boulder the size of a small house rocks from side to side. An earth tremor? No – the boulder is abruptly flung aside, a contemptuously casual gesture by a giant figure that stands directly in your path.

His body is knotted with long silvery scars and in his hand he wields a broken tree trunk that looks puny in comparison to his thick-sinewed arms. But strangest of all is his head, massive even in proportion to his gigantic frame, so that he seems all face, his jutting jaw extending almost to his navel. Hot saliva runs from the corners of his huge lips, sending up hissing vapour as it hits the ground.

'Enceladus,' says Oizys. 'He gave Athena a good fight once.'

Turn and run   ▶ 918

Advance to do battle   ▶ 21

360

'This fountain must be sacred to a nymph,' says a fat man at the front of the crowd. 'I threw in a coin and my wish came true.'

'What did you wish for? An extra chin?' says an old woman, provoking the others to laughter.

They mill around for a few minutes, each in turn going up to the fountain to drop in a coin, their faces screwed up as they concentrate on their hearts' desires.

As the crowd trickles away, the fat man confides to you that it wasn't an ordinary coin that he used to make his wish. 'It was a lava gem. I didn't like to say so in front of everybody as it seems like boasting to tell them I'm rich.'

Throw in a **lava gem** – cross it off your Adventure Sheet and ▶ 240

Too expensive ▶ 806

361

Naft's workman are too busy with their other chores to notice you stealing one small package. Add the **jar of amaranth oil** to your possessions.

▶ 1649

362

'You can't help me!' you shout at the watchman. 'It's the spectre of my own death.'

He backs away, shaking with fear. 'May the gods watch over you,' he says in a strangled whisper.

You hear his stumbling footsteps as he runs off. Overhead, a tangle of leafless branches stretches like a cobweb against the evening sky. Then the soil slips back to cover your face and the last thing you hear is the horrible lullaby the spectre is crooning contentedly in your ear.

▶ **666** but note that your new character will start with 5 Glory because the gods admire your bravery and will ensure the reincarnation of your soul.

363

'So you've seen the error of your ways,' says Nyx as the gale pulls you both towards the tapestry. 'Good. Once we reach Olympus I'll destroy the gods – easy prey now that they're weakened by their battle with the titans.'

'Take a closer look at the tapestry,' you reply, shaking your head. 'I have a friend who can alter reality, and that image isn't Olympus anymore.'

Nyx stares at it. 'Then where – ?'

▶ 559

364

You collapse to the floor and lie helpless. An icy numbness holds you paralyzed. Your lifeblood is spurting out onto the rug.

'Don't worry,' hisses one of the intruders behind his mask, 'you won't bleed to death.' He lights a taper from the fire. 'You'll burn first.'

He quietly and efficiently goes around setting light to series of incendiary packages. Flames roar up the walls, thick smoke adding to the darkness into which you are already sinking.

Cross your possessions off your Adventure Sheet. They will be destroyed in the inferno that consumes the mansion. Also lose the title **The Unexpected Heir**.

'Why..?' It's barely a sigh of escaping breath, but the assassin hears.

'Nothing personal on my account,' he says. 'You put your fingers in the till back in Bridgadoom, I hear, and this is how they wanted to pay you back.'

If you have the codeword *Robber* and die wanting revenge on the burghers of Bridgadoom ▶ **1233**

Otherwise ▶ **111**

365

At first nothingness. Eons wait unpassed. The slip from nonbeing into darkness is marked only by the returning flow of time. Fractions of a second reassemble sluggishly, like hair-thin fragments of finely crushed glass. Minutes roll back, grains of sand like boulders sliding uphill to rebuild the rock-face of eternity.

Still no form, no self, no body. Sounds. Night, fire. Shouts. Movement, a clumsy reeling that creates dizziness even though no sense yet exists of place nor balance. Seaweed and salt spray. Gulls that shriek in the sky. Meat burning over campfires. Blood spilled on rock. Sharp wine, honey, spices. The rustle and snap of canvas tents. Creak of leather armour, jangle of bronze. Lapping of waves in a gusting wind.

A touch of cool cloth on a burning brow. Something insistent, familiar. The familiar is always welcome until it has a name, and that name is agony. Blistering, annihilating, pitiless agony. A howling deep under the earth, screams from a bottomless well, helpless cries pounding in the ears.

The scattered parts of you are drawn together by the agony. Memory. Thirst. Fear. Need. The senses return, vision last of all. A pulse in the veins. The hot dragging of breath in a dry throat. Sinews twisted and tortured. Identity trickles back. You are you. You are here. The pieces of reality spiral, coalesce, snap into place.

Cramp racks your limbs. Every inch of your skin is afire as if you'd been scoured. Throbbing pain in your skull. Ache deep in your bones. But a soft bed under you, fragrant herbs wafting from a lamp, soothing salve cools the pain.

You know who you are. What happened. What you must do.

You try to swing your legs out of bed. Waves of fatigue and nausea press down on you. With a groan you sink back on the pillow.

'Don't try to get up. You're too weak.'

A face comes into focus in the torchlight. Young and handsome, but his look of confident strength seems weighted down by cares beyond his years. He raises your head in one firm hand, using the other to hold a cup of broth to your lips.

It takes all your strength just to swallow. You lie back, grateful for the meaty juice that seems to pour health back into your body.

'Who are you? Where am I?'

'Straight in with the questions, I see. Well, it makes a change from all the groaning. My name is Achilles. This is the Achaean camp on the beach before steep Ilion.'

'Ilion?'

'You might know it better as Troy.'

▶ **1416**

366

Cross off the 50 pyr, which you count out on the desk in front of him. You've got his full attention now.

'What's the furthest item in the warehouse?'

He scratches his neck. 'The *furthest*?'

'Yeah. That'll take you longest to fetch.'

'Oh,' the pyr drops. 'Wait right here.'

He flips the ledger to another page, draws your attention to it with a flick of his eyes, and scurries out of the office.

▶ **1066**

367

'Prove it.'

His grin fades. His bared teeth now look feral and predatory.

'You say you were the one guiding me all along?' you go on. 'That was you, yeah? Not my god? So tell me which labours you set for me.'

'Insolent mortal!'

'Look, I'll make it easy for you. Just name one labour. There were twelve, so surely you can do that.'

'My brother will smear you out of existence. Not even your memory will remain.'

'Still too tricky? How about multiple choice. I'll name three tasks, you tell me which was an actual labour.'

He bellows in rage, a noise to daunt lions. Whoever thought that Sleep would be an easeful god? But you stand your ground. You are, after all, your god's chosen champion.

If Galatea is with you ▶ **1422**
If Chipos is with you ▶ **1653**
Otherwise ▶ **803**

'I should have cut out my tongue before I ever said anything,' he says sadly. 'Now I fear I've ruined our friendship.'

'No, don't say that. You spoke from the heart, and I respect you for that. We will always be friends.'

He seems to come to a decision. 'I've allowed myself to tarry with you too long, putting off the day when I must tell you the secret of restoring the Great River. Let us go now, without delay. We'll walk the valley and at each cataract I'll teach you the rituals you must perform.'

'It can wait. There's always tomorrow.'

He shakes his head. 'I've been selfish. Come with me now, I beg you – or I'll leave, and you can find me when you're ready. Either way, after the words I've just spoken we can't go on as we were.'

Accompany him to Notus   ▶ **333**
Insist that it can wait   ▶ **1371**

Note **48** as your Current Location, then ▶ **1269** and tick the box next to Pan's Column. From now on you will always be able to find your way back here.

You are drawn to the hub of the city, where majestic marble statues proclaim the glory of heroes, politicians debate matters of state, citizens gather to exchange news and opinions, and musicians and artists show off their latest works.

These are the qualities of Apollo, Olympian lord of the founding of cities and colonies. Record on your Adventure Sheet that he is your god.

▶ **452**

He shrugs. 'They done nothing to me, the Ilionians over there. So why am I fighting them? Because they pissed off the mighty Atrides brothers, Agamemnon and Menelaus. Stole their woman, so I hear. Yet isn't that what our leaders do to us, their own men? Any stronghold that falls, they get the pick of the hottest girls, the best wine, the choicest loot. And who won all that for 'em? Yours truly and his mates. They get rich on ransoms every time they sell some son of Ilion back to his family. Again, who is it took those prisoners in the first place? Blokes like me. What's our reward? Scraps, and 'ere's yer spade, now go dig a ditch. Been digging this bloody ditch every few days for years, what good's it done?'

'So you don't see much point in the war?'

'Didn't exactly say that. If we could take that city tomorrow we'd all go home in ships groaning with booty and broads. We need a proper hero in charge, not those greedy maggots who always take care to keep well back from the fighting. If Achilles said boo to either of 'em they'd shit their kilts.'

Ask him something else   ▶ **1261**
Leave him to his work   ▶ **735**

You flick a contemptuous gesture at the decanter. 'Help yourself. I don't drink with people who rob me.'

Orphea shakes her head. 'I'm not here to rob you. I'm bringing you an opportunity.'

'Now I'm really worried.'

'Remember the Pipes of Pan?'

'I'd almost forgotten. But yes, that's another black mark against you. I can still taste that gas.'

'So they left a trap and you sprung it. Hardly my fault. Anyway, I do feel bad about it so I want to give you a chance to get the Pipes after all.'

'The "Lady Rapscallion" charity drive, huh? You know the way out.'

'Not charity. A wager. We play a little game – ' she indicates the three overturned cups on the desk – 'and if you win I'll give you the Pipes of Pan. Remember the legend: "This music can inflame the passions".'

'Oh, I'm already feeling pretty inflamed.'

She ignores you. 'See this ruby. I'll put it under one of the cups like this. Then I move the cups around – is your eye fast enough to follow? Now, if you think you kept track of where the ruby is then we can wager.'

'You're staking the Pipes of Pan. What am I staking?'

'What about… the deeds of this house?'

'A mansion against some pipes?'

'The pipes of a god.'

You pace to and fro, as if weighing up whether to gamble, then dart forward and snatch up two of the cups. 'There! It's not under either of those, so it must be under the other one.'

She stares in dismay. 'That's not how you're meant to do it. You're supposed to pick up the cup you think it's under.'

'What difference? It must be under that one, right? Shall we look?'

She puts out her hand. 'No… er, that's right, it must be there.'

'So I'll take the Pipes of Pan, thanks.'

For a moment she sits stunned, then throws herself back in the chair and laughs. 'The biter bit. That doesn't happen very often. All right, you win. Fair and square isn't how I like to play, but I can't grumble when I'm outwitted, can I?'

▶ 1126

373

The Palace is constantly hosting banquets and other events, so there is a large staff of cooks, stewards and servants, all of whom need supervision.

Your erstwhile major-domo casts a critical look over the Palace catering records. 'There's a lot to be done,' he says. 'I may as well get started right away.'

The Palace officials are delighted. An Iskandrian major-domo is not only seen as more punctilious than other household managers but also more prestigious.

Gain 1 Glory and ▶ 1642

374

The temple nave presents high, blank walls of pearl-white marble. In front of the altar are two pedestals with stone carvings of a pomegranate and a battle-helmet. Normally these items are depicted as being held by the goddess, but here in her principal temple there is no need for an effigy of Athena herself. She is believed to be everywhere.

If Athena is your goddess and you have the codeword *Rohan* ▶ 1568

If you worship Athena and have the title **The Chosen One** you can enter the inner shrine ▶ 106

Otherwise you can:

Pray for a blessing ▶ 498
Ask for healing ▶ 65
Leave ▶ 103

375

'Lord Xechasiaris…'

He's scrabbling around in the bottom of a cedarwood chest, tossing items aside. 'Medals? What use are they? Titles, glory, all that – nothing, if some whippersnapper makes off with your youth. Ah, now here's something.'

He raises his head from the chest. His beard and robes are thick with dust. In his hand he's clutching a sheaf of papers.

You look over his shoulder as he peers at them. They are crude drawings – wagons, blocky people, some scrawled landmarks, mostly drawn in outline with here and there a few vivid scribbles of colour. The way a child sees the world.

'Is that your youth?'

He stares at you, then back at the papers. 'What? Are you demented? Youth doesn't come in crayon and ink. But

there's a clue in this lot.'

'Shall I take them?' You hold out your hand.

His suspicion suddenly melts in a trusting grin. 'Why not? You seem to have your head screwed on. Sort it out. Find my youth for me, eh?'

Get the codeword *Rectangle* and ▶ 1618

376

'You know the noticeboards at the city gates?' says the sergeant. 'There's a missing person case you ought to look into. Tasty reward if you handle it right.'

▶ 1642

377

The arrow catches on the visor of your armour. It's deflected just enough that it doesn't impale your eye, but it does penetrate the eye-slit and leave a gaping wound in your cheek. Gain 1 scar.

Perhaps the archer's aim was guided by Apollo. No ordinary mortal should have been able to injure you at such a distance, not when you wear battle harness forged in the workshop of Vulcan himself.

▶ 1327

378

Sliding between the interstices of reality, you are whisked across vast distances without any perception of time passing. The cocoon begins to rise and as the beetles slow their constant space-warping motion you are borne back out of the ground into open air.

The beetles dart together in a clump, reconstituting the metallic chrysalis which drops back into your pocket.

▶ 222 in *The Pillars of the Sky*

379

The *Sunrise* throws off its mooring ropes and pulls out into empty space. The sails fill with ethereal energy, carrying the ship out from the shores of the Isle of the Dawn and on across the endless shimmering void.

The helmsman brings the prow around on a bearing into infinity. A million tiny lights burn cold and white ahead of you. For now they are just pinpricks in the velvet black immensity of space, but perhaps the day will come when they take on shape and size, when faith is vindicated and they reveal themselves to be other worlds waiting for the explorer's tread.

Ancaeus joins you at the rail, perhaps sharing your thoughts. Even he must struggle with doubt. These are uncharted seas where even the gods' power does not apply and simple hope is your only guide.

'Man's reach should exceed his grasp,' he says, 'or what's a heaven for?'

And so you have chosen to sail on, out of the Vulcanverse. With no hero to oppose her, Nyx will hold sway there forever. You may find other adventures, but it is beyond the scope of this book to tell you what those are. You're on your own now.

380

'You wanted to see me. Here I am.'

He brushes dirt off his gardening gloves. The dark eye-slits of the mask make it hard to tell if he's looking at you or not.

'I like to meet anybody who hangs around the Grumbles. Call it a proprietorial interest.'

Ask about his garden	▶ 1366
Draw attention to his metal mask	▶ 246
Wait for him to say what he wants	▶ 1487

381

You launch yourself out from the parapet and feel a stab of panic as you hurtle towards the ground – until the wings spread, catching the air, and you soar aloft over the peaks that stretch to the north.

If you were with a companion, delete them from your Adventure Sheet. Also remove the **beeswax** that you have used.

Chill updraughts bring a dusting of frost to the feathers of your wings and cause you to draw your garments tighter around you. You begin to descend, selecting your landing spot in the craggy, ice-scoured landscape of Boreas.

Mount Atos	▶ 849 in *The Pillars of the Sky*
Mount Nysa	▶ 12 in *The Pillars of the Sky*
Mount Othri	▶ 344 in *The Pillars of the Sky*
Mount Helikon	▶ 859 in *The Pillars of the Sky*
The Hippogriff's Eyrie	▶ 275 in *The Pillars of the Sky*
The Great Sinkhole	▶ 140 in *The Pillars of the Sky*
The land of the Sarpedons	▶ 566 in *The Pillars of the Sky*
The citadel of the Halizons	▶ 316 in *The Pillars of the Sky*
The western coast	▶ 200 in *The Pillars of the Sky*
The northern coast	▶ 444 in *The Pillars of the Sky*

382

The axe whistles past your ear. It comes so close that you can hear the air being sliced by its blade. With a crunch it hits something right behind you. A hideous hissing cry rings out followed by a frenzied thrashing of horn-hard limbs.

Whirling, you are confronted by one of the giant insects you came across earlier this evening in the palace garden. Its stick-like feelers are plucking at the axe-blade embedded in its face. Even blinded it remains dangerous as its razor-edged legs scythe around wildly.

You seize a belaying pin, sidestep its frenzied attacks, and deliver the *coup de grace*. Stinking yellow fluid sluices out of the wound across the deck.

'Thanks,' you say as the Minotaur tugs his axe out of the still-twitching carcass.

'I didn't think any of those vermin managed to get past me,' he says. 'It came out of the hold. Must've been hiding out there waiting to ambush one of us.'

▶ 231

383

In the heart of the frontline fighting, beset by a dozen Ilionian charioteers, stands the Achaean hero Ajax. His chariot has overturned, his companions lie crushed and bleeding in the wreckage. His enemies wheel around him, jabbing at him with long spears but being careful to stay out of reach of his axe. They look like children beside Ajax's mighty stature, but despite his strength the force of numbers must eventually wear him down.

You see him fall to one knee, scarlet blood gushing from a shoulder wound. But he rises again, the broken shaft of his chariot in his hand, and he hurls it into the path of one of the yelping Ilionians. The man's chariot overturns, he is catapulted into the dust, and as he lies stunned Ajax steps forward to despatch him. That raised axe could cut an ox in two, you think.

But the axe blow does not fall. Ajax is braced motionless, straining at something that has caught his weapon in an iron grip. Only you can see the cause. One of the giant figures, reaching down from the heavens, holds Ajax's blade between her fingers – invisible to all the fighters, but seen by your enchanted vision as a flickering shade against the back of the eyelid, like an image burned into the retina by staring at the sun.

While she holds Ajax transfixed, his foes come rushing on in a pack, baying like hounds that scent a kill.

Attack her	▶ 274
Hold back	▶ 1513

384

Your friend is waiting by your bedside.

'What happened to Daedalus?' you ask, sitting up.

'No sign of him. I waited to see if they hauled anyone else out of the rubble, but it was just you – and the bodies of the family who lived in the house. He's probably crushed under several tons of rock.'

'Maybe.'

When you are well enough to leave the temple infirmary ▶ 625

385

Inchoate darkness closes in, snuffing out the last feeble glimmers of Hyperion's jewelled eye.

'Why do you think Helios got his job?' laughs Nyx.

The effort of dispelling the sun-god's light has clearly taken its toll, but the note of triumph rings clear in her voice. Across the battlefield, her legions are mopping up your remaining allies.

'The war is over,' she says. 'You lose.'

She snaps her fingers. A strand of black vapour curls from them towards you. There is nowhere to run. You shut your eyes. There is a moment of – what? Anticipation? Terror? Acceptance?

Then you are wiped out of existence and the Queen of Night is the unchallenged ruler of all creation.

▶ 666

386

☐ ☐ ☐ ☐

You stumble between the chairs in the dark and reach for one of the Syndics – but you already know this is not the one you seek.

Tick the next empty box above.

You just ticked the first box	▶ 12
You ticked the second box	▶ 1370
You ticked the third box	▶ 1576
Four boxes are now ticked	▶ 1491

387

At dusk a mist rises to hang in a veil between the graves. The damp air is filled with mothbats, which sometimes flutter over the wall into the neighbouring streets. They are thought unlucky, as they roost among the dead.

As you hurry back towards the exit, you meet a cloaked figure standing by an open grave. They beckon you over.

'It'll be dark soon,' you say. 'It wouldn't do to get locked in here overnight.'

'Do you recognize me?'

You peer through the gathering gloom. 'Sorry, I don't think we – '

'I am the spectre of your own demise,' interrupts the stranger. 'Long, long you have kept me waiting here. Behold our final resting place, so inviting – but you, you are always too fickle. You keep running out on death.'

'That has always been the will of the gods,' you protest. 'And who would choose to cross the Styx if they are given the chance to turn back to the realms of life?'

'Enough!' cries the spectre, seizing you with strong grey arms. 'You have frustrated me long enough. Come! The grave's a fine place to embrace.'

So saying, it drags you with it into the open grave and starts pulling in the soil on top of you. You must break free before you are buried alive. Make a STRENGTH roll at difficulty 10 – that is, you need to score 10 or more on the roll of two dice plus your STRENGTH score.

Succeed	▶ 1344
Fail	▶ 1643

388

Over on the roof, the ever-swelling horde of your foes is turning from a slavering mob to an organized army. The vampires, realizing they cannot board the *Sunrise* themselves, are swinging lines attached to grappling hooks. Whenever a grapple catches hold, immediately a wave of gibbering were-beasts comes swinging across.

'We don't have the numbers to fight them off,' you shout over the howling wind.

The Minotaur roars and lays about him with his axe, revelling in the shrieks of his foes and the blood gushing over his face with every blow. 'Count again!' he says, laughing wildly. 'One of my kind is worth fifty of these curs.'

Ancaeus glances back towards the rift that's opening in the sky. 'They only have to delay us long enough for Thanatos to arrive, then it's game over.'

If you have the title **Kissed by a Golden Princess** ▶ 32

If not but you have the codeword *Noble* ▶ 1150

Otherwise ▶ 611

389

'I didn't invite you here, Orphea, you broke in. Say what you want and beat it before I call the night watch.'

'I came to offer you a unique opportunity.'

'I'll bite. What's the con this time?'

'No con. Remember the Pipes of Pan?'

'The time you sprayed me with knockout gas and swiped the prize after shaking hands on an alliance. Sure I remember.'

She spreads her hands. 'Hey, it was the druids who left that gas trap. But look, I'm here to make amends. What I've got in mind is a little game – ' she holds up a small ruby, then indicates three overturned cups in front of her on the desk – 'and if you win I'll give you the Pipes of Pan.'

'And if I lose?'

She bites her lip in thought. 'Good point, you'd have to stake something of equivalent value. How about the deeds of this house?'

'My house against some pipes? That's your idea of a fair trade?'

'The pipes of a god,' she points out.

Agree to the wager ▶ **1379**

Seize her and summon the night watch ▶ **1610**

Just kill her ▶ **987**

390

'If I go with this good captain,' says Eos, 'what will you do?'

A good question. What do you tell her?

'I'll go back, face Nyx, and somehow I'll thwart her plan.' ▶ **576**

'The battle back there is lost. I'm coming with the rest of you.' ▶ **126**

391

'I am the one they are looking for,' says Polymnia.

The leader of the refugees looks dubious. 'We came in search of a mighty champion who will defend our sect from those who persecute us and call us heretics.'

'I will do better than that. As the Muse of Knowledge I will guide you back to good sense.' She turns to you. 'I must go with them for now, but you know where to find me.'

She leads them away.

Delete Polymnia from the Companion box on your Adventure Sheet, then ▶ **806**

392

Look at your codewords. If you have *Radiant* but not *Rough* ▶ **905**; otherwise read on.

It feels like there isn't much time left. Decide quickly where you'll head next.

The nearest gate ▶ **723**

The nearest tower ▶ **171**

The Avenue of the Anvil ▶ **1632**

Your mansion (only if you have the title **The Unexpected Heir**) ▶ **1257**

Your family home (only if you have the codeword *Reverie*) ▶ **1385**

The Academy of Philosophers ▶ **1510**

The Forum ▶ **981**

393

He scribbles a receipt and hands it to you. Delete the **sceptre of Agamemnon** from your possessions and get a **curio credit** in its place.

▶ **828**

394

She starts rifling through the desk, then hurrying round the room throwing anything of value into a small sack. Lastly she opens your safe with insolent ease and takes any cash you left there.

As she runs lightly across to the window, your hand shoots out to grab her ankle, bringing her to the floor with a crash.

'You didn't drink!' she says, more impressed than alarmed.

'I know you couldn't stay one minute alone in a room without drugging the decanter. If you hadn't been so puffed up with your own cleverness you'd have noticed I tipped the glass into the coal scuttle.'

'Puffed up?' She pats her very slim and flat stomach with a look of feigned offence. 'So now what?'

Call the night watch to arrest her ▶ **1610**

Kill her ▶ **818**

Let her go ▶ **546**

395

His gaze is terrible beyond description. No living thing can endure it. You get no third chance.

▶ **666**

396

You overhear a conversation between two scholarly looking women who are buying pastries from a baker's stall.

'I used to like sitting in the shop and reading his latest acquisitions,' says one. 'Rare first editions, some of them.'

'He didn't mind?'

'Well, I bought enough books there, didn't I?'

'And now – what? You don't go anymore. His stock's no good?'

'It's not as comfortable to stay and browse. He never lights the fire and it gets quite cold in there. I miss my old snug reading nest.'

▶ **198**

397

❑ ❑ ❑

Put a tick in one of the boxes above.

One box is now ticked ▶ **563**

Two boxes are now ticked ▶ **210**

Three boxes are now ticked ▶ **158**

398

If you have the title **Repairer of Reputations** ▶ **615**

If not but you have the title **Informant** ▶ **772**

Otherwise ▶ **1232**

399

Nyx throws back her head in a peal of exultant laughter, certain of her victory. Around her pulses a ghastly grey light that hints at cosmic energies at her command. Above, the darkness in the depths of the sky heaves and crawls like an expectant creature waiting to be born.

In this moment you finally understand. What she brings is the threat of unbeing, the sure annihilation that leads to total emptiness forever. Her power lies in humanity's horror of the void. She is night as the source of unreasoning fear, the harbinger of panic even in the hearts of those who never shrink from any danger they can see and touch. She is the foe who cannot be faced. And yet you must face her. For the sake of all existence you must conquer unconquerable Night.

She strikes, a sword of shadow taking shape in her hand even as it swings towards you.

If you have the **Panoply of the Lost Hero** and the codeword *Royal* ▶ 148

If not ▶ 1057

400

The relationship between the Halizons and the Amazons is a complex one. Originally a single tribe, they split into two factions long ago and have since been sworn enemies. Yet there is respect there – grudging, never spoken of – and it's even said that Halizons and Amazons hold secret mating rituals in the high mountains between their lands.

To gain the officer's trust make a CHARM roll at difficulty 8. (Roll two dice, add your CHARM score, and you need a total of 8 or better.)

Succeed ▶ 791
Fail ▶ 1515

401

You throw yourself flat, at the same time lobbing your weapon off to one side.

You prepared this tactic with the Face of Wisdom in case it was needed. Altering the fabric of reality, the Face conjures an illusory double of you with the weapon seemingly in its hand. The tendril of darkness, no longer directed by Nyx, mistakes the illusion for the real you. It snakes around, consumes the illusory figure, and then dissipates.

'Thanks,' you say. 'That was a life-saver.'

'Hey, I thought it was a long shot at best,' says the Face's crabby metal voice out of nowhere. 'Still, it worked.'

▶ 332

402

'There's a sizeable fine against your name,' he says as he consults a fat leather-bound ledger on his desk. Taking a quill, he scores out the entry. 'There. Must have been a misprint, eh?' He gives you a broad wink.

Lose the codeword *Ridge*.

As you're about to leave, the sergeant nods towards the courtyard. 'They're putting on a bit of a drop show. Come back later, if you're interested.'

'A drop show?'

'A hanging.'

▶ 1642

403

The surface of the mirror is black with soot. You breathe on it, intending to wipe it on your sleeve, but the sensation that comes over you is as if your soul were being poured out with your breath.

Your vision swims, distorts, and reforms. A moment of dizziness passes. You are looking at your own face, massively distorted by the grimy glass. You see your lip curl into a sneer.

'So you betrayed us,' says a familiar voice. 'But even though you broke your promise you will help our cause after all, because you have given me a face that my foe will not suspect. So much the better for taking that monster unawares.'

It is the young Domovoi wizard. And yet he is speaking with your voice. Wearing your features!

'What have you done to me?'

You reach for him, and your fists strike hard glass. You hear him laugh.

'You have done it to yourself, oath-breaker. Now your spirit is trapped in the mirror, and you have bequeathed your body to one who will use it with more honour.'

There is something pressing close behind you. It is the essence of nethermost darkness. Here within the depths of the mirror it is your sole and eternal companion.

▶ 666

404

It's dawn. You're woken by the rattle of the key in the tavern door. The locals find you in the middle of the common room, in the smashed wreckage of a wooden table. You ease yourself painfully to your feet, feeling as though you'd been sewn in a sack and kicked down a hillside.

The landlord peers apprehensively into the alcove. He takes a few steps inside, then turns and stumbles hurriedly back, mouth drooping in horror. It looks like he might throw up.

'She didn't make it,' he says at last. 'Probably for the best.'

The locals greet the news with silence. At last the tension becomes unbearable. 'So you'll keep sending it a new victim, will you? Month after month, while you all scurry off and hide in your homes.'

'All we can do,' says the landlord in a lifeless voice, 'until a champion comes who can rid us of the fiend.'

▶ 764

405

No sign adorns the warehouse of Naft the Lean. He isn't reliant on passing trade, preferring to distribute his goods directly to storekeepers and tavernas.

Wooden gates give onto a covered passage that leads to the warehouse yard. Labourers are at work hefting crates and barrels onto a cart. Even before you've asked the question, one of them points a stubby finger at the cabin over the entrance passage. 'Looking for the boss? You'll find him up there.'

You climb a rickety flight of steps. The door is open. Naft is an underfed scarecrow of a man with a face like a clenched fist. You get a sense of his untiring energy from the way he keeps grabbing items off the shelves and darting back to scribble notes in a ledger.

'Come in, come in,' he says, not pausing in his work. 'What can I do you for?'

'Do much trade in amaranth oil? Love-lies-bleeding, some call it.'

'Not my biggest seller, but I have a few customers with standing orders.'

'Can I see the list?'

Finally he glances in your direction, and even pauses in the act of writing something in his sales ledger. 'There's some as would say that sort of information is confidential.'

He's angling for you to make it worth his while. If you can spare 50 pyr for a bribe ▶ 366

Otherwise attempt a CHARM roll at difficulty 9. To do that roll two dice, add your CHARM score, and you're aiming for a total of 9 or better.

Succeed ▶ 696
Fail ▶ 768

406

A young man in well-tailored robes is sitting on the grass. He takes his hand from his mouth and you see a bright red splash of blood.

'Are you badly hurt?'

'Just a nosebleed,' he says, getting shakily to his feet. 'Two fellows wanted my money. I took issue with that and got a poke in the face.'

Help out by bringing in the militia (if you have the title **Public-Spirited**) ▶ 831

Call in a favour from Zinc (if you have the codeword *Robber*) ▶ 116

Not your problem ▶ 806

407

A heavy vibration thuds through the floorboards, followed by the clunk of a bolt springing back. You snap out of the trance just in time to jump aside. A trapdoor opens where you were standing and the rug drops down a deep shaft from which comes a gust of dank chthonic air.

Marija's look of triumph turns to resignation. You stride forward. She crosses her arms over her chest in a gesture that could be supplication or simple modesty. 'Remember you promised it would be quick,' she says, her voice just a breath in the sudden quiet.

▶ 479

408

'Ever notice you can learn a lot about a thing by looking at something else?'

She never picks an opportune moment for one of her elliptical comments. You dash off after the small figure in red and then a thought stops you dead in your tracks.

'What do you mean?' you say to Galatea.

'Well, there then, for example.' She points along the street. 'What do you see?'

There's the girl, her red hood bright against the drab hues of the slums. As she gambols away, you notice the expressions of the people she passes. In each case there's a moment as they look up and catch sight of her face – and then a frown, or a grimace of distaste, or a wide-eyed stare.

'Not what they expected to see, is she?' says Galatea.

Pursue the girl ▶ 20
Let her go ▶ 571

409

The sun blazes in through high, stained-glass windows, flooding the pale stone of the nave with patches of shining colour that make you think of blood, of gold, of a deep forest pool.

If Artemis is your goddess and you have the codeword *Rohan* ▶ 1568

If Artemis is your goddess and you have the title **The Chosen One** you are permitted to enter the inner shrine whenever you wish ▶ 106

Otherwise you can:

Pray for a blessing ▶ 498
Ask for healing ▶ 65
Leave ▶ 103

410

On the path is a puddle of rainwater as clear as a mirror. Glancing down into it you see your own unblemished face reflected there. Note on your Adventure Sheet that you now have no scars.

▶ 674

411

You both go home scraped and bruised after a no-holds-barred fight that becomes a minor legend among the other children.

From that day on Nihakos has a new respect for you. He stops bullying your brother and even goes out of his way to seem as friendly as his terse, untrusting nature will allow.

If you return his friendship, maybe you can influence him to be a better person.

Good idea ▶ 534

No, he doesn't deserve friends ▶ 657

412

If this box ❑ was already ticked ▶ 64; if the box is empty, put a tick in it now and then read on.

The tower looms above you, darkened but just visible against the jet-black sky because of a faint inner glow like the light emitted by phosphorescent slime on the recesses of cave walls.

'Didn't it used to be straight?' says Dunamis.

The tower looks like a length of toffee that some giant has twisted into a phantasmagoric helix. Stranger still, it's slowly moving, writhing about against the sky. You're put in mind of a giant blind worm tasting the night air.

If you have the codeword **Radiant** and not the codeword **Rough** ▶ 905 now; otherwise read on.

The tip of the enormous polyp sways towards you. You pull Dunamis back out of range. 'Somehow I don't think we want to climb that.'

'No kidding. Where now?'

The nearest gate ▶ 723

The Avenue of the Anvil ▶ 1632

Your mansion (only if you have the title **The Unexpected Heir**) ▶ 1257

Your family home (only if you have the codeword **Reverie**) ▶ 1385

The Academy of Philosophers ▶ 1510

The temple district ▶ 1326

The Forum ▶ 981

413

This armour is identical to the panoply. As you recognize it, you realize too that you can't remember the last time you had it with you. Somewhere in your adventures it disappeared – perhaps when you plummeted through time and fell into the sea here by the Achaean beachhead.

Delete the **Panoply of the Lost Hero** from your Adventure Sheet and then ▶ Current Location

'Oaf,' mutters the head. 'Cheapskate. Philistine.'

'Are you talking to me?'

'From this point on – no.'

To go straight to a city location that you already know about, note **31** as your Current Location, then ▶ **1432**

Or you can go:

East ▶ **570**

West ▶ **555**

'Where there is thirst, let them drink. Where there is dust, bring water. In the shrine to Aphrodite you meet the one who remembers the old ways.'

'Will meet, or have met?'

She blinks – an eerie effect with her eyes turned up to show only the whites. 'Time means nothing in prophecy. Past and future and present are one. Next find the lovelorn, the heartsick, the parted ones. Old parchment and bound books – a strange place to look for passion, but it is there as it is everywhere. You are their Mercury, their matchmaker. Let two hearts beat as one. After that, lost honour must be repaired, stolen glory wrested back from hard white hands. You carry the standard back from the palace of the sown men. That is the last.'

She signals for you to leave.

▶ **510**

'Who says I must give her up?' says Agamemnon, scowling at his advisors. 'Achilles, isn't he the one who's been speaking out? No, don't deny it. That man has no respect for me. I've heard he's blaming this plague on my intransigence.'

Calchas, a seer, is the only one with the courage to speak. 'My lord, all of your priests agree…'

'Fine, I'll give her back. Send her with sacrifices and tell her father I want no ransom, just an end to this plague. But hear this – the king of kings cannot go without a prize. If I must give up my concubine, I'll take her replacement from Achilles's plunder. Go to the Myrmidon camp, select the fairest of his slave girls, and say I claim her.'

'Prince Achilles will choke with fury at such treatment.'

'Let him! He must learn who's strongest here. They all must. I take what I want, and only bow to gods.'

Get the codeword *Rage* and ▶ **1529**

Lose 1 from CHARM. Though probably none of your neighbours or servants can think of a better way to solve the dilemma, there is still a sense that you haven't handled it well.

Your new major-domo is naturally delighted, and you give the departing one glowing references to sweeten the pill of summary dismissal. In the weeks that follow you occasionally wonder if you made the right decision. The Iskandrian major-domo demands higher standards of etiquette and decorum than any Vulcanian is accustomed to, with the result that several of your staff hand in their notice.

'It is part of the process, your grace,' the major-domo assures you as he brings your brandy after dinner.

'What process?'

'The process of civilizing this household.'

As he sweeps out, it occurs to you that perhaps not even your own behaviour is quite up to his lofty expectations.

▶ **97**

Look at your codewords and titles. Check a box for each of the following that applies:

❑ The codeword *Rhapsody*

❑ The codeword *Quake*

❑ The codeword *Pumped*

❑ The codeword *Nanny* or the title **Godslayer**

If two or more boxes are now ticked ▶ **875**

If one or none is ticked ▶ **1160**

The scaffold is soon finished. You wait almost an hour. There's a scuffle at the gate and a prisoner is dragged in. He's a very young man, half starved by the look of him, with eyes as big as saucers. His hands are tied behind him and there's a gag over his mouth that muffles his screams of terror. When he sees the fate that's in store for him, he tries to dig in his heels, but the burly militia drag him across the cobbles and up the scaffold steps like a sack of refuse.

'What did he do?' you ask the woman beside you.

'Who cares?' she says without taking her eyes off the prisoner. 'They caught him, that'll do for me. Go on! Stretch his neck! Pull his head off! You're going to dance on thin air, you little bastard!'

She's almost deranged with glee.

Stay to the end ▶ **1551**

You can't watch ▶ **1507**

One of the guests, a scrawny middle-aged woman wearing a dress suitable for an unblushing dryad, is standing a little way off adjusting her makeup. She has put her wineglass and a jewelled hairclip down on a sundial beside her. A young man approaches and touches her on the arm. She turns, flashes him a smile, and tosses back her hair.

As they chat the hairclip lies forgotten on the weathered face of the sundial. They do not see a slim brown arm reach out of the bushes, close unhurriedly around the hairclip, and draw it back out of sight.

You cut up some steps and surprise the robber as she's emerging from the bushes studying her ill-gotten treasure. The rubies cast a bright gleam in merry eyes. She's a girl in her early teens with a gap-toothed grin and the lean limbs of a street thief.

If you have the codeword *Quench* ▶ 138
Otherwise ▶ 1244

421

Get the codeword *Rhapsody*.

'You are right,' agrees Prometheus. 'Once the Queen of Night is defeated, we will dictate our terms to Olympus as their saviours. Zeus will not dare try his old tricks when he sees the allies you have gathered.'

'Brave words, Fire-bringer!' Nyx calls out to him. 'But soon you'll be chained to your rock again, and this time with birds pecking at your eyes and tongue for all eternity.'

If you have the codeword *Quake* ▶ 553
If not but you have the codeword *Pumped* ▶ 720
Otherwise, if you have the codeword *Nanny* ▶ 1637
Otherwise ▶ 1183

422

Tekto and Agrio meet just outside the city gates at dawn. Duelling is frowned upon by the authorities, but they turn a blind eye to it. Some of the sentries at the gate even leave their posts in order to watch.

Both duellists seem equally unimpressed by their seconds' choice of weapons. Several of their first shots go so far wide that you begin to think they are missing each other on purpose.

'What happens if they get through all the arrows without scoring a hit?' you whisper to the other second.

'No idea,' he says. 'I suppose you and I will have to decide.'

Roll two dice:
score 2-6   ▶ 654
score 7   ▶ 1141
score 8-12   ▶ 1499

423

A servant brings a cup of chalky grey liquid that smells of mouldy berries. You drink it quickly before you can have second thoughts, grimacing at the bitter taste and gritty texture. Immediately you feel a creeping torpor robbing you of strength, and hurry to lie down beside the quiescent form of his wife.

'Bring her back to me,' urges the merchant as your eyes begin to flutter.

'I'll try...' You yawn, feeling the soft embrace of the sheets.

'Or stay in the dreamlands, if you fail.'

At least, later on you think that's what he said, but you are already drifting off. The pillows rise about you like banks of white cloud. Silk slides to embrace you, impossibly yielding. There is a scent of narcissus and sandalwood, heady and enticing, that draws you on down moon-drenched slopes. A languorous stretch of warm limbs. A soft and slumbrous sigh –

You are bolt upright in the bed. Your senses are razor-honed. Your heart is thudding as if something had startled you awake, though you can't think what it was.

You are alone in the bed. There is no one else in the room. The house all around is still and heavy with silence. Not even the distant sounds of the street reach your ears.

At the front door you find the house now isolated in a faint mist. Above, around, and below extends a black void in which occasional lights appear and vanish distantly. The street under your feet is a flux of silvery light that bears your weightless dream-self.

Ahead looms a silhouetted skyline of high-peaked rooftops against the long sharp curve of a scimitar moon, though you can still see no buildings. A nightingale's bright trilling song comes from far along the silver road. As you quicken your pace towards it, a gleam of blood-coloured light can be seen inside an oblong in the air that suggests an open doorway.

Find the nightingale   ▶ 501
Investigate the ruby light   ▶ 985

424

Footsteps advance to meet you from the darkened stairwell. Dunamis raises the lantern. The beam illuminates a figure in silhouette. It comes closer, raising its arms in either greeting or threat, but the light doesn't reveal any more detail. It's a creature of living shadow.

'What the hell..?'

'Don't you recognize it?' says Dunamis. 'I can tell from the walk. It's you.'

It's the shadow that was stolen from you in Arcadia, come to have a reckoning with the one it was always destined to follow. It says nothing, but when it drops into a fighting crouch you know. One of you must die.

If you have the title **Sisyphean Taskmaster** and not the codeword *Rhombus* ▶ 200 immediately; otherwise read on.

You and your shadow lunge at the exact same moment. Of course. Roll one die; you can add 2 to the roll if you have the **Panoply of the Lost Hero**, but deduct 1 if your Wound box is currently ticked. The blessing of Demeter, if you have it, allows you to reroll once.

score 1-3   ▶ **666**
score 4-6   ▶ **1602**

425

Get the codeword *Ripple*.

An old blind man takes you by the arm. He is surprisingly strong. 'You'll help an old soldier,' he says.

'What do you need?'

'Not money, if that's what you're worried about. Just steer me to the East Gate. This time of day there are too many carts trundling about, and I'd like to keep my toes.'

As you guide him through the streets, he starts talking about a magnificent city.

'I suppose it is quite impressive,' you say.

'Not this dump!' he snaps, angrily banging his staff on the ground. 'Pay attention, I'm talking about Iskandria. In the old days it was a wonder of the world, palaces and fountains and tree-lined terraces like a home of the gods. All gone now, of course. Nothing to see except a few overgrown stones and miles and miles of mud flats.'

'Conquered, was it?'

'Conquered by time, as we all are in the end. The people there now, they're what's left of the Myrmidons. You know, Achilles's mob. Good job their ancestors can't see how they've turned into a rabble of goat herders, beachcombers, mudlarks and starving farmers. They make a few coins taking tourists round the ruins and spinning yarns about the past.'

'A sad end for a proud race.'

'When you're young, you think strength and glory are everything. But the river of life, it dries up.'

'You mean the Great River, right? Was there a curse or something? Some reason it went away?'

'Don't know. An old mate of mine, name of Loutro, he was always talking about greening the desert.'

'How?'

'He had some madcap notion that some ritual to some goddess would bring the river back. As if prayers ever did anybody any good.'

'This ritual – did he ever do it?'

'Nah. Always had an excuse. Bunch of things he needed to collect first. Guess he never found them, as last I heard

the river bed is still as dry as granny's dugs.'

You look up. 'Well, here's the gate.'

'I'll leave you, then.' He turns to tap his way back along the street.

'But I thought you wanted the gate to Notus?'

He shakes his head. 'That's where you're heading. If you should happen to bump into Loutro, come by and tell me about it sometime. I'm on a bench in the park most afternoons.'

'Who shall I say sent me?'

'Ptolemos,' he says with a final wave of his staff.

▶ **333**

426

You come to. Ancaeus is leaning over you with an expression of frightened wonder. 'For a minute there I thought you were stone dead,' he says.

'For a minute there I was.'

The hold is strewn with dozens of dead insect larvae, a foul pus-like fluid leaking from their squashed and broken bodies. Some of the sailors are bandaging cuts.

'Nasty little devils,' remarks the Minotaur, 'but their mandibles are too small to puncture my hide. Leave me down here for a while and I'll make sure there aren't any left.'

He crashes around in the hold for the next few minutes, finally clambering back up to join the rest of you. 'That's the lot of 'em,' he says. 'Eggs too. Some of the supplies got a bit trashed in the crossfire, though.'

'We need to reach a harbour soon,' reckons the navigator.

▶ **653**

427

They fall like skittles, struggling to get up with the sprawling bulk of the burliest guard pinning them down. You jump on his stomach to make sure he stays winded, then run down the stairs and out into the street, quickly losing yourself in the crowds milling along the Avenue of the Anvil.

▶ **63**

428

If you have the codeword *Quiver* and this box ❑ is empty, tick it and ▶ 283; otherwise read on.

If you do not have the codeword *Quince* and this box ❑ is empty, tick it and ▶ 1073; otherwise read on.

If you don't have the codeword *Quake* and this box ❑ is empty, tick it and ▶ 315; otherwise read on.

'Your destiny lies elsewhere,' says the priestess.

'So I shouldn't return to Boreas?'

'As you choose. Destiny being fulfilled, the god grants you the gift of free will.'

She says nothing more, and as you are now dizzy from the clouds of incense, you back out of her presence and go to get some fresh air.

► **510**

429

You step swiftly to one side, weaving around Enceladus's cumbrous attack. With swift precision you aim a crushing blow to his quadriceps, numbing his left leg. He's reduced to hopping on one foot, but he makes no attempt to defend himself. Roaring in pain and fury, he swings his tree-trunk club at your head. Make a STRENGTH roll at difficulty 9.

Succeed ► **878**

Fail ► **943**

430

'Are you stupid?' snarls Oizys. 'Can't plan ahead? Or is it betrayal you've got in mind? Either way, you'll get a lesson you didn't bargain on.'

She runs shadowy fingers under skin and sinew, dragging her ragged nails along your nerve endings, plucking and pinching at the soft tissues of your innards.

Roll two dice to see which of your attributes she has diminished:

score 2-4 or 10   −1 from CHARM

score 5-6   −1 from GRACE

score 7 or 11-12   −1 from INGENUITY

score 8-9   −1 from STRENGTH

This effect is permanent. Attributes can go negative.

Keep going to the summit anyway   ► **1391**

Turn to the northern slopes   ► **151**

Go to the east slopes   ► **1088**

Search the south side of the mountain   ► **1311**

Look to the west   ► **1413**

431

Cold marble presses into your back. You open your eyes. You're lying in the foyer of the palace. Dunamis is leaning over you. Her lantern gives little light in the shadowy vastness of the hall.

She helps you to your feet. 'You talked in your sleep.'

'What did I say?'

'Best not to dwell on it.' She shivers and glances back along the corridor to the debating chamber. 'Not easy dragging you out of there, I can tell you. Where now?'

Go back and try again ► **846**

Go outside ► **820**

432

A rueful smile plays on Nestor's lips as he strokes his white beard. 'Can the gods ever truly be said to take the side of mortals? They follow their own plans, and a tangled web it is when you consider that some of our heroes here have Olympian ancestry.'

'Still, there must be some gods who favour each side.'

'Aphrodite supports Ilion, of course, because it was Helen absconding with Prince Paris that started the whole business. And Ares always takes the same side as Aphrodite. The twins are for Ilion too, light-bringing Apollo and moon-rising Artemis, but they stand more aloof, knowing that lofty Ilion is doomed to fall.'

'And on your own side?'

'We have Hera, queen of the gods, and with her the support of bright-eyed Athena and world-shaking Poseidon. And Hephaistos too, whom you Amazons know as Vulcan. He it was who crafted that battle-gear you must have seen by Achilles' tent.'

Ask another question   ► **724**

Thank him and leave   ► **735**

433

Note **222** as your Current Location, then ► **1269** and tick the box next to the North Gate. From now on you will always be able to find your way back here.

434

There is a cobbled square to the side of the road. Above it, just centimetres from the ground, floats a green glass pyramid about five metres high. This is the Tomb of Hope, though no one alive in the city can tell you why it has that name.

Around this miraculous structure are gaudily-covered booths from which hedge-wizards and charlatans sell charms. 'Do not fall prey to the Sphinx!' cries one, a skinny fellow whose bright silk robes leave his tattooed arms bare. 'Here are the answers to all the Sphinx's riddles. Only 10 pyr.'

'That's quite a lot to pay for the answer to a riddle.'

He mimes astonishment and injured pride. 'Not just one riddle. Several. And these answers might save your life.'

Pay him 10 pyr ► **651**

If you don't pay and you have the codeword *Reverie* ► **88**

Otherwise ► **695**

435

He hands you the **voicebox remote**. Add it to your possessions.

'Careful not to press the button marked "shrill",' he says. 'That really is high enough to break glass.'

'Ear-splitting?'

He nods. 'Quite literally.'

Sell him something   ▶ 526

Leave   ▶ 325

436

❑

If the box already has a tick in it ▶ 104

If the box is empty, tick it now and then read on.

'The river's come back,' you tell Ptolemos.

'Loutro was right after all, was he? Glad to hear it. And how do you feel about it? Proud of your achievement?'

'Shouldn't I be?'

'Did it make you wiser? Fitter? Bolder? Happier? Helping the Myrmidons get back on the ladder to greatness has to change you as well as them, doesn't it? Or is a good deed its own reward?'

Choose any one attribute (CHARM, etc) that is currently +1 or less and increase its score by 1.

If you have the codeword *Ogle* ▶ 98

If not but you have **blessed fruit** ▶ 261

If not but you have a **bunch of grapes** ▶ 1312

Otherwise ▶ 1283

437

❑ ❑

Do not tick either of the boxes unless you were told to do so in the section you just turned from.

Neither of the boxes is ticked   ▶ 135

One box is now ticked   ▶ 1558

Two boxes are ticked   ▶ 1647

438

There are enough chores to keep you busy on deck. You soon forget all about the noises in the hold.

There is no telling how long you have been sailing through the void. Far off, faint arcs of light in the blackness make you think of wispy sunlit clouds until Ancaeus tells you they are swathes of stars too numerous to count.

'You should get some rest,' he says.

'Is it night or day?'

'Neither means anything out here in the void. When you're weary, lie down.'

You find a small wooden structure in the stern that serves as a makeshift deckhouse. Using your pack as a pillow, you stretch out and are soon fast asleep.

If you have the codeword *Noble* ▶ 202

If you don't ▶ 1254

439

'You have come at last,' says a tall robed man in a crown that bears a blindingly bright gold effigy of the Sun's face.

'Were you expecting me, Your Grace?' you say as you bow your head, for he is one of the Archons.

He nods. 'I hear songs of your great deeds. Also I see that you are unblemished, which is testament to your great skill. Even Heracles had his battle-scars. But what I seek to find out is whether you have wits to match your courage and prowess.

'You know that there are seven of us Archons, each masked with astrological significance. As well as the Sun and Moon, the five planets are represented: swift Stilbon, twilit Hesperus, fiery Pyroeis, bright Phaethon, and mysterious Phainon.

'Once a year we convene for a feast, though there is no food nor drink. Our sustenance is our recital of the deeds we intend in the coming year. We sit at a round table with eight seats, the empty chair bearing the mask of the god Vulcan lest he should deign to join us.

'Pyroeis sits between the Sun and Vulcan. Hesperus is opposite Stilbon. Phaethon is three seats around from the Sun. The Sun is opposite the Moon. Who is sitting directly across from Vulcan's chair?'

Consider your answer:

'Phainon.'   ▶ 597

'The Moon.'   ▶ 865

'Hesperus.'   ▶ 550

440

Note **764** as your Current Location, then ▶ **1269** and tick the box next to the Tavern of the Hero of Temesa. From now on you will always be able to find your way back here.

441

You jump on a horse and ride back towards the churning melee of battle. The sun is high in the sky now and the full fury of both sides has reached a pitch of violence in which reason and order are swept away. All around you come shrieks of despair and terror, jeering taunts, feral roars, exultant cries such as you've never heard from human throats.

You point your mount towards the thickest fighting. Chariots crash and splinter to left and right of you. Spears lock and sway in desperate contests of strength. Hot-blooded horses stamp the plain of Ilion amid the clamour of jangling war-gear.

But now your vision is enhanced and you can see beyond the merely mortal struggle. A myriad darting lights weave continually overhead – figures flitting to a different rhythm of time, messengers from Olympus bringing the whims of the gods to take root in mortal hearts as fleeting moods of jealousy and rage, pity and pride, that change the course of destiny.

Those are the minor deities, those messengers, but you can also see far vaster figures in the form of looming thunderheads and cloud-piercing shafts of sunlight overlooking the milling hordes below. They have the shape of mortals but their substance and scale are beyond imagination. Surely those are the gods themselves, reaching down to bestow luck on one hero, doom upon another.

If you have the codeword *Rage* ▶ **383**

If not ▶ **1034**

442

The artificial beetles spiral down to the floor and remain with their wing-cases open. They are emitting a faint droning sound. Are they recharging? Or just biding their time? There is nothing else in this small chamber so you wait until the beetles take to the air again. As they circle around you weaving the cocoon of gold light, you experience a feeling of control as though your senses extend into the beetles themselves. By concentrating you may be able to steer the motion of the cocoon to take you wherever you want to go. (You will need the appropriate book in the Vulcanverse series to travel anywhere but Vulcan City, of course.)

Return to the throne room ▶ **1048**

Travel to Boreas ▶ **378**

To Arcadia ▶ **1438**

To Notus ▶ **608**

To Vulcan City ▶ **746**

443

The two of you spend a night of athletic passion, finally falling asleep in a sweaty tangle of sheets.

But then comes the morning after. Chipos rings the bell to order breakfast, lying back in bed with a contented smirk that suggests he thinks you are now a couple. Is he right, or was this a one-night stand?

You're in a relationship ▶ **557**

It'll never happen again ▶ **1328**

444

'Yes, this will do the trick,' says Ancaeus, throwing the book open and consulting it as he sketches out a course on his charts.

He shouts orders to the helmsman. The deck tilts as the *Sunrise* alters its heading. In the deep blackness dead ahead you can make out a faint glimmer. 'What is that?' you ask.

'A new dawn for all of us,' he says.

The vessel makes good headway. For a time there is nothing but the slow creak of the ropes, the almost musical boom of flexing timbers, the occasional muttered remark.

The light ahead grows bigger until at last the cry comes from the lookout: 'Land ahoy!'

▶ **346**

445

'Hey, bonce,' you say to the empty air.

The Face of Wisdom's voice pulses on the wind: 'You could at least try to be polite.'

'I'll make an effort in future. For now, could you switch off this joker's battle suit?'

There's a series of clicks as Daedalus's armour unlocks itself and hinges open like elaborate metal origami, leaving him defenceless.

'That's that damned brass head, isn't it?' he says. 'You know I was the one who built it? The trouble with gadgets: no sense of loyalty.'

Try to enlist him as an ally ▶ **1606**

Forget him and return to the battle ▶ **494**

446

'My loyalty is wholly to you, lord, as yours is to great Queen Night, your mother. When you command me to serve her, as you no doubt will, it will be my privilege to be the unquestioning instrument and slave of your will.'

'A good answer,' says a female voice – a voice that

carries in it the pitiless force of scouring winds and a cosmic immensity to threaten the sanity of mortal minds.

Darkness has crept around you. Without you realizing it, Nyx has come, suddenly, like night in the tropics, and the darkness that envelops you is the hem of her robe.

► **1027**

447

'It's three for three,' says Kazala, applauding louder than any of them. 'You're the clear winner.'

'You're taking defeat well,' you reply.

She smiles. 'There'll be another chance. I've got lots of stories.'

The cream of society attends Lady Pemphreda's salon, and your reputation is enhanced throughout the city. Gain 1 Glory and ► **1324**

448

It's a strip of spicy-smelling jerky in a small wooden box. There is a note in barely decipherable script, literacy and calligraphy not being especially prized skills among the Amazons.

After puzzling over the note for some time you decide it reads, *'Centaur heart eat it good for strong.'*

Risk it	► **783**
Chuck it in the bin	► **97**

449

After some haggling it seems that the storekeeper would rather take a service in lieu of cash. 'Money,' he says in a tone of amused contempt. 'What is it but a reminder that gold and silver can be fashioned in much more pleasing forms than coinage? But if I take a service to be granted later, that not only gives me a lever on the future, it is a thing of aesthetic merit. A service is a story waiting to be told.'

If you have the codeword **Robber** and want to offer him a favour from Zinc ► **1356**

If you have a permanent blessing bestowed on you by the goddess Demeter and are willing to part with it ► **1652**

If you have the title **Public-Spirited** and are willing to give him the goodwill you have earned with the city watch ► **1636**

Offer him a **curio credit** ► **855**

Or you could try and interest him in something (► **526**) or leave (► **325**).

450

You pour a couple of drinks and hand her one. 'Here's to us,' she says. 'Much more warming than the icy lake in Hades you pulled me out of.'

'Careful. That almost sounds like gratitude.'

She smiles over the rim of her glass. 'I admit I took you for a sap at the time. But then I got to thinking that it's much nicer being alive, and I've got you to thank for that.'

'I don't like to ask, but what brings you to the big city?'

'Looking up old friends isn't a good enough reason?'

You gaze into the fire. A log splits, sending crackling sparks up the chimney. 'Friends? You call them marks, don't you? Is it warm in here?'

She sits forward, speaking slowly. 'It is warm. Toasty warm. The fire is lovely and cosy, isn't it? Nice to be in here, so warm and so comfortable, when outside there's a cold night wind.'

You throw down the brandy glass and lunge for the window. 'Need... fresh air. You drugged me!'

'Can't hold your liquor? A lot of heroes are like that.'

She watches impassively as you slump to the floor.

Make an INGENUITY roll at difficulty 9. You cannot use an item for a bonus because you are in your nightgown and don't have any possessions on you.

Succeed	► **394**
Fail	► **280**

451

❑

The north-west corner of the city is dominated by the Tower of Ice. If you do not have the codeword *Reverie* and the box above is empty, put a tick in it and ► **647**; otherwise read on.

The tower is clad in white ceramic tiles that catch and splinter the sunlight so that on the hottest summer days it seems to be limned in shimmering ice. The legend is that once Atlas, drowsing at his work, allowed the sky to tilt until part of its weight rested on the top of the tower. This accounts for the long crack that runs up the side, as thin as a hair and only visible when the light catches it at a precise slant.

To go straight to a city location that you already know about, note **451** as your Current Location, then ► **1432**

To go up the tower ► **760**

Or you can go:

East along the Boulevard of the Undine ► **198**

South-east along the Street of the Winds ► **1062**

South down the Boulevard of the Sylph ► **988**

452

Note on your Adventure Sheet that your Current Location is **1238**, then read on.

One blazing hot afternoon, you return home to find

your uncles Nicomachus and Sophos playing a game of psephoi in the cool green shade of the arbour at the side of the house.

You watch them make their moves across the board, each trying to surround the other's playing pieces. Nicomachus squints closely at the board with his one good eye, making his moves with sudden furious decisiveness. He holds the pieces awkwardly in his right hand, which is missing a couple of fingers from an old war-wound, while Sophos sits back, serenely contemplative, a thoughtful smile playing about his white-bearded lips.

Nicomachus places a piece on the holy line in the centre of the board and throws himself upright in his chair with a self-congratulatory snort. Absent-mindedly reaching for a piece to counter the move, Sophos picks up a silver coin from the table in front of him. Seeing his mistake, he laughs and sets the coin aside, taking up a legitimate playing piece instead. But perhaps it has caught your eye, lying there shining in a shaft of sunlight? The face on the coin is that of an insect.

Ask about it   ▶ 165
You're not interested   ▶ 575

453

Zoë's surprise attack throws your foes into panic and confusion. Half of them turn to face her. In the jostling melee, many are pushed over the edge of the roof and fall screaming to the street far below.

That still leaves plenty for you and the Minotaur. Werewolves bound across the gap, claws skittering on the deck as they lunge at you with snapping jaws. Were-apes swing across, balancing nimbly on the rail to rake you with their claws. Ragged-winged gaunts fly overhead like rags tossed on the storm, diving in to attack whenever your attention is elsewhere.

Carried away by the trance-like rhythm of battle, you fail to notice the sagging sheets, the uselessly flapping sails, the screech of tortured gears from the damaged buoyancy rotor. The ship is listing in midair, sinking lower towards the ground. The rooftop towers over you now, making it easy for more of the nightmarish horde to jump across.

You look up to see Thanatos outlined against the storm, his giant hand swinging around to splinter the hull. Crippled, its sails torn and flapping in the wind, the *Sunrise* spins out of control. It lurches to one side. Sailors scream as they are flung overboard. You cling to the wheel as the ship drops in a helpless spiral, breaking up on the ground as surely as if a gale had swept her onto rocks.

You lie stunned in the wreckage. A few people have remained in the street, too paralyzed with terror to run.

One edges nervously past where you are lying, perhaps hoping to bolt and run. Then he turns his face upwards and gives a despairing moan. Slipping on the wet cobblestones, he starts to scramble away. A sliver of deathly white light stabs down, touching him for just an instant, and he is gone. All that remains of him is a wisp of dark vapour that is blown away on the wind.

A colossal foot descends to the street beside you, landing with a tremor that dislodges bricks and sends cracks spreading through the flagstones. Painfully you rise to behold pitiless Thanatos standing like a mountain against the raging storm.

▶ 595

454

'This shop-bought luck you're wrapped about in is tissue-thin,' says Hypnos dismissively. 'Now that the titans have returned, the gods are fighting for their very lives. They have other things to worry about than to grant you second chances.'

With a gesture he strips away your blessings, including **Death's favour** and any **benisons**. Delete them from your Adventure Sheet but keep the permanent blessing of Demeter if you have it.

▶ 1635

455

Mindful of what befell Pemon, you go about the business of blackmail more cautiously than he did. Himera receives one of the letters with an anonymous note saying she will get more of them back if she makes a payment.

Each payment is to be left in a different location around the city. Under a table at a roadside café, behind one of the idols in a temple, inside discarded crates in the fruit market, and so on. You are careful to collect the drop-offs at times when there are crowds around to prevent anyone watching from knowing who picked them up.

It takes a few days, but each time you send back one of the letters you get another payment. In the end you get 500 pyr out of her. A small enough price to pay to preserve her reputation, too.

Cross the **bundle of compromising letters** off your list of possessions and ▶ 1642

456

A knife slices deep into your flesh. If the Wound box on your Adventure Sheet was unticked, put a tick in it now and then ▶ 1023

If you were already injured ▶ 364

457

Three wiry men in black have entered by way of the study window and are discussing their next move in urgent whispers.

'Do you know which room the target's in?' says one.

'Doesn't matter. We'll just torch the whole house. A tragic accident.'

'Sniff. Yeah, but the servants will all die too.'

'Collateral damage. Gelos and Ersi said to make sure, and nothing makes sure like a house on fire.'

Gelos and Ersi – you know those names. They're leading citizens in the village of Bridgadoom in Arcadia, a village of which you were mayor before some accounting irregularities came to light.

The intruders start preparing incendiary bundles which they obviously intend to distribute around the mansion.

Step into the study to confront them ▶	**1369**
Ambush them one at a time ▶	**1476**
Sneak off and find a militia patrol ▶	**1412**

458

The bolts of energy lance towards you, but as Nyx dies they lose force, dissipating in a wisp of black vapour that is torn apart on the breeze.

At your feet, Nyx's body is disintegrating too. It breaks apart like a crust of cold ashes, collapsing in on itself until nothing is left but a dark stain on the ground and a smell of night blooms and ancient dusty vaults.

▶ **332**

459

Make a STRENGTH roll at difficulty 10. You cannot use an item for a bonus to this roll because you are in your nightgown and don't have any possessions on you.

Succeed ▶	**257**
Fail ▶	**219**

460

You attempt a complicated story of court intrigues, but you lose your thread and get a few names wrong and soon dry up.

Kazala is ready to take centre stage. 'Politics doesn't have to be dull,' she tells the assembled guests. 'What if I told you that a plan for lasting peace began with me crouching in a pit in the eastern desert, breaking teeth out of a fossilized dragon while skeletal sentries prowled the dunes? If they'd caught me I'd have been flayed alive. Look.' She pulls her robe off her shoulder to reveal a long scar. 'That's from one time I wasn't quite quick enough. I left some blood behind on the Spartoi's swords that day, but I got away with –' She opens her hand, revealing a few nuts she took earlier from a bowl. 'Well, these are just snacks, but I left the desert with a handful of dragon's teeth.'

'What use are dragon's teeth?' asks a rotund gentleman with a beard like a dirty white octopus. 'I've heard that if you sow them you get a crop of Spartoi, and they're as likely to murder you as do you any favours.'

'Exactly right, sir!' says Kazala, jabbing her finger at him approvingly as if he'd managed to answer a trick question. 'Who'd want such a thing? I wandered high and low wondering what to do with my clutch of dragon's teeth. Such a hard-won prize –' again she displays her scar, giving the men in the audience a longer look at her shapely back – 'I couldn't bear to sell them, though I had no use for them until I came to Sarpedon on the southern edge of the Borean plateau…'

She goes on to tell of negotiations with the council of Sarpedon, but even though the story is winding down now you can see it will be hard to win the audience round. Make a CHARM roll at difficulty 9. You can add an additional +1 to your dice score if you have a Glory of 10 or more.

If you succeed then you somehow get more acclaim for your story, confused as it was ▶ **785**

If you fail then she has won this round ▶ **168**

461

'We don't have personal servants here at the Academy,' Myletes tells you, 'but we do have a very extensive cellar. Does your fellow have any experience with wines?'

'Do you mean the region, domain, grape, or specific vineyard?' says your erstwhile major-domo. 'I am also trained as a sommelier and can advise on wines to accompany a meal.'

Myletes claps his hands in delight. 'When can you start?' ▶ **1544**

462

She struggles with even greater determination as she sees the storm rolling away and daybreak starting to lighten the eastern horizon. Her nails dig deep into your flesh and she lashes out again and again with bruising force. Tick the Wound box on your Adventure Sheet if it wasn't ticked already.

Make a STRENGTH roll at difficulty 9 to hold onto her. (Remember that you cannot use an item to give you a STRENGTH bonus.)

Succeed ▶	**1614**
Fail ▶	**1063**

463

There's a moment of shock and terror as your vision dims. Has the resurrection failed? But no. You feel hard marble underfoot. The smell of rain and wet grass blows in on the evening wind. The bright lights of the ballroom surround you. You are back in Vulcan's palace. There is no sign of the giant insects.

Get the codeword *Rustic* and ▶ **490**

464

The other second is pacing up and down beside a fountain. He is obviously irritated that you're late, and expresses his anger with a tone of cold civility. 'Let's make it snappy,' he says. 'I'm sure we've both got other things to do. What weapons and armour? I've made a list.'

He hands you three proposals. You know Tekto is an accomplished swordsman, so there's a strong incentive to pick the first proposal. But it crosses your mind that he knows you'll be thinking that, so he might be trying to sucker you into making the wrong choice.

The options are:

Sword and heavy armour	▶ **1396**
Bow and arrows with light armour	▶ **422**
Spiked mace with medium armour	▶ **794**

465

For ten years this conflict has raged. Some of the men here were hardly more than boys when it began. Others have grown old, or been crippled and stayed on to watch from the sidelines. And many, of course, fell in battle and have had their embers sent up to the heavens on the roaring winds of funeral pyres.

You see a group of men glancing along the beach in your direction. No doubt they're wondering if you will join in today's fighting – and if so on which side.

Arm yourself for battle	▶ **727**
This is not your fight	▶ **823**
Speak with Achilles	▶ **766**

466

You recognized the thief right away. You track her down in the Street of Ash, where you know she likes to watch the puppet plays. After the show she drops a few coins into the basket in front of the puppeteers' booth.

'Redistributing your ill-gotten gains, Dunamis?'

She gives you a big gap-toothed grin. 'Robbing from the rich isn't a crime, is it?'

'Apparently your moral education missed out a few key points. But I'm not here to try to talk you out of thievery. I don't have the time for that. Just a word to the wise: if you're going to filch purses right under Zinc's nose – '

'Does he have a nose?' She giggles. 'With that mask of his you wouldn't know.'

'Dunamis, listen to me. You need to pay him a percentage.'

'Doesn't seem fair,' she says with a pout. 'What do I get out of it?'

'You get to grow up.'

Take her to see Zinc	▶ **237**
Let her go	▶ **232**

467

A gleam of red light scratches at your eyes. A hectoring voice is shouting something in your ear.

'Go away. I want to sleep.'

'You must wake up. Repeat, wake up.'

Reluctantly you haul yourself into a sitting position. You're on the floor of the ballroom. Outside a storm has turned the evening to pitch darkness. Rain clatters off the veranda. A blaze of lightning, swiftly snuffed out in the murk, is followed by thunder that shakes the building like a giant's hand.

The glowing mechanical butterfly is speaking a recorded message in Daedalus's voice. 'The good news is I saw all this coming. So our team has me, which is a plus. Against that, you've been in slumberland while Nyx and the kids have been firing up a war in heaven. Get with the prog– '

There's a click as the message loop runs out.

▶ **1561**

468

A couple of the Celedons lie broken at your feet, but there are more arriving every minute in answer to the incessant shriek. You have to get this fight over quick.

Make a STRENGTH or GRACE roll (your choice) at difficulty 14.

Succeed	▶ **1256**
Fail	▶ **185**

469

The sailors aren't happy about having a cat on board. 'He's an albatross around our necks,' says the cabin boy.

You lean down to stroke Nectanebo, who stares at you with utter disdain but can't resist purring. 'He used to be a pharaoh,' you say.

'Lock the moggy up,' grunts an old sea salt. 'A cat running loose on deck is asking for trouble.'

If you agree to locking the cat in a cabin ▶ **312**

If not ▶ **729**

470

Long banks of silvery mist press in on all sides. A chill brings the scent of high passes and bracing mountain streams. The mist is swept away. You stand on the slopes of a mountain. Streams froth and gush amid the rocks and grass of the hillside, gentle enough here but rising steeply towards a towering peak. The land around the summit blazes with what you take at first to be a lava flow. Then you see it is ice flooded with red light from the low sun.

A voice whispers in your ear, a female voice with an irritating mosquito-like whine to it. 'Up there, that's Olympus.'

'Who's that?'

'I am Oizys. The Queen of Darkness sent me along to make sure you do what you promised.'

'Where are you?' You whirl around, catching a momentary glimpse of a shadow that slips away behind you.

'I get under people's skin. That's my thing. Nobody gets to see my face, but they all know me well, from the woman in childbirth to the young man on the battlefield to the elderly on their sickbed.'

'What is this, a riddle?'

'I have another name. I am Pain.'

And to prove the point she pokes unseen fingers among the organs of your guts. Sweat springs from every pore as fiery agony doubles you up.

Note Oizys in the Companion box on your Adventure Sheet.

If you have **food of the gods** ▶ 928

If not ▶ 612

471

Lady Pemphreda's guests make a point of setting aside all divisions of rank while attending her salon. Their prejudice in favour of physical beauty, however, is undiminished. You circulate and everyone speaks to you affably enough, but you get the sense of being subtly excluded from their confidence.

Pemphreda herself, who is the soul of tact, steers the conversation onto cosmetics and gives you a sample tub of moisturizing cream. 'Do try it,' she says. 'You are much younger than I, but these are little tricks that one must learn as the years take their toll.'

You rub on the cream and later discover that it has miraculously removed some blemishes you thought you'd carry forever. Lose 1 scar and ▶ 1324

472

You are in the Avenue of the Anvil. Winds howl through the deserted ruins. The sky overhead is blacker than the darkest midnight.

If you have the codeword **Radiant** but don't have **Rough** ▶ 905 immediately; otherwise read on.

Where will you head next?

The nearest gate ▶ 723

The nearest tower ▶ 171

Your mansion (only if you have the title **The Unexpected Heir**) ▶ 1257

Your family home (only if you have the codeword **Reverie**) ▶ 1385

The Academy of Philosophers ▶ 1510

The temple district ▶ 1326

The Forum ▶ 981

473

Agamemnon is a burly middle-aged man with muscles hard as a knotted fist. A long white scar cuts down across one sightless eye and leaves his teeth exposed by a slit in his upper lip that looks like a permanent snarl.

As you arrive at his tent he's haranguing a frail old man who bears the banded staff and regalia of a priest of Apollo. 'Let me not see your face again, Chryses. I've had a bellyful of your reedy whining. Your priestly robes won't save you from my wrath if I find you loitering around the long ships after sundown.'

'Great lord Agamemnon,' says Chryses, cringing so low he is almost kneeling at the high king's feet, 'I pray that all the gods who hold Olympus will grant you victory over Ilion and fair winds back to your homeland. Grant me only one thing, in shining Apollo's name – set my daughter free. I have brought ransom, see.'

He gestures to his attendants and they throw open a dozen chests, revealing a tribute of silver coins, iron bars, animal hides and gems like liquid droplets of red and green light.

'Father…'

'Astynome!'

In the shadow of the tent flap you see a slender young woman, blonde and with a fragile milk-white beauty. Then you notice the leather collar round her neck, like a dog tethered on a leash.

'Get your skinny arse back in there, wench,' snaps Agamemnon, raising his huge sun-bronzed hand. One slap from him looks like it could break her. As she slinks nervously away, he turns again to Chryses. 'What do I want with your paltry gifts when all of Ilion's vaults will soon be open to me? Astynome is mine now. Get used to it. She'll grow old in my court at Argos. She'll slave away in my household and keep my bed warm. Now beat it or I'll have you whipped.'

Intervene   ► 1140

It's not your problem   ► 1624

474

If Current Location is **260** then ► **1125**; otherwise read on.

If you have the codeword *Royal* ► **1295**

Otherwise ► **1173**

475

You stand defiant. 'Even if you strike me down, I'll be back.'

'Not this time.'

'Sure about that?' you have time to say as he throws back his cowl.

You meet the full intensity of Thanatos's unshielded gaze. It is a blistering magnesium glare, like a rip in the world through to the intolerably white light beyond.

If you are female   ► 1225

Otherwise   ► 923

476

'Good!' shouts Nyx over the shriek of the wind. 'You have come to your senses, I see. Let us travel to Olympus, where I will finish off the dying gods and seat myself on Zeus's throne.'

'I'm afraid you're in for a nasty surprise,' you shout back as the two of you are sucked into the tapestry. 'I didn't poison the gods. I restored them.'

► 1053

477

'You may look up, mortal,' says Zeus, his voice so deep you seem to feel it in every fibre of your body. 'We have shielded our splendour so as not to strike you blind.'

Your own god adds, 'You have done us a great service. Now that our strength is restored we will sally forth and drive the titans back into the pit of Tartarus. All the world owes you a debt today.'

'But the world is still in great peril,' you reply. 'Nyx is remaking it as her own realm.'

Zeus points to the lame, hunched god lurking in the colonnade behind them. 'The world of mortals is your creation, Vulcan. Prevent her.'

'I cuh-cannot, father,' stutters Vulcan. 'Nuh-Nyx has wrested control of the matrix that underpins it.'

Zeus turns to you. His aura may be masked, but the fire in his eyes is dazzling enough. 'Your glorious deeds are not over yet, then. You must travel back to the mortal world and stop her.'

'On my own? I've just saved all you Olympians. Nyx sent me to poison you. Didn't you just all admit you owe me?'

'Enough,' booms Zeus. 'The titans are our concern. You are the hero of your age. The mortal world is under your protection. I will send you back to stop Nyx.'

If Bosk is your companion ► **1050**

If not ► **974**

478

You shrug. 'If you need a reason, it's because I don't want to live in a world shaped by you. Look at how you sent along that spiteful termagant to chew on my viscera. You couldn't just trust me. Threats are all you understand. You'll make a terrible ruler.'

She shakes her head, beginning to turn away even as tendrils of darkness snake out from her robes. The tendrils reach towards you like a giant hand. At their touch, the metal goblets and broken chunks of stone strewn over the floor evaporate into nothingness.

'You will not merely cease to exist,' says Nyx softly. 'You will be expunged from reality. You will never have been.'

A strand of black vapour curls towards you. Backed against the wall, there is nowhere to run. You shut your eyes. There is a moment of – what? Anticipation? Terror? Acceptance? Curiosity?

Then you are wiped out of existence.

479

She gets her wish. It's over so fast that her mouth hardly has time to frame a look of surprise before the light fades out of her eyes.

Zinc instructed you to bring her to his garden allotment.

She hardly weighs anything, and carrying a dead body down the street doesn't draw so much as a second glance in the Grumbles. You find him standing beside a shallow grave next to his cabbage patch.

'Turnips, I thought,' he says, nodding for you to put her in the ground. 'All those honeyed words and sweet smiles, it's got to lend the crop a good flavour, hasn't it?'

You cast your eye along the rows of vegetables, noticing for the first time the rich, freshly-dug loam they're growing in.

'Don't want to waste good fertilizer, do we?' remarks Zinc. 'This way, anyone who lets me down gets to make amends.'

Get the codeword *Robber* and ▶ 326

480

❑

Do not put a tick in the box unless you were specifically told to before turning to this section.

If you have just ticked the box	▶ 317
If it was already ticked	▶ 977
If it is empty	▶ 1405

481

You stuff a crumpled rag in Kleistro's mouth to muffle his screams, then with a short piece of iron piping you proceed to shatter his kneecaps. It's hard work, like cracking coconuts, and you work up a sweat before you're done.

Even through the rag he's making quite a racket, so you drag him right to the end of the lane where a stack of mouldering wooden crates hides you from view. There you fling him face-down the ground. Ignoring his squirms and whimpers, you get a firm hold on each of his legs in turn and wrench it the way you'd dismember a boiled crab.

Kleistro lies moaning, his legs twisted beyond the skill of any physician to fix. You roll him over. His face is sickly pale and his eyes are burning coals of pain. Stooping, you tuck one of the playing cards into the front of his jerkin.

'Luck of the draw,' you tell him and walk away.

Get the codeword *Robber* and ▶ 161

482

Your voice carries the ring of authority. Recognizing you as one of the residents of this affluent neighbourhood, the watchmen follow you at a jog back to the mansion.

The three intruders are surprised in the hallway carrying incendiary parcels. Seeing themselves outnumbered, they surrender to the watchmen and are placed under arrest.

'Who paid you to burn my house down?' you ask as they are led away.

'We were paid to kill you,' is the defiant reply. 'Setting fire to the house just seemed like a good way to make it look like an accident.'

'And who wants me dead?'

He shrugs. 'Might as well tell you, seeing as I'm going to hang anyway. Seems you swindled some honest Arcady burghers out of their life savings.'

The watchman holding the man gives him a jab in the kidneys. 'Don't you go talking to your betters that way, scum.'

If you have the codeword *Robber* and want to call in a favour from Zinc to have those Arcadians dealt with ▶ 290

If you prefer to forget about it ▶ 97

483

There must be a way to convince Lord Xechasiaris that it's time for him to move on to the afterlife. What tack will you take?

Try scaring him	▶ 70
Reassure him	▶ 1247
Offer to escort him there	▶ 874

Make him forget (only if you have some **Lethe water**) ▶ 1439

484

Sitting outside a café, you pore over the drawings you got from the forgetful Lord Xechasiaris. Somewhere in these childish scrawlings is the clue to his lost youth. You hold up each page in turn, studying the drawing and comparing it to the colourful regional costumes all around.

If you have either codeword *Quire* or *Petasos* ▶ 975

If not but you have the codeword *Oblige* ▶ 238

Otherwise ▶ 677

485

Something darts between your legs, almost tripping you up. It's the grey cat you were introduced to while queuing at the gate.

'Shoo,' you snap at it. 'Get out of here, cat. You're barely a mouthful for a werewolf.'

The cat stops and looks at you. Its long hair hangs like sodden rags in the rain. It turns and bounds off across the roof, leaping from ridge to ridge.

Behind you, the door to the stairwell shudders as heavy bodies throw themselves against it.

Which way will you try to escape?

Follow the cat	▶ 1185
Climb up the dome	▶ 759

486

Crossing the courtyard of the Academy, you see a light burning in the window of Myletes's study. You take the stairs two at a time. Bursting in, you find him poring over a book as if the end of the world was just a topic for theoretical discussion.

'Oh, there you are,' he says.

You introduce Dunamis but she hangs back bashfully at the door.

'You're going to need to access Vulcan's simulation matrix,' says Myletes. 'Nyx is using it to rebuild the universe in her image. Everything you see outside is just the first phase. It'll only get worse.'

'How, what and where?'

'Good questions,' he says delightedly. 'You probably need Vulcan's diadem. That might fool the system into thinking you're authorized to make changes.'

If you have **Vulcan's diadem** ▶ **1616**

If not ▶ **348**

487

Your foes pour from the roof in an incessant dark tide. Were-apes and werewolves leap with frightening agility, balancing on the ship's rail and snapping at you with slavering fangs. Flying night-gaunts fill the air. Again and again the grapple-cannons fire steel hooks that bite into the ship's timbers, and as each line goes taut a swarm of vampires scuttle across to join the fray.

If you have the codeword *Recursive* ▶ **700** now; otherwise read on.

You give yourself in to the pulse-pounding rhythm of battle, laying about you with weapons and anything that comes to hand. One of the werewolves, its side sliced open by a blow, flops to the deck and tries snapping at your legs. You snatch up a belaying pin, smash its skull to pulp, and whirl just in time to parry the attack of a flapping horror that looks like a giant face with leathery wings in place of ears.

Make a STRENGTH roll at difficulty 16.

Succeed ▶ **1592**

Fail ▶ **256**

488

'Hey, arse-gob!' shouts the foreman of the work gang. 'Yeah, you, Thersites. Get back to work, you lazy sack of wind.'

For a moment you see murderous rage flash in Thersites' eyes as he turns towards his tormentor, but as he looks back to you he drops his gaze diffidently. 'I'd better not hang around talking,' he mutters, taking up his spade.

'You see how it is.'

▶ **735** and tick the box for Thersites before talking to anyone else.

489

The giant sculpted hand has its fingers expressively pressed together, a gesture such as a philosopher might use when making a subtle point. The water sprays from between the fingertips, flashing in the sinking sunlight and turning the surface of the pond into a constellation of shimmering red-gold stars.

From somewhere deeper in the palace grounds comes a chorus of animal shrieks and growls. That way lies the menagerie.

Make a wish (requires 1 pyr)	▶ **1456**
Continue on to the menagerie	▶ **1392**
Back to the rotunda	▶ **1530**
Return to the first courtyard	▶ **750**

490

The bearded man is standing in the doorway to the garden. He raises his big hands and gives you a teasing ovation. 'Quite a fight,' he says. Behind him the storm rumbles and rolls across a cloud-darkened sky.

'Was that a fight?' you say, catching your breath. 'I thought they just wanted to dance.'

He laughs. 'That's the spirit. Better to go cheerfully into the long night than screaming all the way.'

▶ **1263**

491

Dunamis catches you up. 'Where are you going? There isn't any time to waste.'

'Zinc left something for me. I mean to find out what it is.'

She throws up her hands in exasperation. 'It'll keep, whatever it is. The first thing we've got to do is find a way to crack into Vulcan's workshop and get to the gubbins that shapes reality. Then maybe we can use it to fix what's happened to the city.'

'And how do you suggest we do that?'

'Well, I got into the ball by hacking one of the town noticeboards. Couldn't hurt to try that.'

She's got a point	▶ **1274**
Find Zinc's package first	▶ **1346**

492

'You must make your own mistakes,' says Bosk in a voice heavy with regret. 'Soon now it will be shouted out across the world: the great gods are dead.'

Bosk turns and walks away. As he goes he plays a wistful tune on the pipes he wears slung from his belt. It is a melody of autumn shading into winter, of happy times that will never come again. A eulogy to the grandeur of Olympus.

As you watch him go there is a change in the quality of space itself. Time seems to alter its pace. The gods are here.

You gaze up at them like a child who has wandered out into a gathering of grown-ups. It is not merely their size that overawes you. Their presence is wrapped in an aura of unbearable reality, as if a furnace door were thrown open on the fire at the dawn of creation. To look too long on such beings is to risk blindness, madness, annihilation.

But in that glimpse you see they are diminished. The perfect flesh is marred by welts and bruises and cuts. Golden lifeblood stains their majestic finery. Adamantine armour that should be indestructible hangs in battered plates and broken links from their weary shoulders.

Lowering your eyes, you gesture to the banquet laid out on the table.

'Meagre fare...' booms one, whose dissatisfaction makes you think of proud and rage-filled Ares.

'It must suffice,' says a calm female voice, surely Artemis.

'We'll get no more until the titans are driven back to Tartarus,' states the authoritative Apollo.

'And they will attack again soon,' puts in Athena. 'We must be ready.'

A heavy figure comes to the table. A mountain moving. Zeus himself. 'Each take a mouthful. I will take two. Once restored we'll seal the titans back in their pit for all time.'

They quickly consume the food you've left for them. A moment passes. A tracery of dark lines breaks out across the Olympians' skin as if their golden blood has been replaced with ink. They turn to each other, realizing too late that the food was poisoned. Your own deity stares menacingly towards you, raising one hand to blast you with divine fury. You brace yourself, but the attack never comes. Feebly the gods collapse to the metal floor, the darkness spreading over them until they are covered. Their bodies crumble inwards into a broken crust of ashes.

A cold night wind springs up through the open windows, scattering the desiccated remains of the dead gods. Light bleeds out of the sky and a black rainbow appears for an instant in the last red light of sunset. A torrent of rain blows into the hall, black wisps rising from where each drop splashes on the floor. As the wisps multiply and thicken, they swirl together and coalesce into the mighty form of Queen Nyx, now the unchallenged monarch of all creation.

'You have served me well and faithfully and I will reward you,' she says. 'Behold the throne of Zeus. It's mine now. You will sit at my right hand.'

▶ **1594**

493

Another time. You are at the top of one of the city towers. Your father is here too, which is strange as even when you were a child he rarely had time from his work to take you to places around the city. Now that you are almost an adult, you wonder why he has brought you here.

'You will have to look after your mother and sisters,' he is saying. 'Your brother too.'

'I want to see the world,' you say, standing at the parapet and gazing out from the tower across leagues. Even the nearest villages are like toys, their fields like green felt, and the rivers are silver ribbons that connect them to specks that must be even further settlements. The sun is setting. Smoke rises from chimneys in thin threads. The mountains and plains shade off into blue infinity. Night waits in the east, impatient for the day to die.

'It's getting cold,' your father says, drawing his cloak against the wind whistling around the tower. 'Let's go down.'

Then it's days later and he is being carried, wrapped in dyed cloth, along the road to the necropolis. Your sisters and brother are wailing their grief to the sky. Your mother walks in silence, stumbling, her bare feet grey with dust, hardly seeming to know where she is. Neighbours bow their heads in respectful sorrow as you pass.

At the family tomb, the priests chant blessings to speed your father's soul to Elysium. The crowds of mourners depart like the tide going out and you are alone.

'I want to see the world,' you tell the blank stone door of the tomb.

Get the codeword *Reverie* if you didn't have it already and then ▶ **520**

494

Daedalus is no longer a threat. Turning your back on him, you jump down from the parapet to join your allies. The battle for the fate of the universe has begun.

▶ **1533**

495

'Thetis, the daughter of the Old Man of the Sea, a titan who ruled the oceans before the Olympian gods came. Thetis was loved by Poseidon until he learned that her son was destined be greater than his father.'

'I guess that cooled his ardour.'

Nestor nods. 'The gods are ever eager to indulge their

passions, but above all they guard their power jealously. Thetis wed Peleus, king of the Myrmidons. And Poseidon was right to fear. Even with a mortal father, Achilles is the strongest of heroes, the shining champion of our Achaean army. Herakles himself might have hesitated to meet Achilles in battle.'

Ask him something else ▶ **724**
That's all for now ▶ **735**

496

❑

Do not tick the box above unless you were told to do so in the section you have just turned from.

If the box is empty ▶ **620**
If you just put a tick in the box ▶ **435**
If the box was already ticked ▶ **1297**

497

'How can I go back? Look!'

She shows you her hands, wet with the gore of the corpse she has been gnawing on, the nails broken and filthy from scrabbling in the soil of graves.

You clasp her hands in yours. 'I don't say it'll be easy, but you can atone. If you keep on as you are you'll become a monster and your only home will be among the dead. Do you want that?'

'I deserve no better,' she weeps. 'I was a lady, now I am less than a beggar.'

'Are you Xechasiaris's daughter? Where's his spirit, his strength? At the age of seven he stowed away aboard a caravan to distant lands.'

'My father was braver than I am.'

'There are other kinds of bravery. He also fought against his own nature through his whole life. More than anything else he wanted to travel. That was his heart's desire. Instead he stayed out of duty to rule his people wisely and provide for his family.'

'I'm not strong enough.' She hangs her head. 'You say I will become an unclean thing? I say I already am.'

She's so sunk in despair that she's hardly listening. You need a CHARM roll at difficulty 11 to get through to her.

Succeed ▶ **924**
Fail ▶ **205**

498

At the temple of your own deity, blessings cost 10 pyr. In any other temple you must pay 50 pyr.

The god grants you blessings up to the maximum limit of three. Once you have three blessings, you cannot get another until you have used one.

A blessing can be used to reroll a failed check against CHARM, GRACE, INGENUITY or STRENGTH. In any given situation you can only use one blessing, so if you fail the reroll you can't spend another blessing to try again.

When you are ready to leave ▶ **103**

499

He hesitates, a smile of cold amusement on his lips. 'You'll swear fealty to me when you wouldn't to my brother?'

What's your reply to that?
'He's only Sleep. You are Death.' ▶ **1645**
'I swear fealty to Nyx, not to you.' ▶ **1165**
'Because now I see I have no choice.' ▶ **8**

500

He peers at the sceptre without taking it from you. 'Quite hard to put down, isn't it?'

'That's what I've found,' you admit.

'It's not a problem. I can buy it off you. But are you sure you want to part with it? It could be useful.'

You suck your teeth. 'Useful? It's a bit – '

'Imbued with the essence of primordial darkness? Well, obviously, but sometimes you want to fight fire with fire. Or night with night.' He shrugs. 'It's up to you. I can give you credit against a future purchase.'

'What about cash?'

'Not for a thing like that.'

If you want to sell it ▶ **393**
Otherwise ▶ **828**

501

If you have the **Face of Wisdom** (INGENUITY +3) ▶1442
    If not ▶ 301

502

Between two workshops about halfway down the street there is a narrow gap barely wide enough to be called a lane. You notice that people give it a wide berth. That is one of the ways into the dilapidated district known as the Grumbles.

There is also a vast empty plot at the north end of the street near the Plaza. It is strewn with rubble and fenced off with chains attached to a line of stone bollards. It is prime real estate but nobody seems to know why it is vacant or even who owns it.

If you have the codeword *Ruby* ▶ 635

To go straight to a city location that you already know about, note **63** as your Current Location, then ▶ 1432

Or you can go:

North   ▶ 1642
South   ▶ 555
To the prison   ▶ 1089
Into the Grumbles ▶ 771

503

The two of you are walking in the herb garden. It is early morning and the dew still sparkles on the grass.

'It's going to be a warm day,' you say, trying to prompt Loutro to unburden himself. He's had something weighing on his mind for several days. Perhaps longer than that, now you come to think of it.

'I have something I want to say, but I don't know if I should.' He chews his lip. 'It may not be appropriate.'

'In what way?'

'In a sense I am your teacher.'

'I don't think of you that way, Loutro.'

You can't help smiling, but he remains sombre and troubled. 'My duty is to the goddess. I have no right to speak of my personal feelings for you.'

'Ah.' Now you understand. 'You mean – '

'Our comradeship, our friendship. For me they have blossomed into something more. Alas, that love cannot be cured by herbs.'

He stands waiting for your response to his confession. Nervously his fingers pluck at the leaves of a thyme bush, releasing a spicy aroma on the morning air.

What is your answer?

'We can be lovers as well as friends.'   ▶ 25
'Sorry, but I don't share those feelings.'   ▶ 368

504

'In the garden,' she says, 'there are bergamot trees in alabaster pots.'

'I know the ones.'

'Look under the roots. The treasure is there.' The sky is growing pale. 'Now keep your word. Release me!'

Will you?

Yes, of course   ▶ 1036
No, a promise to a fiend means nothing   ▶ 57

Over the next few days your strength returns. You're able to get up and walk around the camp for an hour or two, though you are still quickly fatigued and must return to Achilles' tent to rest.

The black ships of the Achaeans with their curving prows are drawn high up the beach, long sleek hulls gleaming in the sun, nestled in deep furrows of sand, ominous shells from which bloody war has hatched. Beside each group of ships are the tents of the hero who commands them, distinct camps in roped-off enclosures. The camp of Achilles and his Myrmidons is on the furthest end of the shore.

Near the entrance of the Myrmidon enclosure is a suit of armour on a wooden frame. Licked by the sun's rays it gleams like blood and black oil, a work of fanciful art whose helm and breastplate and greaves seem almost to have grown rather than been fashioned by any craftsman's hand.

The massed ranks of the Achaeans fill the beach and the fringes of the plain where battles are fought almost daily. You watch the men drilling, tending their horses, oiling their chariots and polishing the bronze armour they wear into combat. At all times the camp is filled with shouts, song, laughter, the clatter of weapons in training, the drone of prayers by the priests, the lowing of cattle penned for the feasting.

As you stroll through the camp you pass faces that are becoming familiar to you. Old Nestor, the wise counsellor whose cool head has saved the Achaeans from recklessness on many occasions. Crafty Odysseus, persuasive of tongue and sharp in wits. And Thersites, an ordinary soldier whose voice is often heard raised in the ranks to call out what he sees as foolishness by his commanders – even if it means defying Agamemnon, kings of kings and commander-in-chief of this great army.

Talk to one of them ▶ **735**

Pass by and go to Agamemnon's tent ▶ **813**

Or examine the strange armour – note **650** as your Current Location and then ▶ **306**

If you have the codeword *Rhombus* ▶ **903**

If not ▶ **1480**

You come across Sakan and some other officers playing cards in a tavern.

'Want me to deal you in, stranger?' says a lieutenant of the White Guard who notices you standing near their table.

'Your game seems too rich for me, gentlemen,' you say apologetically, going to sit at a table nearby.

They play on. The candles burn down. Drinks are brought. After a while, as fortunes fluctuate, Sakan happens to win several hands in a row. You seize your chance. On your way to the bar to order another drink, you bend down and pick up something from under his chair.

'Excuse me, is this yours?'

'Eh?' He jerks around, scowling at the card you're holding out.

'You must've dropped it.'

'Something wrong here,' says one of the other players. 'That's the Ace of Chalices, but I just played it – see, here it is. There can't be two in one deck.'

'Get away from me, you dog,' snarls Sakan, lashing out with his foot. He doesn't intend to hit you, but what takes him by surprise is the cascade of cards that scatter to the floor from the fold of his boots.

'Oh, like that is it?' says the White Guard officer.

'That accounts for his winning streak,' growls another player. 'You can have luck on tap if you don't leave it to chance.'

'Cheating at cards? Would've been horsewhipped in my day,' blusters a retired guardsman sitting by the fire.

'This isn't how it looks!' snaps Sakan. 'Those cards aren't mine.' But his haughty manner, so appropriate for browbeating and bullying others, only makes his protests sound more defensive.

Snubbed as a cheat by his fellow guards, Sakan cannot remain in the city. A few days later you hear he's taken indefinite leave.

Get the codeword *Rock* and ▶ **1642**

Thick incense-smoke swirls around the idol that stands in the inner shrine, so that when you prostrate yourself and reach up in supplication you see the god's face as if looking down from the cloudy heavens.

'You are ready,' says a voice that seems to speak inside your head.

'Perhaps not yet, O revered one. There is still – '

'All that holds you back is your own want of courage. Go now, as I directed you before, west and south to the hidden palace of the Fire Worker. Make haste, or the Queen with Eyes of Stars will have made her move and then it will be too late for gods or mortals.'

Shaken by the experience of meeting your deity, you pass the priests outside without a word and emerge into the afternoon sunlight.

▶ **103**

509

□

You arrive at the gates in the west wall of the city. If you do not have the codeword *Reverie* and the box above is empty, put a tick in it and ▶ 264

Otherwise read on.

Next, if you have the codeword *Ridge*, note **509** as your Current Location and ▶ 1064; otherwise read on.

The West Gate's pillars are fancifully carved spires of ice that glisten as if on the verge of melting but remain perpetually frozen by the power of Vulcan's reality-warping decree. From dawn till dusk, carts flow into the city bringing furs, livestock, minerals, pinewood and fish from all across the realm of Boreas. As each cart enters the city, the goods in it vanish and are replaced with a glowing quantity of pyr. 'It saves time at market!' says one trader brightly, sweeping up his cash and heading straight for the nearest tavern.

Nearby is a noticeboard that lists various missions that call for special skills and insouciance in the face of danger. 'Good pay if you live to collect it,' grunts one of the gate guards as he sees you glancing at it.

To go straight to a city location that you already know about, note **509** as your Current Location, then ▶ 1432

Otherwise you can take a closer look at the noticeboard, in which case note **509** as your Current Location, then ▶ 56

Or you can go:

North along the Boulevard of the Sylph ▶ 988
East along the Avenue of Ephirus ▶ 613
South along the Boulevard of the Sylph ▶ 325
West out of the city ▶ **509** in *The Pillars of the Sky*

510

The central courtyard is open to the sky, ensuring that the interior of the temple is filled with light. From somewhere in an inner fane comes the enchanting sound of silver chimes.

If Apollo is your god and you have the codeword *Rohan* ▶ 1568

If Apollo is your god and you have the title **The Chosen One** and wish to enter the inner shrine ▶ 106

Otherwise you can:

Pray for a blessing ▶ 498
Ask for healing ▶ 65
Obtain a prophecy (costs 5 pyr) ▶ 996
Leave ▶ 103

511

He nods slowly. 'Achilles said you were from another time and place. More secrets his mother dredged up from her watery abode, no doubt. But why ask me? The affairs of men are my concern, but this is a matter for the Olympians.'

You wait, but he has nothing more to say right now.

▶ Current Location

512

The armour gives a high-pitched whine as it powers back up. Daedalus stretches out his arms and the armour snaps back into place around him as if it was being fitted by invisible hands.

You give him a narrow look. 'You going to behave now?'

'Seeing as you can switch off my toys whenever you like, I'd say – let's kick some titan-queen ass.'

Taking to the air, he sweeps down from the parapet carrying you to rejoin your troops.

▶ 804

513

'I found a switch in Boreas that turns the sun on and off,' you say, 'so I can tell you without any shadow of a doubt that we're living in a simulation.'

▶ 1542

514

You step out behind her, quicken your pace and put your hand on her shoulder, but instead of flesh your grip closes on unyielding metal.

With a brisk, powerful movement she throws off the robes. Hard aureate limbs gleam in the daylight. Her face is sculpted like a statue's, her body constructed of closely-fitting metal plates. Her eyes are the only part of her not made of golden metal. They fix on you, twin orbs of polished glass in whose depths a mechanical iris whirs.

Shock at her appearance causes you to loosen your grip for a moment. Shaking you off, she reaches up towards the sky. Her arm telescopes up and up until her hand seizes the edge of the roof ten metres above. Flakes of mortar fall around you as her metallic fingers dig into the brickwork, then she retracts the arm and is whisked off her feet. Seconds later she swings over the edge of the building out of sight and you hear her loping footsteps dislodging tiles as she makes off with incredible leaps across the rooftops.

A passer-by stops and looks up, then shakes his head disapprovingly. 'One thing about living in Vulcan City I could never stomach. All the damn automata.'

Her discarded silk robe is lying at your feet. 'Did you see anyone wearing this?' you ask him.

'No, but with all those bright colours it's pretty distinctive. You could ask around. Might be less bother just to buy a new automaton, though.'

'She's not mine.'

He glances up at the rooftops. 'Not anymore she's not.'

Make a CHARM roll at difficulty 12 (ie roll two dice, add your CHARM score plus any one bonus for an attribute-boosting possession, and try to get 12 or more).

Success ▶ 91

Failure ▶ 913

515

Septentrional Avenue is one of the wealthiest districts of the city, a wide street lined with well-tended trees and blossom-laden urns. On either side of the street are high walls enclosing raised gardens with large houses beyond.

If you have the codeword *Quark* and this box ❑ is empty, tick it and ▶ 196; otherwise read on.

If you have the title **The Unexpected Heir** and want to go to your mansion ▶ 1353

To go straight to a city location that you already know about, note **515** as your Current Location, then ▶ 1432

Or you can go:

North ▶ 222

South ▶ 1642

516

'Deep breath,' says the turtle, sinking into the pond.

The water swirls around you, greenly dark and full of muffled sounds. There are glimpses of buried statues reclining in glittering sand, drifting kelp that snakes its strands around the wrecks of sunken ships, shoals of startled fish that dart away as you pass.

Your lungs are strained to bursting point as you sense the turtle veering up towards the surface. A moment later you are standing on firm ground. Your clothing is bone dry and there is no sign of any water. You look around for the turtle, catching a fleeting glimpse of a blue light that ripples across the ground nearby and is gone.

If you have the Vulcanverse book *The Hammer of the Sun* ▶ 548 in that book.

Otherwise ▶ 88 in this book.

517

At last you emerge out of breath at the top of the tower. Wind snatches at your clothing. The cold is intense. A starless sky surrounds you.

Far below, the city is an expanse of even inkier blackness. You see a few scattered specks of light that must be where refugees are huddling together in the ruins. Those firefly-faint glimmers only serve to make the darkness more absolute, like ships with little beacons adrift on a vast lightless sea.

'If this is Nyx's idea of a world,' says Dunamis, 'I don't think much of it.'

'This is just the last gasp of the old world,' you say. 'Nyx's version will be much worse.'

Silently you make your way back down the stairs.

▶ 392

518

If this box ❑ is empty, tick it and ▶ 473

If the box above was already ticked and you have the title **Plaything of Agamemnon** ▶ 541

Otherwise, if this box ❑ is empty, tick it and ▶ 1377

Otherwise ▶ 1529

519

You wrench frantically at the levers that control the wings, but it is no good. The ground rushes up and smashes you with numbing force.

You lie stunned in the broken wreckage of the wings. Some people in the street, cowering in archways out of the rain, edge nervously towards you.

'Are you all right?' says one. Then he turns his face upwards and moans in terror. Slipping on the wet cobblestones, he starts to scramble away. A sliver of deathly white light stabs down, touching him for just an instant, and he is gone. All that remains of him is a wisp of dark vapour that's blown away on the wind.

A colossal foot descends to the street beside you, landing with a tremor that dislodges bricks and sends cracks spreading through the flagstones. Painfully you roll over to behold pitiless Thanatos, god of death, standing like a mountain against the raging storm.

▶ 595

520

Having been born and raised in Vulcan City, you know your way around. You can travel to any of these local landmarks:

Your family home ▶ **1238**
The North Gate ▶ **222**
The South Gate ▶ **555**
The East Gate ▶ **333**
The West Gate ▶ **509**
The Forum ▶ **1642**
The Tower of Ice ▶ **451**
Pan's Column ▶ **48**
The Tower of Sand ▶ **570**
The Tower of Riches ▶ **1222**
The Grumbles ▶ **771**
The Necropolis ▶ **674**
The Groves of Dionysus ▶ **806**
The Academy of Philosophers ▶ **1544**
The Tavern of the Hero of Temesa ▶ **764**
The market ▶ **716**
The temple district ▶ **103**
The Tomb of Hope ▶ **88**

However, there are also some places in the city not widely known even to locals. You can only travel to these if the corresponding box is ticked. You need to discover these secret locations in the course of your adventures, at which point you'll be told to tick the corresponding box.

❑ A tunnel straight to hell ▶ **80**
❑ Lady Pemphreda's salon ▶ **898**
❑ Your mansion ▶ **1353** (only if you still have the title **The Unexpected Heir**)

If you don't want to visit any of these locations right now ▶ Current Location

521

She takes you to one side and whispers in your ear so that Xechasiaris cannot hear. 'It's all bluster, of course. Afraid, that's what he is.'

'Of what?'

'The unknown. Whatever waits on the other side, that sort of thing.'

'What do you suggest?'

'Hold his hand.'

▶ **483**

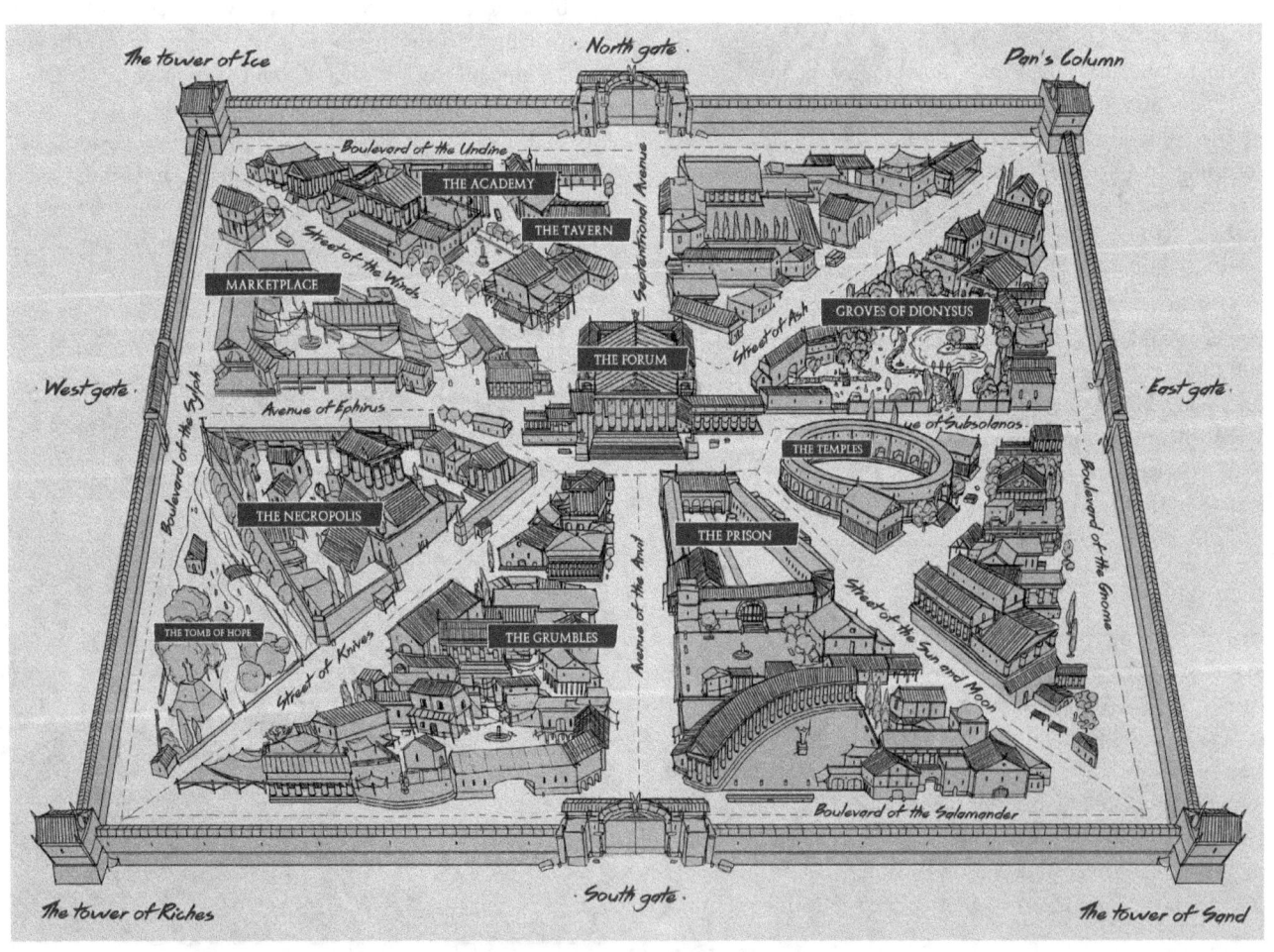

522

You entertain them with the story of your negotiations with the council of the Sarpedons. It could be a dry yarn, bogged down in details of Sarpedon politics and the strategic importance of passes leading into their valley, but you make the most of elements such as dragon's teeth, patrols of fleshless Spartoi, the menace of warlike barbarians on Sarpedon's borders. You make it sound as if invasion was imminent and you brought the council the weapon they needed just in the nick of time.

'If they should ever sow those dragon's teeth,' you conclude, 'it will spell the end of their foes but also of the Sarpedons themselves, and all any visitor to that high valley of Boreas will see moving across the land will be a phalanx of skeletal warriors intent on killing all they meet.'

A shudder goes round the audience followed by a round of applause. You glance at Kazala. She can't hope to win the contest, but she will try her best to outdo you in the final round.

▶ 868

523

More prison guards pile into the passage and you are soon overwhelmed.

'Scum,' says one, spitting out a bloody tooth that you knocked loose. 'I'll take great pleasure breaking you on the wheel.'

You are flung into a filthy cell to await your fate. Lose any money or **lava gems** you were carrying as the guards will help themselves to those and then deny all knowledge of them.

If you have any of the codewords *Rain*, *Rebuke*, *Rhyme*, *Ritual* or *Rock*, or either of the titles **Informant** or **Paladin** ▶ 1076

If not but you have the codeword *Rigor* ▶ 1474

If none of the above but you have Glory of 10 or more ▶ 590

Otherwise ▶ 347

524

❑

If the box above is already ticked ▶ 1016

If the box is empty, put a tick in it now and read on.

A Celedon has shut the doors and is securing them with a padlock. As you approach she looks round, her serene golden face splashed with the fire of sunset.

'Closed for the day, is it?' you ask.

'No one has any further need of the Gallery of Regret,' she replies in perfectly modulated tones.

'Until tomorrow, you mean?'

'No one has any further need,' repeats the bell-like voice. She walks away along the passageway leading to the garden.

Follow her ▶ 1415

Go back to the courtyard by the gate ▶ 750

Go over to the fountain ▶ 489

525

The lady sends away her kitchen servants so that she can speak to you in confidence.

If you have some **ophidiaroot** and this box ❑ is empty, tick it and ▶ 551

If you have **ophidiaroot** and the box was already ticked ▶ 1271

Otherwise she tells you that she's in the middle of cooking a delicate soufflé so doesn't have time to chat. 'Come again soon and tell me all about Arcadia,' she trills as she waves to you from the door. ▶ 1062

526

'What have you got there?' the storekeeper asks.

The **bone flute of Koré** ▶ 802

The **celestial tarbrush** ▶ 4

A **dolphin skin** ▶ 705

A **dragon's egg** ▶ 1588

A **mirror shield** ▶ 1433

A **masterpiece by Apelles** ▶ 60

The **sceptre of Agamemnon** ▶ 500

A **winding key** ▶ 1216

If you have none of the above, you can either look for something to buy (▶ 496) or leave the shop (▶ 325).

527

The dim thudding of your heartbeat stirs again, slowly at first, like a machine left long unused. Sounds penetrate the oppressive silence: an irritable mewling, a chewing noise, the grinding of teeth on bone. A glimmer of light shines wan and tremulous in the cold isolating darkness.

And finally sensation returns – a tugging in your fingers turning to uncomfortable pressure, then searing pain.

You force your eyes open. You are lying on a stone floor. The door stands open, letting a shaft of sunlight into the unlit chamber. You have been dragged from an overturned coffin. A hunched figure squats beside you, gnawing at your hand.

You cry out, reaching feebly to push her away. Her head snaps around, startled eyes staring into yours. Blood and gristle stain her lips.

'You're alive,' she hisses, spitting out a half-chewed fingerbone.

'I know you…'

She jumps away, huddling in the corner of the tomb. 'Don't look at me.'

'You're Xechasiaris's daughter. You came to my house.'

She reacts angrily. 'My house. By rights, mine!'

'What am I doing here?' you say, too weak to argue.

'Buried,' she says with a bitter laugh. 'But not dead. No wonder you were so indigestible.'

There are voices outside. A lantern beam shines through the door. People are coming. Tritona gasps and rushes past them.

'What was that?' you hear someone say.

'A ghoul. Look, here's the corpse she was feeding on.'

The lantern shines right down in your face. 'That's no corpse,' says the first man.

You lose consciousness, vaguely aware of being carried somewhere. Perhaps hours pass before gradually your senses return. Now you are in more comfortable surroundings. A priestess is giving you water from a silver cup. You sit up.

'The tomb police found you and brought you here,' she explains. 'A premature burial? It happens sometimes. You can rest until you're ready to leave.'

You have your possessions, but any money or **lava gems** you were buried with are gone, perhaps taken by the gravediggers or the tomb police who found you. Also tick the Wound box on your Adventure Sheet (if it was not ticked already) and gain 1 scar; Tritona's teeth marks still show on your hand.

Get the codeword *Reef* and ▶ 103

528

An expert thief always takes care to observe what's going on around them, so you are careful to position yourself out of sight in a different hiding place each day. On the first occasion you survey the street from a cart piled high with sacks. The next morning you go up and watch from a rooftop, lying flat behind the parapet and looking through a drainpipe gutter so that nobody glancing up from below will see you.

Your vigil is rewarded on the third day. You're cramped inside one of a pile of crates, peering through a knothole in the wood, when you see a slight young girl who comes up and down the street several times a day. You hadn't taken much notice of her before because she makes no effort to skulk in the shadows, instead racing pell-mell down the middle of the road with whoops of youthful exuberance.

'Hey, fatty, out the way!' she calls to a lumbering priest. He turns, confused, and falters as he sees her trajectory is going to carry her straight into him. At the last minute she skips to one side, bumping off him and running off towards the entrance to the Grumbles.

When she's out of sight you squeeze out of the crate and hurry after the fat priest. 'Your Reverence,' you say, 'excuse my impertinence, but I think you dropped a few coins back there.'

He looks in dismay at his sagging purse. 'It has been cut! Did you see who did this?'

You shake your head. 'No, holy one. But as the gods give they also take away.'

If you have the codeword *Rigor* ▶ 466
If not ▶ 1582

529

If this box ❑ is empty, tick it and ▶ 1122

If the box was already ticked, you are stopped at the doors of the inner chamber by legionaries of the White Guard and the Black Guard who tell you that a parliamentary session is about to begin and all visitors must leave the building.

▶ 1642

530

You hadn't realized how near the enemy vessel was. Its huge cephalopodic prow butts against the Isle of the Dawn, causing the ground to shudder underfoot. The demonic crew are already pouring ashore. They come in a rush, howling and shrieking, spears bristling above a seemingly endless horde.

'Get the goddess to safety,' the Minotaur tells Ancaeus. 'I'll hold them off as long as I can.'

He hefts his axe, swinging it over his head as he sets out across the plain.

Go with Ancaeus ▶ 235
Help the Minotaur ▶ 115
Dive into the pool ▶ 90

531

'You need to restore the farms and the vineyards,' roars Bosk. 'It's only laziness that you didn't get both chores done while you were there. Get back there and see to it.'

'Without even a drink to see me on my way?'

His frown softens. 'All right. Just one drink, then get going.'

He pours you a flagon big enough drown a full-grown cat. By the time you get up from the table your legs are both set on going in different directions and you think you might be better off getting a night's rest before setting off for Arcadia.

▶ 1534

532

The landlord provides you with a strongbox in which you can leave cash and possessions. Record in the box anything you are leaving, or recover items you left here earlier by writing them on your Adventure Sheet and erasing them from the box.

```
ITEMS IN STRONGBOX




















```

When you have finished, the landlord locks the box again. 'Not even the old Hero could get that open without a key,' he says, cracking a rare smile.

▶ 764

533

'Jolly good!' says Bosk, clasping you around the shoulders like a happy bear. 'Well, I've got things to do right now, but come and see me later and I'll put you in the picture.'

He pulls on his breeches and is jogging off across the grass before you think to ask: 'Where can I find you?'

'There's a little tavern by the east wall,' he calls over his shoulder. 'Come through to the garden at the back. I'm there most afternoons.'

Get the codeword **Rye** and ▶ 806

534

You soon get the feeling that Nihakos had been looking for a way to give up bullying the other kids, but he didn't know how until his friendship with you gave him a lifeline.

He is never going to be the sort of person to bare his soul to others, but a couple of times he lets slip how lonely he used to feel. Just hints like: 'When everyone's afraid of you,

that's sort of fine but it doesn't leave you anyone you can hang out with.'

You haven't made him a saint, but you've shown him there's more to life than picking on weaker people. And you've saved a lot of kids from being his victims.

Gain +1 to your CHARM score and ▶ 247

535

The Myrmidon camp is at the far end of the shore. As you stroll back you look across the immense plain towards proud Ilion, whose distant ramparts hang as though daubed in blood against the gathering night. In the other direction, beyond the curved prows of the beached Achaean longships, red sunset sets the sea ablaze. You push aside the tent flap.

If you have the codeword **Rage** ▶ 101

If not but you have the title **Plaything of Agamemnon** ▶ 672

Otherwise ▶ 342

536

Lady Pemphreda's nephew, an eager young lad named Sphikos, has spent the afternoon showing off some magic tricks he learned on a trip to Arcadia. Most are simple conjuring tricks, colourful and showy, but at the end he promises something spectacular.

'See this silken cord,' says Sphikos. 'It could be something you'd find in your grandma's sewing box, you think? But appearances can be deceptive. In fact this silk was once used to tether the cloud on which rested the dragon Kaustikia. It yearns to escape the shackles of gravity and return to the sky. Behold!'

He flings one end of the rope up to the ceiling and it stays there, suspended in mid-air. Sphikos tugs on the rope to show it is taut. He pulls on it with all his strength. Still it hangs there. Then he begins to shin up it.

'Are you going to dust the chandelier?' calls out one of the guests, provoking some merriment.

'A good question!' counters Sphikos. 'What is at the top of the rope? Will I just bang my head on the ceiling? No, for as you see the rope has found a hole in the very fabric of reality.' He extends his arm and it disappears. 'Does it lead to the cloud-tops of Arcady? To the pillared halls of Olympus? Perhaps even to the Empyrean, the heaven in which the first day dawned? Let's find out!'

With those words he scrambles right up to the top of the rope and vanishes. Everyone waits expectantly for him to return with a flourish, perhaps bringing a spray of impossible mountain flowers or a jug of snow from the peaks, but as the minutes drag on their smiles freeze and fade.

'How vexing,' says Lady Pemphreda. 'I really don't have enough nephews to lose one like this. Won't anybody go and fetch him back?'

Do it   ▶ 714
Leave it to somebody else   ▶ 164

537

After a while the beetles again take to the air, quickly spinning their cocoon of golden light around you. You rise back through the solid floor to emerge in the throne room. It seems deserted now, but you don't hang around to make sure. The beetles have clumped back together into the metal chrysalis, which you put in your pocket as you hurry from the room.

▶ 8 in *The Houses of the Dead*

538

You come to with your face in the dust. You must have passed out for a moment, stunned by Celedon's shriek. It feels like you've been kicked in the head by a mule.

The Celedon walks over, her metal feet crunching on the debris-strewn ground. You try to get up but you're still dazed. For good measure she gives you a short banshee blast at close range that leaves you conscious but unable to move a muscle.

▶ 1068

539

Get the codeword **Ratchet**.

The shore of the pool is made up of uneven flat slabs. It resembles clay that has pooled, dried out, and then cracked. You go right up to the water's edge. Luminous mist hangs over the pool, a glowing spray thrown up from the waterfall in the centre. The waterfall pours down from a high crag of rock directly ahead of you, but it falls with an eerie hush, no louder than a stream gurgling in the depths of a shadowy cave.

A shadow moves amid the shining motes of light at the base of the waterfall. As it draws nearer, you see it's a figure stepping over the surface of the pool. The slender frame suggests a young woman, but she keeps her cloak tightly wrapped around her and her veiled face lowered.

She advances out of the torrent of water until she is close enough that you could reach out and touch her. At this range you see that her feet don't make contact with the water; she's floating in the air just above it. Around her the mist of light shines brighter. You have the impression that if she were to cast off her cloak the radiance would be almost blinding.

'Who are you?' you ask.

The veil falls away as she looks up. A narrow face, lambently pale and bearing the tragic beauty of youth. She opens her mouth. For a moment, though her lips move, she makes no sound. Then the words come, so soft that you have to strain to hear her.

'So long has it been since I had company here,' she says, 'I had almost forgotten the power of speech. I am Eos, the daughter of Night.'

What will you reply?

'Do you mean Nyx?'   ▶ 957
'Why are you here?'   ▶ 79
'What do you want?'   ▶ 262

540

As if this fight wasn't hard enough, the Celedons' incessant high-pitched howling makes spots of light flash behind your eyes. You lash out, aiming for their hinged joints in the hope of disabling them.

Attempt a STRENGTH or GRACE roll (your choice) at difficulty 15.

Succeed   ▶ 1256
Fail   ▶ 185

541

Agamemnon carries you into his tent, throws you on the bunk, and mauls you with his hard soldier's hands like he is kneading a lump of dough. Fortunately he's drunk too much to go beyond his rough idea of foreplay. Flopping heavily across your stomach he starts to snore.

Roll him off and leave the tent ▶ Current Location
Wake him ▶ 581

542

She somersaults under the flung poker, coming up in a crouch and jabbing her knife into your thigh before darting away.

If the Wound box on your Adventure Sheet was not already ticked, put a tick in it now and ▶ 656

If you were already injured and you have any companion except Tomyios ▶ 968

Otherwise ▶ 111

543

Half running and half tumbling, you race down the hillside away from the swarm of pyrigons that is blotting out half the sky. Most turn back to the patch of heather where they were feeding, but a few will not be shaken off. They pursue you until you collapse from exhaustion. Settling on your sprawling body, they drive red-hot stings into your exposed flesh.

'Oh! Oh!' cries Oizys. 'Now surely that's quite the most exquisite agony? Mortal, I see you trembling in appreciation.'

Tick the Wound box on your Adventure Sheet if it was not ticked already. Clenching your teeth against the fiery pain, you slap away the insects and stagger to your feet. If only you could swat the irksome Oizys as easily.

'I heard that!' she yelps, giving you a vindictive pinch for good measure.

► 1446

544

You stand entranced, unable to move as a vibration thrums through the floorboards, a heavy bolt scrapes back, and a trapdoor drops open directly underneath the rug where you're standing.

If you have any companion except Tomyios ► 712
Otherwise ► 1227

545

'Look out!'

A commotion breaks out behind you. Shouts. A hideous chirruping sound. Running feet. The swish of a blade. The *thunk* of something hard and heavy hitting the deck.

By the time you look round it's all over. Zoë is standing over the carcass of a giant insect. Its severed halves are still twitching. An oily fluid leaks across the planking, staining it a foetid yellow.

'I saw a bunch of those critters in the palace garden earlier,' you say. 'Thanks, by the way.'

'It came out of the hold,' says Zoë.

Ancaeus comes over for a look. 'Must have slipped past us in all the confusion back there. But why did it stow away and wait till now to jump you?'

► 728

546

'I don't get it,' says Orphea. 'What's your angle?'

'I'm tired and I want to go back to sleep.'

'But…' She seems genuinely confused. 'Where's the fun in that?'

'Where's the fun in being continually bothered by a mad thief? I'm not playing anymore. Find somebody else to annoy.'

Her mouth droops in disappointment. 'All right. My mistake. There's no point if you're not into it. Here – '

► 1126

547

By now there's a milling throng of pursuers pressed right up to the edge of the roof. You can see the pallid, worm-gnawed faces of the vampires, the red eyes and spittle-flecked jaws of the were-creatures, the misshapen features of capering nightmare demons. Baying and snarling, they are so intent on getting to you that some get jostled over the edge and fall flailing to the street far below.

Each time a grapple lodges on the ship's rail, instantly a stream of attackers comes scrabbling along it to get aboard. Careless of the wind, rain and the lethal drop below, their only thought is to continue their wild onslaught. Even the Minotaur, whose blade flashes and spills blood and guts with every swing, must eventually tire and then the monstrous tide will overwhelm the ship.

There's a commotion at the back of the horde, near the stairs up onto the roof. Some of the rear ranks are turning in confusion. A vampire spins, a spear thrust into its chest, and disintegrates in a tattered cloud of dust and rags and old bones. A slim hand reaches out, pulls back the spear, and swings it in a wide arc to keep the nearest monsters at bay.

As the rabble parts you see a lithe figure in studded leather armour. In one hand she has the spear, in the other a sword that's already slick with blood. Behind her are a band of stalwart fighters, each holding their own against the night creatures that come rushing and snapping at them from all sides.

'Zoë..?'

She's too far off to hear you over the raging storm, but she sees your look of recognition and raises her hand in salute. She and her companions swore to come to your aid when you needed it most, and they are as good as their word. You only hope they are enough to swing the tide of battle.

Her surprise attack has distracted the vampires who were manning the grapple-line cannon, but there are still plenty of were-beasts leaping across to the ship. Should you stay to help the Minotaur fight them off, or go to help get the buoyancy rotor working before the *Sunrise* loses any more height?

Stay at the rail to repel boarders   ► 883
Help the helmsman with the buoyancy rotor ► 1498

548

'Tomorrow. Give it another day.'

'I'm not a doll, Achilles. I won't break.'

You meant it as a joke, but he earnestly replies, 'I know. You are braver than any woman I ever met. But rest one more day just to be sure. There will be plenty of heroes of Ilion left to fight when your strength is fully recovered.'

► 203

549

☐ ☐ ☐ ☐ ☐ ☐ ☐ ☐

Tick the next empty box above.

You just ticked the first box ▶ 1211
You ticked the second box ▶ 265
You ticked the third box ▶ 1554
You ticked the fourth box ▶ 681
You ticked the fifth box ▶ 117
You ticked the sixth box ▶ 965
You ticked the seventh box ▶ 1168
You ticked the eighth box ▶ 221
If all the boxes were already ticked ▶ 585

550

'Perhaps I mistook you for another.' The Archon hardly seems to flex a finger, but instantly a servant is by your side. 'Show our guest out.'

▶ 1642

551

You hand over the long dark stalks, which she lays out on a wooden board and smiles over, a gleam of epicurean relish in her eyes.

Delete one **ophidiaroot** from your list of possessions.

'You have to be careful only to use a very small quantity,' you say. 'My chef told me – '

'Oh, no fear on that score,' she says. 'I know exactly how much to use. I will need more than this, though.'

If you have more **ophidiaroot** and want to give it to her ▶ 1271

If not, you tell her you'll call again and ▶ 1062

552

☐

If the box above was already ticked ▶ 833; if the box is empty, put a tick in it now and then read on.

A floor-to-ceiling mirror runs the entire length of one wall of the ballroom. The guests here are chatting urbanely while pretending not to have one eye on their own reflections. A few people move around the marble dance floor, striking languid poses which if enacted with more vigour could be called dancing.

The music comes from more splendidly wrought golden Celedons, this group stroking the silver strings of harps while singing perfectly in tune with their sister automata in the main courtyard.

At the far side of the room, doors stand open onto a patio bordering a garden where carefully clipped hedges enclose luxuriant flowerbeds. You can see more guests out there strolling around the lawn.

A woman lurches past and steadies herself against the table, rubbing her sandalled foot. 'That floor is lethal,' she mutters indignantly. 'I nearly broke my ankle.'

'But, darling,' says her companion, 'it's Sarpedon marble. If you insist on wearing shoes like that to dance in, of course it's going to be slippery.'

Go through into the garden ▶ 1415
Return to the entrance courtyard ▶ 750

553

A mighty wind springs up, roaring and howling through the wreckage of the city. Not only dust and pebbles are whipped up – so strong is the force of the wind that even chunks of rubble roll across the ground.

The wind begins to swirl in a spiral, creating a twister in which the features of a furious bearded face can be seen. 'I am Boreas, lord of the winds!' he thunders. 'Those who would seek to harm this mortal hero must first contend with me.'

If you have the codeword *Pumped* ▶ 720
Otherwise, if you have the codeword *Nanny* ▶ 1637
Otherwise ▶ 1183

554

You get into a scuffle. It's hardly a fight. What courage they have comes from hunting as a pack, picking on lone survivors, or just scavenging from abandoned buildings. None of them has the stomach to face a hardened adventurer like you, but even as you drive them off they lash out in self-defence.

Tick your Wound box unless it was already ticked or unless you have the **Panoply of the Lost Hero**.

'Not so tough now, are you?' yells Dunamis as the looters run off.

▶ Current Location

555

☐

You are at the South Gate. If you do not have the codeword *Reverie* and the box above is empty, put a tick in it and ▶ 990

Otherwise, if you have the codeword *Ridge*, note **555** as your Current Location and ▶ 1064

Otherwise, if you have the codeword *Roar* ▶ 1622
Otherwise read on.

From the wall above the gate dangles a net of mouldered shrouds. Beyond the open doors, which resemble carved coffin lids, drifts a veil of grey mist that is occasionally stirred by a breeze that carries the choking odour of decay.

From time to time a cart comes creaking up the road from Hades and passes between the gates. The guards prod their spears into the cargo to ensure none of the dead are trying to sneak their way back to this side of the grave.

'What goods are brought from Hades?' you hear a man ask in a horrified whisper.

His companion shrugs. 'Sorrow. Resentment. Despair. The cold and hopeless longing for another chance.'

Not far from the gate is a noticeboard on which you can find quests that pay quick cash – if you are short on scruples and willing to stick your neck out. 'Get it wrong and you'll be heading down that road yonder,' says an old woman who sees you contemplating the noticeboard.

To go straight to a city location that you already know about, note **555** as your Current Location, then ▶ **1432**

Otherwise you can see which quests are posted on the noticeboard, in which case note **555** as your Current Location, then ▶ **56**

Or you can go:

East along the Boulevard of the Salamander ▶ **31**

North along the Avenue of the Anvil ▶ **63**

West along the Boulevard of the Salamander ▶ **1649**

South out of the city ▶ **35**

556

The club crashes into you, sending a jolting pain across your back and making your teeth rattle in your skull.

If the Wound box on your Adventure Sheet was already ticked ▶ **1463**

If not, put a tick in it now and ▶ **1446** as you stagger away to a safe distance.

557

Being squired around town by a scruffy reprobate like Chipos does nothing for your reputation. Lose 5 Glory down to a minimum score of 1.

The other side of the coin is that it shows the world that you are confident in your own decisions. You don't care whether anyone else approves. This undoubtedly gives you an edge when dealing with people. Add +1 to CHARM up to a maximum score of +5.

▶ **97**

558

The killer pulled books off the shelf by the handful, presumably looking for something he or she thought might be hidden there. You can find nothing of interest.

▶ **944**

559

The tapestry is a dimensional portal hovering in the air. You are pulled through it along with Nyx. The two of you fall through gulfs of time and space illuminated by flares of cosmic energy. Below is a red vortex of roiling fiery light.

You plunge through into another place. On the far horizon are menacing mountains that flicker with a distant storm. But the entire landscape beneath you is a yawning abyss many leagues across. The very sight of it strikes terror into your heart. Even on Nyx's face you see fear.

'Tartarus!' she gasps.

It is the bottomless pit into which Zeus cast the defeated titans. A void from which there is no escape. The Face of Wisdom reshaped the tapestry to bring Nyx here – the only prison that can hold her. But as you've been pulled in too, what can save you from the same fate?

A giant hand sweeps out of nowhere. Your spirit is caught and swept away. Your final glimpse of Nyx is of a small figure swallowed up in the vastness of the abyss.

Your god holds your essence safe. 'You have done what no other mortal could. The world is free of Night's threat, and her armies now will vanish like the dew in the heat of a bright new day.'

'And what will happen to me?'

'There is no going back to your life. But this is not the end.'

Your deity opens their grip, and suddenly you find yourself in your family home, with your old dog Argos curled up by the fire. How many years has it been since you saw him?

It's getting dark. Aunt Terpe lights a lamp. That's the gift of Prometheus, she tells you, given to mortals so that they need not fear the night.

From outside wafts the sound of laughter and children singing. The door opens. Your parents come in, and behind them your uncles with Aunt Eremia leading your brother and sisters in a playful dance.

A stew bubbles in the pot, filling the kitchen with delicious aromas. The moon rises and warm silver light floods in the windows. The nights here are never long, never frightening. Your family gather you to them around the blazing hearth. You now know you are in the Elysian fields and have no challenges to look forward to, just the reward of an eternity of perfect peace and happiness.

560

'Daedalus!' you call out, recognizing his trim figure alongside the cowled monstrosities who comprise the commanders of the army of night.

He waves to you. 'Hey there. How's the apocalypse

going for you?' He punches the buttons on a metal box he's holding, and in response a massive automaton lumbers forward to stand beside Hypnos and Thanatos. The automaton's hands are huge diamond-edged drills which whine as if eager to tear through the ranks of its foes.

'Great gods, man,' you shout over to Daedalus. 'You can't mean to side with Nyx?'

'Do not judge him too harshly,' says Eros. 'Nyx holds his son's life force as hostage. It's not the kind of love I deal in, but still it is love.'

▶ 1065

561

The intruder has entered through a window opening onto the lawn. One glance is enough to tell you he's no conventional thief. He hasn't touched the silver candlesticks, the fine oil paintings, the crystal decanters on the sideboard. Instead he seems to be searching through cupboards and drawers for something in particular.

Step into the room   ▶ 719
Fetch the militia and have him arrested   ▶ 1241

562

One afternoon you are sitting in your garden when a servant comes to you saying that a sailor is at the door with an important message. Having nothing better to do, you have the sailor brought to you. He is a lean fellow with corded muscles on his bare arms and skin burnished by the sun to the consistency of teak.

'I was on a ship rounding the coast of Arcady,' he tells you, 'when a loud voice could be heard calling for Thamus. That is my name, but I hid below decks till it called a third time, and the captain bade me answer. "Here I am," I shouted across to the shore. Then the voice replied, charging me with a message.'

You notice some greenfly on the roses and call your gardener over to attend to the matter. To Thamus the mariner you say, 'I fail to see why you have brought this unremarkable tale to me.'

'The message astonished us all,' he says doggedly. 'But none knew if the voice spoke true or was a demon of falsity, so the captain resolved that if the wind kept up we would sail straight on for Iskandria, but if there was a calm we would put in at the next port. Thus the decision was left to forces beyond our mortal realm.'

'As a story it lacks tension,' you say. 'Where's the twist? Obviously the wind dropped or you wouldn't be here.'

'Exalted one, you must not make light of this. I have asked around and all tell me you are the one who must hear the message, for only you are thought to have the favour of the gods.'

'And what is the message?'

Thamus gathers his ragged clothes around him with as much dignity as he can muster. 'I repeat it to you now as I declared it when we put into port that day. "The great god Pan is dead." And no sooner had I repeated what the voice had called to me, but all of us aboard heard a dreadful noise, like a multitude in the sky groaning and lamenting with a kind of horrified astonishment.'

'And what do you want for bringing me this message that Pan is dead?'

You turn towards your purse, intending to count out a coin or two for the indigent sailor, but when you look back he is already walking away across the lawn.

Get the codeword **Requiem** and ▶ 97

563

A man in white robes is walking down the middle of the street, gesturing from time to time and talking to nobody in particular.

You stand in his way. He focuses on you with the expression of somebody just waking up. 'What have you done with the Academy?' he asks, blinking in bewilderment. 'And the other two...?'

'They've wandered off their own way, I suppose.'

'But this is a disaster,' he says. 'I have just been expounding a revolutionary new concept in epistemology. Was no one with me to hear it? That priceless wisdom has been lost, scattered to the breeze!'

A shopkeeper leans out of her window. ' 'E's bin up an' down mutterin' nonsense like that all bleedin' day.'

The philosopher breathes a sigh of relief. 'Thank goodness. At least if these ignorant townsfolk heard a little of what I said then I have succeeded in bringing the light of wisdom into their benighted lives.'

'Don't worry,' you tell the shopkeeper, 'I'm sending him back to the asylum now.'

You point the philosopher in the direction of the Academy and advise him not to do any thinking until he's safely home.

▶ Current Location

564

☐ ☐ ☐

The Hero of Temesa is too strong for you. Its grip closes your windpipe and red darkness swirls around your vision. Put a tick in one of the boxes above.

One box is now ticked   ▶ 1470
Two boxes are ticked   ▶ 1434
All three are now ticked   ▶ 1577

565

Get the codeword *Rose*.

Dunamis gives you a few rubies worth 150 pyr. Add that sum to the money on your Adventure Sheet.

'Well, back to the grindstone,' she says, surveying the guests on the lawn.

'Wait. How did you get in? Nobody can see Vulcan's palace unless he wants them to.'

'It's a breeze,' she murmurs distractedly, her eyes fixed on a fat waddling fellow with a large gold clasp on his toga. 'Everything is a simulation, so you just need to tweak the settings.'

'But how did you get access to that level of reality?'

'The noticeboards at the gates. They have links to city locations, so once I figured that out it was just a matter of hacking them to reveal hidden locations like the palace.'

She winks and darts off in pursuit of her next victim.

▶ 808

566

You grab a loose brick from a broken wall and batter her into a shapeless hunk of scrap. She screams all the time, not in fear or pain, for automata have no emotions, but simply because it's her principal weapon – a hideous near-ultrasonic screech that makes your head swim.

Tick your Wound box unless you have **beeswax** to stuff in your ears. (Delete the **beeswax** if you use it.)

'Waste of a good hunk of gold if you ask me,' says Dunamis, gazing at the twisted remains of the Celedon. Sparks shoot out of its broken joints. The unbearable shriek fades to a whine and cuts out.

▶ Current Location

567

'Fortitude and daring are all very well,' says Kazala, 'but we can't overcome everything with main force. Doesn't a hero also have to be able to deal with politics?'

If you have the codeword *Query* ▶ 877
If not ▶ 460

568

If this box ❑ already has a tick in it ▶ 1559

If the box is empty, tick it now and then read on.

'Ptolemos?'

The blind soldier turns his head. 'Who's that?'

'It's Loutro.' He goes forward and takes his old comrade's hand.

'The years have treated you better than me,' says Ptolemos. 'I can tell just from the strength of your grip.'

'That's the goddess's doing, old friend.'

Ptolemos shakes his head. 'Still going on about her, are you? I told the whippersnapper.'

'The Great River will flow again,' insists Loutro. 'Tethys has revealed it. She came to me in my dreams.'

'Well, man, don't stand around here talking. If you're going to do it, do it.'

'It's sad to see Ptolemos brought to that,' says Loutro as the two of you walk away. 'He was so full of life, so vigorous. I remember him with one hand round a buxom wench, a foaming tankard in the other, shaking the tavern rafters with his laughter. It makes me all the more determined to bring the river back to Notus.'

▶ 806

569

There is a change in the quality of space itself. Time seems to alter its pace. The gods are here.

You gaze up at them, a child who has wandered out into a gathering of grown-ups. It is not merely their size that overawes you. Their presence is wrapped in an aura of unbearable reality, as if a furnace door were thrown open on the fire at the dawn of creation. To look too long on such beings is to risk blindness, madness, annihilation.

But in that glimpse you see they are diminished. The perfect flesh is marred by welts and bruises and cuts. Golden lifeblood stains their majestic finery. Adamantine armour that should be indestructible hangs in battered plates and broken links from their weary shoulders.

Lowering your eyes, you gesture to the banquet laid out on the table.

'Meagre fare...' booms one, whose dissatisfaction makes you think of proud and rage-filled Ares.

'It must suffice,' says a calm female voice, surely Artemis.

'We'll get no more until the titans are driven back to Tartarus,' states the authoritative Apollo.

'And they will attack again soon,' puts in Athena. 'We must be ready.'

A heavy figure comes to the table. A mountain moving. Zeus himself. 'Each take a mouthful. I will take two. Once restored we'll seal the titans back in their pit for all time.'

They quickly consume the food you've left for them. A moment passes. Oizys whispers into your ear, 'Perhaps the toxin won't work. Then they'll punish you for your blasphemy.' Your heart skips a beat. Oizys laughs, 'Scaredy-cat. As if my dread mistress would fail. Look!'

A tracery of dark lines is spreading over the gods' skin as if their golden blood has been replaced with ink. They turn to each other, realizing too late that the food was poisoned. Your own deity stares menacingly towards you, raising one hand to blast you with divine fury. You brace yourself, but the attack never comes. Feebly the gods collapse to the metal floor, the darkness spreading over them until they are covered. Their bodies crumble inwards into a broken crust of ashes.

A cold night wind springs up through the open windows, scattering the desiccated remains of the gods. Light bleeds out of the sky and a black rainbow appears for an instant in the last red light of sunset. A torrent of rain blows into the hall, black wisps rising from where each drop splashes on the floor. As the wisps multiply and thicken, they swirl together and coalesce into the mighty form of Queen Nyx, now the unchallenged monarch of all creation.

'You have served me well and faithfully and I will reward you,' she says. 'Behold the throne of Zeus. It's mine now. You will sit at my right hand.'

▶ 1594

570

❑

You are at the south-east corner of the city. Above, where the ramparts join, stands the Tower of Sand, a nacreous spire that gleams liquidly by day and at night stands outlined against the stars like a shaft of cooling moonlight.

If you do not have the codeword *Reverie* and the box above is empty, put a tick in it and ▶ 1481

Otherwise, if you have a **brass head** and the title **Friend of the Nomads** and this box ❑ is empty, tick it and ▶ 180; otherwise read on.

To go straight to a city location that is known to you, note **570** as your Current Location, then ▶ 1432

Other options are:
North up the Boulevard of the Gnome ▶ 161
North-west along the Street of the Sun and Moon ▶ 1324
West on the Boulevard of the Salamander ▶ 31
Go up the tower ▶ 995

571

As you penetrate deeper into the Grumbles, unfinished buildings and unpaved streets of mud are all around. The place is not simply half-built, it only half exists. A wall covered with peeling plaster abruptly ends in a sparking of wire-frame outlines and flickering pixels. A path suddenly disappears in a yawning pit in which nothing can be seen.

Even the inhabitants of this district are not always complete. From time to time you pass someone whose face is a criss-crossing of lines with no skin texture, or a limbless torso that floats along the alleyways gibbering meaningless

barks. 'Expression of woe,' mutters a man who lifts his hood to show there is no back to his head. 'Generalized threatening statement of distrust.'

For whatever reason – lack of interest, lack of architects, lack of money, or lack of materials, or perhaps all those things – Vulcan has left this district only half in reality.

If you don't have the codeword *Reflection* ▶ 850; otherwise read on.

If you have the codeword *Reflection* and want to call on Zinc ▶ 52

Find your way out onto the Street of Knives ▶ 1617
Leave by way of the Avenue of the Anvil ▶ 63

572

A breeze comes in off the sea, bringing a chill to the stifling atmosphere of sun-baked dust that hung over the camp by day. All along the shore, campfires are dying low as the soldiers turn in for sleep. Only a few lanterns mark the sentries who stay on watch until the dawn, protecting the black ships arrayed along the beach. Out in the darkness the sea lies quiet under a canopy of stars.

It would be an almost idyllic scene if not for the ever-present sense of danger, doom and death.

If you have the title **Plaything of Agamemnon** but you don't have the codeword *Rage* ▶ 807 now; otherwise read on.

If the Current Location recorded on your Adventure Sheet is **1500** then ▶ 41
Otherwise ▶ 203

573

'I can't accept this,' he says, shaking his head. 'You're not finished with it.'

'Shouldn't I be the judge of that?'

'We're in a universe ruled by fate,' he says. 'Nothing I can do about it.'

Show him something else ▶ 526
Ask what he has for sale ▶ 496
Leave ▶ 325

574

'No,' insists Prometheus. 'Though I respect you, mortal, and have no love for the Night Queen, I know of old that Zeus cannot be trusted. I shall stand aloof from this war.'

So saying, he withdraws into the sky until all that can be seen of him is a dull fiery gleam behind the rolling black clouds.

If you have the codeword *Quake* ▶ 553

If not but you have the codeword *Pumped* ▶ 720
Otherwise, if you have the codeword *Nanny* ▶ 1637
Otherwise ▶ 1183

575

You recall two events of your youth. They happened on different days, perhaps even different years, but memory is a palette on which the colours mix freely.

The first memory: you are strolling with your Aunt Eremia and your sisters. It is the Street of Ash where the puppet booths are set up. A blaze of green, made from fluttering spikes of grass-coloured paper, catches your eye. The puppet is pushing his way through a verdant forest. 'Clever,' says your aunt, 'but it's been a long time since Arcadia was that lush.'

And now you're in the market with both your aunts. Terpe inspects some peaches, squeezing and sniffing them critically. 'Fresh from Arcadia, lady,' ventures the stall-holder.

'From Arcadia they might be,' says Aunt Eremia with an apologetic laugh, 'but they're not exactly fresh.'

'I thought Arcadia would be your kind of place,' you say to Eremia.

'The great god Pan has forsaken it,' she says sadly. 'The lakes are stinking and choked with algae. Rubbish discarded in the streams. The trees all gnarled and so bare of leaves they look like balding old men.'

'Rank grass spotted all about with worm casts,' adds Terpe. 'So sad. Remember the vineyards, sister? Oh, such rich wines.'

Eremia shakes her head. 'All withered now. Blight got into the grapes. If there's any wine at all to be got there it's sour, and you can't sweeten it with honey because the hives are just abandoned husks.'

'Somebody needs to get the place back on its feet again.'

'But who?' Eremia makes a sweeping gesture. 'They'd need to be bold, resourceful, unflagging.'

Terpe agrees. 'And also be a leader, able to inspire people with a vision of something better – as well as having the administrative skills and the acuity to plan and execute a project on a grand scale.'

In this dream, or memory, or whatever it is, did you answer them?

'I can do all that!' ▶ 1657
Say nothing ▶ 493

576

'Your task will not be easy,' says Eos.

'Overcoming the most powerful of all the titans? You think?'

'Believe me, I do not underestimate the challenge,' she says. 'I can give you only the smallest help in the form of this benison.'

Her eyes shine brighter. You are bathed in a light that warms and invigorates you. If you were wounded, untick that box on your Adventure Sheet.

Also gain the blessing of the dawn. This can be used once, like any blessing, after you fail an attribute roll, but instead of allowing you a reroll it grants you automatic success in the roll you are attempting. Write 'blessing of the dawn (automatic success; one use)' in the Blessings box on your Adventure Sheet.

You shrug. 'It'll have to do. How do I get back to the Vulcanverse?'

Eos indicates the pool below her. 'Dive in. Swim deep. The waters will carry you back.'

No time like the present ▶ 90
Ask her for advice first ▶ 1436

577

You wake from a sound sleep. There was a noise from downstairs. One of the servants? But they all have their quarters in the north wing, and have no reason to be going about the house in the middle of the night.

Tiptoeing out onto the landing, you look over the bannisters. There is a flicker of light on the wall opposite your study. The servants should have doused the fire before going to bed. Somebody is in there.

Sneak down quietly to investigate ▶ 49
Walk in on them openly ▶ 1641

578

'Tonight's the fateful night,' says the gambler, shuffling his deck. 'That's why I brought my cards. It'll be one of those unlucky ladies sitting by the bar.'

You see half a dozen young women sitting silent and fretful. Each must be praying that the cards will pick one of the others to be the demon's next victim.

If you are female and volunteer to take their place ▶ 594
If you want to fight the demon ▶ 1120
Otherwise ▶ 764

579

If you have the codeword *Rug* then you are at a disadvantage and will need an element of bluff to make this work; make a CHARM roll at difficulty 16:

Succeed ▶ 363
Fail ▶ 826
If you do not have the codeword *Rug* ▶ 559

580

A strange sensation gnaws at your mind. Whispers below the range of hearing, hollow feelings of futility, fevered visions of a world cocooned in comforting darkness. The sceptre throbs in your hand like a malevolent living thing.

'Give in to it,' says Nyx. 'There'll be no need to worry anymore about what you have to do, or on which side you must fight. You won't need to think at all. Just surrender and become one with the night.'

To resist Nyx's power you need to make a CHARM or INGENUITY roll (your choice) at difficulty 17. It is a test of the force of your character, a struggle of determination against the terrible gnawing shadow of the abyss in the heart of every soul.

Succeed ▶ 1094
Fail ▶ 175

581

'What is it, my gorgeous concubine?' he mutters contentedly, his words slurred by drink. 'Ah, how I love to see you running in the surf, glistening like a wet otter…'

If you seek a boon, this seems like a good time to ask him.

What do you reply?
'I must get back home.' ▶ 511
'Will you let me make a sacrifice to my god?' ▶ 701
'Let me fight for you.' ▶ 474
'It's nothing. Go to sleep.' ▶ Current Location

582

You grapple the nearest Celedon and with desperate ferocity you haul her off her feet and throw her at another that's dashing towards you. The impact sounds like two huge bells crashing together. They fall like broken puppets, twitching horribly as they try to move limbs that have been twisted out of shape.

Now ▶ 437 and tick one of the boxes there before you read on.

583

Heedless of the long drop to the street, your foes come pouring from the roof in an incessant dark tide. Were-apes and werewolves leap across with frightening agility, balancing on the ship's rail and snapping at you with slavering fangs, while shapeless things out of nightmare flap around on ragged black wings. As you battle to prevent them overwhelming the ship, knots of wizened vampires gather at the edge of the roof, casting grappling hooks improvised from tangled bones and winding-sheets. When a line goes taut they scuttle over on bloodless feet, their long grave-grown nails giving them purchase on the ship's hull.

If you have the codeword **Recursive** ▶ 700 now; otherwise read on.

You give yourself in to the pulse-pounding rhythm of battle, laying about you with weapons and anything that comes to hand. One of the vampires, its mummified entrails trailing from a deep cut, flops to the deck and clutches your legs in a rigor-stiff grip. You snatch up a belaying pin, smash its skull to pulp, and whirl just in time to parry the attack of a flapping horror that looks like a giant face with leathery wings in place of ears.

Make a STRENGTH roll at difficulty 11.
Succeed ▶ 1592
Fail ▶ 256

584

Sphikos turns as you approach. He shows no surprise at your presence here. Everything he has seen already has left him too awe-struck for any more astonishment.

'Do you realize we're at the dawn of creation?' he says. 'Everything that is ever to be is taking shape around us.'

▶ 1044

585

Abruptly there's a change in air pressure that makes your ears pop. At the same time, the wind that has been raging for hours suddenly dies away to a dead calm.

A look of awe appears on Dunamis's face. She's staring up into the sky. Slowly, with a creeping sense of dread, you turn to look. A violet coruscation is blossoming like a new constellation in the night.

'What is it?' she says.

You know. It's the end of the world.

▶ 186

586

'Psst!'

You glance at the bald man, but he and the other guest are deep in conversation about the weather.

'Over here.' A slender arm waves to you from behind one of the pavilions set up on the lawn.

You stroll over. 'Dunamis. What are you doing here?'

'I didn't get an invite so I suppose you'd call it gatecrashing,' she says with a wink. 'See that old bird in the thousand-pyr kicks? See if you can distract her for a minute.'

What do you say:
'You're here to rob people?' ▶ 1520
'How did you get in?' ▶ 338

587

You tell Himera that the blackmailer is dead but you were unable to recover the letters.

'So whoever killed him might now have them?'

You nod. 'It's possible.'

She waves a languid hand towards the door. 'It's a shame you failed.'

As you leave, it occurs to you that you could try blackmailing her yourself. There's a risk, of course, in that you now know her husband is willing to resort to murder.

Do it   ▶ **455**

Forget it   ▶ **1642**

588

The watchmen start bombarding you with questions, unsure whether you are a lunatic or a drunk. By the time you have convinced them to come and investigate, a flickering red glow can be seen far along the street.

'The mansion! It's on fire!'

You race forward into choking clouds of smoke. Neighbours are milling around. 'Oh, thank Olympus you made it out,' says one.

'What about the servants?'

She points. In the high windows you can see writhing figures outlined against the flames. The panes shatter in the intense heat, showering the onlookers with hot broken glass.

By the time a bucket brigade is formed, the roof has already fallen in. Between the bare walls is a roaring inferno, the fire a gleeful mindless entity bent on destruction. The rafters and beams buckle and fall like spent matches. After many hours, the sunrise shows just a burnt-out smoking pile of rubble and ash where your grand mansion used to stand.

Cross your possessions off your Adventure Sheet. They were destroyed in the inferno that consumed the mansion. Also lose the title **The Unexpected Heir**.

▶ **515**

589

'I know that place,' interjects the head. 'But what do you want with engineered lepidoptera when you have a finely crafted cogitating cranium to advise you?'

'Humour me.'

'Look for a brick building in Hades right where the lady said. There's a combination lock puzzle you'll need to solve when you get there. Since you're so dumb I may as well tell you the answer – it's six two one.'

Back to the Avenue of the Anvil ▶ **63**

590

A junior magistrate hears your case. 'It is quite rare to hear of somebody breaking into prison,' she says. 'Especially somebody with such an exalted record as yours.'

Make a CHARM roll at difficulty 8.

Honeyed words   ▶ **832**

Tongue-tied   ▶ **152**

591

Distracted as you are and eager to join the party, it takes you a moment to realize Polymnia has stopped at the gate. When you look back she gives you a wistful half-smile.

'This is where we must part,' she says.

'Really? I think the invitation includes a Plus One.'

She looks up towards the sky. Bolts of red cloud smoulder in the setting sun. 'A storm is coming in which the future of this world will be decided. As the Muse of Knowledge I must remain a neutral observer. Therefore, though we have come far together, now I must recuse myself.'

'Where will you go?'

'If night wins that's the end of knowledge. But you've seen my shrine – mortals rarely visit it in any case.' She turns to go, then hesitates. 'Good luck.'

'I thought you didn't believe in luck?'

You were trying to make light of your parting, but she takes the remark seriously as always. 'I know that some things are unknown, and you must forge your own destiny tonight. I may not walk with you, but if you need me and look inside yourself you'll find the inspiration I bring.'

Delete Polymnia from the Companion box on your Adventure Sheet, then ▶ **941**

592

The restaurant owner is so proud of her culinary skills that she is flattered rather than surprised. She shows you through to a small but spotless kitchen filled with rich smells of roasting meat, baked bread, herbs, and frying peppers.

There are garlands of fruits and vegetables hanging from the rafters: red and green tomatoes bursting with flavour, strings of golden-brown onions, sprays of lettuce, and chillies whose garish colour proclaims their searing taste.

If you have the **Face of Wisdom** (INGENUITY **+3**) ▶ **1314**

Otherwise you spend a few minutes chatting about the cuisines of the different regions of the Vulcanverse before bidding her farewell ▶ **86**

593

A breath of wind briefly stirs the grass, folding the stalks to catch the ruddy light and revealing some scraps of bark lying there. The effect is disquietingly like a face momentarily revealed by a veil blowing aside.

As the breeze dies away, its soughing carries a whisper that drifts off down the mountainside. 'North…'

'Was that you?'

'What?' snaps Oizys.

'That voice.'

'The wind. Plus an overactive imagination. Get moving before I sink my teeth in your succulent parts.'

Decide where on the mountain slopes you'll start your search:

North	▶	**151**
East	▶	**1088**
South	▶	**1311**
West	▶	**1413**

594

Record **123** as your Current Location.

He starts to deal the cards that will decide which girl is to be sacrificed to the Hero of Temesa. You slam your hand down on the table.

'Look, I don't like it any more than you do,' he says, staring across the crumpled cards at you. 'But it's this or a massacre.'

'Don't worry, the "Hero" will get his sacrifice. Me.'

He sits astonished for a moment, then gestures to a few strong men at the bar. 'We've got a volunteer turkey this month,' he says. 'Truss her up, lads.'

'Not so tight that I can't get free,' you tell them. 'And watch where you're putting those hands, buster, or I'll give you a taste of what I'm going to do to the "Hero".'

'Promises, promises.' But they are noticeably respectful as they carry you into the dark, foetid alcove in the wall and lay you out on the cold stone.

At the end of the evening the tavern goes silent and the lamps are put out. You hear everyone shuffling outside, then the thud of the heavy door and the clank of the lock. You are left alone in the gloom to await the demon.

It comes like a rush of soot down a chimney. A stink of wet animal fur, blood-soaked breath, sweat and grave-soil. Its arms reach for you, massive as tree trunks, and it utters a growl that is both predatory and obscene.

With a twist of your wrists you shake off the bonds and reach for a weapon. Make an INGENUITY roll at difficulty 13. (You can reroll using a blessing, if you have one, as the gods admire cunning in a mortal.)

Inspiration shows the way	▶ **639**
Panic makes you hesitate	▶ **163**

595

Thanatos is slender and fiery as a sword against the sky. His outstretched black pinions span the horizon. Scurrying at his heels comes a pack of snarling creatures with lupine snouts and long batlike wings that are folded and pressed against their bodies like wrappings of grey skin. They are the Keres, harbingers of violent death that are drawn to battlefields where they hover waiting to feast on mortal souls.

'It is over,' says Thanatos, his voice easily outmatching the thunder of the storm. 'I bring you quietus. Behold my face. It will be the last thing you see.'

He starts to raise his cowl, turning his gaze towards you.

Offer to join him	▶ **499**
Defy him to the end	▶ **147**

596

You jump to your feet in indignation. 'Try a few weeks as a slave of the Gargareans. Then you'd know what it's like to have reality stomp on you.'

'I say, that's hardly an argument,' says a scholar sitting behind you. 'And please sit down.'

Myletes looks embarrassed by your outburst, but he tries to defend you. 'My friend means that it is hard to accept the concept of the world as a simulation when we see such terrible injustices.'

'Vulcan created this world to be a copy of the real world,' asserts a powerfully-built philosopher who looks like he must juggle kettlebells. 'So why wouldn't he include both justice and injustice?'

'In any case,' says the man behind you, 'injustice is created by human behaviour, not by the rules of nature, so injustice would necessarily exist in every simulation that included human beings. Case in point: thoughtlessly jumping up from your seat without a thought for the people in the row behind.'

'You're all admitting we live in Vulcan's simulation of reality,' you say, quite exasperated now, 'so what's the debate about?'

▶ **1542**

597

'Follow me,' says the Archon of the Sun.

Now ▶ **1337** and tick the box there before reading on.

598

'You going in?' says the head.

'Maybe.'

'Hey, keep your secrets.'

'Why'd you ask?'

'Some things the sentries won't let you keep. You have

to check them in at the gate.'

'What things?'

'Like me.'

'Thought you were unique.'

'Things that enhance you, that compensate for your limitations. Like how I give you advice, make you seem smarter. Maybe you have some other item that boosts your agility or your personality. Such as it is.'

'I can't take things like that into the palace?'

'Finally!' says the head.

If you have the codeword *Ruby* ▶ 1597; otherwise read on.

Enter the palace	▶ 74
Not right now	▶ 722

599

'Now that's tempting.' Agamemnon lets his single eye linger over your well-toned body. He looks from you to Astynome, cringing in a corner of the tent, and sneers. 'You're a much more comely catch than this scrawny slut, Amazon. Tell me you'll take her place in my bed and I'll send her back to her father right now.'

What will you say?

'All right, you can have me instead.'	▶ 847
'No deal. Just set her free.'	▶ 765

600

For just an instant, Nyx's attention is on the motley mob that dares to defy her. To her they are of no more significance than mice challenging a lioness. As her lip curls in scorn, you seize your chance, lunging up at her with all your remaining strength.

If you have the codewords *Rug* and *Rudiment* ▶ 307

If you have *Rug* but not *Rudiment* ▶ 46

Otherwise ▶ 1364

601

A few days later Loutro rises early. He bolts his breakfast and urges you to accompany him out into the streets.

'But where are we going?'

He throws his hands to the sky, filled with excitement but also baffled. 'I don't know! I feel the hand of the goddess guiding me. Come, it's across the Forum somewhere.'

You are amused by his fervour. 'And what will we do when we get there?'

He stops for a moment, wrinkling his brow as if trying to dredge up a distant memory. 'I see a time of darkness and danger. All of this will be swept away.' He gestures at the buildings and people around you. 'But there's a place where

you can leave your belongings for safekeeping, a place that your enemies don't know about.'

He strides on ahead, urging you to hurry, then halfway along the Avenue of the Anvil he comes to a halt. He turns to you with a look of wonder in his eyes. 'The goddess has shown us the way. We're here.'

▶ 872

602

Your hand shoots out, clamping around her slender wrist. You'd imagine from the look of her that you could snap her arm with a single twist, but now that you have hold of her you can feel the potent energy flowing through that undead body.

A massive fork of lightning splits the sky. Over the boom of thunder you hear her threatening you with curses that would turn most people's hair white. Then suddenly she goes from unresisting to violent fury, struggling to break your grip.

You need a STRENGTH roll at difficulty 13 or she'll get free. You have no items currently on your person, having just got out of bed, so you can't use one to give you a STRENGTH bonus.

Succeed	▶ 655
Fail	▶ 1063

603

Stationing yourself a little way down the street, you keep a surreptitious eye on the house. An hour passes, then two, but there is no sign of Autolycus.

If Galatea is your companion ▶ 661

If not but you possess the **Face of Wisdom** (INGENUITY +3) ▶ 1575

Otherwise ▶ 26

604

☐ ☐ ☐ ☐ ☐ ☐ ☐ ☐

If you have the codeword *Planted*, lose it and tick the next empty box above.

You just ticked the first box	▶ 272
Just ticked the second box	▶ 1451
Just ticked the third box	▶ 272
Just ticked the fourth box	▶ 577
Just ticked the fifth box	▶ 272
Just ticked the sixth box	▶ 1201
Just ticked the seventh box	▶ 272
Just ticked the eighth box	▶ 22
Just ticked the ninth box	▶ 272

If you didn't tick a box or if all the boxes were already ticked ▶ 97

605

If you don't have the codeword *Robber* ▶ 1270

Otherwise ▶ 326

606

❏ ❏

Do not tick either of the boxes unless you were told to do so in the section you just turned from.

Neither of the boxes is ticked   ▶ 1454

One box is now ticked   ▶ 44

Two boxes are ticked   ▶ 1305

607

'You seek three that are lost. Look for them in the path of earth and the path of fire and the path that leads to the setting sun.'

She lapses into silence, and after a while starts to snore. You tiptoe out and tell the next person in the queue that there will be no more prophecies today.

▶ 510

608

Unfathomable gulfs of rock surround you in all directions. You lose all sense of time and space until at last the cocoon begins to rise toward the surface. You pass through layers of sand and emerge into the open air under a blistering desert sun. The beetles slow down, flying together into a clump, and the metallic chrysalis reforms itself and drops back into your pocket.

▶ 222 in *The Hammer of the Sun*

609

He looks across the plain, now murky in the dusk, to where the torches of Ilion flare and wink like immeasurably distant stars. 'Why indeed? It's not my war. At my birth it was foretold I must either live a long life without excitement or I could choose glory, the price of which is to burn out and die. And so here I am.'

'Why not get in your ship and sail away? Is glory so much better a fate than just to live?'

He looks into your eyes as if tempted for the first time to abandon his heroic destiny. 'I could enjoy an ordinary life, far from the thrill of battle and the cheering of my men, if only I had one to share it with.'

▶ 572

610

As you step into the tower there's a wrenching sensation as if the whole world just tilted by a few degrees.

Dunamis points into the sky, where a violet coruscation is blossoming like a new constellation in the night. 'What is it?' she says.

You know. It's the end of the world.

▶ 186

611

Your foes keep pouring up onto the roof, swelling a horde of murderous monsters who are now pressed right up to the balustrade alongside the *Sunrise*. You can see the pallid, worm-gnawed faces of the vampires, the red eyes and spittle-flecked jaws of the were-creatures, the misshapen features of capering nightmare demons. Baying and snarling, they are so intent on getting to you that some get jostled over the edge and fall flailing to the street far below.

Each time a grapple lodges on the ship's rail, instantly a stream of attackers comes scrabbling along it to get aboard. Careless of the wind, rain and the lethal drop below, their only thought is to continue their wild onslaught. Even the Minotaur, his blade flashing and spilling inhuman blood and guts with every swing, must eventually tire and then the monstrous tide will overwhelm the ship.

The mainsail is still only half-raised, the wet canvas flapping uselessly in the wind as Ancaeus tugs at the ropes. Not only is there no forward momentum, but the ship is listing and beginning to lose altitude as the helmsman bends helplessly over the buoyancy rotor. But can you afford to help either of them when it means leaving the Minotaur alone to repel boarders?

Stay at the rail to fight off attackers   ▶ 862

Help fix the buoyancy rotor   ▶ 1514

Join Ancaeus in raising the sails   ▶ 1009

612

'The gods have fought off an attack by the titans,' says Oizys, 'but it's only a temporary respite. They are binding their wounds, but without sustenance they can't recover their strength.'

'That's a good thing, isn't it?'

'Better still if they are given food and drink that you have poisoned. Then they will be helpless to resist Nyx.'

'I've got the poison.'

'Smart cookie, aren't you? Now you need the food of the gods to put it on.'

'And where's that?'

Oizys gives you a spiteful flick of pain behind the eyes. 'How do I know? I've never been here before. Somewhere on the mountainside there must be beehives or vineyards or golden apple trees or something. Pick a direction.'

If you have a **heart of oak** ▶ 885

If not but you have a **heart of ash** ▶ 593

Otherwise decide where on the mountain slopes you'll start your search:

North	▶	**151**
East	▶	**1088**
South	▶	**1311**
West	▶	**1413**

613

This is the Avenue of Ephirus. On the south side of the street runs a long wall of white marble, over the top of which stand tall cypress trees. The branches are full of rooks who glare down balefully. Iron gates in the wall admit visitors both warm and cold. This is the Necropolis.

To the north, in stark contrast to that place of eternal silence, is the busy market square, a wide plaza ringed with galleried shops and crammed with stalls, barrows, and rugs where itinerant traders lay out their wares. Odours of spices, perfumes, fruit, meat, fabrics, livestock and liquor mingle with the stench of excitement and life as buyers and sellers harangue, insult, inform, cajole, cozen and charm each other until somehow, amid all the befuddling din, deals are struck and coins and wares exchanged.

If you have the codeword **_Razor_** and this box ❑ is empty, tick it and record **613** as your Current Location, then ▶ **397**

Otherwise read on.

To go straight to a city location that you already know about, note **613** as your Current Location, then ▶ **1432**

Or you can go:

Into the Necropolis	▶	**674**
To the market	▶	**716**
East to the city centre	▶	**1642**
West to the city gate	▶	**509**

614

'I understand a bit about Vulcan's simulation matrix,' you tell Psyche. 'Enough to get a vague sense of what some of these switches and levers do, at least.'

She raises an eyebrow.

'I went to some lectures about it at the Academy,' you explain.

'Well, I'll admit I never thought of you adventurers as having much time for scholarly matters, but that's good. It means that any adjustments I make will be more effective.' She starts turning some dials on the equipment beside her. 'I've managed to isolate this somatic fabricator from the rest of the matrix so that we can use it without Nyx knowing.'

You look at her askance. 'When you say adjustments, are you talking about adjusting me?'

'It's hardly virgin territory. You've been brought back to life, haven't you? Every time you hone your strength or speed, those are changes that the workshop of the gods is making to your basic template.'

Agree to have Psyche modify your abilities ▶ **1545**

Decline the offer ▶ **1171**

615

A scribe with his arms full of scrolls stops you in the corridor. 'I am Lady Himera's secretary, Tyros,' he says.

'I thought I'd seen your face before. How is her ladyship?'

'Fine. She sent me to ask if you wouldn't mind doing her a small favour. It's for her uncle, who recently retired after a long and distinguished career in government.'

This seems to be how high status connections work in Vulcan City. If you do a noble a favour, there may be a sliver of gratitude but mainly you go onto a list of people they can call on for errands.

Refuse	▶	**187**
Agree	▶	**927**

616

You take care to make it a painful lesson for Nihakos. He goes home with blood pouring from a split lip and by the next day he's sporting two black eyes. From then on he leaves you and your brother alone.

Increase your STRENGTH by +1 but reduce one of your other attributes to −1. (You choose which.)

▶ **247**

617

'It sometimes seems as if my whole life has been spent in giving advice.' Nestor sighs and looks past you, seeming to gaze on times long past. 'Yet where are all those great heroes now? As often as not they didn't heed my words, and now the cold clay of Hades is under their feet, the vapours of the Styx chill their every breath. My words are wasted on impatient men.'

'But I am a woman.'

He looks at you and smiles. 'Impatient, though, aren't you? Well, I have advice to give for others to ignore, but think on what I've said.'

He turns and heads back to his own tent. ▶ **735** and tick the box for Nestor there before deciding if you'll talk to anyone else.

618

You climb down the ladder into the belly of the ship. Crates filled with supplies are all around, but they seem to be well secured with ropes and retaining nets.

There's a rustling sound from the gloom at the side of the hold. You go closer, having to squeeze between two wooden boxes. Something small darts around the corner out of sight. A rat? How would that have got aboard? As far as you know, the *Sunrise* has only ever been berthed in high mountains far above the snowline.

Your hand, groping forward in the dark, touches something soft. It feels like a large bunch of grapes. You peer around the crate to see a cluster of translucent yellow nodules. They look like fat grains of rice except that each is as big as a plum. And they're pulsing.

You realize they are insect eggs. But what kind of insect lays eggs that big?

A cascade of small hard objects suddenly rattles down on your head. At first you think it's a sack of woodchips or charcoal. That's before you see that these things are moving –

You're covered in a host of segmented insect larvae, each about as big as your hand. They swarm over you, biting with hard horny mandibles at any exposed flesh. Each bite causes stinging pain that erupts and spreads under your skin. The bites are poisonous.

If you are already wounded, note **426** as your Current Location and ▶ **670**

If you were uninjured, tick the Wound box on your Adventure Sheet and ▶ **1409**

619

'Remember Deucalion? They grow up so fast, don't they. See if you can track him down in Hades.'

'It's a big place.'

'There's a sinkhole between the Acheron and the Black Bayou. I'm sure he told you all this – about rescuing Prometheus.'

'Prometheus?'

'You know, the titan who invented fire.'

'He invented fire? There weren't any flames before Prometheus? Things didn't burn?'

'Stuff got hot, it just didn't combust. Look, I don't want to get into the weeds with you on this. Our end zone here is that Prometheus has been imprisoned by the gods – '

'Because of fire.'

'And some other stuff. He also invented mankind. Anyway, doesn't like the gods, doesn't get on that well with other titans either, so he could be useful. Tricky to deal with, but you've knocked around, you can handle it.'

'Can your intangibility bugs take me straight there?'

'If you like.' He taps a device on his belt and the chrysalis breaks up into the swarm of tiny gold beetles. As they spin around you, you feel your feet lift off the floor. 'You sure you want to go direct to Deucalion? You don't want to pick up anything in the city first?'

What will you decide? (Note that if you choose Hades you must say goodbye to your companion, if any, as no one will voluntarily travel there.)

'Straight to Hades is fine.' ▶ **782** in *The Houses of the Dead*

'Just drop me somewhere in the city for now.' ▶ **31** in this book

620

His long fingers stroke the surface of a polished walnut cabinet. 'I have just the thing for you.'

With a languid sweep of his hand, he swings the cabinet open. Inside, nestling snugly on a mat of green felt, is a palm-sized box with an array of buttons on the front. It seems to be made of some hard, grey, non-metallic material, perhaps the polished shell of a tortoise.

'It's a handy little gadget for retuning the vocal cords of anthropomorphic automata,' purrs the storekeeper.

Buy it ▶ **449**

Maybe another time ▶ **325**

621

Viranos spots you across the parade ground and comes jogging over with a grin on his face. 'I won't ask exactly how you handled things,' he says, 'but I'm forever in your debt.'

'It was nothing.'

'I'll repay you properly if I ever get the chance, but in the meantime I can at least help you make your way in Vulcanian society. Take this invitation to the Street of the Sun and the Moon. Look for a leafy side-street. You'll see a door shaded by cordyline palms. Give the special knock – that's two rapid taps then a more leisurely third one.'

'Sounds very sinister.'

He laughs. 'Quite the opposite. You'll see.'

Add the **gilt-edged invitation** to your possessions if you want it, then ▶ **1642**

622

As the golden maiden runs forward there's a deafening crunch of gears and her limbs seize up. She stands frozen into immobility in the act of reaching for you. You can see her eyes fixed on you, still burning with awareness, but her movements are now excruciatingly slow and her internal machinery is grinding with a sound like gravel being chewed up inside a mincer.

▶ **1408**

623

You have to picture the layout of the chamber from memory and head towards where Zagreus was sitting when the lights went out. You start to feel your way up the banks of seats.

Make an INGENUITY roll at difficulty 15.

Succeed ▶ **153**
Fail ▶ **386**

624

It's that gamine miscreant Orphea, who in a rash moment you saved from drowning in an icy lake. If you'd known what a thorn in your side she would prove to be, you might not have bothered. But what is she doing? Keeping low, you stealthily move closer.

She is sitting at your desk with three upside-down cups in front of her. Taking a small red gem in her hand, she practices putting it under one of the cups. But no – in the gleam of the firelight you can clearly see that as she lowers the cup she palms the gem, sliding it back into the lace frill of her sleeve.

You back to the door and announce yourself with a cough. She looks up sharply, and you spot her annoyance at not having heard you coming down the stairs. But she recovers her poise almost immediately, leans back in the chair, and doffs her feather cap in salute.

'Long time no double-cross,' you say.

'Don't be like that.' She pouts. 'Can't a frenemy drop in for a visit without instant recriminations? Far better to sit with a brandy by the fire and chat about old times.'

She nods at the decanter beside you on a side table. You notice that in spite of her amiable manner she has a poignard buckled at her waist.

Join her in a drink ▶ **450**
Tell her she can pour her own ▶ **372**
No way can she expect hospitality ▶ **1039**

625

The Avenue of Subsolanus is paved with chips of pearlescent stone that occasionally catch the sunlight and throw it back in sparks of rainbow hue. There are few shops here as it is a residential district interspersed with shrines and colonnades.

To the south stretches a broad crescent lined with the temples of the gods that runs all the way through to the Street of the Sun and Moon way off in the distance.

The Groves of Dionysus lie to the north of the street beyond railings entwined with ivy. There the trees form pools of cool dappled shade, and swathes of grass and flowered borders shine under fresh dew.

To go straight to a city location that you already know about, note **625** as your Current Location, then ▶ **1432**

Or you can go:

East to the city gate ▶ **333**
West to the central district ▶ **1642**
Into the Groves of Dionysus ▶ **806**
Towards the temples ▶ **103**

626

The temples are all gone. In their place, a black tower rises up and up into the starless sky.

'The wind's dying down,' notices Dunamis.

You nod. 'Can't you sense that change in the air? Whatever Nyx has planned, it'll happen soon.'

Enter the black tower ▶ **1494**
Leave the temple district ▶ **392**

627

If you have the codeword *Rough* ▶ **27**
If not ▶ **1116**

628

You break out of her clutches and deliver a crushing blow to the side of her face. Her jaw breaks and sags open horribly. The burning stare is undiminished. She doesn't feel pain or fatigue. To defeat the vampire you will have to dismember her carcass with your bare hands.

You wind your fingers around her neck and start to twist. Her own hands, small and pale as they are, sink into your arms with vice-like force and pull her inexorably closer. Her fangs are within inches of your throat. Make a STRENGTH roll at difficulty 10.

Success ▶ **114**
Failure ▶ **1080**

629

'Destiny is not a single length of string,' she says, 'stretched between now and your future self. Rather I see a tangle of possibilities. Before all else, review your opportunities in the land of the Lord of the Dead.'

'So after travelling to Hades and back – then I should free them?'

She shakes her head. 'Go next to Boreas. Find the mariner who builds his hull under the roof of heaven. If you are able to aid him, the prisoners might prove your allies.'

'And if not?'

'What happens along that thread is a knot I cannot unpick.'

She hangs her head, exhausted by the effort of peering beyond the veil of time. You return to the main hall.

▶ **510**

630

'Behold the very literal *corpus delicti*,' says the head.

'You deign to venture an opinion for once, do you?'

'You should be able to form your own opinions. I merely point out that the perpetrator of any act leaves clues, and this cadaver is the embodiment of that act. Consequently you should observe the body, use inductive reasoning to formulate a theory, then proceed to apply deduction. Simple.'

'I don't suppose you'd care to do all that and just tell me the answer?'

The head makes a brassy sniffing noise. 'I leave it as an exercise for my pupil.'

'Not pupil. Owner!'

▶ 299

631

'Yep,' says Ptolemos, chewing his lip, 'that one's the trickiest. Got to get it off the damned Sphinx, as I recall.'

'Which? There are three Sphinxes, aren't there?'

'The proper one,' he growls. 'Human face, like a Sphinx is meant to have, not one of those weird foreign critters.'

'And where is it..?' you wonder, consulting a map of Notus.

'Westernmost pyramid. Don't try any fancy trickery either. Sneaking around in the dark, all that thiefy stuff is for the rubes. Just go right in and let it ask its riddle.'

'A riddle. Of course. And the answer?'

'Oh, would you like me to do the whole blasted quest while you sit cooling your arse on this bench?'

You're not going to get any more hints, so you set off.

▶ 806

632

'You are ready,' says the voice of the god, booming from the brazen idol that dominates the inner shrine.

You bow your head to the cold flagstones. 'Tell me what I must do.'

'Go to the Artificer's palace. I have cleared away the mist that blurred your eyes, that veil of mirage that hides the palace from the sight of all mortals save those he invites to his masked balls.'

'Where is this palace, O divinity?'

'It lies not far to the west from where you now hear my words. Attend the evening's festivities, mingle with the guests. There the Dark Queen and her cohorts will make their first move to seize control of the Artificer's crown.'

You sense the god's presence withdraw back to Olympus, leaving you momentarily bereft like a child abandoned by its parents. Shakily you rise to your feet and make your way back out of the temple.

Get the codeword **Rendezvous** and ▶ 103

633

The drink dissolves all your teeth and washes them in an acidic chalky sludge down your throat. Lucky it's just a dream, but even so you will bear the psychic marks of the experience. Gain 1 scar.

'By gum, that's given you something to chew on,' says Penthé in a husky voice.

She turns and slinks away, guzzling the contents of the hip flask as if it was the finest wine. Just as she reaches the far end of the street, she turns and snaps her fingers, pointing to an ivy-covered hole in the brick wall next to you.

Squeezing through, you find yourself in a garden where a nightingale trills to the silently appreciative moon.

▶ 301

634

The saboteurs thought to strike while the camp was unguarded, not counting on events in the Achaean ranks that have left Achilles sullenly absent from the day's battle. Hearing the flames he erupts from his tent like a tiger inflamed by the scent of blood. His spear and sword flash in the sun. The saboteurs try to defend themselves, but they face the greatest of all the Achaean champions, one who is more than a match for Prince Hektor himself. He makes short work of the attackers, then swiftly summons servants to douse the flames.

As you come down from the rocks you catch his eye. 'You missed all the fun,' he says.

'Did you let any live? We could find out who sent them.'

'Agamemnon would only have ransomed them for gold,' he says, plunging his blood-drenched hands in the sea to clean them. 'It pleases me that he's a little poorer this afternoon than he might have been.'

▶ 1500

635

❏

If the box above is already ticked ▶ 872

If the box is empty, put a tick in it and read on.

A snort of hot breath on your neck startles you. It is a camel, haughtily pushing you aside in its languorous progress along the street.

Two priestesses are sauntering by arm in arm. 'There are no wild camels,' says one, 'but unfortunately there are no tame ones either.' Her companion laughs, but you are starting to get a disorienting sense of déjà vu.

A sun-bronzed man in saffron robes catches your arm. Offended, you are about to pull away when you see he has saved you from tripping back over the edge of a well. 'Be careful, my friend,' he says, passing on, 'even on a sweltering hot day there's such a thing as too much water.'

You glance into the cool interior of the well, and for a moment red lights flit down there in the darkness. There are verdigris-stained metal rungs stapled into the brick walls of the well. Around you, the crowds stream by taking no notice.

Climb down into the well ▶ 1469
Continue on your way ▶ 722

636

'Who have you come to see?' says the sentry at the gate, dropping his halberd to block your path.

'Nobody in particular.'

'On your way, then. No admittance to the barracks unless you know someone in the regiment who can vouch for you.'

▶ 1642

637

You easily slip past the guards patrolling each floor. You soon reach street level and head back to lose yourself in the crowds on the Avenue of the Anvil.

▶ 63

638

Disdaining to ride back into the fray, you listen for a time to the distant hubbub far out across the plain. Men are fighting and dying there, uttering screams and war-cries, but at such a distance all merges into a muddled wordless roar. You turn away and walk along the line of beached ships, sunk in thought, until a sprightly voice breaks in on your daydreams.

'You're having a yourself day, are you?'

You look up, startled. 'Galatea! It's so good to see you again.'

'I can't say the same. For me it's the first time we've met.'

'But – ' You take her hands. 'What are you doing here? Last time I saw you you'd been turned into a statue.'

'That makes sense. After all, I am a statue. I came here looking for sand, but it isn't right sort of beach. Too many pebbles.' She tugs her hands away and takes a few graceful steps as though practicing a dance. 'It's for this.'

She holds up an ivory hourglass.

'I recognize that.'

'In that case one day I'd better give it to you – once I've got the right kind of sand. The little bit I've found here is too grey and coarse. It'll only take you forward, which is the way you're going anyway.'

She flips over the hourglass and the sand starts to trickle through it. Flickering prismatic beams spiral around you. Your feet are lifted from the beach and you feel yourself falling, not only through space but through time.

'I'll catch you up.' Galatea's voice echoes as if down a long tunnel behind you. 'I won't mention any of this next time I see you, though. It'd only get confusing.'

▶ 73

639

The low ceiling here in the alcove makes it impossible to stand upright. You're better off grappling with the demon and trying to take the fight to the floor.

You manage to manoeuvre it into a corner where its longer reach is no advantage. Locking both hands onto one of its thick, furry wrists, you lean back using leverage to bend its arm at the elbow. If you can force an opening, you might get a chance for a decisive blow.

Make a STRENGTH roll at difficulty 10. You *cannot* use a blessing to reroll because the gods will not intervene when a mortal pits themselves against a semi-divine being.

Succeed ▶ 177
Fail ▶ 564

640

A blurred image appears in the depths of the glass pyramid and grows larger. It comes into sharper focus, resolving itself into a figure walking towards you. As she steps out of the pyramid she has grown to full size – a tall, strikingly graceful woman in black robes that shimmer with flickers of reflected light with every slight motion of her body.

'This isn't really my kind of place,' says Pandora, looking around her.

'No? I thought you were a city person.'

'Iskandria is a city. This – this is a stage set. A god's superficial idea of what a human metropolis is like.' She gives an elegant shudder. 'I will not stay long. I came only to give you this.'

You take it from her: **Pandora's Jar**. Note it on your list of possessions.

'You don't think I've got troubles enough?'

She laughs. 'Look around you – the troubles all flew out of it into the world long ago. But Zeus had this made to accommodate all the ills in creation, remember. That's a lot of storage space.'

As long as you have **Pandora's Jar**, you can ignore the limit of twenty possessions at a time. By the miraculous

Olympian construction of the jar you can fit any number of items inside.

| If you have a **brass head** | ▶ 1181 |
| Otherwise | ▶ 242 |

641

'Very heartfelt, a strangling,' she says. 'Surgeons and stone-cold killers use a knife. A murderer might bring a garotte. But to get up close and personal like that – it's a sign of emotions brought to boiling point.'

Examine the body	▶ 299
Look around for the letters	▶ 1431
Make yourself scarce	▶ 988

642

You hesitate a split-second too long. The Celedon's skull-splitting screech lays you flat.

Unless you have any **beeswax**, you are not only stunned but bleeding from your ears, eyes and nose. Tick the Wound box on your Adventure Sheet if it wasn't ticked already.

If you had **beeswax** to plug your ears with then you are not grievously injured, but even so you are dazed and too weak to move.

▶ 1068

643

You're lying on your back. Waves of dizziness swirl around your vision. You must have blacked out for a moment. You are too weak to move and a wet warmth covers your throat and chest.

A weight drops onto your stomach, claws its way up. A hard-featured face stares down at you.

'Still alive,' says the dwarf. 'Soon fix that.'

'Wait,' says the slaver. 'A knife in the eye is too quick. I want this trash to meet a fitting end.'

They take your limp body between them and manhandle you down the stairs. You struggle feebly but loss of blood has left you with no strength. It's all you can do to stay conscious.

The slaver opens a door, strikes a flint, and a wall-bracketed torch flares into life. From the smell of damp stone and effluent this must be the sewer under the building. They carry you down and rest you at the water's edge. As a fresh wave of dizziness clouds your vision, you dimly realize that they mean to drown you – or let the rats eat you alive.

| If you have a **kraken's tentacle** | ▶ 128 |
| If not | ▶ 111 |

644

The last insect monster scuttles to attack. All around you the bushes are swaying in the wind. Rain is falling faster now. Thunder rumbles through the darkening sky. It feels as though creation itself is at war.

Make a STRENGTH or GRACE roll (your choice) at difficulty 10.

| Succeed | ▶ 125 |
| Fail | ▶ 825 |

645

Zinc takes a sealed envelope out of his pocket and hands it to you. 'Don't open this till you get to the big party.'

'Which party?'

'The one at Vulcan's palace.'

You shake your head. 'I don't know where that is.'

'Everybody says that, then one day you're there and it's like you've known it your whole life.' He points at the note. 'Keep it somewhere safe, and remember: no peeking till the night of the ball.'

Get the codeword *Radiant* and ▶ 326

646

'You can just leave me with this old fellow,' pipes up the Face. 'If the world's going to end I'd rather spend my last few hours talking to him.'

'You got it working!' cries Myletes in wonder. 'And to think of all those years I used you as a paperweight.'

'I thought you looked familiar,' says the Face gruffly.

Myletes runs his fingers over the brass skull. 'What a marvel you are. One of Daedalus's most magnificent inventions.'

'Don't mention that guy to me,' snaps the head. 'He switched me off and left me at the bottom of a toolbox for twenty years.'

'You may have an inglorious past, but your destiny is great indeed,' says Myletes. He turns to you. 'Once you've found Vulcan's matrix, leave your metal head connected to it. That will give you remote control of reality – to a very limited degree, at least.'

'Is that useful?'

He nods. 'It might be the only way you're going to survive battle with a titan queen.'

▶ 1290

647

Note **451** as your Current Location, then ▶ 1269 and tick the box next to the Tower of Ice From now on you will always be able to find your way back here.

648

You race along the hall. The intruders are in hot pursuit. Luckily your servants are efficient and the bolts on the door are well oiled – you're outside in a moment and racing down the street. This is a wealthy district with frequent patrols of the city militia. You just have to find them before your pursuers catch up.

Make a GRACE roll at difficulty 10. Even if you have an item that would normally give you a GRACE bonus, you can't use it now because your possessions are back in your bedroom. You have nothing but a nightgown.

Succeed ▶ **30**
Fail ▶ **888**

649

'You cut yourself, you put a bandage on it, don't you?' he says. 'You don't just think, "Oh, it's a part of life, this, so I'll just sit and bleed out." Or if a bull comes at you in a field – '

'You run. I get it. But death is a bit of a bigger proposition than occasional daily hardships. It's not avoidable, it's inevitable. That's the whole point.'

'Getting old – that's not indignity enough? No, on top of that they say your life is done now, that's your lot, move over, you're for the dark. I don't buy it. Since when did Man submit feebly to fate? All of history is the heroic struggle against what's "meant to be".'

If Galatea is with you and you want her advice ▶ **521**

If you possess the **Face of Wisdom (INGENUITY +3)** and want to consult it ▶ **1467**

Otherwise ▶ **483**

650

It is a long walk from here to the middle of the beach where King Agamemnon's tent flies his proud pennant of supreme command.

Talk to one of the warriors nearby ▶ **735**
Go on to see Agamemnon ▶ **813**
Go back to Achilles' tent ▶ **535**

651

He accepts the coins with a fluid sweep of his hand. Deduct the 10 pyr from the money on your Adventure Sheet.

'Now then, listen as if your life depended on it – for one day it may. The answers are man, and coin, and mirror, and wind, and tomorrow.'

'All of them?'

'Would you rather have fewer answers for your money, traveller? I cannot take them back. But I see you are dissatisfied, so I will throw in some advice *gratis*.'

'There is a saying about the value of free advice.'

He shrugs. 'You don't need to act on it. It's only this: when you travel in Notus, before you walk in dreams be sure to arm yourself with a secret.'

'Enigmatic indeed!'

He narrows his eyes. 'Oh, you are hard to please. I think you might be a true hero after all. They always drive the hardest bargains and then come back to grumble.'

Another customer approaches. The wizard gives you a last penetrating look and turns to favour them with his sales patter.

If you have the codeword *Reverie* ▶ **88**
If not ▶ **695**

652

'Would you stand against your mother, the Queen of Eternal Darkness?'

'Of course not,' Thanatos spits back. 'But it is not for the likes of you to split hairs with the gods themselves. I will give you the just reward for your artful words.'

He starts to draw back his cowl.

▶ **147**

653

The *Sunrise* sails on across the Ocean of Night. Distant stars shine icily across the immense gulf. Are there other worlds out there in the blackness of space? Or is it merely an infinite lifeless void?

The sailors are too overawed by their surroundings to indulge in the usual jokes and gripes. For a long time there is nothing but the slow creak of the ropes, the almost musical boom of flexing timbers, the occasional muttered remark.

The rest of the journey passes uneventfully until at last the lookout cries: 'Land ahoy!'

▶ **346**

654

Agrio gets a lucky shot that skewers Tekto through the neck. Blood sprays everywhere as if a tap had been turned on. Your man dies kicking at the dust.

The small crowd of onlookers turn and walk back into the city. Agrio's second seems faintly bored. Agrio himself is weeping. Servants pick up the body and carry it away. There is nothing more for you to do.

▶ **222**

655

Tritona struggles until you fear she's about to wrench your arm out of its socket, but she can't get away.

Abruptly she yields. A crafty look comes into her eyes.

'There's treasure hidden here,' she says. 'A fortune, all yours. If you let me go I'll tell you where it is.'

Agree ▶ 1512
No chance ▶ 462

656

'Had enough yet?' pants Orphea. 'I've got you at a disadvantage, and you know you don't really want to kill me.'

But maybe you do? She has been a thorn in your side ever since you saved her life back in Hades. You size up your chances. She's fast, but you're bigger and stronger. If you could just get your hands on her it would all be over. But there is that knife.

Lunge at her bare-handed ▶ 1362
Give up ▶ 546

657

You spurn him, leaving him even more isolated than before. Maybe he takes out his resentment on other kids, but as long as he leaves you and your brother alone that's not your problem.

Your hard heart shows in the ruthless set of your jaw and the unforgiving steel of your gaze.

Gain 1 scar – not all such marks are physical.

▶ 247

658

Orphea did her best to conceal some of the movements behind the wide lace ruffs of her shirt sleeves, but your eye was quicker than her hands. You are almost certain which cup the ruby is under.

'There.'

She lifts it with a flourish. 'No. It's under this one. Look.'

You stare at the desk, speechless. You were so sure.

She pockets the ruby. 'So I'll take the deeds, assuming your word is your bond. No rush to move out. Anytime tomorrow will do.'

Give her the deeds to the house ▶ 1255
Never! ▶ 1054

659

'Never thought you'd let feelings get in the way of the smart choice.'

Daedalus was halfway through the hatch. He pauses and looks back. 'How do you see that?'

'If I lose here today, Nyx definitely wipes out this reality. She'll be undisputed ruler of the universe forevermore.'

'Right. And if you win, Zeus will step in. Same deal.'

'But that's not a dead certainty.'

'Ninety-nine percent,' he insists. But even as he says it you can see a cloud of doubt in his eyes.

'Smart money plays the odds, right? One percent chance of an outcome where we come out on top – even if it's only that, which I doubt, it's worth shooting for.'

He heaves a sigh. 'I just know this is a mistake. OK then, let's do it before I come to my senses.' He reaches into the hatch and pulls out a bag full of strange devices. 'The gadgets I've got here make Zeus's thunderbolts look like pea-shooters. Kind of glad to have the excuse to use them, if I'm honest.'

'This is it, then,' you say, surveying your forces. 'It's too bad we don't have a catchy rallying-cry.'

'Don't sweat it,' says Daedalus. 'We'll make something up afterwards and say we said it.'

▶ 804

660

He gives a harsh, scornful laugh. 'Forgive me if I don't find your argument entirely convincing. No, I am not going to give up just because some blind authority has decided I've had my allotted span.'

'What, then?'

He looks around. 'I'll travel to all the places I never got to visit when I was alive.'

'It won't end well.'

He shakes his head. 'What does?'

You watch him walk away. Then you make your way back to the Necropolis to give the bad news to his family.

▶ 789

661

'Maybe he doesn't come and go by the front door,' she says.

'What do you mean?'

'Don't thieves sneak about? I'm sure I heard that climbing drainpipes comes into it. And you've got to be a dab hand at the disguises too, like our fellow there.'

'Which fellow?'

'The caretaker. Now didn't you think he had fine straight fingers for somebody that's meant to be all crooked and old?'

Climb up to Autolycus's room ▶ 1359
Keep watching the house from here ▶ 26

662

Kleistro isn't hard to find. He has a small folding table that he sets up at the end of Starbridge Lane, near the East Gate, and fleeces new arrivals in the city with card tricks. You step up and turn over one of the cards.

'The Joker,' you say. 'What are the odds?'

Kleistro pretends not to be rattled, but you sense him instantly go tense. He is a slight, pale-skinned young man with liquid amber-brown eyes half-hidden under an unruly curtain of long black hair.

'Zinc sent you,' he says, not quite managing to hide the quaver in his voice. He has an open, affable way of speaking, a real asset to a con artist.

'Let's take it off the street,' you say. 'No need to distress all these fine upstanding citizens.'

With a firm grip on his arm, you move him back down the lane and into a doorway. 'Have you got the fare for a litter? Only you won't be walking home.'

'Wait.' He sounds breathless now. He tugs at your grip but there's no strength in his fingers. 'Do you want to know what I've done to piss Zinc off?'

Let him tell his story   ▶ 1298
Just get on with the beating ▶ 481

663

The noise of hammers and workmen's shouts echoes across the small cobbled courtyard. They are putting up a scaffold. The noose dangles against the sky, a loop through which some unfortunate soul will soon find their way into eternity.

You watch them work, their tools clanking and clattering against the wooden beams. A few onlookers wait along the side of the courtyard. The mood is like a festival as they chatter among themselves, taking bets on which of the prisoners in the city jail is due for execution.

'They always keep us guessing to the last minute,' a woman with bright, excited eyes says to you.

'I wonder why? It would be easy enough to post a notice on the gate.'

She curls her lip. 'Spoilers? Are you daft? Where's the fun in that?'

Wait to see the hanging   ▶ 419
Leave   ▶ 1642

664

'A windowsill counts as a threshold, doesn't it? So given that the last time we met you were at home among the dead, I don't think I'll be inviting you in.'

Her lip twists in an angry pout, revealing two gleaming fangs. 'We'll meet again,' she says with quiet menace as she withdraws into the ivy.

Let her go   ▶ 1063
Grab her   ▶ 602

665

If you have a companion ▶ 917; otherwise read on.

'Just you, is it?' snaps Ptolemos as you approach.

'How did you know it was me?'

'Everyone else has the good manners not to bother me. So, like I said, you're on your own?'

'Who should I have brought?'

'Don't bring anyone. I don't want to talk to anybody. But you ought to get down to that shrine to Aphrodite in south-east Notus and hook up with my old friend Loutro.'

'Then what?'

He sighs and shakes his head. 'If I had my sight, could've

saved the world three times over by now. You want to restore the Great River, isn't that the plan? Start by walking along the dried-up valley with Loutro. Sort of a psychogeography thing, I think they call it.'

'I'll definitely do that next time I'm in Notus.' You go to sit beside him on the bench. 'I've got some other adventures to tell you about first.'

He slides across, stopping you from sitting down. 'Tell me next time. Right now, go and do the other thing.'

▶ 806

666

That is the end for this character. The final and absolute end from which there can be no hope of resurrection.

Delete everything on your Adventure Sheet including attributes, codewords, possessions, and so forth. Erase any ticks or other records you have written in boxes throughout all the books.

When you are ready to begin again with a new character, pick any of the Vulcanverse books and ▶ 1

667

'What's going on?' you ask one of a crowd of people gathered around some trees at the edge of the park.

'See for yourself,' he says. 'Looks like a glitch in reality.'

A couple of technicians, scholar-priests from the temple of Vulcan, are examining an apple tree which is flickering with incongruous textures: rock, sand, clammy mist. The leaves keep snapping into odd geometric shapes. You glimpse a large eye that appears in a hollow in the trunk, blinks at the crowd, and then closes a lid of bark as if in resignation.

'Keep back,' advises one of the scholar-priests as you step closer. 'Nothing to see here.'

'What are you talking about?' shouts a woman carrying a baby. 'There's plenty to see.'

'Too much, even,' adds a man standing behind her.

'Look, the leaves are turning into feathers!' says another.

The two priests look at each other. 'We'll have to do a full shutdown and boot it back from there.'

He taps a piece of chalk on the slate he has been using to make notes. For a split-second you get the impression of sky and grass kaleidoscoping together in a spiral that diminishes into darkness. A moment later, everything is as it was except that the priests and the tree have gone. The air, previously warm, has acquired a sudden chill. The sun is close to setting.

'What happened?' you ask the man you first spoke to.

He shakes his head as if to clear it. 'What? Why are we standing around here? There's nothing to see. Come on, everyone. The park's closing.'

They wander off, puzzled rather than alarmed. But you remember.

Leave by way of the Street of Ash   ▶ 232
Go out onto the Avenue of Subsolanus   ▶ 625

668

You could act as intermediary. Perhaps Chryses, as a priest of Apollo, would be willing to listen to you. On the other hand, is it seemly for an Amazon to get embroiled in this sordid argument over captive slaves?

Offer to speak to Chryses   ▶ 810
Keep out of it   ▶ 416

669

You leap aside just as something sharp gouges a chunk out of your arm. If you hadn't moved it would have sliced you in half. Tick the Wound box on your Adventure Sheet if it wasn't ticked already.

You get a glimpse of segmented black carapace, spindly razor-edged limbs, scything jaws, multiple eyes like polished coals. It's a giant insect like the ones you saw in the palace garden. It must have crept up behind you and was about to strike when the Minotaur threw his axe.

The axe embeds itself in the creature's head. A gout of foul-smelling yellow liquid spatters you. You're still fumbling for a weapon as the insect rears up to its full height on stiffening legs, gives a horrible hissing cry, shudders, and slumps to the deck. Crippled as it is, you have no trouble finishing it off.

'Should've trusted me,' grunts the Minotaur, pulling his axe out of the twitching carcass.

'Where did the damned thing come from? I saw a bunch of them earlier tonight.'

'I saw it come out of the hold,' says the navigator. 'Must have got aboard during the battle on the rooftop.'

'Strange that it hid away till now,' says Ancaeus, coming over to look at the carcass.

'You're welcome, by the way,' the Minotaur says to you.

▶ 231

670

❑

If the box above is empty, put a tick in it and ▶ 96
If it was already ticked ▶ 867

671

Celedons surround you, their faces remaining blankly impassive as they batter you to your knees. A final blow crashes into the back of your head. You are flung to the ground and lie senseless.

You come round – who knows how long later? Metal hands are dragging you roughly over broken ground. They fling you like a rag doll onto a pile of rubble. You fight to hang on to consciousness. There's no sign of Dunamis – at least she must have got away. The wind has dropped, leaving a dead calm. You must be in the eye of the storm.

Summoning your remaining strength, you struggle to your feet. All over the city darkness is closing in, deepening, streaming from the firmament in rivers of light-extinguishing nullity.

A shadow deeper than the night falls over you. You turn to look up into the eyes of Queen Nyx. She regards you as a tiger might look upon a mouse – barely worth the bother of killing.

'The matrix of reality is almost recast,' she says. 'My world is about to be born. You can do nothing now to prevent it.'

Behind her stand her sons, Death and Sleep. Titans who together even Zeus would hesitate to face in battle. And you are one lone mortal.

▶ 249

672

Achilles is alone in the tent, brooding over a goblet of wine in his hand.

'Why are you sitting in the dark?'

He doesn't turn to look at you. 'So you've given yourself to Agamemnon,' he says thickly.

'News travels fast around this camp.'

'That grasping brute. King of Kings!' Achilles seems to be talking more to himself than you. 'What quarrel did I have with Ilion? They never stole my cattle, never pillaged my lands. We followed Agamemnon for the sake of his family's lost honour. Princes all in our own lands, yet he treats us like his thralls. This war drags on and on while he waits and fills his coffers with the spoils better men bring off the battlefield.'

'So why fight for him?'

He laughs savagely. 'Why indeed? When I think of his hands on you – ugh, it's like a loathsome beast defiling a sacred idol. Henceforth I'll not cut down the defenders of Ilion to feed his rapacious ambition. Here in the camp I'll stay, my men too, and see how Agamemnon's forces fare without the son of Peleus to be their champion.'

Get the codeword **Rage** and ▶ 572

673

'If you've got some good-quality wax and you've got the wings that Icarus's father made for him,' says Bosk, 'you've got all you need to soar.'

'Metaphorically? Sky's the limit, sort of thing?'

He knocks back a pint or two of foaming ale in one great gulp. 'The sky is your oyster. I mean, the air is not just for the birds. How strong is this stuff?'

You shake your head. 'You're talking about actually flying. But where would I start?'

'A high place. For example, the towers at the corners of the city wall. Go up one of those and jump off.' As you walk away deep in thought he adds, 'But put the wings on first, obviously!'

Get the codeword **Raptor** if you don't have it already, then ▶ 1534

674

❏

If you do not have the codeword **Reverie** and the box above is empty, put a tick in it and ▶ 751

Otherwise read on.

The tombs are a jumble of architectural styles and eras. Some are simple gravestones, some overgrown with thickets of weeds while others are tended as well as any garden and have fresh flowers laid on them daily.

The grander vaults are of night-black obsidian, tallow-hued alabaster, stern granite, shining onyx, or marble of many kinds. Some resemble miniature palaces, with colonnades and bronze-barred doors. Others are intricate sculptures that depict scenes from epic battles or else portray the dead person as a conquering hero resplendent on a high pedestal. A few are abstract, just squat blocks displaying enigmatic symbols inlaid with precious metals into the stone façades.

The necropolis is laid out on levels like a rolling lawn, with shaded paths and shrubs that soften the sun by day and leave deep pools of shadow after dark.

If you have the codeword **Rain** and this box ❏ is empty, tick it and ▶ 1443

Otherwise, if you do not have the codeword **Reef** but you do have either **Rabbit** or **Ruffle** and this box ❏ is empty, tick it and ▶ 6

Otherwise if you have 6 scars or more and this box ❏ is empty, tick it and ▶ 387

Otherwise:

Leave by way of the Street of Knives ▶ 1617

Head for the Avenue of Ephirus ▶ 613

675

Given Zinc's reputation you might expect to meet him in a mansion – or the nearest to a mansion that the slums of this part of town have to offer. Instead you're led down an alley so narrow that your shoulders scrape on the damp, algae-slimed walls, emerging at the end into a patch of land enclosed on all sides by crumbling brick buildings. Despite the dreariness of the surroundings, the yard has been cultivated as a vegetable garden with a cabbage patch, a trellis for beans, and a small greenhouse with grubby, cracked panes where tomatoes are making the most of what daylight filters past the high tenement walls.

A man is on his knees working over the soil with a trowel. Noticing you, he drives the trowel into the ground and gets up stiffly. He's not young, but has the physique of one who keeps himself fit. Perhaps you expected Zinc to be a big man, but he's no taller than you. You can only guess at his age because of the mask of hammered tin that completely covers his face. It is a stylized visage such as you have seen worn by the chorus in formal dramas, almost expressionless but for a hint of curiosity or even awe in the rounded mouth and raised eyebrows.

If you have the codeword *Recursive* ▶ 856
Otherwise ▶ 380

676

'True,' says Pug, mulling over your words. 'That's what I told Ancaeus.'

'I don't follow.'

'The last of the Argonauts. He's forever planning one more voyage to match the adventures of old. But you can't steer a ship by looking at its wake.'

▶ 480

677

The drawings that Lord Xechasiaris gave you are in your wallet. You pull them out on the counter as you're paying for a cup of tea at a stall in the market. 'Oh,' says the man behind you in the queue, 'I been there.'

'Where?'

He nods at the drawings. 'The Druid's Shrine in Arcadia. Took your kiddie along, did you? What an artist. How old?'

'At a guess he's about eighty-five.'

The man considers this. 'Second childhood, eh? Well, he's got the colour of those buds to a T.'

You pause in the act of stuffing the papers back into your wallet. Searching through, you find the one he means. A scatter of red spikes on a scrawl of green crayon.

'So you know where this is?'

He blows on his tea. 'I'm heading out that way this afternoon.'

'I'll come with you.'

'It's not a tourist trip. This is business. I'm driving a trade caravan to north-east Arcadia. You want to come along, fine, but it'll cost you.'

You don't think you could find the exact spot on your own, but the price of his guidance is a steep 50 pyr.

Pay him (cross off the money) ▶ 1450
Forget about it ▶ 613

678

If you have neither **food of the gods** nor **poisoned ambrosia** ▶ 430

Otherwise ▶ 1391

679

If Current Location is **260** then ▶ 1125; otherwise read on.

Agamemnon heaves a disinterested shrug. 'Sure, why not? Just remember, I get a third share of any plunder you bring in off the battlefield. That goes for ransom too.'

'I am an Amazon. We fight for victory, not for loot.'

He laughs. 'Noble sentiments, but I've heard of your scrubby little camp out in the desert wastes. If you didn't raid and pillage, you warrior wenches would starve inside a week.'

▶ Current Location

680

'Didn't Loutro tell you what you need to do the ritual?' says Ptolemos as you sit down beside him.

'Three items,' he said.

'I know. He told me about them often enough. A green pearl, a conch horn, and a baby's rattle. So which of those is giving you trouble?'

What is your reply?

'The green pearl.'	▶ 1224
'The conch horn.'	▶ 631
'The baby's rattle.'	▶ 984
'None; I've got them all.'	▶ 1537

681

'Wait up, hotshots. Where's your hurry?'

It's an old beggar folded on a doorstep like a pile of dirty laundry. He peers into your lamplight, rheumy eyes blinking, teeth like stumps of old toffee bared in a leering grin.

'Leave him,' says Dunamis. 'we don't have time.'

'Charity's the first thing on the junk pile when times are tough, eh?' wheezes the beggar. 'Off you scoot, then, chippy. The hounds probably won't bother with a scrap of skin and bones like you anyway.'

Dunamis tugs you on, but you insist on going back to the beggar. 'What hounds?' you ask him.

'Nasty prancing things. Spitting folks like kebabs on those bony arms of theirs. I saw them riding in along of those giants.'

'Giants? He must mean Thanatos and Hypnos,' says Dunamis. 'It's not safe to hang around. We've got to keep on the move.'

'I saw it happen,' says the beggar, talking to you and ignoring her. 'When the darkness came and did all this.'

Get him to tell you more	▶ 1223
You're just wasting time here	▶ 314

682

'I'll have to leave you for a while,' says Galatea after speaking to the refugees. 'Something very important has come up and I need to go with these good people.'

'Saving the world isn't that pressing, you think?'

She gives you a mysterious smile. 'Don't worry, the world won't end until we get there.'

She gathers the refugees together and shepherds them away across the grass.

Delete Galatea from the Companion box on your Adventure Sheet, then ▶ 806

683

There's a wrenching sensation, a moment of vertigo, and you're back on the slopes of Mount Olympus.

'That was dumb of you,' Oizys purrs nastily.

'I'm still stuck with you, then. Might've hoped that resurrection would be like a purgative.'

'Death don't us part, lover. Now, if you don't want me to have to start tormenting you a bit, better get back in the game.'

▶ 1446

684

The delay is fatal. You wrest your leg out of the vampire's grasp, but by then a dozen other clammy bloodless hands have seized you. You are dragged from the parapet. Werewolves close their jaws on your limbs. A weretiger clamps its fangs around the back of your neck. Vampires pile on, holding you fast with the rigidity of the dead.

Struggling under the weight of your foes, you look up in time to see Thanatos step through the rift in space. His fiery sword swings down, shattering the hull of the *Sunrise* like matchwood. Ancaeus and his crew are thrown over the side, their cries drowned out by the roar of the storm.

'It is the master of annihilation!' shrieks a vampire. 'O dread lord, I have served you well these long centuries. Give me the gift of final sleep!'

Descending from the sky, Thanatos flicks aside his cowl and bestows a mere glance of his searing eyes upon the grovelling vampire. There is a blaze like a splinter of the sun. Raindrops burn, the very air is charred, and when the blinding light fades there is nothing remaining of the undead creature. Moans and howls of veneration rise from the throats of the monstrous horde.

Thanatos places one colossal foot on the roof, the other

on the street below. Tiles crack and fall away under his weight. Helpless, you stare up at him where he stands like a mountain against the cloud-tossed sky.

▶ 595

685

Zinc takes an interest in the hourglass which he sees hanging at your belt. He reaches out and touches it almost fondly.

'I had one like this,' he says, 'but it broke. I'd give my time again to get it back.'

You wonder if he expects you to give it to him, but he turns away to snap orders at one of his henchmen and seems to forget all about it.

▶ 326

686

❑

If box above was already ticked ▶ 1272; if the box is empty, put a tick in it now and read on.

In the rear wall is a low portico framing a deep recess like an abandoned hearth. It is traditionally said to be the abode of the Hero of Temesa, a sort of ghost or demon that presumably predates the tavern itself. The story is that he was a wandering traveller who forced himself on a local maiden and was bludgeoned to death by her outraged family. But he returned from the grave and exacted bloody vengeance on his killers, visiting them at night and tearing them limb from limb.

Nor did the ghost's lust for vengeance end there. Having killed all the maiden's brothers, it began murdering random strangers. On the advice of a seer, the locals built a shrine for the demon and agreed to offer up a maiden to it at each new moon. Since then it has caused no more mayhem.

'They pick her by drawing lots,' says a man sitting with a pack of cards, nodding towards the portico. 'She's tied up and left in there.'

'And then what?'

'The tavern is locked up for the night, everyone goes home and locks their doors, and the demon has its wicked way with her.'

'Rapes her, you mean?'

'I don't know about that. None of 'em ever say what happened. In fact, they can't. Come the morning they're either stark mad or else dead of fright.'

If you have the codeword *Pure*, lose it and ▶ 578
Otherwise ▶ 764

687

'Orphea.'

'I prefer Lady Rapscallion these days, but suit yourself.'

'It's good of you to show up at my door. Saves me the trouble of hunting you down.'

'Actually I came in the window, but you're welcome.' She gives you a wry smile. 'Why are you looking at me like that?'

'I'm trying to decide if I'm going to have revenge for the first time you robbed me, or that time you drugged me, or pretending to be an ally so you could make off with the Pipes of Pan, or – '

She daintily covers a yawn. 'Let's not rake over the coals. It's so tiresome. The Pipes of Pan are why I'm here, as a matter of fact. Why don't we sit and chat over drinks and I'll explain.'

She nods at the decanter beside you on a side table. You notice that in spite of her amiable manner she has a dagger buckled at her waist.

Join her in a drink	▶ 450
Tell her she can pour her own	▶ 1251
No way can she expect hospitality	▶ 389

688

Hypnos releases the lightning bolt that had waited trembling above. It arcs across the sky, crashing into the garden where it splits an ancient oak into a fountain of molten sparks. The blast of thunder shakes the building and reverberates off over the city.

The afterimage of the bolt burns a deeper darkness against the heavens. But then the darkness moves, and you see that it is the living embodiment of night, the manifestation of all mortal terrors. Queen Nyx is here.

If Chipos is your companion ▶ 1281
If not ▶ 1027

689

If Tomyios is your companion ▶ 708; otherwise read on.

The flying creatures swarm into the stairwell in a frenzied whirring of leathery wings. They are right behind you. No time to look back. The feral growls of the were-beasts and the insatiate sighs of the vampires echo up from below as you run for your life.

The stairs wind through floor after floor to the very top of the building, a wearying corkscrew. You gasp for breath. Your legs are burning with fatigue. Above is a cupola capped with a lantern through which storm-light flickers down from the night sky. There's a door to the roof. You dive for it, praying to all the gods it isn't locked.

▶ 838

690

The Oracle nods slowly, though whether in approval of your answer or from mere fatigue is unclear. 'Go to the slums where the criminals live. You know their leader. Get to know him better. In doing a service for him you will be reunited with one you saved from a life of misery.'

Bowing, you return to the outer hall.

▶ 510

691

A coven of vampires rush to set up portable cannon along the edge of the roof. Clamping the first of these devices to the parapet, a vampire stabs a button on the side. There's a crack as the cannon flings out a spreading web of grappling lines.

The grapples catch on the rail and immediately a host of werebeasts come scrambling across. The Minotaur chops at one of the ropes with his axe, splintering the rail and sending a string of the creatures howling and tumbling to their doom. But more grapple-lines are being shot across in volley after volley, and there seems no end to the bestial horde.

'Those cannon are Daedalus's inventions,' mutters Ancaeus. 'Nyx must have some hold over him. He'd never serve her willingly.'

You can see more of the cannon being brought up to the edge of the roof. 'We can't match their numbers,' you say, slicing at a were-creature that is clutching at the rail. 'If we're going to get under way it had better be soon.'

If you have the title **Kissed by a Golden Princess** ▶ 278

If not but you have the codeword *Noble* ▶ 1164

Otherwise ▶ 308

692

If you have the codeword **Robber**, lose it unless you also have the codeword **Recursive**.

'What a quandary,' says Autolycus, stroking his chin. 'If I kill you that's just a temporary setback where you're concerned, I hear. And anyway murder isn't my style. But you see what a difficult position you've put me in.'

'You could just return what you stole from me,' you say.

He gives a delighted laugh. 'You're not in a great negotiating position, my friend. I was thinking of a transaction in the other direction. You'd be recompensing me for having to find a new hideout, after all.'

If you have any attribute-boosting items such as **winged sandals (GRACE +2)** he takes them. If not he takes half of all possessions you are carrying, rounded up; you get to pick which items he takes. He also takes any money you have on you.

'I'm not greedy,' he says, 'but a man's got to make a living.'

He ties you up and he and the robot woman hastily pack a few belongings and leave. A few hours later the real caretaker looks into the room. She is a pinch-faced woman with an unhealthily pallid complexion and a shock of black hair like an untidy brush. 'I've come for the rent,' she says indignantly.

'Too bad. I don't think Autolycus is coming back.'

She grudgingly unties you, taking it almost as your fault that she's lost a tenant. Perhaps in a way it is.

▶ 771

693

You grab the watchman's hand and push his wrist into the spectre's grasp. Blindly it seizes hold and pulls him down. Ignoring his cries of terror you climb over him to get back to safety. Rolling across the dew-soaked grass, you see the watchman's flailing feet disappear over the lip of the grave in a cascade of earth.

The spectre must not realize its mistake, or perhaps it was satisfied with any death. Either way, the fresh soil of the grave trembles for a moment and then goes still.

Your split-second decision may have been the rational one, both for yourself and the world, but the gods are unimpressed. They value honour and courage over cold calculation. Lose 5 Glory.

Still, you are alive. Even the dank evening air smells sweet as you head back to the gate and into the teeming crowds outside.

▶ 613

694

'I'm sorry for the inconvenience,' says Pug as the night watchmen lead him off to prison.

'What do you want done with him, your grace?' the officer asks you. 'Beating? Torture? Or for a little extra he could meet with an accident while resisting arrest.'

If you want to bribe them to mete out rough justice, the tariff is 10 pyr for a beating, 25 pyr for torture, or 50 pyr for a fatality. Cross off any money you are spending – or you can disappoint the watchmen and leave Pug's fate for the magistrates to decide.

Closing the door, you head upstairs to bed.

▶ 97

695

Note **88** as your Current Location, then ▶ 1269 and tick the box next to the Tomb of Hope. From now on you will always be able to find your way back here.

696

'Got any saffron?'

Naft almost drops his pen at that. 'Saffron is pretty expensive.'

'You can't get it, then?'

'I can get it. How much do you need?'

'A bag about this big.' His eyes are already close to popping when you add, 'This would be a regular monthly order if you can manage it.'

'That's…' He licks his thin lips. 'It will come to 5000 pyr per bag.'

'I'll need to see a sample before I commit,' you say nonchalantly. 'Just to verify the quality, you understand.'

'Wait right here.' He places his pen down on the desk and darts out of the office. Glancing out of the window you see him hurrying across the loading yard almost rubbing his hands in glee.

► 1066

697

'All I'm going to say,' growls the head, 'is that things are rarely quite what they seem even when you're awake, and that goes double for dreams.'

'So I shouldn't take the job?'

'I'm just here to give information. You want advice, go see your mum. But if you keep your wits about you then it's possible to get something useful from any experience. Just leave your preconceptions at the door.'

The merchant is impatient for your answer. 'Will you help me?' he says in a hushed voice thick with emotion.

Ask him what you'd need to do ► 113

Refuse and leave ► 515

698

Nicomachus takes you to the park and points out an old blind veteran sitting on a marble bench beside a pond. 'That's Ptolemos. Don't let his gruff manner put you off.'

'Oh, I'm used to you, Uncle.'

'I'm a cream-puff in comparison. OK then, you can let me know later how you get on.'

'Are you not coming to say hello?'

'Last time I parted ways with Ptolemos, we swore to kill each other. Can't even remember what the argument was about now, but seeing as we have one good eye between the two of us there's no sense in raking up the past.'

You join Ptolemos on the bench. At first it's hard to strike up a conversation, but his tongue is loosened by the mention of Iskandria.

'Must've been a sight to behold in the old days,' he says. 'Everyone's heard those tales. All gone now, of course. The city walls fell long ago. Nothing much to see except a few overgrown stones and miles and miles of mud flats.'

'What about the Myrmidons?'

'The people there now, I suppose they're what's left of the Myrmidons. Good job their ancestors can't see them. A rabble of goat herders, beachcombers, mudlarks and starving farmers. They make a few coins taking tourists round the ruins and spinning yarns about the past.' He gives a wry chuckle. 'Still, I'm one to talk.'

'Seems a sad end for a proud race.'

'Lesson for us all, kid. You're young, you think strength and glory are everything. But the river of life, it dries up.'

'That was the Great River, right? Was there a curse or something? Some reason it went away?'

'Don't know. An old mate of mine, name of Loutro, he was always talking about greening the desert.'

'How?'

'Oh, he was like you. Looking for curses and portents when most of the time the shit that happens is just random. He had a madcap notion that some ritual to some goddess would bring the river back. Hah, it's been nothing but a trickle of piss in the sand for centuries now.'

'Did he ever do the ritual?'

'Always had an excuse. Special items he needed to collect first. Guess he never found them, as Iskandria is still a stinking ruin on the mudflats last I heard.'

You get up to leave. 'Where would I find him, this Loutro?'

'Down Notus way, if you're serious. Near a lake somewhere I should think. He never did care for sand.' As you walk away he calls after you, 'If you see him, don't forget to come by and tell me about it sometime.

Get the codeword *Ripple* and ► 575

699

You gaze up into the blackness of the tower. Who knows how far it is to the top?

'You could be right,' you agree. 'Got any better ideas?'

If you have **Vulcan's diadem** ► 959

If not but you have the codeword *Rice* ► 1003

Otherwise ► 392

700

In the trance-like fury of battle, even as your limbs react with years of training to parry, slice and crush your enemies, your mind drifts back to a story you were told in childhood. A great hero – was it Jason? Odysseus? – faced unstoppable hordes of sea monsters that were swarming over the side of his vessel.

Yes. It comes to you in a flash. 'Knock out the rail!'

'Huh?' grunts the Minotaur.

He slams his axe into the maw of a leaping werebeast. As he sees what you're doing, the plan makes sense. You smash one end of the rail as the Minotaur smashes the other, and the whole lot goes crashing over the side taking scores of your opponents with it.

'That's only going to buy us a few seconds,' says the Minotaur.

'That's all we needed.'

▶ 1162

701

'Oh yes,' he says, licking his lips. 'Perhaps I'll watch. What savage rites do you Amazons get up to, eh? Cavorting naked before your voluptuous idols, no doubt, to lascivious drumbeats and the strumming of a lyre?'

'Sorry to disappoint. It's just the same kind of praying you Achaeans do, and to the same gods.'

'Huh. You could pretend, at least. No pillow talk, that's the trouble with you Amazon bitches.'

Scowling petulantly, he summons the seer, Calchas, and tells him to take you to see the priests.

▶ 309

702

Get the codeword **Remedy**.

There's a blinding flash and it feels like you've been lifted into the air and flung back by a giant invisible fist. Everything sounds muffled as though your head is wrapped in cotton wool. When you try to get up you find you've been pinned by a broken roof beam. The entire outer wall of the cell has been blasted out and Daedalus is lying in a spreading pool of blood. There's a gaping hole in his chest where he was holding the casket when it exploded. He's groaning so he must still be alive, but maybe not for long.

Shouts and running footsteps break through the ringing din in your ears. You squirm out of sight in the rubble as guards burst in. While they are busy checking on Daedalus, you extricate yourself from the fallen beam and limp down the stairs.

You pass a couple of guards but you are so covered with mortar dust and blood that they don't realize you're not one of them.

'Explosion...' you mutter, pointing up the stairs. You stagger on till you find the door to the outside, steadying yourself against the alley wall till you are back out on the main street.

Tick the Wound box on your Adventure Sheet if you were not injured already. You notice that the metal chrysalis in your pocket has turned back into a **bronze butterfly**, so restore that to your list of possessions and then ▶ 63

703

You dive back, roll, and come up in a crouch. Tritona moves closer, seeming to glide across the room. As you manoeuvre to get in a better position to evade her next attack, you get a shock. Lying on the bed, tossing and crying out in the throes of a bad dream, you see – yourself!

It dawns on you. Your paralysis when trying to attack Tritona, your sluggish reactions, the strange drifting way she moves... You are still asleep. You're dreaming all of this.

You tear away the bedclothes, willing yourself to truly wake up. Instantly you are back in the bed, struggling against the torpor that threatens to drag you down into oblivion. With a sob you leap up, forcing your eyes open. Now you are really awake and you can fight Tritona without any of her hypnotic dream-tricks.

▶ 114

704

You still have two of the creatures to deal with. Here in the bright light of the ballroom they look like monstrously magnified crane flies, their rugose plate armour covered with ridges of razor-sharp spikes that could slice you open with ease.

Make a STRENGTH or GRACE roll (your choice) at difficulty 7.

Succeed ▶ 1399
Fail ▶ 1604

705

He strokes the **dolphin skin** between his fingers. 'Nice leather, this. I can give you 200 pyr for it right now, or maybe you'd rather have credit on a future purchase?'

Take the cash ▶ 1447
Take the credit ▶ 1372
No deal ▶ 828

706

'Now pay attention,' says the head. 'The other second will want to discuss the weapons and armour, and he'll be trying to get any advantage he can. Your man is of slighter build than his opponent, so you shouldn't agree to anything heavier than medium armour.'

'And weapons?'

'Tekto is one of the best swordsmen in the city. You can work out the rest for yourself – I have some cogitations I need to get back to.'

▶ 1471

707

Weightless inside the floating cocoon of light, you are carried into the wall and through the solid bedrock. Time and distance pass in ghostly silence until at last you emerge from a cavern wall. The brimstone stink tells you this is Hades even before you see the familiar broken chains that once trapped Prometheus.

On the uneven rocky floor there are crushed bones, broken wings bigger than a yacht's sails, huge scattered feathers rusty with dried blood – and there, strangely swollen, the eagle's stomach.

You need both hands to lift it. It is like a pouch of cured leather containing something that quivers with a faint pulse. What could Daedalus want with this?

The golden beetles rest to recover their energy, then rise into the air and circle you faster and faster, weaving the cocoon of light in which you are borne back through the cavern walls and the long stretches of magma and rock until you see the sewer pipes and brick foundations of Vulcan City.

You float back up to Daedalus's workshop and as the beetles coagulate back into their metal chrysalis you feel your weight and substance returning. With a grimace you dump the eagle's stomach on a bench.

'Can't think what you want with that.'

Daedalus prods it with a metal probe. 'I'll tell you next time you come. Little idea of mine. It's a long shot, but if it pans out we'll have something pretty special.'

You use the golden beetles once more to float up through the ground, emerging in a deserted side street a safe distance from Daedalus's secret hideout.

▶ 63

708

Tomyios skips ahead of you and flings something down on the steps. Your feet shoot from under you. Thrown backwards, you land with a jarring impact that cracks several ribs. Tick your Wound box if you weren't already injured.

Tomyios giggles and prances around above you, pointing at a banana skin on the stairs. 'Arse over tit!' he sniggers. 'Should be an elf and safety warning.'

You've no time to deal with him now. The hordes of night creatures are right behind you. You lurch painfully to your feet and rush past him.

Pursued by flying demons, werewolves and vampires, you race up the stairs. Higher and higher. Your breath comes in hot ragged gasps. Your leg muscles are on fire. A cupola covers the stairwell above. Through the lantern at its peak comes gusts of cold night air. Just ahead, at the top of

the stairs, there's a door. It must lead to the roof. You lunge towards it.

Delete Tomyios from the Companion box on your Adventure Sheet and ▶ 838

709

Hard stone presses into your back. You are lying on a marble dais. Rising, the first thing you see is a mural of the battlefield at Ilion lit by flickering torches. You are in a circular chamber with a vaulted roof whose air currents stir sluggishly with the mustiness of undisturbed aeons.

'Who are you?'

For a moment you think it was an echo. You turn to see yourself – younger, but recognizably your own face.

'My name is forgotten,' you say, to save explanations.

You remember this meeting. Why didn't you recognize yourself then? The gods have cursed you to be erased from history. Even memory of your own features must have vanished immediately from your memory. When you spoke just now, your earlier self took that to be your name.

'*You* are the Lost Hero.'

'So it seems. Back to redeem myself in the eyes of the gods.'

'This horn… can I use it to summon you?'

You shake your head. You won't need any horn, but to fit with what happened already you say, 'Sure. When the time comes, blow it and I'll be there.'

Nodding, your earlier self fades away. Of course, that too is just how it happened before. You lie back on the dais. You are caparisoned in the Olympian armour and shield forged for Achilles.

Add the **Panoply of the Lost Hero** to your possessions if it wasn't listed there already. Also delete the codeword *Nanny*, then ▶ 73

710

A silver candelabrum stands in the middle of the long banqueting table. On the white marble behind you are puddles of rainwater blown in through the open doors. You watch the candle flames flickering in the wind. They are reflected in the wall-length mirror behind the table.

You see your own reflection, your hand reaching out over the candle. Neither the reflection nor yourself feels anything – of course, because it is just a dream.

Make an INGENUITY roll at difficulty 11 to wake up.

Wide awake   ▶ 906
Still snoring   ▶ 1308

711

Something's not right. You sense it the moment you turn the corner into the street. It's there in the taut, downcast faces of the people coming towards you, and in the way those walking ahead of you suddenly falter in their stride, fall silent, and hurry past on the other side of the road.

The cause is a young officer of the Black Guard, his lacquered armour shining like ink in the sunlight, his sword a sliver of obsidian metal, his cloak a pool of shadow where he sits at a café table staring glumly at a glass of retsina. His proud helm with its sable plume sits in the dust at his feet like a discarded flowerpot.

A few local kids have gathered in an alleyway from where they are able to gawp at him. The adults have the sense to say nothing and move on quickly. At the best of times ordinary people are never eager to attract the attention of one of the elite troops of the city, but the circumstances here are so strange to send a chill of dread right along the street. You might expect to see a Black Guardsman strutting arrogantly by, or snapping his fingers to demand instant compliance from a citizen, or contemptuously dragging some whimpering miscreant to the law court – but to encounter one so sunk in thought as to forget his usual dignity and sit drinking in the street, that's unprecedented. It's like coming across one of the gods picking his nose.

Stop and talk to him   ▶ **1013**

It's none of your business   ▶ **1534**

712

Your friend grabs your arm and pulls you to safety. 'Sorry,' they say, as a slap round your face brings you back to your senses. You watch aghast as the rug flops and tumbles down a shaft into darkness. From far below comes a gust of damp, foetid air.

You stride across the room. Marija sighs. The fight has gone out of her now; she sees the game is up. 'Can't blame a girl for trying,' she says. 'Just remember your promise. Make it quick.'

She raises her chin proudly and you deliver the *coup de grâce*.

▶ **479**

713

If you have the title **Paladin** ▶ **899**

Otherwise ▶ **1337**

714

All eyes are on you. You shrug and take hold of the rope, nonchalantly striking a dashing pose. 'Well, I wasn't doing anything else this afternoon,' you say casually, scaling the rope until your head is just below the ceiling. Where the top of the rope disappears into empty air, you can feel an icy draught.

As you climb the last couple of metres, the murmuring of voices is cut off. Instead of the ceiling of Lady Pemphreda's apartment, above your head now is the high vault of an alien sky. Swirls of white and blue extend off to infinity.

If you have the codeword *Quiver* ▶ **1276**

Otherwise ▶ **1627**

715

If you have the **Face of Wisdom (INGENUITY +3)** and this box ❑ is empty, tick it and ▶ **1599**

Otherwise ▶ **1642**

716

Traders from all over the world come to the city to offer their wares: exotic spices and precious metals from Notus; minerals, ivory and furs from Boreas; herbs and scented woods from Arcadia; and even doomful grave goods and oath-binding Styx water from the melancholy fastness of Lord Hades.

As well as commerce, the marketplace serves as a nexus of news, gossip, jokes and stories. Old friends greet each other with glad cries, swapping reminiscences over a jug of wine. Old foes eye each other sourly, laying out the shelves of their competing stalls as though arraying armies for battle. Romances blossom, rivalries smoulder, fortunes ebb and flow. Here is all of life.

If you don't have the codeword *Reverie* and this box ❑ is empty, tick it now and set **716** as your Current Location, then ▶ **1269** and put a tick in the box there next to the market. Otherwise read on.

If you have the codeword *Rectangle* and this box ❑ is empty, tick it and ▶ **484**

Otherwise, if you have the codeword *Roar* ▶ **741**

Otherwise:

Invest in a trade caravan or check on an investment you made previously ▶ **270**

Buy and sell ▶ **758**

Listen for gossip ▶ **1414**

Leave the market ▶ **613**

717

Hot reeking breath and fetid spittle spray on your face as the werewolf barges you to the ground. Its jaws snap at your failing arms. Behind it, the rest of the horde are closing in with whoops of mad glee.

If your Wound box is ticked ▶ **882**

If you weren't already injured, tick the Wound box now and ▶ **1286**

718

'Why ask me to tell you of Arcadia when you can travel there in moments?'

'I can?'

'Take the wings worn by Daedalus's son to the tower they call Pan's Column.'

You press her with more questions, but her trance has deepened. She no longer sees or hears you. All her attention is now on another world. You quietly leave.

▶ **510**

719

'Can I help you?' you say drily.

The intruder is a man in early middle age. As you entered he was rifling through the drawers of your desk. At least he has the decency to look embarrassed.

'It's rather late to be visiting,' he says.

'Quite. I see you let yourself in.' You nod towards the open window behind him.

'The servants had all gone to bed. I didn't want to be a fuss.' He brushes at the desktop as if wiping away a speck of dust.

You take note of the long, dextrous fingers. 'You could have been a musician instead of a burglar.'

He gives a hollow laugh, and you see the sadness in his eyes. 'You have a keen eye. In fact I was an artist. In a roundabout way that's why I'm here tonight.'

Listen to his story   ▶ **811**

Call the night watch to arrest him   ▶ **1241**

720

A deathly chill permeates the air. Your breath billows in steamy clouds. A slender figure flits from behind a shattered column. Her pale blue skin and icicle hair are as striking as the waves of cold that flow off her.

'I know nothing of mercy,' Evadne says to you. 'Mine is the strength of glaciers and the anger of an Arctic sea. Show me your enemies and I will unleash all my power against them.'

If you have the codeword *Nanny* ▶ **1637**

Otherwise ▶ **1183**

721

If you have the codeword *Recursive* ▶ **1425**; otherwise read on.

As you stand in the street you become aware that people are edging away. You turn to see a group of rough-looking youths swaggering towards you. They are armed with heavy wooden clubs which they slap meaningfully as they look you up and down.

'Can I help you lads?'

'We're collecting taxes for Zinc,' says the leader of the pack.

'And dealing out lumps for those that won't pay,' says his right-hand man, caressing the polished wood of his club.

'It's 10 pyr,' puts in another. 'Cough up.'

What's your reply?

'OK then.'   Cross off 10 pyr and ▶ **1425**

'Piss off.'   ▶ **1118**

722

You are on the Avenue of the Anvil, which runs from the Forum to the South Gate of the city.

To go straight to a city location that you already know about, note **63** as your Current Location, then ▶ **1432**

Or you can go:

North ▶ **1642**

South ▶ **555**

To the prison ▶ **1089**

Into the Grumbles ▶ **771**

To the palace (only if you have the codeword *Rendezvous*) ▶ **1323**

To the well (only if you have the codeword *Ruby*) ▶ **872**

723

The keening of the wind as it sweeps up shattered chimneys and through broken windows sounds like a lament for the city that lies in ruins all around you.

Note **1387** as your Current Location and then ▶ **549**

724

If this box ☐ is empty, tick it and ▶ **1482**

If it was already ticked, roll a die:

score 1-4   ▶ **1482**

score 5-6   ▶ **617**

725

'You think they want it for cooking?' says the Face of Wisdom.

'What else?'

'To lubricate machinery, that's its main use. Take it from one who thinks a lot about these things.'

'Erifili did say something about golden robot women.'

'Careful, you're almost thinking for yourself. OK, if you want to throw a spanner in Autolycus's works, grab a handful of grit and mix it into the jar. That should grind somebody's gears to a standstill.'

Do it   ▶ **949**

Don't   ▶ **76**

726

It's no good. You can't gain altitude. Clawing at the air currents, you skim over the heads of the demonic throng. A vampire reaches up, seizing you in its rigor-hard arms. A were-creature pounces. It snaps at the wings, tearing out a mouthful of feathers. The buckles of the harness strain and give way. You fall with numbing impact to the roof.

Tick the Wound box on your Adventure Sheet if it was not ticked already, then ▶ **882**

727

If you have the title **Plaything of Agamemnon** but don't have the codeword *Royal* ▶ **895**

Otherwise, if you have the codeword *Rage* ▶ **1354**

Otherwise ▶ **327**

728

Zoë introduces you to her Band of Gold, a group of youthful heroes whom she freed from the basilisk's curse.

'We have pledged our undying love to the princess,' declares one handsome youth.

'What, *all* of you?'

'It's platonic,' says Zoë, blushing.

You put your hand on her shoulder. 'In that case, deal me in. You showed up just in the nick of time. I don't think we'd have got away otherwise.'

'Couldn't let you hog all the fun, could I?'

Ancaeus comes over to shake her hand. 'It's a good job you managed to get aboard. We couldn't have hung around.'

▶ **231**

729

You are chatting to the Minotaur a while later when the cat comes shooting out of the hold with a startled yowl.

'He's just seen the biggest rat of his life,' laughs one of the sailors.

You shake your head. 'Not a rat. Something much nastier.'

'Never a dull moment on this boat, eh?' says the Minotaur, hefting his axe. He advances to the open hatch and gazes down into the hold. 'Yuck.'

You peer down. The hold is teeming with a swarm of insect larvae, scores of them. They look like woodlice the size of hedgehogs.

'That's that mutha of a monster was doing down there,' says the Minotaur. 'Laying eggs.'

'They're trying to get out,' you notice. 'Climbing up the bulkhead, the little bastards.'

Closing the hatch, you let out a few larvae at a time. It's a laborious process, but you manage to kill them all without

anyone getting bitten. And perhaps that's just as well, because you notice their vital juices have etched away the timbers of the deck like acid.

▶ **653**

730

You shove him roughly away. He staggers back a few paces, then stops and looks at you with an uncertain expression.

'Beat it. Get out of here. Find your girl and take off.'

'But...' He looks around and you can see he wants to run, but he's torn. 'Why are you doing this? Won't you be in hot water with Zinc for letting me go?'

'I'll tell him you'd already scarpered before I got here.'

Kleistro doesn't need any more persuasion. His qualms of guilt assuaged, he turns and races off down the street like a wild animal given its freedom.

You're not sure what to tell Zinc. Probably a lie. There is some strange bond between the two of you which means you don't think he'd punish you for failing – but why push your luck?

▶ **161**

731

'So you're saying I should move on to give my children and grandchildren a chance? That it's like a tally, and each new living soul means another one has to croak?'

'Well, that is one way to look at it. If none of the dead moved on, the city would soon get overcrowded.'

He nods, bloodless lips twitching in a triumphant smirk. 'Fine. Then let one of my no-good kids get in the grave and I'll keep on living.'

If Galatea is with you and you want her advice ▶ **521**

If you possess the **Face of Wisdom** (INGENUITY +3) and want to consult it ▶ **1467**

Otherwise ▶ **483**

732

'The eyes!' she shouts hoarsely. 'Even its glare is toxic, and to touch it can bring death, though its own blood is an antidote to most ailments.'

'All that is common knowledge,' you point out.

She comes out of her trance and speaks conversationally. 'Do you know that the cockatrice itself can be poisoned by weasel blood? Look for a wedding party.'

'OK... that's counter-intuitive.'

'Weasels at weddings, ferrets at funerals. Everyone knows that too. Anyway, your time's up. Next!'

You bow and return to the main hall of the temple.

▶ **510**

733

'You'll be eager to hear all about our last trip,' says the merchant in charge of the caravan.

To find out how well your investment has done, roll two dice. Add 2 to the score if you have the codeword *Pure*. Subtract 1 if your INGENUITY is 0 or less.

score 2-3	Lose entire sum invested
score 4	Lose 75%
score 5	Lose 50%
score 6	Lose 25%
score 7	Lose 10%
score 8	No gain or loss
score 9	Profit of 10%
score 10	Profit of 20%
score 11+	Profit of 50%

Make a note of any gain or loss, then ▶ **1035**, where you can withdraw the sum recorded in the box after adjusting it according to the result you just rolled.

734

Sakan bends down to pick up the lava gems. He's right next to you but he thinks you're dead to the world. You sit up and in the same fluid motion you push a thin dagger into his ear. He shudders, clutching at the coins and gems, then falls sprawling in the dirt, gives a spasm, and lies still.

You leave the body where it lies. If any militia patrol comes this way they'll take him to be a drunk sleeping it off, so the murder won't be discovered till the morning. Recovering the treasure you used as bait, you hurry away from the scene of the crime.

Get the codeword *Rock* and ▶ **1432**

735

Don't tick any of the boxes below unless you were told to do so in the section you just turned from.

You can talk to anyone below whose box is not ticked.

❑ Nestor   ▶ **933**
❑ Thersites   ▶ **1291**
❑ Odysseus   ▶ **1489**

If all three boxes are now ticked, or if you don't want to talk to any of them ▶ **650**

736

Broken shards of pottery crunch underfoot. You pass buildings that were once thriving smithies, now gutted by fire. Many of the high-peaked roofs show as skeletal timbers, the ancient lichen-grown tiles swept away by storm winds.

If you have the codeword *Ruby* ▶ **7**
Otherwise ▶ **472**

737

'This time I will only hurt you,' spits Oizys. 'Just pain. Just this once, as a warning.'

A flaring aura of light blots out your vision for a moment, like acid dripped on a painting. The pain comes a moment later, a sensation of tearing sinew that ripples through your whole body.

Tick the Wound box on your Adventure Sheet if you were not already injured.

'You know I won't kill you,' moans Oizys ecstatically, aroused by your gasp of pain. 'You can't serve my mistress if you're dead. But I can do worse. I can wither your nerves so that you tremble with uncontrollable palsy. I can dull your wits so that you struggle to remember your own name. I can weaken your limbs till you dodder like a cripple. I can disfigure you so that your closest friends would shudder to look you in the face. Remember that, mortal, next time you think of treachery.'

▶ **1446**

738

❑ ❑

Do not tick either of the boxes unless you were told to do so in the section you just turned from.

Neither of the boxes is ticked	▶ **1111**
One box is now ticked	▶ **956**
Two boxes are ticked	▶ **644**

739

You show him some simple moves, really just tricks such as getting in close so that your opponent can't see to block a blow.

'Don't assume these techniques will always work,' you tell him. 'The best I can say is that at least anyone who picks on you will know they've been in a fight.'

As it turns out, he never has to use what you've taught him. Just the training alone is enough to give him a new sense of confidence. Sensing that, Nihakos gives up bullying him, going off to find a weaker victim.

If you wish, you can adjust any one of your attributes by +1 and adjust another by −1.

▶ **247**

740

'Who says I'm an outsider?'

'Get it over with,' he snarls.

'I mean it. Can you recruit new Murmillos?'

'Murmillones.'

'Never mind the grammar lesson,' you say, grinding your heel against his neck. 'I'm offering you a chance to keep both your life and your honour.'

The obol finally drops. 'Yes, I can induct you as a Murmillo. Only associate membership, mind.'

'But then I could legitimately carry the standard, right? We could say I'm holding it for you.'

He agrees. Get the title **Murmillo Recruit** and make a note next to the **fish-headed standard** that you will lose 5 Glory if you ever sell it.

You bid farewell to the Murmillo, whose name is Atillus, and return to the city.

▶ **555**

741

The market is usually packed shoulder-to-shoulder with jostling crowds of traders and shoppers. This time you notice them open up to give one particular figure a wide berth. It's Lord Xechasiaris.

He's bending to look at a mule hitched to a wagon full of salted fish from Notus. 'And how long have you been doing this job?' he asks it.

You square your shoulders and stride over to him. This won't be easy.

Lose the codeword *Roar* and ▶ **1011**

742

You are woken in the small hours by the metal head, which you are in the habit of leaving on your bedside table. 'Can't you sleep?' it says.

You sit up and light a candle. 'Not if you insist on talking to yourself.'

'I never sleep,' it says. 'What would I dream of, after all? I just watch the curtains and think of what's out there.'

'The city?' You wish the head would shut up and let you doze off.

'The city now isn't the same as the city in the daytime. Night is a place with its own inhabitants, greatest of which are troubled sleep and unresting death. You can forget them during the day, but after dark they move nearer, like prowling predators who have the scent of the kill.'

Now you are fully alert. It's not like the head to speak poetically, and that's worrying. 'What are you getting at?' you ask it.

'Eschatology. The end of days. Night reigned before anything else. Not only before this constructed world of Vulcan's, but before the world of men and even before the world of myth.'

You look at the curtains, already showing a paler outline as the dawn creeps nearer. 'Soon it'll be day,' you tell it. 'Things will look better then.'

'That's not true night,' says the head with something very like a sneer in its tinny voice. 'It gets dark, it gets light, but those are weak reflections of the archetypal truth. Night is all-encompassing oblivion, an end to thought. Do you see why even I fear it? It was night before the cosmos was born. Utter nothingness. This world will sink into it like a pebble into the deepest ocean, and then will be gone forever.'

You snuff the candle and pull the pillow over your head, determined to snatch a little sleep in the few remaining hours of the night. But even though the head says nothing more, sleep does not come and at daybreak you are tired and restless with undefined cares.

▶ **97**

743

Remove the **copper casket of doom** from your list of possessions.

'Curious little doohickey,' says Daedalus, turning the box in his hands. 'What's this combination puzzle? Oh, I get it. The tiles are sized according to a Fibonacci series. Ingenious. So the tile to open it would be this one here.'

He's about to press it.

Warn him   ▶ **1124**
Dive for cover   ▶ **702**

744

Something stirs in your memory. The crack of burning logs in the hearth. For a moment you can almost smell the sharp woodsmoke curling up. It was a fireside tale, the murmur of the storyteller's voice evoking images of a ship sailing through storm clouds high over city rooftops. You sat on their knee watching the flames paint pictures. But who was that? An aunt? An uncle?

A gust of cold wind brings you back to reality. The door to the stairs is splintering. Pallid claw-like fingers are reaching through. Which way will you flee?

Across the roof   ▶ **1185**
Up onto the dome   ▶ **759**

745

'Never figured you for a quitter,' you say. 'An ornery old cuss, sure. But not a coward.'

His eyes flash at that but he bites back his anger. 'I'm the last surviving Argonaut. Got that way by knowing when to cut bait.'

'You can run away if you want. I'm not giving up on the war just yet.' You turn to the Minotaur. 'What about you, beefy? Still got the stomach for a fight?'

He gives a noncommittal grunt. 'Don't need to decide just yet. We'll be putting in at the Island of the Dawn to resupply. Let's talk about it then.'

▶ **781**

746

You drift through regions of rock and magma. There is no sense of acceleration so it is hard to say how fast you're travelling, but you get the impression of flitting across many leagues at incredible speed.

Through the haze of golden light you see sewer pipes, buried ruins, debris from forgotten ages, then you are rising past cellars and up through the street. You come to rest in a deserted alley. The rooftops of the city show narrow chinks of grey sky.

The beetles stop spinning around you and the cocoon dissolves. Clustering together, they combine to form the metal chrysalis, which you slip into your pocket in case you'll need it again.

▶ 63

747

'If you wear Vulcan's diadem, the workshop will open its door to you.'

'But the diadem is missing. The one I saw at the ball was a fake.'

Eos nods. 'Find the one who stole it.'

'They could be anywhere!'

'Finding her is not the hard part,' says Eos. 'But then you must convince her to admit to the theft.'

Ask her something else ▶ 1292
It's time to go ▶ 90

748

'Quiet!' hisses a man in torn priestly robes. 'Can't you hear?'

Everyone stops moving – even the two or three people who had gone to help the trapped woman. There's just the whistle of the wind and the woman's occasional grunts of pain.

'There!' says the priest.

You hear it now. A strange piping ululation sustained by multiple instruments. Or are they voices?

'It's in the breeze! It's coming!' shrieks the priest. And with that they all take to their heels.

The woman still lies trapped under a heavy roof timber. Alone, you could never hope to shift it. You meet her gaze.

'Go,' she whispers. 'Save yourself.'

▶ 233

749

You have a meeting with a noblewoman, Lady Himera, who swears you to secrecy.

'It is a delicate situation,' she begins. 'In my youth I wrote letters to a man I loved. I was too candid in expressing my sentiments. Now these letters have come to light. They threaten my reputation at just the moment that my husband is trying for election among the Syndics.'

'Can you buy the letters back?'

'The man who has them is called Pemon. He wants money, but on a long lease rather than a purchase agreement, if you take my meaning.'

'He's blackmailing you.'

'Ugly word. Will you go to see him? Persuade him to give up the letters.'

'For money?'

She draws a lacquered nail along her elegantly painted eyebrow. 'I'll pay to get them back if I must. Perhaps you'll think of other arguments, though.'

'Where will I find him?'

'He has a bookshop near the Tower of Ice.' She rings a small bell. 'The servant will see you out.'

Get the codeword *Rumour* and ▶ 1642

750

A wintry chill has replaced the summery evening warmth of a few minutes ago. The canvas of the pavilions billows and snaps in the wind. The rose bushes sway, looking less flamboyantly colourful now as the setting sun slides behind mournful clouds.

Glancing suspiciously at the sky, most of the ball guests are heading for the shelter of the colonnade. 'I'm sure I felt a spot of rain,' somebody says in a tone of disbelief. You follow the others into the ballroom.

▶ 552

751

Note **674** as your Current Location, then ▶ **1269** and tick the box next to the Necropolis. From now on you will always be able to find your way back here.

752

You lunge at her. The point of the blade digs into her yielding white skin and for a moment you think it will penetrate. Instead it snaps off.

'I am more than royalty,' she laughs. 'More even than gods.'

Her sword scythes around, splitting your armour which falls in clanging fragments to the ground. Delete the **Panoply of the Lost Hero** and tick the Wound box on your Adventure Sheet if it was not ticked already. If it was already ticked, get the codeword *Rug*.

If you have the **Eye of Hyperion** and want to use it ▶ 1083

If you have the **tapestry of Arachne** and want to use that ▶ 273

Otherwise ▶ 182

753

'I know what it's like to be plunged in endless night,' she says. 'That's how it feels for ever and ever before the spark of life gets put into you. Is that what you'd wish on everybody?'

'Let's not be lectured to by an uppity statue,' says Hypnos. With the slightest of gestures he waves away Galatea's humanity, transforming her back into ivory. She is frozen in the act of reaching to touch your hand.

Remove Galatea from the Companion box on your Adventure Sheet. Does her fate make you change your mind about siding with Nyx?

Yes   ▶ 812
Not at all   ▶ 688

754

The wig-sellers open box after box, but the head sees nothing that strikes its fancy. There are hairpieces that look like meringues, like towers of candy floss, like plaster ziggurats (both ways up), and a spherical wig that seems to be made of red feathers and twists of gold wire.

'None of them are quite me,' gripes the head.

By now you've tried all the shops but one. The bell tinkles as you open the door. There is a strong smell of waxed wood but the shelves are bare. At a table in the middle of the store sits the thinnest man you have ever seen. His lean body is dwarfed by the massive wig he wears, a rainbow-dyed confection that looks more like a cake than a hairpiece.

'Are you a wig-seller?' you ask.

'No,' he says, tilting his head back and sighting along his nose. 'Those other shops deal in mere wigs. I am a *perruquier*.'

'But where's your stock?' You indicate the empty shelves.

He gets up and prances towards you like a huge cricket. 'The creations are not on display.'

'But how will I know which to buy?'

'I will tell you the peruke you need. Is it for your own cranium?'

'No, it's for this grumpy brass noggin.'

He studies the head for a moment. 'I have just the thing.'

He disappears into the back room and returns moments later holding what you take to be a large sleeping rabbit. On closer inspection it proves to be a silky brown wig with dangling corkscrew curls.

'That's the one,' says the head.

'Of course,' says the perruquier loftily. 'Shall I wrap it?'

'I'll wear it!' says the head.

'Hang on,' you say. 'First of all, what's the price?'

The perruquier contorts his face into a lean mask of disgust. 'Oh, so soon we get to the matter of filthy lucre.'

'Cut the spiel. You've got a sale. Just tell me how many pyr you want for it?'

'Pardon?' He bares his teeth in revulsion. 'I would not soil my hands with those ridiculous coins, much less sully my lips by repeating the name. If you have no proper currency, to wit obols, I will take three lava gems instead.'

Buy the wig; cross off 3 **lava gems** and ▶ 173
Leave the shop ▶ 414

755

Here you make your stand, high above the city as the storm flares and pounds from one edge of the world to the other. Gibbering insanely, the hordes of night creatures clamber over each other to crest the dome.

There is nowhere to retreat. No escape route. Outnumbered, you cannot hold them off. They swarm over you. The stench of carrion-breath and grave-soil makes you choke. Dragged off your feet, you tumble down the side of the dome into the press of howling monsters.

▶ 882

756

Entering the darkened Palace of the Syndics, you pick your way carefully through the gloomy halls and echoing corridors to the assembly chamber. Thick darkness hangs in the air like ink, impenetrable even by the light of Dunamis's lantern. From inside the room you can hear the faint stirring of the larval dreams that you saw forming above each syndic's head. What those dreams will become when they are fully formed you can only guess.

Step forth into the darkness ▶ 294
Turn back ▶ 820

757

Your younger brother speaks to you. He is a shadow on the wall, and his voice is as hollow as wind in the chimney. 'Who'd go up on a roof without an hourglass?' he moans. 'You wouldn't know when it was time to jump.'

'I don't understand,' you say. 'Is that a riddle?'

'If it's riddles you want, see a sphinx. See all three.'

His voice rises to a bone-chilling shriek. Unable to listen any longer, you race outside. You thought the sun was shining, but above you the vault of the sky is midnight blue, the stars like white pollen. A nightingale sings nearby.

▶ 301

758

You can buy and sell items at the following prices:

	To buy	To sell
Astrarium	–	200 pyr
Bucket of gypsum	–	70 pyr
Celestial tarbrush	–	600 pyr
Copper ore	140 pyr	70 pyr
Fish-headed standard	–	1000 pyr
Hardwood club	150 pyr	75 pyr
Honey cake	40 pyr	20 pyr
Horn headrest	–	170 pyr
Hornbook	140 pyr	70 pyr
Jar of amaranth oil	60 pyr	40 pyr
Komos cup	–	80 pyr
Laurel wreath	160 pyr	80 pyr
Lava gem	100 pyr	50 pyr
Moon pearls	–	80 pyr
Nemean bagh nakh	–	700 pyr
Pipes of Pan	–	750 pyr
Recurve bow	110 pyr	55 pyr
Sunhat of Hermes	–	750 pyr
Wings of Icarus	–	700 pyr

Leave the market ▶ 613

759

The thunderous clouds boil overhead, their dark mass as heavy as a mountain range suspended in the heavens. As you blunder towards the dome through curtains of icy stinging rain, a sudden, unnatural light shines from within the murky depths of the storm. It is like a portal has opened onto another plane of existence. Through the widening rift you witness a colossal figure pushing its way through into the skies of this realm.

Your instincts tell you it is Thanatos, Death embodied, he whose baleful stare brings ruin with no hope of survival. His long black limbs stretch out, parting the clouds. Alone, you are no match for him. You must flee before he fully materializes.

The door to the stairs crashes open and through it issues a nightmare swarm of pox-eaten vampires and rampant werewolves.

If you have the codewords *Rose* and *Recursive* ▶ 1601
Otherwise ▶ 1197

760

From this high vantage point you can look out across the whole of the region of Boreas. Massive mountains that when seen close comprise unyielding rock and skin-scraping ice, at this distance float on the horizon like smudges of lavender cloud. Indigo lakes and dark green pine forests stretch along the mountain valleys, a strikingly colourful contrast against the snow-covered peaks.

If you have the codeword *Raptor* and both the **wings of Icarus** and some **beeswax** ▶ 1302
Otherwise ▶ 1341

761

Even with Zoë and her band laying into your foes from the rear, their massed ranks are so numerous that they pour from the roof in an incessant dark tide. Were-apes and werewolves leap with frightening agility, balancing on the ship's rail and snapping at you with slavering fangs.

If you have the codeword **Recursive** ▶ **700** now; otherwise read on.

You give yourself in to the pulse-pounding rhythm of battle, laying about you with weapons and anything that comes to hand. One of the werewolves, its side sliced open by a blow, flops to the deck and tries snapping at your legs. You snatch up a belaying pin, smash its skull to pulp, and whirl just in time to parry the attack of a flapping horror that looks like a giant face with leathery wings in place of ears.

Make a STRENGTH roll at difficulty 9.

Succeed ▶ **1592**
Fail ▶ **256**

762

A great crease furrows Prometheus's broad and noble brow. He can see the wisdom in what you say, but his hostility to Zeus and the other gods runs deep. You will need to convince him by making a CHARM roll at difficulty 14. (If your Glory is 18 or more you can add 1 to the number rolled.)

Your words sway him ▶ **421**
They fall on deaf ears ▶ **574**

763

'Thank you,' says the girl, hugging Dydkos's arm. 'If I could tell you the torment my husband has put me through... A husband should be a friend and protector, but he has been more like a sadistic jailer.'

'So you fled into the dreamlands?' you say. You sensed there was something off about the merchant's concern for his wife.

'We are safe here, aren't we, Dydkos?'

The young man nods, placing his hand on hers. 'We are, my love, but if our friend here agrees to help then we needn't hide behind Hypnos's veil forever.'

They look at you imploringly. Will you help?

'Yes. What do you want me to do?' ▶ **1154**
'No. I must go back now.' ▶ **863**

764

❑

If you do not have the codeword **Reverie** and the box above is empty, put a tick in it and ▶ **440**

Otherwise read on.

The tavern consists of a large central hall several storeys high with rooms built out on balconies overlooking the common room. These snugs are connected by a series of wooden staircases that criss-cross the walls of the common room and extend right up to the rafters.

The back wall of the common room is much older than the rest of the building, apparently being the remains of a very ancient temple that still bears carvings in an unknown script – now so blurred that they would be unreadable in any case.

If you do not have the codeword **Rune** and want to ask about the Hero of Temesa ▶ **686**

Otherwise you can:

Pay 10 pyr to hire a snug ▶ **1231**

Go to your strongbox (only if you have the codeword **Rune**) ▶ **532**

Leave the tavern ▶ **1062**

765

'And what's in it for me?' he bellows.

'Apart from saving the lives of hundreds of your men, you mean? Why not try being a leader for once instead of a sleazeball?'

There is silence in the tent. Agamemnon stares at you with a face of thunder. His brother Menelaus has his hand on his sword. Calchas, the seer, backs nervously away. Nestor, the elderly advisor, tries to hide a smile of approval at your words.

Try a CHARM roll at difficulty 9.

Succeed ▶ **1321**
Fail ▶ **1546**

766

You have no quarrel with the people of Ilion, but having been nursed back to health by Achilles you feel duty bound to offer to fight beside him.

If the Current Location recorded on your Adventure Sheet is **140** or **1500** then ▶ **1395**

Otherwise ▶ **548**

767

As he catches sight of his crippled friend, Danu lapses into his native tongue. You know few of the words, but the tone of lament is the same in all languages. Weeping, the two friends embrace each other. They seem to have forgotten you, until Oshi looks up and says, 'May the gods look on you with favour, outlander. You have been a friend to me.'

You shake your head. 'I've done nothing. What can be done?'

Danu takes his friend in his arms and lifts him, carrying him towards the gate to Notus. 'You will not draw your last breath here, my dearest friend. Not in this cesspit of a city.'

'Wait,' you say. 'He doesn't need to die at all.'

Oshi holds up his maimed hand. 'Stay. You have done all I asked of you. Now it falls to Danu to carry me back to the desert. There I can rest my bones and my soul will hunt with my ancestors.'

'You're that ready to die?'

He manages a weak laugh. 'You know better than anyone that death is not the end, and that spirits freed of the weight of earthly flesh can soar among the stars.'

You watch them go towards the city gate. Get the title **Friend of the Nomads**.

To head straight to a city location that you already know about, note **161** as your Current Location, then ▶ **1432**

Or you can go:

North ▶ **333**
South ▶ **570**

768

'You could call it goodwill,' you say. 'Tell me what I want to know and maybe I'll become your newest customer.'

He smiles complacently and turns his attention back to the ledger. 'Betray the confidence of a regular customer in good standing in hope of picking up a bit of walk-in trade? I don't think so.'

'It's only information.'

'Here's some information for you: there's the door.'

If you offer him a 50 pyr bribe ▶ **366**
Otherwise you turn and leave ▶ **1649**

769

You promised the young Guards officer, Viranos, that you would deal with Sakan, the spiteful rival who has been threatening to ruin his reputation. But how?

An obvious way would be to make Sakan himself into a laughing stock. Then nothing he says about Viranos will carry any weight.

Or he could be got out of the way. Perhaps forged orders that will send him on a long voyage where he cannot cause any mischief.

A more certain and permanent solution is simply to kill him, of course, if you have a cold enough heart and steady enough nerve for that.

Ruin his reputation ▶ **1234**
Get him assigned elsewhere ▶ **258**
Murder him ▶ **994**

770

'As a boy, his tutor was Chiron the centaur. He taught Achilles how to wield spear and sword and bow, trained him to run swifter than horses, instructed him in the use of the lyre, and also imparted to him the healing arts that only the centaurs know. If Achilles weren't so important as a front-line fighter, he'd be our chief doctor. I've seen him

replace a man's thumb, almost severed so that it hung by a thread of skin, but he stitched it back and wrapped it in a poultice, and a month later you could barely see the scar.'

'And then there's my own case...'

Nestor nods vigorously. 'When they dragged you from the sea you looked like meat charred on a fire. That one won't want to live, I thought. Yet look now – your skin is without a flaw. The gods must have greatness planned for you, to deliver you to the ministrations of so skilled a healer.'

'I'm not so sure,' you say, gazing out across the grey unending sea. 'The gods have abandoned me in this place, at a time so remote from my own that we do not call it history but myth. What greatness can I achieve here?'

'Perhaps what you learn here you'll take back to your own world. That's the way of the gods, always crooked in their plans. There's no straight path to destiny.'

Ask him something else ▶ **724**
That's all for now ▶ **735**

771

❑

If you do not have the codeword **Reverie** and the box above is empty, put a tick in it and ▶ **1134**

Otherwise read on.

The Grumbles is a confusing rookery of narrow, unpaved lanes lined with ramshackle buildings. Unsavoury types from the four corners of the Vulcanverse have moved in, using planks and rugs to patch up missing sections of roofs and walls, opening up jury-rigged shops, tavernas and food stalls. Knaves, mountebanks and ne'er-do-wells have made the Grumbles their home. It is not safe for ordinary folk. Fortunately, you are not ordinary folk.

If you have the codeword **Rogue** ▶ **1200**; otherwise read on.

Explore the Grumbles ▶ **571**
Exit onto the Street of Knives ▶ **1617**
Exit onto the Avenue of the Anvil ▶ **63**

772

A man approaches and taps you on the arm. 'You have been of service to us in the past,' he says in a confidential whisper.

'And you are – ?'

'We hope you can help out again. It's not a particularly arduous or dangerous undertaking, but it does call for some tact.'

Agree ▶ **927**
Refuse ▶ **187**

773

You notice an opened jar of amaranth oil under the bed and a rag that has been used to clear up some that spilled around the legs of the chair.

'His blankets aren't fake gold,' say the caretaker. 'That's fine Arcady wool. Silk sheets too, look. Damn it, I'm going to start charging him a bit more for this room. Anyway, you want to hang around in case he comes back? Sit down and make yourself comfortable if you like, otherwise I'll lock up again.'

What will you say?

'Fine, I'll wait.' ▶ 922

'I'll come back later.' ▶ 603

774

'There you are!' says a voice. 'We knew we could count on you in a pinch.'

The speaker comes nearer. It's a giant finger as tall as a crane. Of course – Index, foreman of the Dactyls. Behind him are his companions: Thumb, Middle, Ringo and Pinkie.

'What are you guys doing here?' you ask, stunned to see them again after so long.

'We're helping the princess,' says Pinkie bashfully.

'The princess…?'

▶ 184

775

You take one in the face with an elbow strike, feeling a satisfying crunch as his nose breaks. Another thrusts a knife within a hair's breadth of your neck, and you send him reeling with a backfist across the mouth.

Against the third you're not so lucky. His blade cuts into your side, an instant of icy cold followed by searing hot pain. Tick the Wound box on your Adventure Sheet if it was not ticked already.

A surge of adrenaline gives you speed and power. Disarming the third assailant, you drive his own knife up into his throat. He shudders and falls lifeless at your feet.

Now ▶ 1023 and tick one of the boxes there before reading on.

776

Ancaeus turns to you, his beard and hair matted with rainwater. 'Get the halyard onto that winch!' he shouts over the roar of the gale.

You grab the loose end of the rope he's hauling and start winding it onto the winch. Gusts of wind tear at the rope as Ancaeus tries to hold it steady. Blood is flowing freely where the rough fibres have cut deep into his hands, but with his face set against the pain he takes a running jump to seize the halyard further up, dragging it down while you crank furiously at the winch.

The deck lurches to one side. The vessel is now several metres below the level of the roof, making it easier for your foes to jump across. The Minotaur is holding his own for now, but for how long – ?

If you have the codeword **Recursive** ▶ 1437 immediately; otherwise read on.

'We need to get higher,' you yell to Ancaeus.

'It's because we're not moving. She'll gain buoyancy once we're under way.' He staggers back, buffeted by the tempest, and takes hold of the winch. 'The sail's got snagged, can you see?'

He's right. The canvas has caught on a spar, wrapped around it by the wind, and that's why it's not opening.

You can see from Ancaeus's injured hands that he's in no condition to go aloft. 'I'll free it. You stay at the winch.'

Make a GRACE roll at difficulty 12.

Succeed ▶ 859

Fail ▶ 334

777

Lord Xechasiaris's daughter Tritona comes to see you. 'Since we last met I have been travelling in distant lands,' she says. 'There was a time when the notion of sullying my hands with trade would have been as unthinkable as disporting naked in the Forum at noon, but circumstances dictated otherwise. The gods smiled on me and I have restored the family fortune. Now I wish to return to the home where I was happy.'

'You mean this mansion?'

'I will offer you a fair price.'

The sum she has in mind is 10,000 pyr. Are you tempted to sell?

Agree to the deal ▶ 1304

Decline her offer ▶ 952

778

Myletes has been stroking his beard, a sure sign that he is about to come out with a profound thought. 'Let us postulate that a perfect simulation is possible, one that is indistinguishable from "real" reality – whatever that may be. In this simulation, if I stub my toe then the pain appears real.'

'How do we know that such verisimilitude is possible?' objects an old woman with jangling bracelets around her thin brown arms.

Myletes gives her a rather raffish grin. 'It is said that the hero Paris dreamt of Helen of Troy and awoke "armed for battle" as the saying goes. Delicacy forbids – '

The old lady's cheeks go pink. 'That's quite enough of your sauce, Myletes.'

'Yet we must agree that the dream Helen was every bit as arousing as the real Helen, yes? Well then, we must accept the possibility that everything around us is a completely convincing simulation. Now consider probabilities. There is one reality. Within that we might simulate a perfect copy. And within that copy we might simulate another copy, and another. This is the *mise en abyme* effect of infinite reflections in facing mirrors.'

'What of it?' pipes up the old woman, still piqued by Myletes's bawdy analogy.

'Statistically we are therefore more likely to be living in a simulation, of which an infinite number could exist, than in the root reality.'

'I don't know if any of you have seen the employment noticeboards at the gates,' you say, 'but you must have seen how carts are taxed as they arrive in the city. Surely that proves beyond a shadow of a doubt that everything around us is a simulation.'

► 1542

779

You go to the usual table under the arbour, but Bosk is not there.

'I haven't seen him in a while,' says one of the serving girls wistfully.

The landlord is inconsolable. 'My takings have halved since he left town.'

'When do you expect him back?'

He dabs half-heartedly at a beer stain on the counter. 'Maybe never. He said that now Arcadia is back on its feet he's likely to move there.'

► 1534

780

Nothing matches the joy you feel when you are able to leave behind the paved streets and the city dust to race through the park, losing yourself in the scent of blossom and the abundance of greenery, feeling the grass between your toes and watching the sun blaze and swim on the ponds and fountains.

'You have met the goddess,' says your father, seeing the blissful look on your face when you return from an afternoon in the groves.

'Which goddess?' you ask, though you know the answer.

'Artemis, fairest huntress, lady of the lakes and forests.'

On your Adventure Sheet, note that your god is Artemis.

► 452

781

The *Sunrise* sails on across the Ocean of Night. Distant stars shine icily across the immense gulf. Are there other worlds out there in the blackness of space? Or is it merely an infinite lifeless void?

The sailors are too overawed by the prospect of eternity to indulge in their usual banter and grumbling. For a long time there is nothing but the slow creak of the ropes, the almost musical boom of flexing timbers, the occasional muttered remark.

At last the cry comes from the lookout: 'Land ahoy!'

► 346

782

As you are about to take hold of her wrists, she lets go of the pole with one hand and snatches at your clothing. An instant later the force of the wind has torn her grip off the pole and sent her spinning up into the storm-tossed sky.

'Insect!' she cries, her voice tiny in the shrieking gale. 'Worm! Dung beetle!'

You watch her dwindle to a speck among the grey clouds. But did she snatch anything from you before she was swept away? If you have any items that augment attributes, she has taken one. Her order of preference is first CHARM, then INGENUITY, then GRACE, then STRENGTH. If you have multiple items of a given type, she takes the one with the highest bonus. So, for example, if you had a **recurve bow**, **winged sandals** and an **iron spear**, she'd take the **winged sandals**.

The wind blows itself out. You climb out of a pile of leaves and grass cuttings to find yourself in a compost heap at the side of a walled garden. The nightingale starts singing again.

► 301

783

The jerky is as tough as dragon hide. By the time you've finished it your jaws ache from chewing and your tongue feels dry and hot from the peppery spice.

The stomach cramps begin during the afternoon. By the evening you feel sick and sweaty. You tell your cook not to bother with dinner. Taking to your bed, you toss and turn through the night until finally sinking into sleep from sheer exhaustion just as the grey gleam of predawn lightens the curtains. Slowly it gets light and the room takes shape.

There's a tap at the door. Your valet pokes his head in. 'How are you feeling? Do you want breakfast?'

You throw off the covers, leaping up to open the drapes. 'Tell the cook to make a feast. I'm ravenous!'

Increase your STRENGTH by +1 to a maximum score of +5.

▶ 97

784

The syndics crowd round as you demonstrate how the device works. 'See here,' you say, showing them the panel on the front. 'These are different settings for the Speaker's voice.'

A syndic with an extravagantly crimped and waxed moustache adjusts his spectacles and peers incredulously at the controls. 'What in the name of the Muse of Comedy..? "Loud, mute, musical, mumbling, strident, soporific, silly…" What idiot thought we would ever need something like this?'

'Careful,' says the official who first engaged you. 'It was probably Vulcan himself, so technically that's blasphemy.'

Pointing the remote at the Speaker, you press a button labelled 'Authoritative'. When handed a scroll, the Speaker intones: 'Noble syndics, please take your seats.'

'Back to normal,' says the official contentedly. 'Good job.'

It seems he regards service to the city as its own reward, as you aren't offered anything else. Get the codeword *Ritual* and ▶ 1642

785

So far you've each won a round. This third and final story will determine who is the winner of the contest.

If you have the codeword *Quill* ▶ 1069

Otherwise ▶ 144

786

Your sudden attack takes Dydkos by surprise. Fumbling to raise his sword, he is bowled over, but springs nimbly to his feet and circles you on the soft, moon-smoothed grass.

'Keep back, Roxana,' he says to the girl without taking his eyes off you.

If you have a **horn headrest** ▶ 1104

Otherwise, you have the option to use either **attercop silk** (▶ 1607) or **stag antlers** (▶ 1330) if you have them.

If you don't possess any of those items, or decide not to use them, then it's a straight fight and you'll need to make a STRENGTH or GRACE roll (your choice) at difficulty 14.

Succeed ▶ 1149
Fail ▶ 863

787

You follow at a discreet distance until she turns up the Street of Knives. She ducks into the Grumbles, turns down a dank cobbled alley, and goes into a narrow tenement building with high, narrow gables that look like a line of spear-heads against the sky.

▶ 1547

788

If you have the title **Accursed of Ares** and you don't have the codeword *Rohan* ▶ 1221; otherwise read on.

The temple is dominated by a massive granite sculpture of the god that captures a tableau of frozen savagery. Ares is lunging forward, swords in either hand, yelling his battle-cry. On either side of him are his shield bearers Fear and Terror, and on a leash looped around his wrist is the mad Kydoimos, ghastly of visage, the demon of the din of battle. The red stone of these effigies blazes like fresh blood in the shafts of sunlight that penetrate the temple's interior.

If Ares is your god and you have the codeword *Rohan* ▶ 1568

If Ares is your god and you have the title **The Chosen One** you can enter the inner shrine ▶ 106

Otherwise you can:

Pray for a blessing ▶ 498
Ask for healing ▶ 65
Leave ▶ 103

789

Xechasiaris's friends and family are gathered around their ancestral tomb, which is a marble edifice bigger and grander than some townhouses.

The eldest son takes you inside. The walls of the vault are lined with copper doors from floor to ceiling, like filing cabinets except that behind each of those doors rests a sepulchre full of bones.

'All of our forebears are interred here,' he says. 'Except that empty slot there, where our father should lie.'

'What can I say? He wasn't very cooperative.'

'It's unsightly. I think we'll just have to put the empty coffin in there and hush it all up. I'd appreciate you keeping your mouth shut.'

He gives you 50 pyr not to tell anyone that Xechasiaris missed his own funeral. Add it to your money if you accept. Then ▶ **674**

790

Lose the codeword *Robber* unless you also have the codeword *Recursive*.

'Leave it to me,' says Zinc.

A few days later, the whole street is gossiping about the Atreides family's butler, who has unexpectedly handed in his notice. 'He seems almost in a panic to move back home to Arcadia,' says your next-door neighbour, chortling at his own modest pun.

You lose no time in introducing your former major-domo to the head of the Atreides family. 'Thank you,' he says. 'And an Iskandrian too. I was worried we'd be slumming it till I found a replacement. What a godsend.'

'I doubt if the gods had any hand in it,' you say drily.

▶ **97**

791

'Halizon, aren't you?'

He gives you a sharp look. 'What of it?'

'From what I know of Halizons, they don't hide from their problems in the bottom of a bottle. They go out and face them.'

He grabs you by the collar, but more to get your attention than out of anger. 'If I could face this problem – just gimme a sword and put it in front of me – I would. It's not that simple.'

▶ **1153**

792

'So be it. While I have spoken, Ilion has fallen. Achilles died as he knew he would, slain by an arrow shot by Prince Paris but furnished by the gods. Your name was on his lips as he breathed his last.'

'What about Agamemnon?' you have to ask.

'Murdered by his wife after he returned home. Mycenae, his kingdom, has fallen as Ilion fell. Odysseus met his end on a stingray's spine. Now he and the other Achaeans are no longer men but myths.'

You become aware that the curtained walls of the shrine are gone. You are surrounded by darkness. It feels immense.

'The world itself dissolves into story,' continues the voice of your god. 'As men forget the gods, they fashion a new reality of ideas. Hephaistos is the only one with magic to keep our world alive, and now Darkness wants to swallow that as she has swallowed all earlier eons. Have you forged yourself into the weapon I need to oppose her, Amazon?'

You bow. 'Divinity, I hope so.'

'We will see. The time is now. Awaken.'

▶ **73**

793

Xechasiaris dives headfirst into a cedarwood chest, thrashes around inside it as if he was struggling with a hydra, and emerges covered in dust and triumphantly flourishing a handful of papers.

'Did I ever tell you,' he says, throwing an arm around your shoulder, 'about the time I stowed away aboard a trader's caravan and went – oh, now where was it? Somewhere exotic? Doesn't matter. What an experience for a nipper!'

'How old were you?'

He scratches his head, then holds the papers a short distance above the floor. 'This high. Must have been before my seventh birthday. Parents were going wild, of course. I was gone for a month.'

He shoves the papers into your hand. They're crayon drawings that could well have been made by a six-year-old. They show wagons, traders, an enormous blocky figure who could be the *enfant terrible* himself, and a landscape that's hard to identify given the lack of colour.

'Is this… Notus?' You try holding it the other way up. 'Those are hills? Could it be Boreas?'

'Hah. What a trip. Look at this last one. There and back again!'

You'll get nothing useful out of him. The last picture does have a blaze of colour – but is that a flower, a flame, a fruit, a gem? Or something else entirely?

'So you'll see to that,' says Xechasiaris with absent-minded authority.

'I'll – wait, what?'

'Whatever's necessary,' he says, nodding. 'Good stuff. Knew as soon as I laid eyes on you that you're somebody I can count on.'

Get the codeword *Rectangle* and ▶ **1618**

794

The two duellists and a scattering of onlookers wait at the city gate in the predawn twilight. As soon as it is unlocked, they file out to a spot just out of sight of the sentries. Everyone knows that the duel is taking place, but as long as the sentries can turn a blind eye they are not duty-bound to report it to the Syndics.

Agrio is bigger and stronger than Tekto, but each powerful strike of his mace goes wide as your man uses his agile footwork and fast reactions to good advantage. He forces Agrio to stay on the move, tiring him until he sees an opening. His mace catches Agrio under the arm, the spikes biting through his armour, and he reels away and sinks to his knees.

'I yield,' he says through gritted teeth.

Tekto nods, salutes his foe, and turns away as if the duel were simply an inconvenient chore that he has now forgotten. As the two of you walk back to the gate he gives you a bag containing 100 pyr (add it to your money) and assures you of his gratitude.

'I didn't like to show it,' he says with a grin, 'but I've been up all night in a blue funk.'

Get the codeword *Rhyme* and ▶ 222

795

She's quick with the knife, but not quick enough. The tip just grazes your cheek, and then you have both hands either side of her neck in a choke hold. You squeeze, watching her eyes roll up in her head. Her mouth drops open. She struggles weakly for a moment, then there's a clatter as she lets the knife fall. Feeling no resistance in her, you take hold of her jaw and jerk her head around. Her neck makes a sound like a branch breaking.

One of your footmen, woken by the commotion, comes into the room. He looks in horror at the body. 'It's a girl. You've killed her.'

'Believe me, everybody who knew her wanted to do the same. Summon the night watch and tell them to put her in an unmarked grave.'

The ruby she brought is on the desk. It's worth 30 pyr. Add that to your money and ▶ 97

796

Darkness flows from the sceptre along your arm, up across your chest, over your throat, spreading in a lightless film that closes around your face and pours through mouth and eyes and nose into your head.

From the abyss into which you are plunged comes a whispering voice. Is it Oizys? Or Nyx herself? Or is it the voice of your own self-doubt?

'Surrender yourself to the balm of pure darkness,' it says. 'No need to worry anymore about what to do or on which side you have to fight. You won't have to think at all. I will provide for all your needs, all your decisions. Give in. Become one with the night.'

To resist the power of darkness you need to make a CHARM or INGENUITY roll (your choice) at difficulty 18. It is a test of the force of your character, a struggle of determination against the terrible gnawing shadow of the abyss in the heart of every soul.

Succeed ▶ 1163
Fail ▶ 921

797

You have hardly set foot through the gate when a lieutenant accosts you. 'How did you get in?' he demands, eyes wide with outrage. 'Didn't the sentry stop you?'

'There wasn't anyone there.'

He strides to the gate and takes a look to either side, then turns and yells to a sergeant, 'Why isn't there anyone on guard? Any riff-raff could stroll in – no offence. Who's meant to be on duty?'

The sergeant snaps to attention. 'Viranos, sir. But you know the problem…'

The lieutenant sighs and shakes his head. 'This can't go on. When he shows his face, send him to see me.'

The sergeant is told to escort you back outside. 'Nothing personal,' he says. 'The barracks aren't open to the public.'

Ask him about Viranos ▶ 938
Go on your way ▶ 1642

798

Zinc brushes his fingers across the beads of an abacus that rests on the table beside a pile of ledgers. 'Useful trinkets, things like this, and not just for business. You know what I mean.'

You nod. 'Winged sandals, laurel wreaths, and so on. In a pinch they can make all the difference.'

'The really powerful people around here won't let you waltz into their palaces carrying anything that boosts your natural abilities, any more than they'd admit you carrying a deadly weapon. You have to check things like this at the door.'

▶ 605

799

A pattern of striations across the walls of the pass draws your eye. What a less experienced wayfarer would take for scratches on the stone, you see at once to be the scale-armoured grey coils of a huge serpent draped amid the surrounding rocks.

Sensing it no longer has the advantage of surprise, the serpent snaps open its eyes, huge gleaming orbs like magnified pools of algae. It drops its body in heavy loops towards you, but already you are braced for battle.

Make a STRENGTH roll at difficulty 8.

Succeed ▶ 1571
Fail ▶ 1550

800

Remember to cross the 5 pyr off your money.

If you have the codeword *Plundered* but not *Radish* ▶ 1464; otherwise read on.

You tuck into a delicious meal made with fresh ingredients from the fields and forests of Arcadia. If you were injured you can untick the Wound box on your Adventure Sheet, then ▶ 232

801

She did her best to conceal some of the movements behind the wide lace ruffs of her shirt sleeves, but your eye was quicker than her hands. You are almost certain which cup the ruby is under.

'There.'

She lifts it with a flourish. 'No. See, it's under this one.'

You stare at the desk, speechless. You were so sure.

She pockets the ruby. 'So I'll take the deeds. No hurry about moving out. Have breakfast first.'

Give her the deeds to the house ▶ 1255

Never! ▶ 1054

802

If you have either **Sappho's song** or the **Eye of Hyperion** ▶ 284

Otherwise ▶ 573

803

With a petulant gesture he releases the lightning bolt that had waited trembling above. It arcs across the sky, crashing into the garden where it splits an ancient oak into a fountain of molten sparks. The blast of thunder shakes the building and reverberates off over the city.

'Stay benighted in this dream, then,' snarls Hypnos. 'While you slumber, we'll ravish this world and make it our own. I'll wake you when it's time to die.'

He brushes his fingers through his beard, producing a handful of gritty sand which he flicks in your face. For a moment your eyes are red and raw, and when you blink away the tears he's gone.

You walk through the ballroom, the courtyards, the vast echoing halls of the palace. There is the hiss of rain, occasional splinters of lightning in the murky sky, but no sign of other partygoers. Yet as you turn each corner or step through a doorway, you catch glimpses of people vanishing off at the far end of a passage.

A group of guests stand talking in an alcove. You hadn't noticed them. They turn as you approach. Each holds a mask on a stick. The masks are not painted plaster but living faces with soft flapping lips and rolling eyes. When they lower the masks they reveal blank oval heads.

'Who are you?' you demand of them, and it's only now that you realize you are not talking to real people but to a macabre *trompe-l'oeil* painting of ghouls with featureless faces peeling the skin off the heads of corpses they've unearthed.

A servant lopes past you, his gait so low and simian that you almost didn't notice him. 'Where is everyone?' you shout after him.

'Just bringing them up from the cellar. A good vintage, this next lot.'

You go to follow him but it is like wading through treacle. You find your way back to the ballroom, where the wall-length mirror reflects a sumptuous banquet and glittering candelabra – but of your own reflection there's no sign.

You must wake, and quickly. Every minute you spend in this dream world, Nyx and her sons are nearer to carrying out their evil plans. But how can you wake up, when Hypnos himself has closed your eyes?

If you have the codeword *Rose* ▶ 911

If not but you have the title **Earth Mother's Herald** ▶ 1651

Otherwise, if you have a **bronze butterfly** and you have the codeword *Retract* and not the codeword *Remedy* ▶ 467

Otherwise, if you have *Riven* ▶ 1287

Otherwise ▶ 710

804

Lightning crashes across the sky as your champions charge into battle against Nyx's sons Death and Sleep. This is the final showdown, the contest of elemental forces. If your allies can keep the two titans occupied, you have a chance of reaching Nyx herself. And somehow you must find a way to defeat her, or else the world is lost.

If you have the codeword *Romance* ▶ 1317

If not ▶ 418

805

Make a STRENGTH roll at difficulty 8 to see if your back kick is effective. You cannot use bonuses from any attribute-boosting items in this fight because your possessions are upstairs in your bedroom. You can however use blessings.

Success ▶ 1284

Failure ▶ 1023

806

❏

If you do not have the codeword *Reverie* and the box above is empty, put a tick in it and ▶ 1280

Otherwise read on.

Only an ivy-twined iron fence and a row of tall hedges separate the Groves of Dionysus from the streets all around, yet you could almost be standing in the bosky depths of Arcadia. Lakes and streams glitter between the trees. Marble statues and fountains and pavilions gleam like lanterns in the dappled green shade, while broad gardens bordered by well-tended flowerbeds spread colour and scent on the breeze. This is where the weary citizens of Vulcan City come to refresh their spirits, taking a brief respite from the whirl of urban life in this serene parkland.

A fox darts from under the bushes, its bright eyes seeming to follow the gentle flow of the stream. The sound of birdsong and the distant chatter of the bustling city murmur on the air. The sun beats down, casting a warm glow on the sleepy stretches of grass. People stroll and chat, enjoying the fresh air and the peaceful atmosphere.

Look for an old soldier on a marble bench (only if you have the codeword *Ripple*) ▶ 139

Swim in the lake ▶ 1177
Investigate a commotion ▶ 1019
Leave by way of the Street of Ash ▶ 232
Go out onto the Avenue of Subsolanus ▶ 625

807

Get the codeword *Rage*.

Achilles comes to find you. 'So you've given yourself to Agamemnon,' he says thickly.

'News travels fast around this camp.'

'That grasping brute. King of Kings! He's a spoiled bully who must have whatever others cherish. Why did I follow him here? What quarrel do I have with the people of Ilion? They never stole my cattle, never pillaged my lands. We came to save his family's honour yet he treats us like his thralls. This war drags on and on while he waits and fills his coffers with the spoils better men bring off the battlefield.'

'So why fight for him?'

He laughs savagely. 'Why indeed? When I think of his hands on you – ugh, it's like a loathsome beast defiling a sacred idol. Henceforth I'll not cut down the defenders of Ilion to feed his rapacious ambition. Here in the camp I'll stay, my men too, and see how Agamemnon's forces fare without the son of Peleus to be their champion.'

If the Current Location recorded on your Adventure Sheet is **1500** then ▶ 41

Otherwise ▶ 203

808

Behind a long terrace running along one side of the courtyard, doors are thrown open onto a ballroom from which more music comes wafting out.

Directly ahead of you, through an archway leading to the next courtyard, is a round building surmounted by a gilded dome that blazes furnace-white against the evening sky. Beyond it you see water spraying from a fountain of silver-flecked black marble fashioned in the shape of a giant hand.

Go into the ballroom ▶ 552
Enter the domed building ▶ 1530
Take a closer look at the fountain ▶ 489

809

'Of course you'd never bow down and serve Nyx,' you go on. 'After all, you're descended from royalty yourself.'

Daedalus thinks about that. 'Not as rare as you'd think. Most kings have more than their fair share of descendants. It's one of the perks.'

'A bit more recent in your case, though. Aren't you the great-grandson of the first king of Athens?'

He tears his eyes away from the clashing armies below and studies you with narrowed gaze. 'Where are you going with this?'

You've got his attention, at least. If only you can turn it to your advantage somehow. Make a CHARM roll at difficulty 12.

Glib as ever ▶ 1192
Words fail you ▶ 199

810

You arrange to meet Chryses under a flag of truce before the mighty walls of Ilion. Under a windswept sky he comes down the paved ramp that leads to the impregnable iron-banded Scaean Gate.

'You have not brought my daughter back to me,' he says sorrowfully.

'Agamemnon won't give her up. But it's not right that all the Achaeans should suffer because their high king is without honour.'

'If I ask the Shining One to relent and lift the curse, what good does that do Astynome? She's still a captive of that brutish outlander, still abused by him every night.'

'But alive. The plague threatens her too. And I shall see that she is unharmed. You have my word as an Amazon.'

He is hesitant, but he sees that this is the best outcome he can hope for. He agrees to pray to Apollo to end the plague. You return to the Achaean camp.

▶ Current Location

811

'Call me Pug,' says the man. 'I'll make it brief because nobody wants to hear a sob story, and they're all the same anyway. Bad choices. Lost opportunities. Woulda coulda shoulda. If I'd taken another path I'd have been happy, but I took a purse of gold and gave away my love.'

You shrug. 'Plenty of fish in the sea, so I hear. You're not that old. You'll find someone else.'

'I know it's a cliché, the perfect girl,' he says, shaking his head, 'but believe me when I say she was made for me. When the gods brought me back to life –'

'Oh, I do know what that's like.'

'You don't understand. I died of old age. When I came back I thought it was another chance, that the gods had taken pity on me, but they don't know pity. The gods are cruel. They put me here to live out another lifetime without her.'

You cover a yawn. 'I think you need to save this for the magistrates. Not that they'll show any more pity than the gods. "I had a hard life so I turned to theft…" Good luck with that.'

'You haven't been listening,' says Pug impatiently. 'I learned the hard way that riches don't matter. I didn't come here to steal money. I heard you might own a scrimshaw hourglass.'

'And if I did, so what?'

'I could use it. Don't you see? I could use it to go back and change the past.'

If you possess a **scrimshaw hourglass** and are willing to part with it ▶ 321

If not but you have the codeword *Recursive* ▶ 285

Otherwise ▶ 480

812

'I was a fool to think you and Nyx would make better rulers than the gods,' you say, choking with anger and grief. 'With that one act you've shown you're more callous and monstrous than any Olympian deity. Now I'll do everything in my power to make you pay for what you've done to my friend.'

'Bold words for a puny mortal,' he says, raising his huge hand with thumb and forefinger poised an eyelash length apart. 'I could snuff you out as easily as I did your little mannikin here.'

'I don't think so. My deity has been preparing me for this moment.'

Hypnos roars with laughter. 'You thought you were marked out for greatness? Hah! You were chosen precisely because you are of no significance whatsoever. I was the one who chose you. Every time you thought you communed with your god – that was me, speaking to you through your vain dreams of grandeur. The Olympians would never have selected an nonentity such as you to be their hero, which is

why I knew that your god would never notice my deception.'

Give in – your only hope is to join him	▶ 688
Refuse to believe what he says	▶ 1410
Defy him even if you must stand alone	▶ 255

813

Agamemnon's tent is the grandest in the Achaean camp, almost a permanent dwelling with an enclosure of spikes around it, wooden shelters built off to the side, and the high king's pennants streaming from the peak of the roof.

If you request an audience with Agamemnon, note **260** as your Current Location and then ▶ 518

Otherwise you can return to Achilles' tent (▶ 535) or seek out one of the Achaean warriors to talk to (▶ 735).

814

The Palace of the Archons is built on a nexus of lines of cosmological force, monitored at all times by the watchful Fates. Detecting your transgression, they rework the skein of your life on their loom.

You find yourself out on the street, where the sundial in the centre of the Forum indicates that time has been reset to the moment before you set foot in the Palace. The world is as it was before, but you are not. Delete all your blessings (other than the permanent blessing of the goddess Demeter, if you have it) and lose any items currently in your possession that can be used to boost your attributes.

▶ 1642

815

If this box ❑ is empty, tick it and ▶ 1261

If it was already ticked, roll a die:

score 1-4 ▶ 1261

score 5-6 ▶ 488

816

'Here in the city you will confront your ultimate destiny,' says the Oracle in a droning voice. 'There is a masked ball at the palace of Vulcan. I see a theft that threatens the very order of creation. Creatures of the darkness let loose to hunt. A storm that shakes Olympus itself. And you will make the choice that decides the fate of all.'

'Vulcan has a palace here in the city? I've never seen it.'

'He hides it from mortal eyes. When you have earned the right, your deity will uncloud your vision. Now go. Leave me. I have glimpsed the end of time and feel the need for prayer.'

▶ 510

817

You step out into a gallery lit by guttering torches set in iron brackets along the whitewashed wall. There is another door dead ahead that must lead up to the top of the building, but before you can go through there's a shout and a guard comes running towards you brandishing a spiked club. You will need to deal with him fast before his yelling brings others.

Make a STRENGTH roll at difficulty 8. That is, roll two dice, add your STRENGTH modifier including the bonus for any one item, and you are trying to score 8 or more.

Succeed ▶ 1583
Fail ▶ 1045

818

You both rise to your feet, tense and alert as panthers.

'It's like that, then?' she says, whipping out the long knife at her belt.

You nod. 'Pandora must have felt this way when she let the evils out into the world, only in my case I get to put one of them back.'

'Big talk seeing as I'm the one with a weapon.'

You reach back and take the poker from the fire. She'd left it there and the tip is glowing bright yellow. 'Satisfied?'

Swing the poker ▶ 219
Jab at her ▶ 459
Throw it at her ▶ 1020

819

The spider-construct inserts one of its key-shaped feet into the lock and the door springs open.

The prisoner comes forward briskly to greet you. He is a lean, robust man in early middle age, sporting a neatly trimmed beard. The spark of mischief and easy confidence in his eyes suggests he's used to being the smartest guy in any room.

'Hey, so you found your way to the penthouse.'

'All thanks to your – whatever this is.'

'Ari's a crude piece of kit, but the best I could do with the tools available.' He scoops the spider off the wall and inserts a key into its back to rewind it. 'Give me my workshop, I could build you a hive of mechanical bees that make real honey. The coppery taste takes some getting used to, but once you're past that you'll never go back to sugar.'

'So you're – '

'Daedalus, yes. Pleased to meet you.'

If you have the **copper casket of doom** and want to give it to him ▶ 743

If not ▶ 1361

820

Wind whistles across the deserted plaza. All around lie the baleful ruins of the once-proud city.

If you have the title **Paladin** and want to travel to one of the city gates ▶ 1014

If not, decide where you'll head now:

The nearest gate ▶ 723
The nearest tower ▶ 171
The Avenue of the Anvil ▶ 1632
Your mansion (only if you have the title **The Unexpected Heir**) ▶ 1257
Your family home (only if you have the codeword *Reverie*) ▶ 1385
The Academy of Philosophers ▶ 1510
The temple district ▶ 1326

821

Nihakos makes sure to rub your face in the dirt. You limp home with a black eye, but what really hurts is your injured pride.

But, even though you lost, from that day Nihakos stops bullying your brother. Maybe he has found another kid to torment, or maybe he was more worried about the fight than he let on. Even though he beat you easily, bullies don't like to risk anyone challenging them. When intimidation fails, they move onto other victims.

Your reputation soars among the other schoolchildren. 'But I don't get it,' you tell your best friend. 'I lost!'

'Nobody expected you to win, stupid, but you're the only one brave enough to spit in Nihakos's eye.'

Gain 1 Glory and ▶ 247

822

You take a few steps after Sphikos, careful to tread only on the densest masses of vapour. In the crevasses where it has broken apart lie fathomless depths of blue sky. One slip and you would fall forever.

'Come back!' you shout after him.

Your voice is swallowed in the swirling immensity of cloud and void. Sphikos keeps stumbling on towards the slowly drifting bank of cloud.

If Chipos is your companion ▶ 33
Otherwise:

If you have a **conch horn** and want to blow it ▶ 879

If you have a **bronze butterfly** and want to use it ▶ 1368

If you have a **caged canary** and want to set it free ▶ 1259

Or you can chase after Sphikos (▶ 907) or go back down the rope without him (▶ 1248).

823

The Achaeans ride out, war-harness jangling on their chariots, brightly tinted helmet crests fluttering like fabulous plumage, sunlight glancing in dazzling rays from polished bronze cuirasses and burnished shields.

You watch as they sweep across the plain. Against the early morning sun, the walls of distant Ilion look like a painting behind an almost invisible veil. The city's defenders are specks in the golden haze.

The servants and the sick are the only ones remaining in camp. You walk along the line of beached ships, sunk in thought, until a sprightly voice breaks in on your daydreams.

'You're having a yourself day, are you?'

You look up, startled. 'Galatea! It's so good to see you again.'

'I can't say the same. For me it's the first time we've met.'

'But – ' You take her hands. 'What are you doing here? Last time I saw you you'd been turned into a statue.'

'That makes sense. After all, I am a statue. I came here looking for sand, but this place won't do. Too many pebbles.' She tugs her hands away and takes a few graceful steps as though practicing a dance. 'It's for this.'

She holds up an ivory hourglass.

'I recognize that.'

'In that case one day I'd better give it to you – once I've got the right kind of sand. The little bit I've found here is too grey and coarse. It'll only take you forward, which is the way you're going anyway.'

She flips over the hourglass and the sand starts to trickle through it. Flickering prismatic beams spiral around you. Your feet are lifted from the beach and you feel yourself falling, not only through space but through time.

'I'll catch you up.' Galatea's voice echoes as if down a long tunnel behind you. 'I won't mention any of this next time I see you, though. It'd only get confusing.'

▶ 73

824

Note 34 as your Current Location and then ▶ 549

825

Your insectoid opponent rushes at you. You fend off the whirring mouthparts, but the razor edge of a pincer rakes your flesh. A stab of pain lances up your thigh. You twist desperately away, blood spurting out onto the grass.

If the Wound box on your Adventure Sheet was unticked, put a tick in it now and then ▶ 738

If you were already injured, note 1090 as your Current Location and then ▶ 670

826

Bracing herself against the raging wind, Nyx flings a bolt of atramentous energy that incinerates the tapestry. Immediately the gale dies away now that the dimensional portal to Olympus is closed.

'Nice try,' she says. 'But not good enough.'

▶ 182

827

'You won't want to miss this bit,' says the burly giant as a group of female automata file out onto the lawn. 'The ceremony of the crown, they call it.'

One of the Celedons is carrying an iron casket set with fiery yellow topaz. She and the others turn to face the handful of guests who have remained outside. She raises the casket above her head. The sky gives a mutter of rolling thunder.

'In the golden age before time began,' she says in a chiming musical voice, 'the titans ruled and those we call gods were their servants. To commemorate that time, once a year at this sacred ball we reverse our roles. The diadem that symbolizes Vulcan's supremacy is brought out. A mortal is crowned master of all that exists, and servants become masters while those who gave them orders become slaves in their turn.'

She places the casket in front of her and opens it to reveal a shimmering circlet of gold fashioned like curling flames. Vulcan's diadem. But as she lifts it, the diadem crumples in her fingers – not real gold, just a tissue-thin replica of cardboard and gold leaf.

'A fake,' intones one of the other Celedons in a sing-song voice. 'The real diadem has been stolen.'

'It does not matter,' says another. 'We will find it later.'

'Now complete the program,' says the first, discarding the fake diadem. 'It is time for the reversal of roles. The rulers will become the prey.'

Their eyes suddenly switch from a pale blue glow to fiery red. The effect on their sculpted features is instant and dramatic. From creatures of unearthly beauty, they now become hard-faced monsters with no trace of pity or remorse.

'Impressive, eh?' says the big man in his booming voice. 'And wait till you see what they do for an encore.'

The Celedons suddenly start walking towards the guests.

'Is this part of the entertainment?' asks a woman nervously. She gets her answer a moment later when a Celedon reaches her, closes its metal fingers around her throat, and pulls out her windpipe.

Screaming, the guests on the lawn rush for the building

just as the others who were inside press forward to see what's going on. The Celedons stride relentlessly into their midst, striking out at random and using their modulated voices to stun their victims with sonic blasts.

You're about to wade in and help, but the big man touches you on the arm. 'Oh, we have something special planned for you,' he murmurs, pointing across the lawn.

▶ **1556**

828

'Anything else?' he asks.

Sell him another item	▶ **526**
Look for something to buy	▶ **496**
Leave	▶ **325**

829

You race over to join the helmsman. He's bent over a device like a ship's compass. The lid on top of the housing is off, revealing a disk of jagged geometric lines like a spinning knot of molten wires. It makes you feel slightly sick to look at it because of how it's continually shifting, unfolding and refolding, apparently in impossible shapes.

'You have to get your head around it existing in multiple dimensions,' says the helmsman, hesitantly reaching towards the glowing disk with a strangely shaped spanner. 'Got much experience with buoyancy rotors?'

'That what this is? I thought I was looking at a migraine aura.'

If you have the codeword *Recursive* ▶ **1417** now; otherwise read on.

'It's got jolted out of alignment,' says the helmsman. 'See those sparks? It's dragging against the side of the containment vessel. That's why we're losing altitude.'

'And you can adjust it with that spanner?'

He gives a bark of desperate laughter. 'I'm a navigator, me. This is Vulcan-level shit. I've never even taken the top off it before.'

Steeling himself, he drives the spanner into the heart of the machine. There's a protesting screech as the disk grinds against the spanner head. The deck lurches as the ship drops about five metres. Arcs of disturbing light splash and play around your head.

'Little help here…' grunts the helmsman, straining with all his might to twist the disk back into alignment.

Make a STRENGTH roll at difficulty 13.

Succeed	▶ **1318**
Fail	▶ **216**

830

High in the immense black vault of the sky, a bright star flares suddenly. No, not a star – a meteor, hurtling earthwards. Then as it draws closer you see that it is a human figure clad in miraculous winged battle-armour. He swoops to hover directly above you, seizes you with a metal gauntlet, and careens up to a broken parapet overlooking the scene of battle.

'Why don't you sit this one out, sport?'

You recognize that voice. His helmet opens like a metal-petalled flower to reveal the face of –

'Daedalus!'

'How could I miss the big event?' says Daedalus. 'Up here we've got grandstand seats for the end of an era.'

'I'm confused. Didn't I blow you up?'

'Yeah. Did you forget I licked the regeneration problem?' You struggle in his vice-like grip, but you can't break free. 'Don't waste your strength. You're not going anywhere.'

He holds you pinned against a wall with one armoured hand against your chest. Your blows do nothing except bruise your fists.

If you have the codeword *Rudiment* ▶ **230**
If not but you have the codeword *Negate* ▶ **160**
If you have neither ▶ **1315**

831

Normally the militia would make only a half-hearted attempt to find the muggers, but they are capable of mounting an efficient investigation when an influential citizen like yourself starts putting on the pressure. Before sunset there has been an arrest and the young man's purse is returned to him.

'It's really the principle of the thing rather than the cash,' he tells you.

'Well, of course.'

'I mean it. Look, if it won't seem insulting I'd like to make a present of this purse to you.'

Your reply?

'I'm not insulted at all.'	▶ **275**
'No need for a reward.'	▶ **806**

832

'I was just passing the prison, Your Honour, and I saw a side door standing open and unguarded. Naturally I was concerned there might be a jail break. As a good citizen, I went inside to investigate and the guards got a little over-zealous.'

'I see,' says the magistrate. 'And why do you think the guards attacked you?'

'It's not for me to say, Your Honour, although a more suspicious soul might conclude that they were in on the escape attempt. Bribes must be a real temptation when you're on a jailer's salary. Perhaps they didn't want me blowing the whistle on a tasty payday.'

The magistrate orders your immediate release and the arrest of the prison officers who detained you.

▶ 1642

833

A cool breeze blows through the ballroom now and there's a smell of rain. The sky outside has clouded over, but there are still a few hardy guests strolling around on the lawn.

'Didn't they say there would be fireworks?' says a young woman excitedly. She grabs your arm and pulls you out through the doors onto the patio.

▶ 1415

834

Lose the codeword *Regal*.

Nyx looks at you with keen interest for the first time. 'You surprise me,' she says with a delighted laugh. 'And that happens once in a hundred centuries. Why now, with the gods defeated and humanity under my yoke? It is too late to oppose me. Too late to make any difference at all. You want to sacrifice your own life – for what?'

If you have the title **The Liberator** ▶ 226
If not but you possess the **Eye of Hyperion** ▶ 1325
Otherwise ▶ 478

835

It's eerie watching her descend the wall. She seems to float to the ground rather than climbing down. The rain drives out of the darkness with stinging force, the wind howls and buffets the trees, and thunderbolts flash and rumble high overhead. It's like a scene from a play, almost too vivid to be real.

The next thing you know it is morning. You are in bed. Your valet is closing the window. 'The storm blew it open in the night,' he says. 'I'm afraid the carpet is soaked.'

'I thought I got up and shut it,' you say. Or was that all a dream?

Lose the codeword *Ruffle* and ▶ 38

836

The package was sent by Erifili, your head chef at the Palace in Arcadia.

'Here's a golden apple that I picked in the orchard this morning,' she writes. 'An owl has been seen perching on the trees there, so maybe the apple is sacred to Athena. Or it might just be a yellow fungus has got into the skin. I guess the only way to find out is to take a bite.'

You shake the envelope and a large apple rolls out. It gleams on your breakfast plate with a metallic sheen.

Take a bite   ▶ 999
Not a chance   ▶ 97

837

The noticeboard hums, lighting up as you approach. You have only to raise your fingers to the screen for it to provide

you with immediate access.

A message appears: 'RESTORE CITY TO WORKSHOP SETTINGS? Y/N'

'What do you think?' you ask Dunamis.

'Dunno, I never got to this level before. Could be it'll wipe out everyone we know.'

'So that'd be a no, then?'

'Nyx is planning to wipe them out for sure. Might as well roll the dice, eh?'

She reaches past you and taps the screen.

▶ 1503

838

You push the door open against a howling gale and emerge on the palace roof. You have to crouch, bracing yourself so as not to be knocked off your feet. Icy rain stings your face. The wet slate tiles are black mirrors.

Those twisting stairs made you lose your bearings. You look wildly around. Flickers of lightning reveal a massive series of tiled ridges stretching away for hundreds of metres. Somewhere beyond those roof ridges must be the wall overlooking the street. But even if you could reach it that would mean climbing down fifty metres in pouring rain.

A thunder flash detonates directly overhead, splitting the sky and making the stone building shake underfoot. To your left you see the bulk of the high dome that caps the stairwell. The winds howl around it. The dome's metal surface is slick with rain but you might be able to scale it to the stone lantern at the top, which must be the highest peak of this wing of the palace.

Your pursuers are nearly upon you. You hear their howls and gibbering cries echoing from the stairwell. Seeing a loose brick, you use it to wedge the door shut, but it won't hold them for long. There are too many to fight. You'll have to run – but which way?

If you have the title **Earth Mother's Herald** and the codeword *Quiddity* ▶ 485; if not read on.

If you have both the codewords *Recursive* and *Quiddity* ▶ 744; if not read on.

If you have the **wings of Icarus** and the codeword *Recursive* ▶ 1625

Otherwise you must decide your escape route:

Flee across the roof ▶ 1185

Try to scale the dome ▶ 759

839

'Administrator access? Vulcan's crown would give us that, surely?'

Dunamis looks shifty. 'About that. The good news... It was me that took it.'

'I guessed as much. And the bad news?'

'Haven't got it anymore.'

'Who has?'

'One of the Syndics. I think he had some cockeyed notion he could use it to make himself boss of the city.'

Get the codeword *Rice* and ▶ 1549

840

The vampires are rushing to set up portable cannon along the edge of the roof. Clamping the first of these cannon to the parapet, a vampire stabs a button on the side. There's a crack as the cannon flings out several grappling lines. A couple of the grapples bounce off the hull and fall to be winched back for another try, but three of them have caught fast on the rail. Immediately a pack of werebeasts come scrambling across.

'Nyx has the inventor Daedalus on her team,' grunts the Minotaur, glaring at the cannon. 'We can expect more tricky devices like those.'

With a sudden roar he swings his axe at one of the lines, splintering the rail and sending a string of the creatures tumbling to their doom. But more grapple-ropes are being shot across and there seems no end to the bestial horde.

If you have the title **Kissed by a Golden Princess** ▶ 547

If not but you have the codeword *Noble* ▶ 916

Otherwise ▶ 1262

841

'I've got control of Vulcan's matrix,' you explain. 'Once we've dealt with Nyx we can reshape the world however we see fit. There'll be no more need for mortals to bow down to Zeus and his ilk.'

For once Daedalus actually looks impressed. 'I really want to see the look on his big bearded mug when he hears about that. OK, what are we waiting for?'

He slides his armoured visor back down and surges towards the two titans on jets of force that ripple the very air beneath his wings.

▶ 804

842

You join a caravan of wagons that leaves the east gate of the city bound for Notus. As the caravan wends its way south, the climate becomes warmer and drier.

'Don't get too used to the heat,' says your acquaintance as he sees you peeling off layers of clothing. 'We'll be heading up into the hills soon, and it gets a lot cooler.'

The track up to Saesara is indeed welcoming, with fresh invigorating breezes blowing down from the high valleys.

After a couple of days the landscape opens up to a wide vista of fields dotted with villages. Beyond stands the royal palace, dimmed by distance, and behind that the dark ice-crested peaks of the highest mountains.

You notice the smell first, a candy-sweet fragrance on the air. As the wagons roll along the road you round a corner and see an expanse of pale red flowers stretching right across to the next village.

'I only have to catch a whiff and I'm right back here,' says your guide. 'Useful crop, too. Seeds for salads, medicine for toothache, tincture for perfume and potpourri. Symbol of remembrance too, in some quarters.'

'All right,' you say laughing. 'I'm not buying a cartload. I only need one.'

He plucks a few and holds them up so that the reflected sunlight casts a blush across his face. 'You came this far. Might as well have a handful.'

Add the **bunch of poppies** to your possessions. The caravan will stop here in Saesara to trade before returning to Vulcan City in a couple of days. You are given the choice of staying here or accompanying them.

Go back to the city ▶ **333**

Stay in Saesara ▶ **1417** in *The Hammer of the Sun*

843

'Fine, fine!' he says, throwing up his arms in exasperation. 'I only have this whole ship to command, it's not like I'm busy.'

Grumbling, he stamps across the deck and takes a look into the hold. When he turns, the look of red-faced anger has been wiped away. He's pale with shock.

'That – that – that –'

'Take a breath.'

'That insect thing. It's gone and slimed up my hold with eggs.'

'And larvae, by the look of it,' growls the Minotaur, crushing a cockroach-like creature the size of a rat that has just scuttled up from below decks.

Closing the hatch to the hold, you let out a few larvae at a time. It's a laborious process, but you manage to kill them all without anyone getting bitten. And perhaps that's just as well, because you notice their vital juices have etched into the ship's timbers like acid.

▶ **653**

844

Lashing out furiously, you charge through them. They land a couple of hefty blows but you keep going, relying on adrenaline to see you through. It almost works, but then one of the guards hauls off and delivers a roundhouse swing to the side of your head. An explosion of light, then everything goes dark.

If your Wound box is already ticked ▶ **111**

If not, put a tick in it now and ▶ **1127**

845

He gives a shrieking war-cry and leaps across the desk at you, knife held out straight ahead. He's like a human missile. A lesser opponent would have been skewered through the heart, but you block open-palmed with your left hand, driving your right fist straight into his face. His own momentum magnifies the force of the blow and he goes down spitting bloody teeth.

He's trying to get up, but you knock the remaining fight out of him with a kick to the back of the neck.

▶ **253**

846

'Stay here,' you tell Dunamis. You advance into the pitch darkness of the chamber. A soft mechanical hiss and a rhythmic amplified clicking is just audible – the Speaker's voicebox, left untuned when Nyx gave up her possession of its body. It is just enough to orient yourself as you walk forward.

If you have the blessing of the dawn ▶ **992**

If not but you have some **phoenix tears** ▶ **1264**

If not but you have either a **bronze butterfly** or the **hubcap of Helios** ▶ **1665**

Otherwise ▶ **623**

847

Get the title **Plaything of Agamemnon**.

'Send her back, then,' says Agamemnon, flinging Astynome into the arms of the seer, Calchas. 'And you say that will end the plague?'

Calchas nods, but not with absolute conviction. 'It should, my lord, for Apollo's anger will fade when there is no cause.'

'It better,' growls Agamemnon, 'or you'll be the next sacrifice I make.'

▶ **541**

848

A metal-studded club scythes viciously through the air right over your head. If you hadn't ducked it would have cracked your skull right open.

You're facing three trained assassins, you're unarmed, and you're wearing nothing but a silk robe. This could be a tough fight.

▶ **1023**

849

You recount some of your most daring adventures. Kazala stands back with her arms folded, smiling indulgently, until you have finished.

'Very impressive,' she says as a light smattering of applause dies down. 'I've got my work cut out to match that. Ah, I know, there was the time I climbed the mountains of southern Boreas and met the minotaur...'

She proceeds to tell a complicated story involving a door with three locks, each one opened by a metal key that she found in a river. An added wrinkle is that a demon was set to guard each lock, so that when it was opened she needed a protective talisman to ward off the demon's attack. These talismans she found in various clifftop nests. Privately you think the tale has too many digressions to be interesting, and by the time she's got to a gift given to her by some human-headed cows you're hardly listening.

The other salon guests clap politely, then confer among themselves to decide which of you has told the best story. Make a CHARM roll at difficulty 9. You can add an additional +1 to your dice score if you have a Glory of 10 or more.

If you fail the CHARM roll then Kazala is judged the winner and you go onto the next round ▶ 567

If you succeed, you win the first round ▶ 254

850

If your Glory score is 11 or more ▶ 229

If your Glory is between 6 and 10 ▶ 3

Otherwise ▶ 721

851

The predatory scowls of Xechasiaris's family melt at once into smiles. 'Very decent of you,' says one of the brothers, almost going so far as to pat you on the arm. He hands you a purse containing 50 pyr.

As you turn to leave, one of the grandchildren comes over and says bashfully, 'This is for you too,' and pushes a wad of wet chewing gum into your hand.

A cute gesture from an innocent youngster? Maybe not – you notice her brothers and sisters smirking behind their hands. They grow up fast in the city, these kids.

If you have any scars   ▶ 410

Otherwise   ▶ 674

852

As you parry the dwarf's first lunge, your hand almost gets caught in his hood. It gives you an idea. Seizing him by the hood, you swing him around just as the slave trader brings his cleaver scything down. The blade sticks in the dwarf's head as neatly as a butcher chopping up a pig's carcass.

The slave trader's cry of shock turns into a snarl. 'He was my last slave, you cur!'

'I'm surprised he didn't stick that knife in you one dark night, then. You don't really strike me as the kind of boss to inspire loyalty.'

He kicks the dwarf's body off the cleaver and swings at you. You sidestep, feeling the wind as the blade whistles past your ear, and press in close. Then you step back to show him the dwarf's knife sticking out of his chest. He gives a little sigh, almost of surprise, and sinks lifeless to the floor.

If you don't have the codeword *Quiddity* ▶ 28

Otherwise, if you have the codeword *Quench* but not *Rigor* ▶ 1004

Otherwise ▶ 243

853

After a time you realize that the spectre has vanished. It must have decided its work was done. Your lungs are bursting but as long as you are alive you are determined to keep struggling. As you writhe around trying to find a pocket of air, your face brushes against metal bars. There a rusty grating in the side of the grave.

The stifling weight of piled earth presses down, holding you rigid, but you are able to reach into your pocket and draw out the key. Wrenching yourself around in a painful contortion, you manage to find the lock on the grating. The key turns slowly – there, it's open! You push against the bars and squeeze through into a narrow tunnel with just enough air to know you are still alive.

The tunnel is pitch black and reeks of decay. As you squirm forward, fragments of mouldered bone and old shrouds press into your face. There is no way of going back. At last you feel a breeze. There's a chink of grey light in the gloom ahead. The smell of brimstone. You have reached safety of a kind.

▶ 713 in *The Houses of the Dead*

854

You race to the stern, where the helmsman is bent over a device like a ship's compass. He prises off the copper lid on the top of the housing to reveal a spinning disk of tangled geometric lines. It makes you feel slightly sick to look at it because of how it's continually shifting, unfolding and refolding, apparently in impossible shapes.

'You have to get your head around it existing in other dimensions,' says the helmsman, hesitantly reaching towards the glowing disk with a strangely shaped spanner. 'Got much experience with buoyancy rotors?'

'That what this is? I thought I was looking at a migraine aura.'

If you have the codeword **_Recursive_** ▶ **1417** now; otherwise read on.

'It's out of alignment,' says the helmsman. 'See those sparks? It's dragging against the side of the containment vessel. That's why we're losing altitude.' He casts a worried glance at the sails, which hang limply in the rain. 'That and the lack of forward momentum.'

'So you need to adjust it? Is that what the spanner's for?'

'Do I look like a bloody technician? These tools came in the box, but no instruction manual. I don't have a clue how to adjust it. Brute force usually does the trick.'

He lunges for the glittering disk as if it's a rare butterfly he's trying to catch in a net. There's a protesting screech as the disk grinds against the spanner head. The deck lurches under you. Arcs of disturbing light splash and play around your head.

'Little help here…' grunts the helmsman, straining with all his might to twist the disk back into alignment.

Make a STRENGTH roll at difficulty 17.

Succeed ▶ **1318**
Fail ▶ **216**

855

'What goes around comes around,' he says with a scornful twitch of his lips.

'Is my credit any good around here or not?'

'Now, now. No need to get in a huff. Do you want it gift-wrapped too?'

Delete the **curio credit** and then ▶ **496** and tick the box there before reading on.

856

'Now there's a face I haven't seen in a long time,' he says as you approach.

'Have we met before?'

'Maybe, but that's a whole different question.'

▶ **380**

857

The symposium is held on the lawn behind the Academy. Dozens of philosophers are already waiting on the marble benches. Myletes has brought a couple of cushions and hands one to you. 'Good for the head, these talks, but hard on the posterior.'

A fat man with tufts of white hair sprouting from his ears sways his bulk around. 'What's the topic this week, do you know?' he asks Myletes.

Myletes looks a little perplexed, then jumps to his feet. 'I completely forgot – it's my week for chairing the meeting.' He hurries to the front and raises his hands for silence. 'Now, my friends, I have a thesis for us to debate. How do we know that this is reality?'

'The reality of these marble benches is incontrovertible,' calls out the fat man. 'I have the piles to prove it.'

There is polite laughter, though you gather there is a serious contention behind the joke. 'Is the intensity of the experience proof of its reality?' wonders another philosopher. 'I could describe an imaginary meal that would make mouths water, or I could present you with a real piece of stale bread that you would struggle to eat.'

'That's begging the question,' says a beautiful woman in the robes of an Iskandrian. 'How do I even know that I am real?'

'You're asking the question,' ventures a timid man sitting next to her, 'so that much of you at least must be real.'

'We know that our minds are real,' agrees Myletes. 'Because the thought that says, "I am real" must be real. But what of physical form? The sun, the birds, the grass, even these benches that bother Ephrodites's buttocks – how do we know those are not figments of our imagination?'

Join the discussion ▶ **1155**
Listen quietly ▶ **986**
Slip away and leave them to it ▶ **1062**

858

Her attack is sudden and deadly. The next moment you're lying on the rug. It's wet and warm with your own blood. You can't move. The undead creature that was Tritona pounces on you and begins to gorge. The sounds of the raging thunderstorm roll away and all you can hear is the gruesome lapping of her tongue as she drains your lifeblood.

Lose the codewords **_Rabbit_** and **_Ruffle_** if you have them. Also lose 1 from your STRENGTH score, as even after resurrecting you will be permanently weakened by the vampire's bite.

▶ **111**

859

You throw yourself up into the rigging, scrambling up the sheets with frantic haste. To free the sail you have to clamber out to the furthest tip of the yard. The storm-slick timbers and the listing angle of the mast don't make it easy. There is a sheer drop below and at one point a sudden lurch leaves you dangling by one hand. Reaching the snagged corner of the sail, you drag it clear. The sudden snap as it bellies in the wind almost pulls you off the yardarm, but you cling on and watch exultantly as the ship starts to gather momentum and rise past the rooftop and towards the open sky.

Your upwards arc carries you directly towards the colossal figure of Thanatos, looming against the heavens. He extends a giant hand, inexorable as storm-swept clouds, thinking to snatch you out of the air. But the ship is gaining speed. It clears his titanic grip, his fingers closing on empty space directly under the keel.

The ship rises up and up, past growling thunderheads piled up like crags into the sky. Rain pelts the deck. You rise into dank, enveloping cloud and break through to the clear night above where the stars are hard and bright as distant diamonds. Impossibly far below, the streets and buildings of the city are mere toys half-seen in the murk.

Thanatos looks up, his hand raised to draw back his cowl. A moment later and his unshielded gaze would have blasted the ship to atoms, but you are sailing out among the silent constellations. Even death cannot catch you now.

▶ 1067

860

You come back to life. For a moment it's like waking from a very deep and dreamless slumber. You don't remember where you are. Then you feel hard timbers under your back and hear the creak of sails straining against the wind. You sit up to see the deck of the ship, the crew watching you in slack-jawed amazement. And beyond them the infinite blackness of deep space.

The Minotaur points to the still-twitching carcass of a giant insect. 'That's what I chucked the axe at, genius.'

'Remind me to trust you next time.' You get to your feet and take a closer look at the insect's body. 'I saw some other critters just like it in the palace garden.'

'It must have sneaked aboard while we were distracted,' says Ancaeus. 'The damned thing had been skulking down in the hold waiting to jump somebody.'

▶ 231

861

Spluttering with outrage, the priest tells the others to drag you off to prison. There is quite a sizeable mob by now, too many to fight, so you allow yourself to be led away.

You spend a week in prison before a jailer comes to tell you that the real criminal was arrested a few hours after committing the crime. 'So you're free to go.'

'This is a gross miscarriage of justice,' you say as you gather your things.

'Technically,' he says, leading you to the gate, 'we only call it that if a person actually dies in their cell. So in a sense you got off lightly.'

'For a crime I didn't commit in the first place? Sure.'

The jailer points you in the direction of the Avenue of the Anvil, then goes back into the prison and locks the gate. You are left to take stock. If you had any companion except Tomyios they have got tired of waiting and gone home; cross them off your Adventure Sheet. Also tick your Wound box if it was not ticked already, as a week on prison rations has left you severely malnourished.

▶ 63

862

Heedless of the long drop to the street, your foes come pouring from the roof in a relentless black tide. Were-apes and werewolves leap across with frightening agility, balancing on the ship's rail and snapping at you with slavering fangs, while shapeless things out of nightmare flap around on ragged black wings. As you battle to prevent them overwhelming the ship, knots of wizened vampires gather at the edge of the roof, casting grappling hooks improvised from tangled bones and winding-sheets. When a line goes taut they scuttle over on bloodless feet, their long grave-grown nails giving them purchase on the swaying rope.

If you have the codeword **Recursive** ▶ 700 now; otherwise read on.

You give yourself in to the pulse-pounding rhythm of battle, laying about you with weapons and anything that comes to hand. One of the vampires, its mummified entrails trailing from a deep cut, flops to the deck and clutches your legs in a rigor-stiff grip. You snatch up a belaying pin, smash its skull to pulp, and whirl just in time to parry the attack of a flapping horror that looks like a giant face with leathery wings in place of ears.

Make a STRENGTH roll at difficulty 15.

Succeed ▶ 1592
Fail ▶ 256

863

'You're awake, then.'

It's the merchant's voice. You are back in his wife's bedroom.

'I heard the change in your breathing.' He steps over to the bedside, touches a finger to his wife's throat. 'She yet sleeps, so I gather you have failed.'

'Well, it's not as simple as – '

'Here. For your trouble.' He contemptuously tosses you a few coins; add 5 pyr to your money if you deign to pick them up.

He turns his back on you and stands gazing down at his wife's sleeping form. A servant touches your arm and you are shown out of the house.

▶ 515

864

A physician is at your bedside. Before you can turn your head, he's rubbed a thick salve into both your eyes.

'Ow! That stings.'

'The truth hurts,' he says with a chuckle in his voice.

'I can't see you clearly.'

'That will pass.'

He leans over you and in spite of the blurring caused by the salve you get an impression of a youthful face under a wide-brimmed hat.

'You didn't need to stick it in both,' you say. 'The arrow didn't even come close to this eye.'

'Who's the doctor here? Anyway, must dash. I have a million errands to run.' He presses a note into your hand. 'Read this when your vision clears.'

Through the stinging lotion in your eyes, you dimly see him turn and walk into the sun. You blink. He's gone.

Somebody is shaking your arm. It's a servant. 'Lady, shall I fetch you anything while you wait to see a doctor?' he asks.

'I already saw one.'

You get up and walk along the beach. Your vision is clearing now. More than that, everything looks sharper, the colours enhanced. Brilliant white lights dance on the sea. The peeling paint on the Achaean ships is glossily blue-black like lacquer. The banners and tents of the camp are delicate pigments on a celestial palette. You had never truly seen until this moment.

Read the note	▶ 1092
Return to the battlefield	▶ 441
That'll do for today	▶ 638

865

'I foresee you will serve the city in other ways,' says the Archon, escorting you to the steps of the Palace.

▶ 1642

866

You grapple with her, but her slimy flesh sloughs away and your hold on her slips. A gust of charnel breath makes you flinch. Seizing the opening, she smashes a crushing blow to your throat with muscles made tough by rigor mortis.

If you were already injured ▶ 279

If not, tick the Wound box on your Adventure Sheet and ▶ 946

867

'All come to me in the end.'

It is a gentle voice. A hand rests on your brow, a cooling touch after the heat of all your travails. Wings spread against the infinite white void and you gaze enraptured on the most beautiful face you have ever seen. It is Thanatos in his aspect as merciful death.

Delete everything on your Adventure Sheet including attributes, codewords, titles, possessions, and so forth. Erase any ticks or other records you have written in boxes throughout all the books.

When you are ready to begin again with a new character, pick any of the Vulcanverse books and ▶ 1

868

Kazala turns to you and bows as the contest enters its third and final round.

If you have the codeword *Quill* ▶ 1252

Otherwise ▶ 1219

869

'Who's this?' bellows a voice pitched halfway between a laugh and a challenge. 'My old friend! What a bloody long way from home you are.'

'Bosk!'

His huge arms wrap around you. You're almost overwhelmed by his bulk and brawn, his body warmth, and the strong red-blooded scent of healthy, hairy frame and wine-sweet breath. First he draws you to him in a wringing hug, then holds you at arm's length for a good look. His grin is dazzling, eyes sparkling in joy at meeting you here, broad face handsome and brown as a nut. For some reason you hadn't remembered the horns.

You look down. 'Did you used to have..? Have you always..? Those... Er, I don't think I noticed before...'

'Cloven hooves. Call 'em what they are. You know. An old goat, me. Everyone says so.'

He slaps you playfully on the back and it's like being buffeted by a bear. Then, as he ruffles your hair with a hand big enough to crush a coconut, he suddenly stiffens and frowns, peering at a point just behind your ear.

'What's this scrap of shadow? This bothersome blot? Out with you!'

His fingers brush your cheek, there's a slight tug, and he holds up a wriggling thing that hisses like a scalded cat. Bosk pushes her into a wine flask on his belt, prodding to get her all the way down the spout, and drives home the stopper.

'A nasty little chit, that Oizys,' he sighs. 'She'll sour a perfectly good vintage, but at least you're rid of her.'

Delete Oizys as your companion and add Bosk instead.

▶ 54

Your blow lifts him off his feet. He lands flat on his back and doesn't get up.

The mechanical spider gets your attention by clattering its legs to make a sound like flat wind chimes. It has unlocked the door up to the roof and leads the way through, pausing to lock it again behind you using one of the keys attached to its feet. Even when other guards arrive, there's no evidence you came this way.

You make your way up a short flight of steps that brings you to a cell right up under the eaves of the building.

▶ 1397

'Wait up,' says another of the looters, pushing past the leader to peer at you. 'I know you.'

A scrawny rat-haired girl dressed in a stolen satin gown joins in. 'Me too. I seen you earlier. You hauled a stone pillar off that woman that was trapped.'

'Actually it was a pile of bricks and a wooden joist –'

She turns to the other looters and gives an excited account of your rescue efforts. In her retelling, you saved the woman single-handed while fighting off a patrol of Celedons.

The gang leader looks at you, eyes bleary with drink. 'You're a bloody hero, you are.'

'And you're a bloody pig,' says Dunamis, kicking him on the shin.

He looks down dolefully, all the fight gone out of him. 'I deserved that.'

'Then here's your chance to make amends,' you tell him. 'All of you – get out there and round up other survivors. Instead of looting, you can help out with rescue efforts. People need food and clean water. Show them how to get organized and stay a jump ahead of the Celedon patrols. We all have to pull together now.'

Nodding, they head off with a new purpose.

'Think you've reformed them?' scoffs Dunamis, watching them go.

'All we need is for the people of this city to band together against Nyx and her minions. Once she's dealt with, they can go back to picking each other's pockets.'

▶ Current Location

You have come to the mysterious well in which red lights occasionally glimmer and float in the depths – lights that only you can see.

Climb down ▶ 1469
Not now ▶ 722

You cast the net. He fails to see it coming, perhaps because of his encumbering helm or perhaps because of the half-light. It entangles his legs and he falls headlong in front of you. He tries to get up but you plant your foot in the middle of his back.

'Kill me,' he says, panting. 'I cannot live with the dishonour of seeing our standard in the hands of an outsider.'

Finish him off ▶ 1586
Reason with him ▶ 107

'Come with me,' you say.

'Where?'

'To Hades.'

He cannot hide the look of alarm that leaps into his eyes. 'If I go, there's no coming back.'

'Maybe not, but I'll show you the way and you'll see there's nothing to be afraid of.'

For a moment he looks around wildly and you think he's going to bolt. Then he heaves a sigh of resignation and nods. 'Lead on.'

You take him along the Sacred Way and right to the pylons of the underworld. Beyond lies a region of white mist that swirls and pulses as though sentient.

A shade greets him. 'Lord Xechasiaris?'

'Why, isn't that my assistant Molpos? I haven't seen you since – '

'Since I died, my lord. It is good to see you. I am on my way to the Asphodel Meadows, and can take you there if you like.'

Xechasiaris looks around. 'Well, I have no luggage. Is that where I will live – I mean dwell – from now on?'

'Oh no, my lord,' says Molpos. 'That's just for nonentities like me. An honoured soul like yourself will be given a home in Elysium.'

Xechasiaris bids you farewell and sets off towards his final resting place. You wait until the mist swallows him up, then return to the city.

▶ 351

A maelstrom of fighting surrounds you. The clash of weapons, clang of metal armour, jarring impacts of blades on ruptured thews, the crunch of broken bones, the screams, shouted oaths, battle-frenzied roars, ragged gasps of breath – all blur into one deafening cacophony. Bolts of magical energy blister the air. The scent of blood and ichor mingles with the adrenalized sweat of a thousand combatants.

It should be impossible to push through the wall of struggling bodies, yet somehow you stride unimpeded towards your one target: Nyx herself, as cold, remote and beautiful as the face of the moon. She sees you coming and her voluptuous black lips part in a triumphant smile. She opens her arms – strong and supple, huge and white as marble pillars, ready to fold you in a crushing embrace.

'Behold, my new world is almost complete,' she says, each murmured word somehow ringing out clear over the din of battle all around. 'The Darklands are rising. Nothing can stop me now.'

The two of you are face to face in the eye of the storm. You draw back your arm to strike. 'Your dream is a nightmare,' you say, 'and it ends now.'

If you have the **sceptre of Agamemnon** ▶ 39
Otherwise ▶ 399

876

It is not hard to find Pemon's store. The door is locked, but you find a passage leading to the back. A broken pane with a few spots of blood show where an intruder broke it – not long ago, either. The blood is still sticky.

You go along a narrow corridor, nearly braining yourself on the low beams, and duck through a small doorway into the shop itself. The room has the chill of the grave, as there is a grate but no fire has been lit today. The place has been ransacked. Books have been flung off the shelves, the desk drawers broken open, and even some of the floorboards have been wrenched up.

Pemon is lying behind an old desk. His blackmailing days are over; the staring eyes and purple lips tell you all you need to know, even before you notice the deep fingerprints in his neck.

If Galatea is with you   ▶ 641
If Polymnia is with you   ▶ 1501
If you have neither of those companions but you possess the **Face of Wisdom** (INGENUITY +3) ▶ 630
Otherwise decide:
Examine the body   ▶ 299
Look around for the letters ▶ 1431
Make yourself scarce   ▶ 988

877

'I'm very glad you asked me that,' you shoot back, treating Kazala's remark as if it's a line the two of you had rehearsed beforehand. You proceed to tell the story of bringing security to the peace-loving Sarpedons. Kazala stands to one side, confident that she's manoeuvred you into telling a dry tale full of long diplomatic meetings. But you wipe the smirk off her face by dramatizing the hunt for dragon's teeth, hiding behind a pot plant to show how you had to dodge patrols of skeleton warriors in the eastern desert. You even manage to inject a few laughs by having Lady Pemphreda's pet monkey stand in as the infant president of Sarpedon.

'If they should ever sow those teeth,' you conclude, 'it will spell the end of their foes but also of the Sarpedons themselves, and there will be no life left in that high valley of Boreas except for the untiring Spartoi endlessly scouring the land for things to kill.'

A shudder goes round the audience followed by a round of applause. Kazala leans towards you. 'You win this one,' she says. 'But I've been saving my best yarn for last.'
▶ 785

878
❑ ❑
Put a tick in one of the boxes.

One box is now ticked ▶ 429

Both boxes above are now ticked ▶ 151 and tick the box there before you read on.

879

The horn booms out its note, echoing across the nascent universe. Hearing it, Sphikos stops and looks around. He waves when he sees you and carefully picks his way back along the banks of cloud.

When he reaches you he's a little breathless, more with excitement than exertion. 'We're at the dawn of creation,' he says.
▶ 1044

880

It's only after you have torn off the wrapping that you notice the parcel was addressed to Lord Xechasiaris, not to you. It contains a **lava gem**. The accompanying note explains that it's the return on some of Xechasiaris's investments.

By rights you should forward it to Xechasiaris's heirs, but you are not sure where they're living now. Add the lava gem to your possessions if you choose to keep it for yourself and then ▶ **97**

881

Your family home is a shambles. The kitchen table has been overturned. Pots and pans are scattered across the floor. The wind whistles eerily down the chimney, stirring the cold ashes in the hearth.

You call out, but there's no reply. You can only hope that your family managed to get to safety.

'Anything you left here?' says Dunamis. 'If so, let's grab it and go.'

Retrieve some belongings	▶ **1087**
Get going	▶ **1603**

882

Hands as cold as grave-clay seize and hold you. Hot bestial jaws fasten on your limbs. You strain and squirm but you are powerless to break free. You stare defiantly at the leering fang-rimmed smirks of the living corpses, the eager panting jaws of the beasts.

Abruptly they release their grip and fall back, cringing in servility to the one who looms behind you. Slowly you turn.

Half filling the sky, Thanatos forces the edges of reality apart, stepping into space above the city, a god astride the winds. His wings wide-stretched like a rolling stormfront, his smoking sword a rail of lightning at his belt, he comes headlong at you in huge distance-devouring strides.

▶ **595**

883

Even with Zoë and her band attacking from the rear, the massed ranks of your foes are so numerous that they pour from the roof in an incessant dark tide. Were-apes and werewolves leap with frightening agility, balancing on the ship's rail and snapping at you with slavering fangs.

If you have the codeword *Recursive* ▶ **700** now; otherwise read on.

You give yourself in to the pulse-pounding rhythm of battle, laying about you with weapons and anything that comes to hand. One of the werewolves, its side sliced

open by a blow, flops to the deck and tries snapping at your legs. You snatch up a belaying pin, smash its skull to pulp, and whirl just in time to parry the attack of a flapping horror that looks like a giant face with leathery wings in place of ears.

Make a STRENGTH roll at difficulty 10.

Succeed	▶ **1592**
Fail	▶ **256**

884

After a last sweeping gaze across the far blue hills and lush greensward dales, you turn and descend the tower.

▶ **48**

885

A breeze sighs across the hillside, turning the leaves of a solitary tree so that for an instant they make a flickering portrait of a face. You get a flash of recognition, only connecting the image now that the wind has passed to the face of the dryad Karya.

'West...' seems to sigh the wind as it goes.

You look up towards the sun, a blood-red ball suspended in the pearl-coloured sky. Which side of Mount Olympus will you look for the food of the gods?

North	▶ **151**
East	▶ **1088**
South	▶ **1311**
West	▶ **1413**

886

Rather than attempting to duplicate a written order, which would require official seals, you settle for the easier task of sending Sakan a letter purporting to come from his uncle, whom you have heard is a merchant.

'*Dear nephew,*' reads the letter, '*find some pretext for a sabbatical and get yourself over to Thermyra. There are rare black pearls here that you can pay the local brats a few coins to dive for, and they'll fetch you hundreds of pyr each at any market on the mainland.*'

Greed does the job. Sakan applies for a leave of absence and sets out from the east gate a few days later. Thermyra is far out off the southern coast of Notus, and even once he gets there he'll spend months trying to track down the non-existent pearls.

Get the codeword *Rock* and ▶ **1432**

887

If you have a **gladiator's net** ▶ **873**

Otherwise he rushes forward. The sword is a blur in the dim evening light.

Make a STRENGTH or GRACE roll (your choice) at difficulty 10.

Succeed ▶ **1663**

Fail ▶ **1038**

888

There, at the crossroads – the blue lanterns of the night watch. You raise your voice to call to them. There's a slight pressure in your back.

'Hey!'

But it's not even a whisper. You have no breath. No voice. The night watchmen, not noticing you, head on down the street.

You're being held up by the three intruders, mauled by their rough hands. You try to fight them off, but you have no strength. They jeer at your feeble efforts, shoving your limp body back and forth between them. You see dark wet stains on their hands. Your blood.

Two of them support you, turning to drag you back the way you came. Even if another patrol came along, from a distance you'd look like a drunk being helped home. Your legs are like rubber. You can't break away. They haul you up the steps and back through the house to the study, where they finally let go of you.

▶ **364**

889

If this box ☐ is empty, tick it and ▶ **754**

If it was already ticked ▶ **1058**

890

A single Celedon remains. She's still screaming like a metal girder shearing in two, but her face remains a lovely lifeless mask of beaten gold.

Attempt a STRENGTH or GRACE roll (your choice) at difficulty 13.

Succeed ▶ **354**

Fail ▶ **11**

891

The two remaining intruders spread out, coming at you from either side with knives that glitter red in the light from the hearth. They're trained to coordinate their attacks. Clearly these men are professional killers.

Try a STRENGTH or GRACE roll (your choice) at difficulty 10, and you cannot use any items to get a bonus because your possessions are still in your bedroom.

Succeed ▶ **989**

Fail ▶ **456**

892

These people are scared. That's why they're selfish. What they need is a sense of purpose. You have to get them to work together, and the best way to do that is to remind them of the common threat you all face.

'Listen to me,' you say, raising your voice over the howling wind. 'All is not lost. We will fight back against the forces that devastated our city. And we will win.'

'It's hopeless,' sneers the gang leader.

'No it's not. I am the champion of the age, sent by the gods to bring light in this hour of darkness. And I will lead you.'

They want to believe you, but they are frightened. Panic makes it hard to get through to them. Make a CHARM roll at difficulty 15. Add 1 to the number rolled for each of the following:

☐ A Glory score of 15 or more

☐ The codeword **Reverie**

☐ The codeword **Rune**

☐ The title **Godslayer**

If you make the CHARM roll ▶ **69**

If you fail it ▶ **554**

893

You catch hold of an outcropping of rock and swing your legs clear before the serpent can close its embrace.

Make a STRENGTH roll at difficulty 10.

Succeed ▶ **1571**

Fail ▶ **1550**

894

The door slams shut in your face. You tug at it, but the guard has already pushed the bolts across.

'Better give up now,' says the first guard, breathing heavily as he moves towards you. 'Arion'll be coming back with some mates and then you're going to get some lumps.'

Surrender ▶ **1532**

Keep fighting ▶ **1638**

895

Striding to the area where warriors are mustering, you seize the reins of a team of horses.

'Stop her!' shouts one of the commanders. 'The king does not want his concubine to risk injury on the battlefield.'

None of the Achaean soldiers seems in any hurry to try stopping you. The owner of the team, a grizzled veteran called Eumelos, steps forward but when he sees the look of fierce determination in your eyes he gives a grudging nod and waves you to continue. Even so he says, 'These mares were bred by Apollo of the silver bow and – look in their eyes, the savagery there of Ares, bringer of panic. 'Foolish girl, they'll break your neck for you. They'll trample you to a red pulp.'

'They'll soon learn who is mistress,' you say, harnessing the wildly snorting horses to a chariot. 'Not even among the Amazons is there any who can match me in handling a team.'

▶ 166

896

You drive off the last of the Keres – but you know it's only a matter of time before they lick their wounds and come back for revenge.

The fleeing townsfolk pause to stare at you, hardly daring to believe their tormentors have been beaten.

'Don't stand around gawping,' Dunamis snaps at them. 'Find someplace to hide where the next patrol won't find you.'

As they hurry off, one old man lingers for a moment. He reaches out nervously to touch you, as if uncertain that you really exist. 'The gods may have abandoned us,' he says in a thin, wheezing voice, 'but we have a champion with the courage to fight back. Bless you, stranger.'

Gain 1 Glory and ▶ Current Location

897

'Stop and think.'

'Your answer to everything,' you snap back impatiently. 'I can't dawdle here. That little girl needs her father.'

'Little girl?'

'There, in the red cloak. Come on or we'll lose her.'

'So you've caught sight of a small figure dressed in a red cloak. You haven't seen a little girl.'

'What are you talking about? For the Muse of Knowledge you can be really slow on the uptake sometimes.'

'Your mind is filling in too many blanks.' She points to footprints in the mud. 'Large for a little girl, aren't they? Also rather deep. I'd say the person you're following weighs almost twice as much as the average nine-year-old.'

Go after the girl anyway ▶ 20

Let her go ▶ 571

898

You find your way back to the discreetly located entrance to Lady Pemphreda's celebrated salon. The secret triple-knock summons her factotum.

If you have the codeword *Pinot*, lose it and ▶ 1605

Otherwise, the factotum informs you that you have come on the wrong day. His face betrays no emotion, his tone is studiedly neutral, and yet his supercilious satisfaction at telling you this is almost as tangible as if he had leant out of the door and flicked your nose. ▶ 1324

899

If you have the **tapestry of Arachne** and this box ❑ is empty, tick it and ▶ 53; otherwise read on.

The Archon of the Sun has left instructions that you are to be given food and lodging here in the Palace whenever you need it.

If you are injured you can untick the Wound box on your Adventure Sheet. You can also leave possessions and money here to save having to carry them around with you. Write in the box anything you are leaving – or you can recover items you left here earlier by writing them on your Adventure Sheet and erasing them from the box.

```
ITEMS AT THE PALACE




```

When you are ready to leave ▶ 1642

900

Your eyes have had a while to adjust to the darkness, but somehow he parries your blow and immediately counter-attacks with a jabbing cut to your neck.

If you were already injured ▶ 111

If not, tick the Wound box on your Adventure Sheet and then ▶ 1378

901

Lieutenant Tekto has left instructions that you are to be given the hospitality of the officer's mess and a pallet to rest on any time you have need. If you were injured you can untick the Wound box on your Adventure Sheet.

When you are ready to move on ▶ 1642

902

She wasn't as badly injured as you thought. She recovers and throws herself aside in time to avoid your attack.

'Thought I'd really hurt you,' you grunt.

'A flesh wound,' she gasps, keeping one hand clutched to her side.

The firelight from the hearth shimmers along her knife blade as she prowls around looking for an opening.

Throw the poker in her face ▶ 1020

Thrust it straight at her ▶ 459

Swing it like a club ▶ 219

903

High in the immense black vault of the sky, a bright star flares suddenly. No, not a star – a meteor, hurtling earthwards. Then as it draws closer you see that it is a human figure clad in miraculous winged battle-armour. He swoops to hover just overhead. The helmet opens like a metal-petalled flower to reveal the face of –

'Daedalus!'

'Quite a pickle you're in here,' he says, surveying the screeching hordes of Nyx's army and the two towering sentinel-like figures of her sons.

'Thank the gods, you arrived just in time. Distract Hypnos and Thanatos so that I can break through to Nyx and – '

Daedalus holds up his hand. 'Time out. I'm a big fan of your work, you know that. But a deal with Zeus's mob? That's not a whole lot better than handing it all to Queen Afterdark on a platter.'

'Can't we discuss all that once, you know, the world is safe?'

He shakes his head. 'That's no way to stop the apocalypse. You have to think three steps ahead where gods are concerned.'

He's going to take some convincing. If you have the codeword *Rudiment* ▶ 841 now.

Otherwise you will need to make a CHARM roll at difficulty 16:

Succeed ▶ 150

Fail ▶ 1042

904

'If you've got no money to pay me,' you say, 'then suggest something else.'

Autolycus scratches the stubble on his chin. 'Maybe I could teach you some useful tricks. I coached Hercules himself in wrestling, you know.'

He shows you some techniques and stratagems you can apply to a variety of situations. Increase both your GRACE and INGENUITY scores by 1 up to a maximum score of +5 in each.

'I was planning to move on anyway,' he says. 'There's trouble brewing up there among the titans and the gods, and I can see it all coming to a head here in Vulcan City.'

As you leave he is already packing his belongings into a bag. You're sceptical. If there is really to be a war in heaven, it's unlikely he'll find anywhere to hide from it.

▶ 771

905

Get the codeword *Rough*.

'Got a bit of a confession to make,' says Dunamis. 'Back at the ball, I nabbed something out of your pocket.'

'What?'

She pulls it out of her jerkin: a crumpled envelope with your name written on it. 'This letter.'

'I'd forgotten all about that. But why did you steal it?'

She gives a very teenage shrug. 'Had to pinch something. And you being a mate, I couldn't take anything valuable.'

'You've opened it.'

'I recognized Zinc's handwriting. Thought it might have something incriminating.'

'And did it?'

'Nah. Just a load of bobbins.' She holds up the lantern so she can read the note. 'He says something about a chip off the old block, whatever that means. Blah, blah, then "I'd say I'm proud of you for getting this far, but that would be vanity…" Lost his marbles, you ask me. Then, "something you'll need…" Says he's left it somewhere safe.'

'What is it? And where?'

'Listen!' She stuffs the note back into her jerkin. 'There's someone coming. Or some*thing*. We better not hang around here.' She heads off down the street.

Follow her ▶ 1274

Go straight to the Grumbles ▶ 491

906

You become uncomfortably aware of the hard marble floor of the ballroom, the icy trickle of rainwater that has blown in through the open doors, the smell of wet soil outside, and the boom of thunder raging far off in the heavens.

Alert now, you spring up ready to face whatever dangers are here.

▶ 1561

907

The clouds are getting less substantial. As you wade towards Sphikos you are sinking to your ankles, your calves, your knees. And in the gaps where the clouds are drifting apart there's an infinite drop into a limpid blue immensity.

Attempt a GRACE roll at difficulty 7. That is, roll two dice and add your GRACE score (and the bonus from any one GRACE-boosting possession if you have such a thing) and you need to get 7 or more.

Sure-footed   ▶ **584**
Clumsy   ▶ **195**

908

From a portico across the plaza, you observe the other second talking to Agrio, who you notice is considerably bigger and stockier than Tekto.

▶ **1471**

909

You kick the vampire away and leap across to the *Sunrise*. Thrown off-balance as you are, you almost don't make it, but a gust of wind sways the ship just a few paces nearer. Your foot catches on the rail, your shoulder slams into the hard planks, and for a moment you lie there, safe but stunned. A huge hand reaches down, takes yours, and hauls you back on your feet.

You find yourself looking up into a bull's face.

'Clumsy,' says the Minotaur.

'That damned vamp threw me off balance.'

You both look out from the rail to see the crazed vampire gathering its shroud around it. With a howl it leaps from the roof directly towards you.

The Minotaur hefts his axe in readiness, but the ship's mate steps in front of you. 'Ahoy, you bloodsucking swab,' he snarls at the vampire. 'You do *not* have the captain's permission to come aboard!'

The undead fiend is flung back from the side as if it had slammed into an invisible wall. It plunges shrieking towards the ground and you see it turn into a tattered scrap of gossamer shadow that is snatched away on the wind.

The other vampires crouch resentfully at the edge of the roof, daunted by the fate of their comrade. But from behind them come other creatures of the night – loping werewolves ready to launch themselves off the parapet, were-apes that swing across the roof with uncanny agility.

'I don't think that lot play by the same rules,' snaps Ancaeus.

You concur. 'So let's get out of here.'

He looks up at the sails with a scowl. 'She isn't gaining altitude. You two need to buy us some time while I fix whatever's wrong.'

The *Sunrise* floats along the street, stubbornly refusing to climb higher. Chasing along the rooftop in parallel, the horde of monsters keeps pace. You can see the enraged were-creatures getting ready to spring across to the deck. Behind them, vampires are bringing ropes to help bridge the gap.

If you have the codeword *Oasis* ▶ **1508**
If not ▶ **89**

910

He can't help being impressed by your reputation. A commission in the Black Guard carries high social standing and respect, but even so he knows at heart that he's just a glorified police officer, whereas you are a true hero.

'You want the truth, I've been thinking of chucking it in and going home to Boreas.'

He tips back his glass, licking the last few drops, and orders another from the cringing waiter.

▶ **1153**

911

Ticklish fingers probe at your waist. Someone is going through your purse. The effort of prising your eyes open feels like dragging two boulders up the slopes of Hades.

You're on the floor in the ballroom. Outside there's the spit and crack of lightning in a sky the colour of ink. A torrential downpour throws a waterfall of rain across the doors to the garden.

You sit up, coming face to face with the young thief, Dunamis.

'You were robbing me?'

'Loosening your clothing. Isn't that what you're meant to do when somebody passes out?'

▶ **1561**

912

From this high vantage point you look out across the mist-shrouded fires and sluggish rivers of Hades. Beyond a range of black mountains, gloomy and forbidding, the Styx flows, a murky ribbon that carries the dead on their final journey. The air that blows in from the west is heavy with the odour of corruption – and is that faint sound merely the wind, or the distant wailing of despairing souls?

If you have the codeword *Roar* ▶ **23**

Otherwise, if you have some **beeswax** and the **wings of Icarus** and you also have the codeword *Raptor* ▶ **1383**

Otherwise ▶ **1655**

913

You make your way along the street, retracing the route the golden maiden must have taken to Naft's warehouse.

'Did you see somebody wearing this?' you ask a

shopkeeper who is scrubbing his doorstep.

He looks at the silk robe, then at you. 'Nobody's going to tell you anything,' he says in a low voice.

'Why not?'

'She lives with the Wolf Himself, that's why not. If I blab to you, next week I'll open up to find my store has been robbed. If the Wolf gets a grudge against a person, locks aren't going to keep him out.'

▶ 1649

914

The insect-creatures hesitate as they draw level with the wall-length mirror. Perhaps the multiple reflections are confusing to their huge black compound eyes.

Attempt a STRENGTH or GRACE roll (your choice) at difficulty 7.

Succeed ▶ 960
Fail ▶ 1604

915

You find him in the marketplace. The moment you mention the theft he is on his guard. 'Who sent you?' he says, voice rising nervously. 'I won't be intimidated. There are witnesses!'

Offer to pay him off ▶ 1557
Threats are cheaper ▶ 130

916

By now there's a milling throng of pursuers pressed right up to the edge of the roof. Through curtains of slashing rain you can see the pallid, worm-gnawed faces of the vampires, the red eyes and spittle-flecked jaws of the were-creatures, the misshapen features of capering nightmare demons. Shrieking and snarling, they are so intent on getting to you that some get jostled over the edge and fall flailing to the street far below.

Each time a grapple lodges on the ship's rail, a stream of attackers immediately comes scrabbling along it to get aboard. Careless of the wind, rain and the lethal drop below, their only thought is to continue their wild onslaught. Even the Minotaur, whose blade flashes and spills blood and guts with every swing, must eventually tire and then the monstrous tide will overwhelm the ship.

There's a commotion at the back of the horde, near the stairs up onto the roof. Some of the rear ranks are turning in confusion. A vampire spins, a spear thrust into its chest, and disintegrates in a tattered cloud of dust and rags and old bones. A slim hand reaches out, pulls back the spear, and swings it in a wide arc to keep the nearest monsters at bay.

As the rabble parts you see a lithe figure in studded leather armour. In one hand she has the spear, in the other a sword that's already slick with blood. Behind her are a band of stalwart fighters, each holding their own against the night creatures that come rushing and snapping at them from all sides.

'Zoë..?' You turn to the Minotaur. 'She's the daughter of King Midas.'

He grunts. 'Long as she's on our side and can fight, I don't care if she's the daughter of Nyx herself.'

You shout a greeting. Zoë is too far off to hear you over the raging storm, but she sees your look of recognition and raises her hand in salute. You don't know what has brought her here at this moment, or who her companions are, but you'll take all the help you can get.

Her surprise attack has distracted the vampires who were manning the grapple-line cannon, but there are still plenty of were-beasts leaping across to the ship. Should you stay to help the Minotaur fight them off, or go to help get the buoyancy rotor working before the *Sunrise* loses any more height?

Stay at the rail to repel boarders ▶ 883
Help the helmsman with the buoyancy rotor ▶ 1498

917

'If you want to see the world with anyone by your side,' says Ptolemos as you greet him, 'it ought to be my old pal Loutro.'

'Why is that?'

'Try paying attention,' he growls. 'I'm not going to repeat myself. Don't have the breath to spare at my age. Ditch your current partner here and head down to southeast Notus. There's an old shrine – well, a ruined shack, really – that's sacred to Aphrodite, next to a lake – or more of a marsh, in fact. You'll find Loutro there.'

'And I should bring him back here?'

He almost shoves you off the bench. 'Bring him back here? What do I want with him? Go look at the dried-up river bed and listen to what he tells you. Now scram, and take your sidekick with you.'

▶ 806

918

Enceladus's swift feet slap the ground, a rapid drumbeat that you can feel vibrating up through your legs. Who could have thought such a hulking brute could move so fast? You glance back just as his tree-trunk club comes arcing through the air towards you.

Make a GRACE roll at difficulty 10 to dodge his blow and get away.

Succeed ▶ 1446
Fail ▶ 556

919

Eros and Prometheus charge forward. Nyx rakes her nails across the air, tearing a gash in reality which becomes in her grasp a night-black halberd. Sweeping it around in an arc, she parries both their attacks. The clash of titanic weapons sends sparks of scalding plasma careening in all directions, blasting holes in the walls of Olympus. The energies they are conjuring are greater than the death of stars, the collision of constellations. Empty space itself twists and screams in protest.

Even weakened by her fight with the gods, Nyx's strength is as great as theirs combined. You can see it's a battle neither side can win. Their struggle will grow in ferocity until the whole universe is consumed – unless something tips the scales.

The Eye of Hyperion is a globe of yellow amber that fits comfortably in the palm of your hand. You thrust it out towards Nyx. A faint glow at first, quickly it grows brighter. Streamers of white light pour from it like splashes of molten lava. Nyx screams as the light blisters her back and burns away her robes. The smell of charred silk and singeing skin fills the air.

She whirls, quickly conjuring a cloud of darkness that closes around on the Eye like a giant fist. Her face, stark in the blazing light, contorts with pain and effort as she concentrates all her power.

She's fighting the embodied essence of the primordial sun god – and she might win. The cloud of darkness she's summoned is choking off the dazzling beams. But Prometheus and Eros lunge forward, seize her wrists, grapple her to her knees. They force her face nearer to the fiery orb. Unable to shield herself now with her magic, Nyx shrieks as the light burns away her flesh.

The light grows in intensity, a white totality, rebounding from the stumps and pillars of stone all around, filling the air, blazing out to the sky, blotting out all in a glare like the sun's heart.

Nyx can bear it no longer. She is visibly shrivelling in the glare. With a scream like a universe dying, she explodes into a myriad motes that drift and fade in the air like fine cindery ash.

▶ 1170

920

Over on the roof, the ever-swelling horde of Nyx's minions is turning from a slavering mob to an organized army. The vampires, realizing they cannot board the *Sunrise* themselves, are swinging lines attached to grappling hooks. Whenever one catches hold, immediately a wave of gibbering were-beasts comes swinging across.

'We don't have the numbers to fight them off,' you say.

The Minotaur roars and lays about him with his axe, revelling in the shrieks of his foes and the gore that spills over his limbs. 'Count again!' he says, laughing wildly. 'One of my kind is worth fifty of these curs.'

Ancaeus's glances back towards the rift that's opening in the sky. 'They only have to delay us long enough for Thanatos to arrive, then it's game over.'

If you have the title **Kissed by a Golden Princess** ▶ 1373
If not but you have the codeword *Noble* ▶ 142
Otherwise ▶ 55

921

Darkness swells up from within your heart, cracking through the bulwark of your sanity just as a tidal wave sweeps away a coastal town's fragile man-made defences.

Unable to stop yourself, you sprinkle the toxin Nyx gave you onto the banquet.

▶ 569

922

If you have the codeword *Rifle* ▶ 1208
Otherwise ▶ 979

923

Thanatos stands triumphant. Where you were a moment earlier, there is just a curl of ash and vapour that swirls and breaks up on the wind. Nyx's minions howl in savage joy, gloating now that no hero remains to oppose them.

▶ 1488

924

You manage to convince her to accompany you to the Forum, where you send her to the temple of Apollo. There at least she may get a few scraps of food or some coins from citizens anxious to demonstrate their piety.

'What if someone recognizes me?' she breathes timorously, hesitating at the temple steps.

'The rich don't look at a beggar's face. But don't stay dependent on charity, Tritona. Your ancestors must have begun with nothing. Find that strength in yourself and build a new life.'

▶ 1642

925

You strike up a conversation with a merchant who has just returned from Boreas. 'Right up onto the plateau I went,' he tells you. 'Cold as a corpse's arse, so better wrap up warm if you ever go. Anyway, there's this sinkhole – huge, I mean, and filled with a sulphurous hot lake. The

Gargareans live there, perched like sea-birds around the rim of the crater. The vapour rising off the lake keeps the place warm, but it's hideous for all that. Before long I was hankering to get back out over the snowy wastes.'

'You didn't care for it, then?'

'The Gargareans are bastards. The place is dank, cheerless. You never see the sun. There are no bargains to be had in the marketplace, and I'll tell you the worst of it.' He leans closer, dropping his voice. 'They're monotheists.'

'They worship Vulcan, I suppose? Or Zeus?'

'Not even a god,' he mutters darkly. 'A titan. Night herself. Fitting, though. There's a real darkness in their souls, if they have any. They reckon Night created everything, you see. Makes me shiver even to think of it. Anyway, I won't be going back there in a hurry.'

▶ 716

926

Note **1642** as your Current Location, then ▶ **1269** and tick the box next to the Forum. From now on you will always be able to find your way back here.

927

He takes you to an office at the back of the building, where a distinguished-looking old man is madly flinging open cabinets and desk drawers.

'Lord Xechasiaris. I have brought someone to help you.'

Another group of dignitaries is clustered around the doorway. 'Get him to go home,' says one. 'His replacement will be here tomorrow. We need the room.'

They all seem to be waiting for you to do something, so you approach the old man. He gives you a long staring look and then starts tugging at his beard. 'Where is it? I thought it was here, but I can't find it. It's gone. Lost.'

'What, my lord?'

'My youth!' He starts rummaging through a cupboard. Pausing, he turns and glowers at you suspiciously. 'Why do you want to know anyway?'

You're going to have to win his trust. Make a CHARM roll at difficulty 9.

Succeed	▶ 793
Fail	▶ 375

928

'Then you already have what you need,' whispers Oizys's grating voice in your ear. 'Now poison it.'

She wants you to mix the toxin that Nyx gave you into the food of the gods.

Do it	▶ 1564
Refuse	▶ 737

929

The vampires come creeping across the room almost on all fours. At the same time, a horde of ragged fluttering things sweeps in through the open doors from the garden. Needle-sharp fangs show in a whir of black leathery wings.

Outnumbered, you back off towards the entrance. An animal reek of wet fur warns you and you glance around to see a pack of were-beasts loping in from the courtyard. They utter a cacophony of howls and gibbering shrieks that sound like the torments of Hades.

Only one way to go – a set of stairs winding up and up to the top of the palace.

If you have the codeword *Rose*	▶ 1266
If not	▶ 689

930

'Come on!' you call to the wary onlookers. 'Help us.'

A few of them start to edge forward, but then a strange high note rings out over the low moan of the wind. The effect on the frightened townsfolk is immediate. Throwing up their hands, they dart off into the ruins.

'Argh.' The man next to you grimaces and lets the beam drop. 'It's no good. We'll never move it off her before they get here.'

'Who?'

He shakes his head and turns away. The other rescuers are already running off. The woman looks up at you through eyes slitted in pain. 'Too late for me,' she gasps. 'Save yourself.'

▶ 233

931

You plunge from the dome, exulting in the thrill of rushing air as the wings snap out and carry you soaring over the heads of your astonished pursuers. Your sweeping arc carries you directly towards the colossal figure of Thanatos, looming amid the boiling storm clouds. He extends a giant hand, thinking he has you, but as you cross the edge of the roof, updrafts fill the wings and you are borne up and up, past the cowled god of death, higher even than the thunderheads that stretch like crags up into the heavens.

Breaking through the misty upper layers you are clear of the rain. The stars are out waiting to greet you, hard and bright as distant diamonds. Impossibly far below, the streets and buildings of the city are mere toys half-seen in the murk. The lightning strikes that slammed and shook you to your core from here seem only distant sparks.

Thanatos was drawing back his cowl. His gaze would have blasted your soul to atoms, but you are safe here among the silent constellations. Even death cannot catch you now.

▶ 1033

932

Hypnos and Thanatos view your party with open contempt. 'Here on the eve of our triumph I had hoped for a battle to remember,' Thanatos jeers. 'Instead it is as if you have already given up.'

'Some have called you mighty and dreadful,' roars back Eros defiantly. 'Yet I too am Nyx's son, and I say: Death, my brother, today you shall die.'

▶ 1533

933

❑

If the box above was already ticked ▶ 724 immediately; otherwise tick it and read on.

Nestor greets you with a friendly smile. 'Good morning, Amazon. You seem to be recovering quickly under Achilles' ministrations.'

He is a large-bellied, broad-built man. It's only as you get closer that you see the deep creases in his skin and the white hairs on his arms that betray his age. He has outlived two generations, seeing all who were raised with him in youth go down in battle. Now he rules men decades younger than himself. Few would be able to hold onto power as age drained their fiercer spirit, but all his men know that the lord of Pylos is the wisest of lords, fair in judgement, keen and unswerving in analysis.

▶ 724

934

'Hey there, below!' shouts a voice from the sky.

You look up. Through the swirling coruscations of darkness, the hull of a ship is visible. It's the *Sunrise*. Ancaeus is leaning over the rail.

'I knew you'd come back,' you call up to him.

'Don't rub it in,' he growls. 'Anyway, it wasn't my idea. Blame her – '

Beside him is the goddess Eos. She raises her veil and a blistering white light shines down, kindling a greater fire in the core of the Eye of Hyperion.

The light grows, a white totality, rebounding from the city all around, filling the air, blazing high into the starless sky, blotting out everything in a glare like the sun's heart.

Nyx can bear it no longer. She drops to her knees, shrivelling in the glare. With a scream like a universe dying, she explodes into a myriad motes that drift and fade like fine cindery ash.

▶ 332

935

'I'll tell you of a mercy mission that saved a whole community,' you say, 'but first I must speak of the Land From Which None Returns and the fateful day I had to hunt a cockatrice.'

'What's a cockatrice?' asks a man who is dabbing at his nose with a lace handkerchief.

'You know what a basilisk is? Same thing.'

'I've never seen a basilisk,' he mutters.

You press on, describing the slaying of the cockatrice and how you collected its blood, which you used to heal the followers of Kedalion, and how in gratitude Kedalion sent his mechanical workers to restore the sacked city of Iskandria. The story goes down well and there is a smattering of urbane applause at the end.

'Good recovery,' says Kazala in your ear. 'You can always count on that fellow to wreck a good yarn with some damned silly question.'

▶ 1119

936

Get the codeword **Rustic**.

The insects go past and vanish out of sight at the end of the topiary avenue. 'Now is your chance, friend of the wood,' say the dryads in their sighing voices. 'You can slip back to your own world. But beware. A battle of gods and titans is raging towards the slopes of Olympus. Many dangers gather on the storm.'

Thanking them, you emerge from the green spaces between the trees and find yourself once more in the garden. The wind has picked up, flinging a fine cold spray in your eyes, and the setting sun is now blotted out by dark clouds.

▶ 143

937

Is it the crash of thunder that wakes you? The actinic lightning flash that bleaches the outlines of your bedroom? The raindrops lancing against the windowpanes? Or is it the soft insistent voice of the figure at the foot of the bed?

'Open your eyes.'

Rather than a command, her words are a seductive invitation. You emerge sluggishly out of sleep. It feels as though a weight is pressing down on you. You see her standing there and recognition strikes like a thunderbolt: Tritona, the youngest daughter of Lord Xechasiaris, whose house this once was.

'How did you get in?'

'You invited me across the threshold,' she says. 'Once is enough. Now I can come and go as I please.'

Her skin shines like porcelain in the gloom. Her eyes are painted stones that burn with green fire at each flicker of the storm outside. Across her lips curve long slender fangs, a yellowish tinge of corruption on the otherwise perfect face.

'A vampire!'

Your voice is thick with drowsiness. You want to reach out, ring a bell to summon your servants, take up a weapon to defend yourself. You do none of those things. You are held fast by her staring green eyes.

If you have a **horn headrest**　▶ 1131

If not　　　　　　　　　　▶ 87

938

'He's got his troubles, that young man. I don't reckon he's cut out for this regiment.'

'What kind of troubles?'

'What kind? Do I look like a blooming maiden auntie? How should I know what kind? The only thing I care about is he's not doing what he's told to.'

As you walk away, the sergeant must have a change of heart, because he calls after you, 'If you want to hear his tale of woes, look in the taverns along Gnome Boulevard. That's where he slopes off to drown them.'

▶ 1642

939

The Oracle turns her head towards the clouds of blue smoke that billow from the tripods. Following her blank white gaze, you see a figure approaching, seeming a long way off and formed from the trails of fumes in the air. You see him only dimly, yet somehow you recognize him as the dragoman who once showed you around the ruins of old Iskandria.

He speaks in a tone that suggests he is surprised to hear his own words:

'Long ago, a traveller came to Hephaistopolis. Unaccustomed to strong wine and living among others, he got drunk and violated a girl, for which offence he was stoned to death by the locals. But his ghost returned as a werewolf, killing without distinction the people of the city, attacking both old and young. Many wanted to flee, and the city could have been abandoned, but the Oracle of the Bright Lord forbade them to leave, instead commanding them to propitiate the ghost, setting him a sanctuary apart and giving him every new moon as wife the fairest maiden in the city. So they performed the commands of the god and suffered no more terrors from the Hero of Temesa.'

'No more terrors?' you shout. 'No more? What about the maidens?'

You reach out towards the figure, but the motion of your arm disturbs the smoke. It breaks apart and the image is gone.

'What about the maidens sacrificed to this "Hero"?' you ask the Oracle.'

'They do not usually die,' she says. After a pause she adds, 'If you are outraged by this story, it is in your power to set it right.'

Your audience with her is over. You return in silence to the outer temple.

▶ 510

940

If you have the codeword *Numb* and the title **The Apiarist** but do *not* have either the codeword *Rye* or the codeword *Raptor* ▶ 1560

Otherwise, if you have *Raptor* ▶ 718

If not ▶ 320

941

If you have both the **Eye of Hyperion** and the codeword *Radiant* ▶ 1664; otherwise read on.

You step into the vast courtyard, one of a complex of quadrangles, colonnades and gardens that surround the various buildings of the palace. Women pose in extravagant ball gowns that each cost a princeling's ransom: some that are sheer waterfalls of liquid metal, some glittering like cascades of spun glass, some as angular and brightly coloured as festival kites. The men are more simply attired but no less striking, white togas shining in the lengthening shadows of evening like bolts of pristine paper on which imperative laws wait to be written.

Servants with frosted bottles of wine and trays of succulent-smelling delicacies move subtly between the guests – so subtly that you hardly notice their coming and going, even after a glass of fragrant straw-coloured wine appears in your hand. You try to study a waiter's face but the features refuse to stick in memory. It must be another of Vulcan's artifices.

A sweet song is provided as backdrop to the gaiety. On a raised dais stand four golden automata with faces sculpted to express beauty and serenity. Their voices are halfway between the human throat and flutes, permitting a kind of ethereal harmony and purity that no mortal singer could accomplish.

'Exquisite, aren't they?' murmurs a bald man who stands enraptured by their singing. 'Vulcan built these Celedons with his own hand, it's said, because no other voice could do justice to the marvels of the world he'd made.'

As he speaks, against the sublime chorus there comes an ominous bass note: a rumble of distant thunder. The bald man frowns at a dark ridge of sky to the west. 'That's an anomaly,' remarks another guest. 'Doesn't Vulcan always arrange for the weather to be fine on ball nights?'

'Perhaps it's part of a surprise,' wonders the bald man, but he pulls his toga around him fretfully as a chill breeze sweeps the courtyard.

If you have the codeword *Rigor* ▶ 586

Otherwise ▶ 420

942

❑

If the box above is already ticked and you have a **voicebox remote** ▶ 784

If the box is ticked and you do not have a **voicebox remote** ▶ 1032

If the box is empty, put a tick in it and read on.

Soldiers have cordoned off the debating chamber where the syndics usually meet. The morning's usual tide of clerks and petitioners is being turned away, but one of the senior officials recognizes you and waves you through. You follow him to the chamber, where the syndics are standing around with expressions of concern.

'Did they run out of laws to pass?' you ask.

'It's no laughing matter. Come and see for yourself.'

He leads you up to the podium where the mechanic Speaker stands ready to address the chamber. The official puts a scroll on the lectern in front of it. The Speaker reaches robotically for the scroll, unfolds it, and begins to read it out. But instead of the melodious brass-edged baritone with which it normally speaks, it now has a high-pitched lisping voice:

'Noble Thyndicth, pleathe take your theath…'

Suddenly it emits a loud raspberry. The official snatches the scroll out of its hands. The Speaker goes silent, lowering its hands and staring immobile over the heads of the appalled syndics.

'You see the problem. How can we conduct official business with the Speaker talking like that? This chamber would become a laughing stock.'

'Have you tried turning it off and turning it on again?'

He fixes you with a furious glare. 'What?'

'Just a thought.' You shrug. 'Somebody must have tinkered with its voicebox.'

'You think?'

'What I mean is, if it can be set to talk in a silly voice, it must be possible to set it back to its serious voice.'

'I'm glad to hear you say it,' he says, nodding vigorously, 'because that's what we want you to do.'

If you have a **voicebox remote** ▶ 784

Otherwise ▶ 715

943

The club crashes into you, sending a jolting pain across your back and making your teeth rattle in your skull.

If the Wound box on your Adventure Sheet was already ticked ▶ 1463

If not, put a tick in it now and ▶ 1289

944

There are voices outside in the street. 'He's never this late getting up,' someone says.

'Right,' barks a militiaman. 'Is there a back way in? If not we'll have to break it down.'

Time you got out of here. You scurry back outside, remembering to stoop under the low beams in the passage, and hide behind an outbuilding as the customer and militiaman come round and go inside.

Go back and report to Lady Himera ▶ 967

Abandon the mission ▶ 988

945

She pulls off a manoeuvre that's half acrobatics and half desperation, rolling back over the desk and clipping your chin with the toe of her boot as she goes. A flash of light bursts across your vision and you stumble, spitting out a broken tooth. Gain 1 scar.

Orphea is at the window. She looks round at you for an instant, her breath coming in short quivering gasps, too panicked for a clever quip. Then she jumps down to the lawn and runs off.

Later, once you've roused the servants, your valet suggests having bars fitted to the windows. 'She could come back, excellency.'

You shake your head. You saw her face there at the end, the whites of her eyes showing, a small and frightened animal, and you know you've seen the last of Lady Rapscallion.

▶ 97

946

Your fingers sink deep into her cold dead flesh. For all her uncanny strength, you have a firm hold on her now and you're not going to let go. Your gorge rises at the foul reek of the grave. Her grotesque howls and obscene blandishments turn to a pleading whine.

'Let me go. Let me go…'

A glimmer of gold in the sky outside explains what she's afraid of. As the storm rolls away and the black clouds break apart you see the first light of dawn in the east.

'There's treasure. A fortune. Let me go and I'll tell you.'

She claws at you with hands that are stumps of bone

encased in putrid skin. She's getting weaker. The sunrise will finish her off – unless you agree to her bargain.

Offer to release her if she gives you the treasure ▶ **504**
Hold onto her till daybreak ▶ **337**

947

'Some of the doors are pretty narrow,' he says as you set off down the stairs. 'Are you sure you can squeeze your ego through?'

There are patrols of guards on every floor. To get past them all you need to make a GRACE roll at difficulty 9.

Success ▶ **637**
Failure ▶ **1144**

948

The play involves three empty-headed shepherds who keep getting distracted from tending their flocks. Whenever they are at one side of the stage playing cards or getting drunk, a dragon drifts overhead on a large cloud of cotton wool and steals the sheep.

Eventually one of the farmers has the idea of dressing himself in a sheepskin. The dragon scoops him up and he stabs it with a sword, but when he does the cloud breaks apart and he falls – right off the front of the stage. It looks as if he's about to smash into the ground in front of the booth, but his strings go taut and he's hauled back up to take a bow alongside the other puppets.

'I like it when they break the fourth wall,' says the man standing next to you.

'I'm not sure it's exactly that,' says another onlooker. 'It's very meta, though. Classic alienation technique.'

'Alienation? Nonsense. It increases emotional engagement, if anything.'

They go away squabbling contentedly. You notice neither bothered to put anything in the puppeteers' collection box. You can pay a pyr or two if you like.

▶ **232**

949

Get the codeword *Rifle*.

Under the pretence of relacing your boots, you crouch down beside the jar. It only takes a flick of the wrist to remove the stopper. You scroop up a handful of grit from the path. A casual glance around to check none of the workmen are looking, and in a few seconds you've dropped the grit into the oil and refastened the stopper.

▶ **76**

950

The Celedon stalks towards you, her piercing scream rising in pitch as she comes. It feels as if your skull is about to split in two. Fumbling with the remote, you press the mute button.

The Celedon stops dead, stunned at losing her deadly sonic power. You make short work of her, hammering at her metal body with a chunk of rubble until she's no more than a heap of twisted scrap.

▶ Current Location

951

He spits on the **mirror shield** and polishes it with a piece of soft leather until it gleams. 'I can give you 200 pyr for it right now, or credit on future purchases.'

Take the cash   ▶ 1447
Take the credit   ▶ 1372
No deal   ▶ 828

952

'I'm sorry, but I couldn't think of living anywhere else.'

She has the good breeding not to register any disappointment. 'I understand perfectly,' she says. 'Perhaps I will come again with a better offer when my fortune has doubled.'

She leaves. Lose the codewords *Ruffle* and *Rabbit* if you have them and ▶ 97

953

Lose the codeword *Robber* unless you also have the codeword *Recursive*.

A few days later a rumour goes around the streets that an officer of the Black Guard was found to have been in the pay of a notorious criminal. 'Naturally it's all being hushed up,' says a fat tavern-keeper, leaning across the bar to give a garlicky whisper in your ear.

'Surely he'll be punished?' you whisper back.

'Sent to the sinkhole in Boreas, is what I heard. Supposedly it's a mission – special operations, they're calling it, but really it's exile.'

'Is the sinkhole in Boreas that bad?' asks another customer, overhearing the tavern-keeper's words.

'Put it this way,' he says, polishing a glass, 'you'd rather go on a mission to the hole in my ass.'

You have to make sure. 'Who was this guardsman? Do you know his name?'

'A Halizon called Sakan,' says the tavern-keeper. 'Only his name's mud from now on, get it?'

Get the codeword *Rock* and ▶ 1432

954

Emboldened by your defiance, other troops begin to emerge from their hiding places in the ruins, swelling your ragtag army.

If you have the title **Public-Spirited** then the City Watch arrive armed with whatever weapons and armour they could scavenge.

If you have the title **Friend of the Nomads** you are greeted by wanderers from the dusty plains of Notus proclaiming support for their *katoi* friend.

If you have the codeword *Rhyme*, Tekto leads the White Guard to join you, resplendent in their polished armour.

If you have the codeword *Rock* you are hailed by the Black Guard, with Viranos among them. Their lacquered armour and jet-black helmet plumes make Nyx's crepuscular hordes look merely shabby.

If you have the title **Murmillo Recruit** you see a company of Murmillones, Atillus at their head, with their fanciful fish-shaped helmets and swords sharp as the stings of manta rays.

If you possess the **Horn of the Fae**, an eager capering band of dryads, nymphs and satyrs emerge from nowhere, the air around them bristling with enchantment.

'Here is my army, Queen Night,' you call to her. 'You thought to unleash your freakish swarm on a single foe? Guess again. Tyranny always seeks to crush and rule by fear, but the courage of ordinary men and women is not so easily cowed.'

▶ 1339

955

Dunamis shakes her head when she learns that you already know Naft the Lean is the main supplier of amaranth oil. 'Well, just stake out his warehouse,' she says as if speaking to a very small child.

'You can't show me where Autolycus lives?'

'I don't know exactly,' she snaps, masking her loss of face with a show of irritation. 'Do I have to do it all for you? He lives with a clockwork twist, and she needs the oil.'

'A what?'

'Twist and twirl: girl. Oh boy, you're having a slow day, aren't you. Anyhow, go over to Naft's warehouse – it's just around the corner on Salamander Boulevard – and keep watch, and before long Autolycus or the wind-up wench are bound to show. Here, take this, it could be useful.'

She presses a small paper envelope into your hand. Note that you now possess a **packet of emery dust** and ▶ 571

956

Two remain, running forward implacably with no thought but to dismember you in their snapping jaws.

Try a STRENGTH or GRACE roll (your choice) at difficulty 10.

Succeed   ▶ 1206
Fail   ▶ 825

957

Eos nods sorrowfully. 'People believe me to be the child of the Sun and Moon, but they are wrong. It may seem strange, as I am the goddess of the dawn, but my true mother is Queen Nyx.'

Your reply:

'Does she know you're here?' ▶ 79

'Are you my enemy, then? Or a friend?' ▶ 262

958

In the hall hangs a mirror. You are startled to see yourself reflected without any of the blemishes that fate had branded you with. Note on your Adventure Sheet that you have no scars and ▶ 604

959

'I still think we should try and use the noticeboards,' she says. 'If the diadem makes it think we're Vulcan, or at least that he's authorized us to use it, we can crack into the command level and reset reality however we want.'

▶ 392

960

The polished marble floor gives you an advantage. The creatures' chitinous claws can't get any purchase on it, so as they scuttle across the room they have trouble staying upright. One of them, hurrying to outflank you, veers off in an uncontrollable skid and careens into a table, smashing crystal decanters and sending silver plates clattering and spinning across the room.

While it's off-balance, you dart over and despatch it with a thrust that drives in between its exoskeletal plates. It dies twitching in a fountain of colourless, acrid-smelling blood.

▶ 1381 and tick one of the boxes there before reading on.

961

Following the directions you were given, you find a door in a leafy side-street. The secret knock brings a factotum in a yellow robe who takes the **gilt-edged invitation** (delete it from your possessions) and leads you up a narrow staircase of dark waxed wood and into a gallery with high windows facing across rooftops to the park.

Lady Pemphreda's guests are an eclectic bunch – city dignitaries in fashionable togas, diplomats and traders in the garb of distant lands, priests, musicians, poets, gruff soldiers, flamboyant actors, hot-headed youths and liver-spotted elders, sloe-eyed painted dancers with loud excited voices and unadorned ascetics conversing in flinty whispers.

Side chambers open onto the main gallery, allowing groups of guests to slip away for more private discussions and other pursuits. In one you see a woman stretched sleekly on a couch while one satyr plies her with intoxicating fruit and another uses rose-thorns to tattoo her body with lewd signs in an indelible dye. In another chamber, a fat man has lifted his robes and stands ankle-deep in a pot of soil, inviting all and sundry to sprinkle him from a watering can; you are told he is a famous artist. In a narrow book-lined alcove, a poet poses grandly on a footstool to recite odes to a gaggle of bored-looking students.

At the end of the room, you join the line of guests waiting to be presented to Lady Pemphreda, who reclines on a divan festooned with plump silk cushions and sleeping cats. 'I hope you will regard this as a second home,' she says, urbanely presenting her heavily-beringed hand.

You mingle for a while, making some useful contacts and picking up some titbits of intriguing gossip. At last, as the sun sets, servants come to light the lamps and the guests take it as their cue to leave.

Note **1324** as your Current Location, then read on.

If you have the codeword **Reverie** ▶ 520 and tick the box next to Lady Pemphreda's salon.

If not ▶ 1269 and tick the box there next to Lady Pemphreda's salon.

962

Shunning other travellers on the road, you wander through the woods and hills without any destination in mind. Or so it seems, until you become dully aware that you are passing through familiar landscapes. You recognize a stone wall, a post beside the way, a gate. The scent of a honeysuckle bush brings memories flooding back like sudden tears. This is the neighbourhood where you grew up. And there – your throat tightens till you can hardly draw breath – there on the road just ahead are your family. You cannot believe how young your mother and father look. Your aunts and uncles, ghosts from your memory abruptly alive again.

And that child, shrieking merrily as he rides on his father's shoulder. It's you.

There's a tinkling crunch of glass. A sharp pain makes you look down. You didn't notice your tightening grip on the scrimshaw hourglass until it broke. The sand trickles out along with the dripping of bright blood from the cut across your hand. The hourglass is gone but it served the purpose for which Galatea gave it to you – to snatch you from the extinguishing fire of Thanatos's gaze and whisk you back through time. To give you another chance.

Let's look at this from another angle ▶ 1071

'It's not under any of them. You've got it up your sleeve.' You grab her wrist.

A momentary frown of defiance flickers across her face, then she smiles. She shakes her lace ruff and the ruby drops into her hand. 'You're getting smarter, or I'm getting slower.'

You reach into her jerkin and find the **Pipes of Pan (CHARM +3)** in a poacher's pocket. Add them to your possessions. The CHARM bonus is not cumulative with that conferred by a **laurel wreath** or a **golden lyre**.

'I'm getting tired of your shenanigans, Orphea. I could call the night watch and have you arrested, but you'd only come back like a bad penny. Bad pyr, I mean.'

'So what's next for us? Set up in business together? Declare war? Go our separate ways?'

Summon the night watch   ▶ **1610**
You're going to have to kill her ▶ **1650**

Write in the box any items that augment your attributes (that is, give bonuses to CHARM, GRACE, INGENUITY, or STRENGTH) and delete them from your Adventure Sheet.

The gate porters take not only standard augmenting items like the **laurel wreath** or **iron spear**, but also any special-use items that boost your attributes such as the **ring of the Philosopher King** and the **golden dog**.

ITEMS AT PALACE GATE

When you have done that ▶ Current Location

Get the codeword *Recite*.

A crowd of people run screaming around the corner just ahead of you. 'Save yourselves!' says a young woman, pausing to accost you and Dunamis. 'The hounds of Death are coming!'

You can hear how close they are from the sounds – huge bulky bodies loping along the street, the snap of voracious jaws, the squelch of hard spear-like talons driven into human flesh, the eager snuffling and jackal-like barks, the moans of dying victims.

No time to think. Panic is catching. You push past the fleeing crowd and advance to face the threat. ▶ **314**

If you have the codeword *Plenty* ▶ **1485**
If not but you have *Pumped* ▶ **993**
If you have neither, read on.

'You need to get up to Ladon's Lake,' says Bosk. 'It's just north of the Palace, not hard to find, but watch your step as there are some scurvy types running a limestone quarry thereabouts.'

'What do I need to do?'

'The lake's frozen, you see. Unnatural, that. It's something to do with the people exploiting that quarry. See if you can get to the bottom of it.'

The rest of the afternoon passes in a blur, as it often does when you get drinking with Bosk. One of the barmaids wakes you after dark to tell you they are closing up. The evening has turned cold and there is no sign of Bosk.

▶ **1534**

Lose the codeword *Rumour*.

You arrive at Lady Himera's townhouse. As you are waiting in the hall for the servant to call you in, a tall man comes down the stairs. He has a bandage around one hand and a dark bruise across his forehead.

The servant returns to tell you Himera will see you now. 'Who's that?' you ask, nodding towards the tall man.

'Lord Sphingo, the mistress's husband.'

'Has he been in the wars?'

The servant looks sharply at you. 'I believe the master slipped and fell while hanging a painting,' he says sniffily.

If you possess a **bundle of compromising letters** ▶ 1465

If not ▶ 1123

968

You come to as sunrise is spreading an orange-pink glow across the skyline outside the window. You're flat on your back on the rug, which is sticky with blood.

'Ouch…'

'Don't try to sit up,' says your companion, securing a bandage around your wound.

'What happened to…'

'Your assailant? Gone by the time I got here. They must've knocked over that vase getting away, that's what woke me.'

Despite a wave of dizzying weakness, you push yourself to your feet. 'The safe!'

Running to check on your valuables, you discover the worst. The safe has been cleaned out. You retain any possessions marked on your Adventure Sheet because those were stored in your bedroom, but your safe has been ransacked; note **515** as your Current Location and then ▶ 1402 and delete anything written in the box there.

969

You rush forward through the fog. The figure looks up at the last second. Recognition comes too late to stay your blow. You dash her brains out with a stone. She lies dead at your feet, eyes staring from a drawn white face, mouth slack in a final frozen instant of astonishment. It was Tritona, the youngest daughter of the late Lord Xechasiaris. Her expression at the end was of piteous wretchedness, the slime and gore of a half-rotted cadaver slick on her lips, her once-lovely face wizened by privation.

So that was what her life had been reduced to after she left your mansion. Robbing from the dead and feeding on their bodies. Just before you struck, a look came into her eyes that may have been acceptance. Reduced to a ghoul's twilight existence, she must have welcomed death. At least, you'd like to think so.

You stumble blindly until you find the cemetery wall, which brings you at last to the gate. 'I was just locking up,' grumbles the watchman, loosening the chain to let you out.

Too numb with horror to reply, you push past him into the street fighting the urge to be sick. Get the codeword *Reef* and ▶ 1617

970

On the Boulevard of the Undine where the city wall overlooks the verdant land of Boreas, the paving stones are strewn with fresh palm leaves and the smells of the city are swept away by the clean breeze off the woodlands to the north-east.

If you have the codeword *Reverie* and wish to drop in at your home ▶ 1238

To go straight to a city location that you already know about, note **970** as your Current Location, then ▶ 1432

Or you can go:

West towards the city gates ▶ 222

East towards the watchtower ▶ 48

971

What will you ask Eos?

'How can I enter Vulcan's workshop?' ▶ 747

'Where is it?' ▶ 1459

'What dangers will I face before I find it?' ▶ 50

If you have heard all you need to and are now ready to return home ▶ 90

972

'Who do you want killed this time?'

'What, you think we're animals?' says Zinc. 'It's not always about killing. All I need you to do is break a guy's kneecaps.'

'Is he a warlock who'll slap a curse on me? Or a Myrmidon, perhaps, with a score of arena kills behind him? Maybe a demigod who'll tie my limbs in a booby knot?'

Zinc spreads his hands. 'He's just a guy. An irritating little prick called Kleistro.'

One of Zinc's henchmen, a huge militia veteran with a face as broad as a pumpkin, leans over and pokes a thick finger under your nose. 'Putting Kleistro in a wheelchair is what he needs. It'll calm the sumbitch right down.'

You keep looking at Zinc. 'So why don't you send this big ape to do the job?'

' 'Cause this big ape would pull his legs right off,' snaps Zinc in exasperation. He glances at the henchman. 'Piss off, Leukos.' As the burly bodyguard slouches away, Zinc turns back to you. 'I wasted enough time on this. You going to do it or not?'

Take the job ▶ 662

Turn it down ▶ 326

973

Frantic to dispel the light, Nyx lashes you with a fiery net of crackling black lightning. Bolts writhe and curl around you like vicious whips. Blasted and shaken, you struggle to hold the Eye aloft. Its blazing light is weakening her. Your only chance is to keep it thrust out between you and hope that she falls before you do.

Make a STRENGTH roll at difficulty 16 to endure her punishing onslaught.

Success ▶ **458** if you have the codeword ***Rhombus*** and ▶ **1531** if not.

Failure ▶ **385**

974

Zeus raises his hand. A sense of dislocation comes over you. The hall ripples, an image in a pool disturbed by a thrown pebble.

'Wait,' you say as the gods begin to fade, 'where are you sending me?'

'To the Tomb of Hope.' Zeus's voice rolls like thunder. 'You will find your city greatly changed. Now you must be the hope your people need.'

Get the codeword ***Rhombus*** and ▶ **73**

975

A fur trader from the mountains passes your table. Seeing you noticing the long flaps of his hat, he sweeps them up with a rueful smile. 'Hot in this weather,' he says, 'but if the punters don't see you in the appropriate gear they won't pay top prices.'

You riffle through Xechasiaris's pictures. Yes! There's one of a man you assumed just had very big ears, the way a small child would draw him. But those could be the flaps of a fur hat.

And here, another drawing shows a lever on a mountainside with the sun scrawled over in black crayon. There is such a valley, far to the north-west in Boreas.

You call the trader back and show him the drawings.

'Runic incantations, are they?' he says, not wanting to touch them.

'A seven-year-old kid drew them.'

'Oh.' He picks them up, squints at each in turn, then holds up one that shows a blaze of dark red against a white field of snow. 'Hellebore, that is.'

'Have you got any for sale?'

He laughs. 'Bring flowers hundreds of leagues to market? I'd be broke after one trip.' He tosses the drawings down on the table and is starting to walk away when he has an idea. 'If you want to come along on my next trip home you can pick some yourself.'

Accept his offer ▶ **1406**

Decline ▶ **613**

976

It is unsettling to grapple in close combat with a Celedon. Her eyes fix upon you, glassy and full of soulless fury like the stare of a hunting bird. Her metal-banded muscles give her the strength of many men, but she fights without any of the grunts and gasps of breath a living fighter would make.

Make a GRACE roll at difficulty 13.

Succeed ▶ **566**

Fail ▶ **1002**

977

'So what do you want us to do with him, your grace?' asks the officer of the watch.

What's your decision?

'Take him away. I'm going back to bed.' ▶ **97**

'Let him go.' ▶ **1423**

978

Nyx reacts faster than you can move. Her arm sweeps around, knocking your blow aside. In her eyes there's a gloating flash like polished jet. 'Mortal,' she says, 'this has gone on long enough.'

The world flickers. Reality resets. Now your hand is thrust against her chest. Your fingers are closed around the hilt of a dagger. Her essence seeps from the wound like thick tendrils of smoke.

'How…?' says Nyx.

'I have a guardian angel.'

She nods, sensing the Face of Wisdom's interference now. 'You have won. But it'll be your epitaph.'

As she dies, she unleashes a blast of dark energy that rends your very soul. Even the Face's control of Vulcan's matrix is not enough to alter so potent an act. You collapse across her body, knowing that nothing can save your life.

▶ **42**

979

The moment you sit down, the arms of the chair snap around your wrists like manacles. The chair starts to vibrate, then rears up, lifting you clear of the floor. There is a loud clanking sound as the chair transforms itself, metal plates dislocating, swivelling and reconfiguring into the shape of a golden maiden who holds you in a grip you cannot break.

'Now we can talk in a civilized manner,' says the caretaker, pulling off the warty nose that you now see was a rubber fake.

He removes his grey wig and peels off more makeup, straightening as he does so. He no longer looks like an arthritic old man but a lean and wolfish figure in the prime of life.

'Autolycus, I presume,' you say ruefully.

▶ 692

980

This last one is the biggest. You are careful to stay out of reach of its flailing claws, circling swiftly while its chitinous feet scrape and slide on the marble floor of the ballroom.

Attempt a STRENGTH or GRACE roll (your choice) at difficulty 7.

Succeed ▶ 1435
Fail ▶ 1604

981

The stars streak through rents in the frantically sweeping clouds. Looking up past the ruined buildings is like viewing the cosmos from the surface of a dead planet.

Note **1589** as your Current Location and then ▶ 549

982

You fly on. Lacking any sense of time or distance, you begin to grow numb, your mind a blank.

Suddenly a cliff looms right in front of you – an island floating in the emptiness of space. You snap out of your near-trance, shoulders straining as you tilt the wings to gain altitude.

Swooping up the cliff-face, you level off. A twilit landscape of grey crags and silver rivers rushes by below. You heave a sigh of relief at having avoided smashing into the rock. And that's when you fly smack into a tree.

One of the wings snaps in half on impact. You black out for a moment. Fighting your way back to consciousness, you realize you're dropping like a stone. Brittle branches scratch your face. Flapping the remaining wing, it's all you can do to break out of the dive. Fluttering down in a haphazard spiral, you make for a gleaming pool and splash down painfully.

The **wings of Icarus** are dragging you down. You shrug them off (delete them from your possessions) and swim until you reach shallower water and are able to wade ashore.

▶ 539

983

'Surely not,' you say. 'I fight for him.'

Achilles shakes his head. 'He protects Ilion. And the gods do not view loyalty as we do. If your dog bites the wrong person, you kick it. That's how the Olympians view mortals like yourself.'

'And you don't count yourself as one of us?' you say, raising an eyebrow.

'Oh, I'm mortal, all right. But none of the gods dare touch me because of my mother.' He looks up into the sky. 'They are getting too involved in this struggle. War is a mortal folly. When the immortals get drawn in, the very foundations of the universe are at risk.'

'Thanks, by the way.'

He visibly shakes off the introspective mood, flashing you a smile. 'Sorry I took so long. Even one scar is a crime against your beauty.'

▶ 1327

984

'Demeter is the mother goddess – seven children she had, so that brood must have got through a few rattles I'd have thought. Maybe you can find her as she's out in the world searching for her daughter. Last heard of in the north-west of Notus.'

You thank him and set off.

'One more thing,' he calls after you. 'Might be worth taking in a puppet show. You know the booths on the Street of Ash? Some of those plays have a kernel of truth.'

▶ 806

985

Groping your way in near-darkness, you skin your knuckles on a door jamb – cold dank stone under your reaching fingers. Your feet scuff on wet steps. There is a smell of water in the air. The darting red lights, which you now see are airborne fish, throw ripples of light against the dark algae-stained masonry of the walls.

You are at the bottom of a deep well. High overhead there is a circle of amber sunlight with sharp static images that snap from one to another like slides in a magic lantern. A potter's cart laden with wares. A camel. Two priestesses walking arm in arm. A nomad whose lemon-coloured robes blaze against his rich brown skin. The echoing babble of passing crowds echoes down the well from the teeming street above.

A coin falls down the well. You catch it before it hits the water. Get the codeword **Ruby**.

Outside the air is cold on your cheek. You catch a few words spoken in a familiar voice, somewhere nearby but strangely muffled. In the bough of a tree outlined by a blistering white moon, the nightingale continues its song.

Go towards the nightingale ▶ 301
Look for the voices ▶ 1000

986

'We must first consider the kinds of simulated reality that exist,' says an excitable-sounding young man sitting cross-legged on the grass. 'A theatre has a stage set. Not real clouds and mountains, but we accept that they are real when the story grips us. The actors pretend to feel emotions that are not true, and we tremble with anticipation for what will happen. If somebody taps us on the shoulder, we brush them off – thus! "Leave me! I must see what happens to these characters!" But that simulation, although convincing, happens within the wrapper of reality, so to speak.'

'What about a puppet play?' calls someone else.

'I was coming to that,' says the young man, springing to his feet. 'We watch the puppets strutting to and fro and we accept this puppet is dying of love for this other puppet, and these other two puppets are sworn foes. It's only when the curtain drops over the booth and we're asked to pay an obol that reality reasserts itself.'

'You'd know if you were a puppet, though,' Myletes points out.

'Ah yes,' says the young man, 'but how would I know if you are a puppet? And more than that, what if I dream I am a puppet? In the dream it all seems real, and in the dream it no longer matters that I have a head carved of wood with glass beads for eyes. Now I can think, feel, love, hate – and yet I am a puppet!'

A big man is shaking his head. His muscles are so gym-swollen that his academic robes are stretched tight across his chest. 'All of this could merely be a reflection of reality,' he says, 'like shadows on a cave wall. We see the shadows, but not the source of light nor the objects moving in front of it.'

The discussion continues until sunset. You stay for supper with Myletes and then make your way home. Get the codeword *Riven* and ▶ 1062

987

'Tempting as it is to see exactly how you plan to dupe me this time, I've had more than enough of your games.'

You move closer. Orphea must read something in your eyes, because her grin wavers and she backs around the desk, drawing her dagger.

'It's not going to be the night watch, then?' she says.

'Let's face it, you'd just escape and come back and buzz around me again like the irritating human mosquito that you are. It's just going to be easier all round if I put you back in the grave.'

'Fighting talk. But I'm the one with a weapon.'

You reach back and take the poker from the fire. She'd left it there when she stoked up the fire and the tip is glowing bright yellow. 'Satisfied?'

Swing the poker	▶ 219
Jab at her	▶ 459
Throw it at her	▶ 1020

988

You are on the Boulevard of the Sylph. The east side of the street widens at intervals into little squares where marble fountains throw up clouds of dancing prismatic spray in the sunshine. Each square is lined with shops dedicated to a specific trade: glassware, rare books, decorative fabrics, carpets, spices, ceramics, and so forth. And the trade of each square is signified by an ivory statue depicted in a vibrant pose – so that the arcade of the wine shops, for example, is instantly identifiable from the statue of a capering satyr garlanded with vines and carelessly brandishing a wineskin from which carved ivory droplets seem about to spill out to the flagstones below.

If you have the codeword *Rumour* and this box ❑ is empty, tick it and ▶ 876; otherwise read on.

To go straight to a city location that you already know about, note **988** as your Current Location, then ▶ 1432

Or you can go:

North	▶ 451
South	▶ 509

989

You kick a chair into one of them. It only holds him up for a few seconds, but it's long enough to block the other as he cannons into you. The two of you struggle against the desk, knocking papers to the floor. Snatching up a letter opener, you drive it into his eye.

'Just you and me now,' you say to the remaining intruder as he struggles out of the wreckage of the chair.

▶ 1023 and tick one of the boxes there before reading on.

990

Note **555** as your Current Location, then ▶ 1269 and tick the box next to the South Gate. From now on you will always be able to find your way back here.

991

You call at a tall, high-gabled house in the wealthy district along Septentrional Avenue. Outside, rushes and palm leaves have been strewn over the road to muffle the sound of cartwheels.

The servant who shows you in asks you to remove your shoes. You are taken through into a room whose tall latticed windows are curtained, allowing only a few shafts of daylight to penetrate the gloom. As your eyes adjust you make out a canopied bed at the back of the room. Beside it is a man in rich silk robes who is bending to peer solicitously at the occupant of the bed.

'I was told you want somebody to recover a missing person.'

He straightens to his full height, giving a jerk of the head as he turns to you. You get the sense that he is used to snapping orders at underlings, and is softening his usually imperious temper only by conscious effort.

'It is my wife,' he says in a whisper, pointing to the bed.

You crane your neck. She lies there in a deep sleep, a woman with raven-black hair, her absolute stillness in the white expanse of bed linen making her seem like a beautiful doll. She is much younger than the merchant, barely more than a child.

'Her spirit is not here,' he explains in hushed yet urgent tones. 'She has been abducted in her dreams. I need you to enter the dreamlands and bring her back.'

If you are accompanied by Polymnia ▶ 1404

If not but you possess the **Face of Wisdom** (INGENUITY +3) ▶ 697

Otherwise what do you say?

'Why not just wake her up?'	▶ 1210
'Who is her abductor?'	▶ 1110
'How would I enter the dream world?'	▶ 113
'Sorry, but you need to get somebody else.'	▶ 515

992

An unearthly radiance lights up the chamber, swiftly growing until it is as bright and warm as a sunrise. It pushes back the darkness, which writhes resentfully into the far corners. The light limns one of the slumbering Syndics with a golden aura.

'That's Zagreus,' calls Dunamis from the doorway.

You make your way carefully between the seats so as not to brush against the pupating dreams suspended in the air over each sleeper. Each dream has the shape of a nascent figure whose embryonic organs pulse beneath their waxy skin. Their heavy lacertilian eyelids twitch with unknowable thoughts. What happens when those dreams emerge into reality? You'd rather not find out.

Do not delete the blessing; you haven't used it yet. Now ▶ 294 and first tick the box there, then read on.

993

'Freeing Ladon is a grand start!' Bosk gives a shout of triumphant laughter. 'He told you about his brother Alpheus, I'm sure.'

'He did say something.'

'Which means you haven't yet faced that idiot calling himself the Master of Twilight. Fancies himself a son of the goddess Nyx, though why she doesn't blast him for such blasphemy I can't imagine. He's just a deluded mortal with some stupid face paint.'

'So he's a pushover?'

Bosk tugs at his beard. In most people the gesture would seem thoughtful, but he makes it look more like weeding a garden. 'His nightshades certainly aren't pushovers. You're going to need a lightning flint. Those are easy to come by in Boreas – on one of the oread mountains. Mount Nysa, I think it is. Ah, now there's a lass you can't forget in a hurry…'

'No doubt,' you say, distracting him before he drifts off into salacious reverie. 'But then what? How do I find the Master of Twilight?'

'Didn't Ladon explain all that? Careless of him. You know the plateau in eastern Arcadia, well, there's a tarn near the Druid's Shrine. No, I don't know what druids are doing in Arcadia, it's a sign of how far the old place has come down in the world. Anyway, this tarn is all dried up now, but if you snoop around a bit you ought to be able to find Alpheus.'

You pass the rest of the afternoon drinking with Bosk. You have blurry recollections of singing, a dance that spills out into the city streets, climbing some railings and baying at the moon, and the next thing you know you're waking up in a gutter. The rising sun pierces your head with merciless light and your tongue feels like last year's flypaper. There is no sign of Bosk.

▶ 1534

994

If you have the **tunic of Nessus** ▶ 292

Otherwise your only recourse is to ambush Sakan one dark night when he's on his own – but if he sees you coming it's going to be a fight to the death.

Do it	▶ 1490
Not worth the risk	▶ 1642

995

From this high vantage point you can survey the trackless dunes of Notus stretching all the way to the rim of creation. The sun beats down unceasingly, creating a shimmering effect as heat waves ripple across the eastern horizon. Far in the distance to the south, you can make out the impossibly shaped tors of the Land From Which None Returns.

Looking back, you gaze over the close-packed roofs, the wide thoroughfares, the open spaces of the city, the parks and lakes, the acropolis on which stretches the Forum with its palaces, and beyond in the softness of distance the far walls and towers marking the boundary to other lands.

If you have the codeword *Raptor* and also have some **beeswax** and the **wings of Icarus** ▶ 1112

Otherwise ▶ 1246

996

The Oracle is a middle-aged woman incongruously dressed in the tunic and makeup of a young girl. She sits between two braziers supported on tripods. These billow with coloured smoke, and as she inhales the fumes her eyes roll up in a trance.

'I speak with the voice of the far-seeing one.' Her voice is like a boulder rolling over gravel.

'What is in my future?' you ask, prostrating yourself in the presence of the god.

'Mortal fate is a crossroads,' she intones, plumes of indigo smoke snaking from her nostrils across her cheeks and brow. 'Which realm do you seek knowledge of?'

Choose your reply:

'Arcadia.' ▶ 940

'Boreas.' ▶ 428

'Hades.' ▶ 1260

'Notus.' ▶ 1156

'This city.' ▶ 303

997

'Zinc, Zinc…' mutters a sibilant voice. 'Will you betray all that's precious to you?'

'Don't listen to that,' snaps Oizys. 'It's just the wind echoing off the rocks.'

If you have the title **Favoured by Orion** ▶ 799

Otherwise ▶ 5

998

The Keres rear up against the sky, outlined in Dunamis's flickering yellow lantern-light like monstrous carrion-birds or ancient reptiles. They begin a horrible chorus of slavering and yapping sounds as they come eagerly towards you on those long, spike-tipped forelimbs.

You brace yourself for battle, though it seems hopeless against so many. 'Run when you get a chance,' you say to Dunamis.

A desperate cry rings out. The Keres' heads snap around. Running directly towards them is a woman whose elegant robes are torn and smirched with soot. Rings and gold bracelets glitter on her hands. You get a glimpse of her terrified eyes as she looks towards you.

'Go!' she says.

She gasps and goes stiff as one of the Keres impales her on its spear-sharp leg. You start forward, weapon ready,

but Dunamis clutches your arm. 'Don't be a fool. She's bought us a few seconds to get away.'

As you run off down the street, you can't help glancing back. Better if you hadn't. The Keres are savaging the noblewoman's body like dogs with a scrap of meat.

▶ 1175

999

Your teeth sink into the flesh of the apple, releasing a sweet fragrance that conjures up images of tumbling brooks, spring showers, and rolling green fields. It's as though your mind has expanded to encompass the totality of the universe. For a split-second you feel as the gods must, where each current of air or beam of light connects to an infinite network of reality.

The sensation passes, but you are permanently changed by the experience. Gain +1 INGENUITY up to a maximum score of +5.

▶ 97

1000

If you have the codeword *Quill* ▶ 1309

If not but you have the codeword *Nadir* ▶ 1505

Otherwise, if you don't have any of the codewords *Nadir*, *Naughty* or *Prankette* ▶ 1462

Otherwise, if you have the title **Queen's Champion** ▶ 1483

If none of the above apply but you have the codeword *Ozone* ▶ 59

Else ▶ 318

1001

Get the codeword *Ruffle*.

You watch Tritona sweep off along the street, her shoulders proudly squared in spite of her dishevelled appearance. Perhaps she will get over her sense of entitlement and apply herself to making a living, but you suspect not. Once aristocrats begin the slide towards penury, they often sink faster and further than those who are accustomed to work.

▶ 97

1002

Her cry, sharp and cutting as a bird of prey's, stuns you. As you lie helpless, she slashes her metal claws again and again across your face.

If you were not already injured, tick the Wound box on your Adventure Sheet and ▶ 1068

If your Wound box was ticked already ▶ 666

1003

'Seeing as the most useful thing right now would be to get Vulcan's crown – '

'Which you stole.'

'Old news. The thing is, we can get it back if we find the guy I stole it for.'

'And where's he?'

She sighs. 'I'm not a hundred percent, but given that he's one of the Syndics…'

▶ 392

1004

A search of their pockets turns up a **lava gem**, a **winding key** for a music box, and a **honey cake**, which you can add to your possessions. There's also a note written in a crude hand:

'Hey Gulvig, me old mucker, I just found out one of the escaped Iskandrian slaves is living as a street rat right under your nose there in the Grumbles. Stolen goods, that's what she is. See if you can track her down, tan her hide, then sell what's left. If you get her then you owe me a drink. – Yours, Orstil.'

Leaving the bodies for the rats, you make your way back down to the street.

▶ 571

1005

A group of young aristocrats are giggling over the antics of one Philonei, who has the reputation of being rather earnest, awkward and dull.

'She got invited to a gaudy,' says one in an uproarious tone.

'Excuse me… a "gaudy"?'

They look at you askance. 'They're the masked balls Vulcan throws at his palace every now and then,' explains a girl sipping at a tall fruit cocktail.

'Anyhow,' says the first speaker after a pause to commiserate with your ignorance, 'of course they took away her laurel wreath at the door.'

'Surely she got it back after the ball?' says another of the group.

'Naturally, but can you imagine? This is Philonei we're talking about. She's hardly scintillating company even with that laurel wreath.'

'Oh yes. How excruciating for her.'

'For everyone else, you mean.'

They roar with laughter. As they disperse to refill their glasses, you accost the girl with the cocktail. 'Where is Vulcan's palace?' you ask her.

She gives you a wide-eyed look as if you'd just sprouted a tail. 'Right here in the city.'

'Really? I've never seen it.'

'Oh, nobody sees it unless they have an invitation.'

▶ 1324

1006

You drive the last of the Keres off – but you know it's only a matter of time before they lick their wounds and come back for revenge.

Bedraggled survivors emerge from the ruins. There is shock in their eyes but also a growing glimmer of hope. 'They can be killed,' breathes one man excitedly, picking up a broken stick to wield as a club. 'Did you see? Arm yourselves! Next time one of those patrols comes back, we won't be running.'

'We'd better get a move on and save the world,' Dunamis whispers to you as you head along the street. 'Those dopes aren't going to last ten seconds against a pack of death dogs.'

Gain 1 Glory and ▶ Current Location

1007

'So we're stuck until we find Vulcan's crown,' you say, frowning.

'Don't look at me like that. How was I to know we'd need it to save the world? When I sold it to Zagreus, the world didn't even need saving.'

'What do you suggest?'

'We'll have to go back to the Syndics' palace,' she says. 'It's got to be there in the debating chamber. Somewhere.'

'And if it isn't?'

She looks around at the devasted city. 'Then we'll be looking for a needle in a haystack.'

▶ 1549

1008

'I'd have thought you five might have made me a magic sword,' you say to the Dactyls. 'Or failing that, armour that not even Thanatos could hurt me in.'

They look sheepish. 'Sorry,' says Index. 'All we can give you is this. It's one of Kedalion's gadgets that we found lying around our toolroom.'

It's a small matte black tube with a stud on one end. Index explains that you can use it once only to apply a battlefield dressing to a wound. If your Wound box is ticked, use the **epigonic pen** to untick it, and then delete the pen.

Note the **epigonic pen (one-use healing)** among your possessions and then ▶ 1258

1009

Ancaeus turns to you, his beard and hair matted with rainwater. 'Get the halyard onto that winch!' he shouts over the roar of the gale.

You grab the loose end of the rope he's hauling and start winding it onto the winch. Gusts of wind tear at the rope as Ancaeus tries to hold it steady. Blood is flowing freely where the rough fibres have cut deep into his hands, but with his face set against the pain he takes a running jump to seize the halyard further up, dragging it down while you crank furiously at the winch.

The deck lurches to one side. The vessel is now several metres below the level of the roof, making it easier for your foes to jump across. The Minotaur is holding his own for now, but it's only a matter of time.

If you have the codeword *Recursive* ▶ 1437 immediately; otherwise read on.

'We need to get higher,' you yell to Ancaeus.

'It's because we're not moving. She'll gain buoyancy once we're under way.' He staggers back, buffeted by the tempest, and takes hold of the winch. 'The sail's got snagged, can you see?'

He's right. The canvas has caught on a spar, wrapped around it by the wind, and that's why it's not opening.

You can see from Ancaeus's torn hands that he's in no condition to go aloft. 'I'll free it. You stay at the winch.'

Make a GRACE roll at difficulty 14.

Succeed ▶ **859**
Fail ▶ **334**

1010

If you have the codeword *Rhyme* ▶ 901

If not but you have the title **Murmillo Recruit** and Glory of 12 or more and this box ❏ is empty, tick it and ▶ 1660

Otherwise, if you have Glory of 8 or more ▶ 1203

Otherwise ▶ 1253

1011

'You are the late Lord Xechasiaris, former syndic, and right at this minute your family are waiting to bury you.'

'And you are..?'

'I recovered your lost youth, remember? A sniff at a flower petal and it all came flooding back – stowing away on a merchant's cart when you were a child.'

'And now I'm dead?'

'You're in monochrome and you're flickering. Notice how everyone who passes you is making a sign against the evil eye. Look in a mirror and you'll see nothing. You've been deleted from reality, only it seems to have slipped your memory.'

He makes a gesture as if wiping cobwebs from his face. 'So that's why they were carrying me around in that box.'

'And they'd like you to get back in it.'

Xechasiaris straightens to his full height, a look of pride and irritation coming across his face as he remembers everything.

'Put me in a coffin? Never!'

How will you convince him to go back to the necropolis?

'Death is part of existence. It's how things are meant to be.' ▶ **649**

'Consider the circle of life. You've had your turn.' ▶ **731**

'After all your years of service, you've earned this. It's time to rest.' ▶ **1522**

1012

The sensation of coming back to life is less immediately vitalizing this time. You feel groggy, as if woken from a very deep sleep or after a long illness. You rise on shaky legs to find the Minotaur looking down at you.

'We got the lot,' he says. 'And the larvae and the eggs that hadn't hatched yet.'

'Any casualties?'

Ancaeus, a bandage wrapped around a fresh wound on his arm, comes over. 'We lost a couple of men. Who could have guessed those things were stowed away in the hold? It's like discovering you have a canker eating away inside you.'

He goes away shaking his head. The surviving crew, grim-faced, gather up the bodies of the giant insects and cast them overboard into the void.

▶ **653**

1013

It's not easy striking up a conversation. Even half-drunk as he is, the instinct of any Black Guard officer is never to fraternize with civilians. Recognizing his accent as Halizonian, you tell some stories about your travels in Boreas. Those help to break the ice, but if you want him to really open up you need to impress him.

If you have Glory of 10 or more or the title **Paladin** or the codeword *Rune* ▶ 910

If not but you have the title **Champion of the Amazons** ▶ 400

Otherwise you'll need to make a CHARM roll at difficulty 10. (Roll two dice, add your CHARM score, and you need a total of 10 or better.)

Succeed ▶ **791**
Fail ▶ **1515**

1014

'That's the Palace of the Archons,' says Dunamis as you head off across the Forum. 'What do you want there?'

'The Archon of the Sun once told me about a network of secret tunnels that lead directly to the city gates.'

'Fine,' she says. 'But is that where we're going next?'

'Where else?'

▶ 1387

1015

'The beast with five fingers,' she replies at once. 'The hawk's perch. The ring tree. It's all that's left in this world of Calliope's son, who was torn apart by wild women. Trap it with a net, or with glue and a basket, or hunt it with only your hands, as some tickle trout. That takes skill and you would do well to carry an arm with painted leaves on its skin, for it will serve as bait.'

'A severed arm? Where do I find something like that?'

'Not far from here, in Hades, close up against the city wall. What you get from the hunt will stand you in good stead when strings must speak with feeling.'

An enigmatic pronouncement, but that's what you expect from the Oracle. She says nothing more, so you thank her and leave.

▶ 510

1016

A Celedon approaches you, her gait both implacable and graceful. 'The Gallery of Regret is closed,' she says in an exquisitely modulated fluting voice. 'Forgo contemplation. Put aside second thoughts. You are at the Artificer's gaudy. Later there will be fireworks in the garden.'

She points to a narrow passageway that leads through to another courtyard. What makes the gesture eerie is that she is looking into your eyes the whole time with her own gaze empty of emotion.

Go the way she's pointing	▶ 1415
Return to the entrance courtyard	▶ 750
Walk over to the fountain	▶ 489

1017

Gusts of wind thunder across the plaza, forcing you to fight your way forward towards the Syndics' palace. The unlit windows and cracked shell of the dome make it look like no one has been here in centuries.

Dunamis leans close to your ear so she can be heard over the wind. 'I guess it's confession time.'

You give her a hard look. 'I'm not going to like this, am I?'

'It's not all bad news. You know Vulcan's crown got stolen at the ball. Well, it was me that took it.'

'Now that you say it out loud, I'm not even surprised. Was that the good news?'

'No,' she says with a nervous laugh. 'The good news is it was one of the Syndics who paid me to steal it for him. Lord Zagreus, his name is. So maybe he left it here when everything went south.'

The marble flagstones crawl with a soft blue luminance. You approach the gaping entrance to the building. The ghastly cyanic light make the colossal stone portico seem unreal and weightless.

'Let's hope he did,' you say. 'It's our last chance.'

Get the codeword *Rice* and ▶ 1128

1018

A club clips you on the side of the head. The next thing you know you're down on the ground, curling up to avoid the heavy boots and cudgels. It's an efficient beating, carefully judged to be painful rather than crippling. When they see you've had enough they shoulder their weapons and saunter off.

'Thanks for the exercise,' says one, hanging around just long enough to go through your pockets. He cups your chin. You have a blurry glimpse of his grinning face through the blood streaming into your eyes, then a hard right hook sends you spiralling down into darkness.

You come round in a doorway in the Street of Knives with no idea how you got here. Tick the Wound box on your Adventure Sheet. Also lose 20 pyr if you have that much.

▶ 1617

1019

☐ ☐ ☐

If you have the codeword *Riven* then tick one of the boxes above.

One box is now ticked ▶ 667

Two boxes are now ticked ▶ 1552

If all three boxes are now ticked or you do not have *Riven* ▶ 82

1020

Make a GRACE roll at difficulty 11 to see if you're on target. You can't use an item to give a bonus to this roll because you are in your nightgown and don't have any possessions on you.

Success ▶ 1268

Failure ▶ 542

1021

Time passes, all of your childhood years flickering by as if in a dream. The stranger makes regular visits to your home, though never when your family are around; perhaps he is ashamed of his disfigurement. Sometimes he meets you on the way to school and takes you off hunting. He shows you tricks of self-defence, how to spot a lie or tease out a truth, how to look at a problem and figure out ways to solve it. He trains with you in long lung-bursting races, building your stamina. He lets you throw sticks at him to demonstrate how to avoid them with clever footwork.

You remember one time when he's showing you how to climb, searching for the narrowest footholds and crevices in a sheer wall where your fingers and toes can find purchase. It's only when you look down that you see how far up you've climbed.

'You'll rise to greater heights than that,' calls the man. 'One day when you're older, you'll understand. Remember, practice makes perfect.'

On the verge of adulthood your CHARM, GRACE, INGENUITY and STRENGTH scores are all at +3. Record those on your Adventure Sheet.

The stranger tells you other things too. Events that have not yet come to pass. He frames them as stories with advice on what you should do. The details are hazy in this dream-like blur that memory has made of your early life. 'When it counts,' he says, 'you'll know what to do.'

At last the day comes when he must leave. 'I've taught you all I can,' he says, 'and that's worth more than gold.'

'Will I see you again?'

'Who could forget a face like mine?'

Still with one twisted hand clasped around the broken hourglass, he turns and walks away.

Get the codeword *Recursive* and ▶ **1457**

1022

You strike with desperate ferocity, feeling the shock of impact as you score a decisive hit against one of your monstrous opponents.

▶ **1047** and tick one of the boxes there before you read on.

1023

❑ ❑

Do not tick either of the boxes unless you were told to do so in the section you just turned from.

Neither of the boxes is ticked	▶ **132**
One box is now ticked	▶ **891**
Two boxes are ticked	▶ **296**

1024

The first impression is the impact. It's like being punched in the face. Blackness. Vertigo. Then the first nerve-crackles of feeling, which start as a bone-deep ache and a rushing warmth across your face.

And only then the pain, shooting through you like a white-hot poker impaled in your head. Slumped in the bottom of the chariot, you pull on the reins to stop the horses. Only then do you dare reach up.

Your fingers close around the shaft of the arrow sticking out of your eye. You don't stop to think. You have to get it out. Gripping the arrow, you give it a sharp tug. With a sucking noise like a cork being popped out of a bottle it comes loose – taking your left eye with it.

Adjust your GRACE score by −1. Any action involving dexterity is more difficult without the ability to judge distances. Also tick the Wound box on your Adventure Sheet if you were not already wounded.

▶ **1327**

1025

The coin hits the water and the surface breaks into a million glittering silver points of light. Shadows play across it, a half-glimpsed vision in which you see yourself moving guardedly through the rubble of a ruined city. The sky is a swirl of pitch black in which indigo constellations flare and die as time rewinds and the stars go out. A gleam of broken glass proves to be a city noticeboard half-buried by shattered masonry. Sparks crackle from wires exposed by the broken screen. You reach for it and –

The vision disappears and you are once again standing beside a fountain whose cool iridescent spray dances in the late afternoon sunlight.

Visit the menagerie	▶ **1392**
Go back to the rotunda	▶ **1530**
Return to the first courtyard	▶ **750**

1026

Under Psyche's direction, the Dactyls disconnect one of the processing units from the master matrix and wire it up to the Face of Wisdom.

'OK, trial run,' says the Face. 'I've always disliked those boots.'

You look down at your feet. Seconds drag on. There's a hum from the processing unit. Finally one of your shoes changes very slightly. Where the leather uppers used to have black stitching, now it's crimson.

'I can see how that could be a real life-saver,' you say drily.

'Hey, smarty pants, I'm still getting the hang of this,' says the Face.

'We'll make some adjustments,' Psyche assures you. 'In the meantime, since you won't have the benefit of the

Face's advice, you'd better borrow my abacus.'

'Don't you need it?'

She smiles. 'Oh please – as if I couldn't do higher order mathematics in my sleep.'

Delete the **Face of Wisdom** (INGENUITY +3) from your Adventure Sheet and get an **abacus** (INGENUITY +2) in its place. Also get the codeword *Rudiment*.

▶ 1008

1027

Queen Nyx is a majestic figure, towering over you in her gown of night, her flesh blazing like white marble and her eyes darkly glimmering like the gulfs between the stars. Even so, you had pictured her manifesting over the city taller than a mountain, able to raise whole buildings in the palm of her hand.

Without quite meaning to, you say these thoughts out loud: 'I thought you'd be bigger.'

'You mean this?' she says, smoothing her hands down her body. 'It's just a little something I threw on. A reflection in miniature of the real me.'

She demonstrates by clenching her fist. Fingers of darkness close around the moon. Nyx notices the look on your face and laughs. 'Now you know why Zeus himself trembled at the thought of facing me in battle. His thunderbolts are as spent matches falling into the fathomless black ocean of my power.'

'My queen,' you say, taking care with your words now, 'I see the impossibility of opposing you. I am your servant.'

A long time passes as Nyx watches you. You fight back the urge to say something to break the silence. At last she says, 'A fool might think to buy time, then betray me. But you're no fool.'

'No, my queen.'

She turns, surveying the city by night. 'What a feeble imagination that lame god has. See this jumble of toys he calls a world. Given the power to shape reality, is this how you would waste it?'

You start to frame an answer, but she holds up her hand. Black silk flows back like water from an alabaster arm. 'It was rhetorical. That power will soon be mine. I will refashion Vulcan's creation into my own realm. I have only to tie up some loose ends – or rather, you will see to those loose ends for me. Do you know what they are, mortal?'

'I imagine...' You collect your thoughts. Truly it is hard to stay calm when you converse with such an entity. 'I imagine the gods and titans might be a problem, my queen.'

'One of those problems has solved the other,' she says. 'The gods have driven the titans back to Tartarus, from where I freed them, and in doing so have been weakened. If they were given time to recuperate, all of the gods together could prove a serious inconvenience to my plans. Therefore you will go to Olympus and see to it that they never recover.'

'O fuligin majesty, I am one lone mortal!'

'A resourceful one.' She drops a glass vial into your hands. It's like a tiny seed between her fingers, but as big as a pestle in yours. 'Add a few drops of this toxicant to their food and drink. And that is the end of the gods.'

Add the **abysm toxin** to your possessions. Also get the codeword *Regal*.

Nyx lifts the hem of her cloak, the fine silk floating on the air like a bolt of shadow, and sweeps it over you. Enfolded in darkness, you feel the wrench as space and time warp around you. Then the darkness falls away and you are – somewhere else. And alone. (Delete any companion from your Adventure Sheet.)

▶ 470

1028

Once again you enter, pay your respects to Glauco and his family, and wait while the swarm of golden beetles convey you down through the solid floor to Daedalus's secret laboratory below.

'Glad you could drop in,' he says, looking up from his workbench. ▶ 95

1029

The mechanical woman moves with surprising speed, but you're fast too. You weave under her arms and smash a flurry of blows into her at close range, gasping in pain as your knuckles crack against her hard body. You may as well be punching a cast iron stove.

In the cramped space of the room, it's almost impossible to evade both Hypermestra and Autolycus. She gets her hand around one of your wrists and locks it in an unbreakable grip. If she can shackle your other arm you'll be helpless. As you try to twist away, Autolycus delivers a hammer-blow to the side of your head that leaves you groggy. What are you going to do?

Give in ▶ 692

If you fight on you'll need to make a STRENGTH roll at difficulty 16: roll two dice, add your STRENGTH modifier (including the bonus for any one item you are carrying) and you need 16 or more.

Succeed ▶ 1525
Fail ▶ 1273

1030

'You there, what's this jar for?' you say to a passing workman.

'You there, what's your arse for?' he snaps back.

'What do you mean?'

'It's the perfect height for kicking.' He raises his foot as if about to prove the point. 'If you're still lurking around here when I count to ten then I'll show you.'

There's no point making an issue of it. You're just attracting the attention of the other labourers in the yard. You give the man a scowl and walk away as swiftly as you can without sacrificing your dignity.

▶ 76

1031

'Yes,' you say, nodding. 'Why shouldn't I? It's often said the gods are cruel. At the very least they're indifferent to mortals' fate. Perhaps Nyx will rule more wisely.'

'She will do more than that!' says Hypnos with a booming peal of laughter. 'She will fashion a new world of indelible night in which loyal subjects like you will be her trusted lieutenants and all who opposed her will crawl and grope their way in darkness.'

If Galatea is with you ▶ 753
Otherwise ▶ 688

1032

The official who hired you is waiting at the door of the debating chamber. 'Thank the gods you're back,' he says. 'Now the Speaker has started talking to itself.'

'Lorem ipthum dolor thit amet...' comes a squeaky voice from inside the room. You glimpse the syndics sitting with their heads in their hands.

'I don't have any solution yet.'

He stares at you. 'Then what are you doing back here? We need to get this fixed athap – I mean asap.'

▶ 715

1033

You soar up beyond the stars into a sky of unending dark. Impossibly far off, motionless as if pinned to an ebon vault, faint swathes of pinprick golden light mark out the filaments of other universes. The cold of the void makes you shiver, but it is not only a chill of the body. Suspended in this immense blackness you feel a degree of loneliness and insignificance that is almost too much to bear.

If you have the codeword *Quiddity* ▶ 1407
If not ▶ 982

1034

In the heart of the frontline fighting, beset by a dozen Ilionian charioteers, stands the Achaean hero Ajax. His chariot has overturned, his companions lie crushed and bleeding in the wreckage. His enemies wheel around him, jabbing at him with long spears but being careful to stay out of reach of his axe. They look like children beside Ajax's mighty stature, but despite his strength the force of numbers must wear him down eventually.

You see him fall to one knee, scarlet blood gushing from a shoulder wound. But he rises again, the broken shaft of his chariot in his hand, and he hurls it into the path of one of the yelping Ilionians. The man's chariot overturns, he is catapulted into the dust, and as he lies stunned Ajax steps forward to despatch him. That raised axe could cut an ox in two, you think.

But the axe blow does not fall. Ajax is braced motionless, straining at something that has caught his weapon in an iron grip. Only you can see the cause. One of the giant figures, reaching down from the heavens, holds Ajax's blade between her fingers – invisible to all the fighters, but seen by your enchanted vision as a flickering shade against the back of the eyelid, like an image burned into the retina by staring at the sun.

While she holds Ajax transfixed, his foes come rushing on in a pack, baying like hounds that scent a kill.

Attack her   ▶ **1524**

Hold back   ▶ **1513**

1035

Delete the codeword *Pure* if you have it.

Wagons set out daily for the far-flung corners of the world. The merchants are always on the lookout for extra capital to buy goods for their return journey.

You can invest in multiples of 100 pyr. Write the sum you are investing in the box (and delete it from your Adventure Sheet), or withdraw a sum you invested previously after adjusting it for the vicissitudes of fortune (in which case delete it from the box and add it to your Adventure Sheet).

MONEY INVESTED IN TRADE

When you have completed your business here ▶ **716**

1036

She lurches to the window and throws it open. 'It's too late. The night is gone. I haven't time to get back to the graveyard.'

'Then you'll die.'

With a desolate cry she climbs down the ivy and throws herself in a jerking run towards the gate. Better for her if the sunrise does catch her, you think. Death is surely better than clinging to existence as a monster.

Lose the codewords *Rabbit* and *Ruffle* if you have them, then ▶ **38**

1037

You race to the stern, where the helmsman is prising up the copper lid of what looks like a compass or gyroscope. Inside is a spinning disk of tangled geometric lines. It makes you feel slightly sick to look at it because of how it's continually shifting, unfolding and refolding, apparently in impossible shapes.

'You have to get your head around it existing in other dimensions,' says the helmsman, hesitantly reaching towards the glowing disk with a strangely shaped spanner. 'Got much experience with buoyancy rotors?'

'That what this is? I thought I was getting a migraine.'

If you have the codeword *Recursive* ▶ **1417** now; otherwise read on.

'It's out of alignment,' says the helmsman. He casts a nervous glance over his shoulder. 'See those sparks? It's dragging against the side of the containment vessel. That's why we're losing altitude.'

'So we need to adjust it? That's what the spanner's for?'

He snorts. 'Vulcan designed it. The tools came with the gizmo. Too bad he didn't include a repair manual.'

He prods the spanner into the housing. There's a protesting screech as the disk grinds against the spanner head. The helmsman leans back, straining with all his might to twist the disk back into alignment. The friction with the spanner slows it even more. The deck lurches, almost throwing you off your feet. Arcs of disturbing light splash out like molten droplets from a furnace.

You glance back at the rail. The Minotaur is grappling a vampire by the throat as he lays about him with his axe at a press of were-beasts. As the rotor slows its spinning the ship is dropping towards the street. Any moment now the horde of creatures on the parapet will be able to jump down on the deck. For all his ferocious strength, the Minotaur can't fight them all.

'We don't have much time,' you tell the helmsman.

'Uh-huh. Any time you want to lend a hand...'

Make a STRENGTH roll at difficulty 13.

Succeed ▶ **1318**

Fail ▶ **216**

1038

You throw up an arm to defend yourself. His sword slashes you to the bone, but at least you're alive. As you sink with a moan to the ground, he gives you a brutal kick and then wrests the **fish-headed standard** away from you. Cross it off your possessions. Also tick the Wound box on your Adventure Sheet if you were not already injured.

'Be grateful for your miserable life,' he says. 'Normally I would slaughter anyone who profaned our standard with their unworthy hands, but I think you acted from simple ignorance.'

He walks off, leaving you to drag yourself painfully back to the city gate.

▶ **555**

1039

'You're not a guest, Orphea, you broke in. Say what you came for and get out before I call the night watch.'

'I came to offer you a unique opportunity.'

'I'll bite. What's the con this time?'

'No con. Remember the Pipes of Pan?'

'When I got a face full of gas and you took off with the prize? Another alliance betrayed? Oh yes, I'm not soon going to forget that.'

'Hey, the druids left a trap and you sprung it. How's that my fault? But I do feel bad about it so I want to give you a chance to get the Pipes after all.'

'Of course you do. No strings? You're as convincing as a viper with its fingers crossed, "Lady Rapscallion".'

She chuckles at that, indicating the three overturned cups on the desk. 'We just play a little game. If you win I'll give you the Pipes of Pan. See this ruby – I'm putting it under one of the cups like this. Then I move the cups around – whoosh, whoosh, whoosh, is your eye fast enough to follow? Now, if you think you kept track of where the ruby is then we can wager.'

'You're staking the Pipes of Pan. What am I staking?'

'What about… the deeds of this house?'

'A mansion against some pipes?'

'The pipes of a god.'

You pace to and fro, as if weighing up whether to gamble, then dart forward and snatch up two of the cups. 'There! It's not under either of those, so it must be under the other one.'

She stares in dismay. 'That's not how you're meant to do it. You're supposed to pick up the cup you think it's under.'

'What difference? It must be under that one, right? Shall we look?'

She puts out her hand. 'No… er, that's right, it must be there.'

'So I'll take the Pipes of Pan, thanks.'

For a moment she sits stunned, then throws herself back in the chair and laughs. 'The biter bit. That doesn't happen very often. All right, you win. Fair and square isn't how I like to play, but I can't grumble when I'm outwitted, can I?'

▶ **1126**

1040

Sakan steps in, sword drawn back for a thrust. Adrenaline has cleared the drink fumes from his head, but in the near-darkness he fails to see your attack until it is too late. With a gurgle of blood he sinks to his knees, then falls flat.

You drag his body out of sight among the rubbish sacks, recover the coins you placed as bait, and hurry away before a militia patrol comes by.

Get the codeword *Rock* and ▶ **1432**

1041

You dive from the tower, feeling the rush of air as you plummet towards the ground. The wings twitch and spread wide, carrying you out in a long graceful arc that skims the walls of the city and then takes you high up into the sky. The tree canopy of Arcadia stretches beneath you like an endless green sea.

If you were with a companion, delete them from your Adventure Sheet. Also remove the **beeswax** that you have used.

You begin to descend, selecting your landing spot amid the verdant meadows and sun-dappled glades.

The Dales of Leaf and Stream ▶ **266** in *The Wild Woods*

The Summer Palace ▶ **10** in *The Wild Woods*

The Wineries of the Nectar of the Gods ▶ **417** in *The Wild Woods*

The Verdant Farmlands ▶ **270** in *The Wild Woods*

The Druid's Shrine ▶ **463** in *The Wild Woods*

The Woodlands of Ambrosia ▶ **60** in *The Wild Woods*

The eastern shore of Arcadia ▶ **419** in *The Wild Woods*

1042

'The Olympians are happy to sit back while you fight their battles,' says Daedalus. 'Then when you've won they'll step in and mop up.'

'Kind of a cynical way of looking at things.'

'Don't knock it. It's kept me alive this long.' He snaps his visor back down. 'Good luck.'

With a roar of unseen force, he spreads his armoured wings and streaks up into the sky, a gleaming silvery speck that is soon lost to view. Nyx glances up, watching his departure, then turns back to you. 'That Daedalus,' she laughs. 'He could never bring himself to admit when he's scared.'

▶ **1533**

1043

A bell chimes sharply. Myletes glances round at an hourglass perched on the edge of his desk. 'Oh, this contraption might interest you. See how it sits on a measuring scale? When the sands run out, the hourglass briefly registers as heavier than it usually is, and a trigger then rings this bell. I call it my Alerting Chronometer.'

'Maybe "alarm clock" would roll off the tongue easier.'

'Hmm.' He strokes his beard as he considers that. 'Now, the question is what did I set it to remind me of? Oh yes, the metaphysics symposium is just starting. Come on, you won't want to miss it.'

Go with him   ▶ **857**
Make an excuse and leave   ▶ **1062**

1044

From deep in the clouds there's a sky-spitting rumble. You feel a gust of chill thunderous air. Lightning bolts flicker far below, spitting and cracking out of a growing mass of darkness.

'Maybe we shouldn't hang around.'

Sphikos chews his lip. It hadn't occurred to him. 'No, perhaps not.'

Despite the urgency, that looming crag of cloud ahead holds your attention. The blaze of golden light around it is almost unendurable.

'Don't look at it directly,' cautions Sphikos. 'It is the first dawn.'

Too late. The cloud rolls away and pure light fills the world. The cloudscape becomes almost transparent in the glare and you and Sphikos are like figures of candlewax glowing with inner fire.

If you have the title **Hero Without A Shadow** ▶ **1648**
Otherwise ▶ **1306**

1045

He weaves to one side, avoiding your desperate blow, and swings his club into the side of your head with stunning force. The nails set into the club rake your flesh.

If the Wound box on your Adventure Sheet was already ticked ▶ **111**

If not, put a tick in it now and ▶ **40**

1046

You grab the axe out of the air. As you do, you realize the Minotaur wasn't aiming at you but at a point a handspan above your head.

A sharp pain in your shoulder makes you stumble and fall to your knees on the deck. There is a huge insect rearing over you on polished black limbs. Its sharp mandibles are skewered deep in your flesh. It jerks its head back and you see your whole arm torn from its socket.

Red darkness washes over your vision.

Note **860** as your Current Location, then ▶ **670**

1047

❑ ❑

Do not tick either of the boxes unless you were told to do so in the section you just turned from.

Neither of the boxes is ticked   ▶ **1142**
One box is now ticked   ▶ **1613**
Two boxes are ticked   ▶ **1282**

1048

You rise back through the stone floor, emerging in the throne room. The beetles stop whizzing around and the cocoon of light disappears. The room is empty. You cannot tell how much time has passed.

The beetles fly together, combining to form the metal chrysalis as before. You slip it into your pocket in case you need it in future.

▶ **8** in *The Houses of the Dead*

1049

Get the codeword **Rigor**.

You wake in the night to find someone in your room. The thief's step across the carpet makes no more sound than the whisper of catspaws on velvet. Controlling your breathing so that you still seem to be asleep, you watch out of the corner of your eye as the figure slides open each of your drawers in turn, lifting out small items of jewellery and dropping them into a pouch.

The thief creeps over to your bedside. Some valuable trinkets on the night stand, visible in the moonlight, have attracted their interest. A slender hand reaches out.

You seize their wrist. It's thin. You could easily snap the bone. Instead you pull the thief across the sheets. Swinging out of bed, you light the lamp.

'Let me go.' A girl's voice. 'I only wanted money to buy food.'

'You've enough jewellery in that bag to pay for a banquet.'

A black scarf covers her lower face. You tear it off. She's just a child.

'Oh, it's you,' she says.

Recognition takes you a moment longer. 'Dunamis! I didn't free you from slavery just so you could turn to thievery.'

'I didn't have a lot of choice,' she protests. 'It's a long way from Boreas to Notus. If I hadn't learned to fend for myself I'd have starved or been enslaved again.'

'You could have gone to the temples and asked for charity.'

'The temples!' she says scathingly. 'The gods are cruel, not kind. In their hands we're no better off than the puppets you see on the Street of Ash.'

There's a hardness in her eyes that never used to be there, but when she mentions the puppet shows there's a sparkle of childish delight. She has taken some knocks from fate, you can see that, but at heart she remains an innocent.

'If I let you go, will you promise to turn over a new leaf?'

'I wouldn't steal from you anyway,' she says, getting up and rubbing the circulation back into her wrist. Leaving the bag of stolen goods on the bed, she slips over to the window and climbs out. 'See you around.'

▶ 97

1050

'Will you come with me?' you ask him.

Bosk shakes his head. 'My place is in the groves and fields of Arcady. But I will send you with a blessing.'

A tingling sensation ripples through you. Acquire a blessing. It can be used to reroll a failed check against CHARM, GRACE, INGENUITY or STRENGTH. In any given situation you can only use one blessing, so if you fail the reroll you can't spend another blessing to try again.

He uncorks a clay flask and puts it to your lips. 'A good sip of this won't do you any harm either,' he says.

The liquor packs a kick. If you were injured, untick the Wound box on your Adventure Sheet. If you were uninjured, add 1 to your CHARM score, up to a maximum of +5; this bonus will last until the end of your adventure.

Delete Bosk as your companion.

If you have the codeword *Ruby* ▶ 1345

Otherwise ▶ 974

1051

'This is cooking oil, isn't it?' you ask one of the workmen who is busy manhandling a heavy crate across the yard.

He wipes his brow, glad for the excuse to take a break. 'Reckon it's more for machines and that,' he says.

'A lubricant, you mean?'

'Yeah, stops the cogs from seizing up.'

'Is it going to be delivered somewhere?'

'Stuff that's left there is for collection. If the customers don't live far off, or when it's a package small enough to carry like that, they often save on shipping charges by picking it up in person.'

'Or if they don't want somebody to know where they live.'

He nods thoughtfully. 'Yeah, could be.'

Hefting the crate, he totters off towards the waiting cart. It occurs to you that if this oil is intended for use in machinery, you could sabotage it pretty effectively with a handful of grit.

Do it   ▶ 949

Or not   ▶ 76

1052

'Here. For your trouble.' The merchant contemptuously tosses you a few coins; add 5 pyr to your money if you deign to pick them up.

He turns his back on you and stands gazing down at his wife's sleeping form. A servant touches your arm and you are shown out of the house.

Add the **looking glass (403 in *Workshop of the Gods*)** to your possessions. Any time you want to use it, note the section you are at as your Current Location and then ▶ 403 in this book.

You do not have to use it now. Your choices are:

Go north to the city gate   ▶ 222

Go south to the Forum   ▶ 1642

1053

The tapestry is a dimensional portal hovering in the air. You and Nyx are pulled through, hurtling through gulfs of time and space illuminated by bursts of cosmic energy. You plunge towards an oval of golden light.

Now you're standing under the soaring pillared roofs of Olympus. All of the gods are gathered here, restored by the nectar you gave them, clad in armour forged by Vulcan. They are at height of their power.

Nyx stands defiant. 'Come, then. Poison is a coward's weapon. I have no need of it to destroy you all.'

No mortal eyes have ever witnessed such a contest. The deafening fulminant blasts of Zeus's thunderbolts. The blinding shafts unleashed by Apollo and Artemis. The scything sweep of Ares' sword. The corrosive mists wafted by Hades from the banks of the Styx. And against this onslaught, the ebon bulwarks and flames conjured by the Queen of Night.

So great are the energies flowing here that time itself slows, unable to keep up with the clash of gods and titan. At first they seem equally matched. Nyx might even have the upper hand. But the gods know this is their final stand, and on their home ground they refuse to be defeated. They redouble their attacks, driving Nyx back. Her flesh starts to char under the glare of Olympian power. The gods advance, their auras growing in intensity until the blaze is unendurable. You see Nyx open her mouth in a scream as she is swept away into atoms. But the scream goes on, and you realize that it is your own agony, the fate of any mortal who sees the gods in their true form.

The chaos and tumult end. In place of the blistering auras of the gods there's just a soft light of early morning.

You open your eyes to find yourself back at your family hearth. Your parents and siblings are here, and your aunts and uncles, all just as they looked when you were a child. Even your old dog is here. He comes to lick your hand.

You know now where you are. This is Elysium, where the sun never sets. Nyx is gone, the gods are restored, and you have no more challenges to look forward to, just the reward of an eternity of perfect peace and happiness.

1054

'So you're going back on your word?'

You give a scornful laugh. 'I learned from the best.'

'We'll call it quits, then?'

No, you'll have to kill her	▶ 1650
Grab her and call for the night watch	▶ 1610
Let her go	▶ 1506

1055

The creature's weight pins you down. You smell the stink of its hot breath, the reek of its wet fur. Your face is pressed into the puddles and gravel of the roof. Snarling, the were-beast struggles to get its teeth around your neck. You smash your elbow into its face and pull free, ignoring the raking talons clutching at your back.

Scrambling to your feet, you run to the parapet. The baying, gibbering, howling legion of the damned is right behind you. The street is a dizzying drop below. The street is far too wide to jump.

If you have the codeword *Quiddity*	▶ 1299
If not but you have the **wings of Icarus**	▶ 1129
Otherwise	▶ 882

1056

'You and me, we go back a long way, don't we?' says Dunamis.

'Yeah. What happened to the sweet girl you used to be?'

'You haven't heard? Sweet girls finish last. All I'm trying to say is, those Gargarean bastards treated me worse than an animal, and I'd still be there if you hadn't set me free. I owe you. Always will. So can you just trust me this one time?'

'What do you suggest?'

'I'll go get whatever it is Zinc wrapped up for you, but the first thing we have to do is fix whatever Nyx has done to the city. And for that we need one of the noticeboards at the gates.'

It's not often Dunamis lets her guard down and speaks with such sincerity. Maybe you should listen to her.

Go with her to the nearest noticeboard	▶ 723
No, you need that gift Zinc left for you	▶ 824

1057

You twist away but the sword of darkness writhes like a bolt of black lightning, searing your flesh to the bone. Tick the Wound box on your Adventure Sheet if you were not injured already.

Nyx raises her arms, summoning titanic forces to blast you where you lie sprawled at her feet. Before she can strike, lights flicker amid the ruins – more and more of them, like fireflies in the dark. The ordinary citizens of Vulcan City are emerging from hiding, filled now with hope. They come forward, marching defiantly to join your army. Your courage has given them faith that victory is possible.

Each citizen carries a candle or a flaming torch. Individually they are mere glimmers, but together they merge into a bright radiance. For a moment Nyx is distracted, shielding her eyes against the glare. But you can see that it's not enough – no more than a spark that she can snuff out with a gesture.

'Fools,' she says, 'I'll uncreate you all. You will return to the primordial clay.'

If you have the **Eye of Hyperion** and want to use that ▶ 1083

If you have the **tapestry of Arachne** and want to use it ▶ 273

Otherwise, if you have the codeword *Radiant* ▶ 311 and if not ▶ 182

1058

'Back so soon?' says the raw-boned perruquier as you enter his shop.

'About that wig?'

'Wig..? Wig?' He pantomimes looking around for some mystery object, even going so far as to open his desk drawers and peer inside. 'Oh, do you perchance refer to the Number Six Rococo Prodigy, which you so signally disdained to purchase when it was on special offer?'

'Yeah, yeah. So – '

'I have had to raise prices in light of the recent barbers' strike. The peruke you are interested in now costs four lava gems.'

Buy it; cross off 4 **lava gems** and ▶ **173**

No sale ▶ **414**

1059

To Nyx's astonishment, you smite her a crunching blow with the mace. She gives a gasp of pain.

Lose the codeword *Rug* if you have it, then ▶ **399**

1060

'On the Shores of Psamathe, if that's not a tautology, you will find a boat in which you are destined to journey far.'

'Thank you.'

You turn to go, but the Oracle is still speaking. 'To repair it you will need canvas and pitch. The first is easy to find, just walk the Sacred Way northwards along the coast. But as for the pitch… Attend my words. First find a pedlar on the road who will sell you a tinderbox. In the stone quarries you will obtain a net, and when you go fishing with it take whatever you catch. With these things and something to use as a picnic basket, visit the three ancient obelisks.'

'Hold on. I never learned shorthand.'

Ignoring you, she continues: 'Go last to the obelisk in the south, for near there is your encounter with the hawk-headed sphinx, though you can reach it only in dreams.'

'And that – I've lost track – that's to get the pitch to fix up the boat? What about a crew?'

'Your crew are waiting for you.'

'I might need to come back for a recap of all this.'

'Your destiny will not change,' she says, making a gesture of dismissal.

▶ **510**

1061

Get the codeword *Rose*.

'How did you get in, by the way? Nobody can see Vulcan's palace unless he wants them to.'

'Maybe I'm the Chosen One.' She laughs. 'Just kidding. I discovered you can hack the city noticeboards to reveal locations that are normally hidden.'

'If you can rewrite Vulcan's rules for the world, why not just create any jewels you want?'

Dunamis's gaze has fixed on a partygoer wearing a large gold ring, her whole body tensing like a pointer that's spotted a game bird, but then she considers what you've said and turns back to you with an expression of wonder.

'Maybe you could,' she says. 'You'd need access to the deepest level of the simulation. Something that convinced

the system that you had authorization from Vulcan himself.'

You shrug. 'Oh well, there's no chance of that.'

'No. Unless… Hmm. I'll catch you later.' And she darts off across the courtyard.

▶ **808**

1062

Your progress along the Street of the Winds is accompanied by the tinkling of chimes which shopkeepers hang above their doors. On this wide street can be found both the Academy of Philosophers and the Tavern of the Hero of Temesa. For this reason, locals sometimes refer to it as 'Thinkers and Drinkers Street'.

To go straight to a city location that you already know about, note **1062** as your Current Location, then ▶ **1432**

If you have the codeword *Pennywort* you can call on the wife of 'the Grumble King' ▶ **525**

Or you can go:

North-west towards the walls ▶ **451**

South-east to the centre of the city ▶ **1642**

To the Academy of Philosophers ▶ **1544**

Into the Tavern of the Hero of Temesa ▶ **764**

1063

It's eerie watching her descend the wall. She seems to float to the ground rather than climbing down. The rain drives out of the darkness with stinging force, the wind howls and buffets the trees, and thunderbolts flash and rumble high overhead. It's like a scene from a play, almost too vivid to be real.

The next thing you know it is morning and you are lying in bed. Your valet is closing the window. 'The storm blew it open in the night,' he says. 'I'm afraid the carpet is soaked.'

'I thought I got up and shut it,' you say. Or was that all a dream?

Lose the codeword *Ruffle* and ▶ **97**

1064

'There is a fine marked against your name,' says one of the gate guards, accosting you.

'Maybe I've just got that kind of face.'

'Don't get smart. Pay up or sling your hook, got it?'

If you pay the fine of 500 pyr, cross off the money and lose the codeword *Ridge*, then ▶ Current Location

If you are unable or unwilling to pay the fine then ▶ Current Location, but keep the codeword *Ridge* and the guards escort you out through the gate, so you cannot choose any option except for leaving the city.

1065

Lightning crashes across the sky as your champions charge into battle against Nyx's sons Death and Sleep. This is the final showdown, the contest of elemental forces. If your allies can keep the two titans occupied, you have a chance of reaching Nyx herself. And somehow you must find a way to defeat her, or else the world is lost.

If you have the codeword *Romance* ▶ 305

If not ▶ 324

1066

Naft's ledger doesn't list his customers by name but you see that a consignment of amaranth oil is due to be picked up later today. Each item is identified by colour coding, and the symbol for amaranth oil is a red triangle.

As you are leaving, you notice a large jar packed with straw by the side of the loading yard. The label is a red triangle.

Take it with you ▶ 361

Examine it more closely ▶ 293

Leave it where it is ▶ 76

1067

The *Sunrise* soars into the void, accelerating so fast that you have to hold on to the rail to keep your footing. Already you're far above the storm. The lightning strokes that pounded the city are reduced to a distant grey flickering below. A muffled rumble is all that can be heard now of the titanic thunderclaps that made the very walls and streets shake.

You look out from the rail. In all directions there is unfathomable silent darkness. A sense of timeless calm pervades the deck, with only the soft harmonic drone of the buoyancy rotor, the steady creak of timbers, and the musical tautness of the sheets to disturb the hush of infinite space.

Ancaeus strides the deck shouting a barrage of orders, assigning crew members to assess the damage to the ship and patch her up as best they can.

If you have the codeword *Oasis* ▶ 1541 now; otherwise read on.

If you have the codewords *Rustic* and *Noble* ▶ 545

If you have only *Rustic* ▶ 169

If only *Noble* ▶ 728

If neither ▶ 231

1068

The Celedon summons more of her kind. They drag your limp body across the broken ground and fling you down on a pile of rubble. There is no sign of Dunamis. She must have slipped away while the Celedons' attention was on you.

Gradually your strength returns. Enough, at any rate, to stagger to your feet. All over the city darkness is closing in, deepening, streaming from the firmament in rivers of light-extinguishing nullity. The wind that has been raging dies away leaving a dead calm. You must be in the eye of the storm.

A shadow deeper than the night falls over you. You turn to look up into the eyes of Queen Nyx. She regards you as a shark might look upon a minnow – barely worth the killing.

'The matrix of reality is almost recast,' she says. 'My world is about to be born. You can do nothing now to prevent it.'

Behind her stand her sons, Death and Sleep. Titans who together even Zeus would hesitate to face in battle. And you are one lone mortal.

▶ 249

1069

You tell the story of ascending to the mountain peak, finding the Galomoi, and realizing that to cure them of the dry sickness you'd have to give up your precious supply of cockatrice blood.

The story has everything: the arduous climb where any missed handhold would have sent you crashing to the rocks far below, the deserted fortress where you feel an invisible presence, the enigmatic cyclopean telescope, the refrigerated survival pods, the whiff of death when you mention the plague, the conversation with the legendary Kedalion, and your own sacrifice in order to heal the sleeping Galomoi. And then the epilogue in which a grateful Kedalion despatches swarms of clockwork creatures to repair the damage to your city.

'And what about the raiders who sacked Iskandria?' asks one of the listeners. 'Did you find them?'

You wink at him. 'That's a tale for another time.'

▶ 1195

1070

If you have the codeword *Rug* then you are at a disadvantage and will need an element of bluff to make this work; attempt a CHARM roll at difficulty 14:

Succeed ▶ 476

Fail ▶ 826

If you do not have the codeword *Rug* ▶ 1053

1071

One morning you're playing in the kitchen, left to your own devices while your parents are at the market, when the gate swings on its rusty hinges. You hear the crunch of footfalls on the gravel path. Someone is at the open door.

You move protectively in front of your brother's cradle. Your dog, who barks at everyone, rushes outside. 'Careful,' you call out. 'He's liable to bite.'

'This old softie?' says the stranger, allowing the dog to lick his hand.

The stranger is one who must have passed through fire. His face is a disturbing knot of scar tissue barely recognizable as human features. You can't help staring at the sight of his lipless mouth and skull-like nubbin of a nose. His hands too are burned and twisted claws. Even his clothes are blackened, both charred and threadbare. But the dog doesn't bark at him. It wags its tail.

'I don't bite either,' says the stranger.

'You're uglier than Uncle Nicomachus,' you say, transfixed by the ruin of his face.

He laughs. 'Kids don't varnish the truth, do they?'

From his belt hangs the carved ivory frame of an hourglass. The glass itself is missing, the sands long since scattered. 'What good is that?'

'A dear friend gave it to me. I keep it as a reminder of her.'

You're dubious. 'It's bust. You can't use it to tell the time.'

'I know it's early and the future is a clean slate. That's enough.'

'Anyway,' you say, trying to tear your fascinated gaze away from his hideously scarred face, 'who are you? What do you want?'

Maybe he smiles. How could you tell? 'It wouldn't be a lie to say the gods sent me,' he says. 'And here's a funny thing: you and I have the same name. I'm going to be your guardian angel as you grow up. I'll drop in from time to time, but let's keep it as our little secret. We've got a lot to talk about.'

▶ 1021

1072

Your allies fight with bravery and passion. It's not enough. Hopelessly outnumbered, they are swept away by the surging black tide of Queen Nyx's army.

You stand fast in the thick of battle, dealing out a dozen wounds for every one you take, shouting encouragement to your forces until your voice is hoarse. All around you lie the bodies of the fallen.

A shadow falls, winged and darker than the night. You look up into the gaze of Thanatos, which haunts all mortal lives. Your limbs go cramped and icy cold. You watch as your skin loses all lustre, turning bloodless grey in an instant. Thanatos's wings close around you. You know nothing more.

▶ 666

1073

The Oracle's tongue lolls on her lip and her eyes show only the whites. You fear she might be having a fit, but then she speaks. 'Tame the violent, defend the peaceful, cure the wise. This is your destiny in the mountainous realm.'

'Does the lord Apollo offer any hint about how to go about it?' you venture to ask. 'Or where?'

'In a maze where the bull-headed ones once dwelt. On the southern plains of the high plateau. Atop a peak where a one-eyed giant watches the stars.'

That's all she has to say. You return to the main body of the temple.

▶ 510

1074

Swords flash, hewing limbs and heads asunder. Hundreds fall dying but neither your side nor Nyx's can gain ground. The forces are equally matched in strength.

A Myrmidon officer, staggering back to catch his breath, turns to you. 'Show yourself at the head of the troops!' he cries. 'They yearn for their champion.'

He's right. Inspiring leadership can turn the tide of even the most hopeless battle. You hurl yourself into the front line, calling to your soldiers to join you in a push aimed at splitting Nyx's ranks.

Make a CHARM roll at difficulty 13. You can add 1 to your dice score if your Glory is at least 15.

| Fire in their bellies | ▶ 1243 |
| Faint hearts | ▶ 322 |

1075

If you have the codeword *Rhombus* ▶ 287

If not ▶ 181

1076

It helps to have friends in high places, and they soon secure your release. The official story is that the guards who arrested you were trying to shake you down. They are executed to ensure the truth never comes out. Even so, some suspicion lingers and your reputation is tarnished; lose 1 Glory.

▶ 63

1077

'I'm sorry,' you tell him. 'There's nothing I can do.'

'I am the one who should apologize, your grace. I had no right to show up at your door with a metaphorical begging bowl. Of course you have your own staff here.'

'Where will you go?' you ask, showing him to the door.

'Perhaps to the country of the Sarpedons. I hear they are

civilized and looking to expand their diplomatic reach. That means lots of guests and feasts to be organized.'

You're sad to see him go, and even sadder when you notice that your neighbours think less of you for not doing more to help an old and faithful retainer. Lose 1 Glory and ▶ 97

1078

You rush in, exchanging a fast flurry of blows. Sakan blocks and dodges with the skill of a practiced street fighter. As you pull back to recover your breath, expecting him to do the same, he instead hurls himself forward in a desperate lunge. His face is pressed right up to yours, so close you can smell the beer on his breath.

'Nighty-night,' he whispers in your ear.

You look down to see him slowly pulling his blade out of your stomach, twisting it slightly as it comes. As he steps back, you slump to the ground and mercifully you know nothing more.

▶ 111

1079

❑

Do not put a tick in the box unless you were told to do so in the section you just turned from.

If the box is empty   ▶ 1313
If you've just ticked it   ▶ 707
If it was already ticked ▶ 1543

1080

Her fangs sink into your shoulder. She gulps the spurt of blood with a horrible lapping sound. The damage you inflicted on her visibly repairs itself, torn ligaments and broken bones reknitting.

'See how I become stronger as you grow weaker,' she sighs in your ear. 'Like nectar to me is this sweet vein-wine.'

If your Wound box is not ticked, put a tick in it now and ▶ 1612

If you were already injured ▶ 858

1081

A loose rock shifts under your weight. You are flung to the ground. Before you can get back on your feet, the swarm descends on you. There's a smell in the air like scorching cloth. The deafening whirr of insect wings vibrates in your ears. A thousand stings pierce your flesh, each injecting a spurt of fiery venom.

Note that your Current Location is **683** and then ▶ **670**

1082

The immense shaft corkscrews down through aeons of rock. Cascades of dust and pebbles sift down, making the ramp slippery. You have to watch your footing in the dim light filtering up from below.

As your eyes adjust to the gloom, you make out more detail in the walls of the shaft. It's not a regular mathematical spiral but something that looks like the inside of the shell of a titanic mollusc, as if reality itself has been

scrunched up and crumpled aside to make an opening into the belly of the earth.

A hum pulses on the air, a mechanical heartbeat drawing you towards the flickering light. You just keep going down and down. It's like going down to the bottom of the world.

At last you reach the bottom. The top of the shaft now is swallowed in impenetrable darkness. The light comes from beyond an archway, and you step through into a cavern so vast that its roof is like a subterranean sky. The pulsing light swirls from phosphors embedded in the surrounding rock, patches of mauve and green and yellow dancing in almost organic arcs.

Filling this extraordinary space is a machine bigger than any palace, a colossal metal edifice whose rearing central pillar and huge gleaming cables put you in mind of a mechanical octopus. It is from this that the rhythmic hum seems to emanate. You have the sense that, machine though it may be, it is almost a living thing.

Surrounding it are banks of iron-framed devices that stretch for hundreds of metres in all directions. The devices are as big as cottages and laid out in a regular grid like city streets, each covered in lights that flicker like swarms of fireflies in the gloom of a deep forest. Around them spool a complex tangle of thick wires that all feed back into the cables stretching from the master machine.

It is a place of eerie uninhabited automation. Or so you think, but it is not uninhabited. There – a figure moves in the shadows.

If you have the codeword *Ozone* ▶ 774
If not ▶ 184

1083

'What's that little bauble?' Her supercilious smile hardens as she sees the amber globe in your hand. 'Where did you get it?'

'I found it in an idol moment.'

Nyx reacts with desperate speed. Her hands sweep up, summoning a dark mist that billows out around you. You're engulfed in a black void. Ancient fear of the unknown raises the hair on the back of your neck. But you're given hope by the look you saw in Nyx's eyes before the darkness fell. She is afraid.

The Eye of Hyperion begins to glow. At first it's no more than a faint spark, but it grows brighter, golden light streaming from it and pushing back the encircling darkness. Nyx's face, dimly outlined by the light, contorts as she focuses on summoning all her power. Torrents of black nullity pour down onto the glowing Eye. It gutters, dimming, and you fear it's about to be extinguished. But within it lies the essence of the titan of the sun, once almost

the equal of the queen of night. Pulsing, the golden light flares up, resisting Nyx's power for a moment more.

Her face looms huge and white in the abyssal darkness, etched with strain as she summons all her might. Beads of sweat stand out glistening on her brow.

'You will learn,' she mutters between clenched teeth. 'I am Night. I am unconquerable.'

She may well be right. In this struggle between light and dark, she's gradually gaining the upper hand. The beams of light from the Eye are sputtering, growing dimmer, no brighter than a candleflame now in the immensity of utter darkness.

If you have the codewords *Ratchet* and *Quiddity* ▶ 934
If you have *Ratchet* but don't have *Quiddity* ▶ 1355
Otherwise, if you have *Rug* ▶ 973
Otherwise ▶ 1531

1084

❑

If the box above was already ticked ▶ 1549; otherwise put a tick in it now and then read on.

Dunamis brushes brick dust off the surface of the noticeboard. 'We're lucky, it's still working,' she says. 'You can use these doodads to glitch reality.'

She demonstrates by prising off the side of the board and dragging her knife across the exposed contacts. A spark cracks along the metal blade and the screen changes to display a message:

'ENTER DESIRED LOCATION.'

'I use it to get around the city without being seen,' she says. 'But for anything heavy-duty, like sorting out all this chaos for instance, we're going to need administrator access.'

If you have the codeword *Rice* ▶ 1007
If not ▶ 839

1085

'OK, but what's the guarantee there are any more worlds out there? We could sail on forever.'

'According to the legends – ' begins Ancaeus, more in hope than conviction.

'Legends aren't much to go on.'

'What's the choice? The titans and the gods will exhaust their energies fighting each other into submission. Nyx has already seized control of Vulcan's world. She'll remake it in her own image and from there she'll launch a war to subjugate both Olympus and Tartarus. The best place to be by then is the far end of eternity.'

'Have you got enough supplies for a journey like that?'

'I'm an Argonaut. You don't think I've planned ahead?

There's a place called the Isle of the Dawn, right on the edge of the Ocean of Night. We'll put in there and stock up for the voyage.'

▶ 781

1086

You fall from the parapet, feeling the wind's embrace fill the wings. They spread wide, carrying you out in a long sweeping flight that skims the walls of the buildings opposite. But the ground is coming up fast. High as the palace roof is, it didn't give you much altitude to launch from. If you can't pull up out of the dive, your brains will be dashed out on the flagstones below.

Make a GRACE roll at difficulty 10.

Succeed ▶ 1117

Fail ▶ 519

1087

Note your Current Location as **1603**.

If you left any money or **lava gems**, they're not here now. To retrieve other possessions ▶ 319 but roll a six-sided die for each item. On a roll of 1-3 the item has been stolen (cross it off the box at 319); on a roll of 4-6 the item is still here.

1088

If this box ❑ is ticked then ▶ 1212; otherwise put a tick in it now and read on.

The dry grass gives way to scattered rocks across which you have to pick your way carefully. A region of boulders stands out from the hillside like a carbuncle. Navigating a narrow pass between the boulders, you hear an echoing murmur no louder than trickles of stone dust.

If you have the codeword *Recursive* ▶ 997

If not but you have the title **Favoured by Orion** ▶ 799

Otherwise ▶ 5

1089

The sounds of the street fall away as you walk along a narrow lane with high windowless walls of dirty brick on both sides. The prison itself stands at the end of this cheerless alleyway: a glowering edifice of black granite with huge bronze doors spotted with green rust. Far above, narrow cell windows give the inmates their sole glimpse of daylight. A foetid odour lingers in the air, seemingly oozing from the dank mortar and urine-spattered cobblestones. It is the reek of the unwashed incarcerated hordes left to rot behind those unyielding iron bars.

▶ 1301

1090

The chaos of sparks and noise dims. There is a wrench as reality shifts around you. You taste cold rain on your lips. The smell of wet soil and foliage. A storm growls overhead. You are back in the garden of Vulcan's palace. There is no sign of the giant insects.

Get the codeword *Rustic* and ▶ 143

1091

'Mechanical creatures are the hallmark of only a few inventors,' she says thoughtfully.

'Vulcan?'

She smiles. 'Yes, he has made mechanical beings, but usually more sophisticated than this image suggests. As Homer said, "There were golden handmaids who worked for Vulcan, like real young women with sense and reason, able to speak and possessed of strength, skill, and all the knowledge of science that was his to impart." This butterfly seems rather more basic.'

'Then who?'

'There's Vulcan's erstwhile assistant Kedalion, who set up a workshop in north-east Boreas. And the Dactyls of western Notus – except any butterfly they made would be big enough to squash an ox. So I'm guessing this depicts the handiwork of Daedalus himself.'

'And where can I find him?'

'I can tell you the location of his old workshop. It's north of the Delta of Darkness in Hades. But as for Daedalus himself, you'll find him where he wants to be found.'

If you possess the **Face of Wisdom (INGENUITY +3)** ▶ 589

Otherwise it's time to retrace your steps ▶ 63

1092

It is written in the clear, precise hand of a scholar or librarian:

'Dear sister, I send this by the hand of the giver of good things, who will also bestow a gift that I and my beloved send in token of the great debt we owe to you. The balm will allow you to see under the skin of reality to perceive the truth.'

As quickly as you read, the letters fade from the paper. If there was a signature, you don't get to see it before you are holding only a blank sheet.

Return to the battlefield ▶ 441

That'll do for today ▶ 638

1093

'So you're worried Sakan might tell your fellow officers about that.'

'It's just a matter of time. I know him and he's a shit right through to the core. He'll keep the thumbscrews on me till I'm a nervous wreck, then he'll expose me as a coward in front of the whole company.'

'And are you a coward?'

'I don't think so, no. I'd call him out for a duel, but then I'd have to reveal why and it would all come out anyway.'

'If you run home to Boreas you'd only be showing you are a coward.'

'Give me a problem I can face down with a sword, I'll stand my ground. It's backbiting and whispered gossip I've never been any good with.'

'Maybe I can take care of this for you.'

He puts down his glass, looking at you seriously for the first time. 'What are you, a problem solver?'

'Sometimes. Also a problem eliminator. Leave it with me and I'll see what I can do.'

Get the codeword *Rafter* and ▶ 1534

1094

Sweat beads your brow. Your teeth are clenched to breaking point. A defiant snarl wells up from the pit of your stomach as you fling the malevolent sceptre away.

Remove the **sceptre of Agamemnon** from your Adventure Sheet and ▶ 399

1095

A glance down shows you impossibly high off the ground, all the tiny milling soldiers scattered across the plain far below, but even here you are barely level with the giant figure's calf. Time seems to stand still. Straining every sinew, you swing your sword. The blade passes between the shielding curtain of unreality and even as you fall back to earth you feel the tip bite deep into her flesh, scoring a thin line across her ankle from which silver blood streams like liquid radiance.

▶ 1329

1096

The guards were expecting a cut of the money. They take out their disappointment on you, laying into you with fists and boots.

'That's enough, lads,' says the sergeant after a while. 'Don't want to kill the golden goose, do we?' He pats your bruised cheek. 'Hurry back when you've got the rest of it.'

You are tossed out into the street. And as you limp away you realize that you weren't given a receipt, so you still owe the full sum. That hurts worse than the beating.

Tick the Wound box on your Adventure Sheet if you weren't injured already, then ▶ 1642

1097

'Here,' says a voice like chimes in the wind.

A pale hand reaches out of the bushes, beckoning you. A dryad's face peeks out. 'Hurry. They will not find you here within the sapwood.'

She draws you to her. It is not merely like pushing between the clipped foliage. You seem to be inside the vegetation, almost a part of it, looking out through the eyes of the topiary figures as the creatures pursing you come scuttling along the avenue. Their antennae twitch in confusion. They cannot sense you in this hiding-place of the dryads.

If you have any **attercop silk** ▶ 45

Otherwise you can either ambush the insect-things (▶ 155) or else stay in hiding till they've gone (▶ 936).

1098

Delete the **wings of Icarus** from your Adventure Sheet and get the codeword *Retract*.

The spider-robot scuttles ahead to unlock the door to the roof and Daedalus leads the way up, strapping on the wings as he goes. The wind spreads the feathers so that they gleam white against the ultramarine sky.

'Won't we need two sets?' says Icarus as his father wraps his arms around him.

'Short trip, son. Just hang on tight.'

'It's a long way down,' you say, peering over the edge of the roof. 'And don't you need wax to secure the wings?'

Daedalus screws up his face impatiently. 'Everyone's an expert all of a sudden. I made these things, OK? I know what they can do.'

'Thanks for all your help,' says Icarus.

'He means for what you've done so far,' says Daedalus, stretching his wings. 'There's a lot more yet. Come and see us as soon as you can.'

He springs up on his heels and launches over the edge.

'Where?' you yell as they soar away over the rooftops.

'You'll figure it out,' comes a voice already faint with distance.

You watch them dwindle to a speck. They are flying north-east, but just before they reach the tower on the city wall they swoop down, weaving between buildings until you lose sight of them.

Daedalus left the spider-robot behind to guide you back to the exit. You slip past the guard patrols and out into the street.

▶ 63

1099

'You pulling my leg?' He goes from boastful to bashful in a heartbeat. 'I mean, it's not a big mystery. You got that strong jaw, boyish frame, long lean flanks, tits like – '

'Watch it.' You don't like the leer as his gaze traces your physique.

'Hey, you asked. Anyway, it's more about personality with a young buck like him. No doubt he's sweet on your confident stride and firm straight smile. Me, I prefer a wench with more meat on her, not an Amazon with slabs of muscle where a big soft butt should be.'

Change the subject ▶ 1261
Continue on your way ▶ 735

1100

'You should return to the world,' you tell Eos. 'Humankind has never had greater need of a new dawn.'

She shakes her head slowly, though you see it's something she has considered many times. 'My mother has an unforgiving heart. I could never muster the courage to defy her, and now it is too late. While Vulcan and the other gods are distracted by battle with the titans, she has found Vulcan's secret workshop. She is fabricating a new universe in which she will be the supreme ruler.'

'Unless she's stopped.'

Eos nods. 'Humankind has never had greater need of a hero.'

▶ 576

1101

If this box ❑ is empty, tick it and ▶ 204
If it was already ticked, roll a die:
score 1-3 ▶ 204
score 4-6 ▶ 1623

1102

You roll the unconscious man off you, flinging him to one side. You spring to your feet just in time – the other guard's club smashes into the ground where your face was a moment earlier. Planting your boot heel on the club, you step in and slam an elbow strike across his jaw. He grunts and falls to his knees. A second blow lays him out beside his comrade.

The mechanical spider is clinging to the to the final door, which stands open. It beckons you and leads the way up a short flight of steps to a cell in the highest eaves of the building.

▶ 1397

1103

She takes your hand and steps over the sill. Her touch is icy. She is so willowy a figure as to seem almost weightless.

'Dry yourself,' you tell her as you close the window and fasten the catch. 'I'll get the servants to make up a fire.'

'No need to wake them. I'll just have a quick bite and I'll go.'

You turn. Her green eyes gleam like jewels and her lips part in a smile to reveal needle-sharp fangs.

'This is the next career move after ghoul, is it?'

'It's good you can meet your doom with a quip.' She raises her hand, stroking your cheek almost tenderly. Then her fingers close tight around your neck and she draws you towards her eager lips.

The storm batters at the window and casts ripples of rainwater shadow over the walls as you struggle for your life against the vampire you have invited in.

Though she is slight, apparently no more than a frail wisp of a girl, her grip is as hard as cold iron. Make a STRENGTH roll at difficulty 11.

Succeed ▶ 628
Fail ▶ 248

1104

You had the foresight to place the horn headrest on your pillow before falling asleep. Its ancient enchantment intensifies your senses so that the colours and tastes and smells that you are experiencing seem a thousand times more vivid than mundane reality. In each leaf you see the web of chlorophyl veins, in the nightingale's song you feel the tangible patterns of sound that ripple through the air. Your own muscles tingle with a numinous energy that connects you to everything here, giving you a lucid command of the dreamscape around you.

▶ 1149

1105

'Perhaps you know of the Keres,' says Eos. 'People call them the hounds of Thanatos, but they are more deadly than any pack of dogs. Now they roam around the wreckage of Vulcan City seeking out prey.'

'How do I deal with them? Drugged meat? Toss them a bone? Throw a stick?'

She gives you a forlorn smile. 'It's good that you still have the spirit to jest. No one can hope to stand alone against the Keres. Unless you have help, the only recourse is to stay on the move and hope they don't find you.'

Time to leave ▶ 90
One more question ▶ 1292

1106

Much can be achieved in Vulcan City if you have influence and wealthy friends. You have only to make a casual suggestion at the end of a formal dinner party, spend some gold to grease the palms of a few officials, and Sakan is given a mission that will keep him travelling around the furthest rim of the world for years to come.

Get the codeword *Rock* and ▶ **1432**

1107

'What's the guarantee there are any more worlds out there? We could sail on forever.'

'There are legends – ' begins Ancaeus, and you see at once he is drawing more on hope than conviction.

'Legends aren't much to go on.'

'What's the choice? The titans and the gods will exhaust their energies fighting each other into submission. Nyx has already seized control of Vulcan's world. She'll remake it in her own image and from there she'll launch a war to subjugate both Olympus and Tartarus. The best place to be by then is the far end of eternity.'

'This is the Ocean of Night. What makes you think she won't conquer everyone else and then hunt us down just to make sure?'

His shoulders sag. 'I don't know. Perhaps she will. Or maybe we're too insignificant for her to bother about. My responsibility is to my crew, and I don't intend to take them back to certain death.'

'If we're going to undertake a journey into the unknown, we'll need to make repairs first.' You point to the splintered timbers and broken rigging.

Ancaeus nods. 'There's a place out here known as the Island of the Dawn. We can overhaul the ship there. That's if we can find it.'

If you have an **astrarium** and want to let him use it ▶ **1180**

If you have the **journal of the Argo** and show it to him ▶ **444**

Otherwise ▶ **1146**

1108

You open your eyes to bright sunshine streaming through the bedroom window. Beside you, the girl is also awake. She looks around her in alarm, and is about to leap from the bed when her husband steps over and lays a restraining hand on her shoulder. You feel her flinch.

'Are you just going to lie there in bed with my wife?' he says.

He's smiling, but he has to squeeze the joke out like blood from a stone. You throw off the stifling blankets and get up.

'Well… she's safe now, I guess.' The expression frozen on her face doesn't convey safety, though.

'Yes she is,' says the merchant, his tone one of powerful emotion masked and bridled.

He is impatient for you to go. Pressing a purse into your hand, he ushers you to the bedroom door and tells the servant to show you out. 'You have my adamantine gratitude,' he says in parting.

Get the codeword *Rebuke*. The purse contains 100 pyr, which you can add to your money. As you walk away from the house you cast a look back, but the drapes are drawn across the window and there is nothing to be seen.

▶ **515**

1109

Polymnia has eaten nothing, but she holds each dish under her nose to inhale the aroma. 'The amaranth flower is sometimes called love-lies-bleeding,' she says.

'Oh,' says the restaurant owner, 'in that case, yes, I use it a lot. It has a very subtle flavour.'

▶ **191**

1110

'A odious sniffing little mongrel of a man!' Forgetting himself in his fury, he all but shouts the words, and goes pale as his gaze flicks anxiously to his wife's sleeping form.

Dropping his voice till he is almost inaudible, he continues: 'His name is Dydkos. Besotted by stories of my wife's beauty, this upstart spied upon her in a magic mirror and his rancid heart conceived a violent passion to possess her.'

'A wizard, then?'

He gives a soft derisive snort. 'He has a few tricks and trinkets. Lies and blandishments are the major part of his magic. He comes from a travelling people called the Domovoi. They are treacherous rats who live by peddling worthless junk and are known to make off with horses and women.'

He waits while you decide whether to help him or not. His face is impassive, but the inner turmoil of feeling is betrayed by the whitening of his knuckles as he grips the bedstead.

Agree ▶ **423**
Refuse and leave ▶ **515**

1111

The narrow avenue between the rows of hedges prevents the insects from surrounding you. Here they must come at you one at a time. Even so, as you size up their powerful armoured pincers and overlapping exoskeletal plates, you know it will be a desperate fight.

Attempt a STRENGTH or GRACE roll (your choice) at difficulty 10.

Succeed ▶ **1569**
Fail ▶ **825**

1112

Using the wings you could fly to a number of destinations within the desert lands of Notus. To do so you will need a copy of *The Hammer of the Sun*, and you cannot take any companion with you.

Take to the air ▶ **1458**
Not now ▶ **1246**

1113

Beyond a gate in a messily-trimmed hedge there's a door whose green paint is scuffed and faded. You knock and are surprised to find an ordinary family – a plump, apple-cheeked couple with children playing under the kitchen table and a baby squalling in a cot beside the stove.

'Sorry to barge in,' you say, confused. 'I thought this was the home of – '

The woman wipes her hands on her apron, puts a finger to her lips, and points at the floor.

'He's downstairs, you mean?'

You look around for the cellar steps, but you realize you won't need them. The metal chrysalis in your pocket has divided into a swarm of buzzing insects who, as before, have enclosed you in a cocoon of gold light in which you are sinking into the ground.

After a few moments of chill darkness you emerge into a basement where Daedalus is welding a piece of intricate machinery. Seeing you, he drops his tools, pushes back his protective visor, and gives you a broad grin. 'Took you by surprise, did it?' he says, pointing to the floor above. 'Just a security precaution. As far as the neighbourhood is concerned this is the home of Glauco the carpenter and his family. No need for anyone to know I'm even in the city, after all.'

You look around. The room is filled with benches littered with tools and components. On the wall hang the artificial wings you gave him, now attached to a metal harness like a cuirass. More pieces of articulated armour hang on chains from the ceiling, waiting to be fitted together.

'Isn't it the bad guys who are supposed to have underground lairs?' you say.

He cocks an eyebrow. 'We'll come out into the open with a bang when we're ready, you can bet. So let's talk about that.'

▶ **95**

1114

You grab hold of her, your arm levered taut around her neck. 'All your ducking and diving won't help you now,' you hiss in her ear. Then, with a twist of the hips, you jerk her off the ground. Her neck gives with a muffled snap and you feel her go limp.

Flinging the body down, you shout for your servants. They come running, staring aghast at the wreckage the fight has made of your study. Then one of the maids catches sight of the corpse and sinks to the floor in a swoon.

'Clear all this up by morning,' you tell the servants. 'I'm going back to bed.'

▶ **97**

1115

Get the codeword **Ruffle**.

Decide how much money you're giving her and cross it off your Adventure Sheet. She takes the coins without looking at them.

'Keep an obol for the ferryman, won't you?' she says.

'These are pyr,' you tell her.

'Purrs. Oh yes. The new-fangled currency of secrets.' She takes the coins and, standing on your doorstep, throws them to passers-by. 'Here! Crumbs from the table of somebody rich.'

'It's time you were on your way,' you tell her.

She lifts the frayed hem of her gown and flounces off down the street without a backward glance.

▶ **97**

1116

You've gone a few metres down the ramp when you sense Dunamis isn't behind you. Glancing back you see no sign of her. She's gone without a word.

You can't blame her. Forced to fend for herself in the roughest quarters of the city, she's lost the habit of trusting others. If your quest fails there's nowhere for her to flee, but why shouldn't she spend her last few hours in hope? Silently you breathe a prayer, wishing Dunamis godspeed.

▶ **1082**

1117

The slick cobblestones sweep past only inches below your face. The few people who have stayed out on the streets run for cover as you hurtle past. Your upward arc climbs directly towards the colossal figure of Thanatos, looming amid the boiling storm clouds. He extends a giant hand, thinking he has you, but a howling gale fills the wings and carries you up and up, soaring past the cowled god of death, higher even than the thunderheads that stretch like mountain crags up into the heavens.

Breaking through the misty upper layers you are clear of the rain. The stars are out waiting to greet you, hard and bright as distant diamonds. Impossibly far below, the streets and buildings of the city are mere toys half-seen in the murk. The lightning strikes that slammed and shook you to your core from here seem only distant sparks.

Thanatos was drawing back his cowl. His gaze would have blasted your soul to atoms, but you are safe among the silent constellations. Even death cannot catch you now.

▶ 1033

1118

'I hoped you were going to say that,' says the leader with a sharp feral grin. He swings his club at your knees as the others fan out to come at you from either side.

In the cramped alleyways of the Grumbles there's little room to manoeuvre, so this is a contest of simple endurance and brutality. Make a STRENGTH roll at difficulty 9. That is, roll two dice and add your STRENGTH modifier (including any one item bonus, for example from a **hardwood club**) and you need to score 9 or more.

Success   ▶ **1136**
Failure   ▶ **1018**

1119

'To the two best storytellers in the city,' says Lady Pemphreda, raising her glass to you both.

Nobody takes the contest very seriously, not even Kazala herself, but you can't help feeling despondent at having been outclassed. You soon make your excuses and leave.

▶ **1324**

1120

Record **404** as your Current Location.

The cards are dealt and one of the girls is picked for sacrifice to the demon. Watching her being carried helpless and trembling into the dark lair makes you determined to put an end to the Hero of Temesa's reign of terror.

At the end of the evening the customers put out all the lamps but one. At least they have the decency to look abashed. They file out in silence, not noticing you concealed behind a beer barrel. As you hear the heavy lock turn, you emerge from hiding and creep over to the portico in the wall.

The lamplight doesn't penetrate far, but you can see the white face of the girl in the darkness ahead. The alcove is like a deep, disused fireplace with walls of soot-blackened stone. Crouching, you edge forward along the low tunnel and into the chamber that is the Hero's fane. The smell is chokingly strong: a blend of fear-stink, animal fur, burnt wood and decay.

A growl wells up that can be felt through the flagstones underfoot. A shadowy bulk detaches itself from the darkness. Its breath is a charnel reek like a gutted dead thing. Arms as strong as gnarled tree branches reach around you, and in the darkness you get an impression of a twisted, soot-smeared face and clumps of ragged fur.

Unable to stand fully upright in the confined space, slipping on the slimy stone floor, retching with the smell, and mindful that with the girl so close you cannot attack with full ferocity, you realize that this will be one of the hardest fights of your life.

Make a GRACE roll at difficulty 13. You cannot use a blessing in this fight because the gods will not aid a mortal against a semi-divine being, even one as loathsome as this.

Succeed   ▶ **177**
Fail   ▶ **564**

1121

If you have the codeword *Ridge* ▶ **68**

If not and you have the title **Public-Spirited** and this box ❑ is empty, tick it and ▶ **1496**

Otherwise ▶ **663**

1122

If you have one or more scars, or if your Glory is 9 or less ▶ **814**

Otherwise ▶ **439**

1123

You are forced to admit that your investigations have led nowhere.

'On the bright side,' you say, 'the blackmailer is dead.'

'But the letters have not been recovered.' She's not smiling. 'That means I could be threatened with exposure in the future.'

'I don't think the murderer wants money from you.'

'He may exact a price in other ways.' Himera makes a gesture as if brushing away a fly, and you know you have been dismissed.

'I have an expenses sheet,' you tell the servant as he shows you to the door.

'You can leave that with me,' he says, whisking it from your hand. 'I know just what to do with it.'

You turn on the doorstep but he has already closed the door.

▶ **1642**

1124

'Wait. I got it from your nephew.'

'My nephew?'

'Perdix.'

Daedalus shakes his head in astonishment. 'Perdix – huh, that's his mother's name. He always was a deeply confused young man.'

'He set the casket to explode. He told me it was payback for you having pushed him off a roof.'

'Yeah, so I can see how that would look, but he was trying to murder his mom at the time. The genuine Perdix, that was her.' He pulls a handful of needle-thin tools from his belt and quickly disarms the trap. 'It took real genius to build this, too. What a waste of talent that kid is.'

▶ 1361

1125

He considers it for so long you think he has forgotten you. 'Not yet,' he says at last. 'Even Achilles' centaur-taught skills cannot have so quickly restored you to full health. Ask me again tomorrow.'

With that he falls silent, brooding on other things.

▶ 260

1126

With a last rueful sigh, Orphea hands you the **Pipes of Pan** (**CHARM +3**). Add them to your possessions. The CHARM bonus is not cumulative with that conferred by a **laurel wreath** or a **golden lyre**.

'Don't try taking the pipes into Vulcan's Palace, will you?' she says with a crooked smile.

'I don't even know where Vulcan's Palace is.'

'Nobody does till they're invited there. And you won't be allowed in carrying buffs, so better stash them somewhere else first.'

You run your fingers over the smooth polished curve of the pipes. The very texture of them seems to sing of summer breezes amid fields of reeds. Lost for a moment in a reverie of far-off Arcadia, you look up to see Orphea already half out of the window.

'Naturally you can't just use the door like anyone else.'

'Old habits,' she says with a grin. 'We may not meet again this side of the Great Reset, but you've been a worthy – '

What? Saviour? Adversary? Acquaintance? Ally? She leaves you to decide that for yourself, jumping down from the sill with cat-like grace and loping silently away across the moon-silvered lawn.

▶ 97

1127

You are seized and flung into a filthy cell to await your fate. Lose any money or **lava gems** you were carrying as the guards help themselves to those.

If you have any of the codewords *Rain*, *Rebuke*, *Rhyme* or *Ritual* or either of the titles **Informant** or **Paladin** ▶ 1076

If not but you have the codeword *Rigor* ▶ 1474

If none of the above but you have Glory of 10 or more ▶ 590

Otherwise ▶ 347

1128

Inside the building, the corridors that are normally crammed with bureaucrats and petitioners lie silent as an unvisited mausoleum. Ahead are the elaborately carved doors that lead to the audience chamber. You push them open. The feeble blue glow barely penetrates this far inside, but Dunamis's lantern gives enough light to see that the tiers of seats are still occupied. The forty-nine syndics sit slumped around the dais where the mechanical Speaker stands rigid as a shop-window dummy.

'It looks as if they were in the middle of a session and all suddenly fell asleep,' you say.

'Ever sat in on one of their debates?' quips Dunamis, but her attempt at humour sounds a false note in the eerie hush of the auditorium.

As your eyes adjust to the gloom, it's possible to make out translucent forms hovering in the air above each of the sleeping syndics. Their half-formed bodies are folded tubes of smooth flesh and nascent bone gradually taking the shape of limbs, like ghostly embryos.

'They are pupating dreams,' says a tinny voice that rings out clearly in the silence.

The Speaker. Its eyes are turned on you. Eyes that are pools of darkness. Dunamis, normally so bold, clutches at your arm.

'I have possessed this metal mannikin in order to have a last word with you,' says the Speaker – but in a triumphal, sneering voice quite different from its usual calm tones.

'Nyx…'

'Your continued defiance is a bore to me and a waste of your last hours,' says Nyx through the Speaker's voicebox. 'I have already initiated my own rebuilding of the Vulcanverse. The transformation is under way. Soon this will become the Darklands – the whole of reality, my realm forevermore.'

'Yeah? Well I plan to throw a spanner in the works.'

'I see there is no point in trying to reason with you. Go ahead, then. Flail on if it gives you solace. Rage against the dying of the light. In the end, you and all creation will bow before the unconquerable authority of the Queen of Night.'

The Speaker goes silent and sags like a puppet with the strings cut. At the same moment, a pool of inky darkness spreads up the walls of the chamber as though a giant hand were covering a candle. The beam of the lantern is swallowed up. You can see nothing.

Backing away, Dunamis swings the lantern around to

shine down the corridor behind you. 'I can see fine this way. The darkness is only in there.'

You stare into the black void beyond the doors. 'Even so, how can we find Zagreus if we can't see a damned thing?'

'I spotted him just before the light went out,' she says. 'Third row back, sixth seat along.'

Try and find your way in the dark to where Zagreus is sitting ▶ **294**

Leave the palace ▶ **820**

1129

You thrust your arms into the winged harness. No time to worry about waxing the mechanism; you pray the flight will be short enough that it doesn't seize up. You hurriedly fasten the straps, securing at best one buckle in three. It'll have to do.

Poising like a diver on the balustrade, you wait for a strong updraft and launch yourself off into space.

If you have the codeword **Remedy** ▶ **1086**

If not ▶ **1388**

1130

The reply comes like a pulse beating inside your head: 'If you believe the cause is just or the outcome is necessary. Those are the only good reasons to fight.'

'Don't I owe Achilles a debt?'

'His struggle is not yours.'

'He saved my life.'

'He loves you. And he is afire with destiny, that one. A spark of his greatness might ignite you too. That could be an outcome worth fighting for.'

'Still, this war all happened in my distant past. The war against Nyx is what matters, surely?'

'You are my weapon in that other war. Think of this as the furnace. Perhaps you will be forged into something even titans fear.'

'So I should stay?'

'You have a choice as Achilles did. He had to pick between a long and uneventful life or a blaze of glory and an early death. What matters is that you make the choice. That way you earn your destiny.'

▶ **179**

1131

By sheer demonic force of will she tries to pin you where you lie, as a cobra's mesmeric stare is said to hold its prey transfixed. But you are no prey. Drawing on an inexhaustible well of determination, you gather your strength and rise from the bed.

▶ **1659**

1132

There is the rattle and clank of a heavy lock opening. The gates remain closed, but you notice a door further along the prison wall at the bottom of some steps. It slowly swings open. The hairs on your neck bristle as something large and spidery creeps around the edge of the door. But it is not a living spider. It is a clockwork simulacrum with keys instead of feet.

The mechanical spider beckons you with one long limb, then darts back out of sight. By the time you are through the door, it has scuttled to the end of the passage beyond and is unlocking another door. Steps wind up into the interior of the building.

You follow it through a series of doors, passageways and staircases. All around you, muffled by the thick walls, echo the sounds of despair: moans, tortured muttering, screams, angry shouting, the clatter of heavy clubs across cell bars. The barks of nervous command and the snarls of brooding defiance.

By now you must be several storeys above the street. Reaching a heavy oak door, the spider-robot stiffens against the door frame, rotating its head into the passage beyond, antennae quivering. After a moment it holds up one of its hind legs like a raised finger. Detaching that limb, which remains fixed to the side of the door frame like an exclamation mark, it scurries off around the corner on its remaining seven legs.

Wait ▶ **1242**

Follow it ▶ **817**

1133

Closing with her, you pull the dagger from your belt.

If you have the title **Godslayer** ▶ **1484**

If not ▶ **752**

1134

Note **771** as your Current Location, then ▶ **1269** and tick the box next to the Grumbles. From now on you will always be able to find your way back here.

1135

You watch the play long enough to realize that it's one you've seen before. The puppets need a fresh coat of paint, too. Afterwards you mention that to one of the puppeteers as she's packing up.

'No money to repair them, you see,' she says, holding up a very scuffed and dented puppet. 'Most people watch the performance and then wander off without paying. These days everybody thinks content should be free.'

▶ **232**

1136

A metal-capped boot comes at your face. You grab it, twist, and send that attacker flying into the path of another. You twist around just in time to take a powerful strike on your shoulder. It's painful, but it doesn't stop you laying the attacker out with a hard uppercut.

After a short struggle they've had enough. 'Keep your poxy coins if you're that hard up,' sneers the leader.

You grin back at him. He's panting, there's blood all over his teeth, and he'll have a black eye to show for his trouble by tomorrow. He leads the others away, swaggering a little so as not to look like they're running off.

You've come out on top but not unscathed. Tick the Wound box on your Adventure Sheet and ▶ 1425

1137

'Why have you come back here, you blundering worm?' howls Oizys. 'You already searched this stretch of the hillside.'

'There might be more chance of finding something now that I don't have a giant trying to stomp me into the dust.'

'What's that? Self-pity? Rebellion? Try it again and I'll peel your eyes from the inside like two fat grapes.'

▶ 1446

1138

Eros and Prometheus charge forward. Nyx gestures, tearing a rent in the very air, a fathomlessly black gash which becomes in her grasp a night-black halberd with which she parries both their attacks. The weapons clash, sending sparks of plasma careening in all directions. The energies they are conjuring are greater than the death of stars, the collision of constellations. Space itself warps and screams in protest.

Even weakened by her fight with the gods, Nyx's strength is as great as theirs combined. You can see it's a battle neither side can win except at the cost of destroying all of reality. By rights you should be trembling in fear. Any mortal should be paralyzed at the sight of these titans battling. You have no time for that. Running forward, you lift the knife. Nyx is a towering giant. You plant your foot on a toppled urn and jump high into the air towards her. As she turns with flashing black eyes you plunge the dagger into her heart.

Her expression doesn't change at first. Then, as her immortal ebon blood seeps into the air, leaving traces of dissipating vapour like ink spurting underwater, her ferocity gives way to a look of resignation. She glances down. You follow her gaze. The blade of her halberd is buried deep in your breast.

You and she sink together to the floor. 'A glorious end for you, hero,' she whispers. 'To die at the moment the greatest of the titans falls.'

Eros is reaching for you. He's saying something, but the words echo across a gulf that no power can bridge. You can't keep your eyes open. For a short while you're alone with the sigh of your own laboured breathing, until that too fades.

You're at home. Your family home, with your old dog Argos curled up by the fire. How many years has it been since you saw him?

It's getting dark. Aunt Terpe lights a lamp. That's the gift of Prometheus, she tells you, given to mortals so that they need not fear the night.

From outside wafts the sound of laughter and children singing. The door opens. Your parents come in, and behind them your uncles with Aunt Eremia leading your brother and sisters in a playful dance.

A stew bubbles in the pot, filling the kitchen with delicious aromas. The moon rises and warm silver light floods in the windows. The nights here are never long, never frightening. Your family gather you to them around the blazing hearth. You now know you are in the Elysian fields and have no challenges to look forward to, just the reward of an eternity of perfect peace and happiness.

1139

Tick the Wound box on your Adventure Sheet and get the codeword *Rug*.

A maelstrom of fighting surrounds you. The clash of weapons, clang of metal armour, jarring impacts of blades on ruptured thews, the crunch of broken bones, the screams, shouted oaths, battle-frenzied roars, ragged gasps of breath – all blur into one deafening cacophony. Bolts of magical energy blister the air. The scent of blood and ichor mingles with the adrenalized sweat of a thousand combatants.

Sorely wounded, you stumble forward. Nyx stands in the midst of the melee as cold, remote and beautiful as the face of the moon. She sees you coming and her voluptuous black lips part in a triumphant smile. She opens her arms – strong and supple, huge and white as marble pillars, ready to fold you in a crushing embrace.

'Behold, my new world is almost complete,' she says, each murmured word somehow ringing out clear over the din of battle all around. 'The dark is rising. Nothing can stop me now.'

The two of you are face to face. You're almost

exhausted. You'd like to lie down, but if you did you'd never get up again. Somehow, injured and weary as you are, you must summon up the strength to fight her.

If you have the **sceptre of Agamemnon** ▶ 39
Otherwise ▶ 399

1140

'Agamemnon, respect the priest. Take this ransom and give him back his daughter.'

He turns a gaze of smouldering fire on you. 'Found your voice, Amazon? I've heard your screams and whimpers clear enough, keeping us all awake while Achilles nursed you. His bird with a broken wing, you are. Now you're fit enough to strut about the camp, I see, and issue edicts that you imagine kings should heed. Think again.'

'It is not my will you should bow to, but that of the god who strikes from afar. If you dishonour his priest, what fate do you think you will suffer? Even kings must obey the gods.'

'It is not fitting I should give up my gift. All my men have their booty, their treasure and their slave girls. How can their king take less?'

'A king who takes less shows he is greater.'

He snorts like an old bull. 'You're a lawyer, are you, as well as an Amazon? Truth be told, I'd rather this girl Astynome than my wife back home. She's more shapely, better bred, a willing worker – and no sharp tongue on her either.' He examines you with narrowed eyes. 'Unless you'd take her place. With a strapping woman like you to share my bed I'd have no need of a pale little slip like her.'

Agree to take the girl's place ▶ 1477
No way! ▶ 211

1141

Both shoot at the same time and, by the sort of miracle in which many see the workings of the gods, the arrows strike point-to-point in mid-air and clatter into the dust.

There is a moment of stunned silence before both Tekto and Agrio start laughing. It is not just relief and amusement you can hear, but a kind of awe.

'The gods have spoken, brother,' calls Agrio.

'Aye,' agrees Tekto. 'It would be sacrilege to fight on now.'

'Honour is satisfied. Let's get drunk.'

As you are walking back to the city, Tekto catches up and puts a purse in your hands. Add 100 pyr to your money and gain the codeword **Rhyme**.

▶ 222

1142

Each of the Keres is a match for a demigod, and you are facing three of them. Most horrible of all, the dismembered torsos of still-living victims are skewered on their long spear-like limbs, writhing and moaning as the Keres lunge with snapping jaws to attack you.

Attempt a STRENGTH roll at difficulty 17.
Succeed ▶ 1022
Fail ▶ 145

1143

'They'd look a bit inelegant clomping around in a cartload of steel,' you protest. 'Duels are about dignity.'

'Yes, but – '

'Medium armour is the very heaviest I can accept.'

He is reluctant but is unable to come up with a good counter-argument, so is forced to go along with your proposal.

▶ 1633

1144

'Going somewhere?' says a mocking voice.

You were scurrying in a low crouch along a corridor. You look up to see several guards grinning at you. They are all swinging heavy clubs in their hands and look like they're eager for an excuse to use them.

Fight your way past ▶ 1420
Surrender ▶ 1127

1145

Your CHARM score isn't only about cajolery. It's also a measure of how well you can judge the effect of your words on someone, whether that's sweet talk or threats or deception.

You've obviously got the measure of this merchant. A cold sweat breaks out on his brow and he visibility wilts in fear. 'I spoke in haste,' he says, clutching at your arm. 'A little jest, that's all. Of course I wouldn't dream of causing trouble for our friend Moose.'

By sunset he has retracted the charges and Moose is released. When you report back to Zinc, he seems more pleased by the way you handled the problem than at Moose's freedom. 'I said you were smart. You had the sense to ignore that foolishness about confessing. You just went straight to the simplest solution. You're going places, kid.'

Gain the codeword **Robber** and ▶ 326

1146

'It's going to be a long haul,' reckons Ancaeus. He goes to confer with the navigator. Together they draw bearings and start poring over charts, trying to plot a course through the trackless immensity of the void.

If you have the codeword *Rustic* and the title **Earth Mother's Herald ▶ 469**

If you have *Rustic* but not **Earth Mother's Herald ▶ 312**

Otherwise ▶ **781**

1147

You wake to a titanic storm. A thunderclap directly overhead makes the rafters shake. Your first sensations are of cold and wet. The windows have blown open and rain lashes in, soaking your bedclothes. You get up and seize the window, forcing it shut against the screaming gale. Outside, the sky boils with black clouds shot through with molten flares of lightning.

A pale face peeks in from the ivy covering the wall outside – a pretty woman whose hair and clothing is plastered to her by the rain.

'Aren't you going to invite me in?' she murmurs in a lull between thunderbolts.

You know her. 'Tritona – !'

'I'd have come in the front door,' she says, 'but of course I don't any longer have a key.'

This was her family's home until Lord Xechasiaris left it to you in his will.

Get her inside ▶ **1103**

Leave her out in the rain ▶ **664**

1148

Gusts of wind thunder across the plaza, forcing you to fight your way forward towards the Syndics' palace. The unlit windows and cracked shell of the dome make it look like no one has been here in centuries.

'I sold the diadem to a nob, name of Zagreus,' says Dunamis, shouting to be heard over the gale. 'The whole place started falling apart not long after. Zags could be long gone by now.'

You shake your head. 'He won't have left the city. He must have thought the diadem would give him leverage. Probably still does. Reckons he can do a deal with Nyx for it. It's how politicians think.'

The marble flagstones crawl with a soft blue luminance. You approach the gaping entrance to the building. The ghastly cyanic light make the colossal stone portico seem unreal and weightless. ▶ **1128**

1149

You easily overpower your young adversary, flicking his sword into a pond. He lies at your feet, defenceless.

'Wait,' he says. 'You don't understand. I love her.'

You look to the girl for confirmation, but you see she was knocked over in the struggle. She lies unconscious beside a sparkling fountain whose droplets run in reverse, leaping from the water and cascading back into the marble fish-mouth spout.

'Can you be hurt in a dream?' you ask Dydkos.

'Yes, if you accept it as reality,' He rushes to the girl's side. 'Darling, I'm here.'

Take her back to the waking world ▶ **1108**

Agree she can stay here ▶ **1453**

1150

By now there's a milling throng of pursuers pressed right up to the edge of the roof. Through curtains of slashing rain you can see the pallid, worm-gnawed faces of the vampires, the red eyes and spittle-flecked jaws of the were-creatures, the misshapen features of capering nightmare demons. Shrieking and snarling, they are so intent on getting to you that some get jostled over the edge and fall flailing to the street far below.

There's a commotion at the back of the horde, near the stairs up onto the roof. Some of the rear ranks are turning in confusion. A vampire spins, a spear thrust into its chest, and disintegrates in a tattered cloud of dust and rags and old bones. A slim hand reaches out, pulls back the spear, and swings it in a wide arc to keep the nearest monsters at bay.

As the rabble parts you see a lithe figure in studded leather armour. In one hand she has the spear, in the other a sword that's already slick with blood. Behind her are a band of stalwart fighters, each holding their own against the night creatures that come rushing and snapping at them from all sides.

'Zoë?' You turn to the Minotaur. 'Look! It's the daughter of King Midas.'

The Minotaur chops a leaping were-ape off the ship's rail. 'If a warrior princess feels like crashing the party,' he grunts, 'I'm not going to tell her no.'

You shout a greeting. Zoë is too far off to hear you over the raging storm, but she sees your look of recognition and raises her hand in salute. You don't know what has brought her here at this moment, or who her companions are, but you'll take all the help you can get.

Her surprise attack has divided the monstrous horde. Half of them turn to fight Zoë and her men. Others are still leaping from the parapet trying to get aboard, but her arrival has bought you some time. Meanwhile, the *Sunrise* continues to lose altitude.

'I can handle this mob,' shouts the Minotaur. 'Go make yourself useful.'

The crew are still trying to raise the sails, no easy feat in this wind. And the helmsman is struggling to fix the buoyancy rotor. Should you see what you can do to help them, or stay shoulder-to-shoulder with the Minotaur?

Keep fighting at the rail	▶ 453
Help with the rigging	▶ 776
Take a look at the buoyancy rotor	▶ 829

1151

With an eerie rustling the armour begins to stir. At first it seems only to be swaying in the wind. Then the rigid plates begin to vibrate. It twitches, stiffens, and begins to open like a flower in the sun – but a flower whose petals are steel-hard plates, whose colours are metallic reds and blues, flaring gold, shining silver trim.

You stand rooted to the spot as the armour flows off the post where it hung and begins to fit itself around you. The greaves wrap themselves onto your legs, the vambraces snap onto your forearms, the breastplate closes like a protective shell about your torso, and the helm enfolds your head with the whirring and clicking of a finely oiled mechanism. Even Daedalus could not have built something as wondrous as this. It is the work of a god.

Add the **Panoply of the Lost Hero** to your possessions and acquire the codeword **Ramrod**.

▶ Current Location

1152

You are interviewed by a captain of militia who has been investigating Pemon's strangling.

'Lord Sphingo did it.'

'Of course,' he says, nodding. 'Nominative determinism at work. And his motive?'

'To protect his wife's reputation. Or to have something to hold over her. Maybe both.'

You hand over the **bundle of compromising letters**; cross them off your possessions.

'How indiscreet the good lady was in those days,' he remarks after reading a few of the letters.

'Are you going to arrest her husband?'

'No need. With these in the hands of the Syndics, both Sphingo and Himera are politically neutralized.'

'What about justice?'

He laughs. 'Oh, very droll.'

Get the title **Informant** and then ▶ 1642

1153

His story comes out reluctantly, one sip of liquor at a time. He is Viranos, a Halizon whose parents scrimped and saved for years in order to buy him a commission in the Black Guard.

'Of course, it helps to be tall, strong and good-looking,' you point out.

'It cost them all they had,' he says, glowering into his glass. 'It's a great honour back home, being able to say they've got a son in the Guard here in Vulcan City. But I might have to chuck it in.'

'Why?'

'When I was growing up in Halizon, there was this older kid, Sakan. He always picked on me. We got older, both ended up in the militia like every Halizonian youth, but even then he wouldn't let me alone. Anything I did, he'd jump on it and keep on jeering about it until the others laughed at me too.'

'Classic bully. You have to wonder what he found so fascinating about you. Envy, perhaps? Or maybe he loved you but couldn't find any other way to express it.'

Viranos shouts with bitter laughter. 'Don't be a dolt. Some kids pull the wings off insects and throw stones at squirrels. It's not love. Not envy. They're just little savages.'

'Still, you ended up in the Black Guard. The best revenge is to have a good life, right?'

'Except Sakan is in the Guard too,' he says, shaking his head. 'His family are rich, they could buy him a commission without going short. And every day he drops hints about telling the others. I couldn't face the shame.'

'Because he bullied you when you were children?'

'I'm not talking about schoolyard tussles. It was one particular time when we were older. We were both in the Halizon youth militia, like I said. A bunch of us went out on a bear hunt, and all the way Sakan kept telling stories about what a bear would do if it got a man on his own. Pull out your entrails and then play with you for hours, clawing and gnawing a bit at a time, and of course because we were lads he even hinted at – you know, molesting people.'

'I think that's a myth. You're no more desirable to a bear than a bear would be to you.'

'Sure, but we were all young and impressionable and he knew how to work away at insecurities. So we got to a narrow pass and Sakan got us all to set up sharpened wooden stakes. "You're the youngest, so you stay here," he said to me. "The rest of us will go around behind the bear's den and we'll holler and stomp and bang sticks and that'll drive it along the pass. You've just got to make sure you stay in sight. When it sees you it'll charge, but it won't be able to get to you because of the palisade. We'll come up behind and between us we'll be able to kill it with spears and arrows. Just make sure you stay on this side of the palisade, though, 'cause if it gets to you it'll have your innards out faster than your ma could gut a salmon." And then off they all went and I was left there with just the wind and rocks for company.'

You nod, picturing the scene. 'And naturally everything he'd been saying started to prey on your mind.'

'Yeah, he's king of the mind games. I'm standing there, and time passes, and that palisade starts to look awful rickety to me. Would it stop a bear in a killing frenzy? Maybe he'd just bat it aside like matchwood. I start testing the ropes we've used to fix it together. Then I'm worrying if the stakes are sharp enough, and I try to whittle them a bit more, only that means leaning right out through the palisade and I start to think it might collapse.'

'And where are the others? Can you hear them?'

'Way off in the distance. Sounds like they're working their way around like they said, and shouting to each other. I just think how I'd give anything to be out there with them. You know how when your blood's up and you're running with your mates, you can face any threat. It's when you're made to wait alone for danger to come to you that it gets too much.'

Viranos goes quiet and stares broodingly into space, remembering. After a long pause he goes on: 'Suddenly, no warning. I hear a roar behind me and two huge claws seize me by the shoulders. I'm knocked to the ground. I can feel its weight on my back but I'm not thinking straight. All those stories of Sakan's have left me so worked into a knot that the strength goes right out of me. I'm screaming, wailing, pleading, whimpering. I feel the bear's claws prod into my neck and I just piss myself.' He presses his fingers to his eyes as if he'd like to expunge the memory forever. 'Then I look up and the rest of the guys have come up on the other side of the palisade, and I hear a voice in my ear say, "Come on, pretty boy, give a bear a chance." And they're all laughing and I scrabble round to see Sakan wearing a bear's claw on each hand and the look on his face – glee, hatred, contempt, all mixed up with a kind of obscene excitement. I could have salvaged it even then if I'd just got up and punched him on the jaw. But I'd lost my nerve completely, you see. I was so ashamed I just turned tail and ran all the way home, crying like a girl.'

If you have the codeword *Quibble* and not *Quad* ▶ 1376
Otherwise, if you are female ▶ 81
Otherwise ▶ 1093

1154

Dydkos gives you a small looking glass with a film of lampblack obscuring the surface. As you go to wipe it clean, he catches your arm.

'Be careful,' he says. 'It is a trap for the hated one. When you awaken in his house, give it to him. Then Roxana and I can finally be free of him.'

The girl plants a kiss on your cheek. 'We won't forget that a stranger was kind to us today.'

You wondered how you would return from the dream, but now it proves to be simply a matter of willing it. The image of the garden dissolves and swirls away like paints washed down a drain. You are awake in the bed.

The merchant is peering down at you with knitted brows. 'So, you're back. But what about my wife? Still asleep!'

Give him the looking glass ▶ 1572
Keep it ▶ 1052

1155

If you have either of the codewords *Quell* or *Quire* ▶ 513
If not but you have the codeword *Quaff* ▶ 596
If not but you have the codeword *Ordeal* ▶ 1634
Otherwise ▶ 778

1156

'Ah, Notus,' she sighs, her blank gaze seeming to pierce the gulf of distance. 'In the afternoon of time, its pyramids and tall memorials catch the dying sun. What is your question?'

It takes you a moment to collect your thoughts. What do you reply?

'Tell me about the cockatrice.' ▶ 732
'What is the strangest thing to be found in the desert?' ▶ 1015
'What are the three great labours of Notus?' ▶ 415
'What is the best place to set sail?' (Only if you do not have the codeword *Oasis*.) ▶ 1060
'I have no more questions about Notus.' ▶ 510

1157

You hamstring Enceladus's good leg, bringing him crashing to the ground. He writhes around, trying to swat you away with his club, but you easily avoid his clumsy attack and step in to finish him off with a deadly blow to the throat.

▶ 1446

1158

You hear a voice above. The slice of a spade cutting the earth. The soil is pulled away and a hand grips your wrist, pulling you up to safety.

'Are you all right?' asks your companion.

You lie gasping for breath on the damp grass. It is several moments before you can collect your wits enough to reply. Stumbling to your feet, you point towards the exit. 'I'll be fine once we're out of this place.'

The two of you hurry to the gate and out into the street in search of a warm tavern fireside.

▶ 613

1159

You lash out at the nearest one, spearing through fibrous tissue bridging a gap in the chitinous exoskeleton. Your blow cleaves the soft organs within and the creature shudders and falls, slowly curling into a twitching knot of spiny limbs.

But as you step back, a stab of pain runs up your thigh and you look down to see a red gash where the creature bit you before it died. Already the puckered flesh is turning grey from the venom. Tick the Wound box on your Adventure Sheet if it was not ticked already.

Then ▶ 606 and tick one of the boxes there before reading on.

1160

Hypnos fixes you with his gaze that sees into the depths of mortal souls. He raises his hand and a javelin of ice appears from nowhere. It curves across the space between the two armies.

To either side of you, men rush forward, raising shields to fend the javelin away. But how can any physical thing defend against a weapon cast by the lord of dreams? The javelin melts, flows around the upraised shields, and reforms to a lethally hard point that strikes you full in the chest.

If you were already wounded ▶ 18
If you were uninjured ▶ 1139

1161

Your feet glide swiftly across the cold marble of the hall without making a sound. Pressed against the wall, you cautiously edge your head around to look into the study.

If you have the codeword *Prankette* ▶ 624
If not but you have the title **The Embezzler** ▶ 457
If you have neither ▶ 561

1162

There's a cheer from the crew as the sails fill with wind. At the stern, the navigator has the wheel. He spins it and the *Sunrise* sways, rising rapidly up past the hordes on the rooftop and towards the open sky. Your arc carries you directly towards the colossal figure of Thanatos, looming against the heavens. He extends a giant hand, inexorable as storm-swept clouds, thinking to snatch you out of the air. But the ship is gaining speed. It clears his titanic grip, his fingers closing on empty space directly under the keel.

The ship rises up and up, past growling thunderheads piled up like crags into the sky. Rain pelts the deck. You rise into dank, enveloping cloud and break through to the clear night above where the stars are hard and bright as distant diamonds. Impossibly far below, the streets and buildings of the city are mere toys half-seen in the murk.

Thanatos looks up, his hand raised to draw back his cowl. A moment later and his unshielded gaze would have blasted the ship to atoms, but now you are sailing safe among the silent constellations. Even death cannot catch you.

▶ 1067

1163

Lose the codeword *Regal*.

Oizys screeches in fury. Worming her sharp-clawed fingers in among your organs and glands, she begins to tear you away from the inside. 'Savour your last moments,' she spits. 'Every one of them will be spent in crippling agony.'

Choose one of your attributes (CHARM, etc) and reduce it by 1, remembering that scores can go negative. You fall with a gasp, but as suddenly as the pain began it is gone. Recovering, you look up into the face of your deity.

'I have long had a special loathing for that creature. Arise, hero.'

You get shakily to your feet. 'Thank you, your divine majesty. But... what happened to her?'

'She has been evaporated, like ditchwater on a summer's day.'

The other gods are dining on the fruit you brought them. The wounds they sustained in battling the titans disappear. As they are restored to full vigour their auras grow brighter and brighter. You have to cover your eyes. It is like being in the presence of a pantheon of blazing suns.

Remove Oizys from your Companion box and ▶ 477

1164

A gibbering throng of monsters is pressed right up to the edge of the roof. Through curtains of slashing rain you can see the pallid, worm-gnawed faces of the vampires, the eager red eyes and spittle-flecked jaws of the were-creatures, the misshapen features of capering nightmare demons. Shrieking and snarling, they are so intent on getting to you that some get jostled over the edge and fall flailing to the street far below.

Each time a grapple lodges on the ship's rail, a stream of attackers instantly comes scrabbling along it to get aboard. Heedless of the wind, rain and the lethal drop below, their only thought is to press their wild onslaught. Even the Minotaur, whose blade flashes and spills blood and guts with every swing, must eventually tire and then the monstrous tide will overwhelm the ship.

There's a commotion at the back of the horde, near the stairs up onto the roof. Some of the rear ranks are turning in confusion. A vampire staggers, a spear impaling its chest, and disintegrates in a tattered cloud of dust and rags and old bones. A slim hand reaches out, recovers the spear, and swings it in a wide arc to keep the nearest monsters at bay.

As the rabble parts you see a lithe figure in studded leather armour. In one hand she has the spear, in the other a sword that's already slick with blood. Behind her are a band of stalwart fighters, each holding their own against the night creatures that come rushing and snapping at them from all sides.

'Zoë!'

It's the daughter of King Midas, who you restored to flesh and blood after she'd been doomed for centuries to serve as the golden guardian of her father's tomb. She's too far off to hear you over the raging storm, but she sees your look of recognition and raises her hand in salute. You only hope she and her companions are enough to swing the tide of battle.

Her surprise attack has distracted the vampires who were manning the grapple-line cannon. There are still plenty of were-beasts leaping across to the ship, but not so many that the Minotaur can't hold them off. Meanwhile the *Sunrise* is stalled in mid-air and gradually losing altitude. Should you go to help Ancaeus raise the sails, or help the helmsman with the buoyancy rotor?

Get up in the rigging	► **1540**
Help out with the buoyancy rotor	► **172**

1165

'No doubt,' he says balefully, 'for we all are subservient to my most dreaded dam. Yet it sticks in my craw to hear a mortal say it.'

You're going to need a CHARM roll at difficulty 13 to convince him.

Succeed	► **446**
Fail	► **652**

1166

You explore a vast palace with vaulted ceilings like a marble sky, pearl-coloured and shot with veins of gold. The floor is beaten copper that shimmers in the reflected light of the snow that rings the mountain peak. Yet here the aether that you breathe, though so pure that it makes you gasp for breath, carries no arctic chill. There are fragrances of blossom, honey, fresh leaves. The music of dancing fountains and wind chimes drifts softly from far away.

Magnificent as it is, the palace shows signs of a terrible battle. Angry scorch-marks blasted across walls as big as cliff-faces. Chipped bas-relief friezes. Torn tapestries whose beauty is only enhanced by being brutally defaced. Chunks

gouged out of monumental pillars. These marks of damage can only have been inflicted by titanic weapons — swords like storm waves and maces the size of a war-galley's battering ram.

And there is other, more slaughterous evidence of a deathly fight having just taken place here: splashes of golden ichor on the marble walls and lying in still-wet pools on the metallic floor.

The deeper you venture into the palace, the more fragmented and dreamlike it feels. Often you get the sense of entering a room a moment after somebody has left it. Turning down an avenue-sized corridor, you catch a fleeting glimpse of beings too huge for you to fully comprehend, like mountaintops momentarily revealed through a gap in drifting clouds.

'How can I achieve anything here?' you ask Oizys. 'It's like an ant coming to talk to a king.'

'You feel insignificant?' she crows. 'No argument from me on that score. But give it time. You're pushing through from one reality to another. Go with the flow and you'll soon find yourself coming into sync with the Olympians' world.'

Perhaps she's right. Entering a banquet hall, you find the alabaster table only slightly bigger than you'd expect. On this scale you are no longer an insect, more like a child standing beside adult-sized furniture.

Now you hear voices, muttering echoes coming along the colonnaded gallery at the back of the room. Sandalled footsteps are coming closer. The air grows charged with a numinous energy that makes your pulse race and your breath come in shallow gasps. Or perhaps that's just your own nervousness at the thought of coming face to face with the gods.

'Hurry,' urges Oizys.

The golden plates and bowls on the table are empty. But you could fill them.

Put out some **food of the gods**	► **1570**
Serve **poisoned ambrosia**	► **569**
Neither	► **1528**

1167

The first falls, his blood foaming into the surf around your feet. The second lunges in furiously, so hasty for the fray that he slips on the dank seaweed clinging to the shore. You sway back out of the way, his sword clatters against the rock, and you smash his throat with a blow that leaves him gasping his last breath.

A third and fourth race in. Each is easily parried, despatched with blows that splinter bones and tear through flesh. You are getting your second wind now. The pleasure of action after lying so long on a sick bed sends a fire through your veins. You laugh exultantly, and as you do you see fear in the remaining saboteurs' eyes.

'What manner of woman are you?' gasps one, stumbling forward despite his dread. His sword tip trembles as he tries to fend you off.

'Have you never faced an Amazon, you dog? Of course not, for if you had you would already be dead.'

So saying you snap his neck. The others have had enough. On hearing you are an Amazon, they throw down their weapons and flee back to the boats.

▶ 1288

1168

The clang of metal feet rings out along the street. But the oncoming patrol is not a troop of armoured soldiers, but of gold-skinned automata. As they see you, they begin a chorus that quickly swells from exquisite harmony to ear-splitting crescendo.

If you have the **voicebox remote** and want to use it ▶ 77

Otherwise you are surrounded and have no option but to fight ▶ 266

1169

You hear plenty of stories about the crime lord Zinc, who rules the Grumbles with such a blend of ruthlessness, efficiency and romance that it is impossible to say which stories are true and which are mere fancy.

One man, fetching water from a well that smells like a latrine, tell you that Zinc always wears a mask that resembles the face of the mechanical Speaker of the Palace of Syndics. 'You know why? It's because he's actually Vulcan himself and that's how he gets to run both crime and law in this city.'

'What nonsense!' says a woman who is passing with a bundle of laundry. 'Nobody knows what Vulcan looks like, and he could give himself any face anyway, so he wouldn't need a mask. No, the fact is that Zinc is a very rich nobleman who runs the gangs out of boredom with his regular life.'

'Tell you a story,' says a beggar, who is off-duty here in the Grumbles and so has removed his bandages and doesn't bother to affect a limp. 'Zinc and some guys were playing cards one night and one of them made like he was going to whip Zinc's mask off. "'Ere, boss, show us your kisser, won't yer? Can't tell if yer bluffin' when we can't see yer eyes."'

'And did he?' breathes the man with the water pail, eyes widening. 'Pull the mask off, I mean.'

'Course not. He was just taking it as far as he dared,

making a joke of it to show everyone he was like that with the boss.' He holds up two fingers, twisted tight together. 'But I don't reckon Zinc can take a joke, because the next day the guy was fished dead out of this well. His face had been peeled off.'

The man with the pail looks at the well, pours the water back in, and walks away muttering.

'You got the moral of the story?' says the beggar as he too turns to leave. 'Don't mess with Zinc or he'll mess back a lot harder.'

Go west to the Street of Knives   ▶ 1617

Go east onto the Avenue of the Anvil   ▶ 63

1170

'Is that it? She's gone for good?'

Prometheus nods. 'Thanks to your courage, yes. The Queen of Darkness is dead. The Olympian gods are dead. Human beings are in charge of their own destiny now.'

'Well, almost,' says Eros. 'I'd retire if I thought mortals could get by without me to screw their lives up.'

'But what about the titans – ?' you say in sudden alarm.

Prometheus smiles. 'Before I came here I sealed them back into the pits of Tartarus. They only got out last time because it suited Nyx's plans to release them. They'll not escape again.'

You look out of the window, down the now-sunlit slopes towards the mortal world. 'I should get back. Who knows what damage Nyx did to the fabric of reality.'

'That too is in hand,' Eros assures you. 'Psyche is studying the matrix that Hephaistos used to build his "Vulcanverse" so that she can reconstruct it. There might even be a few improvements.'

'What kind of improvements?'

'Knowing her, I expect the world will be a bit less unpredictable, a bit less dangerous, and a bit less exciting.'

'Not much call for heroes, then.'

He sighs. 'I know. It might not appeal to you or me, but what can I say? I love the girl.'

'What now, hero?' Prometheus asks. 'Will you return to this tame and civilized new world?'

'What's the alternative?'

He sweeps his giant arm up to the sky. 'I have been mankind's protector since the dawn of time. Now they are safe, I intend to travel across the gulf of space. Out there are other worlds. Adventures aplenty are waiting. You can come with me.'

Back to Vulcan City for a hero's welcome? Or out among the stars with Prometheus? A future of quiet contentment, or of perils and challenges unknown?

You decide.

1171

If you have the codeword *Ozone* and you possess the **Face of Wisdom** (INGENUITY +3) ▶ 9

    If you have only *Ozone* ▶ 1008

    Otherwise ▶ 1258

1172

You stand in the centre of the room, directly under the dome. Hushed echoes form a background murmur. Galatea hangs back, brushing her hand along the curved wall, and yet you hear her voice as though she were beside you whispering in your ear.

'Troubles aren't really regrets,' she says. 'You can face a trouble; a regret is long gone. If I have any regret it's that I spent so long as a statue when I could have been seeing more of the world. But it's not so easy to turn the clock and change any of that.'

When you rejoin her at the door, neither of you makes any mention of what was said and overheard. Emerging from the rotunda you notice a stone-flagged passage off the side of the courtyard. A group of partygoers come along it laughing and joking raucously, and when you ask where it leads one of them ruffles your hair playfully and says, 'You can get through there to the ornamental gardens. I'd come with you, but three's a crowd.'

    Go along the passage to the garden   ▶ 1415

    Back to the main courtyard   ▶ 750

    Look at the hand-shaped fountain   ▶ 489

1173

'No, I don't think so,' he says.

'I'm an Amazon. My place is on the field of battle.'

'You've been listening to lover boy.'

'Who?'

'Achilles. Think I haven't noticed him making moon eyes at you? But you're my trophy bitch. Your place is here in my bed. What would it do to my reputation if you come back all bruises and scars? You've got to stay unblemished and beautiful. For daddy.'

    ▶ Current Location

1174

'Hey there,' you say to the empty air. 'Liquefy his battle suit, would you?'

The Face of Wisdom's voice pulses on the wind: 'An occasional please wouldn't kill you.'

'Hey, I recognize that snitty tone!' says Daedalus. 'I built that brass braincase, and now – oh.'

His armour suddenly turns to water and splashes to the ground. Daedalus is left soaked and shivering. He's no longer a threat. Turning your back on him, you jump down from the parapet to join your allies. The battle for the fate of the universe has begun.

    ▶ 1533

1175

The door has been kicked in. Looters have ransacked the house. Shards of glass crunch underfoot. The air is thick with a heavy, choking stench – someone has set the drapes on fire.

    Look around for items you left here ▶ 1204

    Stay on the move ▶ 1285

1176

You look around for Dunamis. She's already running. Chasing after the vanishing pool of lantern-light, you hear the Celedon's plangent shriek rising to an unbearable pitch. Pressure grows inside your skull and it feels like the sound is loud enough to liquefy your innards.

Make a STRENGTH roll at difficulty 15 to keep going. You can add 4 to your dice roll if you have any **beeswax**, which you jam into your ears to block out the noise – but delete the **beeswax** if you use it.

    Succeed   ▶ 183

    Fail   ▶ 538

1177

If you have neither the codeword *Rye* nor the title **Steward of the Summer Palace** and this box ❏ is empty, tick it and ▶ 1343; otherwise read on.

The water is exhilaratingly cold. You swim until your limbs are glowing with inner warmth, afterwards lying stretched on the grass bank to let the sun dry you off. If you have the codeword *Pure*, lose it and 1 scar (if you have any).

    ▶ 806

1178

The vampires come creeping across the room almost on all fours, their shrouds draped over near-skeletal frames. At the same time, a horde of ragged fluttering things sweeps in through the open doors to the garden. Needle-sharp fangs show in a whir of black leathery wings.

Outnumbered, you back off towards the entrance. An animal reek of wet fur warns you and you glance around to see a pack of were-beasts loping in from the courtyard. Thick saliva drools from their slavering jaws.

'The stairs!' yells Dunamis.

As the two of you run towards the stairwell, she grabs a leg of roast lamb from the buffet table and tosses it to you.

'What's this for?'

'A mutual friend told me you might need it,' she shouts back. 'Also something about rain in a drainpipe. He said you'd understand.'

If only you did. Waving the roast meat at the pursuing were-beasts, you race after her.

▶ 1266

1179

You hurtle towards the giant figure, weapon stretched out ahead of you, a human missile. She stirs and the iridescent fabric of her robes shifts, moving in front of you. Her clothing looks so soft, so insubstantial, that it can give no protection – but it moves her from the mundane world to the empyrean realm unreachable by mortals. Your frenzied attack is spent on empty air. You are falling.

A giant hand catches you. Struggling, you make ready to fight against it, but then you see it is not Aphrodite who has hold of you. You hear the voice of your own god, a tone that allows for no opposition.

'Now you would contend against the gods themselves. Good. But here is not the place for it. This war is already lost in the fog of legend. Go back to your own time, and use this fighting spirit against the most terrible deity of all.'

Giant fingers close, sealing you in silent darkness.

▶ 73

1180

A look of delight shines on Ancaeus's habitually surly face as he examines the clockwork device. Suddenly he gives it a sharp wrench. The casing snaps open, rotates with a mechanical clicking sound, and settles into a configuration you've never seen before.

'Don't break it,' you say in alarm.

'So what? You're never going sailing with it again,' he says with a laugh. 'Those seas are already gone. What we need now is to use it in a way it was never designed for – navigating *outside* the stars.'

Lose the **astrarium**. But perhaps it was a sacrifice worth making. The *Sunrise* makes good headway across the void. For a while there is nothing but the slow creak of the ropes, the almost musical boom of flexing timbers, the occasional muttered remark.

At last the cry comes from the lookout: 'Land ahoy!'

▶ 346

1181

'An interesting device, that. One of Daedalus's toys.'

'What does it do?'

She reaches out her hand. A spark leaps from her fingers; it makes you jump. 'Now that its power is restored you'll find it quite useful.'

Delete the **brass head** and in its place get the **sulky head**.

It opens its eyes and stares at you in something like outrage. 'I refuse to be of any use in this condition. Look at me, flaunted for all and sundry to see, and here I am as bare-headed as any peasant oaf. If you want my cooperation you'd better find me a wig. And a nice stylish one, mind, not some mangy mop you'd see on a fat old matron.'

'Oh yes,' says Pandora. 'It can also be quite crochety.'

'I'm right here!' snaps the head.

▶ 242

1182

He sets the **dragon's egg** on a bed of wool and examines it closely. 'I can give you 200 pyr for this right now, or a line of credit on future purchases.'

Take the cash   ▶ 1447
Take the credit   ▶ 1372
No deal   ▶ 828

1183

If you have the codeword *Root* but not *Remedy* ▶ 506

If you have both *Root* and *Remedy* ▶ 830

Otherwise, if you have the codeword *Retract* ▶ 1075

If not but you have the codeword *Remedy* or the title **Soul Bearer** ▶ 932

If you have none of the above ▶ 560

1184

The Oracle suddenly opens her eyes wide, sputtering in outrage. 'Preposterous!' she shouts.

'What is it? What did you see?'

'If you find a thief stuck a hole in the ice, you have to rescue her, even though letting her drown is really all she deserves.'

'Good to know.'

'Sometimes this job disgusts me,' says the Oracle. 'What's the point of choice if you're going to be railroaded? In fact, I shouldn't do this, but here's something from the temple vaults.' She shows you a golden lyre. 'I'll give you this if you promise to let the little minx freeze to death in the lake.'

Seems a bit cold-blooded, and there's obviously a bit of personal animosity at the root of this. You're not sure if Apollo would approve. On the other hand, it is a free **golden lyre (CHARM +2)**. Add it to your possessions if you agree to the Oracle's terms.

'Any other tips?' you ask her.

'Don't let the gods shove you around,' she says bitterly.

'Look at me, getting out of my skull on toxic fumes every day so as to be a vessel for prophecy. It's a kind of abuse, if you think about it. Also, I shouldn't have to still be doing it at my age. It's a young woman's job.'

The conversation is skirting the edge of blasphemy, so you make an excuse and bow out.

▶ **510**

1185

Swollen storm clouds roll overhead – swirling crags of darkness that press down with the weight and solidity of a mountain range. As you scramble over the first roof ridge, a flare of unearthly light breaks amid the clouds. It's like a door opening onto another cosmos, and beyond the widening split above you see a giant figure emerging, pushing its way from another plane of reality into the skies of this world.

Without being told you know that it is Thanatos, Death incarnate, whose gaze brings annihilation without hope of returning. You are not ready to confront such a foe. You must get away before he is fully materialized.

And you have a more pressing problem. The door to the stairs smashes open and through it pours a nightmare horde of vampires and bounding werewolves.

If you have the codewords *Rose* and *Recursive* ▶ **1593**

Otherwise one of the were-beasts leaps on your back. You must throw it off quickly before the others bring you down. Make a STRENGTH roll at difficulty 9.

Succeed   ▶ **1055**
Fail   ▶ **717**

1186

Lose the codeword *Regal*.

The gods limp into the room. Some are supporting others whose injuries have left them too weak to walk unaided. Their once-perfect flesh shows the marks of many wounds. Golden lifeblood stains their majestic finery. Adamantine armour wrought to be all but impervious to damage now hangs in battered plates and broken links from their weary shoulders.

'Pan,' says Zeus. 'Have you brought us nectar from Arcadia?'

Bosk shakes his head. 'There are no immortal fruits or wines to be had, O Thunderer, now that Nyx is spreading her pall of darkness over the world.'

Zeus nods. 'Then we must fight on as we are. The titans are no more at full strength, their main might spent. As long as Nyx does not attack at the same time, we can yet force them back into the abyss.'

'And my friend here is just the one to keep her busy,'

says Bosk, giving you a slap on the back.

You give him a nervous glance. 'You'll come too, though, right?'

He shakes his head. 'My place is in the groves and meadows of Arcady. The city, that's your territory. Hold still now. I'll send you back.'

He takes a set of pipes from his belt and begins to play a rapid, skirling tune. Faster and faster he plays, the music getting higher and higher in pitch, and with each note the image of the hall and the Olympians shudders and swims. You have a sense of drifting like the melody, out from the hall, away from the palaces of the gods, across the slopes of Olympus and down again to the mortal world.

Down and down and down...

Delete Bosk from the Companion box on your Adventure Sheet and ▶ **73**

1187

'Do you ever bother making a plan?' barks a tinny voice from your backpack.

'Oh, you're piping up now, are you?' you say over your shoulder.

'I'd have said something before if I could see where we're going,' says the Face. 'You've already got the diadem. Better pull your finger out before everything goes down the shitter.'

'What do you suggest?'

'Find a noticeboard, genius. You'll find they're advertising for somebody to save the world.'

▶ **820**

1188

Myletes gives a yelp of excitement and starts pacing around the room as he reads aloud from the scroll.

'It's useful, then?' you say.

'Priceless. Each of these sayings is a meditation which could spark an entire afternoon of debate. For instance, listen to this one: "He that fears death either fears that he shall have no sense at all or that his senses will not be the same as in life. Whereas – " '

You raise a protesting hand. 'That's fine. I dipped into it already. Read enough to last me a lifetime.'

Myletes's jaw drops open. 'Don't you want it back?'

'You keep it. Seems like it's found a good home.'

For once he is speechless. He rushes around the study lifting bundles of papers until he finds a round mango-sized object which he presses into your hands. It is a human head sculpted from a dull golden metal.

'It's one of Daedalus's creations,' he explains.

'Daedalus studied here at the Academy?'

'Not for long. He became frustrated at what he saw as too much theory and not enough practical invention. But he left a few trinkets behind in his workshop.'

You weigh the object in your hand. It feels too light to be solid metal all the way through. When you shake it there's a faint rattling of cogs and gears.

'What does it do?' you ask Myletes.

He shrugs his thin shoulders. 'Unfortunately Daedalus didn't leave any documentation behind, so nobody has any idea.'

Myletes remembers he has to give a lecture so you bid him farewell for now. Delete the **Precepts of Chiron** and get the **brass head** in its place.

▶ 1062

1189

You feel around the hearth and up the chimney, where your fingers brush against a package wedged between two loose bricks. It contains the **bundle of compromising letters**. Add them to your possessions and ▶ 944

1190

Note **103** as your Current Location, then ▶ **1269** and tick the box corresponding to the temple district. From now on you will always be able to find your way back here.

1191

Slipping away through the fog, you blunder your way between the graves until you reach the necropolis wall, feeling your way along it until you come to the gate.

The watchman was just locking up. He grumblingly removes the chains so you can leave. 'Another minute and you'd have been in there all night,' he says. As you pass close by he sees the look stamped on your face, and his truculent mood changes to fear. 'Did you see a ghost?'

'No, a ghoul,' you mutter tersely before hurrying away along the street.

▶ 613

1192

'Just seems to me that if you're going to rule all of creation it ought to be as a king.'

'Like Zeus only more so? Good point. I'll be sure to put "valued consultant" on your tombstone.' He transforms his armoured helmet into a crown. 'OK, I hereby proclaim myself monarch of gods, men, titans and all the other stuff. No need for formality – you can call me "your maj".'

If you have the **kingslayer dagger** ▶ 1228
If not ▶ 199

1193

A shaft of sunlight catches the dancing spray of the fountain, reflecting and bathing you in a golden glow. The fat man, sensing the presence of the divine, falls to his knees.

You feel a current of numinous energy coursing through you. Add 1 to any attribute (CHARM, GRACE, etc) up to the maximum possible score of +5.

As the light fades back to normal, you see the fat man is weeping. 'I wasted my wish,' he groans. 'All I asked for was for the nymph to cure my flat feet.'

'A healthy diet would have done that,' you tell him.

▶ 806

1194

You bludgeon the automata with anything that comes to hand – bricks, broken timbers, chunks of scattered masonry. You cannot kill what never lived to begin with, but you batter their joints so out of shape that they are unable to move. They lie in the road, broken mannikins whose limbs jerk and twitch with faint grinding sounds.

Their faces remain impassive, sculpted golden masks of exquisite beauty. One of them opens her mouth, but whatever she has to say to you goes unheard now that her voicebox is inactive.

'We're running out of time,' says Dunamis, dragging you away.

▶ Current Location

1195

Having won two out of three rounds, you are presented with the storyteller's trophy – a vase with a few flowers in it, swept up from an alcove by your opponent and handed over with a whimsical flourish.

'We'll have to have a rematch,' she murmurs in your ear over the applause.

'Give me a chance to get out there first and have some more adventures.'

▶ 1324

1196

'All right,' you say. 'I'll join your side. If this has been a sham all along then the gods can't care what happens to mankind. I'll help you destroy them.'

'You won't regret it,' says Hypnos with a booming peal of laughter. 'Queen Nyx will fashion a new world of indelible night in which loyal subjects like you will be her trusted lieutenants and all who opposed her must crawl and grope their way in darkness.'

If Galatea is with you ▶ 170
Otherwise ▶ 688

1197

Rain drives into your eyes. Blindly you stumble against the dome and start to drag yourself up it. A flash of lightning shows that some of your pursuers have got ahead of you and are scurrying towards you around the curve of the dome.

Above you, across the towers and rooftops of the city, Thanatos has almost pushed through the gaping rent in space. His gigantic form fills half the sky. It seems as though he is hatching from a mythic amnion to become born as a physical presence in reality.

Make a GRACE roll at difficulty 13.

Succeed ▶ **1389**

Fail ▶ **882**

1198

A familiar figure is wandering ahead of you, a human speck in the colossal marmoreal immensity of the Forum.

'Lord Xechasiaris!'

He turns, peering at you with a puzzled frown. 'Is that who I am?'

Lose the codeword *Roar* and ▶ **1011**

1199

❑

Do not tick the box unless you were told to do so in the section you've just turned from.

If you have just ticked the box ▶ **673**

If it was already ticked ▶ **779**

If the box is empty, read on.

Bosk is chatting to a bevy of giggling barmaids. With his big arms around their waists they look like a line of dolls. He shoos them away when he sees you.

'Tell me about your travels,' he says, his voice reverberating richly in the foliage-sheltered arch of the arbour. 'Setting the world to rights yet? Or poor neglected Arcadia, at least, yes?'

If you have the title **Steward of the Summer Palace** ▶ **966**

If not, read on.

You have to confess that you've made no progress in restoring the land of Arcadia to fertility.

Bosk's disappointment is palpable. 'Better start with the basics, then. You'll have to refurbish the Summer Palace before you can get anything else done.'

'Yes, I – '

'Have you spoken to King Nyctimus yet?'

'Well, it – '

'He'll explain it all. Obviously you need to hire Lefkia first of all. A lick of paint and some replastering, make the place shipshape, then crack on with the real challenges.'

Bosk calls for more wine and the rest of day swirls into a riot of singing and dancing until the tavern closes for the night.

▶ **1534**

1200

Pressing through the cramped alleys and jostling crowds of unwashed slum-dwellers, you catch sight of an unwonted flash of bright colour against the drab greys and browns. A red cape.

'Get out of the way.' You quicken your pace. You round a corner just in time to see the small hooded figure skipping off down a narrow side-street.

It can only be the café owner's daughter, the one who escaped from slavery in Boreas.

If Polymnia is here and you want her advice ▶ **897**

If your companion is Galatea ▶ **408**

Otherwise:

Give chase ▶ **20**

Let her go ▶ **571**

1201

If you have the codewords *Reef* and *Rabbit* ▶ **937**

If you have just *Reef* ▶ **1147**

Otherwise ▶ **777**

1202

If this box ❑ is empty, tick it and ▶ **14**; otherwise read on.

You spend a pleasurable hour or so filling Myletes in on what you've been up to and hearing his own news. For all that he is a philosopher given to abstruse theorizing, his lively sense of humour makes the conversation sparkle, and you are sorry when he says he has to get back to work.

▶ **1062**

1203

You are turned away at the gate by sentries with polearms. 'It's a question of security,' says one apologetically.

The other glances around to check no officer is nearby before adding, 'One of the lieutenants here has got into a spot of bother. Matter of honour, like. He's going to need somebody who isn't a guardsman to help out.'

'Check out the noticeboard at the city gates,' says the first sentry out of the corner of his mouth.

▶ **1642**

1204

Note your Current Location as **1285**.

The looters have been pretty thorough. Any money or **lava gems** are long gone. To retrieve other things you left here ► **1402** but roll one six-sided die for each item in turn. On a roll of 1-5 the item has been stolen (cross it off the list at **1402**); on a roll of 6 the looters overlooked it and it's still here.

1205

A marionette with winged heels and a wide-brimmed herdsman's hat prances across the little stage. He is the god Hermes, and the play consists of various vignettes in which mortals have their plans disrupted by the god, until somebody armed with an enormous set of bagpipes blows his hat off. Hermes chases it as it darts and flits around the sky, provoking gusts of laughter from the people who have gathered to watch the show.

'It used to be a fart, not bagpipes,' complains one disappointed onlooker.

'That wasn't suitable for children,' says a woman at the front. 'Too rude.'

'Rude?' he scoffs. 'Children love rude!'

You can pay a pyr for the performance if you want. Contributions seem entirely voluntary, though, and most of the audience disperse without paying anything.

► **232**

1206

Another of the foul creatures falls to your powerful blow. Its limbs jerk in horribly puppet-like death throes. The screech it emits from gill-like flaps is not the cry of any living thing but more like steam bursting under pressure from a broken kettle.

► **738** and tick one of the boxes there before reading on.

1207

You straighten up, approaching her through the agitated tendrils of fog. 'Tritona, have you come to this?'

She recoils, scrabbling away a short distance and hiding her face in her hands. 'Don't look at me. I've disgraced my family name, corrupted myself, enraged the gods. I shouldn't be allowed to live.'

What will you reply?

'You're right. I'll make it quick.' ► **19**
'It's never too late for redemption.' ► **497**

1208

The chair begins to vibrate, and the arm rests move as if to encircle your wrists, but with a harsh grinding sound it suddenly seizes up. You turn to see that the 'chair' was actually the female automaton. She is now frozen in the act of metamorphosing back into her human-like form. Her golden carapace is locked in mid-transformation like a beetle with its wing-case badly folded. Very slowly she continues to move, the metal plates of her limbs and body trying to swivel back into place, but every centimetre she stirs brings a sound like gravel going through a mincer.

The caretaker flings aside his cane. He's standing straighter than before. Another one who wasn't what he seemed to be – but of course, as the world's greatest thief he would naturally also be a master of disguise.

'Autolycus,' you say.

► **1408**

1209

You'll need to make both a powerful leap and a your mightiest blow. Attempt two rolls, STRENGTH and GRACE, both at difficulty 10.

Both rolls are successful ► **1095**
Either or both fail ► **1179**

1210

He starts back in alarm, raising his hand sharply, and for a moment you think he means to strike you.

'That is the very thing we must not do!' he hisses, struggling to keep his voice to a whisper. 'I have consulted the Oracle. With my wife's spirit so far away, her sleeping body is an empty vessel. If she were woken now then any passing ghost or demon might be pulled from the ether to possess her. Why do you think I have taken all these measures to ensure she is not disturbed?'

Ask what you need to do ► **113**
Decline and leave ► **515**

1211

A house has collapsed into the street. Over the keening of the wind come the faint, desperate cries of a woman who is buried under rubble. A few people have crept out of the ruins to help, heaving aside chunks of broken masonry while casting nervous glances along the street. Others hover nearby in doorways, watching anxiously, torn between helping the rescuers or staying ready to run. If they all joined in it would be easy to free the trapped woman, but fear keeps most of them in hiding.

Convince them all to help ► **269**
Join in the rescue – lead by example ► **66**
Ignore it – you have more pressing concerns ► **233**

1212

You come across the carcass of the slain dragon.

'Dolt, you've been here already!' Oizys screeches with derisive laughter like a drill skidding across torn steel.

'Worth checking,' you insist.

'The world is winding down,' she hisses. 'Hurry, or you'll get left behind.'

To emphasize the point she nibbles some shreds of flesh from your vital organs. Roll two dice to see which of your attributes is affected:

score 2-4 or 10   −1 from CHARM
score 5-6   −1 from GRACE
score 7 or 11-12   −1 from INGENUITY
score 8-9   −1 from STRENGTH

Remember that attributes can go negative. After adjusting the score on your Adventure Sheet ▶ 1446

1213

One of the other guests in the queue holds up a long-haired grey cat in a tiny mask.

'This is Nectanebo,' he says. 'He used to rule Notus.'

'You mean he was human in a previous incarnation?'

'No,' says the man. 'Nectanebo has always been a cat, but the people of Notus in olden times were not prejudiced against feline pharaohs.'

The porters ask you to hand over any attribute-boosting items 'to prevent cheating at the gambling tables, dishonestly achieved seduction, or other peccadilloes of that sort.'

Note 207 as your Current Location and then ▶ 964

1214

Your mother is subdued, greeting you with a desolate look. She seems to have aged years since you last saw her. Distracted, she doesn't even hear your account of your most recent exploits. She leaves household chores unfinished and goes to sit gazing out of the window.

Your sisters explain. 'Our brother is dead,' says the eldest. 'He was found by the roadside, way out in Notus. Robbers had stabbed him through the heart.'

'But if it was robbers,' says your youngest sister, 'why did they cover the body? And they didn't steal anything.'

'His tongue was cut out!' snaps your third sister, her eyes flashing. 'Isn't that cruel enough?'

If you have the codeword *Quad* ▶ 295
If not   ▶ 1411

1215

You're about to ask Eos something when the Minotaur shakes your arm, almost pulling you off your feet in the process.

'Hey, it's attached at the shoulder!' you say.

He points off into the void. 'We've got company.'

Far off in the glittering darkness of space, something is moving. Ancaeus raises his telescope. You see his jaw tighten. He hands the telescope to you.

The object jumps into focus. It's a squid, dark and bloated, hauling its way through the aether using its writhing tentacles.

'That's odd,' you say.

'Look again,' says Ancaeus grimly. 'The size of the thing.'

He's right. All along its flanks are hordes of Nyx's underlings — demons with black chiropteran wings and sickle-shaped horns, clinging to the squid like marines to the rigging of a warship.

'It must be bigger than an Iskandrian quinquereme!' you gasp.

'At least two, three hundred crew,' grunts the Minotaur. 'Figure a quarter of them are warriors.' He looks at you. 'Got anything else to ask the goddess, I'd make it quick.'

One more question   ▶ 971
Get moving   ▶ 176

1216

'I don't have a use for it,' he says, 'but maybe you'll have a use for this.'

Reaching under the counter he brings out a small music box decorated with gold leaf, pearls and opals in the form of astrological symbols.

'How much?'

'Oh…' He affects a nonchalant air. '100 pyr, let's say. Or I'll always take a credit note.'

Buy it   ▶ 356
Not interested   ▶ 325

1217

Get the title **The Unexpected Heir**.

'I'm not unreasonable,' you tell them. 'Just be sure you've cleared out your belongings by this evening.'

Note 674 as your Current Location, then ▶ 520 if you have the codeword *Reverie*, or ▶ 1269 if not, and tick the box next to 'your mansion'.

1218

'I cannot tell a lie,' you announce to the officer on duty at the White Guard barracks. 'I robbed the spice merchant and then I framed Moose for the crime.'

He peers at you suspiciously. 'Then how come the merchant picked Moose out of a line-up?'

'I disguised myself to look like him.'

'That's some make-up kit you got. Moose is two metres tall after a close haircut and he outweighs most wild hogs.'

He stares at you a moment, then throws up his hands. 'Oh, what do I care? You're so keen to get yourself locked up, be my guest.'

You are sentenced to a month in a squalid prison cell. Lose 3 Glory as you emerge with a tarnished reputation, but Zinc is pleased that you got Moose off the hook.

Gain the codeword *Robber* and ▶ 63

1219

'I was high in the mountains of north-east Boreas,' begins Kazala, 'where I had come seeking the fabled cyclops. But when I looked up and saw it outlined against a frost-bright sky awash with stars, I knew that it was far stranger and more mysterious than I could have imagined. And so began the most thrilling escapade of my career.'

She goes on to relate a story of a deserted citadel high in the mountains, where automated servants swept and cleaned but no life stirred. A flashback to the western Badlands of Notus involves her stalking a cockatrice, slaying it in battle, and draining its blood to use as an antidote for sickness and poison.

You hardly listen to the rest of her tale as you're trying to concoct an equally enthralling yarn from some of your old adventures. Make a CHARM roll at difficulty 10. You can add an additional +1 to your dice score if you have a Glory of 10 or more.

Success means that your tale is deemed the more exciting ▶ 447

Failure means that the applause Kazala gets is louder ▶ 1195

1220

You race over to join the helmsman. He's bent over a device like a ship's compass. The lid on top of the housing is off, revealing a disk of jagged geometric lines like a spinning knot of molten wires. It makes you feel slightly sick to look at it because of how it's continually shifting, unfolding and refolding, apparently in impossible shapes.

'You have to get your head around it existing in multiple dimensions,' says the helmsman, hesitantly reaching towards the glowing disk with a strangely shaped spanner. 'Got much experience with buoyancy rotors?'

'That what this is? I thought I was looking at a migraine aura.'

If you have the codeword *Recursive* ▶ 1417 now; otherwise read on.

'It's got jolted out of alignment,' says the helmsman. 'See those sparks? It's dragging against the side of the containment vessel. That's why we're losing altitude.'

'And you can adjust it with that spanner?'

He gives a bark of desperate laughter. 'I'm a navigator, me. This is Vulcan-level shit. I've never even taken the top off it before.'

Steeling himself, he drives the spanner into the heart of the machine. There's a protesting screech as the disk grinds against the spanner head. The deck lurches as the ship drops about five metres. Arcs of disturbing light splash and play around your head.

'Little help here…' grunts the helmsman, straining with all his might to twist the disk back into alignment.

Make a STRENGTH roll at difficulty 8.

Succeed ▶ 1318

Fail ▶ 216

1221

You are forcibly ejected from the temple, not by the priests themselves but by an invisible force.

'How am I to supposed to rid myself of this curse if I can't even enter the temple?' you ask the sentry-priests who stand at the top of the steps.

'Go and do great deeds,' they advise you. 'The Bane of Mortals suffers you to live, so use that gift to please him.'

'Doing what?'

One of the sentries leans to whisper in your ear. 'I'm not supposed to say this, but if you consult the Oracle in the temple of Apollo she can give you some useful tips. Don't say I sent you.'

▶ 103

1222
❏

The Tower of Riches casts a baleful shadow over the south-west corner of the city. If you do not have the codeword *Reverie* and the box above is empty, put a tick in it and ▶ 1398

Otherwise read on.

To ascend the tower ▶ 912

To go straight to a city location that you are already familiar with, note 1222 as your Current Location, then ▶ 1432

Or choose to go:

North along the Boulevard of the Sylph ▶ 325

North-east along the Street of Knives ▶ 1617

East on the Boulevard of the Salamander ▶ 1649

1223

'Like a tide it was. Black and high as the sky. I saw it rolling over the rooftops. And maybe it was my fancy, but I saw it taking the shape of a hand, a hand as big as heaven clutching the stars away. On it came across the city. I was hanging around the rich quarter – where the giving's good, you know – and I saw it. A wave of darkness flooding on and nothing to stop it. Everyone screeching and running, but I could only drag myself – see this leg? Could've been trampled, those fat lords and ladies lifting their robes and squealing like pigs for the slaughter. So I just lay there and I saw that dreadful tide break over the houses with a burst of dark unearthly foam and it passed on and the buildings were left standing, just about, but oh, they were changed, all desolate and ramshackle, enchanted ruins such as you come upon in dreams. That's when I knew that Nightfall had poured over Now.'

'Anything else?'

'What more is there to say? There are new rulers now and anyone who wants to survive had better pick a side.' He smirks, a curious expression midway between triumph and self-disgust. 'I've picked mine, see.'

A shadow falls over you. The beggar's tale was just a ploy to keep you here. 'We've got company,' says Dunamis, her voice catching in fear.

You turn.

▶ 314

1224

'Perhaps you're working too hard.'

'How do you mean?'

'You need to kick back. Take some time out, enjoy life a bit, and remind yourself what you're fighting for.'

'I have a feeling you have something specific in mind.'

'It was me, I'd go and do the tourist thing down Iskandria way. Take a guided tour, get a meal, maybe have a swim.'

That's all he has to say, so you thank him and set off.

▶ 806

1225

Thanatos stands triumphant. Where you were a moment earlier, there is just a curl of ash and vapour that is snatched away on the wind. Nyx's minions howl their victory to the skies, gloating now that no hero remains to oppose them.

If you have the codeword *Omen* or bear either the title **Champion of the Amazons** or **Amazonian Queen**
▶ 365

Otherwise ▶ 127

1226

Seeing you fall, your troops fight on with bravery and passion. It's not enough. Hopelessly outnumbered, they are soon swept away by the surging black tide of Queen Nyx's army.

All around you lie the bodies of the fallen. Stricken by the essence of uttermost darkness, you are only numbly aware of the catastrophe. With great effort you raise your head. Nyx stands over you, her sword of living night poised to strike.

You manage to force out a few words through pain-gritted teeth. 'Do your worst, foul queen of hell…'

She smiles. 'Don't worry, I will.'

The sword slices down in a short and lethal arc.

▶ 666

1227

Dank air rushes past you. The air is thick with a foetid smell of soil, wet stone, mould and decay. Your breath is slammed out of you as you hit a torrent of black surging water and are flung and battered along lightless tunnels until finally swept up on the edge of a cistern.

Tick the Wound box on your Adventure Sheet if you were not injured already. Gasping, dazed and half-drowned, you drag your bruised body along a narrow shaft into the daylight.

A group of elegantly dressed patricians recoil from the sight of you. And not just the sight. One of them pinches his nose and steps gingerly closer. 'Are you a creature of the Stygian realms?' he says.

You wipe the stinking slime and mud off your clothes and get unsteadily to your feet. The grand marble buildings, the neatly trimmed trees and the fine white robes of the passers-by create a disorienting contrast to your ordeal in the sewers. 'Stygian? Why, is this the Elysian Fields?' you mutter, stunned.

'No,' he says. 'You're on Septentrional Avenue, just along from the theatre.'

▶ 515

1228

The knife is tucked in your belt. Closing your fingers around the hilt, you drive the blade into his unprotected throat. His hand jerks up and with the augmented strength of his armour he crushes the **kingslayer dagger** – cross it off your Adventure Sheet. But it's too late to save him. His blood comes spurting out in bright gouts.

'No point trying to regenerate,' you say. 'That was the knife that slew Agamemnon, and there's no defying the power of myth.'

'What really smarts…' gasps Daedalus, sinking to his knees, 'is being outsmarted…'

The armies are gathered. You jump down from the parapet to join your allies. The battle for the fate of the universe has begun.

▶ 1533

1229

The Oracle speaks rapidly, as if barely able to keep up with the visions the drugged incense is giving her.

'You'll need to find the hydra king and get the garden key. Squash the spiders in the Slimeswamp – vinegar will help. And obviously you need to find the wings of Icarus, which I see are cross-referenced with another prophecy. Anyway, that's about it for the labours of Hades.'

She runs out of breath and goes silent, slumping like a doll with its strings cut. A fat, matronly doll in an unbecomingly youthful dress.

You tiptoe out so as not to wake her.

▶ **510**

1230

Get the title **Soul Bearer**.

The strands of hair break easily. The ghost-like figure blunders out, dissolving into motes of silvery light that settle on the waiting beetles and are absorbed.

That seems to be the signal that galvanizes the beetles back into action. With a high-pitched whine they rise into the air and begin circling you faster and faster. The cocoon of golden light forms again and you feel a wrench as you slip out of reality and into the interstitial world where time, space and mass do not exist.

Without any command from you, the cocoon begins to float into the wall of the chamber, carrying you through stone and soil – to where?

▶ **746**

1231

A snug costs 10 pyr unless you have the codeword **Rune**, in which case the landlord refuses to accept payment and you can get it for free.

You climb rickety wooden steps beside the rough plastered walls up to a gallery where your snug sits, a wooden cabin wedged up under the rafters like a wasps' nest. But inside are cushioned benches, rugs, and even a small stove that gives a welcome feeling of warmth.

Servants bring up a succession of dishes: minced olives and prawns baked on seashells and flavoured with herbs, then clear soup to cleanse the palette before a pot of mushroom-stuffed quails with fresh bread and side dishes of buttered vegetables, followed by spiced sausages and pickles, culminating in the main course of roast venison in a sharp fruit sauce accompanied by barley and salad, and ending with cakes, nuts, small oranges, grapes, and mint-filled chocolates. Each course is accompanied by jugs of fine wine, ale, chilled sherbet, buttermilk or water according to your preference.

'Always the same meal,' says the landlord as he oversees the clearing of the table, 'but we get no complaints.'

If you were injured, untick the Wound box on your Adventure Sheet.

▶ **764**

1232

'Ah, there you are.'

Lost in contemplation of the extraordinary architecture of the building, it takes you a moment to place him. 'Lieutenant Tekto. Good to see you.'

'Got any spare time at the moment? There's a job you might be interested in.'

'What kind of job?'

He laughs. 'You're right to be wary, but it's nothing risky or underhand. Just a simple matter of helping out a retired syndic.'

What do you say?

'All right.'   ▶ **927**

'Not interested.' ▶ **187**

1233

You come to your senses. A hard stone bench presses into your back. You feel cold, stiff and uncomfortable – which are all good signs. After a moment of savouring the taste of fresh air you sit up and rub the circulation back into your limbs.

You still have your codewords, blessings and titles. Cross off your companion, if you had one, and lose any money and possessions you were carrying. Also untick the Wound box on your Adventure Sheet and gain a scar.

'Alive again, I see,' says a familiar voice distorted by a metal mask.

'Zinc... Where am I?'

The room is lit by a single globe of waxy white light set into the ceiling.

'My personal bootleg reviv clinic. I store my identity template here as a safeguard. The clinic doesn't get a lot of use these days, mind you, because I'm not as reckless as I used to be.'

Memories are coming back. Smoke, flames, blood. 'They burned my house down!'

'Hired muscle sent by those tight-asses from Bridgadoom,' says Zinc. 'Never could stand that place. They don't know how to take a joke.'

'They'll pay for this.'

'Best revenge is a free resurrection, isn't that right?'

'Yeah, thanks for that.'

He gives you a long look from behind his impassive metal mask. 'Gelos and Ersi are the two ringleaders.

They're staying at a dive on the other side of town. I've got some guys keeping an eye on them, so now you better decide. You want them taken care of, or will you let it lie?'

What do you say?

'I want them dead.'   ▶ **290**

'They're not worth the bother.' ▶ **326**

1234

If you are female   ▶ **1403**

    Otherwise   ▶ **507**

1235

'Clock's still ticking,' remarks Daedalus, adjusting the screws on a device clamped to the bench.

You look around the workshop. 'I don't see a clock.'

'Funny. The doomsday clock. If we're not ready then it won't be worth turning up for the end of the world.'

'This is about that eagle's stomach again.'

'It'll take you five minutes.'

He taps some buttons on the device he's building. The metal chrysalis on your belt emits a bleep and unfolds, breaking up into a swarm of tiny glowing insects that surround you in the intangibility field.

Agree to the mission   ▶ **1079** and put a tick in the box there before reading on.

Refuse and he'll send you back up to the surface a few streets away so as to cover your tracks ▶ **63**

1236

'We're not in Hephaistopolis anymore,' she says.

'Then where are we?'

'If I had to guess…' She looks at you quizzically. The white brume underfoot continues to shift.

'Yeah, take a guess!'

'We're at the beginning of things. This cloudy substance is hyle, the primordial stuff from which all things are destined to form. The light that's currently hidden by that mountain of hyle is the first dawn.'

'Why is it all drifting apart?' you ask.

'It's expanding. Hephaistos's code matrix will then cause it to take shape as trees, deserts, lakes, and so on.'

'Are we safe?'

'Oh no. If we stay here, the ground will give way under us and we'll fall out of Hephaistos's program altogether. I imagine we'd not only cease to exist, we never would have existed.'

▶ **822**

1237

There's nothing in the drawers but old bills. The murderer must have searched it too as they are scattered and crumpled. Was the murderer looking for the same thing you are, or did they just kill him for money?

▶ **944**

1238

The house where you grew up is on the Boulevard of the Undine. Your spirits lift as you come in sight of the familiar porch gate, the doorstep worn smooth by generations of your ancestors, and the apple tree you used to swing on as a child. Wherever you travel in the Vulcanverse, it is always comforting to return here.

If you have the codeword *Ostrich* and this box ❏ is empty, tick it and ▶ **1214**; otherwise read on.

Your mother has a loaf of freshly baked bread and a bowl of hot soup waiting for you. She always seems to know when you are coming. You enjoy a fine meal and, if you are injured, you can untick the Wound box on your Adventure Sheet.

You can also leave possessions and money here to save having to carry them around with you. To do that, note that your Current Location is **970** and then ▶ **319**

To leave the house ▶ **970**

1239

Where will you go now?

Agamemnon's tent   ▶ **518**

Achilles' tent   ▶ **535**

Neither – sleep on the beach   ▶ **572**

1240

The Archon of the Sun walks you to the entrance hall in person, drawing astonished glances from the guards. 'Without that music box, the machinery of state must grind to a halt,' he says.

You look out over the thousands of rooftops of this great city. 'If it's out there, I'll find it and bring it back.'

▶ **1642**

1241

The intruder doesn't put up a struggle or try to run away, much to the disappointment of the watchmen who would have appreciated a bit of excitement to relieve the boredom of their patrol.

'I am sorry about this,' he says to you as they tie his hands behind him.

'Don't take any notice of his patter, your grace,' says the officer of the watch. 'They all turn contrite once the game's up.'

Now ▶ **480** and put a tick in the box there before reading on.

1242

You wait, every muscle tense. Footsteps approach along a corridor. A door starts to swing open and you get ready for a fight, until a shout rings out and the guard mutters a curse before turning without noticing you and going back the way he came.

A tap on your shoulder makes you jump. It's the mechanical spider, now reattached to its eighth limb. It beckons for you to come through a final door and up a short flight of steps to a cell under the highest eaves of the prison.

▶ **1397**

1243

With a collective howl that sounds like the magnified last breath of a dying man, the centre of the army of night gives way, turning to flee in the face of unbridled ferocity from your troops.

You throw yourself through the gap in the foe's collapsing ranks. Towering before you like an obelisk stands Nyx herself. 'Come!' she shrieks. 'Embrace your doom!'

You race towards her, a defiant war-cry on your lips, but even in the white heat of battle there must be some qualm deep in your heart. Can a lone mortal really hope to best the Queen of Darkness Incarnate?

▶ **344**

1244

'What do you know, caught red-handed,' she says, holding the ruby hairclip up for you to see before she drops it in her pocket.

'That's a bold attitude for somebody in your situation.'

'Old turkey-neck back there won't even miss it. Probably got a half dozen more of them at home. Boyfriends and hairclips both.'

You can't help smiling. 'I'd have put a mousetrap in my pocket if I knew it was going to be that kind of party.'

'I'm Dunamis, by the way.' She hesitates, perhaps wondering if she can run past before you catch her. 'Look, you can have a share.'

Take half of the hairclip's value to keep your mouth shut ▶ **565**

Insist she gives it back	▶ **300**
Let her go	▶ **1061**
Throw her out	▶ **358**

1245

Agamemnon rakes his fingers through his beard, grimacing as he considers your request. 'What you've got to understand, Amazon, is that we've only got a certain amount of goodwill with the gods. Can't keep bothering them with requests or they might turn against us.'

You can see where this is heading. He's angling for a bribe. 'What do you want?'

It turns out he'll let you talk to the priests if you give him gifts – two items, which you must cross off your possessions. He wants **lava gems** by preference, but if you can't give him those he'll accept anything else.

Give him two possessions ▶ **309**

Not right now ▶ Current Location

1246

Taking a last look out over the blistering sun-washed sands, you turn and descend the tower.

▶ **570**

1247

'You imagine death as something monstrous,' you tell him. 'A dreadful doom that bears down on every living thing from the moment of its birth, like a predator waiting to snap its jaws around your throat.'

'I never said – '

'It isn't like that. Death is a place of peace, not icy fear. You'll stroll over the Elysian Fields and bask in the warmth. And what is that warmth? It's the love and respect of all your future generations.'

Make a CHARM roll at difficulty 7 to convince him – but subtract 1 from the dice roll for every five scars. (So if you have twelve scars, for example, you'd have to subtract 2 from what you roll.) Your argument is more convincing if you don't bear the harrowing marks of death yourself.

Succeed	▶ **47**
Fail	▶ **660**

1248

You slide back down the rope into Lady Pemphreda's salon, glad to be breathing ordinary air and perfume and pipe smoke rather than the thin crystalline ether of the cloudscape.

'And my nephew?' asks Lady Pemphreda, affecting nonchalance.

'I think he's happy where he is,' you say.

The rope drops in a limp coil on the floor beside you. The other guests turn away, disappointed not to have witnessed an act of derring-do.

'Bit of a damp squib, that last trick,' says an officer of the Black Guard, and you can't help taking it as a criticism.

Lose 1 Glory and ▶ **1324**

1249

Get the codeword *Rifle*. Under the pretence of relacing your boots, you crouch down beside the jar. It only takes a flick of the wrist to remove the stopper. You pour in the contents of the packet Dunamis gave you. A casual glance around to check none of the workmen are looking, and in a few seconds you've refastened the stopper.

Delete the **packet of emery dust** and ▶ **76**

1250

The sun appears over the trees, sending a blaze of warm clean light through the rain-spattered windows.

The effect on the vampire is ghastly. With a sound like a foul drain clearing, she spews maggots onto the carpet. Corruption spreads over her like a mould, turning the rotted white flesh a poisonous dark grey. Her eyes sink and shrivel in her sockets. Her hair falls away in clumps.

With a last shudder and a gust of foetid breath that might be either a curse or a sigh, she collapses into a shapeless mound of decayed bones and dirt-smeared rags.

The smell lingers for days, even after you've had the rug removed and burned. Finally you have to move to another bedroom. The door to the room where you slew the vampire is kept locked, and after a time the servants take to calling it Tritona's chamber. Thus in death she returns as a presence to the house she was exiled from in life.

Lose the codewords *Rabbit* and *Ruffle* if you have them and ▶ **38**

1251

You fling a contemptuous gesture at the decanter. 'Help yourself. I don't drink with people who rob me.'

Orphea shakes her head. 'I'm not here to rob you. Quite the reverse. I'm here to give you the Pipes of Pan.'

'Shall I count my silverware now, or after I call the night watch to arrest you?'

'Who's woken up in a grump? I'm talking about a wager. We play a little game – ' she holds up a small ruby, then indicates three overturned cups in front of her on the desk – 'and if you win I'll give you the Pipes of Pan.'

'And if I lose?'

She bites her lip in thought. 'Of course, you'd have to stake something of equivalent value. I know, what about the deeds of this house?'

'My house against some pipes? That's your idea of a fair trade?'

'The pipes of a god,' she points out.

Agree to the wager	▶ **1379**
Seize her and summon the night watch	▶ **1610**
Just kill her	▶ **987**

1252

You tell the story of ascending to the mountain peak, finding the Galomoi, and realizing that to cure them of the dry sickness you'd have to give up your precious supply of cockatrice blood.

The story has everything: the arduous climb where any missed handhold would have sent you crashing to the rocks far below, the deserted fortress where you feel an invisible presence, the enigmatic cyclopean telescope, the refrigerated survival pods, the whiff of death when you mention the plague, the conversation with the legendary Kedalion, and your own sacrifice in order to heal the sleeping Galomoi. And then the epilogue in which a grateful Kedalion despatches swarms of clockwork creatures to repair the damage to your city.

'And what about the raiders who sacked Iskandria?' asks one of the listeners. 'Did you find them?'

You wink at him. 'That's a tale for another time.'

▶ **447**

1253

Two tall sentries cross their polearms as you approach the gate. 'No admittance,' says one, staring straight ahead. 'Hop it.'

▶ **1642**

1254

While you are deep in slumber, a horde of giant insects creeps up from the hold. The crew are taken unawares and many are dead from poisonous bites before they even realize what is happening. The rest fight desperately but finally are forced to flee in a small lifeboat. In the confusion, you are forgotten.

The ship is soon overrun by the insectoid monsters. Feathery feelers touch your face. Glistening mandibles are poised over your throat. You never wake up.

▶ **666**

1255

Lose the title **The Unexpected Heir** and note that your Current Location is **515** .

She gives you time to pack your things. Collect any money or possessions you had stored at ▶ **1402** but you do not get the opportunity to rest and recuperate. Leave as soon as you have retrieved what you're taking with you.

1256

You grapple the nearest Celedon. It's like wrestling a statue. She bends you back with muscles that have the strength of metal cables. In desperation you haul her off her feet and throw her at another Celedon that's dashing towards you. The impact rings out like two huge bells crashing together. The automata fall like broken puppets, twitching horribly as they try to move limbs that are now bent out of shape.

▶ **17** and tick one of the boxes there before you read on.

1257

You pass a mansion half-hidden by foliage. Behind the railings, tossed by the wind, branches thrash wildly to and fro giving the impression that the trees are screaming in panic.

Note **1175** as your Current Location and then ▶ **549**

1258

Psyche comes with you to the bottom of the ramp. 'You saw that Nyx's rebuild of reality is almost complete,' she says. 'But we haven't really talked about what will happen if she isn't defeated before then.'

'I can guess.'

'It will mean a universe of endless night, with each person separated from the rest – alone forever in a world without either light or hope.'

You look up the shaft. 'And I'm supposed to take her down single-handed. I was really hoping for a better plan.'

'You won't be on your own,' says Psyche. 'I've sent word to Eros. He's coming.'

'Isn't he more of a lover than a fighter?'

'His power is as great as Thanatos or Hypnos,' she assures you. 'Greater, to hear him tell it.'

'Well,' you say smiling, 'that's love talking. Good luck, Psyche.'

'And good luck to you,' she calls after you as you ascend the shaft. 'For the sake of the world you'll need it.'

The shaft seems even deeper going up. All you can see above is unyielding dark, so it takes you by surprise when you finally reach the top. The wind that has been raging has dropped, leaving a dead calm. You must be in the eye of the storm.

A shadow deeper than the night falls over you. You turn to look up into the eyes of Queen Nyx.

'At least you've saved me the trouble of finding you,' you shout, trying to make your voice strong enough to hide a tremor of fear.

'What brave words,' says Nyx. 'I will see to it they are engraved on your tombstone.'

Behind her stand her sons, Death and Sleep. Titans who together even Zeus would hesitate to face in battle. And you are one lone mortal.

▶ **249**

1259

You open the cage and release the **caged canary**. Cross it off your list of possessions.

Tweeting wildly, it flies up, a yellow spot in the vast blue sky. Sphikos sees it too, and then catches sight of you. As if suddenly aware of the danger, he haltingly makes his way along the piled banks of white cloud to join you.

'You know where we are?' he says, his eyes bright with something between panic and joy. 'This is the beginning of creation.'

▶ **1044**

1260

If you have neither codeword *Naughty* or *Nadir* and this box ❏ is empty, tick it and ▶ **1184**; otherwise read on.

If you don't have the title **Grief Stricken** and this box ❏ is empty, tick it and ▶ **1360**; otherwise read on.

If you don't have the codeword *Noisome* and this box ❏ is empty, tick it and ▶ **336**; otherwise read on.

If you don't have the codeword *Nomad* and this box ❏ is empty, tick it and ▶ **1229**; otherwise read on.

'You have achieved much in Hades,' says the Oracle. 'Other regions of the Vulcanverse are available.'

That is all she will tell you. With a muttered prayer of thanks you return to the main hall.

▶ **510**

1261

Thersites is eager to stop and chat, if only because it gives him an excuse not to get on with other chores. You can ask him any question below for which the box is unticked – first tick the box, then turn to the section indicated.

❏ 'What do you think of the war?' ▶ **371**

❏ 'Why do you think Achilles took it on himself to nurse me?' ▶ **1099**

❏ 'That armour by the Myrmidon tents – where did it come from?' ▶ **1386**

If all the boxes are now ticked ▶ **488**

1262

By now there's a milling throng of pursuers pressed right up to the edge of the roof. You can see the pallid, worm-gnawed faces of the vampires, the red eyes and spittle-flecked jaws of the were-creatures, the misshapen features of capering nightmare demons. Baying and snarling, they are so intent on getting to you that some get jostled over the edge and fall flailing to the street far below.

Each time a grapple lodges on the ship's rail, instantly a stream of attackers comes scrabbling along it to get aboard. Careless of the wind, rain and the lethal drop below, their only thought is to continue their wild onslaught. Even the Minotaur, whose blade flashes and spills blood and guts with every swing, must eventually tire and then the monstrous tide will overwhelm the ship.

Should you stay to help the Minotaur fight them off, or go to help get the buoyancy rotor working before the *Sunrise* loses any more height?

Stay at the rail to repel boarders ▶ **1461**
Help fix the buoyancy rotor   ▶ **1037**

1263

There is no sign of the guests slaughtered by the robot handmaidens only minutes ago. Not only are the bodies gone, there's no blood either. He sees your confusion and says, his deep voice softer and more mellifluous now, 'No distractions here. I have brought you into my realm so that we can talk.'

'What have we to talk about?'

'Allegiance. Self-interest. The fulcrum of choice.' He glances up towards the rumbling storm, which seems muted now. Lightning flashes out of the heart of the storm but he holds up his hand and the bolt is frozen in mid-strike, a fork-shaped scar of light against the livid roiling of the sky. 'There. Let us not be disturbed by time until this discussion is finished.'

'Your realm? Where is that?'

'I am Sleep, as you have guessed. My brother is Death and our mother is Night Eternal. As we speak, beyond the world a battle is being fought that will decide the fate of all existence. The titans have escaped from Tartarus and they are fighting the gods of Olympus. This storm is just the outer fringes of that mighty struggle whose ripples are warping reality itself.'

'The gods have beaten the titans before.'

He gives a peal of laughter like the tolling of an enormous bell. 'And they will again. Zeus and his kin will overcome the titans and slowly force them back towards the abyss of Tartarus. But they will be weakened. And that's when we shall strike. With both gods and titans gone, Queen Nyx will hold illimitable dominion over all.'

'And what has that to do with me?'

He removes his mask, revealing deep slumbrous eyes and a broad smile like a big beast of prey that has caught the scent of blood.

'Join us,' he says.

Your reply?
'Yes.'   ▶ **1031**
'No.'   ▶ **1472**

1264

You had almost forgotten the tears. Pulling out the vial in which you keep them, you pour out the remaining droplets and rub them into your eyes. Your vision changes. Now you can see the outlines of the room and the sleeping figures as if they were sketched in white ink on black paper.

You make your way between the seats, careful not to brush against the pupating dreams that are visible now as grey blurs. They hang suspended in the air over the sleeping Syndics, each taking the shape of a nascent figure whose embryonic organs beat out a febrile pulse beneath its waxy skin. Their heavy lacertilian eyelids twitch with unknowable thoughts. What happens when those dreams emerge into reality? You'd rather not find out.

Cross the **phoenix tears** off your list of possessions, then ▶ **294** and tick the box there before reading on.

1265

You are helpless to attack her directly. The intensity of her stare radiates a palpable force that prevents you getting closer. But you can still move. Reaching down, you take hold of the edge of the rug and tug it with all your might.

She falls back, but not stumbling as you expected. Rather, she drifts away as if weightless, like a puppet on strings, swaying around slightly so that eye contact is broken. With a roar you run in, closing with her before she can renew her hypnotic charm.

▶ **61**

1266

'You can get out that way,' you tell Dunamis, pointing to a narrow window off the stairs.

'What about you?'

'I'm too big to squeeze through.'

'How are you going to get away?' she says as you give her a leg up.

'I'll figure it out. Hurry!'

You push her through.

▶ **689**

1267

Enceladus comes rushing at you from a clump of trees, a hurtling mass of bone and muscle with a face as big as a boat's prow squashed down upon his heavy chest and shoulders.

There is no time to get away. You must stand and fight.

▶ **21**

1268

Orphea gives a satisfying howl of pain as the poker gashes her just above the eye. In shock, she drops the knife and staggers back whimpering.

No time to find another weapon. You rush in to press

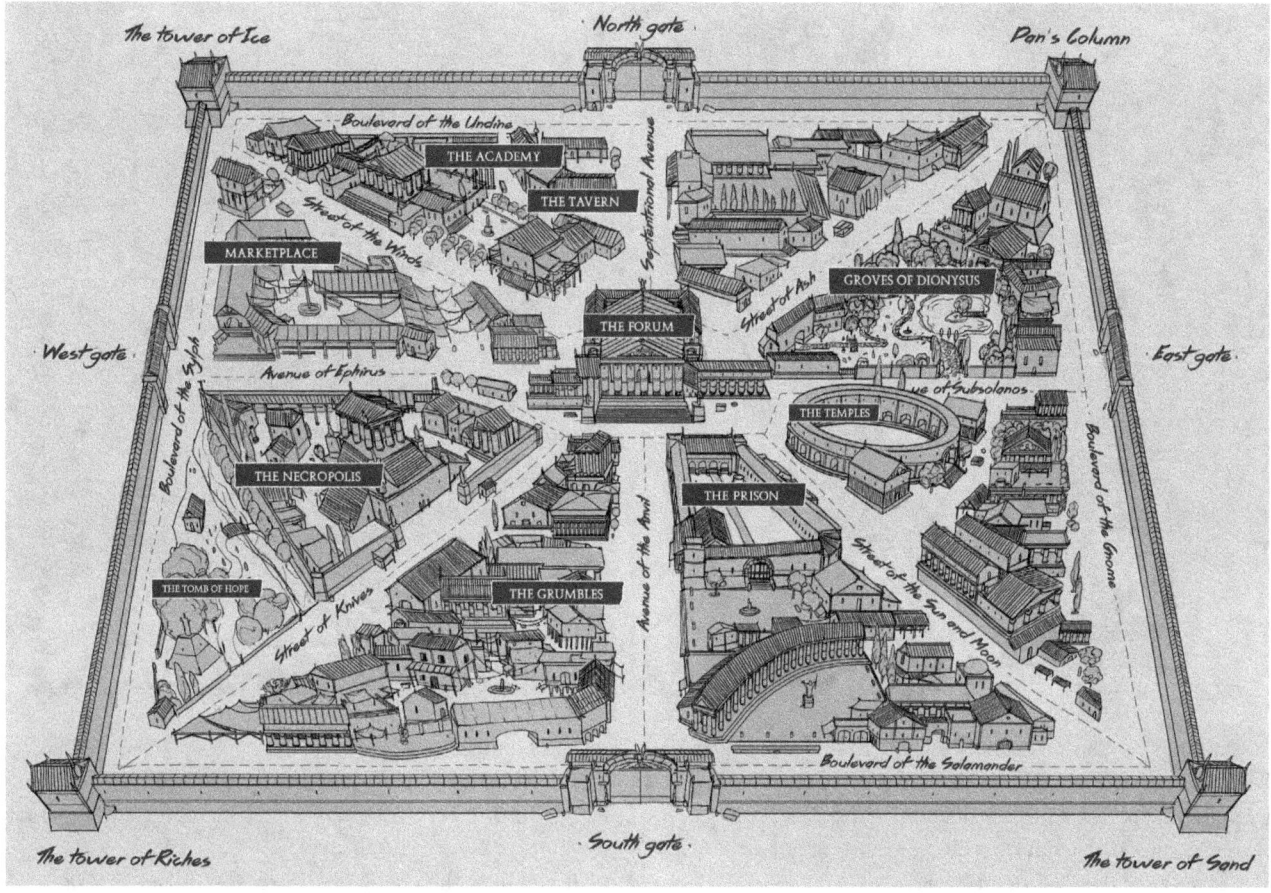

your attack before she has a chance to recover. Make a STRENGTH roll at difficulty 6 without any item bonus.

Success ▶ **1114**

Failure ▶ **945**

1269

You can travel to any location for which the box is ticked, as those are the places in the city that you are familiar with. (You don't get to tick a box unless specifically told to do so in the course of your travels.)

- ☐ The North Gate ▶ **222**
- ☐ The South Gate ▶ **555**
- ☐ The East Gate ▶ **333**
- ☐ The West Gate ▶ **509**
- ☐ The Forum ▶ **1642**
- ☐ The Tower of Ice ▶ **451**
- ☐ Pan's Column ▶ **48**
- ☐ The Tower of Sand ▶ **570**
- ☐ The Tower of Riches ▶ **1222**
- ☐ The Grumbles ▶ **771**
- ☐ The Necropolis ▶ **674**
- ☐ The Groves of Dionysus ▶ **806**
- ☐ The Academy of Philosophers ▶ **1544**
- ☐ The Tavern of the Hero of Temesa ▶ **764**
- ☐ The market ▶ **716**
- ☐ The temple district ▶ **103**
- ☐ The Tomb of Hope ▶ **88**
- ☐ A tunnel straight to hell ▶ **80**
- ☐ Lady Pemphreda's salon ▶ **898**
- ☐ Your mansion ▶ **1353** (only if you still have the title **The Unexpected Heir**)

To stay where you are ▶ Current Location

1270

☐ ☐ ☐ ☐

'The problem with running a business like mine is that a lot of criminals are dumb,' says Zinc, returning to one of his favourite themes. 'I like you because you're smart. You remind me of me at your age – only maybe not so pretty.'

Tick the next empty box above.

You just ticked the first box	▶ **1609**
Just ticked the second box	▶ **1598**
Just ticked the third box	▶ **972**
Just ticked the fourth box	▶ **271**
If all the boxes were already ticked	▶ **326**

1271

'This is marvellous, just what I need,' says the lady, dropping the plants you've brought her into a jar.

Cross the **ophidiaroot** off your list of possessions. Also lose the codeword *Pennywort*.

'I hope your husband will enjoy it.'

She gives you a beaming smile. 'Oh, I don't think he'll ever complain again. Now, I must reward you for your kindness. I have some coins here – but perhaps a payment would seem crass? I could offer you a gift instead.'

You can either take 150 pyr in cash, two doses of **tincture of healing** (each cures 1 wound), three applications of **Iaso's balm** (each removes 1 scar), or up to six pieces of **beeswax** if you have room on your Adventure Sheet to carry them. She leaves the choice up to you.

'Do you mind slipping out the back way?' she says, taking you to the kitchen door. 'We must be discreet.'

'If I find myself back over in Arcadia, would you like me to bring any more?'

She shakes her head. 'I think by the next time you pass this way I'll have moved somewhere nicer. Perhaps a little cottage by the sea. I'm expecting to come into some money, you see. Goodbye.'

▶ **1062**

1272

'Back, are you?' says the man with the deck of cards.

'You've got a good memory for faces.'

'No, I read it in the cards. You and the Hero have unfinished business.'

In the rough-hewn stone of the rear wall, the portico leading into the Hero's lair is as black and forbidding as an open grave.

If you have the codeword *Pure*, lose it and ▶ **578**
Otherwise ▶ **764**

1273

There's a metallic clang as the golden maiden gets a firm grip on your other arm too. Immediately you know you're beaten. It's like being held in iron shackles. You kick back at her but only succeed in bruising your heels on her unyielding shins. She straightens to her full height with an inexorable grinding of ratchets and gears, bending you back until your feet are lifted off the floor and you are dangling helplessly.

Autolycus wipes a smear of blood off his chin where you caught him with a good blow. He grins, looking more than ever like a wolf.

'Call it a draw, then?' you say.

He laughs. 'Hey, that's the spirit. Now, what am I going to do with you?'

▶ **692**

1274

Wind screeches through the ruins. The only relief from pitch darkness comes from guttering fires that have broken out in some of the empty buildings.

Decide where you're heading:

The Academy of Philosophers ▶ 1510

The temple district ▶ 1326

The Forum ▶ 981

The nearest gate ▶ 723

The nearest tower ▶ 171

The Avenue of the Anvil ▶ 1632

Your mansion (only if you have the title **The Unexpected Heir**) ▶ 1257

Your family home (only if you have the codeword *Reverie*) ▶ 1385

1275

'You have pledged yourself to the Olympians,' says Prometheus, stooping so that his eyes are more nearly level with your face. You can feel the force of his words like the rumbling of foreshocks that precede an earthquake.

'I didn't have much choice.'

'Zeus sentenced me to an aeon of torment for siding with humanity against his brood. I will not join your cause only to restore their supremacy.'

What will you say to change his mind?

'Once Nyx is defeated we can renegotiate with Olympus.' ▶ 762

'Nyx is far worse than they are.' ▶ 220

'If you're scared to fight, just say so.' ▶ 1591

1276

Wherever this place is, its pure atmosphere is toxic to the creature clamped around your brow. It relaxes its grip and slithers away, mewling horribly. You look down but the creature remains invisible, stirring the white vapours that spool and snake around your feet with its death throes. You are conscious that the dull pain in your head, which had become your constant companion, is finally gone.

Lose the codeword *Quiver* and ▶ 1627

1277

'Wake up! Wake up!'

You're being violently shaken. A swaddling caul of sleep falls away and you realize that you were dreaming. You are still lying in bed. Your companion is leaning over you, clutching your shoulder and shouting.

'My friend, you're hurting me.'

'Get up! Look!'

'I dreamt a beautiful vampire was about to drink my blood.'

'Beautiful?' cries your companion in a voice thick with horror. 'It is a monster. See.'

You look where he's pointing and in a split-second you're on your feet, heart pounding with adrenaline. Because only the vampire's appearance was a dream. The rest is all too

true. You see the vampire now as she really is – not a pale and beautiful woman, but a rotted corpse with maggots writhing in her pock-marked cheeks and lustreless eyes that leak brown slime. Clammy strips of dead flesh hang from her bones. The room is filled with the stench of decay.

She lurches forward, swollen grey fingers reaching for you, her lipless teeth clacking eagerly. With your companion backing you up, you must fight this monstrosity. Make a STRENGTH roll at difficulty 9.

Succeed ▶ 946

Fail ▶ 866

1278

With a shock you realize, 'It's gone.'

'What?' says the priestess.

'The blessing that Demeter gave me. I've lost it.'

She gives a scream, her eyes brimming with fear and sorrow. 'But that means… the goddess has been killed!'

Delete the permanent blessing and ▶ 1619

1279

Pandora materializes as before out of the depths of the glass pyramid.

Not for the first time, you wonder if she has physically transported to Vulcan City or whether this is just a holographic projection. But to know for sure you'd have to reach out and touch her, and that feels as though it would be an unacceptable liberty.

If you have a **brass head** ▶ 1181

Otherwise ▶ 242

1280

If you don't have title **Initiate of the Tethysian Mysteries** and Loutro is not your companion, set **425** as your Current Location.

Otherwise set **806** as your Current Location,

Then ▶ 1269 and tick the box next to the Groves of Dionysus. From now on you will always be able to find your way back here.

1281

'I'm out of here!' yelps Chipos.

He tears off across the garden, trips over his own feet, and falls to lie sprawling at the Night Queen's feet.

'Don't get up,' says Nyx.

With a sweep of her hand she turns Chipos into a puddle of ink-black water on the lawn. Raising her robes fastidiously, she steps over the puddle. You could swear you hear it whimpering very softly to itself.

Delete Chipos as a companion and ▶ 1027

1282

A single Ker remains, snarling with insensate fury as it snaps and claws at this stubborn mortal hero who has the temerity to fight back. Drawn by the sound of battle, wary onlookers creep out of the ruins. Seeing you holding your own against Thanatos's hunting dogs makes them dare to hope that all is not lost.

'You can do it!' shouts Dunamis, scurrying up onto an overturned cart to lob pebbles at the monster.

Attempt a STRENGTH or GRACE roll (your choice) at difficulty 15.

Succeed ▶ 1631
Fail ▶ 145

1283

'You should go and say a prayer of thanks.'

'I'll drop by the temple later.'

'Not here, dummy. In Iskandria.'

'They're the ones who should be thanking me.'

'All right, so go and bask in the adulation, then. And maybe the gods will see to it that you bump into an old friend.'

That's all he will say, but not for the first time you feel sure he knows much more than he lets on.

▶ 806

1284

The heel of your foot sinks into his solar plexus. There's a retching sound and he goes down like a punctured balloon. He's out of the fight but that leaves two more.

▶ 1023 and tick one of the boxes there before reading on.

1285

'Where now?' says Dunamis.

The nearest gate ▶ 723
The nearest tower ▶ 171
The Avenue of the Anvil ▶ 1632
Your family home (only if you have the codeword *Reverie*) ▶ 1385
The Academy of Philosophers ▶ 1510
The temple district ▶ 1326
The Forum ▶ 981

1286

Your last chance. In seconds the whole pack will be on you. Make a STRENGTH roll at difficulty 13.

Succeed ▶ 1055
Fail ▶ 882

1287

Philosophically speaking, the whole world is Vulcan's simulation anyway. A dream is just a simulation within a simulation, so the idea that you might be trapped in sleep is entirely illusory.

Armed with this insight, make an INGENUITY roll at difficulty 9 to wake up.

Succeed ▶ 906
Fail ▶ 1308

1288

In the late afternoon, as the troops start returning to camp, word of your fight spreads quickly and priests come to inspect the site where the saboteurs landed. Seeing the marks of three keels on the sand, they confer and then turn to the king. 'The Amazon blunted the trident of the god Poseidon,' declares the high priest.

'Poseidon?' growls Agamemnon. 'Even I know he fights on our side.'

The priest shakes his head. 'Poseidon favours the Achaeans, true, but he harbours resentment for Achilles because the swift-footed prince's grandfather was the first god of the sea.'

'So they were only out to burn the Myrmidon ships,' you hear Agamemnon say to one of his aides.

Get the codeword *Royal* and ▶ 1500

1289

Staggering from the impact, it is all you can do to avoid the follow-up blow as he swings the club back through its infinity-shaped arc.

'Time it right and you can jab him as you twist away,' howls Oizys, shrieking with mad glee. 'Get it wrong and it'll be pain, pain, pain.'

Make a GRACE roll at difficulty 11.

Succeed ▶ 878
Fail ▶ 1463

1290

Bidding Myletes farewell, you exit the Academy onto the Street of the Winds. Dust and scraps of paper fly past on the roaring gale. Pulling your collar tight against the biting cold, you make for your next destination:

The nearest gate ▶ 723
The nearest tower ▶ 171
The Avenue of the Anvil ▶ 1632
Your mansion (only if you have the title **The Unexpected Heir**) ▶ 1257
Your family home (only if you have the codeword *Reverie*) ▶ 1385
The temple district ▶ 1326
The Forum ▶ 981

1291

❑

If the box above was already ticked ▶ 815 immediately; otherwise tick it and then read on.

'You're her,' are Thersites' opening words. He is one of a gang of men who've been ordered to dig a defensive trench along the seaward side of the plain. Talking to you gives him an excuse to take a break.

'I am she.'

Thersites leans on his spade in an awkward posture that keeps his forearm across the lower part of his face. Catching a glimpse of his uneven yellow teeth you realize he's self-conscious about his appearance, so you gaze across the plain towards Ilion while chatting with him.

Now tick the box above and then ▶ 815

1292

❑ ❑

If you have the codeword *Quiddity*, tick one of the boxes above before reading on. If you don't have *Quiddity*, leave them unticked.

No boxes are ticked   ▶ 971
One box is now ticked   ▶ 1215
Both boxes are ticked   ▶ 530

1293

As you eat, Achilles strums a lyre and sings. It takes you a few moments to recognize it, a song you sometimes heard in the marketplace of Iskandria.

'I'm no musician,' he says, stopping mid-verse and setting the lyre aside. 'The only tunes I learned are bashed out on swords and shields.'

His diffident grin is unexpected, so at odds with his reputation as the fiercest of the Achaean warriors.

'Do you miss your home?'

He looks into the campfire. 'I can hardly remember it. It sometimes feels like this war has been my whole life. I never knew any finer feelings until...'

'Until?' you say, when the silence has stretched too long.

'There'll be a battle tomorrow,' he says, changing the subject. 'You could fight if you like.'

'Do you want me to?'

'You are an Amazon, my princess. Your will is your own. But as you've asked me, I'd rather you fought with caution. Do not fling yourself too far into the fray. Whatever honours Zeus tempts you with, take care not to lose your head in the joy of battle. Don't carry the fight to the walls of Ilion. Turn back once the foe are kept from our fleet.'

'That doesn't sound much fun,' you say, meaning it in jest.

Achilles answers in a troubled voice. 'If the gods who never die see you deep in battle, magnificent and triumphant on the field, I fear they will come down from Olympus to intervene. They might be jealous of your prowess, and no mortal survives the spite of the gods.'

▶ 41

1294

The Archon of the Sun gives such a violent start on seeing the music box that his high gilded crown nearly topples off. Hurrying to the console in the domed chamber, he winds the box and as the tune plays he adjusts the controls of the room's mechanism. At last, satisfied that the settings are correct, he throws the master switch. There's a soft hum that builds into the opening notes of a breathtakingly haunting melody. The celestial symbols slide across the walls, ascending towards the top of the dome amid constellations of jewels. As you watch you feel a chill like the night breeze under the stars, until you realize it is no physical sensation but the stirring of wonder. This is a device built by Vulcan himself.

'I will not forget your service to the city,' says the Archon. 'From this day you are an honorary official of the Palace and can come and go as you please.'

Remove the **Box of the Music of the Spheres** from your possessions and get the title **Paladin**.

As he is walking you to the entrance hall, the Archon points out a staircase. 'That goes to the vaults, where we'll be sure to keep the music box secure from now on. If you should ever need them, there are also secret tunnels down there that lead direct to the city gates. Very handy for coming and going when you don't want said comings and goings to be the stuff of gossip.'

▶ 1642

1295

Agamemnon considers it. 'You did shatter Poseidon's trident.'

'Huh?'

'That's what they're calling it. That business with the three raiding ships. So I figure there's no keeping you off the battlefield now. Just don't get any scars on that beautiful bod.'

He gives you a parting slap on the rump.

▶ Current Location

1296

A crowd has gathered around a giant blue turtle that has surfaced in the middle of a lily pond. Fixed in the middle of its back is a chair plated with snail shells and small pebbles.

'You're here,' says the turtle, snapping its leathery beak impatiently as you push to the front of the crowd. 'Let's get going.'

Climb on its back ▶ 516
Walk away ▶ 806

1297

'There's nothing you'd be interested in,' he says.

You scan the shelves, crowded almost to overflowing with all manner of curiosities. 'Nothing at all?'

He leans forward, beckoning you with a lean bony finger. 'Save your money,' he says confidentially. 'It's all junk.'

Sell him something ▶ 526
Leave the shop ▶ 325

1298

'Growing up back home, Parthena was the girl next door. I'd see her every day playing on the seashore as I helped my dad pull in the day's catch. She was a couple of years younger than me and pretty as coral in the sun.'

You laugh. 'So the con man has the soul of a poet. Maybe you'll be able to earn a crust spinning yarns like this in the marketplace, kid. The crippled legs might even be an asset.'

'It's not a yarn,' he retorts hotly. 'I love her. She loves me. But she wanted to act in the theatre and she came to the city to study. We agreed I'd save up some money and then join her, but while I was scrimping away back in Notus he got his hooks into her. Your boss. Parthena had trouble making ends meet and he put her to work. Pimped her out as one of his whores. Oh, you didn't know that, huh?'

You shake your head. 'I didn't ask.'

Kleistro is still shaking with fear, but a wry smile curls his lip at that. 'Why would you care, someone like you? Just doing Zinc's dirty work, aren't you? Well, you can guess the rest. I turned up here, found Parthena ashamed to face me. She was living in squalor, most of her earnings taken by your boss, half the time with bruises from being slapped around by clients. Or if not clients then enforcers like you driving her out on the street to work harder. I begged her to come home with me. That's why I'm sharping a little cash off these out-of-towners, to make enough to pay our way back home. But when Zinc got wind of it he wasn't happy. Didn't want to lose the income my beloved brings in. So he tells you to rough me up.'

'Bit more than a roughing-up,' you point out. 'He could just send a street thug for that. I've got to do some surgical maiming.'

Kleistro's shoulders slump. 'Let's get it over with,

then. I'm through. You might as well kill me. I don't want to live seeing my love degraded by a bloodsucking parasite like Zinc.'

Go through with the job ▶ 481
Relent ▶ 730

1299

You turn to face the horde of night-creatures. Your back is pressed against the stonework of the parapet. The werewolves snarl and snap, hungry to taste raw flesh. The vampires are more wary, slinking round to try and encircle you. They have you at bay and there is nowhere to run. All you can do is strike out at random and do your best to fend them off for as long as you can.

A rumble from behind you, audible even over the din of the storm. The rooftops on the other side of the street erupt in a tsunami of broken tiles. Thrusting through the shattered roof comes the prow of a ship. A flying ship. Its keel ploughs through the exposed rafters, dislodging an avalanche of bricks that go crashing down to the street far below.

With sails straining against the gale, the ship heaves out on empty air, an impossible bulk of timbers, cables and canvas defying gravity hundreds of feet above the ground. As it draws level with the palace roof, the ship swings around as if coming in to dock. You feel the jarring impact as the hull slams into the building and slides ponderously by with a scrape of tarred wood against stone.

You see the name painted on the prow: *Sunrise*. It stirs a memory of a shipyard built improbably on a mountain peak. A familiar figure waves to you from the rail.

'Ancaeus!'

'What are you standing there gawping for, dummy?' he shouts back. 'Jump!'

Taking advantage of your distraction, a werewolf leaps for your throat. You turn just in time, diving to one side. It goes flying over your shoulder. Its snarls turn to yelps as it falls to its doom below.

The others are closing in. You don't wait around. Springing onto the parapet, you brace yourself for the leap over to the *Sunrise*'s deck. But as you do a vampire lunges, clutching at your ankle and throwing you off-balance.

Make the jump anyway ▶ 909
Wait and regain your footing first ▶ 684

1300

Get the codeword **Robber**.

It doesn't take you long to spot how the pickpockets are doing it. It's a team of three. Two of them stage an argument in the middle of the street with one acting the role of a drunken bully who picks on a much smaller and better-dressed man. As people hurry past, relieved not to be the target of the drunk's attention, a third accomplice bumps into them and lifts their purse.

You let yourself be the mark, but when they open the purse they've stolen from you they find no money, just a note saying that if they don't start paying a cut of their takings to Zinc then they'll each be losing a few fingers and that will put paid to their pickpocketing career.

It does the trick. Next time you see Zinc he pats you on the cheek. 'There's that pretty face,' he says. 'Good job. I'll find something more challenging for you next time.'

If you have the codeword *Recursive* ▶ 645

If not ▶ 326

1301

❑

Do not tick the box above unless you were told to do so in the section you have turned from.

If the box is blank ▶ 1332

If you just put a tick in the box ▶ 1382

If the box was already ticked and you have the title **Soul Bearer** but not the codewords *Remedy* or *Retract* ▶ 1132

Otherwise the prison guards come out from a postern gate swinging heavy studded clubs. 'Don't loiter around here unless you want us to find you a room,' they snarl. You go back to the main road ▶ 63

1302

Using the wings you could fly to several points within the mountainous realm of Boreas. To do so you will need *The Pillars of the Sky* (the fourth book in the Vulcanverse series) and you cannot take any companion with you.

Take to the air ▶ 381

Not right now ▶ 1341

1303

There's a broken door-jamb lying on the pavement. You pick it up, hefting it like a club. The weight feels comfortably dangerous.

As the Celedon approaches you give her a mirthless grin. 'Come on, then. Let's see how tough that metal hide really is.'

Try to outwit her ▶ 223

Head-on attack is the best defence ▶ 976

1304

Add the 10,000 pyr to your money. Lose the codewords *Ruffle* and *Rabbit* if you have them and also lose the title **The Unexpected Heir**.

'You'll want to pack,' says Tritona. 'There is no rush, but I'd appreciate it if you're out by the end of the week.'

▶ 97

1305

The sky is filling up with heavy black clouds. Chill gusts drive a fine spray in your face.

With two of the insect-creatures down, at least you don't have to have eyes in the back of your head. But your single remaining adversary looks like the biggest.

Try a STRENGTH or GRACE roll (your choice) at difficulty 13.

Succeed ▶ 174

Fail ▶ 1587

1306

'Astounding,' says Sphikos, his voice just a breath in the infinity of creation.

Feeling the clouds softening under your feet, you grab him and start back towards the top of the rope. 'Let's get home now while we still can.'

Urging him onto the rope first, you follow to the sound of polite applause. You are back in the salon breathing the homely aromas of perfume, tobacco, coffee and cake. For a moment the unearthly electric scent of the cloudscape lingers, then Sphikos gives a tug on the rope and it is pulled back, closing the dimensional portal forever.

'How very kind of you to bring him back before tea,' says Lady Pemphreda, ruffling her nephew's hair.

Get the title **Witness of the First Dawn** and ▶ 1324

1307

The refugees are dressed in dusty clothes and have their belongings tied up in bundles of rags. They are going from person to person asking for help.

'We don't want foreign beggars in our city,' grumbles a woman out walking her dogs.

'We are not beggars,' protests one of the refugees in the cultured accent of an Iskandrian. 'We do not want your money. We ask only for help in finding the one we seek.'

If Polymnia is your companion ▶ 391

If you are accompanied by Galatea ▶ 682

Otherwise they hurry on across the park and are soon out of sight ▶ 806

1308

Your slumbers are disturbed by a needle-sharp pain at your throat. Struggling against waves of sleep, you force your eyes open. You are stretched on a marble slab – no, on the cold hard floor of the ballroom. The smell of wet soil is not from your dream of being buried alive but comes from the rain driving into the lawn outside. You shiver at the chill wind blowing in through the open doors. The palace shakes to the crash and mutter of the storm now raging high in the heavens.

You turn your head. A face presses close to yours. Its skin is grey and has a slick sheen like week-old fish. You gag on an odour of breath that suggests dead things lying in stagnant water. Its teeth are thin yellow splinters tipped with fresh bright blood – a vampire. It was snuffling curiously at your neck. That's what woke you.

Seeing you stir, it makes a sound deep in its throat like insects scuttling in a drainpipe. Bonelessly it swings away from you and sweeps across the ballroom floor to join a group of figures crouching around something limp.

Tick the Wound box on your Adventure Sheet if it was not ticked already and ▶ **1561**

1309

In the middle of an empty plaza stands a tall, stately man in scholar's robes. As you get closer you see that his skin is blue under a coating of frost.

'To think I complained about dreamless sleep,' he says through chattering teeth. 'The dreams that arise out of nothingness are far worse.'

'Can dreams come from nothing?' you find your voice saying.

'Anything can.' He seizes you by the arms, and you can feel the icy cold of his grip. 'Inchoate darkness is the void from which anything can arise. Do you see? Reality is just a skin on the surface of the dark. It can pop, like a bubble, but the darkness is always there ready to sweep away one reality and replace it with another.'

'Got any advice?' you say. 'I'm at sea here.'

He considers that for a moment. 'If you want to get ahead, get a wig.'

There is something dark and huge in the sky above. You can't bring yourself to look up, but Kedalion does and his face registers horror. You press your hands to your eyes, hearing his panicked footsteps as he runs away. The ominous presence follows him, leaving you at the entrance to a leafy arbour with just the nightingale's song to guide you.

▶ **301**

1310

You lie flat among the rocks and watch as the saboteurs move swiftly along the shore. Their goal is the fifty trim ships of the Myrmidons, dragged high up onto the sand and propped with wooden bulwarks, festooned with lean-tos where the soldiers' supplies are kept.

The torches soon send licking flames along the dry hulls. Smoke rises, ink-thick, unfurling in billowing clouds above the Myrmidon tents.

If you have the codeword *Rage* ▶ **634**
If not ▶ **1548**

1311

Over a large stretch of the southern hillside the grass seems to be covered in dark burrs. At your approach they rise into the air, a seething mass of insects with filmy wings.

'A pyrigon swarm,' Oizys says with obvious relish. 'Ooh, stay right where you are. The pain is said to be delicious.'

'Easy to say when you're not the one who'll be feeling it!'

You take to your heels, but the swarm gives chase. Make a GRACE roll at difficulty 12.

Succeed ▶ **543**
Fail ▶ **1081**

1312

'Want a grape? Loutro gave them to me.'

'To stuff your face with?' says Ptolemos, brushing your hand away. 'And don't feed me like a baby. I'm blind, not senile.'

'You don't know what you're missing,' you say, savouring the sweet succulence of one of the wine-dark grapes.

He snorts, a kind of laughter. 'You're the one who's missing all the hints, dummy. Didn't Loutro tell you to go and get them blessed?'

'How do you know?'

'I know Loutro. It'll be at that place where you first met him, that shrine to Hephaestus's wife.'

You start to talk about something else, but Ptolemos has lost interest. After a time he grunts, 'You still here?'

Best to leave him when he's in that kind of mood.

▶ **806**

1313

If this box ❑ is ticked then ▶ **1235** immediately; otherwise put a tick in it now and read on.

'Quick recap,' says Daedalus. 'The Caucasian Eagle was the big bird Zeus commanded to peck out Prometheus's liver every day.'

'Big is putting it mildly. I've seen smaller elephants.'

Daedalus snaps his fingers. 'That's the one. I need you to bring me its stomach.'

'You might be disappointed. There wasn't a lot left of

the eagle once Prometheus had finished with it.'

'Peeved, was he? Still, I think you'll be able to find the piece I want.'

'What do you need it for?'

He gestures at dozens of blueprints and schematics pinned to the walls. 'Save-the-world stuff. We can get into all that later, first let's see if the stomach is salvageable.'

'You want me to go to Hades now?'

'If you're not too busy. It won't take long. I can send you by beetle express.'

He gestures and the metal chrysalis at your belt breaks apart to become a swarm of glowing golden insects.

If you agree to fetch what he wants ▶ **1079** and put a tick in the box there before reading on.

If you decline the mission, he directs the beetles to carry you back up through the ground to a nearby street ▶ **63**

1314

You pause beside a shelf crammed with jars of cooking oils.

'This is what I fried the crêpes in,' says the owner, handing you one of the jars. 'Notice how light it is.'

'Let me take a look,' pipes up the metal head in your backpack.

'Oh,' says the owner, alarmed.

'It's all right,' you tell her, placing the Face of Wisdom in front of the jar of oil. 'Just a fancy gadget I picked up on my travels.'

'Certainly looks like amaranth oil,' says the head, studiously ignoring your jibe. 'The viscosity and colour are right.'

'Nothing to say about the smell?'

'Take a look up my nostrils. Just cogs and wires.'

'It doesn't much smell of anything much,' says the restaurant owner, still staring in amazement at the metal head. 'Just a faint aroma like cut grass.'

'Yep. That's amaranth oil.'

'We call it love-lies-bleeding oil,' insists the owner.

'Of course. You're just a cook – mmph,' says the head as you stuff it back in your pack.

▶ **191**

1315

You struggle, but Daedalus holds you in an adamantine grip. You are forced to watch helplessly as your allies are slaughtered on the field of battle.

Standing amid the carnage, surrounded by the baying hordes of her army, Nyx surveys her new realm. She beckons to Daedalus.

He salutes her, then turns to you. 'You'll appreciate I need to play along with her for a while longer.'

'No doubt,' you say, sick with despair at the fate of your friends.

'I knew you'd understand.' So saying, he closes his mechanically augmented fingers and tears out your throat.

▶ **666**

1316

If you have the codeword **Robber**, lose it unless you also have the codeword **Recursive**.

Autolycus cannot hide a smirk. 'How long do you think they'll be able to hold me?' he says as you march him across town to the Office of the Watch.

'They'll have your clockwork girlfriend as a hostage too, don't forget, and I'll tell them to keep her unwound. So if you break out you'll have to leave her behind.'

The city militia are pleased to have the world's greatest thief delivered to their door. Get the title **Public-Spirited** and ▶ **1642**

1317

Look at your codewords and titles. Check a box for each of the following that applies:

❑ The codeword **Rhapsody**
❑ The codeword **Quake**
❑ The codeword **Pumped**
❑ The codeword **Nanny** or the title **Godslayer**

If three or more boxes are now ticked ▶ **875**

If two or fewer are ticked ▶ **1160**

1318

A final howl, a spitting of sparks – the spanner is torn out of your hands and flung off with enough momentum to disembowel a cyclops – and the disk of the buoyancy rotor snaps into perfect alignment. Now, instead of a mess of jangling strands, it spins up to a blur of light, the sound settling to a modulated hum that is almost soothing.

With a stomach-flipping lurch, the *Sunrise* bobs up past the rooftop and towards the open sky. Your upwards arc carries you directly towards the colossal figure of Thanatos, looming against the heavens. He extends a giant hand, inexorable as storm-swept clouds, thinking to snatch you out of the air. But the ship is gaining speed. It clears his titanic grip, his fingers closing on empty space directly under the keel.

The ship rises up and up, past growling thunderheads piled up like crags into the sky. Rain pelts the deck. You rise into dank, enveloping cloud and break through to the clear night above where the stars are hard and bright as distant diamonds. Impossibly far below, the streets and buildings of the city are mere toys half-seen in the murk.

Thanatos looks up, his hand raised to draw back his cowl. A moment later and his unshielded gaze would have blasted the ship to atoms, but you are sailing safe among the silent constellations. Even death cannot catch you now.

▶ 1067

1319

'Where didn't he travel to?' says the head.

'Lots of places.'

'Yes, obviously, but there's one particular region you might expect a dead man to have on his mind.'

▶ 133

1320

The curio shop has windows as thick as bottle glass and a door that rattles a clapperless bell as you step inside. The interior is filled with polished wooden cases, each containing colourful artifacts from around the world. There are crystal globes filled with sand from distant shores, jewellery wrought to the tastes of vanished tribes, and incomprehensible trinkets from empires of the distant past.

The shopkeeper, stooped and thin but with a surprisingly youthful face, stands behind the counter in a pose that suggests he has been waiting for you. Half-closing his eyes, he smiles and spreads his arm out in an expansive gesture, inviting you to stay and browse.

Look for something to buy ▶ 496

Offer something for sale ▶ 526

1321

'Hah!' Agamemnon explodes in a gust of laughter. 'You Amazons, you don't mind what you say. Hear her, Melelaus? Tongue as sharp as most men's swords.'

'So I'll send her back to her father. Agreed?'

'Yes, go on.'

Now that you've called his bluff, he has lost interest in Astynome. You usher her from the tent and tell her to return home.

▶ 1529

1322

Tick the Wound box on your Adventure Sheet if it was not ticked already.

The crew are all experienced fighting men. Under your orders they quickly form into defensive ranks and muster behind the Minotaur, whose thick hide makes him almost impervious to the insect-creatures' pincers. With Zoë and her men advancing from the other side, you surround the insects. The fight is long and exhausting, but finally you have slaughtered every last one.

'Don't relax just yet,' says Ancaeus. 'There are still larvae and unhatched eggs below decks.'

He gives orders to sterilize the hold, gathering up the eggs and wriggling larvae and casting them overboard into the void.

▶ 653

1323

As you approach what most people take to be a vacant lot there is a ripple in the air – in fact, in the very fabric of reality. A veil of illusion is drawn away and you behold the palace of Vulcan as it shimmers into solidity, a majestic structure with high walls enclosing a complex of buildings and courtyards.

The closer you get the more the palace takes on weight and substance as if from empty air. Now you can see sentries in glittering armour, bright pennants streaming from the adamantine ashlar walls, sweeping marble arches decorated in rainbow mosaic, and high windows with frames of orichalcum, ivory and gold. The palace stretches up and up until, far above, ornate sky-piercing towers and gleaming-tiled roofs overlook the city.

If you have the **Face of Wisdom** (INGENUITY +3) and this box ❑ is empty, tick it and ▶ 598; otherwise read on.

Enter the palace ▶ 74

Not right now ▶ 722

1324

The Street of the Sun and Moon has an air of exclusivity. Though the townhouses here are not showily grand, there is an aura of wealth and taste visible in the architecture and the clothing of the residents.

A long curving promenade of sparkling marble flagstones sweeps north-east from here all the way to the Avenue of Subsolanus. Along this broad crescent stand the mighty houses of the Olympian gods. Some of the grander buildings are connected by arched bridges of veined marble that span the street below, sparing the highest echelons of the nobility the indignity of rubbing shoulders with the crowds.

If you have a **gilt-edged invitation** ▶ 961

To go straight to a city location that you already know about, note **1324** as your Current Location, then ▶ 1432

Or you can go:

North-west towards the centre of the city ▶ 1642

South-east towards the watchtower ▶ 570

Along the crescent of the temples ▶ 103

1325

'What's that you have there?' Her mocking smile hardens as she sees the amber globe in your hand. 'Where did you get that?'

'I found it in an idol moment.'

She wastes no more time on words. Her hands sweep up, summoning a dark mist that billows out. Instantly the hall is flooded in lightlessness, a primal void that stirs atavistic fears of the unknown. But you are no stranger to fear. You've learned to accept it as an inevitable companion to danger, and to endure it and keep on going.

Also, you're given heart by the last look you saw in Nyx's eyes before the darkness fell. She too is afraid.

The Eye of Hyperion begins to glow. At first it's no more than a faint spark, but it grows brighter, golden light streaming from it and pushing back the encircling darkness. Nyx's face, dimly outlined by the light, contorts as she focuses on summoning all her power. Torrents of black nullity pour down onto the glowing Eye. It gutters, dimming, and you fear it's about to be extinguished. But within it lies the essence of the titan of the sun, once almost the equal of the queen of night. Pulsing, the golden light flares up, resisting Nyx's power for a moment more.

Her face looms huge and white in the abyssal darkness, etched with the strain as she summons all her might. Beads of sweat stand out glistening on her brow.

'Weakened as I am by the effort of killing the Olympians,' she mutters between clenched teeth, 'yet you will see I am unconquerable.'

She might be right. In the battle of light and dark, she's gradually gaining the upper hand. The beams of light from the Eye are sputtering, growing dimmer as the void swallows them up.

The glow becomes weaker and weaker, no brighter than a candle flame now in the immensity of utter darkness.

Then – glimmers appear like birthing stars, reflecting and rekindling the fire in the heart of the Eye. It burns brighter now, increasing unstoppably, a blinding nova that drives Nyx back. The hall around you blisters away into a white totality, but not before you see mirrors that have angled down from the walls and ceiling. They are magnifying the intensity of Hyperion's jewelled eye till it outshines the dawn of the universe.

Nyx can bear it no longer. She drops to her knees, shrivelling in the glare. With a scream like a universe dying, she explodes into a myriad motes that drift and fade like fine ash.

With a click the mirrors retract into the wall. Beside the panel that controls them stands the god Vulcan, supported by metal braces around his misshapen legs. His face, twisted by deformity, would be ugly in a mortal, but in a god even ugliness is beautiful.

'Everyone forgets about me,' he says. 'It's a curse and a blessing.'

► 281

1326

A lone, skeletal tree creaks as the wind tosses it to and fro, its silhouette clawing hopelessly at the roiling black clouds above. The air is gritty with the taste of pulverized bricks and charred wood.

Note **626** as your Current Location and then ► 549

1327

You are led back through the ranks to a medics' tent near the beach. Even so early in the morning, already the casualties are piling up. The sand is sticky with blood from which rises a sweet smell like a butcher's shop. The air carries an aroma of healing herbs and the acrid pungency of woodsmoke from braziers used to heat the saws and knives that the physicians use on the most grievously hurt. Strangely there's not much noise, just the urgent muttering of the physicians and the occasional gasp of pain from one of the men waiting to be treated. The loudest sound is the rhythmic surge and suck of waves against the shore.

'I can't waste time here,' you tell the soldiers who have carried you to a wooden cot. 'I need to get back out on the plain.'

'Plenty of time for that, Amazon,' says one as they leave you. 'Usually we fight until sunset. Let these healers wash out the wound and get a poultice on it. The battle will still be in full swing when you get back.'

If you have the codeword *Nanny* and don't have the codeword *Royal* ► 1573

Otherwise ► 864

1328

You push Chipos out of your bedroom before the servants are up, but he's not the sort to keep a conquest to himself. He obviously brags about it to anyone who will listen, because you notice the maids giving you odd looks at breakfast. Then it dawns on you that he's probably slept with all of them too.

Later, as you and your major domo go over the household accounts, you can't help but notice a slight frostiness in his manner. He clearly thinks you've demeaned yourself. And as word spreads through the town it's clear that others disapprove too. You pass a couple of neighbours who cut you dead, turning their faces to a shop window to avoid saying hello.

'With a servant,' you hear one of them say.

'I've seen the fellow,' chuckles the other. 'Filthy looking wretch. I hope she had a good bath afterwards.'

Lose 2 Glory down to a minimum score of 1.

▶ 515

1329

Her shriek rings out into the sky, louder than ten thousand voices. Like a crack through the world, it silences the struggling armies. Soldiers stand stock-still, staring up, straining their eyes to see beyond the veil that hides the gods. The goddess, recoiling from your attack, stumbles and falls in the way that mountains crumble, or avalanches detach and slide out of the sky – slowly, inexorably, terribly.

You land sprawling on the plain and scramble to get out of her way. The huge figure blots out the sun and even the armies see her now. They recover their wits and scatter as the goddess crashes down in their midst. The rocks of the plain shear and split with the impact, throwing up a bank of dust across the hills. Chariots are flung like jumbled toys.

Then time speeds up again and the sprawled god is gone, furious with indignation and shame, and for an instant the world pauses as all present see with wild eyes that it is possible for human hands to strike a blow against the immortals.

Rising to your feet, you look around. The shock on people's faces tells you that was a deity you toppled. Both Achaeans and Ilionians, their quarrel forgotten, stare aghast at you.

'What's the matter with you all?' you say. 'See, you don't have to let them control your lives. We can fight back against the – '

▶ 1527

1330

Moving back out of range of Dydkos's rapier, you step under the boughs of a willow tree. The leaves enclose you like a tent, hiding you from his eyes while you strap the antlers to your brow.

With slashes of his sword he cuts through the foliage. You see him blink in astonishment.

'What is it, my love?' says the girl.

'The one who attacked me has gone.' He steps forward and pats your neck gently. 'There's only this deer.'

'Are we safe?'

He looks to and fro, scrutinizing the bushes. 'They could be hiding anyway. But I have an idea. Quickly, darling, get up on the deer's back. It will carry you to safety while I look for that interloper.'

He lifts her onto your shoulder. They both think you are

a deer, and as you draw a cloven hood across the turf you could almost believe it yourself.

Ride off with her ▶ 1108

Dispel the illusion and reveal yourself ▶ 349

1331

Odysseus gives a short burst of laughter. 'I should say not! He was only fifteen years old when we first landed on this beach.'

'That's young to go to war.'

'Yes...' He grimaces, stroking his beard. 'You see, it was foretold that we'd never conquer Ilion unless Achilles was with us. So I went and found him and sort of talked him into it. His mother wasn't at all pleased. Her being a sea nymph, I always wonder when I board a ship whether it's going to be wrecked or not.'

Change the subject ▶ 204

Bid him farewell for now ▶ 735

1332

A bright patch skitters across the dark brick wall opposite the prison. Glancing up, you see a dazzling flicker from one of the windows. Somebody up there is signalling you with a mirror tilted to catch the few beams of sunlight that penetrate to this dreary corner of the city.

A closer look at the patch of reflected light on the wall reveals an image – a butterfly with cogwheel wings. It must have been scratched out of the surface of the mirror. But what does it mean?

If you have a **bronze butterfly** ▶ 208

If not but you have the codeword *Neural* ▶ 1401

Otherwise if Polymnia is your companion and this box ❑ is empty, tick it and ▶ 1091

Failing all the above you can only make your way back to the Avenue of the Anvil while pondering the message's meaning ▶ 63

1333

There's no letter inside the package to indicate who sent it, just a slender book of stories so pithy that they are barely more than aphorisms. Nonetheless as you read them you feel a warm sense of empathy with the foibles of the characters depicted. There are vain donkeys, greedy squirrels, haughty cockerels, crafty frogs, miserly beetles, and several dozen more such oddities – yet all the stories are really about humanity, not animals, and they leave you with insights you can apply in your daily life. Gain +1 CHARM up to a maximum score of +5.

▶ 97

1334

'Huh, I was only doing you a favour, girl,' he says, leaping out of bed. 'You don't know what you're turning down.'

You sit up and give him a long look in the moonlight. 'I can see exactly what I'm turning down, thank you.'

He storms out in a huff. The next morning when you come down for breakfast, the servants tell you that he has packed his bags and left. Delete him from the Companion box on your Adventure Sheet.

▶ 97

1335

You break her neck with a single powerful blow, then fling the poker back into the fire and call for your servants. They come running.

'Take that away,' you say, nodding towards the body as you go back to bed.

'What should we tell the militia?' asks your valet.

'Tell them I fished it out of Hades but I decided to throw it back.'

▶ 97

1336

'What floats downriver and needs its nappy changed every few hours?' says Daedalus.

'Is this a riddle?'

'Show is better than tell. Why don't you go take a cruise along the Styx.'

'The river Styx? In Hades?'

'Hey, you make it sound grim. There are barges you can hire. It's glamping, really.'

'And what am I looking for when I get there?'

'Some people say babies are cute.'

You sigh. 'It's a long way to Hades.'

'I can send you straight there if you like.' Daedalus indicates the chrysalis, which at his gesture again dissolves into the swarm of glowing gold insects.

'That could work,' you say as the cocoon of light surrounds you and starts to lift you back towards the surface. 'By the way, I keep meaning to ask: how *do* these beetle things make me intangible?'

'Actually they discorporate you atom by atom and rebuild you at your destination.' He waves his hand. 'Forget I said that. Better not to think about it. So, do you want to go straight to the Styx, or back up to the city? I'll get the tootlebugs to take you somewhere random – again, just as a precaution in case you were followed.'

Which do you prefer? (If you choose Hades you must say goodbye to your companion, if you have one, as nobody will willingly travel there.)

'Direct to Hades.' ▶ **145** in *The Houses of the Dead*

'Somewhere in the city will do for now.' ▶ **1649** in this book

1337

❑

Do not tick the box above unless you were told to do so in the section you just turned from.

If the box is empty   ▶ **529**
If you just put a tick in the box   ▶ **1455**
If the box was already ticked   ▶ **1441**

1338

Crossing the hall, you catch up with Lord Sphingo.

'I don't think we've been introduced,' he says severely.

'We have a mutual acquaintance. A bookseller who has recently retired from the business.'

He says nothing, but for a moment there is murder in his eyes.

'I think he would have wanted you to have these,' you say, handing over the letters. Delete them from your list of possessions.

He scans the contents. 'Interesting. You'll take something for your trouble?'

'If you insist, my lord.'

He gives you three **lava gems** (add them to your Adventure Sheet) and shows you out.

▶ 1642

1339

With stirring cries, your troops surge forward, rushing against the massed ranks of night-demons like a mighty wave crashing against jagged black rocks. Snarls and screams fill the air along with spurts of blood and ichor. Neither side can give ground. This is a desperate battle to the bitter end.

Going down the boxes below, tick all the ones for which you have the corresponding codeword, title or item. Note that the Amazons and the Fae are stronger than the other units, and so count double.

❑ ❑   The title **Amazonian Queen**
❑   The title **Public-Spirited**
❑   The title **Friend of the Nomads**
❑   The codeword *Rhyme*
❑   The codeword *Rock*
❑   The title **Murmillo Recruit**
❑ ❑   The item **Horn of the Fae**

If 6 or more boxes are ticked   ▶ **1243**
If 4-5 boxes are ticked   ▶ **1074**
If 3 or fewer boxes are ticked   ▶ **78**

1340

You get talking to a number of important-looking folk who flatteringly address you as an equal. You learn later that it is a rule of Pemphreda's salon that guests leave their notions of social status at the door. The ensuing camaraderie does not extend to the servants, who hand out the drinks and snacks with an air of lofty disdain.

If you have the codeword *Rectangle* ▶ 1005
Otherwise ▶ 1615

1341

After a last look at the distance-blurred crags and luminous fields of ice and snow, you turn and descend the tower.

▶ 451

1342

'The Olympians are happy to sit back while you fight their battles,' says Daedalus. 'Then when you've won they'll step in and mop up.'

'Kind of a cynical way of looking at things.'

'Don't knock it. It's kept me alive this long. Good luck, hero.' He jumps down through the hatch and pulls it shut behind him.

Nyx watches him go with a sneer on her lips. 'That Daedalus,' she laughs. 'He could never bring himself to say he's just scared.'

▶ 1533

1343

A bushy-bearded man, burly as a bear, wades out of the lake taking great gulps of air and slapping his broad, hairy chest. 'Taste that morning breeze!' he bellows. 'Fresh as it used to blow off the meadows of Arcady, before that poor realm went to seed.'

'You don't care for fields and forests, perhaps?'

He snorts like a bull. 'It's because I care too deeply that I never go back to Arcadia now. There's a blight on the land and to see it gives me heartache. Why else would I come to this city? Bricks and mortar, dust, stink, the press of crowds, the noise of commerce – these things give me no pleasure, I assure you. I'm Bosk, by the way.'

He folds your hand in a grip of iron. You introduce yourself, wincing. 'Can't anything be done to put Arcadia to rights?'

Bosk grins – a friendly smile, but still a smile with something savage in it. 'That would call for a hero,' he booms. 'D'you know any?'

The breeze and the birdsong in the trees is stilled as you think about your answer:

'Me, I can do it.' ▶ 533
'Sorry, can't help.' ▶ 13

1344

You wrench yourself free and scrabble up out of the grave, kicking at the cold arms that are trying to drag you back. Sprawling across the damp grass, you kick lumps of earth back into the grave on top of the spectre.

'You cannot escape me forever,' it howls into the mist as you run off. 'We have eternity together.'

You blunder your way through the mist just in time to slip out of the gate before it's locked for the evening.

▶ 1617

1345

You turn back towards Zeus. 'I'm ready.'

Bosk puts a meaty hand on your shoulder. 'One more thing before you go. You know that well in the Avenue of the Anvil? If you left anything there, don't forget to go and retrieve it before you take on the Night Queen.'

His words echo around you. His face, the hall, the assembled gods of Olympus – everything swims and fades and you feel yourself falling through the void between worlds.

Get the codeword *Rhombus* and ▶ 73

1346

If you have the codeword *Quench* ▶ 1056
If not ▶ 824

1347

After dispelling the glowing cocoon that brought you here, the tiny mechanical beetles settle to the floor.

You are in a small chamber with no obvious exits. In the centre is a cage of what looks like intertwined black hairs, the long strands forming bars around a strange prisoner. He is translucent, barely visible except when he moves to shake the bars of the cage. He seems to be struggling with all his might, but though the strands of hair seem fragile he is barely able to move them.

Snap the bars to free him ▶ 1230
Leave him trapped ▶ 537

1348

You crawl between the gravestones until you are close enough to see the figure clearly between drifting banks of fog. It is no undead monster, just a thin young woman dressed in grave-soiled rags.

'It's only like eating an ortolan,' she's muttering to herself between grisly mouthfuls. 'No more shameful. Got to live. Think of suckling pig. The mould – no, no, it's finest truffles. Soil must do when there's no salt. Needs must, needs must.'

Your heart leaps in horror as you recognize her – Tritona, the late Lord Xechasiaris's youngest daughter. You turned her away from your door when she came as close to begging as her pride allowed. So this is what she's been reduced to – not only stealing from the dead, but feeding on their rancid flesh.

Speak to her, she deserves pity ▶ 1207

Attack her, she needs to die ▶ 19

1349

You are both tiring. The only sounds in the study are your ragged breathing and the careful tread of your feet as you circle each other.

Throw the poker in her face ▶ 1020

Thrust it straight at her ▶ 459

Swing it like a club ▶ 219

1350

Daedalus takes up his tools. 'Well, I've got work to do and no doubt you've got hero things you need to get on with.'

'No more errands?'

He grins at you. 'I'll take it from here. Don't worry, the world's safe in our hands.'

He claps his hands and the gold beetles whip through the air around you, curving space in on itself in a glowing energy field that carries you up in a bubble that slips through the spaces between atoms and deposits you in a street on the far side of town.

▶ 325

1351

Your own deity brings you into the presence of the gods of Olympus. With their power restored they are once again far beyond your perception. You have a sense of vast marble halls, like the view an ant might have of an earthly palace. The amethyst blue of the sky, the sculpted whiteness of the clouds, the sunbeams like solid shafts of gold, the invigorating chill of the air, the waft of sublime perfumes – this is an intensity of reality that almost burns your senses.

'My mortal has recovered the world from the Night Queen,' says your deity.

'That is good. The titans are imprisoned again. Disorder is banished. All is as it should be.'

Zeus waves his hand, perhaps. You sense that he has already lost interest.

You have only fleeting impressions of the faces of the gods, too huge and numinous for your mind to comprehend. You feel yourself drawn away. Your surroundings swirl, melt, reform. Now you no longer stand in the rarefied air of Olympus but back on the streets of

Vulcan City

'Too much to expect the gods to be grateful, huh?' says Dunamis when you speak to her later.

'Who needs a reward from them? We set out to defeat Nyx and we succeeded. Whether the gods acknowledge it or not, we saved their big holy arses.'

'Even so,' she says, scowling, 'I wouldn't have minded a hundred blessings or a casket full of lava gems or something.'

'It's a reward you're after? Come outside.'

With an arm around her shoulders, you lead her to the door. Vulcan City is once more the noisy, teeming, chaotic, wonderful melting pot of old. You make your way along the street.

A vendor waves, pointing to the wares on her stall. 'Delicious pastries.'

You press on through the crowds of people.

'Hello, love.'

'Five pyr? Five? I'd be cutting my own throat.'

'Was it the second left, or the third?'

'But, Dad, I want to see the puppets.'

'Look at these prices. You'd need to be Midas.'

'Hey, I'm walking here!'

You push through a group of travellers from Arcadia who are so dazzled by the sights of the city that they aren't looking where they're going. 'Oops, sorry,' says Dunamis, bumping into one.

'See what I'm talking about?' you say. 'The gods are like infants: selfish, vain, given to tantrums, moved by petty whims. Let them sit up on their remote peak and imagine they rule us. They have none of this – this glorious, surprising, adventure-filled mess we live in.'

You turn to her. There's a bag of coins in her hand. Where did that come from?

'Fancy a drink?' she says.

1352

A traveller arrives at the door. At first you take him for a beggar, so ragged and dusty are his clothes, but when he greets you it is in the unmistakably refined tones of your former major-domo.

'Your grace,' he says in a choked voice, bowing deeply, 'I have often thought of you as I tramped the flinty roads that lie between here and far-off Iskandria. It gladdens my heart to see you have restored your fortunes after that deplorable business. The rank ingratitude!'

He is too discreet to describe the way you were evicted from your palace overlooking Iskandria's azure bay, though the look you exchange says that you both remember it all too vividly.

He has obviously fallen on hard times, and as you reminisce about happier times part of your mind is racing to think of some way to make it up to him. Obviously to offer him any position in this household below the rank of major-domo would be insulting, but you already have a perfectly capable factotum. A gift of cash? But then you would be treating him like the beggar you first assumed him to be.

Appoint him as your new major-domo ▶ 417

Give him some money – decide how much, cross it off your Adventure Sheet, and ▶ 67

Try to find him a position in another household ▶ 1646

Tell him you can't help ▶ 1077

1353

Your mansion is a tall building of lustrous green marble and white stucco. A sparkling fountain in the forecourt freshens the air as you approach. Beyond a heavy bronze gate, steps lead up to a door framed by Corinthian columns.

If you have any scars and this box ❑ is empty, tick it and ▶ 958

Otherwise ▶ 604

1354

One of the Myrmidons helps you to secure the straps of your armour. 'It can take quite a battering in the thick of melee,' he says. 'Last thing you want is your breastplate falling off at a crucial moment.' You give him hooded stare and he blushes. 'I didn't mean… my lady…'

'At ease, soldier, I'm messing with you.' You throw a glance at Achilles's tent. 'Still angry?'

'Not at you. In fact he told me to assign you the best horses for your chariot. He would… It would go hard with him if you were hurt out there, my lady.'

'With me too, but I don't plan on taking any punishment, just dishing it out.'

▶ 166

1355

Just as it seems that all is lost, a faint light penetrates the veil of darkness that Nyx has summoned.

'Look!' cries a voice. And as the light grows brighter, both your own allies and Nyx's demonic minions stop fighting and gaze up into the sky.

A beautiful golden angel is descending out of the night. A nimbus like a new dawn surrounds her. It is the goddess Eos. She smiles her tranquil smile and a blistering white light shines down, kindling a greater fire in the core of the Eye of Hyperion.

The light grows, a white totality, rebounding from the transformed buildings all around, casting a blinding incandescent blaze that makes the assembled hordes look like figures of glowing white wax. The combined radiance of Eos and Hyperion fills the air, blazes high into the starless sky, blots out everything in a glare like the sun's heart.

Nyx can bear it no longer. She drops to her knees, shrivelling in the glare. With a scream like a universe dying, she explodes into a myriad motes that drift and fade like fine cindery ash.

▶ 332

1356

Lose the codeword **Robber** unless you also have the codeword **Recursive**.

'Just go round to the Grumbles whenever you want to call in the favour,' you tell the storekeeper.

He smiles complacently. 'Oh, I know Zinc. It's not the first time I've bought a favour from him.'

Now ▶ 496 and tick the box there before reading on.

1357

As the coin hits the water, the surface breaks into a million glittering silver points of light. Shadows play across it, a half-seen vision in which you see your own hand magnified to the size of the sculpture. You are at bay on a high place, surrounded by a legion of the things that skulk in darkness: baying werewolves, vampires with bloodless faces eaten by grave-mould, and flitting demons with wings of stretched ink-blue skin. Yet though your foes are a savage multitude, you stand your ground with no fear of them. In your fingers you are holding the hourglass as the last sands trickle through. And as the last grain falls –

The vision disappears and you are once again standing beside a fountain whose cool iridescent spray dances in the late afternoon sunlight.

Continue on to the menagerie ▶ 1392

Go back to the rotunda ▶ 1530

Return to the entrance courtyard ▶ 750

1358

The till is just a tin box on the counter. It's open; the killer must have prised the lock. But he or she wasn't here to rob the place – there are 50 pyr that have been left untouched. Add the sum to your cash if you want.

▶ 944

1359

You find a derelict tenement block a few doors along from Autolycus's building. The staircase is rotten but it takes you most of the way to roof level. Getting out onto a ledge, you shin up a drainpipe, climb a sloping roof, and find yourself almost opposite Autolycus's digs. You have to get across to the roof of his building, and the drop below is dizzying, but it's an easy leap. A tile dislodges under your feet, skittering down over the edge. A moment later there's the crash of it breaking several storeys below.

No sense in waiting. If Autolycus is here he can't have missed that. You throw up the window and swing inside.

He's ready for you but hasn't bothered to arm himself, even though there is a knife on the table. You also notice the walking stick, false whiskers and greasepaint that made such a convincing disguise. Now he isn't infirm and bent-backed. In fact he looks to be in the prime of life, as limber as a wolf and just as confident.

'Hypermestra,' he says to the golden android standing behind him. 'Grab this intruder, will you.'

If you have the codeword *Rifle* ▶ 622
If not ▶ 1029

1360

'To enter the Mourning Fields in Hades is not easy for one who still feels the joys of love and laughter in their heart. You must know pain and loss, and only then will you be welcome among the dead.'

'Seems like a high price to pay for a dubious reward,' you say.

'Suffering is the wages of life. You can avoid it by not caring, but that is an even heavier burden. Your path takes you to the headwaters of the Styx, where Niobe will meet you.'

'How long will she wait? Do I have to go there right away?'

'Take your time. Niobe will be there till time and space are folded back into the blueprints of Vulcan's workshop, whence they came.' She gestures for you to leave.

▶ 510

1361

You now notice another man lying on a bed of straw at the back of the cell. His eyes are open but unseeing. His chest rises and falls with shallow, monotonous breaths. The resemblance to Daedalus is unmistakable even though he must be twenty years younger.

'And that's my son, Icarus,' says Daedalus. 'Let's just get body and soul together and you can say hello.'

He touches a series of buttons on a metal box on the table. In response the chrysalis vibrates in your pocket, breaking apart into a swarm of metal beetles that fly out and start circling Icarus where he lies on the bed. A shimmering silvery glow forms between them, a ghostly image of the prone figure, that settles onto Icarus's skin and is absorbed. He gives a gasp and sits up.

'Dad! It's Nyx! She's inside the compound! She – ' He looks around at the cell, heaves a sigh. 'She got me, didn't she?'

Daedalus nods. 'She's been holding your soul to ransom for months now. That's why it's been convenient for us to be locked up here. There's not a lot she could force me to do for her while I'm in a cell. But now you've got your soul back – thanks to this obliging stranger – we can see about getting out of here.'

'There's a lot of guards between here and the exit,' you tell them. 'Even with all your spiderbot's keys, it won't be easy getting past them, especially not all of us together.'

'We won't go that way,' says Daedalus. He points up. 'The roof. You brought the wings, didn't you?'

If you have the **wings of Icarus** and want to hand them over ▶ 1098

If not ▶ 1666

1362

You try to fool her by pretending to be out of breath. It doesn't take much acting. She's as close as she's going to get, and you've got to avoid that blade in order to grapple her.

Make a GRACE and then a STRENGTH roll, both at difficulty 7. You can apply blessings to the rolls if you have them, but not item bonuses.

Succeed in both ▶ 795
Fail either roll ▶ 1497

1363

'Now!' screeches the slave trader, running in with his meat cleaver raised in both hands. His bald head and hate-contorted face shine in the gloom like a theatrical mask depicting vengeance.

At the same time the dwarf comes in low, jabbing with his wickedly sharp knife. Wounded as you are, you will need all of your fighting skill to take them both on at once.

Make a STRENGTH roll at difficulty 10.
Succeed ▶ 852
Fail ▶ 643

1364

'Impossible!' gasps Nyx as your blow skewers her dark heart. 'No mortal can harm me.'

'Mortal I am, but I am also the Godslayer.'

She sinks to her knees, the dark ichor that fills her veins pouring out from the wound like ink. But even as you step back, she raises her hand and unleashes a searing bolt of magical energy. You cry out, charred to the very core of your soul, and fall dying across Nyx's lifeless form.

▶ 42

1365

A beggar reaches out a bandaged stump, gesturing to the wooden bowl in front of him. In Vulcan City you have to harden your heart to such unfortunates, so you are quickening your pace when you recognize the language in which he is muttering.

You stop and look back. He has the narrow squint, sun-scoured face, and ritual scars of a nomad of northern Notus.

'I know you,' he says.

'I have hunted with your people.'

He shows you his disfigurements: a missing leg, a missing hand, the other lacking several fingers. 'I hunt no more,' he says.

'What happened?'

'I fell under the power of my foes. They were *katoi* and did not treat me with honour, as you see.'

'What can I do to help?' You consider putting coins in his bowl, but it would seem almost an insult.

'Somewhere in the city is my partner, Danu, who I was to meet here. Take the knife from my belt. He will recognize it.'

You take the **bone knife**. Its hilt is hard and cold in your grip; add it to your possessions.

As you are leaving, it occurs to you to ask, 'Where will I find your friend?'

He stares up at the sky. 'Orion favours you. He will guide your steps.'

To go straight to a city location that you already know about, note **161** as your Current Location, then ▶ **1432**

Or you can go:

North ▶ **333**
South ▶ **570**

1366

'You've obviously got green fingers.'

He glances at the rows of cabbages. 'Man's got to have a hobby.'

'I'm just surprised you can get anything to grow here.'

The masked face looks into yours. 'There's a knack to it. Maybe you'll find out.'

'A reward? If I behave myself?'

'Oh no.' You hear a dry chuckle echo behind the tin faceplate. 'The only people who learn that secret are the ones who displease me very badly indeed.'

▶ **1487**

1367

'I always loved this vase,' she says, lifting it carefully from the hall table.

It is of pink-tinged alabaster, light as a maiden's blush, and so delicately thin that the light makes her hands visible through it. The narrow neck is just wide enough for the stem of a single rose.

'Good choice. It is a very fine piece.'

CRASH!

'That's what you have done to our family,' she says, sweeping a hand at the shattered pieces of the vase. Her eyes flash and her voice is like an angry swan. A moment later she is back out of the door and marching haughtily down the street.

'I'll fetch a dustpan and brush,' says one of your footmen, quite unperturbed by the drama even though you realize that he must have been Tritona's servant once.

▶ **97**

1368

The butterfly rises into the air, spirals around your head, and flits in erratic jerking sweeps across the shifting cloudscape to Sphikos. As it alights on his shoulder he gives a start, amazed, and looks around to see where it came from. Seeing you, he waves and hurries back, taking care where he treads on the endlessly shifting ridges of vapour.

'I was surprised to see anything here,' he says as he reaches you. 'We're at the dawn of time. Nothing is supposed to have formed yet.'

▶ **1044**

1369

A furtive sound behind you – there's another of them creeping up for a sneak attack. You hear his soft intake of breath as he braces to swing.

Duck ▶ **848**
Kick backwards ▶ **805**

1370

Something stirs in the darkness above you. Long fingers soft as wax probe your face. The whisper of a dream in your ear awakens atavistic terrors you thought to have left behind you in childhood…

You are lying on a stone slab. Above you soars the triangular vault of a vast pyramid chamber. You hear the swish of sifting sand. The grating of stone on stone. Huge ponderous masonry blocks are sliding into place over the exits. Somehow you know that the pyramid is being sealed and will remain undisturbed for millennia. It will become your tomb if you don't get out. But in your nightmare you are unable to move. You can only lie there and listen to the stone blocks inexorably closing all around you.

Lose a total of 2 points from your attributes: CHARM, GRACE, INGENUITY or STRENGTH. You can decide which attribute is affected, and if you wish you can take 1 point from two different attributes. Then ▶ **431**

1371

Loutro goes to his room and swiftly packs a few belongings. 'Think kindly of me,' he says at the door.

'Always. Where will I find you?'

'The usual place.'

You go to embrace him but he flinches away, embarrassed, and turns to hurry off along the street without another word.

Remove Loutro from the Companion box on your Adventure Sheet, then ▶ **97**

1372

He records the transaction in a notebook and gives you a copy. Add the **curio credit** to your possessions and delete the item you've just sold him.

▶ **828**

1373

By now there's a milling throng of pursuers pressed right up to the edge of the roof. You can see the pallid, worm-gnawed features of the vampires, the red eyes and spittle-flecked jaws of the were-creatures, the misshapen features of capering nightmare demons. Baying and snarling, they are so intent on getting to you that some get jostled over the edge and fall flailing to the street far below.

There's a commotion at the back of the horde, near the stairs up onto the roof. Some of the rear ranks are turning in confusion. A vampire spins, a spear thrust into its chest, and disintegrates in a tattered cloud of dust and rags and old bones. A slim hand reaches out, pulls back the spear, and swings it in a wide arc to keep the nearest monsters at bay.

As the rabble parts you see a lithe figure in studded leather armour. In one hand she has the spear, in the other a sword that's already slick with blood. Behind her are a band of stalwart fighters, each holding their own against the night creatures that come rushing and snapping at them from all sides.

'Zoë?' You turn to the Minotaur. 'Look! It's the Princess of the Golden Band.'

The Minotaur chops a leaping were-ape off the ship's rail. 'A little helping hand can't hurt,' he grunts.

Zoë is too far off to hear you over the howling wind, but she sees your look of recognition and raises her hand in salute. She and her companions swore to come to your aid when you needed it most, and they are as good as their word.

Her surprise attack has divided the monstrous horde. Half of them turn to fight Zoë and her men. Others are still leaping from the parapet trying to get aboard, but her arrival has bought you some time. Should you stay to help the Minotaur repel boarders, or go to help get the buoyancy rotor working before the *Sunrise* loses any more height?

Keep fighting at the rail	▶ **761**
Help with the buoyancy rotor	▶ **1220**

1374

She points to the stack of letters, refusing to touch them herself, and the servant throws them on the fire. Delete them from your Adventure Sheet.

'You have done a good job,' she says. 'Though actually killing Pemon was a little extra service that I didn't expect.'

'But that wasn't – '

She holds up her hand, yawning. 'It is of no consequence. You will find your reward in that pouch. My servant will show you out.'

Get the title **Repairer of Reputations**. On the doorstep you count your money. She has paid you 200 pyr. Add it to your cash and then ▶ **1642**

1375

Ancaeus turns to you, his beard and hair matted with rainwater. 'Get the halyard onto that winch!' he shouts over the roar of the gale.

You grab the loose end of the rope he's hauling and start winding it onto the winch. Gusts of wind tear at the rope as Ancaeus tries to steady it. Blood is flowing freely where the rough fibres have cut deep into his hands, but with his face set against the pain he takes a running jump to seize the halyard further up, dragging it down while you crank furiously at the winch.

The deck lurches to one side. The vessel is now several metres below the level of the roof, making it easier for your foes to jump across. The Minotaur is holding his own for now, but for how long?

If you have the codeword ***Recursive*** ▶ **1437** immediately; otherwise read on.

'We need to get higher,' you yell to Ancaeus.

'It's because we're not moving. She'll gain buoyancy once we're under way.' He staggers back, buffeted by the tempest, and takes hold of the winch. 'The sail's got snagged, can you see?'

He's right. The canvas has caught on a spar, wrapped around it by the wind, and that's why it's not opening.

You can see from Ancaeus's injured hands that he's in no condition to go aloft. 'I'll free it. You stay at the winch.'

Make a GRACE roll at difficulty 17.

Succeed ▶ 859
Fail ▶ 334

1376

'This guy. He doesn't by any chance have a crow's beak tattoo on his face?'

Viranos stares at you. 'No, that's Belus. Why?'

'Just wondered if this could be a two birds with one stone type situation.'

▶ 1093

1377

Agamemnon is raging at his advisers. You already know why. Plague is sweeping through the Achaean camp. Men lie on their cots moaning, faces bathed in sweat. Doctors hurry from tent to tent, but they are too few and their medicines bring no more than a brief respite from the pain. At the far end of the beach, soldiers are building pyres on which to burn the bodies of those men and animals that succumb to the dreaded disease.

'Does nobody have a cure for this pestilence?' bellows Agamemnon.

'What poultice can we apply, what herbs can we burn to drive off the displeasure of a god?' says the king's brother, Melelaus.

'Even if we set sail now,' puts in the general known as Little Ajax, 'we may not escape death.'

'Set sail?' Agamemnon batters his fist against the table in front of him, scattering battle plans. 'You think I'll abandon the siege now? That I'd let the plague defeat us where Priam's forces could not?'

'What can we do?' says old Nestor, who never fears to say what others are thinking. 'By keeping the girl and insulting her father, Chryses, you have incurred the wrath of Apollo. His unseen arrows land among us.'

If you are a worshipper of Apollo ▶ 668

If not, you can:

Advise Agamemnon to return the girl ▶ 599

Stay out of it ▶ 416

1378

'I'm going to piss on your corpse,' says Sakan, dropping into a fighting crouch. Even in the gloom, you can see the eager bloodthirsty light in his eyes now that you're wounded.

Make a STRENGTH roll at difficulty 9. Remember that being wounded means you take an extra −1 modifier to this roll.

Success ▶ 1040
Failure ▶ 1078

1379

'All right. So where do the ruby and the cups come in?'

'Like so.' She puts the ruby under one of the cups. 'Now I move the cups around – here, there, back around. Is your eye fast enough to follow? Think you know which cup the ruby is under?'

Roll two dice and add your INGENUITY – just your innate INGENUITY score, without adding any bonuses for items. You can use a blessing, if you have one, to reroll once.

score 4 or less ▶ 215
score 5-11 ▶ 658
score 12 or more ▶ 963

1380

'Which way did you turn in your dream?' asks Dydkos. 'When you came to find us?'

'Right, I think, if this was the door I came through.'

'Sometimes I have the gift of second sight. It's telling me you found the well between worlds.'

'There was a well…' You shake your head. 'Dreams. Vivid at the time, but you wake up, they're gone.'

He looks along the street. 'It's hard to find that place, but just as there are vaults that let you move things between life and death, the well allows you to retrieve items from this reality when you have been carried elsewhere.'

'OK, that makes even less sense than finding a lost person in a dream, but I'll go along with it.'

'Right would take you south from here.' He looks along the street. 'I don't know, it might be worth seeing if you can find it again. Farewell.'

▶ 515

1381

❑ ❑

Do not tick either of the boxes unless you were told to do so in the section you just turned from.

Neither of the boxes is ticked ▶ 914
One box is now ticked ▶ 704
Two boxes are ticked ▶ 980

1382

As you unfold the butterfly's wings, it begins to glow. Rising into the air it flutters higher and higher until it is level with the barred window where you saw the mirror flashing. A hand reaches out and draws the butterfly inside.

Minutes pass. You eye the prison gates, knowing that if the guards spot you hanging around they'll chase you off.

Or even arrest you.

The butterfly returns, settling on your shoulder, and now it begins to play back a recorded message – but one much longer than any you have been able to impress on its memory cylinder.

'I am Daedalus,' says the recorded voice. 'I am imprisoned in the highest tower of this building along with my son Icarus.'

'And you want me to help you escape.'

'Two points,' the butterfly's message continues. 'First, this is a recording of my voice, so don't bother answering back. Second, don't assume I need anyone to break me out of here. I could escape any time I like, but if I did so then I could be compelled to serve the titan Nyx, Mother of Darkness. She has imprisoned my boy's soul in a cage and while she holds power of life and death over him, I would be forced to do her bidding. Therefore it suits my purpose to stay in my cell until Icarus's soul is freed. That's where you come in. Whoever you are, you're obviously resourceful or you wouldn't have been able to follow my blueprint for the mestramaton. And you must be familiar with Hades. So what I need is for you to find Nyx's throne room beneath the volcano across the Plains of Howling Darkness and there recover Icarus's soul. Then come back here.'

'Hades, volcano, throne room, soul. Got it.'

'Do this if you believe in the cause of Mankind. No longer are we to be either pets or prey to the gods and monsters of antiquity. Now is the time to strike a blow for freedom, for the sake of all humani– '

There is a click as the butterfly's memory cylinder reaches the end. Stiffening, it folds its wings tightly around its body to form a hard tubular casing. You don't know what that signifies but it might be needed so you stow it in your pocket. Daedalus – if that's really who the message came from – has given you a lot to think about.

Get the codeword *Restore*. Remove the **bronze butterfly** from your list of possessions as you cannot use it now it has turned into a chrysalis. There is nothing else to be done here, so you retrace your steps to the Avenue of the Anvil.

▶ 63

1383
Using the wings you could travel across the miasmal skies of Hades and alight at a safe landing place of your choice. To do that you will need the Vulcanverse book *The Houses of the Dead*, and you cannot take any companion with you.

Take to the air ▶ 29
Not now ▶ 1655

1384
You wait, wishing furiously, but nothing happens. The lava gem lies at the bottom of the fountain, gleaming like a droplet of honey against the algae-spotted grey marble.

You reach for it. The fat man waves his hands in horror. 'You cannot take back what you've offered to the nymph,' he says in shocked tones.

Nonsense – take it back ▶ 1644
He's right, it would be sacrilege ▶ 51

1385
The moon and stars are lost in thick shelves of cloud that race by overhead, as though the sky itself were desperate to escape what is going to happen here tonight.

Note **881** as your Current Location and then ▶ 549

1386
He spits into the trench. 'Vulcan made that. Impervious to any ordinary weapon, so I heard. Who's he give it to? The golden boy, the champ. Achilles is who I mean. And him a sodding demigod already. What's he need with miraculous armour? Give it to one who needs it, that's what I say. But no, in this world the rich get richer.'

'So it's Achilles' armour? Why does he leave it out in the open like that?'

'To show he doesn't need it. Why strap on Olympian battle-gear when you've got prophecy armour? Achilles won't die till Ilion falls, and that's as sure as the sun coming up. His old ma the sea-goddess got Zeus himself to promise it. That armour on its rack there, sitting in the wind and rain, that's him saying, "Bring it on, Ilion!"'

Try another tack ▶ 1261
Walk away ▶ 735

1387
The city gate looms out of the darkness, monumental columns of shattered stone standing out starkly in the light of burning buildings. The noticeboard's screen gleams like a slab of polished obsidian, surrounded by debris but undamaged.

If you have **Vulcan's diadem** ▶ 837
If not ▶ 1084

1388
The wings snap out, straining like a ship's sail against the wind. You launch yourself off the parapet just as taloned hands clutch at you. They're too late. You twist around in mid-flight, laughing at the frustrated faces of your pursuers.

The danger isn't over yet. As you swoop across the sky, a blast of furnace-heat swims through the air around you.

On the rooftop opposite are a dozen golden androids who between them are manhandling a wide cannon-like weapon to point at you. The mouth of the weapon glows angry red. It's a heat projector. No one but Vulcan himself could have built such a thing, except perhaps the inventor Daedalus. Of course! He designed the wings. Who better to contrive a weapon to counter them?

The remaining wax evaporates instantly in the heat. The ailerons seize up. The wall of the building opposite is dead ahead and you can no longer steer. Angling downwards in a desperate attempt to lose height before the crash, you see a few figures in the street far below, pointing up in alarm. A moment later you slam into the wall. The wings splinter on impact and you drop in a rapid spiral like a broken leaf. The ground rushes up and smashes you with numbing force.

You lie stunned in the broken wreckage of the wings. A colossal foot descends to the street beside you, landing with a tremor that shakes the surrounding buildings and sends cracks spreading through the flagstones. Painfully you roll over to behold pitiless Thanatos, god of death, standing like a mountain against the raging storm.

▶ 595

1389

Strong buffeting winds tear at your limbs as you desperately scramble up the side of the dome. The blinding rain makes you gasp – it's like icy gravel flung in your face. From below comes the cacophonous shrieking of Night's legion of monsters.

A growl. You feel the shock as a were-beast's jaws snap shut on your ankle. Its teeth don't penetrate your boot, but its weight tugs you back. You lose your grip, slithering over the wet copper dome. With a cackle of glee a vampire lunges for you, thirsty for the taste of hot living blood.

To break free you need to make a STRENGTH roll at difficulty 12.

Succeed ▶ 108
Fail ▶ 882

1390

You go to stand in the centre of the room, directly under the dome. Hushed echoes form a continual hum. After a moment you hear a whispered voice in your ear:

'No need to keep hassling me. I'm playing the field till I hear what she's offering. And you can tell her I know what I'm worth, all right? I won't be bought for peanuts. Now piss off.'

You look around. Chipos is just outside the door, swigging wine from a glass he's just taken from a waiter's tray. The waiter is walking quickly away.

'Didn't get a glass for you,' he says as you rejoin him. 'Figured you'll probably want to keep a clear head this evening. Me, I can drink whole flagons of the stuff and it never has any effect.'

Glancing over his shoulder you notice a stone-flagged passage off the side of the courtyard. A group of partygoers come along it laughing and joking raucously. You ask where it leads but they sweep by, so engrossed in each other that they ignore you.

'Oi, you wankers,' yells Chipos. 'Answer when somebody's talking to you. Where's that passage go?'

They look back, faces blank with astonishment. 'Er… the ornamental gardens,' says one.

'Thank *you*,' snaps back Chipos.

Go along the passage to the garden ▶ 1415
Back to the first courtyard ▶ 750
Look at the hand-shaped fountain ▶ 489

1391

The climb is long and arduous. You find a rhythm and stick to it, one foot after another, trudging up and up. The incline gets steeper and the hardy grass gives way to bare flanks of rock. Now you are half walking and half climbing, picking your way along narrow tracks. The air grows colder, gusts of thin air wafting down off the ice above.

Now you are crunching across fields of snow set ablaze by the low red sun. Your breath comes in gasps at this altitude. And perhaps it is not only the altitude. No mortal has ever before set foot on this part of the mountain. There is nothing welcoming for ordinary humans in the habitat of the gods.

Lulled as you are by fatigue, cold, and the rarefied air, your arrival at the halls of Olympus takes you by surprise. A staircase built on titanic scale rises up through walls and palaces that look to have been shaped out of the living rock of the peak. All around lies a limpid skyscape stretching to the horizon.

Clambering with effort up the mighty steps you come to something like the forum of a city as it would be seen by a mouse. Palaces huge as cumulonimbus clouds loom over you.

If you have the codeword *Rye* and do not have *Requiem* ▶ 869

Otherwise ▶ 1166

1392

The reek of the place is a physical thing, a wall of musk and sweet secretions and nonhuman sweat that greets you as you arrive at the menagerie complex. It's almost overpowering: damp straw and dung, pungent fur, half-chewed carcasses, and the sharp tang of urine.

Low buildings of brown granite enclose a welter of creatures never encountered together in the wild. Cheetahs and lions face wide-eye ibex and glowering dromedaries. Bronze bars keep predator and prey apart, but the roars and growls of hungry savagery and the terrified mewling show that a massacre of the imagination is happening ceaselessly all around.

Floridly coloured songbirds and chattering albino monkeys make a cacophony against the disgruntled trumpeting of mammoths in a pit lined with blocks of ice. In one small cage a panther prowls restlessly, confined to the point of derangement. It has chewed off the tip of its own tail, an angry blot of red meat against the black fur. Reptiles creep coldly watchful around a glass case almost opaque with steam. In another case, fragile butterflies like flakes of rainbow flutter between the boughs of a bare tree.

Beside the gravel path there is a coil of **attercop silk**, which the menagerie keepers weave into nets for recapturing animals that get loose. Add it to your possessions if you take it.

Go back:

To the fountain	▶ 489
To the rotunda	▶ 1530
To the courtyard by the gate	▶ 750

1393

Your voice carries the ring of authority. The watchmen instinctively respond, following you at a jog back to the mansion.

The intruders are surprised in the hallway carrying incendiary parcels. Seeing themselves to be outnumbered, they surrender to the watchmen and are placed under arrest.

'Why didn't you run for it?' asks the officer of the watch.

'Thought you'd figure this one for a drunkard or a nutter,' says one of the intruders, nodding at you. 'We been paid to burn the place down and we reckoned we had enough time to see the job through.'

'Who paid you?' you ask as they are led away.

'Can't you guess? Some honest burghers down Arcady way who you skunked out of their life savings.'

The watchman holding the man gives him a jab in the kidneys. 'Don't you go talking to your betters that way, scum.'

If you have the codeword **Robber** and want to call in a favour from Zinc to have the Arcadian burghers punished ▶ 290

If revenge doesn't interest you ▶ 97

1394

He strokes the bristles of the **celestial tarbrush**, then fastidiously wipes his fingers on a cotton handkerchief. 'I can give you 200 pyr right now, or credit on future purchases.'

Take the cash	▶ 1447
Take the credit	▶ 1372
No deal	▶ 828

1395

If this box ❑ is ticked then ▶ 134; otherwise put a tick in it now and read on.

'If you feel fully recovered,' he says, 'then there's nothing to stop you fighting.'

'That's all I wanted to know.'

You're about to walk away when he adds, 'I will not tell you to be careful, because one warrior does not tell another warrior to take care. But if we were only a man and a woman, I would say it then. And I would add that if any harm came to you, I'd pour ashes on my head and scream the wind hoarse, and then I'd wage a war to make all this seem like children's squabbles. On that day Ilion would have a hundred widows. The city walls themselves would weep to see the slaughter I'd carry to their gates. The air would go black with funeral smoke, and King Priam would have no sons left to hold us back.'

You nod, fighting a smile. 'Then I'd better make sure I come back in one piece.'

If the Current Location recorded on your Adventure Sheet is **1500** then ▶ 41

Otherwise ▶ 140

1396

The two duellists meet at dawn. The heavy armour hampers Tekto, preventing him from making full use of his better footwork and dexterity. His opponent is clearly much less skilled in swordplay, but his greater strength means he can just batter away until finally he knocks Tekto down and forces him to yield.

'I'm afraid I didn't do a very good job,' you say to Tekto as you are walking back to the Forum after the duel.

He shrugs, wincing at a sprained muscle in his shoulder. 'I'm alive, which is not nothing.'

He gives you a purse containing 30 pyr, which you can add to your money.

▶ 1642

1397

If this box ❑ is empty, put a tick in it now and ▶ 819

If it was already ticked ▶ 1658

1398

Note 1222 as your Current Location, then ▶ 1269 and tick the box next to the Tower of Riches. From now on you will always be able to find your way back here.

1399

Another of them comes for you, its horn-hard claws skittering on the polished floor. That slows it up just enough. You drive your weapon under its thorax, prising between the hard plates of its armour to pierce the fibrous meat within. A colourless blood oozes out, slowly at first and then in violent spurts. There is a chirruping shriek and the creature folds on itself like crumpled origami.

And that leaves just the one.

▶ **1381** and tick one of the boxes there before reading on.

1400

A sense of vertigo, a dislocation, and suddenly you're back in the Achaean camp. The tents flutter in a cold sea breeze as dusk falls. The surf rattles and sighs between the pebbles. Out on the far horizon, a red furrow like a bloodstain leaks from the setting sun across the bronze water.

A squad of Achaeans are carrying a limp figure atop their outstretched arms like a fallen hero being borne to a funeral pyre. They take her to Achilles's tent and lay her down on a trestle. You are swept closer with no more volition than a leaf swept by the wind.

The figure has your face. You reach out. Soul and body reunite. You fight to return to life. You suck air into your lungs. Open your eyes. With a roar of defiance you throw yourself up off the trestle.

'Well,' says Achilles, 'that wasn't bad for your first day's battle.'

Seeing that your efforts have left you dizzy, he puts a hand on your shoulder to steady you.

'I'll be all right,' you say. 'But I suspect my god won't want me causing any more trouble.'

'The priests have already said as much.'

You nod. 'I must go to the shrine. I think now I'll be able to go back to where I came from.'

If you don't already have the **Panoply of the Lost Hero**, Achilles awards it to you. 'I have cherished our brief time together,' he says. 'When I am but a shadow in the underworld, all glory gone, remember me.'

▶ **357**

1401

You don't have a **bronze butterfly** on you, but you know how and where to make one, having seen the blueprints in Daedalus's workshop in Hades.

A guard is scowling at you from the postern gate of the prison, so you make your way back to the Avenue of the Anvil.

▶ **63**

1402

You can leave possessions and money here to save having to carry them around with you. Write in the box below anything you are leaving – or you can recover items you left here earlier by writing them on your Adventure Sheet and erasing them from the box.

```
ITEMS IN MANSION




```

When you are ready to leave ▶ Current Location

1403

You find Sakan drinking one evening in a tavern. You make eye contact as you pass his table. That's all it takes for him to think you're interested. When the tavern closes, he follows you down the street, grabs you and pulls you down a side alley.

'Don't scream or I'll knock out all your teeth,' he hisses in your ear.

As he reaches to yank off your clothes, you seize his arm and put him in a painful wrist lock. Halizon men are used to pushing their womenfolk around, and him being drunk makes it even easier. A little pressure forces him to his knees.

'Bitch,' he snarls through gritted teeth. 'Just you wait. Agh!'

'Sorry, can't hear you. Speak up.'

'Ow! No, please… Let go.'

You apply a bit more pressure, then when he's doubled up in pain you cosh him over the back of the head. While he's out cold, you strip him naked, gag him, truss him up like a turkey, hang a placard round his neck, and leave him outside the White Guard barracks to be found in the morning.

The next day you pass a couple of regular militiamen gossiping about it. 'You hear about that guy Sakan in the Black Guard?' says one.

'Yeah. Apparently he picked up a girl in a dive somewhere and she handed him his ass.'

'Had to have been an Amazon. They hate his sort.'

'What's become of him since?'

'Slunk off back home to Boreas with his tail between his legs, I heard. Let's face it, whoever did that to him he could never live it down.'

'It was the message round his neck that was the cherry,' says the other militiaman.

He leans to whisper it in his colleague's ear and they both roar with laughter. Over the coming days you hear dozens of different versions of what was written on that placard, but only you know for sure.

Get the codeword *Rock* and ▶ 1642

1404

She draws you aside. 'There's real danger in what he's asking. Sleep is the brother of Death. They are, as you know, the twin sons of Night.'

'You don't think I should do it?'

A smirk rather than a smile. 'A bit late in the day for you to start listening to my advice, isn't it? Anyway, almost everything you do is dangerous. You must balance risk and reward. Perhaps entering Hypnos's realm will forearm you against his wiles.'

'Will you come with me?'

'Into the dream world? No, the atmosphere there is toxic to me. But I have heard reports of a place between the waking world and sleep, denoted in dreamers' tales by a ruby-coloured light, and if you come across that I'd be interested to know more.'

The merchant is impatient for your answer. 'Will you help me?' he says in a hushed voice made hoarse by emotion.

Ask him what you'd need to do ▶ 113
Refuse and leave ▶ 515

1405

'Well, you've heard my tale of woe,' says Pug, stepping over to the window. 'With your permission, I'll go out the same way I came in.'

Shut the window behind him and go back to bed ▶ 97
Summon the militia to arrest him ▶ 694

1406

You are given a seat on one of the wagons that trundle out of the city a few hours later bound for Boreas. Over the next few days the air grows colder and takes on the sharp fresh smell of high meadows and snowfields.

You grow ever more impatient as the caravan stops from time to time to sell goods and resupply, but at last you are approaching the slopes of the north-west. While the other traders are making camp, the caravan driver leads you up a valley sparkling with ice.

'There.' He points to a flower with sharp flame-shaped petals the colour of a fresh bruise.

'Striking.'

'Smell it.' He squeezes a petal, working it between his fingers to bring forth a musky aroma.

'Why is it called hellebore?'

'What am I, the Muse of Knowledge? Maybe it's because elks eat it. You mustn't, though. It's toxic.'

Add the **hellebore flower** to your possessions. The caravan driver says he'll be taking the route back to Vulcan City tomorrow. 'You want to come with, or stay here?'

Go back to the city ▶ 509
Stay in the valley ▶ 621 in *The Pillars of the Sky*

1407

Something catches your eye. A faint speck moving against the static backdrop of stardust. Veering towards it, you swoop closer until you can see startled sailors crowded along the rail. It's a ship, adrift in the endless heavens.

You circle, spiralling down, and come to rest on the deck.

'Oh, it's you,' snaps the captain grumpily. 'I might have guessed.'

'Ancaeus! Last I saw of this ship, it was perched on a ledge on Mount Helikon.'

'Told you there were other seas than the ones you catch fish in. Now you see what I was talking about.'

A weighty slap on the back sends you staggering. 'Little hero!' bellows the Minotaur. 'You got away, then.'

You shake his huge hand. 'You're here too. This is quite a reunion.'

'We were coming to haul you off the palace roof,' says Ancaeus. 'His idea, not mine. I guessed you'd have your own escape plan already worked out.'

'I'm not sure you could exactly call it a plan,' you reply. 'But I'm glad I ran into you. We'd better figure out how we can defeat Nyx and her sons.'

Ancaeus gives you a sidelong glance. 'Come again.'

'When we get back to the Vulcanverse.'

'We're not going back,' he says with a snort. 'This is a one-way voyage. We're going to find a new home somewhere out there and hope that Nyx never comes looking for us.'

What do you say?

'That's crazy talk.'   ► **745**

'You've got a point.'   ► **1085**

1408

'What have you done to Hypermestra?' gasps Autolycus.

'Just slipped some grit in her lubrication. Nothing that can't be fixed by taking her apart and giving all the parts a good cleaning. But for now you'll have to face me without your lady robot for backup.'

'You fiend,' he says, staring aghast at the golden maiden as she struggles to move despite the grit clogging her every joint.

'It's best not to get attached to possessions. Especially not other people's possessions, which brings us to why I'm here.'

► **1468**

1409

There are too many to fight off on your own. Covering your head, you blunder away from the chittering swarm. You bang your shins on a crate, stumbling blindly, and by luck you find yourself at the bottom of the ladder. You scramble up it as fast as you can, swatting the larvae away, and roll out onto the deck.

Several of the crew come running over, staring in horror at the few larvae that clung onto your clothing and that you are now stomping into a gruesome paste.

'Close the hatch!' you shout as a few more of the larvae find their way up from the hold.

The Minotaur slams the hatch shut with a contemptuous sweep of his huge arm. 'That's what that stinkin' insect must've been doing down there,' he snorts. 'The mutha!'

Letting a few of the larvae out at a time, it's an easy matter to finish them off. The liquid that oozes out of their crushed bodies stains the deck an unpleasant dark green. The cabin boy scrubs for hours but it doesn't come off.

'All ships have their battle scars,' says Ancaeus philosophically. 'Iason had to replace the entire quarterdeck of the *Argo* after harpies shat all over it.'

► **653**

1410

'Prove it.'

His grin fades, leaving just the bared teeth of something vicious and predatory.

'You claim you were the one guiding me all along? Pretending to be my god?' you go on. 'So tell me what labours you set for me.'

'Insolent mortal!'

'Look, I'll make it easy for you. Just name one labour. There were twelve, so surely you can do that.'

'My brother will smear you out of existence. Not even your memory will remain.'

'Still too tricky? How about multiple choice. I'll name three tasks, you tell me which was an actual labour.'

He bellows in rage, a noise to daunt lions. Whoever thought that Sleep would be an easeful god? But you stand your ground. You are, after all, your god's chosen champion.

► **803**

1411

You sweep the floor, do the laundry, and cook a meal. Your mother picks at her plate abstractly but has no real appetite.

To store possessions or money here or to collect items that you left for safekeeping, note your Current Location is **970** and then ► **319**

Or leave your mother to her grief ► **970**

1412

You unlatch the door and slip out into the street. Hurrying along the road, you hear voices. A blue lamp flashes against the wall from a side street. It's a patrol of the night watch – half a dozen stalwart fellows with cudgels.

'Ah, officers – '

It's only as you raise your arm to accost them that you remember you've come out in just a nightgown. This will take some fast talking.

To convince them to pay heed to what you're saying, you need to make a CHARM roll at a difficulty of 20 minus your Glory score. For instance, if you have Glory of 11 then the CHARM roll is at difficulty 9. You cannot use an item such as a **laurel wreath** or **golden lyre** to influence this roll, but you can use a blessing to reroll.

The gift of the gab   ► **482**

Tongue-tied   ► **588**

1413

The declining light of the sun, which on the snow of the peak burns like a raw red wound, here touches the gentle meadows of the western slopes with a honey-coloured light. A fragrance of succulent fruit fills the air. The breeze stirs the leaves of an orchard, bringing snatches of distant music that are as quiet as murmured endearments that caress and soothe the soul. In such a place it is almost possible to forget that the world's fate teeters on a knife's edge.

'I was expecting to fight a guardian,' you say, looking around.

'Gift horse, meet mouth,' sneers Oizys.

'That doesn't even – '

'Enough chitter-chatter. Get what we came for.'

You reach up and pluck an armful of fruit. Add **food of the gods** to your possessions.

'Now sprinkle it with the toxin,' Oizys's insinuating voice whispers in your ear.

Do it   ▶ **1564**

Refuse   ▶ **737**

1414

If you don't have the codeword *Quark* and this box ❑ is empty, tick it and ▶ **925**

Otherwise read on.

You get talking to some merchants who are swapping tips about the best prices. It soon becomes a game of one-upmanship.

'You know that fishing town on the west coast of Boras?' says one. 'I can get fish there for 5 pyr and sell at Treycross in Arcadia for 15 pyr.'

'You must make a lot of trips,' laughs a rival. 'Stinky trips too, in hot weather. I'll tell you a bargain. In Hades you can find lava gems selling at 90 pyr each.'

'The Amazons will sell at that rate,' says a third merchant, scornfully flicking his camel whip. 'You can buy them at 80 pyr from the lakeside market in Notus.'

'Oh sure. If it's open,' spits another. 'But where's the best price to sell? The Spartoi will give you 120 pyr, but that's not a trade route you want to travel too often.'

'I got a caged canary off a pedlar in Notus,' says a merchant dreamily. 'On the Sacred Way, this was. I only paid 50 pyr.'

'Canaries? You can get 'em for free,' says the first man dismissively. 'Now I'll tell you what's never worth buying, and that's phoenix tears, but if you have any then that fishing town I mentioned is the place to go. Those yokels will pay up to 90 pyr each.'

▶ **716**

1415

The ornamental garden consists of terraces of lush green lawn, each as perfectly level as a palace floor. Roses bloom like jewels in the dusk beneath the coiling branches of old plane trees. You stand on a path of powdered coral that shines and sparkles. The scents are of sense-caressing jasmine, sweet pomegranate, and the warm spice of limes. From the ballroom comes the sound of singing, a choir of perfectly tuned golden throats.

Paper lanterns are strung across the entrance to the glittering ballroom. The breeze has picked up, making the lanterns sway, and partygoers are heading inside clutching their gowns and togas. 'This weather really is too bad,' you overhear somebody complaining to an automaton with a blandly smiling face.

The lawn is covered in discarded wine glasses and plates with half-eaten delicacies. The pond is rippling in the breeze. Only a few guests remain outside to brave the elements. Most are taking shelter indoors now that cold drops of rain are flicking down out of a dark grey sky.

On the far side of the lawn is an avenue of topiary monsters, hedges artfully trimmed to look like crouching sphinxes, a flock of harpies, a minotaur with bunched foliage muscles, and a hydra's rearing fan of heads poised to strike. At the far end of the topiary avenue, a marble pavilion is just visible.

You become aware of an insistent tapping sound. In one of the lanterns above the patio, a crane fly has taken shelter from the impending rain and is batting against the paper sides.

'A refuge can become a prison,' says a deep voice at your shoulder.

He is a big, barrel-chested man whose full beard shows from behind the grinning mask he wears.

'Not worried about getting wet?'

He gives a rumbling laugh. 'Scurry inside like those timid mice? You and I have faced greater threats than raindrops in our time.'

What will you reply?

'Have we met?'   ▶ **331**

'What mask is that you have on?'   ▶ **214**

'Excuse me, I can't stop to chat.'   ▶ **827**

1416

Untick the Wound box if you were injured. Also your skin is completely unblemished despite your ordeal; lose any scars you had acquired. Whoever treated your injuries must have been a miracle-worker.

'You fell from the sky,' says Achilles. 'It was three days before you'd let anyone near you and all that time you were screaming.'

'But how did I get here?'

'Perhaps Aphrodite, who favours the side of Ilion, wanted to distract me from the war, so she dropped a beautiful woman in the sea right by my camp.' He laughs. 'I'm joking, but that doesn't mean the gods didn't send you. You are an Amazon, aren't you? Zeus may mean for you to join the war against Ilion.'

You shake your head. 'I have another battle to fight, and I need to get back to it. I was brought here by a device. An hourglass.' You gesture towards your belongings, which he has piled up beside the bed.

'This?' Achilles points to pieces of broken glass that still hold a little sand. 'It was in your kitbag but it looks as if it's been in a furnace.'

'Hotter than any furnace. The gaze of Thanatos.' You sink back with a groan. 'How will I get back now?'

Achilles gives you a long and searching look before he replies. 'There's no doubting your resilience and courage. I've seen ample evidence of those in these past days as you've fought your way back to health. You'll find a way. Now rest.'

Delete the **scrimshaw hourglass** from your possessions and ▶ 505

1417

The radiation that flickers around the spinning disk is almost hypnotic. Looking at it stirs a dim half-memory of a story you were told in childhood.

'Give me that.' You take the spanner from the helmsman.

'Knock yourself out. Got a plan?'

'As I see it, the thing's out of whack.'

'True that. So?'

'So we whack it.'

You raise the spanner with both hands and bring it down with all your strength on the edge of the disk.

▶ 1318

1418

Your little brother comes and stands over you. 'You are a bad dog,' he says.

'I'm not a dog!' you bark.

'Always too far this way or that way, that's you. Can't find a middle path and stick to it.'

'Throw me a bone. I've looked out for you my whole life.'

'Then prove it. Don't bury me in the back garden.'

He goes to get your leash, but you don't see why you should put up with being taken for a walk by your kid brother. Running outside, you find the day has drained away and all the stars are suspended in an infinite sea of ink. You want to howl at the moon, but you're ashamed of being thought a dog so instead you sit quietly listening as a nightingale sings.

▶ 301

1419

She's skilled at sleight of hand, but you're wise to such tricks. You are almost certain which cup the ruby is under.

'That one.'

She lifts it with a flourish. 'No. It's here, see.'

You stare at the desk, speechless. You had your eye on her the whole time. How could you have got it wrong?

She pockets the ruby. 'So I'll take the deeds, assuming you don't want to welch. No need to move out right away. Anytime in the morning will do.'

Give her the deeds to the house ▶ 1255
Never! ▶ 1054

1420

You lower your head and butt the biggest guard in the stomach, hoping that his weight will bowl the others over while you get away. It won't be easy. Make a STRENGTH roll at difficulty 13.

Succeed ▶ 427
Fail ▶ 844

1421

'Ah, Sivi, that gorgeous girl,' says Bosk, going misty-eyed as he reminisces. 'Those lissom limbs like saplings, tresses luxurious as wine-burdened vines, eyes that are woodland pools caught by sunlight's shaft. I can taste the honey now.'

'From her apiary?'

'Apiary?' He looks at you. 'Oh yes, she keeps bees, of course, in the Ambrosial Woods. Well, that's the problem right there. She'll need a queen bee. I seem to remember there's often a swarm around the Atlas tree on the stretch of the old road south of Boreas. And then of course there's all the pesky bears. Dumb brutes, they crack open a hive to slurp the honey and naturally the bees don't hang around after that.'

'What do you do about the bears?'

'Sad to say, that's one of the problems you can really only solve the hard way.'

He gets you to try a honey ale that goes down smoothly enough but soon has your head swimming. You decide to call it a day while you can still walk.

► 1534

1422

'That's why you'll lose,' she says to Hypnos. 'You think mankind are cringing slaves. Any show of force and they'll roll over. But life is precious, and it's brief, and because of that we know that freedom matters. For all your power you can only threaten mortals with death, and they know that death is their inevitable fate anyway. That's why we'll defy you whatever the consequences.'

He looks at her in irritation. 'What do you mean, "we"? Did you forget so soon, mannikin? You are no mortal. You're but a piece of sculpted ivory that was granted a semblance of life.'

He flicks his fingers, and in that single gesture Galatea's humanity is instantly stripped away. She stands frozen, once again just a lifeless statue. She had been turning to you to exchange a last look and you saw the light go out of her eyes. For a moment you stand as immobile as Galatea herself. Then cold horror gives way to hot rage.

'You'll pay for that,' you say, lunging for him. 'I'll defy you – you and your whole noxious brood. I'll see you cast down into the pit of Tartarus if it's the last thing I do.'

His laughter is savage. 'The last thing you do will be a lot sooner than that.'

Delete Galatea from the Companion box on your Adventure Sheet and then ► 803

1423

The night watchmen scratch their heads, not for the first time bemused by the whims of their betters.

'May the gods reward your kindness,' says Pug.

'I doubt if the gods even recognize kindness,' you say. 'Where will you go now?'

'Back to Notus. That's where I learned my trade as a sculptor.'

'Iskandria?'

He shakes his head. 'The peninsula west of there.'

'Is that because of the stone quarries down that way?'

Pug gives you a strange look. 'I don't work in stone. I

thought you knew. I carve my statues out of ivory. Well, thank you again and goodbye.'

Pondering his parting words, you go back to bed.

► 97

1424

Agrio's second sends a note asking you to meet him in the Forum at noon, when the two of you can agree the terms of the duel.

If you have the **Face of Wisdom** (INGENUITY +3) ► 706

If not, decide if you will:

Go early	► 908
Arrive on time	► 1471
Keep him waiting	► 464

1425

❑

If the box above is empty, put a tick in it and ► 1169

Otherwise you can go:

West onto the Street of Knives	► 1617
East to the Avenue of the Anvil	► 63

1426

The Keres are the personification of violent death. By reputation even one is a formidable foe, and this is a whole pack. One look at those snapping teeth and sharp bony claws tells you there are too many to fight. Grabbing Dunamis, you head towards the park.

'We can't outrun them,' she says as you vault the railings and set off across the grass.

She's right. They are bounding after you on swift legs. Their glittering eyes see easily in the dark and with their keen hearing you can't hope to hide from them in the bushes.

Dimly you can make out a silver gleam ahead. It must be the lake. You head towards it, crashing through shrubbery and into a grove of trees. In the near-total darkness Dunamis's lantern is barely able to illuminate the swaying branches overhead. Close behind you hear the low panting of the Keres as they fan out to surround you.

One of them gives vent to a long warbling howl. The others snarl exultantly, tasting the night air for a scent of their prey. You put an arm around Dunamis. She has already drawn a dagger. It will be no more use than a pin against those monsters.

And then – a creak of wood. Branches twist like human limbs, ushering you both into a small space that's opened up in an oak tree. The bark swings shut behind you, nestling you tight inside the tree trunk.

Hardly daring to breathe, you hear the Keres snuffling

around the tree. They can't figure out where you've gone. Finally, with disappointed growls they give up, loping back to the street in search of easier prey.

'*We have aided you as we promised,*' says Dunamis in deep and laboriously slow tones. She slaps a hand to her mouth in surprise and adds in her own voice, 'Whoa! Where did that come from?'

'It's the Great Green Ones,' you explain. 'They don't have minds or mouths of their own so they use mortals to speak through.'

'I don't much like it!' protests Dunamis, then immediately adds in a gravid voice, '*Still less would you have appreciated being eaten alive by Death's hounds, little flesh-thing.*'

'That'll do,' you tell the unseen totem spirits. 'We're grateful for your help, but if you keep using her brain like that she's liable to throw up.'

The door in the oak creaks open and you step out into the fresh air. Together you hurry across the deserted park towards the nearest street.

▶ 881

1427

'He is our greatest warrior in attack, just as Big Ajax is mightiest in defence. Have you seen him run across a battlefield? He can outpace a chariot, racing on to strike a new foe even before the one he has just slain has fallen to the ground. Some say that's because Zeus gifted him with the swiftness of Arke, the disgraced messenger of Olympus who sided with the titans.'

'What do you think?'

'He presses his attacks with reckless courage because his mother revealed to him what is fated to be. He will die after Ilion falls, not before.'

'Who is his mother?'	▶ 495
'How was he able to treat my wounds?'	▶ 770
Ask about something else	▶ 724
Thank Nestor and leave	▶ 735

1428

Your muscles tighten as instinct takes over. There's no time to waste. You are the camp's lone defender in this crucial moment. You have to intercept these saboteurs before they reach the ships. You scramble over the rocks, careless of bruises and scrapes, and slide down to plant yourself in the middle of the narrow strand that connects the cove to the main shoreline.

The crashing waves and the distant clamour of the battle make a strange contrast with the near silence of the saboteurs as they come around the rocks and catch sight of you. They crouch, weapons drawn, scurrying forward

without a word. They don't want to risk alerting any sentries in the camp. Your own breath comes in gasps. Running on wet sand all morning has already tired you after the long days of illness. But you are the only one who stands between them and the unguarded ships.

The narrow stretch of sand here means that they must come at you one at a time. Make a STRENGTH roll at difficulty 8.

Succeed	▶ 1167
Fail	▶ 85

1429

Taking fright, the spider scuttles off into the bushes, leaving you with a sturdy length of **attercop silk** as strong as ship's cable. Add it to your possessions if you want to keep it.

Pushing your head between the bushes, you see a young man and woman walking barefoot on the lawn. She has a face you recognize, though you have never seen her awake. The apple-green moonlight sets a rim of pale lambency around her raven-black hair.

'Must we always stay in this garden of night, Dydkos?' she says, her voice a breathy murmur barely audible over the nightingale's song.

Eavesdrop on what they're saying	▶ 218
Step out of the bushes to speak to them	▶ 1639
Attack the young man	▶ 786

1430

The dark blue vapour casts twisting, snakelike shadows across her pallid face. 'That which is lost requires to become found,' she intones.

'Sounds like philosophy.'

'The god has granted you insight. Go to the Academy. There you will learn what you must do.'

She points to the door. Bowing, you return to the main body of the temple.

▶ 510

1431

The shop door rattles. 'Hey, Pemon! Open up!'

You duck down behind the counter. A face presses up to the glass. 'Are you in there?'

The door rattles again. The customer swears and stomps off. But you'd better not hang around. If he saw anything suspicious he might come back with the city militia.

Search the shelves	▶ 558
Search the desk	▶ 1237
Search the chimney	▶ 1189
Look in the till	▶ 1358
Get out of here	▶ 988

1432

If you have the codeword *Reverie* ► 520

    Otherwise ► 1269

1433

If you have the codeword *Nanny* and also you either possess some **cockatrice blood** or have the codeword *Quill* ► 951

    Otherwise ► 573

1434

The demon uses its soot-covered talon to tattoo degrading messages all over your face and body. Gain 3 scars and lose 3 Glory. (Glory cannot go negative.)

    ► Current Location

1435

It lunges towards you, lifting its pincers to strike down at your head. Instead of backing away, you dive directly at it, twisting in mid-air so as to hit the floor on your back. Momentum carries you sliding under the creature's thorax. Thrusting upwards with all your strength, you burst the smaller plates of chitin along its belly, slicing through the soft inner organs. Fetid slime and pale viscous blood gush out in a torrent.

Rearing high on its extended legs, the creature emits a horrible chirping hiss and collapses in a shuddering mass to the floor.

    ► 490

1436

'How can I hope to hold my own against the power of titans?' you ask her.

'You must steal the fire of the gods. By that I mean the fire of Vulcan's workshop in which he shaped the world.'

You're ready   ► 90

You need more information   ► 1292

1437

A flash of lightning stirs some long-forgotten memory of childhood. Somebody – one of your uncles? – told you a story of a ship in danger of being wrecked in a storm.

'Where are you going?' shouts Ancaeus as you race past him towards the prow.

'The mainsail's about to snag,' you call back. 'We'll never get it up. Help me raise the jib instead.'

He hesitates, but with the winch abandoned he has no hope of raising the heavy mainsail. Gesturing to his small crew, he follows you to the cable that hoists the smaller headsail.

'Hope this will give us enough thrust,' he grunts as he heaves on the line alongside you.

'Trust me. In this gale a handkerchief would be enough to get her under way.'

As the jib catches the wind it snaps taut. The *Sunrise* leaps forward, gathering altitude as it gathers speed.

Your upward arc carries you directly towards the colossal figure of Thanatos, looming against the heavens. He extends a giant hand, inexorable as storm-swept clouds, thinking to snatch you out of the air. But the ship is gaining speed. His fingers close on empty space directly under the keel.

The ship rises up and up, past growling thunderheads piled up like crags into the sky. Rain pelts the deck. You rise into dank, enveloping cloud and break through to the clear night above where the stars are hard and bright as distant diamonds. Impossibly far below, the streets and buildings of the city are mere toys half-seen in the murk.

Thanatos looks up, his hand raised to draw back his cowl. A moment later and his unshielded gaze would have blasted the ship to atoms, but now you are sailing high among the silent constellations. Even death cannot catch you.

    ► 1067

1438

Unfathomable gulfs of rock surround you in all directions. You lose all sense of time and space until at last the cocoon begins to rise toward the surface. The hum of the beetles' incessant motion drops an octave as you are carried back up out of the ground into open air. The scents of blossom, foliage and meadow grass mingle on the breeze.

The beetles fly together in a clump, reconstituting the metallic chrysalis which drops back into your pocket.

    ► 222 in *The Wild Woods*

1439

Cross off a dose of the **Lethe water**.

'And this will make me forget?' He smiles. 'That hasn't been my problem for the last few years. More the reverse.'

'Even so, you remember too much about life – the food you like, the wines, the people whose company you enjoy, the music that sets your feet tapping, the fragrance that brings back your youth. They're what's shackling you to this plane of existence.'

He nods and raises the vial to his lips, drinking it back in one gulp. As he turns to say something more, you find you can see right through him. His voice comes from far away: 'The bright day is done...'

For a moment his outline hangs like dew in the early morning, and then he's gone.

    ► 351

1440

Eros and Prometheus charge forward. Nyx rakes her nails across the air, tearing a gash in reality which becomes in her grasp a night-black halberd. Sweeping it around in an arc, she parries both their attacks. The clash of titanic weapons sends sparks of scalding plasma careening in all directions, blasting holes in the walls of Olympus. The energies they are conjuring are greater than the death of stars, the collision of constellations. Empty space itself twists and screams in protest.

Even weakened by her fight with the gods, Nyx's strength is as great as theirs combined. Prometheus and Eros cannot give up, but neither can they hope to defeat her. Cosmic forces swirl around them in an ever-increasing vortex of destruction. The struggle grows in ferocity until the whole universe is consumed by the conflagration.

Among the silent atoms drifts the dying spark of your consciousness. There is no deity to resurrect you this time. The void swallows you up along with all of creation. The future is an eternity of nothingness.

1441

An official fetches the Archon of the Sun. 'You're back at last,' he says, lifting his long robes in bunched fists so he can hurry along the corridor to meet you. 'Tell me you have good news.'

If you have the **Box of the Music of the Spheres**
▶ **1294**

Otherwise ▶ **1240**

1442

Somebody is with you. You get the impression it's your uncle Sophos, though he is walking just behind you and you don't see his face.

'Doesn't red mean stop where you come from?' he says.

'Where I come from?'

'The nightingale's song is diamonds and gold, but don't disdain rubies.'

You look round and he's an owl that flies off. Nearby is the open door, opening on a dark interior where red lights flicker and swim.

Investigate the lights   ▶ **985**
Go on towards the singing bird ▶ **301**

1443

You come across a funeral party standing disconsolately in the drizzle. There are three brothers and three sisters, accompanied by their spouses and children fidgeting in stiff mourning clothes. Perhaps the dismal weather makes you feel their sorrow more keenly, because as you pass the group you nod respectfully and say, 'Sorry for your loss.'

You're walking on, but one of them calls you back. The oldest of the brothers, by the look of him. 'What do you know about it?' he demands.

'What?'

'Our loss.'

'I don't know anything about it.'

It's only now that you notice the empty coffin resting by the side of the path. The lid lies on the grass with a scattering of red poppies over it.

'That loss,' says the man. 'We've lost the body.'

'Can't help you there. I don't even know whose funeral this is.'

'Our father's,' says one of the other brothers. 'That was the plan, anyway. The addle-headed old fool was losing his memory even when he was alive, but since he died he's got worse. Now he's forgotten he's dead and wandered off before we could bury him.'

'And we're paying the pallbearers by the hour,' interjects one of his sisters. 'The inconsiderate old goat.'

'Who was he, your father?'

'Lord Xechasiaris,' snaps the youngest brother.

'I didn't even know he was dead.'

'Neither does he!'

The eldest sister, a plump matron in early middle age, smiles at you coquettishly. 'You could help us find him…'

Agree   ▶ **335**
Refuse   ▶ **674**

1444

Lose the codeword **Robber** if you had it unless you also have the codeword *Recursive*.

You make short work of Autolycus using his own knife. After a lifetime of narrow scrapes, the look in his eyes as the end comes is one of simple astonishment. He falls back across the bed, blood spraying up through his fingers, and soon lies still. You can safely leave the body where it is; murder is common enough in the Grumbles that nobody will bother to investigate.

It takes you several hours to dismantle the golden maiden. Under the metal plates that comprise her skin you find an ingenious array of pistons, cables, gears, springs and flywheels. Not all of them are gold alloy, so you discard the scrap metal and keep only what you can melt down for treasure.

The head is last. Using a screwdriver to take it apart, you become aware of an aggravated whine like a wasp in a bottle, very faint, as if whatever spark remains of her consciousness is trapped in there raging against the dying of the light. You gaze into her polished glass eyes and there's a whir as her ocular motors seem to focus on you.

Lifting off the top of her skull, you tug out the wires and crystals embedded there. A spark cracks across the broken circuit, and immediately the faint hum stops. The eyes darken and grow dull. She is dead – if indeed you could ever say she lived.

It doesn't take you long to find a buyer for the golden metal, which turns out to be worth 1000 pyr. Add that sum to your money, set **63** as your Current Location, and then ▶ **1432**

1445

You throw yourself into a slide, kick his legs out from under him, and fell him with a punch to the jaw as he falls.

So far so good. But now the other guard is running up behind and you're prone on the floor with the unconscious guard's weight pinning you down. Try a STRENGTH roll at difficulty 10.

A Herculean effort ▶ **1102**

A feeble flop ▶ **523**

1446

You stand on the flanks of Mount Olympus. The air makes you gasp; it is almost too cold and pure for mortal lungs. Ahead, in the dazzling blaze of sunset glancing off the snow of the peaks, stand the majestic palaces of the gods.

Climb towards the summit ▶ **678**

Or you can explore the slopes of the mountain:

To the north ▶ **151**

To the east ▶ **1088**

To the south ▶ **1311**

To the west ▶ **1413**

1447

Add 200 pyr to your money and delete the item from your possessions.

▶ **828**

1448

You throw up your arm in a desperate block, but though you shrug off the brunt of the attack you can't avoid the spikes that rip long bloody chunks out of your flesh. Dizzy with pain, you hear shouts and running footsteps from behind.

If the Wound box on your Adventure Sheet was already ticked ▶ **111**

If not, put a tick in it now and ▶ **523**

1449

You jump up, grab one of the rafters, and kick down with all your strength. The floorboards give way, tumbling through in a cascade of damp plaster and splintered wood to the room below.

The slave trader is taken by surprise. Too late to check his headlong rush, he runs into the hole in the floor and falls with a sickening crunch on the floor five metres below. As he lies there moaning and clutching his broken ankle, you let go of the beam and drop onto his chest. It's a soft landing made all the more satisfying by the crack of ribs.

Snatching up the slave trader's cleaver, you put an end to his screaming. The dwarf looks down through the gap in the ceiling and hisses. You hear his feet scurry across the loft space and down the stairs. You are ready to greet him with a broken plank in the face. As he spits teeth, you slice his throat with the cleaver. His blood is no redder than the hooded cape he wears.

If you don't have the codeword *Quiddity* ▶ **28**

Otherwise, if you have the codeword *Quench* but not *Rigor* ▶ **1004**

Otherwise ▶ **243**

1450

As a paying guest, you get to travel along with the caravan without having to pitch in and do any work. You sit on the rear wagon, idly swinging your legs and watching the city walls dwindle into the distance.

'Quite a holiday for you,' grumbles one of the traders that evening as she hammers tent stakes into the ground.

'An expensive one,' you tell her. 'Perhaps a bit less pepper in tonight's stew? Just a suggestion.'

To be sure, it is pleasant to brush off the dust of the city. The air off the woods and meadows is clean and fresh, the slow swaying of the wagons restful, the herbs that go into each meal restorative. If you are injured you can untick the Wound box on your Adventure Sheet.

After a week the caravan takes a trail up onto the downs. Your guide comes to see you. 'Sometimes you can see the sea from up here,' he says.

'When will we reach the Druid's Shrine?'

'We already passed it. But here's what you came for.' He hands you a **rosebud**; add it to your possessions. 'That thick lemony scent always makes me think of Arcadia.'

'Maybe it'll jog my patron's memory.'

'You heading straight back?'

'What else?'

'If I were you I'd hang around here a few days. Why rush back to the rat race when you can doze away the afternoon in a hayrick making daisy chains?'

Go back to Vulcan City ▶ **222**

Stay in Arcadia ▶ **463** in *The Wild Woods*

1451

A visitor arrives at the door one morning just as you're getting ready to go out. She is a distraught young woman whose once-fine clothes are patched and threadbare.

'You don't recognize me,' she says, her tone caught between defiance and hopelessness. 'I'm Tritona, the youngest daughter of Lord Xechasiaris whose house this was.'

Invite her in	▶ **1516**
Give her a little money	▶ **1115**
Tell her to go away	▶ **1001**

1452

'Quite a responsibility, being a parent,' says Daedalus.

'Says the guy who pushed his nephew off a roof and nearly killed his son testing some prototype wings.'

He shrugs. 'It's a learning curve.'

He's obviously busy with whatever machine he's building, so after a while you use the golden beetles to return to the surface, taking care to drift laterally a few streets to shake off anyone who might have followed you here.

▶ **570**

1453

She gives a soft moan and opens her eyes.

'I dreamt I woke up,' she says, starting in alarm.

'Don't worry, my love,' says Dydkos. 'You're safe.'

'And I will not take you back,' you assure her. 'I see now that your story is not as your husband led me to believe.'

▶ **763**

1454

The creatures scuttle nimbly to and fro on their long segmented legs. You must be careful not to let them surround you, and you're not even sure your blows will penetrate their armour plates. This will be a tough battle.

Attempt a STRENGTH or GRACE roll (your choice) at difficulty 13.

Succeed	▶ **1159**
Fail	▶ **1587**

1455

The Archon of the Sun leads you to the inner chamber of the Palace, a circular room whose domed ceiling is inlaid with jewels representing stars and planets. Seven thrones are set around the wall.

He goes to a seven-sided console in the centre of the room. He touches a switch and with a meshing of great gears the dome starts to rotate, each section moving on separate bands so that the celestial objects shift relative to each other. At the same time the opening notes of an ethereal piece of music fill the air – but only for a moment, and then the music disintegrates into a discordant crashing and grinding and the rotating mechanism judders to a halt.

'You see why we need your help.'

'Not really my field. Have you called a mechanic? Could be it just needs a spot of oil.'

He shakes his head, a movement made majestically sedate by the need to balance that tall solar crown. 'There is nothing wrong with the mechanism itself. It requires tuning to the correct melody for each season, which can normally be accomplished with these sliders and dials here. Those melodies were handed down to us by Vulcan on a music box, which we locked away for safekeeping. After a while, rather than bring the box up from the vault four times a year, two of us would memorize each melody. It worked for generations, but this season we've got a problem. The Archon of the Moon and I were both supposed to know the Phthinoporonian melody – '

'The what, now?'

'The tune for autumn. But I've developed tinnitus and the Archon of the Moon admitted that he's tone deaf and all music sounds like cats wailing to him. So we sent down to the vaults for the music box and – '

'And it's gone.'

'Yes. How did you know?'

'Why else would you be talking to me?'

He nods, again with great care so as not to upset his carefully balanced crown. 'Can you help?'

'It's a big city.'

'The music box might have been stolen any time in the last twenty years. It's been that long since we needed to send for it. But I have a feeling it was taken quite recently. We had to let a servant go, a bald Gargarean cook. Rather a shifty individual. I didn't trust him an inch.'

If you have the **Box of the Music of the Spheres** ▶ **1294**

Otherwise ▶ **1240**

1456

You throw a single coin into the water. Cross it off the money recorded on your Adventure Sheet.

If you have the **scrimshaw hourglass** and do not have the codeword *Recursive* ▶ **1357**

Otherwise ▶ **1025**

1457

Memory is a kaleidoscope of thoughts and images, sometimes experienced as if in the present moment and sometimes as if those events happened to someone else. The faceless stranger is gone from your life, but it still feels as if he's a constant presence.

If you have the codeword *Reverie* ▶ 452 in this book.

Otherwise, decide which region of the world will be the starting point for your adventures:

Arcadia ▶ **459** in *The Wild Woods*
Boreas ▶ **992** in *The Pillars of the Sky*
Hades ▶ **459** in *The Houses of the Dead*
Notus ▶ **1696** in *The Hammer of the Sun*

1458

You launch yourself off the wall, spiralling down at dizzying speed, then stretch your wings and feel the stomach-flipping wrench as you swoop up high into the sky. Far below, the endless sands and age-broken ruins of Notus go racing past.

If you were with a companion, delete them from your Adventure Sheet. Also remove the **beeswax** that you have used.

Selecting a landing spot, you begin to descend through rolling waves of heat. Already the wax is melting – you touch down not a moment too soon.

Iskandria ▶ **182** in *The Hammer of the Sun*
The shores of Psamathe ▶ **328** in *The Hammer of the Sun*
The kingdom of Saesara ▶ **64** in *The Hammer of the Sun*
The cataract of Tethys ▶ **1592** in *The Hammer of the Sun*
The cataract of Oceanus ▶ **1452** in *The Hammer of the Sun*
The Land From Which None Returns ▶ **1375** in *The Hammer of the Sun*
The east coast of Notus ▶ **200** in *The Hammer of the Sun*

1459

'No one has ever seen Vulcan's workshop,' you say.

'What lies in the very centre of the universe?' asks Eos.

'Is this a trick question? Vulcan City, if the maps mean anything.'

She nods. 'You must look in the city for a way to enter the workshop of the gods.'

'It's a big place.'

'Where would you normally look for information? It's the first thing any visitor to the city sees.'

If you have the codeword *Ruby* ▶ 1563

Otherwise you can set off now (▶ 90) or ask her for more information (▶ 1292).

1460

If you have the codeword *Royal* ▶ 1151

If you don't have *Royal* and this box ❑ is empty, tick it and ▶ Current Location

Otherwise ▶ 43

1461

The massed ranks of your foes seem limitless. They pour from the roof in an incessant dark tide. Were-apes and werewolves leap with frightening agility, balancing on the ship's rail and snapping at you with slavering fangs, while shapeless things out of nightmare flap around on ragged black wings. As each grappling hook crunches and bites into the ship's timbers, vampires scuttle across the taut line with ghastly moans of blood-lust.

If you have the codeword *Recursive* ▶ 700 now; otherwise read on.

You give yourself in to the pulse-pounding rhythm of battle, laying about you with weapons and anything that comes to hand. One of the vampires, its mummified entrails trailing from a deep cut, flops to the deck and clutches your legs in a rigor-stiff grip. You snatch up a belaying pin, smash its skull to pulp, and whirl just in time to parry the attack of a flapping horror that looks like a giant face with leathery wings in place of ears.

Make a STRENGTH roll at difficulty 12.

Succeed ▶ **1592**
Fail ▶ **256**

1462

You pass a red-headed girl who is sitting on cobblestones beside a puddle. She seems to be fishing, only her rod is a long flute and she is using musical notes as bait instead of worms.

'You're not likely to catch anything like that,' you remark as you go by.

'You're one to talk,' she jeers.

'That's a bit personal,' you say.

She squints up at you. 'Maybe I have you mixed up with somebody else. Aren't you the sort of person who leaves somebody to die so you can steal their stuff?'

'I don't think so.'

'You ought to know for sure. Decide how you want to be remembered: a carrion crow and a thief? Or a hero with a conquering tune to play?'

Her mention of a tune reminds you of the nightingale's song, so you turn away and push through a gap in a wall, emerging through a trellis of ivy into a secluded garden.

▶ 301

1463

Enceladus's club splinters with the force of impact as he slams it down directly on your head. A burst of caustic light flares behind your eyes – and then darkness that pulls you down and down into an endless abyss.

Note that your Current Location is **683** and then ▶ **670**

1464

The owner comes over, wiping her hands on her apron, and asks how you're enjoying your meal.

'It's delicious. Such subtle flavours.'

She nods, pleased that her cooking is appreciated. 'We use only the finest herbs of Boreas and Arcadia and I get the spices brought here from far-off Iskandria.'

'And these crêpes – superb, so succulent yet also crispy. Do you fry them in amaranth oil?'

She looks puzzled. 'No. Is that used in recipes? I've never heard of it.'

If Polymnia is your companion ▶ 1109

Otherwise you can finish your meal and leave (▶ 86) or ask to see the kitchen (▶ 592).

1465

Will you give the letters to:

Lady Himera?	▶ 1374
Her husband?	▶ 1338
The authorities?	▶ 1152
Or to no one?	▶ 587

1466

If you have the codeword *Numb* ▶ 1199 and put a tick in the box there.

If you don't have *Numb*, read on.

'Honey isn't the only useful thing to come out of those hives,' Bosk tells you.

'Not so much profit in candles, though.'

'Candles? Who's talking about candles? There's something much more interesting you can do with all that wax. Now, listen – put that wine mug down, you need to remember this. In Hades, between the volcano of death and the Phlegethon river, you'll come upon a tomb with two caryatids supporting the entrance. Descend below that tomb and you may find the wings that Icarus used to escape from Krete.'

'They didn't do him much good, as I recall.'

'Because he didn't have beeswax of the quality that your hives produce. Use that to lubricate the wings and you can fly anywhere you want. Only one snag – you'll need to best a ridiculous beast that calls itself Lockjaw, or Mantrap, or something like that.'

'Any tips?'

'Find a workshop where you can build a metal butterfly. That's somewhere in Hades too. I know, it sounds like a kiddie's toy, but it's exactly what you'll need to beat the monster.'

The talk of Hades throws a dampener on your revels, so after a couple of drinks you make your excuses and leave.

▶ 1534

1467

You excuse yourself for a moment and step out of earshot to talk to the head.

'He sounds self-assured,' it declares in its crackling tinny voice, 'but he's just afraid of moving on.'

'Probably you're right, but what do I do about it?'

'Simple. If he's scared of death, you've got to make him more scared of life.'

▶ 483

1468

'Think about it,' says Autolycus. 'Most of the problems in life come about because of misunderstandings about money.'

'Exactly. You found some money of mine and you misunderstood that it didn't belong to you.'

He shrugs. 'I'd give it back, but as you can see from my accommodation I'm temporarily low on funds. In any case, fixing what you've done to Hypermestra will cost at least that much.'

'Or I could melt her down for scrap and that would just about cover what you stole.'

He gives you a guarded look. 'I wouldn't do that if I were you. Not unless you plan on killing me.'

Well, what's it to be?

Kill him	▶ 1444
Bargain with him	▶ 904
Hand him in to the city police	▶ 1316

1469

Record **722** as your Current Location.

For any possession you left in the well on a previous visit, roll a die. On a score of 1 that item has been stolen; on a score of 2-6 it is still there. Roll separately for each item.

▶ 252

1470

Get the title **Walking Wounded**. Also tick the Wound box on your Adventure Sheet if it was not ticked already.

As long as you have the title **Walking Wounded**, you cannot recover from wounds by any means. Salves, resurrection, rest, or the intervention of your god – none of these will work. Any time that you are told you can untick the Wound box, ignore it.

▶ Current Location

1471

You stride up to the other second outside the barracks of the Black Guard. The two of you quickly set a date for the duel in two days' time outside the north gate at dawn.

'We also have to arrange the details of weaponry and suchlike,' he says.

Tekto has told you that he considers himself a better swordsman than Agrio, so you propose swords.

'Very well,' he agrees. 'Now, as to armour. We don't want them risking a fatality, so I suggest heavy plate.'

Agree ► **1396**
Demur ► **1143**

1472

'Never,' you say. 'Why would I join the losing side? The gods aren't going to let Nyx set herself up as a tyrant over all creation. Do you really think Zeus and the others, even weakened by battle, would give in to the likes of you?'

'Brave words,' he says, raising his huge hand with thumb and forefinger poised an eyelash length apart. 'I could snuff you out right now.'

'I don't think so. My deity has been preparing me for this moment.'

Hypnos roars with laughter. 'You thought you were marked out for greatness? Hah! You were chosen because you are of no significance whatsoever. I am the one who chose you. Every time you thought you communed with your god – that was me, speaking to you through your vain dreams of grandeur. The Olympians would never have selected an nonentity such as you to be their hero, which is why I knew that your god would never notice my deception.'

Give in and join him; if your god doesn't care why should you? ► **1196**
Refuse to believe him ► **367**
Defy him even if you do stand alone ► **1492**

1473

Cross off the **phoenix feather** and get the codeword *Root*.

'You know what this has in common with the other thing you brought me?' says Daedalus.

'Birds.'

'Not the eagle's stomach. That wasn't what interested me. It was what was inside it.'

It takes you a moment. 'Prometheus's liver?'

'Exactly.' He straps a magnifying glass on his head and studies the feather. 'Like the gods, the titans are able to ignore the rules of reality. Prometheus had his liver pecked out every day but it always grew back. What does that remind you of? The phoenix. There's something in the code of both – the underlying magical structure, you might say – that lets them overwrite their own destruction.'

He looks up. The magnifying lens makes his eye seem huge and all-seeing. 'You see where I'm going with this. If I can isolate that regeneration property, that's better than the gift of fire. It would give me the same power as the gods.'

For a moment you're speechless. 'You're taking Prometheus's liver and you're *weaponizing* it?'

Daedalus smiles to himself, entranced by his vision of what is to come. 'We don't need gods or titans anymore. Their time is over. It is the time for man to become the creator of things – and I will be that man.'

If you have a **copper casket of doom** and you want to give it to him ► **213**
Otherwise ► **1350**

1474

One moonless night you hear a scrape of boot leather on rough brickwork. A face appears at the window, outlined against a spray of stars.

'Dunamis!'

'In the flesh. Here – ' She hands you a key. 'Wait till it kicks off, then head down through the kitchens.'

'Till what kicks off?'

'You'll know.' She starts to climb back down.

'Wait. Where are the kitchens?'

'Follow the stink and the rats. You can't miss 'em.'

An hour later there's an uproar on the floor below. Inmates begin shouting, banging their water-mugs against the bars, smashing up their beds. Running feet in the corridor outside tell you that your guards are joining in to quell the riot. You unlock your cell door and find your way down to the kitchen following the slops of gravy and vermin-gnawed scraps on the stairs.

A couple of prisoners are waiting for you. One of them holds up a sack of potato peelings. You climb into the sack and between them they haul you outside, tossing you on a pile of garbage in the yard. A cart arrives and carries you jostling through the deserted streets to a rubbish dump outside the city gates. At dawn you crawl out of the sack and make your way home. You are tired, stiff, and covered in reeking slime but at least you're free.

If you have the codeword *Robber*, lose it unless you also have the codeword *Recursive*.

► **555**

1475

'Where do you think he'll have got to?' you ask her.

'When you lose something, it pays to look in the last place you saw it. Same principle applies to people – even the dead ones.'

► **133**

1476

You wait in an alcove down the hall. Before long one of the men comes along carrying a bundle of oil-soaked straw. As he starts tiptoeing up the stairs, you cosh him with an ornamental candlestick and drag him to a closet.

A minute later another of them scurries along the hall with a similar bundle. He glances up the stairs, but as you're creeping up behind him he suddenly whirls, warned by some sixth sense. You see his eyes widen in surprise, though he says nothing.

You lunge, but he's already racing back towards the study, still without making a sound. Armed with the first intruder's knife, you give chase.

▶ **1023** and tick one of the boxes there before you read on.

1477

Get the title **Plaything of Agamemnon**.

A half-stupid, half-crafty look of rapacious delight softens Agamemnon's ugly face as he runs his hands over your body. 'Oh yes, you'll do,' he says.

The old priest steps forward. 'Then, lord, my daughter..?'

'Take her and piss off!' roars Agamemnon. 'What do I want with that skinny bit of scrag-end now I've got this beautiful bitch here?'

Chryses bows to you in gratitude as he takes Astynome's hand and leads her from the camp. 'I shall make an offering to the Archer on your behalf, lady,' he says.

Gain a blessing. It can be used to reroll a failed check against CHARM, GRACE, INGENUITY or STRENGTH. In any given situation you can only use one blessing, so if you fail the reroll you can't spend another blessing to try again.

Now ▶ **518**

1478

If you have the codeword *Quench* ▶ **528**

Otherwise ▶ **1300**

1479

You are caught in the monster's coils. It's like the grip of Atlas, an unstoppable contracting clutch that squeezes your flesh and grinds your ribs to breaking point.

If you have a **jar of amaranth oil**   ▶ **157**
If not   ▶ **251**

1480

High in the immense black vault of the sky, a bright star flares suddenly. No, not a star – a meteor, hurtling earthwards. Then as it draws closer you see that it is a human figure clad in miraculous winged battle-armour. He swoops, hovers, then drops beside you, and the helmet opens like a metal-petalled flower to reveal the face of –

'Daedalus!'

'You started the party early, I see.' There's a bleep and a whine as strange mechanisms within Daedalus's armour begin to charge to full power. 'Got some uninvited guests we need to kick out first, though.'

▶ **804**

1481

Note **570** as your Current Location, then ▶ **1269** and tick the box next to the Tower of Sand. From now on you will always be able to find your way back here.

1482

Nestor is willing to talk about anything you like. You can ask him any question below for which the box is unticked – first tick the box, then turn to the section indicated.

❑ 'What side do the gods take in this war?' ▶ **432**
❑ 'How can I return to my own time?' ▶ **345**
❑ 'Tell me about Achilles.' ▶ **1427**
If all the boxes are now ticked ▶ **617**

1483

A slim woman comes rapidly towards you with a long, sinuous gait. Just as you open your mouth in greeting, she delivers a stinging slap across your face.

'Harsh,' you say, rubbing your jaw, 'considering I got you out of a hole.'

She gives you a sweet, drowsy-looking smile and pulls out a hip flask. 'No hard feelings, little bean. Have a drink.'

She uncorks the flask and a wisp of acrid green vapour rises out, stinging your eyes. 'Is this safe to drink?' you ask.

She sneers. 'Safe? Who cares about safe? Live dangerously.'

Drink up   ▶ **633**
Go looking for the nightingale   ▶ **301**

1484

The blade snaps against her ebon armour. She sneers, 'That trinket is for mortals who style themselves royalty. I was Queen before creation itself.'

Then she gives a soft grunt and looks down to see your other weapon buried deep in her belly. Black ichor gushes from the wound.

Nyx slumps to her knees. 'Impossible…'

'You underestimated me, Night Queen. Not Kingslayer am I, but Godslayer.'

'If I must die, so will you!'

Screaming in fury and despair, she conjures licking black flames, trying to engulf and destroy you in a last encircling band of darkness.

If you have the codewords *Rug* and *Rudiment* ▶ 310

If you have *Rug* but not *Rudiment* ▶ 267

Otherwise ▶ 458

1485

If you have the titles **Archon of Agriculture** and **Archon of Wines** and you also have the title **The Apiarist** ▶ 1466

If you have both the first two titles but not **The Apiarist** ▶ 1421

If you have only one of the two titles **Archon of Agriculture** and **Archon of Wines** ▶ 531

If you have none of the titles listed above, read on.

'Great progress!' roars Bosk lustily. 'This calls for a drink.'

'Yes, but before we dive into another jug of wine and I lose hours of my life, could we just go over what needs doing next?'

He gives a deafening peal of laughter and claps you on the back. You've had beatings that were more gentle.

'You need to get the farms and vineyards up and running,' he says. 'That'll pay for upkeep on the Palace. Start at the wineries.'

'That's your answer to everything.'

He stares at you in wide-eyed astonishment for moment, then bursts out laughing. 'Ah, you know me so well. Let's get drunk.'

The next thing you know it is dawn and a light drizzle is falling, awakening a cool earthy scent from the ground. You must have fallen asleep under the arbour. There is no sign of Bosk.

▶ 1534

1486

You stare at him in disbelief. 'Run away? You can't be serious. Nyx has launched a war of absolute conquest. We're the only ones left to fight her.'

'Wise up,' growls Ancaeus. 'Back there on the roof – *that* was the war, and we lost. I didn't pull you out of there as a tactical withdrawal. All that's left for us now is to find a new home far away from Nyx's realm.'

'So you're willing to sail off and leave the world to be despoiled by the Night Queen?'

'It's Vulcan's simulacrum of the world, remember. Most of those people you want to save, they're not even real.'

'Have you ever loved? Hated, even? If something or someone matters enough to make you care, they're real.'

After an uneasy silence, Ancaeus says, 'Anyway, we need to make repairs. We can't do that while under sail.'

Your own tone is also a little more conciliatory after the heated argument a few moments ago. 'Surely there's nowhere you can find a berth out here?'

He looks out into the void ahead. 'There's one place. The Island of the Dawn. If I can find it.'

If you have an **astrarium** and want to let him use it ▶ 1180

If you have the **journal of the Argo** and show it to him ▶ 444

Otherwise ▶ 1146

1487

'There's a café round the back of this building.' He jerks his thumb over his shoulder, indicating a crooked tenement of dingy yellow brick. 'If you're looking for me, I'm usually there in the afternoon.'

He turns back to his vegetables, taking up the trowel and lowering himself stiffly to a crouch. As he does, his sleeve rides up giving you a glimpse of burned and puckered flesh around his wrist.

'You want to see me again?'

There's a long pause and you wonder if he's heard you. 'If you plan on hanging around this part of town, you should check in from time to time.'

He makes a casual gesture. Immediately a henchman comes forward to escort you out of the Grumbles and back onto the streets.

Get the codeword *Reflection* and ▶ 63

1488

You are on fire, in agony, blind, flung headlong, oblivious of everything but the winds roaring around you that are not any normal gale but the howling storm of protesting, sundered time.

Do you cry out? Scream? The sound is snatched away by years that surge and flow behind you as you fall back helplessly into the past. And through it all, in fingers blistered and seared to stumps by Thanatos's stare, you are clutching something tight. The hourglass.

Silence and darkness for a while. You must have passed out. You come to only to find the pain has been patiently waiting for you. There is moss under your head. The scent of leaves and blossom. Insects and woodland animals scurrying in the bushes.

Numbed by burning agony that blots out thought, you lie helpless in the forest. Day and night flick across the sky, uncaring of your ordeal. It feels as if your every nerve is being picked out of the skin and tortured at needlepoint. At last thirst brings you back to full consciousness. You crawl across the moss to a pond, drink, and in the jangling ripples you see the melted ruin of your face. It is the last time you will ever look at your reflection.

Delete all companions, titles, possessions, scars, wounds, codewords (apart from the codeword **Reverie** if you have it), money, and blessings (including permanent ones). Restore your attribute scores to 0. Do not delete the god you worship.

Next remove anything stored in caches, townhouses, strongboxes, vaults, etc, and erase marks in tickboxes. Do that for all the Vulcanverse books.

In short, erase *everything* from your Vulcanverse books and your Adventure Sheet apart from your god and the codeword **Reverie** if you have it.

Then ▶ 962

1489

❑

If the box above was already ticked ▶ **1101** immediately; otherwise tick it and read on.

'Stay, Amazon,' calls Odysseus on seeing you. 'I'd like a word, if you have time.'

'Lord Odysseus,' you say, 'it was you I was looking for. You have the reputation of being the cleverest of the Achaeans.'

'Go on.' His wide, easy smile and sharp eyes give an impression of lively intelligence. 'Was there something you wanted to ask me, lady?'

'How did I get here? Just for starters.'

'Is that really the question you want to ask?'

'Not so much as: how do I get back?'

'Only the gods know that.'

'OK. Thanks,' you say sarcastically.

Odysseus gestures to take in the beach, the army, the plain, and the far-off walls of Ilion. 'This is the age of heroes. The gods aren't so far away.'

▶ 1101

1490

Note your Current Location as **625**.

Taking a shortcut back to the barracks one night, a little the worse for drink as he often is around payday, Sakan comes across a trail of gold coins that look to have spilled from a split purse. Stooping to pick up each coin as he goes, he follows the trail into a blind alley where he sees a drunk lying on some piles of refuse beside a few lava gems.

The moon is half-hidden in clouds, there are no street lamps in this part of town, so little light penetrates into the narrow alley. Sakan comes unsteadily closer, peering at the faint gleam of the lava gems. You wait, breathing stertorously like any unconscious drunkard, listening as his boots squelch in the mud of the alley.

Make an INGENUITY roll at difficulty 10. That is, roll two dice and add your INGENUITY modifier, including any bonus for one item in your possession, and you need to score 10 or more.

Succeed ▶ 734
Fail ▶ 162

1491

Invisible hands reach out of the darkness to take hold of you. They sweep you off your feet, hurtle you at breakneck pace out of the chamber and along the corridor, and fling you down the palace steps with brutal force. You land painfully on the hard flagstones of the plaza. Tick your Wound box if you weren't already injured.

Dunamis catches up to you. Her mouth is open as she gazes in awe at the sky. You notice a change of air pressure as presages a thunderstorm. The wind that has been raging for hours has dropped. Rolling over, you look up to see a violet coruscation blossoming like a new constellation in the night.

'What is it?' she says.

You know. It's the end of the world.

▶ 186

1492

You laugh scornfully, and for the first time Hypnos looks astonished.

'You think I'm doing this for the gods?' you say to him. 'The gods don't care what happens to mortals. Nor do the titans. Let them destroy each other. As for your mother – human beings have been in fear of the dark too long. Prometheus gave us fire to banish those fears. I oppose you because it is mankind's destiny to drive back superstition and hate. That's my reason for siding with the forces of light.'

If Galatea is your companion ▶ 1422
If Chipos is with you ▶ 1653
Otherwise ▶ 803

1493

Instead of opening the cocoon to let you out, the beetles begin to fly about even more furiously. Their motion creates a high-pitched whine that sets your teeth on edge. After several minutes, the cocoon starts to rise again, floating up through solid rock until you reach the throne room. Then the beetles abruptly peel away, flying off into the darkness.

▶ **486** in *The Houses of the Dead*

1494

If you possess the **sceptre of Agamemnon** ▶ 610

If not but you bear the title **Hero Without A Shadow** ▶ 424

Otherwise ▶ 94

1495

Somebody proposes a story contest and, as a newcomer to the group, your name is put forward. 'I expect you have dozens of spellbinding adventures to tell us about,' says your opponent, a lissom and sardonically smiling woman called Kazala who wears a peacock feather in her hair and has a reputation as an explorer.

Everyone gathers around the two of you. It's like the circle of onlookers who gather to watch a duel, only this battle will be fought with words.

The hubbub of excited chatter fades away. They are waiting for you to begin.

If you have the codeword *Quarter* ▶ 1565

If not ▶ 849

1496

The sergeant on duty greets you warmly. 'I'm glad you dropped by.'

If you have the codeword *Ruby* ▶ 328

If not ▶ 376

1497

You were watching the point of her blade, but instead she flips the poignard around in her hand and cracks the pommel hard across your brow. An explosion of stars behind your eyes swirls and dies, carrying you down into a pit of uttermost darkness.

▶ 280

1498

You race to the stern, where the helmsman is bent over a device like a ship's compass. He prises off the copper lid on the top of the housing to reveal a spinning disk of tangled geometric lines. It makes you feel slightly sick to look at it because of how it's continually shifting, unfolding and refolding, apparently in impossible shapes.

'You have to get your head around it existing in other dimensions,' says the helmsman, hesitantly reaching towards the glowing disk with a strangely shaped spanner. 'Got much experience with buoyancy rotors?'

'That what this is? I thought I was looking at a migraine aura.'

If you have the codeword *Recursive* ▶ 1417 now; otherwise read on.

'It's out of alignment,' says the helmsman. 'See those sparks? It's dragging against the side of the containment vessel. That's why we're losing altitude.'

'So you need to adjust it? That's what the spanner's for?'

'What am I, bloody Daedalus? I dunno how to adjust the bugger. Brute force usually does the trick.'

He lunges for the glittering disk as if it's a rare butterfly he's trying to catch in a net. There's a protesting screech as the disk grinds against the spanner head. The deck lurches under you. Arcs of disturbing light splash and play around your head.

'Little help here...' grunts the helmsman, straining with all his might to twist the disk back into alignment.

Make a STRENGTH roll at difficulty 11.

Succeed ▶ 1318

Fail ▶ 216

1499

Tekto looses an arrow. A white-fletched shaft quivers in Agrio's eye socket. He gives a cry that sounds more like surprise than pain, staggers a few paces, then falls like a sack of rocks. There is surprisingly little blood.

'What gave you the idea of bow and arrows?' asks Tekto as you and he walk back into town.

'Um... divine inspiration,' you say. 'Apollo looks with favour on archers.'

'Strange.' Tekto scratches his head. 'Agrio worshipped Apollo too.'

'The ways of the gods are not for us to understand.'

He nods and, as the two of you part, hands you a purse. Add 100 pyr to your money and get the codeword *Rhyme*.

▶ 1642

1500

Clouds of dust above the plain, helmet plumes swaying, bronze armour blood-flamed in the sunset – a moment in amber as the Achaean troops rest after their exertions of the day.

There is feasting and rejoicing at the spoils seized, the armour and horses taken from fallen foes, the hostages led back for ransom. But also sadness, for around every campfire are empty places where comrades who rode out eagerly this morning will not be returning.

If you have the codeword *Ramrod* ▶ 1239; otherwise read on.

Go to talk to Agamemnon ▶ 518

Examine the strange armour in the Myrmidon camp ▶ 306

Seek out Achilles in his tent ▶ 535

Find a patch of sand where you can sleep ▶ 572

1501

'Just look at his fingernails,' she says, tutting. 'All that soot.'

'I daresay he'd have scrubbed with soap if he'd known he was going to be found dead.'

'Sarcasm is often a cover for ignorance, you know that? And booksellers are always scrupulously clean. They're handling expensive books all day long. If they get the pages dirty, it spoils the merchandise.'

Look around for the letters ▶ 1431
Make yourself scarce ▶ 988

1502

'That knife,' says a man, whirling to face you on the street. 'Where did you get it?'

He wears the lion-skin cloak of a nomad of the northlands of Notus. 'You must be Danu,' you say, handing him the **bone knife**. Cross it off your list of possessions.

His quarrelsome look softens to an expression of concern. 'My friend Oshi was supposed to meet me a month ago. I have been searching the city for him, but these streets are not like the clean plains of our homeland. There are no tracks to follow, no signs in the wind. It is like pushing through spiders' webs.'

'He's on the Boulevard of the Gnome, south of the city gate.' You catch Danu's arm. 'Prepare yourself. He's in a bad way.'

He sets off down the street.

Follow him ▶ 767
Let him go ▶ 198

1503

For a moment, nothing happens.

And then – is that a deep, subsonic rumbling? Something unseen but felt through the soles of your feet, a flutter in your bowels, a stirring of hair on the back of your neck.

It grows, shaking the ground now. Dust sluices down from the jumbled masonry blocks of the city gate. Chunks of mortar are dislodged and bounce across the street. The ground starts to tilt as fissures open up. It's like standing on an ice floe that's breaking apart underneath you.

Dunamis crouches beside the noticeboard, clinging onto it with both hands. Her eyes are wide and white.

'Should we run?' she says.

'Run where?'

The sound drowns out even the wind now – a churning, twisting, grinding snarl of rock moving against rock. In front of you, an area hundreds of metres across begins to slump downwards. Buildings already half-ruined topple into the yawning crater. You and Dunamis can only watch in awe as titanic stone cogs rotate and descend, opening a winding funnel-shaped chasm deep into the earth.

You stand on the lip of the shaft. It spirals down into darkness. Far below, a nimbus of glowing light flickers rhythmically, suggestive of a disembodied heartbeat.

Dunamis peers over the edge. 'There's a ramp. Sort of. It's pretty narrow. Maybe you're meant to go down.'

You drop a pebble. It bounces off the side, fleetingly visible as a speck against the misty glow, and is soon swallowed by distance. If it hits the bottom you don't hear it.

What's down there? And are you willing to find out?

Descend into the pit ▶ 627
Wait here ▶ 585

1504

If you possess a **fish-headed standard** ▶ 201; otherwise read on.

The notice directs you to meet a man called Tekto in a tavern near the east gate. Tekto tells you that he is an officer of the White Guard. 'Recently I was sent to arrest a lieutenant of the Black Guard for – well, never mind, it doesn't matter what for. This man, whose name is Agrio, became enraged because I found him at a noble lady's salon. As he couldn't very well complain about the general who ordered him placed under arrest, the moment he was free again he challenged me to a duel.'

'And you want me to do what? Dissuade him? Threaten him? Kill him?'

'Of course not! Preposterous as his challenge is, regimental honour is now involved. I need you to act as my second. Meet with Agrio's second and agree what weapons and armour we will use in the duel.'

'Obviously you don't expect me to do it for honour alone. I'm not a member of either regiment.'

'If I win, I will pay you 100 pyr.'

'And if you lose?'

'Then my savings will have to pay for my funeral.'

Agree ▶ 1424
Refuse ▶ 333

1505

You are pushing against a roaring wind. A girl calls to you, and you look around to see her clinging to a pole with both hands, her feet off the ground like a flag flapping in a gale.

'Everything gets swept away in a storm like this,' she yells.

'You could let go. Just see where the wind takes you.'

'That's your way of living, not mine. Seeing as you seem to have both feet firmly on the ground, genius, why don't you give me a hand? Otherwise I'll be the next leaf on the autumn bonfire, gone as sure as a straw hat in a high wind.'

Help her ▶ **782**

Continue looking for the nightingale ▶ **301**

1506

You look round to see her already half out of the window. 'Naturally you can't use the door like anyone else.'

'Old habits,' she says with a grin. 'We may not meet again this side of the Great Reset, but you've been a worthy –'

What? Saviour? Adversary? Acquaintance? Ally? She leaves you to decide that for yourself, jumping down from the sill and loping silently away across the lawn. For a moment her silhouette appears on the wall, outlined by the moon, and then she's gone like a ghost.

She left you the ruby, which is worth 30 pyr. Add the money to your Adventure Sheet and ▶ **97**

1507

You glance at the spectators. They are crouched and eager, aroused to a savagery of anticipation. The faces of rank beasts, not humans with any claim on an immortal soul.

Rather than wait to see the end of this sad spectacle, you hurry out of the gate.

▶ **1642**

1508

'We've got to get under way,' says Ancaeus, his face taught with urgency. The ship is swaying on the wind, incredibly floating fifty metres above the ground, but seems unable to make headway.

The Minotaur smashes his axe into the face of a slavering werewolf as it leaps across from the roof. 'Take your time,' he says. 'I can do this all day.'

'How can I help?' you ask.

'There's the rigging,' says Ancaeus, 'but we've got that covered.'

He jerks his thumb towards a thick-set man standing bashfully off to one side.

'Elos!' It's your first mate.

'Aye, skipper,' says Elos, pointing out the rest of your crew up in the rigging. 'All the lads are here. When Captain Ancaeus said he was setting sail to find you, we didn't want to miss out on the fun.'

'Catch up later!' snaps the Minotaur, booting another werebeast off the rail as he scythes his axe to cut a grapple-line that the vampires have flung across.

You glance back towards the roof. A horde of vampires, werewolves and other night creatures are swinging ropes to try and snag the ship. Their numbers are swelling every

minute as more of them pour up the stairs or scuttle from chimneys to join the monstrous ranks.

The *Sunrise* lurches and drops a couple of metres. 'We need more lift!' shouts Ancaeus. 'Helmsman, stoke up the buoyancy rotor.' He turns to you. 'If we lose altitude they won't even need ropes to get aboard. They'll just be jumping down on us from the roof.'

Directly astern along the street, your attention is caught by the rent in the air you noticed before. It's larger now and a greyish-blue glow flickers around the edges. Rain is sucked towards it and thrown out in hissing gobbets. In the midst of the searing light, a giant shadowy shape is wading or clawing its way through the pulsing light.

'Thanatos,' you say, catching Ancaeus's arm.

He nods grimly. 'We don't have much time.'

If you have either or both of the codewords **Retract** and **Remedy** ▶ **920**

If you have neither ▶ **840**

1509

The Oracle nods slowly, though whether in approval of your answer or from mere fatigue is unclear. 'There are those who make their living stealing the wealth of others. Go to the district where they dwell. Make the acquaintance of their leader. In serving him you'll be reunited with a child you once saved from slavery.'

You are puzzled. 'But why is that important?'

'The child's fate and yours are intertwined. Now go. You have heard as much of the future as the Lightbringer cares to reveal through me.'

▶ **510**

1510

Storm-ragged moonlight paints the ruins with flitting shadows, turning the familiar streets into a chilling vision of nightmare. You hurry past shattered and smouldering buildings with the uneasy sense that something is watching you from the empty windows.

Note **93** as your Current Location and then ▶ **549**

1511

'You're too valuable to me as you are,' you tell the Face, stuffing it back into your knapsack.

'That's flattering, but – mmph.'

'Talkative little bonce, isn't he?' says Index.

▶ **1008**

1512

'In the garden,' she says, 'there are bergamot trees in alabaster pots.'

'I know the ones.'

'Look under the roots. That's where the treasure is.' The sky in the east is growing pale. 'Now keep your word. Release me!'

Will you do as you promised and let her go?

Yes ▶ 835

No ▶ 24

1513

Achaean warriors hurtle past you, rushing to Ajax's aid, and you lose sight of them in the press of battle.

The next few hours pass in a torrent of blood and screams, furious action followed by long periods in which you roam seeking a fresh foe. Throughout the afternoon you're aware of the gods stooping over the plain, now and then reaching down to pluck a favourite out of harm's way or guide a spear to end a life they have decided has run its course.

'It makes a mockery of all mortal endeavour!' you rage at your comrades as you stand shoulder to shoulder against a phalanx of Ilionian troops.

'What?'

'The gods interfering like this.'

You gesture up into the celestial throng, but of course he can see nothing. Only you perceive the condescending smile of watching deities who tower over the two armies like waterfalls pounding down over a spray of scattered droplets.

A gigantic hand reaches down, sweeping you up off the plain. Squinting into the blaze of divine light, you see the features of your own god.

'It is time for you to go back,' booms a voice louder than storms or eathquakes.

The god's fingers close and you are in darkness.

▶ 73

1514

You race to the stern, where the helmsman is prising up the copper lid of what looks like a compass or gyroscope. Inside is a spinning disk of tangled geometric lines. It makes you feel slightly sick to look at it because of how it's continually shifting, unfolding and refolding, apparently in impossible shapes.

'You have to get your head around it existing in other dimensions,' says the helmsman, hesitantly reaching towards the glowing disk with a strangely shaped spanner. 'Got much experience with buoyancy rotors?'

'That what this is? I thought I was getting a migraine.'

If you have the codeword *Recursive* ▶ 1417 now; otherwise read on.

'It's out of alignment,' says the helmsman. He casts a nervous glance over his shoulder. 'See those sparks? It's dragging against the side of the containment vessel. That's why we're losing altitude.'

'So we need to adjust it? That's what the spanner's for?'

He snorts. 'Vulcan designed it. The tools came with the gizmo. Too bad he didn't include a repair manual.'

He prods the spanner into the housing. There's a protesting screech as the disk grinds against the spanner head. The helmsman leans back, straining with all his might to twist the disk back into alignment. The friction with the spanner slows it even more. The deck lurches, almost throwing you off your feet. Arcs of disturbing light splash out like molten droplets from a furnace.

You glance back at the rail. The Minotaur is grappling a vampire by the throat as he lays about him with his axe at a press of were-beasts. As the rotor slows its spinning the ship is dropping towards the street. Any moment now the horde of creatures on the parapet will be able to jump down on the deck. For all his ferocious strength, the Minotaur can't fight them all.

'We don't have much time,' you tell the helmsman.

He nods. 'Any time you want to lend a hand…'

Make a STRENGTH roll at difficulty 15.

Succeed ▶ 1318

Fail ▶ 216

1515

'You can talk to me,' you say, patting his arm. 'A trouble shared is a trouble halved. Waiter, another bottle of retsina here.'

He glowers across the top of his glass at you. 'I'm just trying to enjoy a quiet drink. You want to keep bothering me, though, I'll be happy to haul you off to jail.'

'For what? For taking an interest in another's problems?'

'For attempting to bribe an officer of the Guard. Now beat it.'

▶ 1534

1516

Get the codeword *Rabbit*.

'Kind of you,' she says, stepping into the hall.

'How can I help you?'

Ignoring your question, she looks around. 'You redecorated.'

'Lord Xechasiaris's tastes were a tad old-fashioned. All those tapestries and painted statues.'

She gives a sudden shudder than could be distaste or the chill of the marble hall after the heat of the day outside. 'It's your home now,' she says, fixing you with an unblinking stare.

'It's what he wanted. We must respect his last wishes.'

This is excruciating. You'd like to get rid of her, but you're not sure how.

Offer her some money ▶ **1115**

Tell her she can take one ornament as a memento ▶ **1367**

Just tell her you're busy and have her shown out ▶ **1001**

1517

'Gods bless you, sir,' you say, adopting a servile tone. 'But you're makin' a hades of a din. If you're goin' to burgle the ol' place, couldn't you do it quiet, like? You might wake my employer.'

How convincing is your act? Make a CHARM roll at difficulty 7. Do not use any item to get a bonus to the roll; all your possessions are currently in your bedroom upstairs.

They think you're a servant   ▶ **167**

They're not taken in   ▶ **1369**

1518

'Too bad,' sighs Dydkos, 'but there's nothing I can do.'

The girl is distraught. 'Must I go back to him? No, I can't.'

'It won't be so bad, dearest.' Dydkos plucks a dandelion from the lawn and twirls it in his fingers. It looks like a tiny constellation of stars. He puffs his cheeks, and the constellation swirls through the scented night air.

'She loves me – '

'Of course I love you.'

'See each little seed.' He's talking to you. 'Thistledown light, soft as smoke, worlds swirling in a deep billowing dream. Each sweep of the clock – ' he blows again, scattering more microscopic seeds – 'brings you closer to waking up, and up, and up...'

It's a test of emotional intelligence. Attempt a CHARM roll at difficulty 9.

Succeed   ▶ **1596**

Fail   ▶ **863**

1519

Using the wings you could fly to several points within the bucolic realm of Arcadia. To do so you will need the Vulcanverse book *The Wild Woods*, and you cannot take any companion with you.

Take to the air   ▶ **1041**

Not now   ▶ **884**

1520

'You say it like it's a bad thing,' she chuckles. 'But didn't you rob the Gargareans when you set their slaves free?'

'They enslaved people like you by conquest, remember. They had no right to keep them.'

She rolls her eyes. 'And you think her over there bought that ballgown with the sweat of her brow? Or baldy digs ditches to pay for those gold rings he's flashing around?'

'Here I was thinking you were just a pickpocket. Turns out you're a striking a blow for justice, eh?'

'Look.' She opens the pouch at her belt to show you the things she's filched already: a filigree bracelet, a couple of silver brooches, and emerald earrings that flash with green fire in the sunset. 'Recycling a bit of their ill-gotten wealth is only fair.'

Escort her out of the palace ▶ **358**

She's got a point   ▶ **1061**

1521

'Any priest can tell you that. Make an offering. Say a prayer. Show them you're a humble mortal who needs their help. Gods always smile on those who flatter their sense of pride.'

'What about you?'

He nods knowingly. 'I prefer to rely on my own wits. Those I can count on. Gods are too fickle, and their gifts always come at a price.'

Ask him something else   ▶ **204**

That's all for now   ▶ **735**

1522

'Now it's a prize, is it?' he says. 'To lie quiet and still in a wooden box while the damp soil gets in and maggots feast? I don't see you being in any rush to die the long death.'

'The gods keep sending me back because I have to save the world. It's kind of an exception.'

He laughs. 'Tell me this. "It was a beautiful story with a satisfying ending" – would you settle for that epitaph?'

If Galatea is with you and you want her advice ▶ **521**

If you possess the **Face of Wisdom** (INGENUITY +3) and want to consult it ▶ **1467**

Otherwise ▶ **483**

1523

The earth is pressing down on your chest. It's impossible to move. You can barely breathe. The spectre holds you in an iron grip. You struggle to break free but the weight of the soil is too overpowering.

Is this it? A moment of dread and helplessness is momentarily relieved as you hear a voice above. Could it be the night watchman on his rounds? You try to scream, but dirt fills your mouth. Even so, you manage a moan that must penetrate through the loose-packed soil. There's the sound of digging. Then the dim light of the evening sky.

You blink the dirt out of your eyes. Yes, it's the night watchman.

'Get me out of here,' you gasp.

'Hang on there.' He pulls away more of the soil. 'Give me your hand.'

You reach up but the spectre also frees one arm, groping around to get a better hold on you. Its bloodless fingers brush the night watchman's hand. And that's when an unworthy thought enters your head: let the spectre take him, not you. If you give in and sink down into permanent death then the fate of the whole world is in peril. But no one will miss the night watchman.

Let the watchman take your place ▶ 693

Accept your own final demise ▶ 362

1524

You race your horse towards the giant figure. It swims in and out of reality before your vision. As you draw close her scale becomes clear. This is a colossus you are attacking, but there's no chance to back out now.

Running across the battlefront, swifter than any horse or chariot, comes Achilles. Seeing your plan, he comes alongside your horse and throws away his shield, offering his left hand as a stirrup for your foot while cutting down foes with his other hand. You step off, and as you make your leap Achilles braces his powerful shoulder muscles, giving you a boost that launches you up towards the gigantic figure.

'Fly, my princess,' you hear him shout. 'Strike and show the gods that we mortals are not mere gnats. We bite back!'

A shimmering aurora hangs around the giant figure, the billowing gossamer folds of her celestial robe that shield her from sight of mortal eyes. You must aim your blow between those folds, at the fleeting moment her marble-white flesh is exposed.

If your Glory score is 18 or more ▶ 1095

Otherwise, if you have the codeword *Royal* ▶ 1535

Otherwise ▶ 1209

1525

Stumbling backwards into a shelf, your fingers close around a screwdriver. You swing it around in a swift arc, driving the point through the golden maiden's ear. Her scream knifes the air and a jolt of electricity kicks up your arm, throwing you back. Sparks and smoke are pouring from her head, along with an acrid charring smell.

'Hypermestra!' cries Autolycus, rushing to help her.

You take advantage of his confusion to break a table over his head. The table is plated in fake gold alloy, giving it more than enough heft to knock him off his feet. The golden maiden is stumbling around, flailing blindly, with the screwdriver still sticking out of the side of her head. Her screaming goes on and on, like a kettle that's been left to boil over. You put paid to that by wrapping the handle of the screwdriver in a cloth and giving it a firm twist. There's a sound like a lead weight dropping inside a metal bucket. Her limbs spasm and she freezes into immobility.

Groaning, Autolycus gropes around and finds the edge of the bed. He hauls himself up and sits there clutching the bump on his head. He looks dazed, all fight gone out of him now.

▶ 1468

1526

'I can't just go to sea,' you explain. 'I don't know where we are in relation to the world I knew. And it's more than an ocean that separates me from my own time and place.'

He sighs. 'Ask the gods. It's always the gods. We're just playing pieces in their games.'

'But how do I speak to the gods, when they have the prayers of thousands of men pouring in their ears?'

'You'll need the intercession of the priests. Speak to Agamemnon.'

▶ 572

1527

What just happened? A blinding flash of light. The pungent scent of a thunderbolt. You felt a wrench like soul and body parting. Where did everybody go? You whirl around. You are no longer on the dusty plain of Ilion. There is cold white marble underfoot. The reek of blood and sweat has gone, and in its place are delicate perfumes. Instead of men's shouts and horses snorting, the distant sound of music wafts on the pure air.

'She cut me,' says a voice from above. 'It hurts!'

You squint into a blinding light that's brighter than an open furnace – the sun, but never have you seen it so close. Against the blistering, roiling gold of its surface, shadowy mirages take the shape of giants.

'Oh Aphrodite,' says another of the voices, also female, reverberating in the immensity of the marble dome above, 'seven acres you covered when you fell. The plain of Ilion's not as comfortable as the couch you like to drape yourself on, eh? I can see that after this you'll shudder at the thought of war. A mortal felling the goddess of love! That's a song they'll sing.'

A rumbling male voice says, 'That we cannot have.'

'Exactly, father,' says Aphrodite. 'She must be killed. Crushed. Blotted out of history.'

'Are we so petty?' says another of the gods. 'Heroism once was lauded, not punished.'

'True.' The older god, whom you take to be Zeus, regards you from the heart of the empyrean radiance. 'Amazon, we note your courage, but the story of the Godslayer is not one we can allow mortals to tell.'

'A cut on her leg, that's all!' you protest. 'I didn't slay any god.'

Zeus says, 'You will.'

Get the title **Godslayer**.

If you have the codeword *Royal* ▶ **241**
If not ▶ **1400**

1528

Sharp teeth gnaw at your innards. Gasping, you stagger and fall. Through a mist of pain you see the gods. They are gazing down on your writhing form with the fleeting curiosity with which you might take notice of a wounded mouse.

Even in the throes of agony, you see the gods are weakened. Their once-perfect flesh shows the marks of many wounds. Golden lifeblood stains their majestic finery. Adamantine armour wrought to be all but impervious to damage now hangs in battered plates and broken links from their weary shoulders.

The pain intensifies. It feels as if you are being eaten by rats from the inside.

'You have failed our dread and thestral sovereign,' screams Oizys into your ear. 'Now suffer the deserts of incompetence.'

If you were already wounded ▶ **666**

If not, tick your Wound box now and ▶ **136**

1529

'Well then, Amazon, speak your piece. I have a hundred demands on my time.'

What will you say to Agamemnon, commander of the Achaeans?

'I need to return home.' ▶ **511**
'I wish to make a sacrifice to the gods.' ▶ **1245**
'Let me fight on your side.' ▶ **679**
'Forget it. We'll talk another time.' ▶ Current Location

1530

❏

If the box above is already ticked ▶ **524**

If the box is empty, put a tick in it now and read on.

'That's the Gallery of Regret,' you overhear a guest saying to her companion as they stroll arm in arm towards the fountain.

'Shall we go in?'

'You might not like what you hear,' she says. 'Tradition says you can solve your troubles by speaking them aloud under the dome, after a princess in ancient times confessed she didn't care to marry the wealthy lord to whom she was pledged. She was overheard by a young prince who rescued her from her fate.'

Her friend laughs wickedly. 'You don't want to be rescued from your fate, do you, my dear?'

You step inside. It is a circular chamber of honey-yellow stone that glistens in the light filtering through narrow amber windows. Above is a lofty brass dome that magnifies whispers from any part of the room and brings them back to someone standing in the centre.

If Galatea is your companion ▶ **1172**
If Chipos is your companion ▶ **1390**
Otherwise ▶ **75**

1531

As Nyx's power weakens, the jewelled Eye burns ever brighter. Its intensity increases unstoppably, a runaway nova that drives her to her knees and grows until it outshines the dawn of the universe. The scene around you blisters away into a white totality.

Nyx can bear it no longer. She is shrivelling in the glare. With a scream like a universe dying, she explodes into a myriad motes that drift and fade like fine cindery ash.

You are slumped on the ground. You have no strength left. Even the pain has gone. You feel as if your own body has disintegrated too.

'You did it,' says a voice. Eros is beside you. Others too, eager to congratulate you. You're only dimly aware of them. The Eye is returning to normal, but that's not the only reason for the fading light. You realize that Nyx's final blasts have inflicted wounds that nothing can heal. You defeated her at the cost of your own life.

▶ **42**

1532

The guard relaxes when he sees you're not going to fight on. He licks his lips nervously, one ear cocked for the sound of the other man returning with back-up.

A metallic clink makes him jump. 'What the hell – ?'

The mechanical spider scurries out of the torchlit shadows beside him. He reacts in horror, backing away from it wide-eyed.

Taking advantage of his distraction, you slip through the door opposite where you came in. A moment later the spider joins you, rushing around the corner in a flurry of limbs and locking the door with one of the keys on its feet.

The guard starts hammering on the other side of the door, but when he tries his own keys they don't seem to work. The spider beckons you to follow, leading the way up a short flight of steps to a cell in the very eaves of the building.

▶ 1397

1533

Lightning crashes across the sky as your champions charge into battle against Nyx's sons Death and Sleep. This is the final showdown, the contest of elemental forces. If your allies can keep the two titans occupied, you have a chance of reaching Nyx herself. And somehow you must find a way to defeat her, or else the world is lost.

If you have the codeword *Romance* ▶ 324

If not ▶ 1317

1534

The Boulevard of the Gnome runs the length of the city's eastern wall. When the wind is in the right direction the street is filled with fresh leaf-smelling air and the scent of blossom from Arcadia.

If you have the codeword *Razor* and this box ❑ is empty, tick it and record **1534** as your Current Location, then ▶ 397; otherwise read on.

If you have either or both of the codewords *Quad* or *Queen* and this box ❑ is empty, tick it and ▶ 711; otherwise read on.

To go straight to a city location that you already know about, note **1534** as your Current Location, then ▶ 1432

Visit a tavern garden (only if you have the codeword *Rye*) ▶ 1199

Or you can go:

North ▶ 48

South ▶ 333

1535

You'll need to make both a powerful leap and your mightiest blow. Attempt two rolls, STRENGTH and GRACE, both at difficulty 9.

Both rolls are successful ▶ 1095

Either or both fail ▶ 1179

1536

If you have the **Face of Wisdom** (INGENUITY +3) and this box ❑ is empty, tick it and ▶ 1187; otherwise read on.

'There's no point going back to the Syndics' place,' says Dunamis.

'You got a better idea?'

She pulls a face. 'I haven't got a worse one.'

▶ 820

1537

'Remind me, which of us is blind?'

'Huh?'

'That pond over yonder, is it the Cataract of Oceanus?'

'No, but – '

'Are we in a park in the middle of the city, or are we in northern Notus?'

'The park, obviously.'

'Well, now you know where you've gone wrong, don't you, kid?'

Ptolemos has nothing more to say, so you bid him farewell.

▶ 806

1538

You pledged to save the world on behalf of the Olympian gods. Do you mean to turn it over to them now?

'There's another way,' says Eros, joining you at the front of your band of allies. 'Psyche can reprogram Vulcan's matrix to create a bubble universe alongside this one. The world you deliver to the Olympians could just be a simulation of a simulation.'

'Fob them off with that? But none of the people in that simulation will have free will. They'll just be puppets.'

Eros laughs. 'And you think the Olympians will notice? They've never given two pyr for the wishes of mortals.'

Do as Eros suggests ▶ 84

Keep your oath to Zeus ▶ 1351

1539

Moose is sent down for several years. You figure that Zinc probably isn't happy about that, and you are proved right a few days later when half a dozen ex-gladiators jump you outside a tavern and deliver a short but severe punishment beating.

Tick the Wound box on your Adventure Sheet if you weren't injured already. Also lose any money and **lava gems** that you are carrying, which they confiscate for their trouble.

'The boss says it's not personal,' says one, looking down at you lying on the cobblestones.

'Well, technically he said it was heartfelt but he'd forgive you in a few days,' puts in another over his shoulder as they stroll off.

'Tell him the feeling's mutual,' you call after them, gingerly probing a tooth that you think they've knocked loose.

▶ 988

1540

Ancaeus turns to you, his beard and hair matted with rainwater. 'Get the halyard onto that winch!' he shouts over the roar of the gale.

You grab the loose end of the rope he's hauling and start winding it onto the winch. Gusts of wind tear at the rope as Ancaeus tries to hold it steady. Blood is flowing freely where the rough fibres have cut deep into his hands, but with his face set against the pain he takes a running jump to seize the halyard further up, dragging it down while you crank furiously at the winch.

The deck lurches to one side. The vessel is now several metres below the level of the roof, making it easier for your foes to jump across. The Minotaur is holding his own for now, but for how long – ?

If you have the codeword *Recursive* ▶ 1437 immediately; otherwise read on.

'We need to get higher,' you yell to Ancaeus.

'It's because we're not moving. She'll gain buoyancy once we're under way.' He staggers back, buffeted by the tempest, and takes hold of the winch. 'The sail's got snagged, can you see?'

He's right. The canvas has caught on a spar, wrapped around it by the wind, and that's why it's not opening.

You can see from Ancaeus's injured hands that he's in no condition to go aloft. 'I'll free it. You stay at the winch.'

Make a GRACE roll at difficulty 14.

Succeed ▶ 859
Fail ▶ 334

1541

Your six loyal shipmates are working alongside Ancaeus's own crew.

'That Ancaeus bloke was as good as his word, skipper,' says your first mate. 'He said he was coming looking for you, that's why we signed on with him.'

'And I'm glad you did, Mister Elos.'

They nod their heads in the bashful way of plain-speaking honest men. 'What are your orders now, cap'n?'

'It's Ancaeus's ship. He's the captain. Do what he tells you for now.'

If you have the codewords *Rustic* and *Noble* ▶ 545
If you have only *Rustic* ▶ 169
If only *Noble* ▶ 728
If neither ▶ 231

1542

'Oh, of course it's a simulation in that sense,' says an aristocratic philosopher who has chosen to remain standing throughout the debate. 'Everyone knows that Vulcan created the world. But is it a simulation of a simulation? And if this isn't real, what is reality?'

'A simulation of a simulation?' says Myletes. 'Can you define your terms?'

The aristocrat dips one sandalled foot in the pond beside him. 'Is this water? Or is it a physical construct of Vulcan's, by which I mean another substance that resembles water? Or is everything an illusion and I only think that my foot is wet?'

The discussion continues until sunset. You stay for supper with Myletes and then make your way home. Get the codeword *Riven* and ▶ 1062

1543

'You know about the phoenix? Lives in the Aetnaean mountains north of Notus? Course you do. Everyone's heard of the phoenix. I'm going to need one of its feathers.'

If you have a **phoenix feather** to give him ▶ 1473

If not, he programs the glowing beetles to transport you to a nearby street, and you drift up through the ground ▶ 1617

1544

❏

If you do not have the codeword *Reverie* and the box above is empty, put a tick in it and ▶ 15

Otherwise read on.

The Academy of Philosophers is not a single building but an entire campus of courtyards, auditoriums, residential halls, meeting rooms, covered walkways, a refectory and a library, all set amid green manicured lawns where the scholars can stroll, think and discuss their ideas in peaceful contemplation.

If you have either codeword *Namesake* or *Nihilism* and this box ❏ is empty, tick it and ▶ 122; otherwise read on.

If you have the title **Giant Slayer** and you want to call on Myletes ▶ 188

Leave the Academy ▶ 1062

1545

There is a recessed bay on the side of the machine. It looks a little like an open sarcophagus but you try not to dwell on that. At Psyche's direction you back into it.

'Make sure you're in contact with the copper veins at the back of the pod,' she says. 'Ready? Don't move...'

She pulls a lever. Arcs of crackling plasma dance around you, sending a burning sensation flowing through your limbs. You look down to see an actinic glow emanating from inside you, so intense that your skeleton and muscles can be seen silhouetted under your skin. Instead of agony, the feeling it gives you is of being reborn.

'This is the true fire of the gods!' you shout over the noise of the machine.

Psyche is peering intently at a bank of dials. You can see her counting down. She slams the lever back and the galvanic arcs flicker and fade. The machine goes quiet.

'All done,' says Psyche.

Increase your attributes (CHARM, GRACE, INGENUITY and STRENGTH) to +5. If all four attribute scores were already at +5, you can increase one attribute of your choice to +6.

If you were injured, untick the Wound box on your Adventure Sheet.

Also, acquire two blessings. Each blessing can be used to roll again when you fail an attribute check but only once in any given situation, so if you fail the reroll, you can't spend another blessing to try again.

► 1171

1546

'I should have you whipped, Amazon.'

'Try it, please. On that instant everyone will see the colour of your blood. You with your savage dog's face but the quailing heart of a deer. I notice you never buckle on armour when your men go out on the plain to do battle. You sit here, a bloated sack of wine with a bevy of young girls – and those you had to seize in war, for no woman would lie with you of her own will. Yes, go get your whip. I'll choke you on it.'

Agamemnon stands as though struck by one of Zeus's bolts, stunned and speechless. The others turn away, embarrassed to bear witness that he dares no answer to your challenge.

Nestor leads you out of the tent. 'Next time he sees you, he'll pretend to have forgotten all about it. But you have made an enemy there, lady.'

'Hey, I've got titans for enemies. A preening pustule like him counts for less than a drop of piss in the ocean.'

► Current Location

1547

Get the codeword *Rink*.

A narrow staircase of dark waxed wood leads up through the crumbling, half-derelict building. On each floor there are several rooms, most of them housing more than one family. You have to step over toddlers left to play on the landing while their parents are busy with whatever jobs the denizens of the Grumbles have.

'Looking to rent a room?' says a cracked old voice. You look up to see a bent-backed caretaker hobbling downstairs

towards you. The cane he uses to support his doddery legs is almost as gnarled as he is.

'Looking for a man named Autolycus,' you say.

He points up the stairs behind him. 'He's in the garret room at the top. Don't think he's in right now, though.'

'What about the woman who lives with him?'

The caretaker frowns, puzzled. 'I had the notion he lives alone. He only buys food for one.'

'That makes sense.'

'You can wait in his room if you want.' The caretaker pulls out a bunch of keys and leads the way up the stairs to the garret.

Follow him ► 225
Tell him you'll come back later ► 603

1548

Seeing the ships ablaze, the saboteurs scurry back to their own vessels with arms full of plunder from the Myrmidon tents.

At the end of the day, the soldiers return weary from the battle. Achilles and his companions survey the ruin of their camp. Having spent their fury out on the plain, they have none left to rage at this fresh misfortune.

'Go to the other kings,' he tells his companions. 'Borrow what we need to repair the camp.'

'What about the ships?' says his friend Patroklos, staring aghast at the smouldering hulls like the ribs of slain titans. 'How will we get home?'

'Time enough to worry about that later. We never needed that many ships anyway. For half of us at least this was always a one-way journey.' Seeing you, Achilles' sombre look breaks into a smile of relief. 'There you are! Praise the gods. I feared the reavers who despoiled our camp might have done you harm.'

► 1500

1549

To access the underlying code of reality you will need **Vulcan's diadem**, but for the time being you can at least use the board's rapid-transit function to teleport to another location:

The nearest tower ► 412

The Avenue of the Anvil ► 736

Your mansion (only if you have the title **The Unexpected Heir**) ► 1175

Your family home (only if you have the codeword *Reverie*) ► 881

The Academy of Philosophers ► 93

The temple district ► 626

The Forum ► 1589

1550

The dragon-like head sways in front of you, tongue darting in and out in a rapid mesmerizing flicker. As it lunges, you bring your hand up to drive deep into the softer flesh of its throat, where there are no scales to protect it.

If your timing was a split-second quicker, you would have avoided its bite. The teeth grind down on your arm, losing strength as the monster's life-blood ebbs away, but still sharp enough to grate against your bones.

If you were already injured, record your Current Location as **683** and then ▶ **670**

Otherwise, tick your Wound box now and ▶ **1446**

1551

Just before the drop, the guards reluctantly remove the condemned man's gag. Tradition demands that he be free to call out to the gods, whether they heed him or not, as the soul exits the body with the final breath.

Instead of a prayer he cries, 'It's in the trees! Catapulted west! The eye! The light that – '

His feet are kicked off the platform. The rope snaps taut. His words are choked off and he dangles there, kicking and writhing, as his eyes pop out and his face turns from purple to black.

'Didn't break his neck,' remarks the woman beside you. There's relish in her voice. 'That's good. It's cheating when they go quick.'

Mulling over the criminal's last words, you return to the Forum.

▶ **1642**

1552

Two or three out-of-towners are roping off a patch of grass, while a larger group of people are yelling at them to get lost.

A big man with a crewcut shakes his fist. 'You can't close off an area of the park like that, you dopey yokels.'

'Get back to where you came from,' shouts a woman who is spitting with fury. 'We don't want your sort around here.'

You ask the outlanders what they're doing. 'We only want to fence off this small area for a week or two,' says their leader. 'We are worshippers of the capricious god Sabazios. See, he has cast down a gift to remind us of his whims. It would be sacrilege to touch it.'

He points to an apple lying on the grass.

'A miracle,' breathes a scrawny young woman who is tying off the rope.

'You muddle-headed foreigners,' snarls someone in the crowd. 'Since when is a windfall apple a miracle?'

The leader of the outlanders turns with raised arms. A preacher's zeal lights up his eyes. 'Friends! Yes, it seems but a windfall apple. But see – there is no apple tree!'

Something stirs dimly in your memory. 'Didn't there used to be..?'

'No apple tree!' he insists. 'The rope is for your own protection. That apple is the sign of the great god Sabazios, who would instantly curse any who touched it.'

At that moment a fox bounds out of the trees, grabs the apple, and runs off. The outlanders stare, shoulders sagging in dismay. The crowd disperse with peals of scornful laughter. But all you can think about is a fleeting memory of an apple tree with bark that looked like stone and leaves of twisting shapes.

▶ **806**

1553

If you have the codeword *Remedy* ▶ **276** immediately.

If not and this box ❑ is empty, tick it and ▶ **1113**

If you don't have *Remedy* and the box was ticked already ▶ **1028**

1554

How often have you had to jostle your way along these streets through a bustling crowd of shoppers and traders? Now the city is shrouded in darkness and seemingly deserted. The beam from Dunamis's lantern shows a scene of blasted ruin. Some houses look as if a titan had stamped on them. Others have sagging roofs and lopsided beams as if from long years of neglect.

You see a few fires, perhaps lit by survivors, but there is no sign of life. Perhaps, like the people you saw before, they are hiding out in the rubble too scared to show themselves.

Dunamis grabs your arm and points. Up ahead, outlined in silhouette against a guttering brazier on the street corner, is a woman. From her outline she appears to be naked. Taking her for a refugee, you call out.

She turns towards you just as the light from the lantern strikes her. It reveals the ingot sheen of her skin and the cold alien beauty of a metal mannikin. Her eyes reflect the light as flat panes of quartz. Approaching swiftly, she opens her golden lips and utters a shrill cry.

'A Celedon!' says Dunamis.

If you have the **voicebox remote** and want to use it ▶ **77**

Otherwise you can make a run for it (▶ **1176**) or stand and fight (▶ **1303**).

1555

'It's a shame the old fellow never got to travel,' she says wistfully. 'Wanderlust was in his soul from an early age. All the stories he heard from traders bringing their wagons from the corners of the world. Think how hard it is to give up your dreams like that.'

'A lot of us have notions when we're seven that we've forgotten about in adulthood.'

'Oh, you never wanted to be a hero, then?' She shakes her head. 'I don't think something like that ever leaves you. It stays buried in there calling to you, fainter and fainter but it's always there. Think about the time you met him. It wasn't decades of boring old duty that he wanted to talk about, it was crayon drawings of distant lands.'

▶ 133

1556

There's a frenzied thrashing in the bushes. Scuttling forth on long thorny legs come three huge insectoid monsters whose smooth armoured carapaces will turn all but the mightiest blows. Their coal-black eyes fix on you and they come rushing across the lawn. Their sharp chitinous claws dig easily into the turf, giving them the purchase to move swiftly to surround you.

Stand your ground and fight	▶ 606
Retreat indoors	▶ 1578
Head to the avenue of topiary figures	▶ 119

1557

'It's easy to be mistaken,' you tell the merchant. 'For example, you thought my friend Moose was robbing you, and all he wanted was a loan. He should've been clearer about that, but surely we can avoid the unpleasantness of a trial? Look, here's your money back plus interest.'

The spice merchant looks at the coins you've counted out. It's an overcast day, but they seem to gleam with a light of their own. He licks his lips.

'What a silly misunderstanding!' he booms, suddenly ebullient. Sweeping the coins into his hands he adds, 'I'll explain to the authorities that I got the wrong end of the stick. But please impress on Mr Moose that he needs to be more straightforward when dealing with honest citizens in future.'

By the end of the day Moose has been released and Zinc is satisfied. 'To be honest it was a little bit of a test,' he admits. 'I wanted to see if you'd solve the problem the dumb way or whether you'd use your initiative. Here's money to cover what you paid the merchant. Much better to handle it that way than all the bother of confessions and jail sentences.'

Gain the codeword *Robber* and ▶ 771

1558

You have incapacitated a couple of the Celedons, but there are more arriving every minute in answer to the incessant shriek. You have to get this fight over quick.

Make a STRENGTH or GRACE roll (your choice) at difficulty 13.

Succeed	▶ 582
Fail	▶ 259

1559

'Keep putting it off, don't you?' calls out Ptolemos as you approach his bench.

'How did you know it was me?' says Loutro, surprised.

'That hesitant tread. You can't think of an excuse for not having got on and done that blamed ritual.'

'I thought you didn't believe in it anyway.'

'Not the point. If I had my sight back and I believed in something, I'd be off this minute. I wouldn't let the days pile up behind me like dung heaps.'

They exchange a few reminiscences, but you can tell Loutro is stung by his old colleague's rebuke. 'He's right,' he admits as you walk away, 'I'm clinging to my companionship with you when I should be doing the task that Tethys has set me.'

'To restore the river?'

'No. To teach the one who will restore it.'

▶ 806

1560

Get the codeword *Raptor*.

'If you still have the wings of Icarus,' says the Oracle, 'you can use them to travel to the outlying realms of the Vulcanverse.'

'How?'

'Go to the top of one of the four towers in the city wall. Affix the wings to your body with beeswax. Then you will soar like a bird.'

'And where should I fly?'

She draws her hand across her face as if lowering a veil. 'As to that, trust to fate for guidance. Now go.'

▶ 510

1561

Half a dozen figures clad in tattered, dust-covered clothes are hunched around the punch bowl. There's a sound of urgent lapping like thirsty animals at a waterhole. To one side of the room there's a stack of very old lichen-spotted coffins. The discarded nails and torn rotted wood tell you that the coffin lids have only recently been prised open.

You go closer. You can see your own reflection in the wall mirror, and the punchbowl whose scarlet surface is rippling, but the mirror shows no sign of the figures themselves.

The air is thick with the reek of mildewed clothing and decayed flesh. Sensing you, they turn furtively. Their faces are dusty and shrivelled, wax noses and ears replacing what was eaten by rats or the pox. Something red and sticky dribbles down their chins. The punch bowl is filled to the brim with fresh frothing blood. The drink they've taken from it is slowly reinflating their shrunken veins, which wriggle and swell visibly beneath the papery skin.

Where did that blood come from? You remember the guests torn apart by the Celedons. The bodies are gone, but there are gory drag-marks across the marble floor.

'This punch is no good for quaffing,' says one of the vampires in a plaintive, reedy voice. 'Not enough body.'

Their eyes fix eagerly on you.

If you have the codewords *Rose* and *Recursive* ▶ 1178
Otherwise ▶ 929

1562

Note **333** as your Current Location, then ▶ **1269** and tick the box next to the East Gate. From now on you will always be able to find your way back here.

1563

'Remember once that in a dream you found the well between the worlds?' says Eos. 'Perhaps you left some things there. If so, the first thing you do on returning to the Vulcan City should be to retrieve them.'

Seek more advice ▶ 1292
Get going ▶ 90

1564

Delete both the **food of the gods** and the **abysm toxin** and replace them with **poisoned ambrosia**.

Tittering horribly, Oizys urges you up the mountainside towards the glittering palaces of the Olympians.

▶ 678

1565

You tell the story of your ascent into the mountains – the jagged grey peaks, the gritty sleet skittering on the wind, the mysterious doorway sealed by multiple locks and guarded by a demon of darkness, the gloom of the labyrinth, and finally turning a corner and coming face to face with the minotaur.

Your audience are by this time completely transported by your tale. They are crouching as they listen to you, as if the low tunnel of the labyrinth were pressing down overhead. Some are even shivering at the imagined cold. As you describe the minotaur, one or two give little yelps of alarm and have to sit down.

'It came right at me. Thud, thud, thud.' Lowering your head, you mime the minotaur's massive, relentless tread and the listeners in front of you lean back in alarm in case you stomp right through them.

'What did you do?' squeaks a man nearby.

By luck he has a prominent nose. You reach out and give it a light pinch.

'What did I do? I clipped a ring on its nose and ever after it was as meek as a lamb.'

He gives a little shriek. Everyone else laughs in relief, and after the initial shock passes he joins in, rubbing his nose. 'Well, I had to ask,' he says with a grin.

There is polite but enthusiastic applause. 'I can't match that,' says Kazala with a decorous bow. 'Round one to you.'

▶ 254

1566

Spitpuddle Row is a dank and noisome alley even for the Grumbles. You watch the building where Marija lives and are surprised when she comes out. Instead of the furtive, pinch-faced, scurrying wretch you'd been led to expect, she is a handsome woman clad in elegant gold-threaded silk.

She sees your shadow on the muddy ground and looks up to see you blocking her way. She nods, apparently having expected this moment.

'You'll make it quick?' she asks, biting her ruby-painted lip.

'You know Zinc. It's just business with him.'

Marija looks around. 'Not here in the street. Let's go to my room.'

Fair enough ▶ 268
Just kill her right now ▶ 479

1567

The Keres spread out to encircle you, picking their way through the rubble like huge grounded bats. You glance around. There's one escape route, but if you turn your back the nearest of the Keres will surely impale you on its spear-like forelimb.

A figure is charging at the Keres from the rear. He gives a bellowing war-cry to get their attention. In the dim lamp-light you see that he wields a sword in each hand and his skin is tinged blue.

'Glaukos!'

One of the Keres lunges at him, snarling in frustration as its needle-sharp teeth glance off his bronze-hard flesh. The others turn, forgetting you in their impatience to despatch this impudent new foe.

Glaukos pitches into battle swinging his swords to left and right. You see at once that he can't hope to last more than a few seconds. The Keres will bring him down by sheer weight of numbers, then drive their hard spiky claws even through his gorgon-hardened skin.

You reach for your weapon and start forward. 'Don't be an idiot,' snaps Glaukos. 'The fate of the world depends on you. Get going!'

He's right, though it's with heavy heart that you grab Dunamis and run off down the street. You vow that Glaukos's sacrifice will not be in vain.

▶ Current Location

1568

Lose the titles **Accursed of Ares** and **Unfriended by Apollo** if you have either of them. Also lose the **obsidian sword** if you have it.

You have no need to explain yourself to the priests. They recognize your aura of destiny as surely as if a beam of celestial light were shining down on you. The high priest takes you through to the inner shrine and leaves you alone to commune with the god.

Incense curls and snakes from copper braziers, thickening into veils of hazy golden light that hang around you. The muffled, vault-echoing murmur from the outer shrine recedes. Cool air, sharp and clean, brushes your cheek, parting the haze of incense-smoke to reveal a vision of a hillside carpeted in green grass. Streams plunge and spray among the rocks. Far up towards the summit are clouds in which the towering shapes of palaces can be glimpsed beyond a dazzling boundary of sun-glancing ice.

'You have passed all the tests I set.'

'Who's there?'

You turn, looking all around, but there is only the wind in the trees, the splashing of the brook – and from very far off the transcendent melody of a empyrean choir, barely in the range of earthly hearing.

'The twelve labours are done,' continues the voice. 'You have proven yourself my worthy champion. Now you stand on the slopes of immortality. But there remains a challenge more dangerous than any you have faced so far.'

'A challenge beyond the powers of the gods?' you reply, perhaps from defiance, perhaps pride, perhaps fear.

'There will be a battle here too,' says the voice of your deity. 'The war is coming to the very gates of heaven. To have any hope of survival we must fight the Queen of Night on all fronts. Your part is to face the foe in the mundane realm, for Night desires to wrest control of Hephaistos's creation.'

'Why must I fight her alone?'

'You will not be alone. In achieving the labours I set you have made friends who will stand by you. And as my champion you will fight with the blessing of the Olympians themselves.'

'When will the battle begin?'

'Soon. Go out into the city. Hone your body and your wits to weapon-keenness. Gather your war gear. When you know yourself to be ready, return to my temple and I will tell you what must be done.'

The distant singing swells, rising in pitch impossibly. The golden radiance of the sky grows brighter until it is a blaze against which you are forced to close your eyes.

A moment later, still dazzled, you emerge from the inner shrine. Priests and worshippers alike stop what they are doing and stare along the nave towards you. They watch you pass in silence as you make your way to the pillared entrance. The streets outside still teem with people. The streets lie all around as far as the city walls. The sun shines as before, the clamour and smells of the city are unchanged. And yet you have the feeling that everything has been transformed. As if the world ceased to exist while you dreamed of Mount Olympus and now has been remade exactly as it was before.

'That one has met the god,' somebody says in an awed whisper from the nave behind you.

Lose the codeword *Rohan* and gain the title **The Chosen One**, then ▶ 103

1569

You lash out at the first of them, spearing through the fibrous tissue bridging a gap in the chitinous exoskeleton. Your blow crushes the soft organs within and the creature shudders and falls, curling up into a twitching knot of spiny limbs.

A stab of pain runs up your thigh. You look down to see a red gash where the creature bit you before it died. Already the puckered flesh is turning grey from its venom. Tick the Wound box on your Adventure Sheet if it was not ticked already.

▶ **738** and tick one of the boxes there before reading on.

1570

'You must poison it,' Oizys snarls in your ear.

| Do as she says | ▶ **569** |
| Refuse | ▶ **112** |

1571

The dragon-like head sways in front of you, tongue darting in and out in a rapid flicker. At the exact moment it lunges, you bring your hand up to drive deep into the softer flesh of its throat, where there are no scales to protect it.

Thrashing its coils against the rocks, the serpent writhes and lashes out blindly. Most horrible of all, it howls curses and prophecies in a hundred strange rustling voices, only falling silent when you heft a boulder and bring it crunching down on the long reptilian head. It lies twitching in a spreading lake of blood and pulped brains.

'That was Ladon,' purrs Oizys, taking a depraved pleasure in the brutal violence of your battle. 'All the classic monsters are getting squashed these days. It's going to be a whole new era.'

► 1446

1572

'What's this?'

'A window onto the dreamlands. In it you can spy on what your wife is doing.'

'Huh. It's covered in soot.' He scowls, breathes on the blackened surface, and wipes a handkerchief over it. For a moment he stares into the glass, astonished, then in less than the blink of an eye he's gone, and in his place stands the young man, Dydkos.

'Wake up, darling,' he says, shaking the sleeping girl. 'It's all over.'

Her eyes flutter open and she stretches languorously. 'Is it true? I hardly dare believe I'm not still dreaming this.'

'He's gone, all right. All the way to the bottom of the dream.'

Dydkos shows her the mirror, then hands it to you. In its depths you can just make out a small, flickering figure blundering through what seems to be an unlit cavern. It is the merchant.

'Now what?' you say, handing back the mirror. 'He's an important man in this town. People will soon notice he's missing.'

Dydkos smiles. 'My people are not the arch-wizards that some make us out to be, but I know a few magic tricks.'

At that moment a servant taps on the door. Dydkos strides over, drawing his hand across his face as he goes. As he opens the door he already wears the merchant's face and speaks with his voice. 'Don't disturb us now,' he tells the servant. 'Go and tell the cook to prepare a meal. Your mistress is awake and she is famished.'

When the servant has gone, Dydkos reverts to his real form. 'I can only keep that illusion going for a few minutes at a time, but it will be enough. Roxana and I will live here, and people will think us a quiet married couple who keep mostly to ourselves.'

'How can we ever thank you?' says Roxana. 'It seems an insult to offer you money, but if this is of use then please take it.'

She hands you a box of coins worth 100 pyr; add them to your money if you accept them. Also gain the codeword **Rebuke**.

'We owe you a debt that can never be repaid,' they say as they show you to the door.

If you have the codeword **Ruby** ► 1380
Otherwise ► 515

1573

A figure leans over you. Your vision is watery and unfocussed, so that you see the newcomer's face as only a blur of disjointed features and jagged pinpricks of sea-flung sunlight.

'Nothing we can do for you, I'm afraid,' the stranger says.

'Nonsense. It's just a scratch.'

You try to sit up, but your strength has drained away. Gently the stranger presses you back against the bed. 'You're out. It can't be helped. A prophecy conflict error. The easiest way to balance the books is to say you died as a result of your injuries.'

'What are you… talking about…?'

You're so drowsy. Getting hard to stay awake. Could you have lost that much blood? Darkness encroaches at the edges of your vision, and the last thing you're aware of is the presence of your god.

► 73

1574

'But Nyx controls the workshop of creation. How are you going to fight her when she sets all the rules?'

'Nice try,' says Daedalus with an appreciative nod, 'but my regeneration ability trumps that. Vulcan's simulation of the world is built on top of the essence of the gods and titans.'

'How can you be sure?'

'You know, you might be right. Instead of hanging out here to watch the show, I need to get down into the nuts and bolts of Vulcan's machine and rejig it to do what I want.'

'Exactly.'

He starts to tighten his grip on your windpipe. 'Of course, that does mean I don't have any more time to waste on you.'

'Wait,' you gurgle. 'I can help you.'

'Don't worry, I'll figure it out. I usually do.'

His armoured fingers are digging into your throat. You can't breathe. A wave of dizziness drags you into oblivion.

► 666

1575

'I don't like to resort to clichés,' says the head, 'but they say you should set a thief to catch a thief.'

'Ideally, yes. But it's just us, so we'll have to make do.'

'Then you should try thinking like a thief.'

'For instance?'

'If you were a thief, you might not come and go by the front door. You might sneak about, bound across rooftops, climb down drainpipes, things like that. So why not try it and see if that helps?'

Climb up to Autolycus's room   ► **1359**

Keep watching the house from here   ► **26**

1576

A sensation like cobwebs brushing over your face. With a shudder you realize that the embryonic dream above you has pushed free of its caul. Soft boneless fingers, probing. A faint, mewling voice rusting in your ear. An over-sweet smell like honey left in a dank cellar.

The darkness seeps away. You are staring out at a sea of expressionless faces. You try to speak – no sound comes. You raise your hand to attract their attention. It's a lump of painted wood lifted by a piece of string.

Now you're moving, but without volition. The strings drag your clattering feet across the felt-covered stage. On either side of you hang canvas flaps. You are in one of the puppet booths that used to be found on the Street of Ash, before the city became a ruined warzone in the onslaught of Night's hordes.

Screaming inside, but unable to speak or move except as the puppeteer directs, you act out a drama of the end of the world in which a lone mortal struggles in vain against the unstoppable might of the titan queen.

Lose 3 points from your attributes: CHARM, GRACE, INGENUITY or STRENGTH. You can decide which attributes are affected, and you do not have to take all 3 points from the same attribute.

► **431**

1577

Choose one of your attributes (CHARM, GRACE, INGENUITY or STRENGTH) and reduce it by 1. Attribute scores can go negative.

► Current Location

1578

Torn and broken bodies stain the white marble floor. The surviving partygoers have all fled into the entrance courtyard, where you can hear terrified shrieking as they stampede towards to the gate.

The Celedons are standing in the middle of the ballroom scanning for victims. Each time they catch sight of themselves in the long wall-length mirror they jerk as if about to attack, then it seems they recognize their own reflection and continue looking around. For some reason they are taking no notice of you.

The three giant insect-creatures have you firmly fixed in their faceted gaze. They lurch rapidly towards you across the ballroom, spiky limbs and claws scything the air.

► **1381**

1579

From the shape of the package you think somebody has sent you a walking stick or a club, but when you tear off the wrapping paper you find it is a narthex stalk consisting of a hard rind around a core of cottony white pith. A smell of singed vegetation wafts out. There are smouldering embers buried among the pith.

A note is wrapped around the stalk: cursive letters burned into a scrap of hide. It reads:

The time approaches. Be ready. I will be there when you need me. – Prometheus'

The stalk heats up, releasing a cloud of hot fumes. As you inhale them, it is like being struck by lightning. You take a step back, almost tripping over a low table, yet instead of falling you plant your hand in the middle of the table and execute a perfect back flip, landing gracefully beside the maid.

'Shall I serve breakfast now?' she asks, unfazed.

Gain +1 GRACE up to a maximum score of +5, then ► **97**

1580

The Celedon steps warily closer. Her moulded face shows no expression but you can see by her careful movements that she's reluctant to get within range of your heavy club.

Instead of lunging at her, you throw the club down with a sob. Seemingly overcome by terror, you turn and scramble across shattered blocks of masonry into the interior of a ruined building.

The Celedon marches forward. You stop short and turn to face her. She thinks she has you cornered. Framed in the doorway, she unleashes her scream. The arch above her, no longer supported by a door-jamb, gives way under the sonic vibrations and she is buried under a half-tonne of bricks.

Dunamis emerges from hiding. 'If they're all as dumb as that one, we're laughing.'

You gingerly prod the golden foot that's sticking out of the rubble. It doesn't move. 'I was lucky. We can't count on that trick working every time.'

► Current Location

1581

Swift-footed and fierce, the Amazons come to your aid, running in close formation with their bows and spears ready. Without any need for a command, so instinctive is their battle drill, they come to a halt and fall in beside your other troops.

'Hail to you, Majesty!' the Amazons shout as one, a voice to strike terror into their enemies' hearts.

'Phoebe, it is good to see you,' you shout to your chamberlain. 'And Tekmessa, I see. Are you ready for a battle royal?'

'It is a good day to die, Majesty!' cries the ferocious Tekmessa, to cheers from the other Amazons. 'Let me kill a score of them and I'll go to Hades' arms exultant.'

▶ 954

1582

Get the codeword *Rigor*.

You find the girl a few streets away buying sweet buns from a roadside stall.

'Sugar will rot your teeth.'

She whirls, wide-eyed, jam from the bun running down her chin. 'You!'

You're as startled as she is. Life on the streets in Vulcan City has made her leaner, sharper and certainly grubbier, but you recognize her all the same as the girl you freed from slavery among the Gargareans.

'Dunamis! You were supposed to go straight home to Iskandria. Not take up a career as a thief.'

She shifts her feet guiltily, looking more like a naughty little girl than a master criminal. 'I only rob the ones that look like they can afford it.'

| Take her to see Zinc | ▶ 237 |
| Let her go | ▶ 1617 |

1583

You duck his clumsy swing and come in under his guard, striking for his throat to prevent him calling out. He rolls back gasping and you lay him out flat with a second blow.

The spider runs back along the wall, stands poised over the prone guard for a moment, then jumps across to the final door and leads the way through. A short flight of steps brings you to a cell right up under the highest eaves of the prison.

▶ 1397

1584

❑

If you have the codeword *Rock* and the box above is empty, tick it and ▶ 621

If you have the codeword *Rock* and the box above was already ticked ▶ 1661

If you don't have *Rock* but you have the codeword

Rafter and this box ❑ is empty, put a tick in it and ▶ 769

If you don't have *Rafter* and this box ❑ is empty, tick it and ▶ 797

Otherwise ▶ 636

1585

He shudders. 'You make life sound as cruel as death.'

'Crueller. Life is change, death is stasis. Change can be good or bad, but stasis holds no surprises.'

As doubt takes hold, his outline flickers and blurs. He recedes, becoming fainter and fainter as he finally gives in to death.

His family may still be waiting at the Necropolis. You make your way there.

▶ 351

1586

You quickly despatch the Murmillo with a lethal strike to the neck. To avoid complicated explanations, you strip off his scale armour and helmet and throw them into the bushes. Carrying his body back to the sentries at the gate, you report that you were set upon by a robber in the twilight.

'Sounds like self-defence,' says the sergeant in charge. 'Dump the body there and we'll bury it in the potter's field.'

▶ 555

1587

An insectoid foe is the most terrifying of all, having no mind to feel fear. It rushes at you. You fend off the whirring mouthparts, but the razor edge of a pincer rakes your flesh. A stab of pain lances up your thigh. You twist desperately away, blood spurting out onto the grass.

If the Wound box on your Adventure Sheet was unticked, put a tick in it now and then ▶ 606

If you were already injured, note 1090 as your Current Location and then ▶ 670

1588

If you have either the **bag of Aiolos** or the codeword *Petasos* ▶ 1182

Otherwise ▶ 573

1589

If you have **Vulcan's diadem** ▶ 1536

Otherwise, if this box ❑ has already been ticked ▶ 756; if the box is empty put a tick in it now and read on.

If you have the codeword *Rice* ▶ 1148

If not ▶ 1017

1590

Lieutenant Tekto doesn't look happy when you ask him to pull some strings and get Moose released, but it's too insignificant a crime to argue about. With a grimace like he's swallowing a mouthful of vinegar, he orders the charge struck out and Moose is released.

Success comes at a cost. Tekto thinks a little less of you now he knows you're working as an enforcer for a crime boss. Lose 1 Glory. You can only hope that Zinc's goodwill is worth the damage to your reputation.

Get the codeword *Robber* and ▶ 1642

1591

'Oh, I am fearful – even I, who am Zeus's older cousin, who have seen constellations born and burn and die, who created mankind and brought them fire – even I shudder to face the Queen of Night, just as Zeus himself goes in fear of her.'

So saying, he withdraws into the sky until all that can be seen of him is a dull red gleam, like a phantom face stamped against the immensity of the heavens.

If you have the codeword *Quake* ▶ 553
If not but you have the codeword *Pumped* ▶ 720
Otherwise, if you have the codeword *Nanny* ▶ 1637
Otherwise ▶ 1183

1592

In a momentary lull in the fighting, you turn for a moment to the Minotaur. Bodies are piled around him on the deck. He has the torn guts of some creature dangling from his horns.

'You're covered in blood,' you tell him.

He snorts. 'It's all right. Most of it's not mine.'

On the rooftop, another wave of monsters are bracing to spring across. But their eager, murderous grins turn suddenly to looks of dismay. You feel the deck lurch and press up under your feet. The *Sunrise* is gaining altitude.

▶ 1162

1593

You whirl as you run, heaving the roast meat Dunamis gave you towards the slavering were-beasts at your heels. They fall on it ravenously, snarling and fighting over the succulent morsel. They've forgotten all about you.

But the vampires haven't. They lope on gleefully, scrambling ahead to try to cut you off from the edge of the roof. They lunge towards you, pallid stalk-like arms clutching for your flesh.

The rain runs gurgling along an intricate maze of lead gutters and drainpipes snaking down the side of a chimney.

You lash out, dislodging a downspout so that it falls athwart the roof ridge. The vampires titter smugly, thinking you meant to strike one of them, but when they try to pursue you they find themselves held back by an invisible force. They cannot cross the running water in the pipe.

It delays them for a few seconds, that's all. You race to the parapet. The street is a dizzying drop below. The street is far too wide to jump.

If you have the codeword *Quiddity* ▶ 1299
If not but you have the **wings of Icarus** ▶ 1129
Otherwise ▶ 882

1594

Now that she has despatched the gods of Olympus, the surviving titans aren't bold enough to challenge Nyx's rule. With her sons Sleep and Death beside her she consigns the titans back to Tartarus.

The Vulcanverse is remade as the Nightlands, a place of perpetual darkness where every mortal is trapped, blind, afraid, as terrifyingly isolated as their ancestors were before the gift of fire.

Queen Nyx, who now holds illimitable dominion over all, looks upon what she has wrought and is pleased. To you, seated on the floor beside her eternal throne, she says, 'Harken. Now is the time of endless fear for Man, huddled around a guttering fire listening to the direst creatures of his imagination howling in the outer dark. A time when shadows crawl along the cave wall, when buried instincts boil in the depths of troubled minds. That caress of terror's sharp edge is the only thing that wakes mortals from listless wallowing in their own squalid appetites to become truly alive – when they tremble, hearts pounding, breathless, frantic at the approach of things that wait in the void.'

She considers her own words and smiles.

It is a fate you helped her bring about. And as you sit here you begin to wonder – are you her follower, her champion, her trusted lieutenant? Or are you merely a house pet, the last free mortal that she keeps to remind herself of the sweetness of victory?

Which is it? You decide.

1595

You stab at the buttons but to no avail. The **voicebox remote** is out of power.

Their combined screams are growing in intensity, causing a pulsing pressure inside your skull.

If you have any **beeswax** ▶ 341
If not ▶ 17

1596

You turn, sleepwalk your way to a flowerbed, and curl up on the soft soil.

'What happened?' sys the girl.

'Hypnosis.' Dydkos sounds surprised. 'I thought they'd vanish when they woke up. You don't normally keep your form in the dream world when you stop dreaming.'

Through almost-closed eyelids you sense her standing over you. 'Sound asleep,' she says.

'Sound awake, rather,' says Dydkos with a laugh. 'Anyway, you're safe for now. I don't like that the dream-self is still here, though. Wait while I fetch a book from my caravan. There may be a charm I can work that will send them back permanently.'

Waiting for his footsteps to recede across the grass, you leap up, seize the girl, and will yourself to wake up for real.

► 1108

1597

'You're meant to be so smart,' you say to the head. 'What do you suggest?'

'You know the well back there...'

'With the red lights at the bottom?'

'You can stash things in that well.'

'Got plenty of places I can stash things.'

'You asked my advice. Take it or leave it.'

Go to the well   ► 635
Go into the palace   ► 74
Continue down the street ► 722

1598

'There's a woman called Marija the Sobstress,' says Zinc. 'Lives on Spitpuddle Row. She needs to go away.'

'Anywhere in particular?'

He looks at you, the impassive tin mask seeming to size you up. 'Six feet down is far enough.'

'Oh.' Murder is always a conversation stopper. 'What's she done, this Marija?'

'She's got into my bad books,' says Zinc. 'Not enough? You'd like a good reason. Kiddy fiddler, psychotic killer, whips her slaves, something like that. No, she's just a rat. She ratted on my business interests. She's got to go. You don't want to do it, fine. I'll get someone else.'

What do you say?

'I'm not an assassin.'   ► 326
'OK, her days are numbered.' ► 1566

1599

'The Speaker probably came with a manual,' growls the head. 'Not that any of them will have read it.'

'Did you come with a manual?'

'Witty. I don't need one, being self-maintaining. You're going to have to find the Speaker's control unit, which I bet these idiots slung out years ago.'

'Where would I start looking?'

'The syndics assumed it was junk, so I'd try the junk shops. Isn't there one near the Tower of Riches?'

► 1642

1600

The moment you enter the inner shrine, you know that your deity is no longer here. The sense of numinous presence which formerly pressed in around the edges of reality is gone.

One of the priests runs in shrieking, face contorted in panic.

'You can't be here!' you say. 'I must commune with the god.'

'It is too late,' says the priest, collapsing in a whimpering heap in front of the god's effigy. 'Too late for anything now. The day is done. We are for the dark.'

You look out into the nave to see the sky close up under a pall of atramental darkness. Night sweeps down like a storm upon the world and there is no safe refuge for mortal or immortal. The dominion of Nyx has begun.

► 666

1601

You still have the roast lamb Dunamis gave you. You turn as you run and throw it to the snarling werewolves hard at your heels. Forgetting about you, they fall on the meat with ravenous howls, snapping and fighting for a share.

You reach the dome. At its highest point is a capstone where you might make a stand. The rain runs gurgling along an intricate maze of lead gutters and drainpipes. As you reach to brace your weight on a pipe, a trio of shroud-wrapped vampires emerge around the side of the dome. Their bloodless grey arms snake out to entangle you, seeking to hold you until the rest of the horde gets here.

You lash out. Your blow sends a downspout clattering off the side of the dome. It drops straight as a sword between you and the oncoming undead. They sneer, believing you have missed them, but their needle-sharp smiles turn to looks of dismay when they find themselves unable to close with you. The running water in the pipe stands in their way, a barrier no vampire can cross, and they must go around.

It buys you seconds at most. The copper surface of the dome is slippery with the rainwater sluicing off it, but you have the strength of desperation. You scramble up the side,

slipping and skinning your shins, and at last you claw your way to the top. From here you can see the whole city cowering under the fury of the storm. Across the rain-lashed roof, converging on you from all sides, comes the hellish rabble of night creatures, surging around the base of the dome like a dark tide. And beyond them, vast and terrible against the roiling clouds, comes Thanatos, the angel of death with his sword that even the Olympians fear.

If you have the **wings of Icarus** ▶ **193**
Otherwise ▶ **755**

1602

Your shadow-self sinks silently to the floor, melts into an ink-black puddle, and reforms as a regular and obedient shadow attached to your feet as it should be.

Lose the title **Hero Without A Shadow** and ▶ **392**

1603

You take a last glance around the house where you grew up. Out in the street, you hesitate as you try to decide where to go now. Dunamis tugs at your arm. 'Let's get moving,' she says.

The nearest gate ▶ **723**
The nearest tower ▶ **171**
The Avenue of the Anvil ▶ **1632**
Your mansion (only if you have the title **The Unexpected Heir**) ▶ **1257**
The Academy of Philosophers ▶ **1510**
The temple district ▶ **1326**
The Forum ▶ **981**

1604

An insect-creature leaps forward, jaws snapping, and in twisting to avoid it you are caught a slashing blow from the claws. Red blood splashes across the pale marble floor as you stagger back.

If the Wound box on your Adventure Sheet was unticked, put a tick in it now and then ▶ **1381**

If you were already injured, note **463** as your Current Location and then ▶ **670**

1605

☐ ☐ ☐ ☐

If Tomyios is your companion ▶ **1620** immediately; otherwise read on.

You are admitted to the salon. If you have more than 5 scars ▶ **471** immediately; otherwise put a tick in one of the boxes above and read on.

If one box is now ticked ▶ **1340**
If two are ticked ▶ **1495**
If three are ticked ▶ **536**
If all four are ticked ▶ **343**

1606

'You just don't play well with others, do you?'

He actually laughs at that. 'Says the person who literally tried to kill me with a bomb.'

'Maybe we should put our differences behind us, given how things have moved on recently,' you say, pointing to the ranks of night creatures swarming behind Nyx's banner.

He thinks about it. 'Fair point. But you see how it is. My

armour's just sitting here like a pile of junk. Not a lot I can do without it.'

Reactivate his armour ▶ **512**
You can't trust him ▶ **494**

1607
You truss him up, winding the webbing around him so tightly that he can neither move nor speak. Delete the **attercop silk** from your Adventure Sheet.

The girl hammers her tiny fists on your back. It's no more troublesome than being pelted with corks. You take her in your arms and will yourself back to the waking world.

▶ **1108**

1608
There are rose-covered trellises along the back of the patio. Grabbing a section, you tear it free of the wall and hurl it onto one of the insect-things just as it makes a rush towards you. Entangled in the debris, it stumbles, its pincers caught up in the broken wooden frame.

You drive your weapon up under its thorax, prising between the hard plates of its armour to pierce the fibrous meat within. A colourless blood oozes out, slowly at first and then in spurts. There is a chirruping shriek and the creature folds on itself like crumpled origami.

That leaves one.

▶ **606** and tick one of the boxes there before reading on.

1609
'There's a pickpocket who's been plying their trade on the Street of Knives, right around the corner from here,' says Zinc, stirring heaped spoons of sugar into coffee that's as hot and black as tar.

'I'll keep an eye on my money, then.'

'It's my money I'm thinking about.'

He looks at you. Is he smiling? Frowning? Indifferent? You wonder how he's going to drink the coffee until you see him fit a short silver tube to his mask's lips. He bends over the cup and sucks up a mouthful.

'So this pickpocket – not one of your people?'

'I don't mind independent operators. Free enterprise is the key to a thriving criminal network. But they need to pay their dues. This new pickpocket is too much of a lone wolf. So I want you to keep an eye out, find them, and have a word about them paying a ten percent cut to be allowed to keep on – ' He waves his hand. 'You know.'

'Thieving?'

'Breathing.'

Say you'll do the job ▶ **1478**
Tell him it's not for you ▶ **326**

1610
Keeping a firm hold on Orphea, you yell for your servants and they fetch a militia patrol. As the militiamen snap shackles on her wrists she gives a yawn.

'This is an inconvenience,' she says.

'It's only for a few years,' you tell her.

'Years?' She laughs. 'I love you for your naivety, do you know that?'

The watchmen shove her to the door, causing her to stumble against one of them. 'No need to be so rough, fellas,' she says. As they take her down the street she turns and gives you a broad wink.

When you return to your study you find she left the ruby on the desk. It's worth 30 pyr. Add that to your money and ▶ **97**

1611
Noticing the shops on the first gallery, the head perks up. 'Finally,' it says.

'See something you like?'

'One doesn't buy a wig the way you might choose a tart. Let's go up and take a look at their wares.'

Buy a wig ▶ **889**
Walk on by ▶ **414**

1612
She lashes out. The attack is casual, almost dreamlike, but at the same time bewilderingly fast. Her nails rake towards your eyes. Make a GRACE roll at difficulty 9 to dodge.

Just quick enough ▶ **703**
Too slow ▶ **858**

1613
One Ker howls and dissipates, but the others fight on with redoubled strength, furious at being defied by a mere mortal.

Make a STRENGTH or GRACE roll (your choice) at difficulty 16.

Succeed ▶ **1022**
Fail ▶ **145**

1614
The sun appears over the garden wall, sending a blaze of daylight through the drenched and sagging ivy.

Tritona's mouth forms a perfect O of surprise. You feel the shudder that runs through her. As the sunbeams touch her face she dissolves like a painting being washed away by turpentine. You are left holding empty air.

It isn't worth going back to bed. Famished after your ordeal, you call your servants to prepare a hearty breakfast.

Lose the codeword *Ruffle* and ▶ **97**

1615

Two elegantly-robed officials are wedged in a corner discussing a confidential matter. They don't object to you joining them, and even go out of their way to draw you into the conversation.

'I suppose you've heard all about Xechasiaris,' begins the older of the two.

'Actually, I... who?'

'He's just retired from his post as syndic,' says the other official.

'In theory, yes,' says the first with an ironic laugh. 'Only he doesn't seem to remember retiring.'

'Senile.' This said with a shrug.

'Let's not be uncharitable. He's been in the job since before the three of us were born. After a run like that, retirement takes some getting used to.'

'All I know is it's causing a lot of headaches at the palace.'

'Why is that?' you venture to ask.

They both look at you in surprise. 'I thought you knew all about it. Xechasiaris won't vacate his office. Makes it very difficult for the next chap.'

'Or gal.'

'What they need – what they really need, is somebody who can apply tact, charm and determination in equal measure. Get him out of there forcefully and fast. But with delicacy.'

The younger official sucks his teeth. 'Not easy to find, somebody like that.'

'A fixer, I mean.'

'Miracle worker, almost.'

They start talking about other administrative matters and you make your excuses and leave.

▶ 1324

1616

'Then you've already done the hardest part,' says Myletes. He strokes his beard. 'Well, no, perhaps I exaggerate. The hardest part will be entering the matrix, reconfiguring it, and then dealing with Nyx when she shows up to destroy you. Still, the diadem is a jolly good start!'

If you have the **Face of Wisdom** (INGENUITY +3) ▶ 646

Otherwise ▶ 1290

1617

The whole length of the Street of Knives wears a sinister aspect. The tall, narrow houses are cramped together, the upper stories jutting out over the street to leave the ground in perpetual shade. Moss hangs in dank tufts from the sagging, high-peaked roofs. There is a dark slimy look to the houses here, as if soot and mist have seeped into the brickwork. Behind dingy windows of bottle-thick glass, distorted faces leer out at passers-by.

The cobblestones underfoot are slick with slime. A runnel down the middle of the road is the only drain. The smells are rank: human waste, sweat, rotten fruit, and the occasional whiff of decay. Most people who have to pass along this street quicken their step and keep a handkerchief pressed to their face.

Halfway along the street, a winding alley veers off into the warren of slums known as the Grumbles. Opposite, on the northern side of the road, wide gates in a white marble wall open onto the Necropolis.

To go straight to a city location that you already know about, note **1617** as your Current Location, then ▶ **1432**

Or you can go:

South-west towards the city wall	▶ 1222
North-east to the Forum	▶ 1642
Into the Grumbles	▶ 771
Into the Necropolis	▶ 674

1618

If you have the **Face of Wisdom** (INGENUITY +3) ▶ 159

If not but Galatea is with you ▶ 102

Otherwise ▶ 187

1619

The priestess suddenly lets go of your arm, takes a few faltering steps as though she's forgotten what's happening, and then runs off after the others.

'It's all falling apart,' says Dunamis. 'If we're going to do anything we'd better make it soon.'

▶ Current Location

1620

The moment the factotum opens the door, Tomyios thrusts his bare buttocks towards him and emits a fruity-sounding fart.

'I cannot admit you while you are accompanied by this creature,' says the factotum, holding his nose. 'Last time you were here, he urinated in the punchbowl, shaved Lady Cassia's head while she was taking a nap, and committed an atrocity involving the cockatoo which has left it with a permanent stutter.'

Tomyios picks his nose, proudly shows you both the bogey, then wipes it on the factotum's tunic. 'Snot your day,' he giggles.

The door is shut in your face.

▶ 1324

armour's just sitting here like a pile of junk. Not a lot I can do without it.'

| Reactivate his armour | ▶ 512 |
| You can't trust him | ▶ 494 |

1607

You truss him up, winding the webbing around him so tightly that he can neither move nor speak. Delete the **attercop silk** from your Adventure Sheet.

The girl hammers her tiny fists on your back. It's no more troublesome than being pelted with corks. You take her in your arms and will yourself back to the waking world.

▶ 1108

1608

There are rose-covered trellises along the back of the patio. Grabbing a section, you tear it free of the wall and hurl it onto one of the insect-things just as it makes a rush towards you. Entangled in the debris, it stumbles, its pincers caught up in the broken wooden frame.

You drive your weapon up under its thorax, prising between the hard plates of its armour to pierce the fibrous meat within. A colourless blood oozes out, slowly at first and then in spurts. There is a chirruping shriek and the creature folds on itself like crumpled origami.

That leaves one.

▶ 606 and tick one of the boxes there before reading on.

1609

'There's a pickpocket who's been plying their trade on the Street of Knives, right around the corner from here,' says Zinc, stirring heaped spoons of sugar into coffee that's as hot and black as tar.

'I'll keep an eye on my money, then.'

'It's my money I'm thinking about.'

He looks at you. Is he smiling? Frowning? Indifferent? You wonder how he's going to drink the coffee until you see him fit a short silver tube to his mask's lips. He bends over the cup and sucks up a mouthful.

'So this pickpocket – not one of your people?'

'I don't mind independent operators. Free enterprise is the key to a thriving criminal network. But they need to pay their dues. This new pickpocket is too much of a lone wolf. So I want you to keep an eye out, find them, and have a word about them paying a ten percent cut to be allowed to keep on – ' He waves his hand. 'You know.'

'Thieving?'

'Breathing.'

| Say you'll do the job | ▶ 1478 |
| Tell him it's not for you | ▶ 326 |

1610

Keeping a firm hold on Orphea, you yell for your servants and they fetch a militia patrol. As the militiamen snap shackles on her wrists she gives a yawn.

'This is an inconvenience,' she says.

'It's only for a few years,' you tell her.

'Years?' She laughs. 'I love you for your naivety, do you know that?'

The watchmen shove her to the door, causing her to stumble against one of them. 'No need to be so rough, fellas,' she says. As they take her down the street she turns and gives you a broad wink.

When you return to your study you find she left the ruby on the desk. It's worth 30 pyr. Add that to your money and ▶ 97

1611

Noticing the shops on the first gallery, the head perks up. 'Finally,' it says.

'See something you like?'

'One doesn't buy a wig the way you might choose a tart. Let's go up and take a look at their wares.'

| Buy a wig | ▶ 889 |
| Walk on by | ▶ 414 |

1612

She lashes out. The attack is casual, almost dreamlike, but at the same time bewilderingly fast. Her nails rake towards your eyes. Make a GRACE roll at difficulty 9 to dodge.

| Just quick enough | ▶ 703 |
| Too slow | ▶ 858 |

1613

One Ker howls and dissipates, but the others fight on with redoubled strength, furious at being defied by a mere mortal.

Make a STRENGTH or GRACE roll (your choice) at difficulty 16.

| Succeed | ▶ 1022 |
| Fail | ▶ 145 |

1614

The sun appears over the garden wall, sending a blaze of daylight through the drenched and sagging ivy.

Tritona's mouth forms a perfect O of surprise. You feel the shudder that runs through her. As the sunbeams touch her face she dissolves like a painting being washed away by turpentine. You are left holding empty air.

It isn't worth going back to bed. Famished after your ordeal, you call your servants to prepare a hearty breakfast.

Lose the codeword *Ruffle* and ▶ 97

1615

Two elegantly-robed officials are wedged in a corner discussing a confidential matter. They don't object to you joining them, and even go out of their way to draw you into the conversation.

'I suppose you've heard all about Xechasiaris,' begins the older of the two.

'Actually, I... who?'

'He's just retired from his post as syndic,' says the other official.

'In theory, yes,' says the first with an ironic laugh. 'Only he doesn't seem to remember retiring.'

'Senile.' This said with a shrug.

'Let's not be uncharitable. He's been in the job since before the three of us were born. After a run like that, retirement takes some getting used to.'

'All I know is it's causing a lot of headaches at the palace.'

'Why is that?' you venture to ask.

They both look at you in surprise. 'I thought you knew all about it. Xechasiaris won't vacate his office. Makes it very difficult for the next chap.'

'Or gal.'

'What they need – what they really need, is somebody who can apply tact, charm and determination in equal measure. Get him out of there forcefully and fast. But with delicacy.'

The younger official sucks his teeth. 'Not easy to find, somebody like that.'

'A fixer, I mean.'

'Miracle worker, almost.'

They start talking about other administrative matters and you make your excuses and leave.

▶ 1324

1616

'Then you've already done the hardest part,' says Myletes. He strokes his beard. 'Well, no, perhaps I exaggerate. The hardest part will be entering the matrix, reconfiguring it, and then dealing with Nyx when she shows up to destroy you. Still, the diadem is a jolly good start!'

If you have the **Face of Wisdom** (INGENUITY +3) ▶ 646

Otherwise ▶ 1290

1617

The whole length of the Street of Knives wears a sinister aspect. The tall, narrow houses are cramped together, the upper stories jutting out over the street to leave the ground in perpetual shade. Moss hangs in dank tufts from the sagging, high-peaked roofs. There is a dark slimy look to the houses here, as if soot and mist have seeped into the brickwork. Behind dingy windows of bottle-thick glass, distorted faces leer out at passers-by.

The cobblestones underfoot are slick with slime. A runnel down the middle of the road is the only drain. The smells are rank: human waste, sweat, rotten fruit, and the occasional whiff of decay. Most people who have to pass along this street quicken their step and keep a handkerchief pressed to their face.

Halfway along the street, a winding alley veers off into the warren of slums known as the Grumbles. Opposite, on the northern side of the road, wide gates in a white marble wall open onto the Necropolis.

To go straight to a city location that you already know about, note **1617** as your Current Location, then ▶ 1432

Or you can go:

South-west towards the city wall	▶ 1222
North-east to the Forum	▶ 1642
Into the Grumbles	▶ 771
Into the Necropolis	▶ 674

1618

If you have the **Face of Wisdom** (INGENUITY +3) ▶ 159

If not but Galatea is with you ▶ 102

Otherwise ▶ 187

1619

The priestess suddenly lets go of your arm, takes a few faltering steps as though she's forgotten what's happening, and then runs off after the others.

'It's all falling apart,' says Dunamis. 'If we're going to do anything we'd better make it soon.'

▶ Current Location

1620

The moment the factotum opens the door, Tomyios thrusts his bare buttocks towards him and emits a fruity-sounding fart.

'I cannot admit you while you are accompanied by this creature,' says the factotum, holding his nose. 'Last time you were here, he urinated in the punchbowl, shaved Lady Cassia's head while she was taking a nap, and committed an atrocity involving the cockatoo which has left it with a permanent stutter.'

Tomyios picks his nose, proudly shows you both the bogey, then wipes it on the factotum's tunic. 'Snot your day,' he giggles.

The door is shut in your face.

▶ 1324

1621

There is a change in the quality of space itself. Time seems to alter its pace. The gods are here.

You gaze up at them like a child who has wandered out into a gathering of grown-ups. It is not merely their size that overawes you. Their presence is wrapped in an aura of unbearable reality, as if a furnace door were thrown open on the fire at the dawn of creation. To look too long on such beings is to risk blindness, madness, even annihilation.

But in that glimpse you see they are diminished. The perfect flesh is marred by cuts and bruises. Golden lifeblood stains their majestic finery. Adamantine armour that should be indestructible hangs in battered plates and broken links from their weary shoulders.

Approaching the table, the gods devour the food you brought. As they eat, their wounds disappear and their auras grow brighter and brighter. You have to squint to bear the blazing light.

'Do we have you to thank for this, Pan?' they say to Bosk as they are restored.

'No, my buddy here.'

'The mortal?'

'A cut above that. This is my good friend, the hero of the age.'

Your own deity squints thoughtfully across the table at you. 'The face does look faintly familiar.'

'But all mortals look the same,' sighs Hera.

Lose the codeword *Regal* and ▶ 477

1622

A forlorn figure stands at the gate watching travellers setting off for the south. 'Is it the underworld you're making for?' he asks, grabbing one by the arm.

'No,' replies the man, shaking off his grip. 'We'll all get there soon enough without having to hasten the journey.'

A woman pushing to get by turns and stares at the imploring figure, whose face is chalk white. 'You look as if you've just come back from there,' she says, mouth curling in disgust.

You step in. 'Lord Xechasiaris, may I have a word?'

'Xechasiaris..?' he mutters, confused. 'Is that who I am?'

Lose the codeword *Roar* and ▶ 1011

1623

One of Odysseus' men comes with a report. Distracted, Odysseus surveys the army and looks out across the plain. 'Excuse me, lady. I must attend to our attack plans for tomorrow.'

'You're going to try and take the city?'

He smiles. 'It's been years. As long as Prince Hektor leads the Iliad forces I doubt we'll get as far as the walls. That's why it would help to have another hero on our side.'

He bows and hurries off towards his own ships. ▶ 735 and tick the box there corresponding to Odysseus before deciding if you'll talk to anyone else.

1624

The priest walks mournfully away, dragging his feet as though millstones were bound to them. As he goes he casts many looks back towards the high king's tent, surely hoping for a glimpse of his captive daughter, but she is nowhere to be seen.

You follow him a while along the shore, though he is so sunk in his own despondent thoughts that he takes no notice of the many Achaean warriors he passes. Gradually his look of sorrow hardens into one of anger. He stops and looks out to sea, brandishing his staff aloft.

'Hear your servant, shining lord of the silver bow,' he mutters. 'If ever I built a shrine to please your heart, or burned oxen in sacrifice on your altars, now answer my prayer. Loose your shafts of pestilence upon the Achaeans, let them pay for the tears I've shed today.'

For a moment Chryses stands proud, arms upraised towards the distant horizon, exultant in his power to commune with the god. Then his years catch up to him again. Hunched over in despair, he totters away.

The smell of meat roasting on campfires reminds you it is getting late. The sun is low over the sea and, still weak after your long ordeal, you could use a rest.

▶ 535

1625

An incident comes back to you, a moment of childhood that stirs and rises suddenly out of the deeps of memory. A blustery day in spring. Grass rippling over the curve of a hill. You were flying a kite. Somebody was with you – an aunt? an uncle? – and as they helped you spool out the line they told a story about a hero with mechanical wings who launched themselves to safety from a high dome.

A gust of cold wind brings you back to reality. The door to the stairs is splintering. Pallid claw-like fingers are reaching through. They'll be on you in seconds. Which way will you try to escape?

To the edge of the roof ▶ 1185
To the top of the dome ▶ 759

1626

You scramble back down to the beach, careless of the scrapes you take from the rough rocks.

If you have the codeword *Rage* ▶ 282
Otherwise ▶ 178

1627

Everything about this landscape is alien. You're not even sure if it is land in any normal sense. The terrain curls overhead in long smoky plumes, like a crashing wave frozen into extravagant outcrops of white foam at the moment it hit the shore. The ground underfoot is soft, yielding, more congealed cloud-stuff than solid earth. Against the unending blue of the sky, a distant white crag of cloud rolls slowly against a hidden blaze of light that limns it in blinding gold. The air has the fresh dewy smell of very early morning.

Movement catches your eye. A dark speck in the misty contours of cloud. It can only be Sphikos, but he was barely a minute ahead of you. How did he get so far off?

Then you see that the white substance on which you stand is itself moving, great floes of vapour breaking and drifting asunder. Sphikos is being carried away from you towards the unendurable glare that is temporarily eclipsed by that vast bank of cloud.

If Polymnia is your companion ▶ 1236
If not ▶ 822

1628

There is a recessed bay on the side of the machine. It looks a little like an open sarcophagus but you try not to dwell on that. At Psyche's direction you back into it.

'Make sure you're in contact with the copper runes at the back of the pod,' she says. 'Ready? Don't move…'

She pulls a lever. There's a crackling sound, ending in a slam like a metal door crashing shut. Other than a faint tingling and an acrid odour, you don't notice anything.

'Is that it?'

Psyche nods. 'All done.'

You have acquired two blessings. Each blessing can be used to roll again when you fail an attribute check but only once in any given situation, so if you fail the reroll, you can't spend another blessing to try again.

'In a small way we just made history,' says Psyche proudly as you step out of the machinery. 'Blessings always came from the gods before today. Those blessings you have are the first ever made by mortals.'

'Let's hope they're enough to make a difference.'
▶ 1171

1629

From this high vantage point you look out over the rolling meadows and dense forests of Arcadia. A gust of wind brings the fragrance of wildflowers, snatches of birdsong, the drone of bees, the scents of sun-warmed wheat and rich forest loam.

If you have the codeword **Raptor** and possess some **beeswax** and the **wings of Icarus** ▶ 1519
Otherwise ▶ 884

1630

You race to the stern, where the helmsman is prising up the copper lid of what looks like a compass or gyroscope. Inside is a spinning disk of tangled geometric lines. It makes you feel slightly sick to look at it because of how it's continually shifting, unfolding and refolding, apparently in impossible shapes.

'You have to get your head around it existing in other dimensions,' says the helmsman, hesitantly reaching towards the glowing disk with a strangely shaped spanner. 'Got much experience with buoyancy rotors?'

'That what this is? I thought I was getting a migraine.'

If you have the codeword **Recursive** ▶ 1417 now; otherwise read on.

'It's out of alignment,' says the helmsman. He casts a nervous glance over his shoulder. 'See those sparks? It's dragging against the side of the containment vessel. That's why we're losing altitude.'

'So we need to adjust it? That's what the spanner's for?'

He snorts. 'Vulcan designed it. The tools came with the gizmo. Too bad he didn't include a repair manual.'

He prods the spanner into the housing. There's a protesting screech as the disk grinds against the spanner head. The helmsman leans back, straining with all his might to twist the disk back into alignment. The friction with the spanner slows it even more. The deck lurches, almost throwing you off your feet. Arcs of disturbing light splash out like molten droplets from a furnace.

You glance back at the rail. The Minotaur is grappling a vampire by the throat as he lays about him with his axe at a press of were-beasts. As the rotor slows its spinning the ship is dropping towards the street. Any moment now the horde of creatures on the parapet will be able to jump down on the deck. For all his ferocious strength, the Minotaur can't fight them all.

'We don't have much time,' you tell the helmsman.

'Any time you want to lend a hand…'

Make a STRENGTH roll at difficulty 10.

Succeed ▶ 1318

Fail ▶ 216

1631

If you have the codeword *Recite* ▶ 896

If not ▶ 1006

1632

Tiles crash down from a roof that's been torn open by the wind. The stench of uprooted drains hangs heavy in the air. You step over a motionless bundle that could be a pile of rubbish or a dead body – you don't stop to find out which.

Note 736 as your Current Location and then ▶ 549

1633

The duellists meet outside the city gate as the sun is rising. Agrio is much bigger and stronger than your man. Heavy armour would have favoured him, but medium harness leaves Tekto free to make full use of his superior agility and swordsmanship. He quickly scores a harsh red scar down the side of Agrio's face, ending the duel. The two of them go off arm in arm for breakfast.

Get the codeword *Rhyme*.

Later that day Tekto sends a servant to find you with a purse containing 100 pyr. Add it to your money.

▶ 1642

1634

'I was in Iskandria when it was sacked by raiders from the sea,' you say. 'Thousands lost their homes and loved ones. Others later starved. With so many witnesses to such a calamity, how can anyone doubt it really happened?'

'But how do you know those people were real?' counters a man in the robes of an Arcadian scholar. 'I might dream of the death of millions, and wake in a sweat with their screams still ringing in my ears – but that wasn't reality, it was just too much cheese.'

'No, no,' shouts a strapping middle-aged woman with a rich, booming voice, 'the point is that for the duration of the dream each of those imagined souls felt real terror. A perfect copy of the world is indistinguishable from the real world. And do we not all agree that this world around us, this garden and the Academy and the streets beyond right as far as the coast and the sea beyond – that this is all Vulcan's simulation?'

▶ 1542

1635

'Now don't waste any time monologuing, boss,' advises Chipos. 'Quick death, that's what's needed here. Heroes don't give in, and they always seem to find exactly the right fabled thingamajig to turn the tables on you.'

'Be silent,' growls Hypnos.

'No, listen. I can read secret signs, me. When I go out, it's like everything is shouting prophecies at me. Stars, wind, birds and cats and stuff – they're all omens if you know what to look for.'

'I could overlook your treachery, despicable as it is,' Hypnos growls at him, 'because at least you are toadying to the winning side. But your inane chattering is too exasperating to tolerate a moment longer.'

He reaches out, grabs Chipos by the hair, and yanks. It's like a conjurer performing a trick quicker than the eye can follow. You don't see the transformation, but now where Chipos was standing there is a skinny mongrel dog. Hypnos kicks it away and it whines, running a short distance and then slinking back to cringe beside him.

'That's better. Keep quiet, and when we've conquered the Vulcanverse I might find you the bone of a lesser god to gnaw on.' He strokes his beard. 'Oh, but we'll need a new word, won't we? Not Vulcanverse but Noctiverse.'

'Dream on, Sleep,' you say. 'Nyx will never rule over mankind. I'll see to that.'

▶ 803

1636

'Mention my name to the militia,' you say. 'I'm in their good books, so they owe me one.'

'What I'm about to give you is worth far more than a garland and a place in a parade,' he says.

Lose the title **Public-Spirited**, as you realize your social capital with the city watch will only go so far. Then ▶ 496 and tick the box there before reading on.

1637

You glance back at the battling hordes. Though you have won past, the alliances you've made are barely enough to hold the line – and that line is failing. But there is one hope left. You had almost forgotten it, but now you see it at your belt and clutch at it. The Horn of the Lost Hero.

You raise it to your lips. Its sound echoes across the battlefield, giving pause to your enemies and hope to your allies. But the echoes fade away and the Horn crumbles to dust.

As your enemies renew their attack and you are about to lose all hope, she comes – from nothing, suddenly just there. Lethia, the Lost Hero, lost no more. Her memory is reborn in your mind, in the minds of your allies, and by the shudder that goes through their ranks, in the minds of your enemies as well. They know her: the champion who toppled a god.

'I told you I would come,' she says.

▶ 1183

1638

He grins. 'I was hoping you'd see it that way.'

He launches himself forward, more daring now that he knows back-up is on the way. His club scythes towards your head with bone-crushing force as you step in and swing at him.

You need to make a STRENGTH roll at difficulty 8.

Success ▶ 870

Failure ▶ 1448

1639

Dydkos jumps in front of the girl, his hand reaching for the rapier at his side.

'No need for that, unless you want the dew to rust your blade.'

He squints at you suspiciously. 'Has he sent you to bring her back?'

What's your reply?

'Yes, she'll have to come with me.' ▶ 1518

'No, she can stay here after all.' ▶ 763

1640

You point the remote, stabbing frantically at the mute button. The Celedons' deadly voices fall silent. It makes them hesitate, but only for a moment. They rush towards you and chop with forge-hardened limbs.

Make a STRENGTH or GRACE roll (your choice) at difficulty 15 to beat them.

If you succeed ▶ 1194

If you fail, tick the Wound box on your Adventure Sheet and ▶ 671

1641

The intruder looks up as you enter the study. 'You're a light sleeper, then,' they say with a wry smile.

If you have the codeword **Prankette** ▶ 687

If not but you have the title **The Embezzler** ▶ 353

If you have neither ▶ 719

1642
❑

The Forum is the central plaza of the city, built on a majestic scale. An entire town could be fit on the broad sweep of white marble, which is bordered by a double row of columns two storeys high.

If you do not have the codeword **Reverie** and the box above is empty, put a tick in it and ▶ 926

Otherwise, if you have the codeword **Roar** ▶ 1198

Otherwise read on.

The Forum is dominated by the two palaces of government. These stupendous marble edifices are like the dwellings of the gods, declaring their power in every pillar vast as a tree trunk, in the blocks of masonry that even titans would strain to lift, in the monumental steps that all must labour to climb, and in the precious metals beaten into gleaming roof tiles that seem to rival rather than merely reflect the sun.

Some say there is a third palace, even more resplendent than these seats of mortal authority, and that is the home of Vulcan himself. You have yet to meet anyone who can tell you where in the city that is, and the popular belief is that Vulcan clouds all mortal minds so that you might walk past his palace every day and never know it, even though it is more magnificent than any other building in the Vulcanverse.

Beside the palaces are the barracks and parade grounds of the two regiments of elite guards, who are mustered only in times of great danger, and the humbler offices of the militia who deal with day-to-day policing.

To go straight to a city location that you already know about, note **1642** as your Current Location, then ▶ 1432

Alternatively you can visit:

The Palace of the Syndics ▶ 187

The Palace of the Archons ▶ 316

The Barracks of the Black Guard ▶ 1584

The Barracks of the White Guard ▶ 1010

The Office of the Watch ▶ 1121

Or you can go:

North on Septentrional Avenue ▶ 515

South on the Avenue of the Anvil ▶ 63

East along the Avenue of Subsolanus ▶ 625

West on the Avenue of Ephirus ▶ 613

North-east on the Street of Ash ▶ 232

North-west on the Street of the Winds ▶ 1062

South-east down the Street of the Sun and Moon ▶ 1324

South-west along the Street of Knives ▶ 1617

1643

The more you struggle, clawing desperately at the side of the grave, the more the earth presses down, smothering you. You open your mouth to scream but it is clogged with the wet, clay-like soil and all you manage is a whimper. The spectre winds its arms around you, hugging you in the foetid darkness. You no longer have the strength to break free. It is impossible to breathe. Your eyes are blinded by the earth. Panic wells up as you realize this is the end.

Or is it..?

If you have any companion except for Tomyios ▶ 1158

Otherwise, if you have an **iron key** ▶ 853

Otherwise ▶ 1523

1644

Put the **lava gem** back on your Adventure Sheet. As you walk away, you can still feel the biting chill of the water. A sharper chill runs up your spine as you realize you have been cursed. Lose all your blessings (including the permanent blessing of Demeter, if you had it) or, if you have no blessings, permanently reduce the maximum number of blessings you can hold by one.

▶ 806

1645

You can't see Death's eyes under the cowl, but the curl of his lips tells you that it was the right answer. 'Remember you are my creature now,' he says quietly.

You wonder for a moment why he spoke under his breath, but you get your answer as a booming thunderclap rattles the heavens. Stepping out of a swirling portal that has opened in the sky come Queen Nyx and her other son, Hypnos.

▶ 1027

1646

The uniquely specialized skill set of a good major-domo means that there are not many vacancies. He must be discreet, methodical, untiring in his dedication, with zealous attention to detail and a grasp of savoir-faire at least equal to that of his employer.

You ask around among the city's great and good, but in every case these households have staff who have been with the family for years. 'Anyway,' one aristocrat confides to you, 'I'd never be able to relax in my own home with an Iskandrian running the staff. I'd think I wasn't good enough for him.'

If you are to find your former servant a job, you're going to need to pull some strings.

If you have the codeword **Robber** and want to enlist Zinc's help ▶ 790

If you have the codeword **Ritual** and want to find him a job at the Palace of the Syndics ▶ 373

If you have the codeword **Riven** and want to see if Myletes needs a servant ▶ 461

Otherwise ▶ 1077

1647

A single Celedon remains. She glances at the wrecked bodies of her fallen sisters, convulsing weakly as their gears spill out onto the ground, but her graven metal features show no trace of feeling.

Uttering a shrill cry like an attacking swan, she lunges at your throat. Attempt a STRENGTH or GRACE roll (your choice) at difficulty 12.

Succeed ▶ 354

Fail ▶ 259

1648

In the obliterating white glare of the first dawn, Sphikos's shadow is like a bolt of black cloth spread out to infinity. You of course cast no shadow, having lost it to a demon of night in the wilds of Arcadia.

Far off in the distance something is tumbling through the sky. A ragged scrap of darkness, a blot against the refulgent blue. It is swept nearer, jerking and dancing on unseen winds. Now you can see its outline – a struggling figure, living and yet flat as crumpled paper.

It hurtles headlong towards you. At the last minute you duck. There's a tug as it hits, followed by a sense of wellbeing. You hadn't realized anything was missing until you felt whole again. Now, beside Sphikos's shadow there is a second one. Yours, restored to you and reattached because night could not stand against the coming of time's first dawn.

Lose the title **Hero Without A Shadow** and ▶ 1306

1649

The Boulevard of the Salamander runs east to west in the lee of the city's south wall. The wall is built out in a pentice that stretches halfway to the buildings on the north side, so that the line of twisted brick pillars that support the pentice runs along the middle of the street.

If you have the codeword **Razor** and this box ❑ is empty, tick it and record 1649 as your Current Location, then ▶ 397

Otherwise read on.

If you have the codeword **Radish** and this box ❑ is empty, tick it and ▶ 405

Otherwise read on.

To go straight to a city location that you already know about, note **1649** as your Current Location, then ▶ **1432**

Or you can go:

East   ▶ **555**
West   ▶ **1222**

1650

She reads the look in your eyes. 'Oh, it's like that.'

With her free hand she whips the poignard from her belt and scores it across the back of your hand. Surprise rather than pain makes you loosen your grip. She twists away, dropping into a crouch.

'I don't think of this as murder,' you say. 'I'm just putting you down like a troublesome animal.'

She cocks an eyebrow. 'Excuse me, but I'm the one holding a weapon.'

You reach over to the hearth and snatch up the poker. She must have used it to bank up the fire, because the tip is red hot. 'Happy now?'

She grins fiercely. 'To the death.'

Swing the poker like a mace   ▶ **219**
Thrust it like a dagger   ▶ **459**
Throw it at her   ▶ **1020**

1651

You wake to find a small pink tongue rasping at your ear. It's the masked cat you saw at the gate earlier.

'Nectanebo, isn't it? Where's your owner?'

You sit up, reaching to stroke the cat, but it darts away under a tablecloth. You're in the ballroom. You get up stiffly, your limbs cramped after falling asleep on the hard marble floor. Outside there's the spit and crack of lightning in a sky the colour of ink. A torrential downpour throws a waterfall of rain across the open doors to the garden.

▶ **1561**

1652

Lose your permanent blessing.

'That's the gift that keeps on giving,' says the storekeeper with a smirk. 'Still, I don't think you're going to be disappointed.'

Now ▶ **496** and tick the box there before reading on.

1653

Chipos steps over to stand beside Hypnos. He looks sheepish but refuses to meet your gaze. 'Sorry,' he says, 'but I can see which side my bread's buttered. I'm going to have to side with the winners.'

Remove Chipos from the Companion box on your Adventure Sheet. Hypnos throws him a kind of curdled smirk. He obviously has no interest in Chipos, but it gives him some satisfaction to see your friend abandoning you.

'You're a fool, Chipos,' you say. 'They'll crush you along with everyone else.'

'Yeah, but only after they crush all you fancy-pants hero types.' Now he does look up, and you're taken aback by the resentment blazing in his eyes. 'Got to watch this one, boss,' he says to Hypnos. 'Got all kinds of boons and whatnot from the gods, special favours and that.'

If you have any blessings, benisons, or **Death's favour** ▶ **454**

Otherwise ▶ **1635**

1654

The spider diligently spins a web between the branches of a sprawling plane tree. The resulting net is big enough to wrap around an elephant, so you are not very surprised when a girl comes along picking night blooms and, stumbling into the web, is held fast.

As she struggles, she only succeeds in wrapping herself in a cocoon of silken strands. The spider darts out of the corner of the web, and now you see that the jewel-bright pattern on its back is like a face. It's the face of the merchant who sent you here.

'Quickly, fool,' he hisses. 'If you delay, that gypsy wizard Dydkos will find and free her.'

He's right. Her muffled cries have brought a young man who is even now rushing towards you across the grass.

Grab the girl and wake up ▶ 1108

Kill the spider and free her from the web ▶ 763

1655

Turning with a shudder from the stygian murk that roils above the landscape of the afterlife, you make your way down the tower.

▶ 1222

1656

He makes up his mind when he sees you running towards him. He's backing out of the doorway and you'll have to be quick to stop him closing it before you reach him.

Attempt a GRACE roll at difficulty 10.

Succeed ▶ 1445

Fail ▶ 894

1657

Did your aunts say anything in reply to your boast? You only remember their secret smiles. But later – how long later? – they told you of a tavern nestled against the city's eastern wall.

'If you find yourself in the garden there one afternoon,' says Aunt Terpe, 'and you hear the sound of singing, go and look into the arbour.'

You have an image of a bearded man with broad shoulders, sweat glistening on his chest under an open shirt, eyes flashing with dangerous merriment. He is sitting with a brimming wine jug in front of him. Greenery filters the afternoon sun in his thick brown hair. Bees drone amid the blossom whose sweet perfume fills the warm air.

The wooden seat in the arbour creaks under his powerful bulk as he sways crooning a song of meadows and brooks and woodlands. Then suddenly he stops singing,

looks around with an expression between anger and delight, and points a meaty finger at you. 'There you are!'

'My aunts sent me,' you stammer.

'What's this? Modesty? I won't have modesty. Fate brought you to me!'

He pours another goblet of wine. It's strong and dark and unlocks thoughts of hot sun, light rain, and fresh green growth.

Hesitantly you accept the goblet. 'I don't know if I should.'

'You can call me Bosk,' he says in his booming voice, and curls of ivy stir in the heavy air as he spreads his arms wide, inviting you to join him.

You wake up in the park around midnight, still drunk, and somehow find your way home. The morning stabs you between the eyes and when your mother puts breakfast on the table it's all you can do not to throw up.

'Painting the town red?' says Aunt Eremia.

'Green, more like.' You nurse your aching head. 'Sorry, I don't know what I'm talking about. Might have had a bit too much to drink.'

'Now, what's this?' says your mother, giving your aunts a disapproving look, but they remain a picture of innocence.

'The strangest thing...' you go on. 'I think I promised to do something, but I can't remember what.'

Get the codeword *Rye* and ▶ 493

1658

Daedalus and Icarus are waiting for you in their cell. Daedalus is tinkering with a gadget on the table. 'Still need those wings,' he says, without looking up.

'Your spider-thingy has a key to every door in the place. Why not walk out?'

He puts the gadget down. 'Because I've got one of the most famous faces in the Vulcanverse and I wouldn't get a hundred metres without being recognized.'

'What's the objection?' Icarus says to you. 'You want the wings for yourself? Possessions aren't going to mean a thing if the titans destroy reality.'

If you have the **wings of Icarus** and are willing to hand them over ▶ 1098

If not ▶ 289

1659

The storm batters at the window and casts ripples of rainwater shadow over the walls as you close in a death-struggle with the vampire.

Though she is slight, apparently no more than a frail wisp of a girl, her undead body is animated by the overpowering vigour of the eternally damned. You wrestle with her and her grip is as hard as cold iron. Make a STRENGTH roll at difficulty 9.

Succeed ▶ 628
Fail ▶ 248

1660

You strike up a conversation with a White Guard officer called Tekto, who is looking for a second to represent him in a duel. 'Recently I was sent to arrest a lieutenant of the Black Guard,' he explains. 'This man, whose name is Agrio, became enraged because I found him at a noble lady's salon. As he couldn't very well complain about the general who ordered him placed under arrest, the moment he was free again he challenged me to a duel.'

'What was he arrested for?'

'A minor breach of discipline. He's headstrong, but that's irrelevant. I need you to act as my second. Meet with Agrio's second and agree what weapons and armour we will use in the duel.'

'Obviously you don't expect me to do it for honour alone. I'm not a member of either regiment.'

'If I win, I will pay you 100 pyr.'

'And if you lose?'

'Then my savings will have to pay for my funeral.'

Agree ▶ 1424
Refuse ▶ 1642

1661

You learn that Viranos is out on patrol. 'Can't say when he'll be back,' the officer on duty tells you, 'but he left word that he hopes to bump into you at Lady Pemphreda's salon one of these days.'

▶ 1642

1662

The parcel contains the **Pipes of Pan (CHARM +3)**. Add them to your possessions. The CHARM bonus is not cumulative with that conferred by a **laurel wreath** or a **golden lyre**.

There is no note. 'Who could have sent it?' you wonder aloud.

'Obviously a friend who holds you in high esteem, excellency,' murmurs your major-domo as he gathers up the wrapping paper.

▶ 97

1663

You knock away the sword and, as he stands gaping in astonishment at your skill, you sweep his legs from under him. He is at your mercy.

Finish him off ▶ 1586
Try reasoning with him ▶ 107

1664

Lose the codeword **Radiant**.

You had almost forgotten the note Zinc gave you. He told you to read it when you got to Vulcan's palace. You tear open the crumpled envelope. A small slip of paper falls out.

'You're going to have a blast,' it reads. *'Or that's what happened to me, anyway, when I was last there. If I've got one piece of advice it's to seize the moment. Don't wait around till everything's perfect. It's never perfect. When it comes time to jump, just jump. Now get in there and party. Zinc.'*

You turn the paper over but that's all he wrote. Enigmatic advice – but that's typical of Zinc.

▶ 941

1665

The item gives off a glow that penetrates the darkness just enough for you to see your way. You are careful not to brush against the pupating dreams that are visible now as grey blurs. They hang suspended in the air over the sleeping Syndics, each taking the shape of a nascent figure whose embryonic organs beat out a febrile pulse beneath its waxy skin. Their heavy lacertilian eyelids twitch with unknowable thoughts. What happens when those dreams emerge into reality? You'd rather not find out.

▶ 294 and tick the box there before reading on.

1666

'I figure you could probably use a spare one of these now the original has morphed into an intangibug chrysalis.'

He grabs a replacement **bronze butterfly** from his workbench and tosses it to you. Add it to the possessions on your Adventure Sheet.

▶ 289

1667

Over the next few days, a stream of people come to see you with requests for how the world should be run.

'Milk shouldn't go off,' says one.

Another: 'The sky could flicker when it's about to rain. Then we'd have time to go and get an umbrella.'

'Why not have shoes regrow the way skin does?' suggests another. 'One pair of boots could last a lifetime.'

'Folly!' cries a man in the queue behind him. 'You would ruin the livelihood of the city's cobblers.'

'Not to mention cordwainers,' calls a voice from further down the line.

You turn to your friends. 'This is getting exhausting. I don't mind saving the world, but I don't see why I should have to rebuild it.'

'You're the hero of the age,' says the Iskandrian ambassador. 'It's only to be expected that the people would look to you, their saviour.'

'I could sort it out, if you can't be bothered,' puts in Dunamis casually.

'No way. You'd be sitting on a mountain of rubies and nobody else would have a coin to their name.'

Eros has an idea. 'Leave it all to Psyche. She'd like nothing better than to tinker around in Vulcan's workshop.'

You chew your lip. 'What kind of world would she make, though?'

Eros laughs at that. 'Less unpredictable, less dangerous, less exciting. She'll call it an improvement, naturally.'

'Not much call for heroes in a world like that,' you say with a sigh.

'There are other worlds,' says a familiar voice from the doorway.

'Kedalion!'

'News of your victory even reached me,' he says, sweeping magisterially past the grumbling citizens waiting in line.

'I feared you were dead, old friend.'

He strokes his beard to conceal a self-satisfied smile. 'That's what I wanted Nyx to think. And now you are restoring the Vulcanverse as you once restored Iskandria? Wonderful.'

You draw him to one side. 'Never mind that. What do you mean, there are other worlds?'

'I've seen them. You remember my telescope. Out there among the stars — a million worlds waiting to be explored. And all of them could use a hero.'

The next day your friends look for you in vain in Vulcan City. There is no word of you in Iskandria. At the Summer Palace in Arcadia or the fishing villages of the Borean coast there is no sign. Not even among the wanderers on the banks of the Styx are you to be found.

But if anyone were to look up at night at the constellations, and gaze with the all-penetrating sight of imagination, they would know that your adventures still continue, out there in the reaches of infinity.

Adventure Sheet

NAME

COMPANION (maximum of 1)

ATTRIBUTES   SCORE

CHARM

GRACE

INGENUITY

STRENGTH

WOUND

−1 from all attribute rolls
when ticked

TITLES

MONEY

GOD

GLORY   SCARS

POSSESSIONS (maximum of 20)

BLESSINGS (maximum of 3)

CURRENT LOCATION

Codewords

- ❑ Rabbit
- ❑ Radiant
- ❑ Radish
- ❑ Rafter
- ❑ Rage
- ❑ Rain
- ❑ Ramrod
- ❑ Raptor
- ❑ Ratchet
- ❑ Razor
- ❑ Rebuke

- ❑ Recite
- ❑ Rectangle
- ❑ Recursive
- ❑ Reef
- ❑ Reflection
- ❑ Regal
- ❑ Remedy
- ❑ Rendezvous
- ❑ Requiem
- ❑ Restore
- ❑ Retract

- ❑ Retrieve
- ❑ Reverie
- ❑ Rhapsody
- ❑ Rhombus
- ❑ Rhyme
- ❑ Rice
- ❑ Ridge
- ❑ Rifle
- ❑ Rigor
- ❑ Rink
- ❑ Ripple

- ❑ Ritual
- ❑ Riven
- ❑ Roar
- ❑ Robber
- ❑ Rock
- ❑ Rogue
- ❑ Rohan
- ❑ Romance
- ❑ Root
- ❑ Rose
- ❑ Rough

- ❑ Royal
- ❑ Ruby
- ❑ Rudiment
- ❑ Ruffle
- ❑ Rug
- ❑ Rumour
- ❑ Rune
- ❑ Rustic
- ❑ Rye

Notes